·EX·LIBRIS·

READER'S DIGEST

CONDENSED BOOKS

DAWN
by Susan Hunt-Wulkowicz

READER'S DIGEST
CONDENSED BOOKS

VOLUME 4 1996

THE READER'S DIGEST ASSOCIATION, INC.
Pleasantville, New York

READER'S DIGEST CONDENSED BOOKS

Editor-in-Chief, Books & Home Entertainment: Barbara J. Morgan
Editor, U.S. Condensed Books: Tanis H. Erdmann
Executive Editor: Marjorie Palmer
Managing Editors: Thomas Froncek, Joseph P. McGrath, James J. Menick
Senior Staff Editors: Dana Adkins, Anne H. Atwater, M. Tracy Brigden,
Catherine T. Brown, Thomas S. Clemmons, Maureen A. Mackey,
Angela H. Plowden-Wardlaw, Ray Sipherd
Senior Editors: Linn Carl, Christopher W. Davis, Catharine L. Edmonds, Paula Marchese,
Ayesha Pande
Associate Editors: Laura E. Kelly, Mark Poirier, Amy M. Reilly
Managing Editor, Copy Desk: Jeane Garment
Assistant Managing Editor, Copy Desk: Maxine Bartow
Senior Staff Copy Editors: Jeanette Gingold, Tatiana Ivanow, Marilyn J. Knowlton
Senior Copy Editors: Claire A. Bedolis, Daphne Hougham, Charles Pendergast,
Miriam Schneir
Senior Associate Copy Editors: Barbara Booth, Alexandra C. Koppen, Arlene Petzal
Editorial Administrator: Donna R. Gataletto
Art Director: Angelo Perrone
Executive Art Editor: Soren Noring
Senior Art Editor: Clair Moritz
Assistant Art Editor: Stephanie Brauer
Director, Book Rights: Virginia Rice

International Editions

Executive Editor: Gary Q. Arpin
Senior Editors: Bonnie Grande, Eva C. Jaunzems, Antonius L. Koster

Reader's Digest Condensed Books are published every two to three months at Pleasantville, N.Y.

The condensations in this volume have been created by The Reader's Digest Association, Inc., by special arrangement with the publishers, authors, or holders of copyrights.

With the exception of actual personages identified as such, the characters and incidents in the fictional selections in this volume are entirely the products of the authors' imaginations and have no relation to any person or event in real life.

The credits that appear on page 576 are hereby made part of this copyright page.

CONTENTS

NOTORIOUS
Janet Dailey

In the town of Friendly, Nevada, the lives of some people are about to change forever:

Eden Rossiter, the beautiful young owner of Spur Ranch, struggling to free herself from her notorious past.

Duke DePard, the embittered cattle tycoon who's determined to break her at any cost.

Kincade, the mysterious stranger who has drifted into town looking for work—or so he says.

When their paths cross, it's more than just Nevada dust that gets stirred up. . . .

Chapter I

THE town of Friendly, Nevada, shimmered in the heat haze of an August afternoon. The distorting waves were kind to the time-ravaged buildings that flanked the main road through town, wrapping them in a veil that hid the crumbling and peeling of age. A battered bullet-scarred sign on the outskirts claimed a population of seventy-two, but the number of boarded-up storefronts and abandoned buildings made that number suspect.

A lone pickup with Texas tags limped into a combination service station, garage, and welding shop. Dust caked its black exterior, and steam hissed from beneath its hood. Inside the station, the ding-ding from the gas-hose bell roused Hoague Miller from his contemplation of a calendar photograph of a mountain lake. He rocked forward in his office chair to look out, indifferent to the squeals of protest it made at the shifting of his nearly three hundred pounds.

A stranger stepped out of the truck, tall and trimly muscled. A straw cowboy hat shaded a face that was all lean planes, hard angles, and the beginnings of a five o'clock shadow. He moved to the front of his truck with that slow, rolling gait of a cowboy.

Strangers were rare in Friendly—it was too far off the beaten path. Most maps didn't even list it. Impelled by curiosity, Hoague Miller maneuvered his considerable bulk out of the chair and headed for the pumps, bypassing the scattered innards of an ancient Jeep that waited to be put back together. Only a fool or a cowboy worked in this heat, and Hoague Miller was neither.

The tall stranger had the hood of his pickup raised. If he noticed Hoague Miller waddling toward him, jowls swaying, he gave no sign as he swiveled to idly survey the town.

A dust devil came out of the sage flats and sent an empty beer can clattering down the street. The stranger observed it and murmured, " 'Thus the whirligig of time brings in his revenges.' "

Hoague frowned in puzzlement. "What's that you say?"

The man turned back and gave him a sleepy-eyed look that almost concealed the hard, cold blue of his eyes. "Just quoting a line from Shakespeare," he replied with a shrug.

"Shakespeare?" Hoague took a closer look at the stranger. "Are you one of those poem-writing cowboys?"

On the wrong side of thirty, the stranger had a rider's narrow hips and wide shoulders. The pale track of an old cut was visible on his right temple. His hair was the tawny color of a mountain cat, and the man looked about as dangerous—until he smiled with an indolence that had Hoague relaxing. "I can't say that I am," the stranger said.

"Thought maybe you was, knowing Shakespeare and all." Hoague peered under the hood. "Looks like you got a busted radiator hose." He pulled a handkerchief from his pocket and mopped at the perspiration flowing down his face.

"Yeah." The stranger nodded. "How long to fix it?"

"Well . . ." Hoague scratched his jaw. "I got a couple of other jobs ahead of you. Two or three hours, I'd say."

"There's no rush," the stranger said, and shifted his gaze to the high desert country surrounding the town. Here was the West of legend, subtle in its grandeur and awesome in its vastness, a land of broad, undulating valleys clumped with sagebrush, riven with dry arroyos, and walled by saw-toothed mountains. A banner of dust boiled up in the hot air. It was the only stirring of life to be seen for miles. The stranger watched it a few seconds, then faced his truck again. "Where can a man get something to eat here?"

"The Lucky Starr, just down the street." Hoague motioned toward a two-story building on the corner.

With a parting nod the stranger moved off in the direction of the building. There were no clouds to filter the streaming white light of the sun. He narrowed his eyes against its brilliance and pulled the brim of his straw Resistol lower on his brow.

The sun-bleached sign above the building identified it as the "Lucky Starr Hotel and Casino." A second sign announced it was "Always Open." An old planked sidewalk wrapped the structure on two sides, and a roof shaded the walk.

The stranger paused in the shade and swept his gaze over the town again. An old yellow dog lay sprawled along the edge of the road, panting in the full glare of the sun. Across the way a woman walked out of a dual post office and grocery, capturing his attention. Long-legged and slim, she wore a man's white shirt, open at the throat, and faded denims that hugged the curves of her hips. A flat-brimmed hat sat low on her head, and her hair was the dark, rich shade of expensive Swiss chocolate, its length bound behind her neck to fall in a gleaming tassel halfway down her back. She tapped her riding quirt against her leg in a show of impatience. Beneath the gesture was the impression of a pride that wouldn't bend. Watching her, the stranger felt a stirring of interest and immediately killed it. As he swung toward the entrance to the hotel casino, the woman moved off in the opposite direction.

Cool air whispered over him when he walked inside. The place reeked of stale tobacco smoke and spilled liquor. To his left, steps led to a second floor. An arched opening on his right led into a lounge-and-casino area. He moved toward it.

The front windowpanes were painted green to keep out the sunlight, and slot machines were racked up in front of them to further block the outside light. In the near corner a set of drums sat on a raised platform. The far corner was taken up with a couple of black-jack tables, a roulette wheel, and some poker tables. Scattered in between was a collection of scarred bar tables and chairs.

A once impressive mahogany bar anchored one side of the long room. A woman in white leggings and a teal silk blouse sat on a bar-stool counting bills from a cash drawer. Her shoulder-length hair was the soft blond color that came from a bottle. When the stranger walked in, her almond-shaped eyes made a slow study of him.

"Come on in and take a load off, cowboy. As you can see, you got the place to yourself." Her voice had the low, raspy quality of a purring cat. It matched her feline features—wide, slashing cheekbones and a jawline that came to a sharp point at her chin.

"Thanks." He touched a finger to his hat and headed for the bar.

With a slight lift of her head she called out, "Hey, Roy! You have a customer out front."

A portrait in a gilded frame hung between the shelves of the back bar. It showed a sultry blonde in a slinky gold dress crooning into a microphone—a younger, softer version of the woman on the barstool. "That's me, Starr Davis," her smoky voice confirmed. "The portrait was done during my days as a singer in Reno."

"The clubs in Reno are a long way from this place—in more than just miles," the stranger observed with dry humor.

Her smile echoed his sentiments. "You've got that right, cowboy." Starr Davis slipped a stack of bills into an envelope. "But it's the old story. I found myself with a kid to raise and no father. Show business is not the most stable career, so I looked for something else and found this." The gold bracelets on her arm jingled as she waved a hand at their surroundings. "I got it for a song."

His glance made a slow sweep of the empty tables and came back to her. "Bad song, I'd say."

She laughed in her throat, taking no offense. "At the time, there was talk they were going to put a highway through here to Oregon. It turned out to be just talk." She called out again, "Roy!"

A withered, bone-thin man pushed his way through the swinging doors at the far end of the bar. The smell of grease rushed into the room with him. The man slipped behind the mahogany bar and advanced toward the stranger, an expression of utter indifference on his face.

"What do you have to eat?" asked the stranger.

In answer the man slapped a plastic-covered menu on the counter. "That says we got breakfast anytime, but we ain't. I shut the griddle off three hours ago."

The stranger ordered a T-bone steak. Roy grunted an acknowledgment and disappeared into the kitchen.

"Roy has a real sunny disposition, doesn't he?" the stranger remarked with a faint smile.

"Draws customers for miles." Starr Davis's full lips curved in a small answering smile as she slid off the stool and carried the money drawer to the cash register behind the bar.

The stranger moved to one of the bar tables. He settled his long frame into a chair and removed his hat.

Starr Davis poured herself a cup of coffee and eyed the stranger. "You're new in town, aren't you?"

"Just drove in," he confirmed.

"I thought so." When she walked out from behind the bar with the cup, the stranger pushed back a second chair, inviting her to join him. "I'm good at faces. I would have remembered yours."

His wasn't a face a woman would forget. He wasn't handsome exactly, but he had the kind of tough, go-to-hell good looks that challenged women and broke hearts. At forty, Starr had lost all illusions about life and men. Yet looking at this man, she wished she'd met him fifteen years ago. That made him dangerous.

"What brings you to a forgotten corner of Nevada like Friendly?" She studied him over the rim of her cup.

"A busted radiator hose." He didn't elaborate. Roy came out of the kitchen carrying a plate of greasy home fries and a T-bone steak that hung over the sides of its platter. He shoved the food in front of the stranger.

"The town's pretty quiet. Are there many ranches around?" the stranger asked Starr.

"The Diamond D is the biggest. Are you looking for work?"

"Right now I'm not looking beyond this steak, a hot shower, and a month's worth of sleep."

As he sliced off a chunk of steak, the cuff of his left sleeve rode back, exposing a recent scar. Noticing it, Starr remarked, "That looks like a fresh cut. What happened to you?"

"I got thrown from a bronc and broke my wrist. It took a surgeon who was good at jigsaw puzzles to piece it back together."

"You must have been laid up for a while."

"A while." He nodded and continued to eat.

When he finished his meal, he kicked back in his chair and lit a long, slim cigar. It was half smoked when the muffled beginnings of a racket came from outside, a low rumble that grew steadily louder.

"Sounds like the Diamond D's moving cattle," Starr said.

The stranger brought the chair down on all four legs and stood up. "Think I'll have a look." With the cigar clamped between his teeth, he tossed some bills on the table, then scooped up his hat and headed for the door at an unhurried gait.

Outside, the heat hit him first, then the choking dust churned up by the stream of bawling cattle that came out of the desert and filed down the middle of town. The stranger leaned a shoulder against a post at the edge of the planked walk to watch.

At the intersection an outrider on a bald-faced roan horse positioned himself on the hotel's side of the street. Two other riders covered the opposite side. One was a gawky kid, barely in his teens. But it was the tall, big-shouldered man on the steel-gray horse next to the kid who drew the stranger's interest. There was an air of authority about him that said he was the boss of the outfit. In his hand he carried a bullwhip, the length of it uncurled to the ground.

The dust haze grew thicker as the main body of the herd entered town, accompanied by more riders, slapping coiled ropes to keep the cattle moving. The stranger wasn't the only spectator. Others had ventured out of the air-cooled buildings to watch. Those across the street from the stranger were obscured by the dust fog that hung over the herd, but the tall brunette coming down the street toward him wasn't. She was the same slim, well-built woman he had seen earlier.

She stopped at the corner directly across from him, her attention on the man on the gray horse. For an instant there was something challenging, almost defiant in her stance; then she stepped off the curb and angled across the dirt road toward a small false-fronted building separated from the hotel casino by a narrow alley.

A sharp, explosive sound cracked across the backs of the cattle. The stranger turned toward it. There was another harsh pop and an arm motion by the man on the gray horse. The river of beef bent in the middle, veering away from the snapping whip. In that same pitched-off instant, the stranger saw that the near cowboy on the roan horse was out of position. The dirt road to the north lay open.

Pressed from behind by riders and from the side by the veering herd, a dozen cows bolted for it. The rest followed. Not ten feet away was the woman. She had her back to the street, completely unaware of the cattle rushing toward her.

"Look out!" the stranger shouted.

As the brunette glanced back, he took a step toward her, but his path was already blocked with brown hides. There was no way he could reach her on foot. She started to break for the corner building, then saw she wouldn't make it. Stopping, she turned and faced the onrushing cattle, tall and slim and straight. She lifted her quirt and brought it smartly down on the nose of the nearest steer. It swerved, creating a wedge of space. Wielding the quirt like a slashing sword, she forced the cattle to flow around her with a coolness the stranger would have applauded if there had been time.

But time was the enemy. Any second the crush of cattle could overwhelm her. The stranger looked around for help. The closest rider was the cowboy on the roan horse, his back to the woman, oblivious to her plight. In a flash the stranger was off the porch and catching at the horse's reins. Before the cowboy could offer a protest, the stranger grabbed a handful of shirt and pulled him out of the saddle. Catching hold of the saddle horn, the stranger swung onboard, pulled the roan around, and aimed for the woman, still valiantly lashing out to defend her ever diminishing space.

The roan needed little urging to plunge into the opening she had created. Bending low in the saddle, the stranger hooked an arm around her middle and swept her up. She immediately struck out at him with her quirt. "Let me go!"

Fighting to control his rearing mount, the stranger dodged the slashing quirt. "Hang on, dammit!" She went motionless for an instant, then grabbed hold. He dragged her fully onto the saddle and guided the roan to the side of the road.

Satisfied that the danger was over, he lowered her to the ground, then swung out of the saddle himself. He saw at once she wasn't as tall as he had thought. It was an illusion created by the way she held her head and by the soldier-straight line of her back. Her face was away from him, and her hat hung down her back, caught by the throat string around her neck. Dust coated her clothes and skin, but she seemed unharmed. "Are you all right?" he asked.

She turned on him, her eyes flashing fire. "Don't you dare pretend to be concerned! Those cattle were deliberately turned on me. If this is some new scare tactic, it didn't work. Do you hear?"

She was trembling. Her face was alive and beautiful in its rage, and he felt the edge of sexual awareness kick through him like the explosive heat of excellent whiskey. " 'O tiger's heart wrapped in a woman's hide.' " He murmured the apt quote from *Henry VI.*

"What?" She frowned, then shook off her momentary confusion. "Get on your horse and go tell DePard he failed."

His eyebrow shot up in idle curiosity. "Who is DePard?"

That stopped her. She glanced at the roan with the Diamond D brand on its hip, then back at him. "You don't work for DePard?"

"Is that who owns the horse? I never took the time to ask when I borrowed it." He gave the roan a slap on the rump, sending it trotting off.

Her eyes narrowed on him. "You must be new here."

"I landed in town about an hour ago."

She slowly nodded. "That explains it, then." She looked away and immediately stiffened when a trio of riders pulled up, led by the big-shouldered man on the steel-gray horse. The young kid was on the man's right, his boy-soft features streaked with dust and sweat. The third rider had a purple birthmark that covered most of his left cheek. He had not the size of the big man, but the impression was still one of lean toughness and sharp cunning.

But the man on the gray dominated the group. Past middle age and showing gray hair below his hat brim, he had all the earmarks of a large cattle owner, with such a man's accustomed sense of un-challenged authority. He had broad features and a thick mustache sprinkled with gray. The glitter of hatred in his eyes was almost tangible, and all of it was directed at the brunette. "You're a very lucky woman." Venom coated his voice.

"That galls you, doesn't it, DePard?" she shot back, fearless and defiant. "If you want to get rid of me, you'll have to do better than trying to run me down with a bunch of cattle."

The third rider surged forward. "You smart-mouthed little—"

As the stranger stepped forward to intercept the threat, the man called DePard issued an order that silenced the rider.

"You're smart to keep Sheehan on a short leash, DePard," the brunette said.

"Shut up," DePard snapped, then threw his glare at the stranger. "You're the one who took Jenkins's horse."

"It seemed the thing to do at the time." The stranger looked up at the man with calculated indifference.

"You must be new here."

"Does it matter?" Amusement edged the corners of his mouth.

"Not much. It just means you don't know what you're sticking your nose into."

"I thought I was sticking it into your face."

DePard was shocked into silence. The young kid took up the cudgel. "You better watch what you say, mister. You're talking to Duke DePard. He owns the Diamond D and half this town."

"Is that a fact?" the stranger drawled, unimpressed. "I don't know about the Diamond D, but from what I've seen of this town, it isn't something I'd brag about owning."

"Then clear out!" DePard roared the warning and dug his spurs into the gray, hauling back on the reins and spinning the gelding around. As one, the trio rode back toward the main herd.

The brunette examined the stranger with new interest. "You just made yourself an enemy," she warned. "DePard isn't going to forget this. And, believe me, he has a long memory."

"So do I."

A hint of a frown briefly marred the smoothness of her forehead. "Who are you?"

"The name's Kincade," he said after an instant's hesitation.

"Are you looking for work?"

He grinned and shook his head. "I'm not broke yet."

She gave him a rueful look and nodded. "When you are, try the Spur Ranch, north of town about thirty miles."

"Who should I ask for?" Kincade suddenly wanted a name to go with her face. Maybe because he had rescued her or because he admired her courage . . . or maybe because he was remembering how she had felt in his arms, the lightness of her body.

A hint of annoyance showed in her face. "Ask for the boss."

"Is that you or your husband?"

"I don't have a husband."

Women ranchers weren't uncommon, but the majority took over the role following the death of their husband. Assuming she was a widow, Kincade said, "I'm sorry."

"I'm not." Without another word she walked off.

He watched her a moment, curious and not wanting to be. Turning, he saw Starr Davis outside the Lucky Starr. She met his gaze, her expression faintly amused and wholly cynical. Unhurried, Kincade wandered back to join her.

"That was not a smart move," Starr remarked, yet there was a glint of admiration in the look she gave him.

"I gathered that." He nodded and glanced after the brunette. "Who is she?"

Starr looked down the street in time to see the woman enter the boot-and-saddlery shop. "She is trouble, in capital letters, for anyone fool enough to side with her against DePard."

"Why? What did she do?"

Her lips curled in a feline smile. "She killed his brother."

"What?" His gaze whipped back to her. "Was it an accident?"

"It was no accident. It was a deliberate act. DePard is convinced she shot Jeff in cold blood. Naturally, she claimed self-defense."

"Which was it?"

Starr laughed, a low and throaty chuckle. "You don't strike me as a fool. Take a look around. This town survives solely on the business DePard throws it. Believe me, cowboy, you don't disagree with a single thing he says. Whatever comes out of his mouth is gospel."

His mouth quirked, wryness tugging at a corner. "Something tells me you are a very smart lady."

"Smart enough to lick the hand that feeds me, not bite it."

"Are you his woman?"

Starr released another throaty laugh, rich with amusement. "He may think so, but I wear no man's brand, cowboy."

It was the second time within a handful of minutes that a woman had disavowed any ties. Kincade thought of the brunette again and that intriguing blend of beauty and bravery, pride and strength. It was a combination that could ignite a man's imagination—and his interest. Kincade acknowledged the flaring of his own.

Chapter II

A WHIP cracked as DePard rode by on his big gray horse, pushing the last of the herd through the intersection. The young kid rode beside him. He lifted a hand and flicked it in Starr's direction in a small wave. She waved back, her eyes soft, that cynical edge gone from her expression. "That's my son, Rick," she said to Kincade.

The herd moved out of town, but the dust continued to hang in the air. A lanky cowboy crossed the street and stepped onto the planked walk. He touched his hat to Starr, then looked at Kincade, a grin splitting his freckled face. "Looks like I pulled into town just in time to catch all the excitement. That was some piece of work you did getting that gal out of the path of those cattle."

"Thanks." Kincade cut short the praise and pushed out a hand. "The name's Kincade."

After an instant's hesitation the cowboy recovered and shook hands. "Mine's Walker, but most folks call me Rusty."

"For obvious reasons," Kincade said, glancing at the brick-red color of the cowboy's hair visible below his hat brim. Then he swung to include Starr. "Meet Starr Davis, owner and namesake of the Lucky Starr Hotel and Casino."

"Now, I am really pleased to meet you, ma'am. The air-conditioning in my truck quit on me, and as you can see"—Rusty Walker glanced at his sweat-ringed shirt—"I have a powerful need for a hot shower. If you've got an empty room in that hotel, I'll take it."

"They're all empty," she told him.

"I think I'll take one as well," Kincade spoke up.

"In that case, you can both follow me." Starr turned and led the way to the door.

AN OSCILLATING fan whirred from its corner perch on the counter, blowing around air that smelled of new leather and old polish. Eden Rossiter turned her face to the fan, savoring the rush of air and the illusion of coolness it produced.

A new hand-tooled saddle sat atop a wooden rack near the counter. More saddles, mostly used, hung from ropes fastened to the ceiling. An array of tack lined one wall of the shop. On the opposite wall, shelves of boots and shoes shared space with hooks holding leather chaps, rifle scabbards, and saddlebags.

Eden glanced beyond the grimy windowpanes at the street, her mind flashing to that moment on the road when the cattle boiled around her. If that stranger hadn't reached her when he did . . .

She took a deep, steadying breath to quell the sudden churning of her stomach and concentrated instead on her rescuer. She remembered his hard, beard-shadowed face and the deep bronzing of his skin. There had been a ridge of callus on his hands, and he had handled the horse with the skill of someone born in the saddle.

The stranger Kincade had cowboy written all over him, a member of that restless breed who jumped from ranch to ranch, following the drifter's circuit that laced northern Nevada and eastern Oregon and twisted into parts of Arizona, Montana, and Wyoming. Eden knew his kind well. Yet the feeling lingered that he was a cut above the others. DePard certainly hadn't intimidated him.

She was about to decide he didn't care about anything. Then she remembered the way he had looked at her with eyes that were too direct, disturbing in their intensity. Men had looked at her with woman-hungry eyes before. But this time she had felt a slow heat radiate through her, a heat that she had thought she had become immune to long ago. She was annoyed to discover she wasn't.

The sound of footsteps came from the back room. A stocky middle-aged woman came through the curtained doorway carrying a pair of old boots, resoled and polished to a high shine. "It was just as I thought. Your boots were still in back, but they are finished." Rosa Winters set the boots on the counter. "I'll fetch your bridle, and you'll be all set." She took down a bridle with a new leather throatstrap from one of the wall shelves and laid it on the counter, her dark eyes fastening on Eden. "I saw what happened out there. The man who rescued you—who was he?"

"Some stranger named Kincade."

"I knew it couldn't have been one of DePard's men, not if he wanted to keep his job." She gave a long sigh, heavy with despair. "Hatred is an evil sickness. Like a cancer, it spreads over time. It has been almost fourteen years since his brother, Jeff, died, and I have watched DePard's hatred for you grow year by year until he is eaten up with it. He will never rest until you are punished." She lifted a hand toward Eden in a beseeching gesture. "Sell your ranch, Eden. Go from here before he destroys you."

"I will not sell." The very idea was unthinkable. Spur had been the Rossiter home for four generations. The house she lived in had been built by her great-grandmother. Her roots were anchored deep in the desert soil. She would never willingly give up the ranch.

"You are a fool, Eden Rossiter." Rosa shook her head. "DePard is too powerful. No one can stand against him for long."

"People have been predicting my downfall for years. I'm still here." She dug some bills out of her jeans pocket. "How much do I owe you?"

"Twelve fifty." Rosa's expression was grim with disapproval. "You know it was DePard who made sure your permit wasn't renewed to graze cattle on government land, don't you?"

"I guessed it." Eden laid thirteen dollars on the counter and waited for her change.

"Now you have more cattle than your land can support, and you can't find a shipper to haul them to market. DePard told all the local companies that if they haul your cattle, they will never haul for him again." Rosa slipped the money into the cashbox under the counter and gave Eden two quarters in change. "People are saying that if you can't get your cattle to market, the grass on your land will be grazed to the roots within two months."

Eden reached for the bridle and boots. "They forgot to factor in my hay surplus." With it, Eden had calculated she had about three months. After that . . . Desperation clawed at the back of her throat. She fought it off, telling herself she would find a solution.

"I know someone who might haul your cattle," Rosa said.

"Who?"

"My brother-in-law hauls livestock in Oregon. I could speak to him for you."

"Does DePard know about him?"

"I doubt it. Jerry is just getting started." Rosa's expression sharpened in concern. "You can't tell anyone how you found out about Jerry. DePard owns this building—and most of the equipment."

"This will be strictly between you and me," Eden promised. "Tell your brother-in-law the sooner he can get here, the better."

"I'll call Friday morning and let you know what he says."

Eden left the shop and headed for her truck, parked on the town's main street. As she passed the Lucky Starr, she saw the stranger Kincade carrying a duffel bag into the building and instantly remembered the hard pressure of his arm around her. Blocking out the memory, she threw her boots and bridle onto the front seat of the ranch pickup, then climbed in and started up the truck.

The dirt road leading north from town ran straight for a distance, then swerved to angle across the undulating sage flats toward a gap in the craggy mountains to the west. Eden followed it. The windows of her truck were rolled down. A hot wind, spiced with the scent of sage, tunneled into the cab. Typically, Eden met no other vehicle as she drove through the vast emptiness of the high desert country. Out here, there were no emergency services. Help was invariably hours away—a fact Eden knew only too well.

Her eye was drawn to the rutted track that branched away from the dirt road and clawed its way up a mountain slope. Halfway to the top, it disappeared onto a wide volcanic bench, stippled with green. Hidden from view was a hot spring that bubbled to the surface and collected in a series of small rock pools. The site was a favorite haunt of teenagers out to chugalug a few beers or score with their steadies.

As Eden passed the spot where the track joined the dirt road, she tightened her grip on the steering wheel. From this point it was exactly seven miles to the ranch and more than twenty to town. The distances were forever etched in her memory.

If only she hadn't snuck out of the house that night fourteen years ago. . . . If only she hadn't agreed to meet Jeff. . . .

If only . . .

SHE drove as fast as she dared over the rough road, her breath coming in panicked sobs. Her hands, wet with blood, were slick on the steering wheel. Jeff DePard lay beside her, sprawled at an awkward angle. Blood soaked the front of his shirt and the compression bandage she had tied over the ugly bullet hole in his chest.

"Where's the turnoff to the ranch?" Her whispered words held a silent plea. Shaking all over, Eden probed the darkness beyond the reach of the truck's headlights. She had to get to the ranch. Her grandfather would know what to do. She looked down at Jeff, whispering tightly, "You can't die. Damn you, you can't."

BUT he had.

And before that night was over, she had been charged with first-degree murder. DePard had made certain of that. In his eyes she had caused the death of the brother he had raised like a son, and for that she deserved to be punished. Harshly.

During the three years of legal wrangling that preceded her trial, DePard spread the story that she had killed his brother in a jealous rage after she had caught him with another woman. When a jury in faraway Tonopah returned a verdict of not guilty, DePard was outraged over what he saw as a blatant miscarriage of justice. The grief and bitterness he felt had festered over time into full-blown hatred and a need for vengeance that had become a raging thirst.

Where would it all end? Eden wondered as she drove into the home yard of Spur Ranch.

Desert hills rose behind the site, forming a natural break against winter winds. A spring-fed stream meandered through it on its way to the sage prairie beyond. Summer heat had reduced its flow to a trickle, but no Rossiter had ever seen it go dry, a rare thing in desert country, where a constant water supply was a valuable commodity.

Bypassing the corrals and outbuildings, Eden headed for the hacienda-style house, a two-story affair roofed with corrugated iron, now rusted a deep reddish brown and shaded by century-old cottonwood trees. Against the green of the trees the thick adobe walls had the look of old parchment, faded and grainy with time. Wooden verandas stretched across the front of the house on both levels, and the dun of the desert ran all the way to its front steps. The house was simple and solid, built to last. For Eden it was the heart of Spur. She could not imagine ever leaving it.

An old stock dog, a blue heeler named Cassius, trotted out to meet the truck when Eden pulled up. He carried the scars from fights with coyotes and other varmints that dared to invade his territory. In size the dog wasn't much, weighing a scant fifty pounds, but he had the heart of David, ready to take on any Goliath.

"Hey, Cash, how are you doing?" Eden stepped out of the truck and reached for the boots and bridle.

The dog replied with an excited whine, then froze in a stance of alertness and pointed his ears at the screen door. It sprang open as Eden's older brother, Vince, charged out of the house, a look of concern in the handsome cast of his features.

"Am I glad to see you. Are you all right?" He caught her arms and made a worried inspection of her.

"I'm fine," she began, but Vince had already come to the same conclusion.

"Do you know how close you came to getting killed by those cattle?" he demanded, angry now.

"How did you find out about that?"

"I got a phone call a few minutes ago." He let go of her and stepped back, sweeping off his hat and running a hand through his thick dark hair. "I've been worried sick. How could you let something like that happen?"

"*I* didn't. It was DePard." Eden made that clear, then conceded, "I never dreamed he would try something like that in broad daylight."

"He's out to get you, Eden," Vince muttered, "and he isn't going to stop until he does."

"What should I do?" Eden demanded in exasperation. "Grovel at his feet and beg for mercy?"

"No. I want you to get out of here while you're still in one piece."

"I will never give up Spur."

"There is no reasoning with you." He turned and stalked off.

Suppressing a sigh, Eden headed for the house. This argument was an old one. Eden knew that if control of Spur had passed to Vince following their grandfather's death seven years ago, he would have sold it on the spot. Vince had never felt her attachment to the ranch. To him it was a source of cash, one he was eager to exploit.

The thick adobe walls kept the temperature inside several degrees cooler. Eden left the bridle and boots by the front door, then crossed the wood floor and entered the main room. The odor of old smoke drifted from the arched fireplace, wide enough to roast a whole steer in. Fat easy chairs filled the space in front of it, their cushions faded. Spur marks scarred the room's hardwood floor, and the area rug had a path worn into its design. It was the living room of a working ranch, yet for all its signs of use and abuse, the room had a sense of comfort that touched all who entered it.

Unconsciously Eden responded to it and slipped off her hat to let it swing from her fingers by the throatstrap, some of the tension leaving her. Her glance strayed to the antique oval-framed picture on the wall of a woman dressed in a long riding skirt, a wool jacket, a flat-crowned hat, and dusty boots. She wore a holstered gun belted around her slim hips, and held the reins of a tall, rangy horse.

Eden studied the photograph of her ancestor Kate Rossiter, the woman who came west as a bride of fifteen and eventually built Spur into a successful ranch with little help from her often absent husband. Gold, silver, copper—it hadn't mattered to Daniel Rossiter. With each new rumor of a strike, he had taken off, leaving Kate to run the place.

"I guess Vince takes after your Daniel—always chasing the dream of hitting it big," Eden murmured, a weary resignation in her voice. Vince was back, but like Kate, Eden didn't fool herself into believing he would stay. She was on her own against DePard.

A FORD Bronco led a small convoy of pickup trucks with stock trailers in tow over a graveled road. The vehicles slowed as they approached the Diamond D Ranch. Duke DePard sat in the Bronco's passenger seat, his gaze directed out the side window in a sightless stare. Forty-year-old Matt Sheehan was behind the wheel, the cow boss at the Diamond D for the last fifteen years, second in power only to the man beside him.

Thirteen-year-old Rick Davis rode in back, tired and sweaty, every muscle aching, unaccustomed to long hours in the saddle moving cattle from one section of the range to another. Yet at the same time he was filled with exhilaration. He kept reliving the experience, dwelling on the moments of high action, like the time a young steer had bolted and he had chased after it at full gallop, leaping over sagebrush and plunging into gullies. Rick was fairly bursting to recount those moments. Only the fear that he might sound to DePard like some dumb town kid held him silent. Duke DePard's opinion of him mattered more than anything else to Rick.

When the Bronco swung between the twin pillars of stacked rock that marked the ranch's entrance, DePard broke the silence. "Call ahead and let them know we're on our way in."

"Right." Sheehan picked up the radio mike.

Rick thought of the string of communication towers that linked the farthest reaches of the Diamond D Ranch, which stretched across two and a half million acres, a checkerboard of private holdings, government grazing and leased railroad land. It was that kind of forward thinking that made Rick look up to the older man. Duke DePard was quick to embrace modern technology. Computers tracked the ranch's income and expenses; airplanes reduced the number of man-hours spent in the saddle during roundups; satellite dishes kept him up to date on market trends.

At the same time DePard lived by a set of Old West codes. He demanded absolute loyalty and gave it, too. And he believed a man's family and his good name were to be defended against the smallest slight. Rick admired that about him, although it wasn't something he would admit to his friends.

Sheehan braked to a stop in front of the main house, a long, low, rambling structure built of wood, glass, and rock. Rick was a step slow climbing out of the Bronco, his sore muscles screaming in protest. DePard gave him a knowing look. "A little stiff, are you?" he observed, his mouth tightening in a smile of dry amusement.

"It's nothing." Rick feigned a shrug of macho indifference and did his damnedest to walk naturally when DePard and Sheehan headed for the front door.

"You did a good job today." DePard made the remark almost as an afterthought. As praise went, it was scant, but Rick Davis flushed with pleasure. Fatherless, he ached for a man's approval. It was Rick's secret fantasy that his mother would marry Duke DePard, a hope he cherished each time he saw them together. Rick had stopped asking about his natural father years ago. He never got a straight answer from his mother. He knew nothing about his father, not even his name. He had heard talk that he was Jeff DePard's bastard. But he was afraid to ask about it—afraid to find out it wasn't true. He wanted to be a DePard. This way he could believe he might be.

He followed the two men inside, past the sunken living room, to the corner den. DePard went directly to the built-in bar next to the stone fireplace. "How about a Coke, son?" He opened a small refrigerator.

"Coke will be fine, sir."

DePard set a cold can of Coke on the bar counter, then took two glasses from a back shelf and filled them with ice. Rick picked up the Coke can, popped the top, and took a long, deep swig from it, then wandered back to the room's center.

Sheehan saw him pause before a grouping of photographs on the wall. All showed the handsome face of Duke DePard's long-dead brother, Jeff, the tribal stamp of a DePard evident in his strong, square jaw and broad features. His eyes had a wicked glint, and his smile was reckless, irresistible. There was no doubt Jeff DePard had been a hell-raiser and a charmer, as well as a star athlete and straight-A student. Talk had been that Duke was grooming his little brother for a career in politics. Some had even made bets that Jeff DePard would one day be Nevada's youngest governor.

Idly Sheehan studied the photos on the wall. It had been years since he had been inside a church, but he couldn't shake the feeling that he was looking at a religious shrine. Only the prayer candles were missing.

Sheehan turned a speculating glance on Rick Davis. The rumor that he was Jeff DePard's son had been fueled by the interest Duke had taken in both the boy and his mother, Starr Davis. Sheehan looked for, but couldn't find, a physical resemblance to the De-Pards. The boy had his mother's angular features and pointy chin. Which didn't mean he wasn't Jeff's illegitimate offspring.

Ice clinked against the sides of the glass Duke DePard offered to Sheehan. He held a second one, filled with whiskey and water. As Sheehan lifted the whiskey drink in a silent toast, the doorbell rang. Below its strident sound came the familiar slip-slap of the house-keeper's thongs as she hurried across the foyer to answer it.

Rick's eyes rounded, staring in surprise, when Vince Rossiter charged into the den and headed straight for DePard. "You've gone too far, DePard," Vince declared, his body rigid with anger. "My sister nearly got killed this afternoon because of you."

At a signal from Duke, Sheehan took Rick by the arm and led him from the room, closing the door to the den behind them. Rick could no longer hear what was being said, only the murmur of voices punctuated by the sound of Rossiter's raised in anger. What was going on?

Chapter III

REVITALIZED by a three-hour nap and a hot shower, Kincade came down the steps and headed into the casino lounge.

Starr Davis smiled when she saw him. She wore a body-hugging black dress that flared about her legs as she walked toward him with a smooth, sinuous grace. "I was beginning to think you were going to spend the evening in your room alone," she said in greeting.

"Not hardly," Kincade responded, his glance drifting to the succession of buttons and loops that ran down the front of her dress.

"You shaved." Starr touched him because she wanted to, trailing her fingers across the smoothness of his cheek.

"I needed it." Along with the shower and nap, Kincade could have added, but didn't. "I intended to see if my truck was fixed, but I saw from my window a 'Closed' sign hanging on the door."

"Hoague usually locks up around five. He'll be in here later. You might as well sit down and have a drink. What can I get you?"

"A beer." Kincade sat down at a bar table, facing the doorway.

When Starr returned with his beer, the red-haired cowboy Rusty Walker strolled into the lounge, spotted Kincade, and wandered over. "Care if I join you?"

"Not at all." Kincade nodded at an empty chair.

"Thanks." Rusty sat down, then rubbed a hand over his stomach. "I need to put some food in this stomach of mine."

"The same goes for me," Kincade said.

Starr turned toward the bar. "Roy, bring these gentlemen some menus."

Roy came out from behind the bar, grumbling under his breath. He tossed a pair of plastic menus on the table. "We still ain't got breakfast," he announced, and walked off.

"Jolly fellow," Kincade murmured, then looked up when the door opened and Hoague Miller propelled his ponderous bulk into the lounge. The smile on his face fled the instant he noticed Kincade.

"Did you get the radiator hose fixed on my truck?"

"Yeah, it's fixed." Hoague's expression was cold. "But the station's closed for the day. You can come by around seven in the morning and settle up what you owe."

Something in the man's body language suggested he expected an argument from Kincade, but Kincade didn't give him one. There was a hint of swagger to Hoague Miller's lumbrous gait when he joined a handful of his cronies at the bar. All smiled their approval at the way Hoague had handled the stranger. Totally indifferent to them, Kincade picked up his menu.

An hour later, finished with his meal, Kincade settled back in his chair, drew a cigar from his shirt pocket, and lit it. The clump of booted feet heralded the arrival of more customers. Kincade's attention swung to inspect the trio, centering first on the teenaged boy, who quickly distanced himself from the others.

"Hey, Mom, I'm back," he said to Starr Davis as she came forward to welcome the group.

She looked at her son with a mother's pride. Well on his way to becoming a strapping young man, he topped her by a good two inches. Starr reached up and brushed an imaginary strand of hair off his temple, needing an excuse to touch him. This was her child. She wanted the best for him, no matter the cost. She looked up at the other two men, directing a smile at Duke DePard.

In a western-cut suit, with his silver hair tamed into order beneath a black hat, DePard looked every inch a range lord. "Your son has worked up a man's appetite, Starr."

"Have *you?*" The smoke in her voice and the smolder in her eyes injected a whole new meaning to the phrase.

DePard released a low chuckle. "I don't recall a time when my appetite hasn't been healthy," he declared with a trace of smugness.

"Good." Her smile lengthened in silent promise before she turned back to her son. "Why don't you run your things up to your room, Rick?" She waved a hand at the duffel bag he carried, then hooked an arm around DePard's and clutched it with both hands the way a lover would. "I have our table all set."

Starr didn't include, either by look or gesture, the foreman of the Diamond D, who hovered nearby like some malevolent shadow. DePard, however, showed no such inclination as he glanced at the man. "You'll join us, Sheehan," he stated, giving no one an option.

But Sheehan had spotted the stranger. He pointed Kincade out to DePard with a nod of his head. DePard turned, his expression hardening. He flicked a censorious glance at Starr. "You should be more particular about whom you serve."

She made a quick, nervous attempt to soothe him. "Now, Duke—" she began.

But he pulled his arm free of her and walked to the stranger's table. A tense silence gripped the room. "How come you're still in town?" DePard challenged.

Unmoved, Kincade released a puff of cigar smoke. "My pickup had a busted radiator hose. I had to get it fixed." He gave DePard an amused stare. "It should be ready in the morning."

DePard swung about. Before his searching gaze located Hoague Miller, Hoague was on his feet. He darted an anxious glance at DePard and pawed in the side pocket of his coveralls. "Fixed that hose this afternoon, Mr. DePard. Got his keys right here." He produced them from his pocket and pushed them onto the table in front of Kincade. "Your truck's outside the garage. Pick it up anytime."

DePard fixed another hostile look on Kincade. "There. Now you have no more reason to stay."

Amusement still tugged at the corners of Kincade's mouth. "I've already paid for a night's lodging here. I think I'll use it."

The room hummed with shocked murmurs. No one defied De-Pard. Conscious of his audience, DePard showed only a rigid composure. "I wouldn't stay where I wasn't welcome," he warned.

"No, you probably wouldn't," Kincade agreed in a lazy drawl that drew even more wide-eyed looks.

DePard's temper flared, hot and bitter. He fired a glance at the red-haired cowboy sitting at the stranger's table. "You with him?"

Rusty pulled back with a startled look. "Me?"

"Rusty here had the misfortune of arriving in town about the same time I did," Kincade inserted. "I guess you could say we're two strangers passing the time away with some idle talk."

Starr came up and laid a soothing hand on DePard's arm, feeling the rigid contraction of his muscles. "Misfortune is the perfect word to describe all this, Duke," she said, keeping her voice husky and warm. "Kincade had barely been in town an hour when you drove your cattle through. He couldn't know the true situation."

To her relief DePard listened. "I suppose ignorance is an excuse of sorts."

"That's real big of you," Kincade murmured with mock sincerity, and raised the cigar to his lips, holding it between his teeth.

DePard studied him with sharpening eyes. "You don't look like a fool, Kincade. But you talk like one. For now, I'll overlook it." De-Pard shifted slightly, sure of himself again. "If you're looking for work, come out to the Diamond D tomorrow and we'll hire you on."

Kincade lowered the cigar. "Isn't that curious? Do you know, that is the second job offer I've had today."

"What outfit offered you work?" DePard frowned in anger, already guessing the answer.

"Spur," Kincade replied with a faint, slow smile.

"You'll work for the Diamond D, or you'll work for no one." De-Pard snapped the threat. "Make no mistake about that."

"I hear you talking." Kincade tapped the ash from his cigar.

DePard looked at him for a long, measuring second, then nodded. "You will," he stated, then turned and walked straight to the table he always occupied and sat down.

Sheehan pulled out the chair next to him. "You want me to do something about that stranger's smart mouth, Mr. DePard?" His voice was couched low.

DePard weighed his options. If he failed to come down hard on the stranger for this small show of defiance, would the locals see it as a sign of weakness? Could it give one of them the idea he could act against DePard's wishes with impunity? If one did, DePard would have no choice but to deal harshly with that individual. Which would create ill will among the rest over an injury to one of their own. However, if he made an example of the stranger, the reaction would likely be a general nodding of heads and an I-could-have-told-him-something-like-that-was-going-to-happen attitude.

DePard glanced sideways at his foreman. "Rough him up some, but make sure he's still able to travel. I want him out of town by morning. And do it outside," DePard added. "Not in here."

"Right." Sheehan got up from the table with an expression of surly pleasure and headed for the back hall, where the rest rooms and public telephones were located.

AROUND nine o'clock a man stopped by Kincade's table. "Are you the one who calls himself Kincade?"

"I am," Kincade admitted with a slight frown.

"There's a guy wants to see you. He's waiting outside."

"What does he want?"

"Hey, I'm just the message boy," the man declared with a careless grin, and moved on.

A faint chill fiddled through Kincade's nerves. It was the way a sense of trouble always came to him. But curiosity got the better of him. He left the table and headed for the front door.

Outside, he swept his gaze over the town's main street. Here and there a light glowed from a storefront window. Beyond, night closed around the town, and there was a waiting stillness. Nothing stirred.

"Kincade." The furtive whisper came from his right.

Turning, Kincade studied the solid darkness beneath the roofed walkway. "Step out where I can see you."

A plank creaked as the silhouette of a man in a rolled-brim hat emerged from the shadows. Unable to see the man's face, Kincade hesitated. "Who are you?"

"Not so loud," the man hissed, and motioned for Kincade to come closer as he retreated to blend again with the shadows.

More curious now than wary, Kincade followed the man. "What did you want to see me about?"

The words were barely out of his mouth when two figures sprang at him from the darkness, seizing his arms. Before he could shake loose, a fist slammed into his midsection, doubling him over. Again and again blows hammered his face, ribs, and stomach. There was a roaring in his ears as pain dulled his senses. At last his legs buckled, and he sank to his knees.

"Stand him up," a voice said.

The hands hauled him upright and shoved him against the wall of the building. Kincade tried to brace himself for the next blow. When it failed to come, he forced his eyes to open.

"You're not such a tough guy anymore, are you?"

Kincade recognized the jeering voice. DePard's foreman. The one with the large birthmark on his face. The man loomed closer. "Stay away from the Rossiter woman. Do you hear?"

"Rossiter?" Kincade repeated the name, grabbing at it and struggling now to concentrate. "Is that—"

His jaw and chin were seized in a talon grip that cracked his head back against the building. Color exploded behind his eyes.

"Don't play dumb with me, Kincade. It won't work," the foreman snarled. "Now hear me and hear me good. Come morning, you better be long gone from this town."

Light from an open door suddenly flooded the walkway as a man stepped out of the Lucky Starr. In one glance he took in the scene and called out a sharp "Hey, what's going on?" He rushed forward.

The foreman swung to block the red-haired cowboy's advance. "You're reading this all wrong, mister," he taunted smoothly. "Your buddy here must have had too much to drink. He fell and banged himself up. We were just helping him to his feet, weren't we, boys?"

The two men backed up his claim.

"Yeah, and coyotes guard sheep, too," Rusty scoffed. "I think you've *helped* him enough. I'll take over now."

"You heard him, boys," Sheehan said, smiling his contempt. "Give him his friend."

With a hard yank the men jerked Kincade away from the wall and pushed him straight at Rusty. Rusty staggered back under his weight but managed to keep them both upright. Sheehan laughed softly and strolled on by, followed by his snickering cohorts.

BY THE time Kincade reentered the Lucky Starr, pain jabbed him in a dozen different areas. He walked slightly hunched forward, a hand clamped on Rusty's shoulder for support.

Intent on reaching the staircase to his room, he never saw where Starr came from. One moment there was nothing between him and the stairs; the next, she was in his path. She made a quick visual inspection of him, her lips tightening their line.

Kincade tried to smile and winced, discovering a cut along the inside of his mouth. He saw movement with his peripheral vision. He swung his head toward it. A handful of bar patrons had gravitated closer for a better look. DePard was in the forefront, coldly satisfied with what he saw. Kincade saw the Diamond D foreman a discreet distance behind DePard. "You might hear two different stories. If you did," Kincade said to Starr, "DePard's man would tell you I had too much to drink and fell."

"Did you?" The deadly soft challenge came from DePard.

Kincade opened his mouth to reply, but it required too much effort. He swayed a little.

Starr intervened. "It doesn't matter." She motioned to Rusty. "Take him up to his room." Starr pivoted, her skirt flaring, her voice lifting. "Roy, bring me the first-aid kit from behind the bar. The rest of you, go back to your drinks. The excitement's over." She treated DePard to a cool, critical look. "Was that necessary?"

"It was," he stated as Roy arrived with the first-aid kit. "Make certain he's fit to travel."

"I will." With the kit in hand, she climbed the stairs.

The second-floor room measured a scant eight by ten, with most of that space taken up by an old iron bed. Kincade sat on the edge of the bed, his muscles slack and his head tipped down while Starr examined the egg-size knot on the back of his head.

"The skin isn't broken," she said, drawing back.

Kincade reached up to check it himself and sucked in a wincing breath when he touched a tender spot. Rusty saw it and grimaced in empathy. "They didn't waste any time banging you around," he said. "You weren't gone more than a couple minutes."

"He mentioned a name," Kincade said. "It sounded like Rossiter."

"Rossiter?" Rusty echoed.

"Eden Rossiter." Starr supplied the rest of the name. "She's the woman you foolishly rescued today."

"The notorious owner of Spur, the one who killed DePard's brother," Kincade recalled in a dead-flat voice.

"Killed his brother?" Rusty repeated. "Are you kidding?"

"Not hardly." Starr gave him an amused look. "She shot Jeff out of jealousy when she learned he was seeing someone else."

"You make it sound like she killed him in cold blood." Rusty frowned. "If she murdered him, why isn't she in prison?"

"Her grandfather Jed Rossiter gets the credit for that. A ranch hand working for him saw Jed slap the hell out of Eden when he found out she shot the boy. Before the sheriff got there, he ripped her clothes and staged it to look like Jeff assaulted her. Then he hired one of the best criminal lawyers in Nevada. He not only stalled the trial for three years, he also convinced the judge that it would be impossible to get an impartial jury here. The trial was moved to Tonopah. By then she had her story down pat."

"There were no witnesses to the shooting?" Kincade asked.

"None," Starr replied. "As often happens with a jury, the fact that the DePards owned one of the largest ranches in Nevada and that Jeff was extremely handsome and popular went against him. The jury preferred to believe the worst of someone who, as the saying goes, had everything. It didn't matter to them that Jeff could have had his pick of women, he didn't have to force himself on anyone."

"Where's her grandfather now?" Kincade wondered.

"He died a few years back and left control of the ranch to Eden." Starr reached into the first-aid kit. "That cut on your cheek could use a bandage."

"It's okay." Kincade waved off the suggestion.

Starr took an antiseptic wipe from the kit. "If you don't want a bandage, at least let me clean it."

She curved a finger under his chin to tilt his head up. Kincade obeyed the pressure, his gaze coming up to examine her face. "Why are you doing this?" he asked. "DePard isn't going to like it that you're up here tending to my wounds."

Her mouth lengthened in an ironic smile as she dabbed gently at the trickle of dried blood on his cheek. "Maybe DePard sent me."

"To make sure his message was hammered home, I suppose," Kincade guessed.

"And what do I tell him?" Despite the lazy smile on her lips, her eyes were sharp and watchful.

"Tell him I got his message, that come morning, I'll be checking out and looking at Friendly in my rearview mirror."

Starr nodded. "I'll tell him. I'm almost sorry you'll be leaving, but it's best." Her eyes softened. "Take care of yourself, Kincade."

Rusty opened the door for her. Starr walked out, leaving a trace of her cologne in the air. As soon as she left, Rusty turned an amused look on Kincade. "So you're leaving in the morning, are you?" he said, not buying a word of it.

"First thing." Kincade nodded, a smile forming. "Eden Rossiter has a job waiting for me at Spur."

Chapter IV

DIRT fanned out behind the speeding pickup in a long tan plume. In all directions there was nothing but wide-open emptiness, dotted with clumps of sagebrush. Kincade glanced at the odometer. He should be coming to the ranch turnoff any time now. A small wooden sign on the last cross fence had read SPUR RANCH, J. ROSSITER.

He was watching for it and still almost missed it. The lane was little more than a pair of ruts that swung up a low hillock on his right. Braking, Kincade swung the wheel, and the pickup bounced onto the track, jolting his battered ribs despite the Ace bandage that girdled them.

The road snaked in and around a succession of foothills, then made a final swing into a shallow canyon, walled on three sides by long, gentle slopes. A stand of cottonwood trees made a splash of green at the head of the canyon. Kincade headed for the two-story adobe house nestled among them. An old cow dog bounded from its shade, hackles raised as it barked an alarm.

Kincade stopped in front of the house and climbed out of the cab. The dog stood between him and the house, growling a warning. Kincade noticed the scars on its coat and chose not to test the old dog's mettle. "Hello! Anyone home?" he called to the house.

There was no answer. The rumble of a tractor came from somewhere in the distance. The old blue heeler swung its head toward the east, then faced Kincade again, baring its long yellowed teeth.

"Is that where they are, fella?" Kincade turned, as the dog had, to locate the tractor.

A rough track curved from the house toward a set of holding pens with a loading chute. Beyond the pens the gold of a hayfield gleamed in the morning sunlight. An old tractor chugged into view, pulling a flat rack loaded with a dozen square bales.

Kincade crawled back into his truck and headed for the hayfield. Ahead, the tractor slowed, and two men hopped off the wagon and began tossing hay bales onto it for a third person to stack. Kincade parked at the edge of the field and stepped out of the truck. The sun was in his face, and the smell of cured hay mingled with the odor of dust and sage.

The driver of the tractor saw Kincade first and hollered something to the others, his words lost under the growling of the tractor. A figure appeared from behind the rack's growing stack of bales. It was Eden Rossiter. She had on a black tank top that showed the ripeness of her figure. A hat shaded her eyes, but Kincade knew the instant she saw him. It was like a leap of something electric between them.

The connection was broken when she turned and signaled to the driver to stop, then issued an order to one of the men tossing bales. He nodded and climbed onto the wagon. She passed the hay hooks to him, then jumped to the ground and proceeded toward Kincade.

Kincade met her halfway and touched a finger to his hat. "I'm looking for the boss."

"You found me." She inspected his bruised jaw, the cut on his cheekbone. "I trust you landed a few punches of your own," she remarked as she stripped off her leather work gloves.

"Not a one. It's hard to hit back when two men are holding you."

"DePard," she guessed with sudden grimness.

"His foreman."

"Same thing." She shrugged off the minor discrepancy. "Is that job offer of yours still open?"

"Why would you want it now?"

"Because DePard ordered me not to work for Spur. Naturally, that's just what I want to do. Call it a character flaw." It was Kincade's turn to shrug. "Do I have the job?"

"You're hired." Eden stepped forward to shake on it. His calloused hand engulfed hers. She felt a little involuntary jolt of something she would neither name nor acknowledge, and pulled her hand free, thumbing it toward the field. "Go start pitching bales."

TOSSING forty-pound bales awakened every sore muscle Kincade had. When a halt was called at noon, he was ready for a break. He climbed onto the rack and rode it as far as his pickup. He jumped to the ground, and Eden Rossiter motioned to one of the other ranch hands. "Go with Kincade, Al. Show him where to eat."

A short, stocky cowboy who had passed his prime several years ago hopped off the wagon. A tired smile rearranged the deep lines in his ruddy face. "Your truck is bound to offer a smoother ride for these old bones of mine than that hayrack," he declared.

"I hear you," Kincade replied, and struggled to ignore his own aches as he pulled himself into his truck.

The cowboy crawled in the passenger side. "I remember when I could work from dawn to dusk with never a break. Now they can't come often enough." He glanced at Kincade. "The name's Al Bender."

"Mine's Kincade." He started up the truck.

Al Bender ran an inspecting eye over him. "You ain't worked around these parts before, have you, Kincade?"

"First time."

"I thought so." He motioned for Kincade to drive straight ahead. "The cook shack is that way."

The ranch kitchen was a small one-story building built of adobe, like the others. Flies beat at the screen door. Inside, a radio blared a Willie Nelson song about Pancho and Lefty. Kincade parked the pickup in front and climbed out. Al pulled open the screen door and walked in. Kincade followed, his stomach rumbling as he inhaled the yeasty aroma of freshly baked bread.

Al walked past the long table, flanked by wooden benches, to the kitchen area. Over his shoulder Kincade glimpsed an old woman with straggly gray hair standing with her back to them. Al walked up to the woman, reached past her, and turned down the radio. The woman spun to face him, brandishing a long, serrated bread knife.

"What're you doing sneaking up on a body like that?" The voice was deeply pitched and rough. Kincade had his first clear look at the cook's profile and the gray stubble of a beard on his face—and revised his first impression. This was a man, not a woman.

"That was a damn fine thing to do," the cook complained to Al. "I could have killed you with my knife."

"If you didn't play that radio so loud, you would have heard me," Al countered. "I hope you fixed plenty of food. The boss hired a new man." Al waved a hand at Kincade. "His name's Kincade. And this character, believe it or not, is the cook. His real name is Frederick Daniels, but we call him Wild Jack. He claims his grandfather was a Sioux war chief. There's about as much chance of that as there is of me being related to the pope."

The old cook turned toward Kincade, a gleam lighting his eyes. "You bring any whiskey with you maybe?"

Kincade shook his head. "Sorry."

The cook grunted his disappointment. "All this dust gives me a bad cough," he said, then proceeded to force a cough to prove his claim. "You got any cough syrup maybe?"

"Sorry."

"Maybe some mouthwash to kill germs?"

"Nope," Kincade replied, seeing the connection.

"Damn fine shame," the cook mumbled, and shoved his knife onto the counter, turning away. On bowed and spindly legs he walked to a cupboard by the range top and opened a door, revealing a store of condiments and spices. Gnarled fingers closed around a tall, narrow bottle of vanilla. A quick twist, and the lid was off. In three long gulps the cook drained the bottle. He squinched his face up, shuddered, then released a gusty sigh. "Much better." He tossed the empty bottle into a dented metal trash can near Kincade.

Kincade heard the clinking of glass hitting more glass and peered into the trash can. Along with the one Wild Jack had just thrown in, there were two more empty bottles of vanilla extract. Kincade looked at Al, then nodded to the wastebin. "Your cook is guzzling vanilla."

"When you're desperate for booze, you'll drink anything, I guess," Al said. "At least with the vanilla he can still function. If Wild Jack gets his hands on a bottle of whiskey, he goes off on a binge that lasts for days." The cook walked by with a basket of homemade bread. Al snatched a slice and bit into it. "He's a crazy old coot, but he can cook," he said between chews.

The screen door opened, its creaking hinges heralding the arrival of the rest of the ranch hands. The youngest of the group, a tall, skinny kid, spotted Kincade and said, "The boss said you're to come to the house after you get done eating. You need to fill out some forms if you wanna get paid, so you better not forget."

"I won't." Kincade smiled to himself and joined the others, stepping over the long bench to take a seat at the table.

A FOOTPATH wound through the cottonwoods, linking the outbuildings with the main house. Kincade moved along the path, a toothpick between his teeth, and his stomach full after a satisfying meal of country-fried steak and mashed potatoes.

Approaching the house, he caught the sound of voices raised in anger. He recognized Eden Rossiter's with no difficulty. But it was the second voice, a man's, that he focused on, his stride quickening, a feeling of urgency gripping him.

The footpath stopped at the corner of the wooden veranda. Eden Rossiter stood in the veranda's shade, arguing with a man in a wine-red shirt. The old cow dog sat at her feet. It growled to warn her of Kincade's approach, but she paid no attention. "The answer is no," she stated in a voice that vibrated with anger. "It has always been. And it always will be."

"Don't be a fool," the man erupted. When she started to turn away, he grabbed her arm. "You can't win. You—"

Kincade cut him off. "What's the problem here?" The question was addressed to Eden Rossiter, but Kincade had eyes only for the man in the wine-red shirt.

He was five ten, with wide shoulders that tapered to a slim waist and hips. Dark hair curled from under his hat brim, and a dark mole marked his left cheek. He was good-looking in that smooth, pretty-boy way some women liked. But the dark eyes he turned on Kincade were angry. "This is private. Do you mind?" he snapped.

"My mother told me I never minded when I was a kid. Seems a bit late to start now," Kincade replied.

Eden started to tell Kincade that his help wasn't required, but the words died on her lips when she saw the look on his face. All expression was channeled into his eyes, turning their blue color into something cold and deadly. He held her brother's eyes as he would have gripped a man's shoulders with his hands.

"I think you better let the lady go!"

Vince released a laugh of disgust, but he let go of her arm. "Who is this guy, Eden?"

"He's the new man I hired."

"Well, tell him to get lost."

"Why don't *you* tell me?" The challenge came softly, but it carried no less threat.

Vince drew back, his gaze narrowing to take a closer look at Kincade. "Have we met somewhere?"

Kincade gave a small shake of his head. "Maybe I look like somebody you know."

"Maybe." He stared at Kincade an instant longer, then turned away. "The hell with it. I'm going to town." He stalked off, heading for a blue-and-white Ford pickup, waxed to a high shine. A second later the engine roared to life and the tires spun.

When the pickup pulled away, the tension that had bunched Kincade's muscles began to ease. He sensed Eden's gaze on him and turned to meet it.

"Don't tell me that guy works for you?" Kincade studied her face, noting the mingling of small delicate bones and firm muscles. Without a doubt she was a beautiful woman.

"Vince?" There was a faint shrug of her shoulders. "He comes and goes as he pleases."

"Vince—is that his name?"

"Yes. Vince Rossiter. He's my brother." Eden saw him draw back in obvious surprise.

Kincade flashed her a quick, guilty grin that was potent and disarming. "It looks like I butted into a family squabble. I hope it wasn't about anything serious."

"He wants me to sell the ranch," she replied, and was instantly irritated at herself for telling Kincade that.

"And you don't," he guessed.

"I don't."

"Do you and your brother own the ranch together?"

"In a way, yes. But make no mistake. I have sole authority here." With that she turned on her heel and headed for the door. "Come inside and fill out those payroll forms."

Kincade followed Eden into the main living area of the house. She headed straight for an old rolltop desk, which sat in a corner alcove. Kincade watched as she swept her hat off, then reached back to pull out the confining rubber band, shaking her hair loose with a toss of her head. Her dark hair fell in glossy waves onto her back. She picked up some papers from the desktop's cluttered surface, then searched through the pigeonholes for a pen. "If you would fill out these forms . . ." She handed the pen and papers to Kincade.

He took them and sat down in a big easy chair. After scanning the first sheet, he picked up the thin volume of poetry Eden had left on the coffee table. "Is it all right if I use this to write on?"

"Of course." Eden sat down at the desk.

"Robert Frost." Kincade identified the author of the well-thumbed book. "He was my sister's favorite poet."

Eden made a noncommittal sound, acknowledging his remark, and began sorting through yesterday's mail. The last thing she wanted was a discussion with Kincade about his sister or the interest they shared in the works of Robert Frost. To her relief Kincade didn't pursue the subject.

In short order he completed the forms and walked back to the desk. "Here you go," he said. In the next breath he asked, "Who is the woman in the picture?"

When Eden looked up, she saw his attention was directed at the framed photograph of Kate Rossiter on the wall. "My great-grandmother Kate Rossiter. She built Spur—virtually single-handedly."

A note of pride had crept into her voice, and there was a softness in her expression that Kincade hadn't seen before. "What about her husband? Or was she a widow?"

"No. Most of the time he was off prospecting somewhere, chasing his dream of a big strike."

"Shakespeare called it 'saint-seducing gold,' " Kincade remembered. "Gold fever claimed many a victim back in the Old West."

"It still does today, only in different ways."

Kincade had a strong suspicion she was referring to her brother. He turned back to the photograph of the ranch's matriarch. "Your great-grandmother wore that gun like she knew how to use it."

"From all accounts she did."

His glance traveled over the woman in the picture. "It's clear you take after her."

Eden came to her feet, bristling with challenge. "Why? Because I shot someone?"

"Actually"—Kincade pushed his hat to the back of his head, a rueful smile edging his mouth—"I was talking about the physical resemblance: the dark hair and eyes, the hint of fine bones, the proud way you carry yourself."

Eden looked away, color rising in her cheeks. "My mistake," she said. "I thought you were referring to . . . something else."

"I heard about the shooting," Kincade admitted. "I also heard the jury acquitted you of any wrongdoing."

"That's right. They did." She looked up, her eyes cool with challenge. "Is that a problem for you?"

"Not a bit." He swung his glance back to the framed photographs, this time his attention focusing on the second one. It pictured a man in his fifties, with hard features chiseled in stern lines. "The man—is he Kate's husband?"

"Her son and my grandfather Jed Rossiter."

"I take it both your parents are dead."

"My mother died when I was four." Eden focused her eyes on the payroll forms to make certain all the information had been filled out. "After her funeral my father brought Vince and me here. He had a job that kept him on the road." She didn't tell Kincade that her father had left and never come back. For a long time Eden had thought that if she was a good girl and minded her grandfather, her father would return. But he didn't. "He was killed in a car crash in Nebraska shortly after I turned sixteen."

"So you were raised by your grandfather?"

Eden nodded. "He was a good man."

"He looks a bit on the stern side," Kincade remarked.

Eden chose not to reply. In some respects her grandfather had been a hard taskmaster, a strong believer in work and discipline, although Vince had suffered more from that side of him than she had. She had always known that behind his gruffness, her grandfather had a loving heart. But that wasn't something she cared to discuss with a stranger. She let the silence build between them, conscious of his gaze traveling over her.

"You have beautiful hair," he murmured unexpectedly.

A breath later Eden felt his fingers tangling with the ends of it. She went stone-still. A dozen different emotions ripped through her like leaves in a storm, every nerve jumping to life.

"I've never been able to resist a woman with long hair."

Regaining control, Eden turned a withering look on him. "Really? I have never found anything about a man I *couldn't* resist." To her irritation he looked more amused than repentant. "If you are wise, Kincade, you will remember I'm the boss—and forget I'm a woman."

"*That,* Miss Rossiter, would be impossible."

"Try," she snapped, and turned back to his papers. "The pay is six hundred a month, plus room and board, and a bonus if you're still here after a year." She doubted he would be—ranch hands seldom were. She shuffled through his forms to a section he had failed to fill out. "I need the name and phone number of a relative to contact in the event of an accident or emergency."

"I have no family left."

Eden looked up in surprise. It was as if a shutter had come down, closing all expression from his face. "Your parents are dead," she guessed, then remembered. "You mentioned your sister. What about her? Is she dead, too?"

He nodded. "Some time ago."

"What about a friend?"

"I said there's no one. As far as I'm concerned, you can write your own name in there," he said.

"All right." A little uncertain, Eden set the forms aside and glanced at the wall clock. "The boys should be at the barn now, unloading the hay. It's time we joined them."

Outside, they set off along the trail to the barn, the old cow dog trotting alongside Eden. Kincade gazed at the desert hills rising in the distance. "How much land do you have?" he asked.

"All in all, about seventy thousand acres."

"How much of that is federal?"

"None. We lost our grazing permit," she told him, then added with wry cynicism, "DePard has low friends in high places."

Kincade chuckled, finding her sense of humor unexpected. But her assessment of DePard matched his own. "Somehow that doesn't surprise me. From the little I saw, I'd say the man is out to get you." He glanced sideways to study her reaction.

"I know," she replied calmly.

"Is that why your brother wants you to sell?"

"That's one of his reasons."

"And the other?" he prompted.

"Money. According to the terms of the will, Vince is entitled to a share of any profits. But I'm not selling." As they approached the barn, she began issuing orders to the men gathered around the hayrack. "Connors and Hart, get those bales unloaded and stacked. Deke, give them a hand. Al, I want you and Kincade to head back to the field and pick up the rest of the bales."

As soon as the rack was empty, Al Bender climbed into the tractor seat. Kincade stood beside him, braced against the fender, as Al fired up the tractor and headed back to the field. "One thing you can say about the boss," Al declared. "She works as hard as the next man."

"I don't think the same can be said for her brother."

Al snorted in disgust. "Talk about someone who's completely worthless. He only shows up around here when he wants money, which is most of the time."

"What does he do with his money?"

"Gambles most of it away. Believe me, with Vince for a brother and DePard for an enemy, she hasn't got a chance of making it."

"Then how come you're working for her?"

"It's a job. At my age they're hard to come by." Al gave him a sidelong study. "How come you hired on?"

Kincade smiled. "Maybe I wanted to even the odds."

Al looked at him like he was crazy.

Chapter V

WHEN the sun rose Friday, a bank of low clouds blackened the sky to the west. It rolled slowly toward Spur, heavy with the promise of drought-breaking rain. By the time the morning chores were finished, clouds had blotted out the sky.

Eden headed back to the house, the old cow dog trotting at her side. "It looks like rain, Cassius," she said. "Let's hope so." The dog wagged its tail in seemingly vigorous agreement. Eden laughed. "Sometimes I think you understand everything I say, Cassius."

When she opened the front door, the dog slipped in ahead of her and went straight to the kitchen, flopping on the rug in front of the sink. Eden poured herself a cup of coffee and carried it to the open window. She watched as the first fat drop of rain pelted the dusty ground. Another fell, and another. Then the rain poured down, falling in straight crystal filaments.

Relief washed over her. As long as this rain kept up, there would be no outside work, which meant she wouldn't have to come up with a reason to stay around the house to wait for the call from Rosa Winters. Eden sent up a silent prayer that Rosa's brother-in-law would agree to transport her cattle to market. She glanced at the wall phone, wishing it would ring. Instead she heard Vince clumping down the stairs. Eden stiffened, the memory of the angry words they had exchanged the previous day rushing back.

He came into the kitchen. "Is it raining outside?"

"Yes." She took a sip of her coffee and continued to face the window. "There's some coffee in the pot if you want a cup."

"No, thanks. It may be your idea of fun to sit around the kitchen and listen to the rain, but it isn't mine."

His scorn set her teeth on edge. Silently counting to ten, she turned from the window. "I suppose you're going into town again."

"Well, I'm sure not going to stick around here," Vince mocked, then hesitated, regret flickering through his expression. "Look, why don't you come with me? We could drive into Winnemucca, grab a bite of lunch."

She shook her head. "I have a bunch of bookwork piled up."

"There's always something, isn't there?" Vince glared, his temper boiling again. "Can't you see this place has—"

"Stop it, Vince," Eden broke in. "I don't want to get into another fight with you. If you're going, go. But don't say another word about selling this ranch."

"You're as muleheaded as the old man. Nobody can reason with you," he fired back. "Forget it. I'm out of here."

Eden heard the front door slam. At the same instant the phone rang. Moving quickly, she grabbed it. "Spur Ranch."

It was Rosa Winters. "I spoke to my brother-in-law," she told Eden. "He will haul your cattle. He can have his trucks at your place Tuesday morning at nine o'clock if that is good?"

"It's perfect."

"I will tell him. Remember— Someone has come into the shop. I must go." The line went dead.

Eden returned the receiver to its hook and sank onto the kitchen chair, laughing and crying softly at the same time. The old cow dog padded over to her and pushed its graying muzzle under her hand. Eden rubbed the top of the dog's head. "We did it, Cassius," she declared. "DePard isn't going to get the best of us this time."

IT RAINED off and on for most of the morning. After the first heavy shower the rest were light drizzles. Around two o'clock Eden finished the last of the bookwork.

She had settled in a lawn chair on the veranda, enjoying a rare quiet moment, when she saw a rider coming in. The man sat loose in the saddle, a high-crowned hat on his head. Sunlight glinted off a pair of round steel-rimmed glasses. It was her cow boss, Bob Waters, a full-blooded Paiute. Eden rose to meet him.

He swung his mount broadside as he neared her. "The windmill at Flat Rock is busted." He broke the news without expression, dust dulling the jet black of his hair. "Shaft's broken. There's maybe six inches of water in the tank."

Flat Rock was the ruins of an old mining camp. Years ago Jed Rossiter had tapped into its well to water his stock. The water source made it good grazing ground; it was where she had put the cattle she planned to ship next week.

Eden wasted no time giving orders. "Tell Wild Jack to stock up the chuck wagon, and have Deke wrangle the cavvy. We'll round up the cattle at Flat Rock and drive them back here to the home meadow." Where the gathering pens were, but she didn't say that. "We'll leave in the morning at first light."

"Done." Waters touched his spurs against the horse's belly, sending it forward at a trot. Eden was about to go inside when she heard Vince's pickup.

"What did Waters want?" he asked when he joined her. She explained about the windmill.

"Flat Rock is about a mile from Diamond D's west boundary," he remarked.

"I know."

"Are you thinking DePard sabotaged that windmill?"

"I wouldn't put it past him," Eden replied.

"Neither would I. That's what bothers me, sis. DePard is out to break you. You can't win against him, not in the long run. And I don't want to see you lose everything. That's why I want you to sell the ranch. Now. While you can still get some cash out of it."

"Don't you mean while *you* can still get some cash out of it?"

"I would be lying if I said I didn't want my share out of the deal. Put yourself in my shoes. How would you like it if I invested all our money in some venture you knew was going to lose?"

"I don't see it that way, Vince."

"That's because you've gone stubborn on me and refuse to listen to reason."

"No. I just refuse to sell the ranch. I'm not going to run away."

"It isn't running. Think about it, sis. You could start over, make a new life for yourself."

"Look, Vince, even if I put this ranch on the market, what makes you think DePard won't block the sale?"

"Because he wants you gone from here. He would prefer to ruin you, see that you walk away with nothing. But if he can't do that, if you put the ranch up for sale, he would have the satisfaction of believing he had forced you out."

Eden sensed this wasn't idle speculation. "You've talked to him about this, haven't you?" she accused, her temper flaring.

Vince laughed, but it was a little too forced. "Whatever put a crazy idea like that in your head?"

Looking at him, Eden felt the hurt become stronger than the anger. "I can't trust anyone, can I? Not even you."

"That isn't true," Vince said, then changed tactics. "Look, if I did wrong, I'm sorry."

"You're always sorry."

"Hey." His voice was soft and coaxing as he caught her wrists and pulled her hands toward him. "The other day with DePard and the cattle—that changed things. DePard's started to play rough, Eden. Real rough. You are my sister, all the family I've got. I don't want anything to happen to you. If that means talking to DePard or convincing you to swallow your pride and sell the ranch to get you out of danger, then I'll do it. Can you understand that?"

"Yes." That she understood and believed. In many ways Vince was selfish, but she never doubted that he loved her and would do anything to protect her—even going to DePard.

MAGENTA streaks creased the sky as the setting sun unleashed a vivid, dramatic prelude to the night. Kincade paused beneath a cottonwood tree near the ranch house and made a slow survey of the vast landscape before him, the rain-washed air bringing a sharpness and clarity to the scene, intensifying the green of its grasses, the amber-gold of its soil, and the purple of its far mountains.

Kincade leaned a shoulder against the trunk and lit a cigar. From the corral came the squeal of a horse and a flurry of hooves as the pecking order was reestablished in the cavvy. Then all was quiet.

Kincade turned his attention to Vince Rossiter's blue-and-white pickup, parked in front of the house, his eyes narrowing in thoughtful study. The front door opened, and he lifted his head in instant alertness, then relaxed when he saw a hatless Eden Rossiter walk out. She strolled to the end of the veranda, then wandered beyond it. The old cow dog ranged alongside her.

Eden halted some thirty feet from where he stood, presenting her profile to him as she looked out across the open country, rather like a monarch surveying her kingdom. Obviously pleased with what she saw, she smiled faintly and reached back to pull off the confining band around her hair. She shook her head, letting her hair fall loose down her back. Visibly relaxing, she slipped her fingers inside the back pockets of her jeans and breathed in deeply, filling her

lungs with the rain-freshened air. Kincade deliberately failed to make his presence known, satisfied simply to observe Eden Rossiter when she wasn't wearing the mantle of ranch boss. He suspected she had allowed few men to see the woman underneath the boss.

But the old cow dog caught Kincade's scent. With hackles raised, the dog growled and fixed his gaze on Kincade.

"What is it, Cassius?" Eden glanced idly at the dog. In answer it took a crouching step toward Kincade and growled again. Half turning, she peered into the shadows beneath the cottonwood, then stiffened. "Who's there?" she demanded.

"Kincade." He tossed his cigar away and moved out of the shadows toward her. "It's beautiful out, isn't it?"

"Yes." She concealed a smile when the blue heeler, as expected, darted over to block Kincade's path before he came too close to her. The dog growled another warning, this time showing its teeth. "That's enough, Cassius," Eden said.

"Cassius," Kincade repeated. "Did you name him after the Roman general or the boxer Cassius Clay?"

"The boxer," she admitted, watching as Kincade crouched down to let the dog smell the back of his hand.

"You may not be a heavyweight like Muhammad Ali," he told the dog, "but there's no doubt you're a fighter." He straightened after the dog had sniffed his hand, and backed two steps away.

To Eden's surprise the dog trotted off, something it never did unless it had known the person with her for a long time. She wasn't sure if the dog's action was a sign of trust or old age. Whatever the case, she remained wary herself as she eyed Kincade. The brim of his hat threw a shadow across his eyes, hiding them from her, but she felt their gaze on her. She was unsettled by it. And by him.

He looked to the west, where the sun had just slipped below the horizon. His expression turned thoughtful. "You know, this isn't the kind of a country a person can call beautiful," he mused. "In fact, a few days ago I thought it was the most desolate land I had ever seen. But there's something about it that pulls you under its spell."

Eden nodded her understanding. "I know. To a lot of people this is the middle of nowhere. But to me it's the middle of everything. I wouldn't want to live anywhere else."

Kincade studied the glow of pride in her dark eyes, his attention drawn once again to the classic lines of her features. Eden Rossiter was beautiful, her brows naturally arched and her eyes outlined by a thick fringe of lashes. "For anything to survive out here, I imagine it has to sink its roots deep," he observed.

"I suppose that's true," she admitted. "I know mine are."

"I think it's true of the ranch house as well." He gestured toward it. "It looks like it grew here."

"In a way it did," Eden replied, smiling as she gazed back at it. "All the materials used to build it came from right here on Spur." The pull of the century-old dwelling was strong, drawing Eden toward it. She paused at the end of the veranda and ran her hand over an upright timber worn smooth with age. "Most old homes get torn down or simply deteriorate," she said, then smiled as she recalled, "Jed—my grandfather—claimed this house would never crumble, because it was held together with Rossiter blood."

"You're kidding?" Amusement riddled his voice, but it was the warm, sharing kind.

"I'm not," she assured him. "According to family legend, there was an accident while mixing the materials for the adobe. Kate Rossiter was badly cut and lost a lot of blood, so much blood that there was a red cast to that batch of adobe. Kate supposedly ordered her workers to use the bricks from that mix to lay the cornerstone for the house."

"That's quite a story," Kincade remarked. "It's one of those you want to believe whether it's true or not."

"It was definitely my favorite story when I was growing up," Eden admitted. She lifted her face to the darkening twilight air, savoring its stillness, then said softly, "I couldn't sell this ranch. It would be like tearing out my soul." She glanced at Kincade, angry with herself for telling him about her feelings. Watching his face, she missed the upward reach of his hand as it slid around her neck and his mouth came down on hers. She hadn't anticipated this, and she hadn't guessed his mouth would be this warm.

Kincade tightened his fingers on the back of her neck. Other women would have leaned toward him in response or pulled away in refusal. But she stood there, stiff as a schoolgirl. Beneath his hand he felt the heavy beat of the pulse in her neck. He knew it wasn't wise to be distracted by her, but he pressed for more, delving deeper—and tasted her inexperience. It rocked him. Kincade drew back, trying to reconcile this new discovery against the sight of the full-blown woman before him.

Her face had paled, and there was a glimmer of fear mixing with the anger in her eyes. Pride kept her head high as she brought the back of her hand to her lips. But he noticed she made no attempt to wipe away the sensation of his kiss as she strode past him into the house.

HANDS gripped her shoulders. Eden fought them, only to be shaken harder. "Eden, wake up."

She jerked back as if struck, and cringed into the pillows. Her eyes were wide with fear as she stared at her brother.

"It's me, sis," Vince murmured softly. "Are you okay?" He sat on the edge of her bed, clad in jeans, his dark hair tousled from sleep.

"Yes." But she felt anything but okay. She dragged herself into a sitting position and drew her knees up, resting her forehead on them. Nausea rolled her stomach while she pulled in deep, long breaths and fought her way back to reality.

"When did the nightmares start again?" Vince asked.

"This is the first . . . in a long time." At least two years, maybe three. Eden wasn't sure.

"Do you want me to sit with you awhile?"

"No." She shook her head. "I'm sorry I woke you."

The mattress shifted when he stood up. Reaching back, he cupped her cheek in his hand. "You can holler for your big brother anytime. Want me to leave the light on?"

"Please." Eden managed a wan smile. It died the instant Vince walked from her bedroom.

She gathered up the spare pillow and hugged it tight as she leaned back against the maple headboard, the sick, scared feeling slowly receding. Why had the nightmares started again after all this time? She had the uneasy feeling she knew the answer. The kiss. She had liked it. The warmth of it. The evocative sensation of it.

She had liked being kissed the other time, too. She had liked it a lot . . . at first. She slid down between the covers and curled into a tight ball, moving gently from side to side, trying to rock herself to sleep, just as she had done when she was a little girl.

Chapter VI

In the gray light that precedes the breaking of the sun above the horizon, Eden set out for Flat Rock with Vince and the ranch hands. The chuck wagon led the procession, with the cook perched atop an old truck seat, a tall-crowned hat on his head, his long gray hair streaming onto his shoulders. The bed wagon followed, with Connors at the reins. The cavvy brought up the rear, Deke riding point, while Kincade rode drag to keep the stragglers moving. The rest ranged between the wagon and the remuda.

Passing the holding pens just beyond the ranch headquarters, they headed across the basin, a large saucer-shaped hollow planted with tough range grass. Vince brought his horse alongside Eden's. "You're making a mistake moving the cattle here," he said. "You'll need every bit of this graze come winter."

"They won't be on it long."

"You're dreaming, sis," Vince said critically. "DePard has all the shippers around here in his hip pocket. They're never going to haul the cattle to market for you."

"I know. That's why I contracted with an Oregon outfit."

"What?" Vince reined in.

"They'll be here Tuesday morning at nine to start loading." Eden kept her horse moving, calling the blue heeler to her horse's side.

Vince spurred after her. "When did this happen?"

"Yesterday."

"Why didn't you tell me?"

"I would have if you hadn't been so busy trying to convince me to sell." She sent her horse into a canter. Vince didn't follow.

It was past noon when they reached the ruins of the old Flat Rock mining camp. A few crumbling remains of foundation marked the locations of former structures. A windmill stood guard over it all, its blades churning uselessly in the morning wind. A small bunch of cows stood around the metal tank at its base, sucking at the few inches of murky water that covered the bottom.

No time was wasted setting up camp. Wild Jack fired up the propane stove and started the midday meal. The cavvy was driven into the permanent trap by the windmill and left to graze. The rope corral was off-loaded from the bed wagon, and the mess tent was erected next to the chuck wagon. Each rider set up his own canvas teepee and stowed his gear. Then it was back to the trap with rope and halter to select a horse for the afternoon's work. Kincade chose a lean and rangy cream-colored mustang with a jet-black mane and tail, and short black stockings.

The noon meal consisted of beef hash, accompanied by fresh-baked biscuits and wild honey. But it was the steaming hot apple cobbler that had everyone coming back for seconds. Except Kincade.

Instead he refilled his coffee mug and took up a position directly opposite Vince. He puffed on a cigar and watched Vince through the curling smoke. After a moment Vince noticed him.

He bristled instantly. "What are you looking at?"

"Nothing." Kincade took the cigar from his mouth and said slowly, "Absolutely nothing."

Rossiter's eyes narrowed, not liking the sound of that. "Do your looking in some other direction," he retorted. "Hey, Wild Jack," he called, and raised his cup. "Pour me some coffee."

Before the cook could lift the pot from the stove, Kincade suggested, "Why don't you get your own?"

The mess tent went silent. Muscle corded along Vince's jaw as he lowered his cup and stared hotly at Kincade. "You better watch that mouth of yours, mister," he told him. "One of these days somebody's going to ram a fist in it."

A smile dented the corners of Kincade's mouth. "That's possible."

"You're looking for trouble. Why?" Vince demanded.

"Who? Me?" Kincade countered.

"Yes, you." Vince walked over to the cook's wreck pan and tossed his dishes in, then stalked off.

The afternoon orders were simple: Each rider was assigned a section, and told to search thoroughly and push all cattle back to the trap.

Alone in the camp, Wild Jack cleaned up the dishes, drank half a bottle of vanilla extract, and began preparations for supper. Late in the afternoon he hauled himself onto the old truck seat and watched for the dust that would signal a rider returning to camp.

Eden was the third one in, driving twenty head of stock into the trap with the help of the cow dog. She was gathering her gear together when she saw Vince approaching with less than a dozen head. She waited until he had driven the bunch into the trap, then said, "Is that all the cattle you found?"

"That's it." He looked irritable, preoccupied with something as he lifted a neckcloth to wipe the sweat from his face.

"But you had Big Meadow in your section," she said, frowning. "You should have found three times that number."

He swung his head toward her, his eyes black with temper. "Are you saying I don't know how to do my job?"

"No. I'm saying you should have found more cattle."

"You know everything. You go look." For a hot run of seconds he glared at her, then wheeled his horse away. "To hell with this."

Eden grabbed his reins. "Where are you going?"

"To town," he snapped. "It's Saturday night, and I'm going to have a few beers and some laughs at Starr's."

He dug his spurs into the horse's belly. Eden let go of the reins, and Vince whipped the horse into a gallop, heading toward town.

Deke stood at the corral staring after him with a wistful expression. He said nothing. No one worked at the ranch long without becoming accustomed to Vince's abrupt goings and comings.

A haze of dust hung over the backs of the forty head of cattle Kincade herded toward the trap. As he approached it, he glimpsed someone galloping away.

Scenting water, the cattle trotted through the open gate. Kincade reined in and stroked the mustang's neck for an afternoon's work well done. The mustang swung quickly at the touch of the rein, as if eager to go back out. "End of the day, fella." Kincade envied the animal's stamina. It had been a long time since he had spent an entire day on a horse, and he could feel the soreness in every muscle.

He spotted Eden busying herself with saddle and gear, ignoring him a little too completely, as she had all day. He knew the memory of the kiss was there between them. Once that step was taken, once that invisible line was crossed between a man and a woman, there was no going back from it and no forgetting it. Every time she looked at him, she would remember that kiss, just as he did.

His gaze lifted to the dust hanging in the air, the rider already lost from view. "Who's that?" he asked Deke.

"Rossiter."

"Rossiter? Where's he headed?"

"To Starr's for a beer."

"A beer, huh? Where's town from here?"

Deke looked in the general direction of Friendly. "Oh, fifteen or twenty miles southwest."

Kincade hesitated a moment, then nudged the mustang forward.

"Where're you going?" Deke frowned.

"To get a beer," Kincade called back, and pushed the horse into a ground-eating trot.

VINCE rode up to the Lucky Starr. His weary horse stumbled to a halt near a corner post supporting the overhang. Vince swung out of the saddle and hastily tied the reins to the post.

Starr Davis was at the big mahogany bar when he walked in. She saw him, hesitated fractionally, then fixed a big purring smile on her face and went to meet him. "If it isn't the proverbial bad penny back again," she mocked. "What's it going to cost me this time?"

"That's no way to talk," Vince chided with a grin. "You know I always make things right."

"You usually do." She nodded. "One way or another."

"So how about it? Are you going to buy this bad penny a drink?"

"Don't I always?" Starr took his arm and led him to the bar. "Roy"—she rapped a hand on the counter—"give this man a drink on me."

"Draw me a cold one, Roy." Vince pulled a crumpled twenty-dollar bill from his pocket. "And keep them coming until I tell you to stop." He pushed the money at Roy, then turned to face Starr. "So tell me, how's my lucky Starr these days?"

"Better than ever," she replied, and ran an assessing eye over him. "The same can't be said for you. You look like you've been rode hard and put up wet."

"That is a fact." He picked up the frosty mug Roy set in front of him. Lifting it, Vince saluted Starr. "Here's to generous women." He drank down half of it in one long guzzle, then lowered the mug and called to Roy, "Throw the thickest, juiciest steak you've got on the grill for me, will you?"

"Burn one," Roy hollered into the kitchen.

Vince turned sideways to survey the crowded room. "Where's the kid? I don't see him around."

"At a friend's house watching horror movies."

"That wouldn't be my idea of fun," Vince declared.

"He isn't like you. Thankfully," Starr murmured.

"That's good. I'd hate to think of anybody getting the kind of luck I've been having lately." He studied the crowd. "It looks like you've been invaded by the Diamond D. Is DePard around?"

"Over there, playing poker." With a nod of her blond head Starr gestured at a table in the far corner.

"How are things going between you and DePard?"

"I see him whenever it can be arranged," Starr replied. "He has become very fond of Rick."

Vince squared around to face the bar, resting both elbows on it. "A kid needs a man in his life. Someone he can look up to and admire." He glanced back at the corner table. "You better grab DePard if you can."

"I intend to."

He gave her an assessing look. "You'll do it, too." He turned to study his beer. "Does the kid ever ask about his father?"

"Not anymore."

Vince nodded, then flashed Starr one of his patented smiles that had melted many a heart. "You say they're playing poker? Would you stake me fifty dollars in chips? I promise I'm good for it."

"Don't worry. I'll make sure of that."

"Hey, Starr!" someone yelled. "Come deal us some blackjack."

"Be right there," she said, and moved away from the bar.

Vince tracked her with his eyes, then gathered up his beer and carried it to a bar table.

ROSSITER'S lathered horse gleamed wetly in the light that spilled from the Lucky Starr. An ear swiveled in tired interest when Kincade reined the mustang alongside it.

Stiff and sore, he lifted himself out of the saddle. He loosened the cinch, then pulled the bandanna from his neck and soaked it with water from his canteen. He wiped the dust from the mustang's nostrils and washed its mouth, squeezing water into it. Finished, he tied the reins to the post, then checked Rossiter's horse, running a hand down its chest and feeling the steamy heat beneath its wet coat. The canteen on Rossiter's saddle was empty. "Something tells me you didn't get a drop of it," Kincade murmured to the horse. He soaked his bandanna with water from his canteen and repeated the previous procedure. Then he headed into the casino.

The noise was deafening after the silence of the desert night. He spotted Rossiter at a bar table, slicing into a huge steak. Kincade's stomach growled at the sight. He started for the bar, then changed direction and crossed the length of the room to the narrow hall. A cowboy came out of the men's room, giving his zipper a final tug. Kincade stepped aside to let him pass, then went in to wash off some of the day's sweat. At the sink he turned both faucets on full force, took off his hat, and bent down to wet his face. He was drying his face and hands on the towel roll when the door opened and Rusty came in. His thatch of brick-red hair was tucked in under a towering chef's hat, and a long bibbed apron, stained with grease, was tied around him.

"What are you doing in that getup?" Kincade frowned.

"I'm the new cook." Rusty grinned. "I ordered a steak and hash browns last night, like always. But this time I told Roy to chop up some peppers and onions in my potatoes. He told me that if I didn't like the way he cooked, I could fix my own. So I did. Next thing I knew, Starr was offering me a job."

Kincade pushed his hat back on. "There's a couple of horses out front. If you get a chance, take them some water."

A sandy brow shot up. "You rode in?"

"Yeah."

"You hungry?"

"Starved."

"I'll throw a steak on for you," Rusty said. Kincade left the men's room. Rossiter was still busy with his food and never noticed Kincade when he took up residence at the end of the bar.

Finished with his meal, Vince leaned back in his chair. Roy brought him a fresh beer. Vince took it and sauntered over to the blackjack table, where Starr was dealing. She shoved a slip of paper at him. "Let's keep it legal," she said.

Vince signed the IOU and pushed it back. Starr counted out a fifty-dollar stack of chips, and Vince drifted off to the poker table, where Duke DePard sat facing the room. His expression was a study of grim concentration, his thick, bushy brows drawn together, hooding his eyes. His mouth was in its usual stern line, half hidden by the heavy mustache that covered most of his upper lip.

Idly Vince clicked the chips together in his palm. "Mind if I sit in for a few hands?" He pushed an empty chair back from the table without waiting for permission. "I feel lucky tonight."

"The table stake's fifty," DePard told him.

"I know the rules, Duke." Vince let his chips clatter onto the table as he sat down.

DePard pointed a finger at one of the other players. "It's your deal, Ernie."

"The game's five-card draw, jacks or better to open." Ernie split the deck and began shuffling the cards together.

"Ante up, boys. Ante up." Vince tossed a chip into the pot and pushed his hat to the back of his head, strands of dark, wavy hair falling onto his forehead.

Curious that Rossiter would be playing poker with his sister's archenemy, Kincade finished the last of his steak and went over, taking his beer with him. Two other cowboys were slumped against the wall, watching the game. Kincade joined them, the angle giving him a view of both Rossiter and DePard.

"Looks like you've had a hard day, Rossiter," DePard observed.

"You're looking at the sweat of honest toil." An easy grin split Vince's mouth as he fanned the hand dealt to him.

"Is that a fact?" DePard seemed unimpressed.

"Yep." Vince discarded two cards from his hand, then sent DePard a sly look. "We're gathering cattle out at Flat Rock."

DePard's interest sharpened. "What for?"

"To ship to market, of course." He held up two fingers to the dealer and trapped the cards that sailed across the table.

"Right." DePard sounded both amused and smug. "And who do you figure will ship them?"

Vince took his time answering as he studied his cards. "An outfit out of Oregon." Vince watched DePard's reaction out of the corner of an eye. The man had gone still. "She's outfoxed you, Duke."

"If it's true." DePard looked at the cards he'd been dealt, then tossed some chips into the pot. "Ten to you, Bill."

"Oh, it's true." Vince nodded. "The trucks will be at the ranch Tuesday morning at nine." The two players on his right folded. Vince pushed a stack of chips into the pot. "There's your ten, and ten more."

"Too rich for me." The other player threw in his hand.

DePard pushed more chips into the pot. "I call."

Vince spread his cards on the table, face up. "Three tens with an ace high. Read 'em and weep."

Out of the next five hands Vince won three. Kincade watched as Vince stacked the chips from his last win, then rapped the table. "Come on, Murphy. It's your deal."

"Deal me out." DePard collected the small stack of chips in front of him and stood.

Startled, Vince looked up. "Quitting already?"

"Your luck's running too good for me." The corners of DePard's mouth pulled into a smile that didn't reach his eyes; they remained hard. With a swing of his big shoulders he left the table.

Kincade watched as DePard spoke to a cowboy in a spotted cowhide vest sitting at a bar table. The man had a large purple birthmark on his face. It was Sheehan, DePard's foreman, the one who had worked Kincade over.

Sheehan stood and followed DePard out of the lounge. Thoughtfully Kincade redirected his attention to the poker table. Vince lost the next hand. When he picked up his beer mug, he saw it was empty. He glanced at the cowboys along the wall. "One of you guys tell Roy I need another beer."

"Tell him yourself." The phrase, almost an echo of the one Kincade had used on Vince at the noon meal, brought Rossiter's glance slicing to him.

Displeasure, born of mutual dislike, immediately darkened his face. "What are you doing here?"

"Having a beer." Kincade raised the nearly empty mug.

"Have it somewhere else," Vince snapped.

"I like it here."

Vince made an effort to ignore him and concentrate on the next hand. But over the next hour the stack of chips in front of him went steadily down. "Looks like you've run out of luck," Kincade observed.

Rossiter placed both palms flat on the table and pushed his chair back, his eyes darkening with a sultry anger. "When I want your opinion, I'll ask for it." He stood up and swept a glance over the other players at the table, forcing a smile. "Another time, boys."

He headed for the bar. Kincade ambled in the same direction. Vince ordered a fresh beer, drank a couple of swallows, then noticed Kincade. Irritation flickered through his expression. He slapped a hand on the counter in a gesture of finality, then swung away. As he headed for the door, he called cheerfully to Starr. She responded with a wave of her hand.

After the front door closed behind Rossiter, Kincade settled up his tab and left. Outside the casino, he saw both horses still tied to the post. Rossiter was nowhere around. Kincade moved toward the horses, his boots making a heavy sound on the wooden sidewalk. The mustang lifted its head, its ears pointing to Kincade. Then it swung its nose toward the corner of the building. Kincade wasn't surprised when Vince stepped out of the shadows a second later.

"Why are you following me?"

" 'Suspicion always haunts the guilty mind,' " Kincade remarked, quoting Shakespeare. "Do you have a guilty mind, Rossiter?"

"No." The answer was quick. A little too quick. "Why would you think that?" He frowned. "I know you from somewhere, don't I?"

"Like I said before, we've never met."

Confused, Rossiter shook his head, then went to his horse and yanked the reins loose from the post. He pulled himself into the saddle and kicked the horse into a lope out of town.

Chapter VII

FROM somewhere in the distance came the rumbling growl of diesel engines. The crew had driven the cattle from Flat Rock back to the ranch the previous day. Now Kincade was perched atop a fence rail when he spotted a billowing swirl of dust off to the west. His glance strayed to the loading chute, where Eden stood with her brother. Cattle lowed in the pens behind Kincade—three-hundred-and-fifty-odd head ready to ship.

The diesel roar grew louder as a tractor-trailer rig came into view. A second truck followed, slowing to a stop when it drew level with Eden. The name "J J Trucking, Fields, Ore." was stenciled in black on the driver's door. Eden climbed onto the cab's running board. The man behind the wheel was in his late forties, with a hard-used look about his face. "Jerry Jones," he said by way of introduction.

"Eden Rossiter."

"Right. Sorry I'm late." He spoke with the resignation of a man who had become used to Lady Luck frowning on him. "These gravel roads . . . It took longer than I figured."

"We're ready to load as soon as you're in position."

"Won't take but a jiff," he said, and popped the clutch.

Eden hopped to the ground and stood back. True to his word, the man had his trailer backed up to the loading chute in minutes.

Bob Waters and Al Bender rode into the fenced alleyway between the pens. Leaving the mustang tied outside, Kincade swung off the rail and, when both riders were in position, unlatched the gate to the first pen of cattle. The pair walked their horses into the pen and began hazing the cattle out. Two more men were at the chute to keep the cattle moving up the ramp to the trailer. Pushed from behind by the hazing riders, red-coated hides soon filled the alleyway, bawling in confusion. With a clatter of hooves the first of them went up the chute.

Over the din a loud report rang out. There was no mistaking the explosive crack of a high-powered rifle. "What the—" Al Bender's muttered oath was cut off by a second shot, followed by the nasty ping of a bullet ricocheting off the steel rim of a truck tire.

In the scramble for cover, both riders piled off their horses and the two men at the chute shot over the top, dropping into the pen with the cattle. There was another shot and the thwack of a bullet penetrating a rubber tire.

Crouching low, Kincade worked his way through the milling cattle. He reached Bob Waters as a bullet slammed into the truck body. "Where is the shooter? Have you spotted him?" Kincade took cover behind Waters's horse.

"Up on that ridge." With a bob of his head Waters indicated the boulder-strewn slope a short distance from the holding pens.

Ducking down, Kincade peered under the horse's neck and caught the flash of sunlight off a rifle barrel. Behind him Vince shouted, "Eden, for God's sake, get down!" Kincade turned and saw Eden near one of the saddled horses outside the corral. "What are you doing?" Vince yelled again when Eden jerked a rifle from its scabbard and swung herself into the saddle.

Giving no answer, she wheeled the horse away from the pens and kicked it into a gallop. Kincade had a fairly good idea of where she was headed and why. "The little fool," he muttered, and made a quick dash to the fence. Vaulting it, he untied the mustang and climbed aboard. In one stride he had the horse in a full run. He spotted Eden circling to the far side of the slope. Taking a direct line, he raced to intercept her.

Intent on the gunman somewhere on the hillcrest, she never heard Kincade until he was almost on her. Bending low, he grabbed her reins and pulled both horses to a halt.

"What the hell are you doing?" The mustang sidled nervously under him as another shot rang out.

Eden flung up her head at the sound, then glared at Kincade. Behind all the anger was something wild and desperate. "Let go of my horse." She tried to yank the reins out of his grasp.

"Not until you start using your head. You can't go up there."

Suddenly Kincade found himself staring into the barrel of her rifle. She levered a bullet into the chamber. "Get out of my way." She sounded cool and steady and deadly.

Kincade considered the various things he had learned about her and took a chance. "Or what?" He held her gaze. "You'll shoot me? That shouldn't be hard. You've killed a man before."

She went white, and her eyes turned bright with pain. His taunting words had cut deeper than he'd expected. But they had given him the advantage he wanted. He grabbed the rifle out of her loose grip. With her reins now free, she whipped her horse around and sent it up the hill at a lunging gallop. Kincade gave chase.

He was out of the saddle before the mustang came to a stop. But his raking glance found no one on the ridge except Eden. She was on the ground making her own search. Extending his sweep, Kincade saw a man on horseback streaking toward the next hill. Eden spotted him at almost the same moment and grabbed up her reins to mount. "He's getting away."

"Unless you know how to track, he's gone." Kincade caught sight of something black and white as the man disappeared behind the hill. A vest maybe. DePard's foreman had worn a spotted vest at Starr's. A coincidence? Kincade doubted that. He scanned the ridgetop. A low boulder near the edge gave a commanding view of the pens below. An area of grass around the base of it had been flattened. "He might have crouched over there," he said to Eden. "I don't see any spent shells, but he could have taken them with him."

When she made no response, Kincade turned back to her. Her rigid stance radiated anger. He glanced at the rifle in his hand—her rifle. "Here." He held it out to her. She took it without a word and jammed it back in the saddle boot. He suspected he knew the reason for her anger. "That remark I made about killing a man," he began. "I only said what it took to stop you. I'm sorry."

She whirled on him, her eyes like chips of hot black ice. "You're fired. Pack your things and get out."

"I'm not going anywhere," he told her with the same harshness she used on him. "I am staying right here on Spur."

"No, you're not. You're fired! Do you understand? I don't need you here. I don't want you here."

"Why?" he shot back. "Because you're a woman and I make you feel like one?"

"No!"

"Liar." He seized her shoulders and hauled her roughly against him, bringing his mouth down with bruising force.

She answered with a violence of her own, kicking, hitting, twisting to get free. But her struggles died when the anger in her changed to something else. Needs, longings sprang up fresh and terribly strong. She wanted to give way to them and feel—just feel.

Breaking away from the drugging heat of his mouth, Eden lowered her head, trembling, bracing herself to feel savage fingers tangling in her hair and jerking her head back up. When it didn't happen, when all she felt was the brush of his lips on her forehead, she pulled free and walked quickly to her horse. On legs that weren't quite steady, she climbed onto the saddle and reined the horse toward the slope. By the time she reached the bottom of the hill, she had pieced back together her scattered composure.

"Are you all right?" Vince came to meet her, holding the horse's head while Eden dismounted.

"Of course." She made a visual examination of one of the tractor-trailer rigs, trying to assess the extent of damage.

"Who was it? Did you see him?" Vince asked.

"Just a man riding away." Eden heard the crunch of booted feet on the gravelly soil. Kincade was behind her. She fixed her gaze on the grim-faced stock hauler striding toward her.

"I used your phone to call the sheriff." He jerked a thumb toward the house. "They're sending someone right away."

Eden doubted Sheriff Lot Williams would be in any great hurry. He and Duke DePard were second cousins.

"What's the damage?" she asked Jones.

"Six flat tires on both rigs, and this one's out of commission with a bullet hole in the radiator."

"What about the other one?"

"It's just a matter of switching tires from this one to it."

"How long will it take?"

"Couple hours, I suppose."

"My men will give you a hand," she said. "The sooner we get it done, the sooner we can start loading cattle."

"Not in my trailer you're not," the man told her. "I don't want anyone taking potshots at me again."

"The sniper is gone. I saw him ride off myself."

"Yeah, and for all I know, he could be waiting somewhere along the road."

Panic rose, threatening to surface. Eden battled it back. "You agreed—" she began.

"That was before I found out the kind of man you have for an enemy," he cut her off. "You failed to mention that, but your boys told me all about it when the shooting finally stopped."

Eden wanted to plead with the hauler to reconsider, but pride wouldn't let her beg. "You're easily intimidated, Mr. Jones," she said, trying to shame him into changing his mind.

He reddened, but didn't budge. "Say what you want, but that bullet could just as easily have punctured the fuel tank. Hire yourself someone else."

"Very well." Eden stiffly turned away.

Vince laid a comforting hand on her shoulder. "I'm sorry, sis." The gentleness in his voice was almost her undoing. She had come too close to success for it not to affect her. For an instant, tears blurred her eyes.

"I really thought you had a chance of beating DePard this time," he said.

DePard. The mere mention of his name drove away the tears and brought back the anger. She swung around. "No one knew I was shipping cattle this morning. How could he have found out?" Too late she saw Kincade standing there.

"Maybe somebody told him," Kincade suggested, and deliberately looked at Vince, then turned and led his horse to the pens.

It was the way Vince watched him, the angry look on his face that made Eden suspicious. "You went to town Saturday night," she remembered. "Was DePard there?"

"He might have been. What of it?" he asked testily.

"Did you tell him we were shipping cattle today?"

"All right, so maybe I did." Vince became indignant. "Maybe I was proud of the way you outmaneuvered him."

"You should have waited until *after* the fact to do your bragging," she told him angrily. "You should have realized he would try to find some way to stop me."

"Do you think I'm not sorry?" He caught her shoulders, a pained look in his eyes. "You scared the hell out of me when you went charging up that hill. If anything had happened to you, I could never have forgiven myself. This is all my fault, and I know it."

"Don't." She couldn't deal with his feelings of guilt. Not now. Not when she had so many other problems.

Abruptly Vince dropped his hands and stalked off.

Close to an hour after the shooting, a sheriff's car rolled into the ranch yard. Eden recognized the tall, gaunt frame of Lot Williams, but she made no move to approach him. The stock hauler went to meet him. Eden watched the two converse. Jones did most of the talking, punctuating his remarks with a lot of arm waving and hand gesturing at the flat tires and the ridge.

The sheriff listened with an expression of steely indifference, a contrast to the cold fury he had shown Eden that long-ago night when he had walked into the kitchen after seeing Jeff's body. She had sat at the table, haunted by horrible images that wouldn't go away. At intervals, light from the ambulance and patrol cars had flashed across the window, adding their own nightmarish quality to the moment.

Even though she had already told her story once, Lot Williams had demanded that she tell it again. He had interrupted her constantly, grilling her on every detail, twisting everything she said. Her torn blouse, the scratches and bruises on her skin had meant nothing to him. Then he had taken her in. Wrenching her arms behind her and snapping the handcuffs on her wrists, he had marched her to the patrol car.

Every time she saw Lot Williams, she relived the events of that night, the forty-eight hours in jail. But she wasn't seventeen anymore. She wasn't scared and confused. When Sheriff Williams walked over to her, Eden met his piercing eyes without flinching.

"Jones tells me somebody used his trucks for target practice this morning," he said.

"That's right."

"I understand you took a rifle and went up there after him."

"I had the rifle." Kincade came over to her side. "The lady was unarmed."

His glance swung to Kincade. "And who are you?"

"Kincade." He pushed his hat to the back of his head. "I work for Miss Rossiter."

"What happened when you got to the top of the hill?"

"We saw a man riding away," Eden replied.

"What did he look like?"

"Average build," Kincade began. "He had on a dark hat, a dark plaid shirt, and a vest of some kind. He was on a bay horse."

Lot Williams studied him more closely. "Could you recognize the man if you saw him again?"

Kincade shook his head. "I never saw his face."

The sheriff nodded and glanced at the ridge. "I'd better go take a look." He turned to Eden. "I'll need a horse."

"You can use that sorrel." She pointed to a white-stockinged horse tied to a fence rail. He nodded and crossed to the animal. Eden knew he was only going through the motions of an investigation.

"Something tells me the good sheriff isn't going to find one darn thing," Kincade remarked idly.

Angry, Eden turned to him. "If you hadn't interfered, I would have made it to the top before Sheehan got away."

His eyes narrowed on her. "You know who it was?"

"I know who it had to be. So does the sheriff. But thanks to you, I can't prove it." She turned sharply on her heel and walked off.

KINCADE rapped lightly on the screen door. No voice called for him to enter. The only sound from inside was the faint rustle of pages. He started to knock again, then changed his mind and walked in. Finding the living room empty, he crossed to the kitchen, making no attempt to silence his footsteps.

Eden sat at the table, poring over a trio of telephone books. A pad of paper was next to them, with a list of names and phone numbers scribbled at the top. She was totally oblivious to his presence. Something held him silent as his glance traveled from the tightly gripped pencil in her hand to her troubled eyes and the tight, compressed line of her mouth.

This was an Eden Rossiter Kincade hadn't seen before. Nowhere was there a trace of the volatile temper he had occasionally glimpsed. Instead she had the look of a woman struggling desperately to survive. Seeing her like this awakened all his protective instincts.

She dragged in a long breath and lifted her head, freezing when she saw Kincade. "What do you want?"

"I hear Connors and Hart quit." Kincade came the rest of the way into the kitchen. "Am I still fired?"

"Are you certain you still want to stay? I can't guarantee the shooting this morning was an isolated incident."

Before he could reply, the phone rang, startling both of them. Eden swung away to answer it. "Spur Ranch." She turned to look at Kincade. "Yes." A faintly puzzled look entered her expression. She looked at the phone and hung up. "That was for you. It was the cook at Starr's. He said you lost something and that you'd better come get it because he wasn't sure how much longer it would be there."

"Must be my pocket knife," he lied, feeling the weight of it against his thigh. "I noticed it was missing a couple days ago. I'd better go get it," he said, turning away.

Alone in the kitchen, Eden noticed how much emptier the room seemed without his presence, how much louder the silence.

"IT's about time you got here, DePard."

Hearing Vince Rossiter's voice, Rusty hurried to the swinging doors that opened from the kitchen into the casino lounge. He inched them open a crack and peered through the slit.

DePard was with Vince. He said something to Rossiter and gestured to the far side of the room. Rossiter briefly balked, then went with him.

A second later Rusty felt the weight of a hand settle on his shoulder. Swinging around, he found Kincade behind him.

"You scared the bejesus out of me," he hissed.

"I saw Rossiter's truck outside," Kincade said. "What's up?"

"Rossiter and DePard are sitting at the corner table. Rossiter seems a might testy."

"With cause." Kincade gave Rusty a capsulized account of the morning's sniper incident while he switched places so he could see the pair for himself. The two were still talking, DePard calmly and Rossiter with a lot of angry gestures.

Suddenly Rossiter's voice came clearly above the sound of the jukebox. "Dammit, DePard, if she gets hurt, you'll pay for it!"

Amused, DePard stood up. "Don't make threats you can't back up, Rossiter." He squared his shoulders and walked out.

Vince paled and remained in his chair, head bowed.

Stepping back, Kincade eased the swinging doors shut. "I suspect Rossiter has been feeding DePard information on his sister's plans. I know for a fact that he told DePard where and what time we would be loading cattle this morning."

Rusty frowned in confusion. "Rossiter told him that and then comes in here and corners him, raving about how he doesn't want his sister hurt? That doesn't make a whole lot of sense."

Kincade didn't understand it any better than Rusty. "Eden told me once that her brother was trying to convince her to sell the ranch. His half would probably amount to a tidy sum."

"I guess he figured that if DePard started making things uncomfortable for her, she might be more easily talked into selling. Only DePard made it hotter than he figured."

"That's possible." Yet Kincade had the feeling that that wasn't the whole story.

DePard had a drink waiting for Sheehan when he walked into the study at Diamond D headquarters. "To a job well done," DePard told him and clinked his glass against Sheehan's. "Lot Williams called. Both trucks suffered damage, and the hauler has refused to ship her cattle. After today she won't find anyone else willing to take the chance."

"Rifle bullets tend to deliver a loud and clear message." Sheehan downed his whiskey in one big gulp.

"They certainly do." DePard smiled. "They shook Vince up. I just came from a meeting with him at Starr's."

"What did he want?"

"Nothing, really. He made a lot of noise about being concerned for his sister's safety." DePard shrugged it off.

"Then he'd better convince her to leave."

"That's what I told him. He's worried she'll find out he's feeding us information. You're to meet him Friday afternoon at Saddletree Creek, along our west fence line."

"I'll be there," Sheehan promised.

Chapter VIII

THE sun was a full, blistering blaze, scorching the land and everything on it. If there was a breeze, Kincade couldn't feel it. Stripped to the waist, sweat streaming from every pore, he labored to secure the windmill's new shaft in place. A ruddy-faced Al Bender held it in place while Kincade tightened the last bolt.

It had been three days since the shooting. Three days spent at a myriad of tasks that were the province of the ordinary ranch hand, tasks that required him to be everything from welder and veterinarian to mechanic and common laborer.

Finished, Kincade rocked back on his heels and wiped at the sweat with the back of a gloved hand. "That should do it." He pushed to his feet, dropped the wrench in the toolbox, and peeled off his leather gloves. A water jug sat in the sliver of shade next to the water tank. Kincade scooped it up and guzzled down half before passing it to Al.

"Hell can't possibly be this hot," Al declared, and tipped the jug up, pouring most of the water into his mouth and letting the rest stream over his red face.

"Amen." Kincade dragged his shirt off the wooden support. Using it as a towel, he wiped the sweat from his face and neck, then ran it over his chest and stomach before he tossed it back on the crown post. When he turned back, he saw Al staring at the long scar that curved across the side of his rib cage.

"Nasty scar," Al observed. "How'd you get it?"

"A bull." Kincade pushed his hat back on.

"You rodeoed?" Al asked.

"I tried my hand at it," which was one way of saying he had ridden the professional rodeo circuit full-time for the last ten years. He didn't remember much about his short ride on the bull called Nine One One, but he remembered the bull had pitched him over its shoulder. He had landed on his back, dazed by the impact. When he had opened his eyes, he had seen the bull's cloven front hooves taking dead aim at him. Reflex had kicked in to move him out of their path. He had almost made it. "I think I broke a couple ribs that time," he recalled.

Al took a can of Red Man out of his pocket and settled a wad of tobacco between his cheek and gum. "Ever compete at the big rodeo in Reno?"

"A few times."

"I went a couple times myself," Al said. "In fact I saw a guy win the bare-bronc event one time. From Texas he was, like you. As I recall, his name was K. C.—K. C. Harris. A tall, lanky guy with dark blond hair."

"I can't say that I know him." Kincade held Al's gaze, aware he had been recognized. "Can you?"

Al thought about that for a long minute, then turned and spit. "No." He rolled the chaw to the other cheek. "I can't say that I do."

Kincade relaxed a little. "Thanks."

"I guess you have your reasons." Al waited to hear them, but Kincade had no intention of telling him.

Instead he moved to the ladder. "Let's see if we can get this working." Kincade started up the windmill's tower. Fifty feet from the ground, he swung onto the wooden platform beneath the fan's eight-foot steel blades. At this height a hot wind blew, tugging at his hat. He pushed the straw Resistol more snugly on his head, welcoming the stir of air.

The securing cables groaned with the strain of holding the blades motionless against the wind. Kincade released one, then the other. The wind caught them, and the blades slowly picked up speed. He called down to Al, "She's loose. Any water in the tank yet?"

"A trickle."

"Helluva view up here." Kincade made a slow sweep of the vastness.

"You can have it," Al yelled from below. "If God wanted man to be that high, He would'a made his legs longer."

Kincade's chuckle was drowned out by the moan of the wind through the blades and the creaking of gears.

"Got a good flow out of the pipe now," Al announced. "Looks like we got 'er fixed."

Kincade swung onto the ladder to make the long descent to the ground, while Al collected the toolbox, threw it in the back end of the pickup, and climbed in behind the wheel. As soon as Kincade was in the cab, they took off toward the ranch house. The buildings were a low form in the distance when Kincade spotted a rider in a bright blue shirt cantering toward them. "That looks like Rossiter."

"Yeah. I wonder where he's going."

"Let's find out." Kincade reached over and gave the horn two quick blasts.

Vince reined his horse off to the side and waited for the pickup to draw abreast of him. Al stuck his head out the driver's-side window. "Where you off to?"

"Thought I'd check the east fence line. Why? Do you need something?" When he glanced past Al and encountered Kincade's eyes, a wariness leaped into his expression. A wariness and something that looked suspiciously like guilt. He broke the eye contact with a quick turn of his head.

"Nope. Don't need a thing," Al told him.

"In that case, I'll catch you later." Vince backed his horse away from the pickup and turned it east. A jab of his spurs sent the chestnut bounding forward, tail swishing.

Al watched him a minute, then shook his head as he eased the truck forward. "I never figured he'd volunteer to ride fence."

"What do you mean?" Kincade shot him a curious look.

"Rossiter's never been one to turn his hand to ranch work since the old man died."

Kincade was skeptical that Vince had turned over a new leaf. Back at the ranch, he grabbed a bite to eat, threw a saddle on a bay gelding, and rode out, taking the same trail Vince had used.

At midafternoon Kincade topped a ridge of low hills and scanned the empty expanse of sage below, searching for a telltale lift of dust that would mark the passage of horse and rider. Off to the east and south he found it. The sun caught the electric blue of the rider's shirt, confirming it was Vince. Kincade put the bay down the slope.

A gully cut a path across the valley floor. Reaching it, Kincade rode the bay over the embankment and sat back as the horse slid on its haunches to the sand-and-gravel bottom. After traveling some distance, he saw a fence swoop across the gully a good quarter mile ahead. He searched and found a slight slope to the opposite bank. A moment later the bay scrambled over the top.

The instant he cleared the gully, Kincade spotted Vince next to the boundary fence, barbed-wire strands separating him from a second rider. At this distance Kincade couldn't see the second man clearly, but the spotted vest of black-and-white cowhide was unmistakable. Kincade lifted the bay into a trot.

VINCE faced Matt Sheehan across the fence. "You give DePard my message, Sheehan." He tried to inject a note of authority in his voice and make it sound as if he were in control.

"I'll do that, all right." Sheehan nodded.

"Dammit, she's called anyone who has a vehicle with more than four wheels, and struck out every time. He has her boxed."

"It could be he'll think it's time to tighten the box."

Vince felt a cold sweat break out. "She's not to get hurt. One hand touches her, and all bets are off."

Sheehan was unimpressed by the threat. "You're already in the game, Rossiter. DePard's paying you money for information. There's no pulling back just because you don't like the cards dealt." His glance slid past Vince, his eyes narrowing. "Who's that?"

Kincade was within fifty yards when Vince's head jerked around, his glance running to Kincade. Vince wheeled his horse and rode to meet him, while Sheehan turned his horse parallel to the fence line and nudged it into an ambling trot.

Vince swung his horse to block Kincade. "What are you doing here?" His voice was hot with anger.

Kincade glanced at the departing rider. "I could ask you the same question. Who's your friend?"

A flicker of unease crossed Vince's expression. "He works for the Diamond D. He was checking fence, like me."

"That's a fancy vest he's got. Looks like one of a kind."

"Could be, for all I know." Vince was defensive.

"Has your sister found someone to haul her cattle?"

The question appeared to startle Vince. "No. Why?"

"Is that what you told DePard's man?"

Vince glared at him for a white-hot second. "I've taken all I'm going to take from you, mister. If I turn around and catch you behind me one more time, you'll regret it." He buried his spurs in the chestnut and took off. Kincade reined the bay after him. All the way back to the ranch he stayed within sight of Rossiter's dust.

The chestnut was in the corral when Kincade arrived. Vince was nowhere in sight. Kincade dismounted, pulled his saddle from the bay's wet back, then turned the gelding loose in the corral. Saddle and gear in hand, he headed for the barn and its tack room.

After the sun's glare the shadows inside seemed deeper, blacker. Old hay rustled underfoot. The chink of his spurs rang loud in the stillness. Kincade had taken no more than a dozen steps when Rossiter's voice rang out in challenge. "You followed me for the last time."

Kincade hesitated a step and searched the cloaking darkness until he located Vince's shape. He stood blocking the door to the tack room, legs spread, hands on his hips.

"I'm going to find out who the hell you are if I have to beat it out of you," Vince declared.

"You talk a lot, Rossiter." Kincade resumed his even pace, walking straight at the man, feeling the blood heat in his veins.

"You'll find out how much is talk," Vince began, but Kincade never let him finish the threat as he heaved the heavy saddle at him. It hit Rossiter in the chest, drawing a grunt of surprise and pain. He staggered backward and came up against the tack-room door. Kincade waded in after him with cocked fists.

Cursing savagely, Vince threw the saddle aside and lunged at him, coming in under Kincade's swing and wrapping both arms around his middle, driving them both to the floor. They grappled in the hay, rolling in a tangle of elbows, knees, and fists. A right to the jaw knocked Kincade sideways. Light exploded in his brain. His head reeled with pain, but pain was an old companion. He had ridden with it, competed in the throes of it too many times to let it stop him. He got his hands under him and pushed up, his hat gone, dislodged in the scuffle.

Rossiter's dark face loomed before him, lips curled back. A second later Kincade was rocked by another hard right to the jaw that staggered him to his knees. "Had enough?" Vince asked.

Kincade looked up through the sweat that stung his eyes, letting his head clear. "Not hardly," he said in a voice that showed the extent of his exertion.

A horse whinnied outside, but Kincade was deaf to the sound, blind to everything but the sight of Rossiter in front of him. Straightening, he feinted suddenly and lashed out with a right. Vince caught it coming in. Watching his face, Kincade knew the blow had hurt him. Maddened by a fighting lust, he pressed harder. With both hands he slammed short wicked hooks to Rossiter's head, then sliced his cheek to the bone with an overhand right.

Vince went down, blood streaming. Dazed and beaten, he lifted a hand to the deep cut on his cheek and stared in disbelief at the blood on his fingers. Dumbly he looked at Kincade.

"What's going on here?" Eden's voice broke in between them.

Chapter IX

PIVOTING on a heel, Kincade saw Eden framed in the opening of the barn's double doors. He knew the moment she saw Rossiter sitting on the barn floor. Her whole body stiffened for a taut second; then she moved swiftly across the space. "Vince, what happened?" She sank to her knees next to him. "Dear Lord, you've been hurt." She pulled a handkerchief from her pocket and pressed it against the gash on his cheek to stanch the flow of blood.

The fight went out of Kincade. He let his fists sag to his sides, fingers slowly uncurling.

"I'm all right." Half irritated, Vince pushed her hand away and held the cloth himself, but she stayed, helping him up when he stood.

Her eyes were black and cold when she turned to Kincade. "You did this."

"You're damned right I did." He felt no remorse, only regret that Eden knew he had injured her brother. He was aware she would hold it against him, and the only thing he wanted her to hold against him was her body. Desire was precisely what he felt when he looked at her. Maybe it was the freshness of battle that put it there. Or maybe he would always feel it every time he looked at her.

Her expression turned colder. "You are fired."

This time Kincade didn't try to argue with her.

"No." Vince stunned them both by speaking up. "He stays."

"What—" she began.

He cut her off. "I don't know why he's out to get me. But I want Kincade where I can keep an eye on him. I don't want to wonder where he is or when he might turn up." He scooped up his hat and walked out. Eden stared after him, tiny lines creasing her forehead.

Instead of relief Kincade felt tired and sore. He saw his hat lying among the hay rubble. Avoiding her eyes, he started to walk away. He was close to her, close enough that she had only to reach out and catch his arm. The slight pressure stopped him in his tracks.

"What was the fight about?" Her voice was stiff, riddled with pride. "He owes you money, doesn't he?"

Kincade looked at the hand on his arm. It was tanned and strong, yet it still had the small shape of a woman's hand. "He doesn't owe me one cent."

"Then what do you want with him?" she demanded.

He lifted his gaze to her face, centering his attention on her lips, soft and full, slightly parted. If she didn't already hate him, Kincade knew she soon would. The knowledge pushed him into taking what he could have now. Abruptly he swung toward her and took a closing step. She backed up and came against the wooden partition of a stall. In one move Kincade had her pinned against it, an arm on either side of her head. Her heart increased its beat—from anticipation or fear, Eden wasn't sure which.

He stared down at her, things shifting inside. "What makes you so certain it's your brother I want and not you?" he murmured. "Lord knows, I can't seem to stay away from you."

Eden noticed the change in his look. His eyes intensified to a shade that took her breath away, hot and blue like the Nevada sky. "Don't," she said. But there was no conviction in her voice. He rubbed his lips over hers and felt them quiver in response. It was all the invitation he needed. He brought his mouth down, devouring hers. She told herself she didn't want this, that she didn't need this. It was a lie. She wanted to touch him, feel his hard, flat muscles. She gave in to the urge. When she sank against him, Kincade lowered her onto the bed of hay in the stall.

Eden had convinced herself it could never be like this. Not for her. Not after what happened. Yet for the first time she wanted a man completely, as a woman. Then, as her body responded to his kiss, the fear came back. Other sounds and sensations came flooding in. "No!" She struggled in panic. "Don't touch me. Don't!"

She struck out with her fists, and Kincade grabbed her wrists in reflex. "Dammit, Eden." He dragged her to him, but all the bitter accusations died on his tongue at the sight of her ashen face. The terror in her eyes was real, as were the tears.

"Take it easy." He relaxed his grip. "I'm not going to hurt you."

"Then let me go." Her throat was tight, her voice hoarse with it. "I don't want you to touch me."

His temper rose and had to be fought down. "I don't force myself on women. I'm going to let you go. Okay?"

The instant he released her wrists, she scooted backward in the hay. He kept his hands in front of him, fingers spread as proof he meant her no harm.

She scrambled to her feet, trembling visibly. She pressed close to the wood partition and inched her way along it, her eyes never leaving him. When she reached the end, her glance darted to a pitchfork propped against an inner wall, then back to him. He could almost see her mind working, trying to decide if she could reach the pitchfork before he could. Kincade suddenly understood her fear.

"The story you told was true, wasn't it?" he said softly. "DePard's brother tried to rape you."

She reacted sharply to his words. Her pride surfaced with a rush that stiffened her spine and squared her shoulders. "Am I supposed to care whether you believe me?" There was bitterness in her voice. "I don't need pity from you or anyone else."

"No," he agreed. "But you are entitled to respect."

A flicker of surprise showed in her eyes, followed by confusion and lingering distrust. With an admirable display of control she turned and walked toward the sunlight that streamed through the barn's tall opening.

Reaching down, Kincade picked up his hat. Anger rose up in him, hot and bitter with loathing. And all of it directed at a dead man—Jeff DePard.

WHEN Kincade came out after the evening meal, Vince was outside the ranch kitchen. A Band-Aid closed the cut high on his left cheek, and one eye was nearly swollen shut. The other ranch hands threw questioning looks at both of them, but nothing was said.

"Surprised to see me?" Vince murmured.

"A little." Kincade studied the damage he had inflicted.

"I told you I would keep my eye on you from now on," Vince reminded him. "Get used to it."

The next morning, when Kincade rode out on his day's assignment, he looked back and saw Vince following a hundred yards behind. The second day was the same as the first, with Vince always somewhere in Kincade's vicinity. On the third day Kincade decided to change the routine.

He rode north and west from the ranch, lifting the sorrel horse into a lope. A covert glance confirmed that Vince followed.

The ranch's western boundary reached deep into the desert mountains. Slowing his pace, Kincade searched for a place that would suit his purpose. Close to midafternoon he found it.

A tangle of boulders and fallen timber created a screen on the downslope of a saddleback. Beyond it was a grassy bench, shaded by junipers. He walked his horse past the screening deadfall, then turned the sorrel to stand parallel with it. Concealed from view, he waited for Vince. For long minutes the only sounds were the stamp of his horse and the whisper of a faint wind through the junipers.

The sorrel caught the first rumor of activity along their back trail and signaled it to Kincade with an alert pricking of its ears. Kincade gathered up the reins, his muscles bunching in anticipation.

A horse's nose bobbed into view. Kincade charged out from behind the natural blind. But it was Eden, not Vince, astride the horse. Startled, she hauled back on the reins. Kincade did the same, swearing silently at the glare of alarm in her eyes.

"Sorry. I didn't mean to surprise you like that." He studied her face, drawn again by that unusual mingling of strength and vulnerability. These last three days he had done his best not to think about her. Now he realized she had been on his mind the entire time.

"You're supposed to be checking the tank at Red Butte. That's almost a mile from here."

"This section of the ranch is new to me. I thought I'd look around." The explanation was plausible, but he wasn't sure she believed him. "Where are you going?"

She hesitated before answering. He watched the minute shift of expression on her face, the quick transition of light and dark in her eyes. "I came to check on the broodmares." Eden felt the heat of his glance and the disturbance it created within. She waited for the fear to come, but all she felt was a shivery need and an achy regret.

"Where are the mares?"

"There's a hanging valley about a half mile from here. I usually can find them there."

At that moment her horse swung its head toward a distant point along the ridge and sent out a ringing neigh. Looking back, Eden saw a horse and rider posed on a high curve of the saddleback two hundred yards away. She recognized Vince. She looked at Kincade, then at the deadfall with dawning understanding.

"You thought I was Vince." A moment ago she had believed Kincade had sought her out deliberately, that he had wanted to see her. She used anger to cover her mistake. "You were lying in wait for my brother, weren't you? Why?"

Kincade ran his fingertips over his bruised right jaw. "This isn't something I started."

"But you'll finish it, won't you?" Bitterness mixed with her anger. "Right or wrong, you'll strike back, and you won't be satisfied until you've crushed him."

"Are you talking about me or DePard?"

Pride lifted her head and covered her like a hard finish. No emotion showed through. A tap of the quirt, and her horse moved out briskly. Kincade swung his horse alongside.

Not a word was exchanged as they rode through the mottle of junipers. On the other side the way narrowed, and Kincade reined his horse in behind Eden's. Single file, they climbed the rocky defile, the silence between them lengthening and changing into something simple, more comfortable.

It was the land's influence, its indifference to human emotions, like anger. This vast Nevada land bred silence into those who spent much time in it, took the hurry out of them and stretched their vision to take in its far distances. Riding through it, Kincade's gaze wandered over the craggy tops of its mountains and explored the wide sweep of its desert floor, then came to a stop on Eden.

Her shoulders made a straight line in front of him, her hips swaying slightly with the motion of the horse. She was like this land—strong and resolute. Like it, she could be hot one minute and cold the next. And like it, she had a fragility that wasn't readily apparent.

When the trail widened, Kincade moved up to ride alongside her. They rounded a mountain, and the valley spread out before them—a wide grassy meadow cupped high in the rocks. Cottonwoods and willows grew along the banks of a spring-fed stream that rippled its way through it.

The horses were there. Kincade counted nine mares, all with foals nearby. Eden's horse nickered a greeting, and a young colt charged out to meet them. At a midway point the colt stopped and reared up, its small hooves pawing the air, its head tossing with the mock ferocity of a herd stallion defending his band.

Amused by the display, Kincade glanced at Eden. "I think we're being warned off."

A smile edged the corners of her mouth, echoing the humor he found in the scene. "I think you're right."

A big pinto mare whickered to the colt. When it continued its challenging antics, the mare trotted out. As she neared the colt, her ears snaked back. The next minute she was on it, head low, teeth bared. The colt squealed with the first sharp nip and rushed for the safety of the other horses, looking very much like a sulky child.

The sight drew an exchange of glances and a laugh from both of them. The glow of the shared moment was in Eden's eyes as she urged her horse forward to ride slowly through the scattered band of mares, Kincade ranging alongside.

The big pinto watched them. White, with patches of brown, she was stout and heavily muscled. She tossed her head, her ears going back, warning Kincade that he was getting too close. He started to rein his horse around her, then pulled up to stare at the mare's mismatched eyes—one blue, one brown. He knew that horse. . . .

THE big pinto stood in the bucking chute, ears swiveled back and brown eye rolling to catch the movement above and behind her. Kincade straddled the chute directly above the pinto, adrenaline surging through his system.

"Our next rider is K. C. Harris from Big Springs, Texas. K.C. is sitting in first place in the saddle-bronc competition, but he's drawn the great bucking mare Miss Fortune. I have to tell you, folks, this horse had been the *misfortune* of many a rider."

Tension hummed in the chute as Kincade lowered himself onto the mare. His weight touched the saddle, and he felt the knotting of muscle that humped the pinto's back. Kincade toed into the stirrups and double-checked his grip on the rope. The mare swung her head to the side, showing him a blue eye and the patch of brown on her neck shaped exactly like a child's mitten.

The heavy beat of his pulse drummed in his ears; the smell of rosin, horse, and sweat was strong around him. Every nerve had an edge to it. Kincade rocked back in the saddle, his free arm aloft and his hat snug on his head. He knew the mare's reputation, and he knew in his gut he could ride her. He gave a nod to open the gate.

The husky pinto shot into the air, exploding out of the chute like a rocket, a thousand pounds of compressed energy determined to rid itself of the man on her back. True to habit, the mare went straight for three high-kicking jumps, and Kincade raked his blunted spurs over her shoulders with each leap. The horse came to a sudden stop, pitching Kincade forward against the pommel. Cat-like, the pinto leaped sideways, twisting in midair. Kincade fought to stay in the saddle. With the next bone-jarring jump he sailed over the mare's neck. He threw out his arms and landed wrong, catching his left hand underneath him. Something snapped, and a white bolt of pain shot through him.

He came up, cradling his left arm, teeth clenched against the pain. Free of her rider, the horse relaxed into a gallop. On the way to the pens behind the chutes, the mare went past him. He caught the flash of a blue eye and swore there was a glint of laughter in it.

IT WAS there now; so was the mitten-shaped patch of brown on the pinto's neck.

"What's wrong?"

Caught up in the memory of that afternoon five years ago, Kincade answered without thinking, "I know that mare. That is Gus Holt's top bucking mare, Miss Fortune. That wasn't what we called her, though. To us she was No Score, because that's what you usually got when you drew her."

"You rodeoed professionally?"

He hadn't intended to reveal his past to her, but it was done. "All my life practically." Kincade continued to watch the mare. "I was four when I rode my first Little Britches Rodeo. After that it was all I wanted to do. It was my dream to ride in the National Finals Rodeo. Five years ago I was one win away from it when I climbed aboard Miss Fortune here. She tossed me off as easy as you please. I broke my riding arm and lost any chance of qualifying that year."

Looking back on those years when he had traveled the rodeo circuit, Kincade realized how very long ago those days seemed. The dream of becoming a national-champion bronc rider had no allure for him anymore.

"What made you give up rodeoing?"

"I didn't have much choice. I broke my riding arm too many

times." He flexed his left hand. "It can't take that kind of punishment anymore."

"So you traded the rodeo circuit for the ranch circuit." Eden didn't believe that even as she said it. He had the look of a man with a purpose, a mission.

"Something like that."

"You won't be satisfied with this kind of life for long."

"Maybe not." He shrugged. "I heard the mare was injured and had to be destroyed. How did you end up with her?"

"I sent letters to several rodeo stock contractors, letting them know I was starting a breeding program and asking them to contact me if they had any aged or injured mares they wanted to sell. Mr. Holt called me after the mare had the accident—it wasn't serious enough to warrant destroying her."

"A breeding program." He looked at the horses scattered over the valley. "You mean all these broodmares are—"

"Former rodeo stock, bareback or saddle bronc." Eden finished the sentence for him and relaxed a little when she saw the gleam of interest in his eyes. "We all know a horse passes certain traits on to its get. For some it's speed. In others it might be endurance."

Kincade picked up the thread of her thought. "And you believe that just as some horses are born to run, others are born to buck." His mouth curved in a smile. "What kind of results have you had?"

"One four-year-old turned out to be a good ranch gelding, and four three-year-olds we'll be trying out this winter."

Eden nudged her horse into a walk. Kincade did the same. But he wasn't ready to drop the subject. "What stallion are you using?"

"My ranch stallion. I'd like to get a stallion that's a proven bucker. I heard about one in Oklahoma this past spring. Vince checked it out for me, but the stallion was part draft horse. If the colts he sired didn't buck, they would be too big and clumsy for ranch work."

"You must be talking about Rod Bucher's stud Loco Louey."

"You know the horse?" She glanced at him in surprise.

"Just about every cowboy and stock contractor on the circuit knows Bucher and his stud. That stallion is vicious, the closest I've ever seen to a true man-killer."

"Vince never mentioned that," Eden murmured.

"Maybe he had other things on his mind."

Eden gazed at the sweep of land before them. Rodeo had been a part of him, just as this land was part of her. To be torn from it, to be forced to leave it would be a torture too horrible to imagine.

Kincade pulled up. "What lake is that?"

She looked in the direction he indicated, and smiled at the ghostly shimmer of water to the north. "It's a mirage. That's the southern edge of Black Rock Desert, a playa really. It's a dry lake bed that once was part of prehistoric Lake Lahontan, which covered much of the Great Basin fifty thousand years ago."

"How big is it?"

"Roughly seventy miles long and as much as twenty miles wide."

"And on the other side of it?"

"Another mountain range and, beyond that, the plains of Oregon. Imagine crossing that desert in a wagon pulled by oxen, then facing the mountains to reach the Oregon plains. To travel that same one hundred miles today by car would take maybe two hours. By oxen it must have taken—" She stopped, silenced by the thought that flashed in her mind. She stared at the desert mirage and the far-off mountains. The Oregon border lay just beyond them.

"What is it? Is something wrong?"

Eden turned. "No, nothing is wrong. You'd better go check that tank at Red Butte. I have some checking of my own to do."

She swung her horse away and headed back to the ranch.

THE sun was well below the horizon. Only a knife-edged ridge of amethyst remained in the western sky as the truck's light beams sliced through the gathering shadows. Eden drove straight to the house and climbed out of the truck. She was hot and tired after the long drive cross-country, yet exhilarated. There was a lift to her steps when she crossed the porch. She caught a whiff of fried onions, and hunger pangs struck. Her nose followed the delicious scent to the kitchen, where Vince was standing at the stove, spatula in hand, dishing a hamburger steak smothered in onions onto a plate.

"I'll forgive you anything if you tell me you fixed enough for two." She swept off her hat and shook her hair loose.

He threw her a glaring look. "Do you realize how late it is? Where the hell have you been?"

Eden wanted to tell him. She wanted to tell Vince the whole plan. But she couldn't take the chance he might let something slip, the way he had before. "Is that your way of telling me you didn't cook enough for me?"

"I already have food put aside for you." In irritation Vince lifted a lid off a plate to show her the food. "You could have left a note saying where you were going." He carried both plates to the table.

"You're right. I should have. Now, can we save your brotherly lecture until after dinner? I'm starved." Ravenous, Eden dug in.

They ate in silence. When they were finished, Vince leaned back in his chair, fastening his dark gaze on her. "You never said where you were."

"Everywhere." She faked a slight grimace. "And if you know where we can hire a couple more men, let me know. I've decided to start the fall roundup tomorrow." She gathered the dirty plates into a stack and carried them to the sink.

"It's early."

"And we're short of help. It could take us twice as long." If they did a normal, thorough job of it, which Eden didn't intend for them to do. She wanted to make one fast sweep of the ranch and be done in two weeks. DePard would expect her to be tied up over a month, and that's what she wanted him to think.

"What will you do with the cattle after you round them up? You can't ship them anywhere. DePard has you boxed in."

"I'll cross that bridge when I come to it." She went back to clear the table.

"There won't be any bridge. DePard has torn them all down. You're doing all this for nothing."

Rather than argue, she glanced at the bandage on his cheek. "How's the cut healing?" Eden opened the refrigerator and put the condiments away.

"Fine." Vince trailed after her when she crossed back to the sink. "I saw you with Kincade this afternoon. You looked pretty chummy."

"Not really." She was instantly on guard against both her feelings toward Kincade and Vince's subtle prying. "We just rode out to check the broodmares."

"Did he say anything about me?"

"No. Mostly he talked about himself. He used to compete on the rodeo circuit. You remember that big pinto mare I bought? Miss Fortune? He rode her once."

"He was a rodeo rider?"

"That's right. As a matter of fact, he knows that stallion you checked out for me in Oklahoma."

She went on, but Vince had stopped listening, his mind racing, rejecting, yet always returning to the same chilling possibility—the one that made sense of so many things. Sweat broke across his brow, the seeds of panic sprouting. He edged toward the door.

"Vince?"

He turned with a start. "Sorry. It's hot in here. I need some air."

Outside, he paused on the front porch and dragged in a shaky breath. The chrome on his pickup reflected the glow of the house lights. As he dug into his pocket for the keys, a voice came out of the shadows. "Going somewhere, Rossiter?"

He froze, fear heightening his senses. He caught the aroma of cigar smoke and saw the burning tip glowing from the shadows like a red eye. Kincade, a.k.a. K. C. Harris, moved out of the shadows and into the pooling light from the house. Vince stared at his face— the high cheekbones, the sharp jaw. It was there, the resemblance to Marcie. He had the same blue eyes and tawny-blond hair. Why hadn't he seen it before?

"What do you want?" He had to force the question through the constricted muscles in his throat.

Kincade idly flicked the ash from his cigar. "I thought it was time to remind you who was following whom."

Vince turned on his heel and went back inside the house, straight into the darkened living room. He made his way to the window by the gun cabinet and peered out. Kincade was a black shape in the shadowy darkness.

Pushed by worry, Vince swung from the window and raked his fingers through his hair. He propped a hand against the locked gun cabinet. For long minutes he stared at the rifles inside without seeing them. Slowly his eyes focused on the one Eden had taken when she went after DePard's man, shooting from the ridgetop. His expression cleared. Straightening, he turned and left the room. "I'm going to Starr's for a beer," he called to Eden as he went out the door. He climbed into the pickup and took off down the lane.

A mile down the track, the reflection of headlight beams flashed in his rearview mirror. Vince smiled when he saw them. "That's right," he murmured. "You just keep following me."

A HALF-DOZEN customers were in the Lucky Starr when Vince walked in. At the bar, Roy spotted him and said something to Starr. She turned, the movement setting the acres of fringe on her green shirt to swaying. "Well, if it isn't Mr. High, Wide, and Handsome himself," she declared, coming to greet him. She ran a glance over his face, a curious frown forming. "What happened to you?"

Vince hesitated, then lied masterfully. "Same old story, Starr—a jealous husband and no back door."

Her laugh was short and husky. "You always were an excellent liar, Vince. I'm not sure you would recognize the truth if it hit you in the face. Or is that what happened?"

"It doesn't matter." He glanced over his shoulder. Kincade would be walking through the door any minute. He didn't have much time. "I need you to do me a favor, Starr." He put an arm around her shoulders and steered her toward the bar.

"What kind of favor?" she asked with her usual caution.

"Get a message to DePard. Tell him I need to meet Sheehan the day after tomorrow at Eagle Gulch crossing at ten a.m. sharp. It won't be easy for me to slip away, and I won't have time to wait for him. Have you got that?"

"I've got it, but why not call DePard yourself?"

"I don't have time to explain. Will you do it? It's important."

"I'll do it."

"I knew I could count on you." Vince winked, then pointed her toward the stairs and her office on the second floor. "Go call him now."

The front door opened, and Kincade walked in. Starr spotted the bruises on his face and shot Vince a telling glance. "Looks like you landed a few punches of your own."

"One or two." He smiled.

She headed for the stairs, issuing a greeting to Kincade on the way. Relaxed, Vince signaled Roy for a beer. He was still smiling when Kincade walked up and leaned on the mahogany bar top.

"Pour the man a beer, Roy"—Vince motioned to Kincade—"and put it on my tab."

"I prefer to buy my own," Kincade stated.

"Suit yourself." Vince lifted his mug, hefting it toward Kincade in a mock salute before turning to a group of men sitting at a bar table. "Hey, Hoague, what do you say we get us a poker game going? I feel lucky tonight."

Two hours later Vince gathered up his winnings and sauntered over to the bar, where Kincade still stood, idly nursing a beer. "I'm ready to leave," he said, then winked. "Are you?"

Chuckling softly, he slapped Kincade on the back and headed for the door on legs that weren't too steady. Kincade paid for his last beer, then pushed away. Braced for trouble, he went out the door and immediately stepped to the side. But Vince wasn't lying in wait for him. Still cautious, Kincade edged toward the corner.

A truck motor turned over and caught. Kincade rounded the corner in time to see Vince's pickup pull away and head out of town.

Rusty came out of the shadows of the alleyway, the white of his bibbed apron standing out in the darkness. He glanced after the departing truck. "How's it going?"

"I'm not sure." Kincade took out a cigar and lit it.

Rusty skimmed his face with a glance. "Maybe you should drop this, Kincade," he suggested. "Marcie wouldn't like it. You know that."

"Marcie was too tenderhearted."

"Yeah, but don't forget—what goes around, comes around, Kincade," Rusty warned.

"In that case, Rossiter has a lot of grief coming."

"And you're going to see that he gets it."

"That's right."

"How? Have you figured that out?"

"Not yet," Kincade admitted. "But there's something he wants or something he dreads—something that will make him suffer more than anything else. When I find out what that is, he'll pay. If you don't want to help, go back to Oklahoma."

"I wouldn't be much of a friend if I walked away just because I think you're wrong. And you are wrong, Kincade."

"We'll see."

"You make it damned hard to be your friend, Kincade. But whether you're right or wrong, I'm going to be here if you need me.

And you'd better call me if you do, or you'll find out what this red hair on my head is all about. You hear me?"

Kincade nodded. "Loud and clear."

"Good." Rusty stalked off, disappearing into the alleyway.

Chapter X

THE dawn stillness was broken by the swelling sounds of activity in the ranch yard—the groan of saddle leather taking a rider's weight, the clump of hooves, the clatter of wagons rolling out.

Eden stood off to one side, impatient for the crew to be gone. The bed wagon lumbered closer, with Vince at the reins. He motioned for her. With her nerves screaming at yet another delay, Eden went over to him. "What do you want? You're holding up the others." She sent a quick glance at Kincade and the riders behind the wagon.

"Why aren't you coming with us?" Vince frowned.

"You have a short memory." Eden struggled to conceal her irritation. "I told you last night that I had to pick up supplies."

"You did? When?"

"After you got home from Starr's, where you had too many beers. I'll catch up with you tomorrow at Big Timber Canyon." As Eden turned to walk away, Kincade saw a packet of papers slip out of her hip pocket. He spurred his horse over to retrieve them.

"Eden, wait up." He swung out of the saddle. "You dropped something." Kincade saw they were maps of Nevada—one a state highway map, the other a detailed map of secondary roads. Both were folded open to the same section, and both had a series of X's in various places. "Treasure maps?" he joked when Eden came back.

"Of course not." She yanked them out of his hand. "They're ordinary road maps."

They might be road maps, but her attitude suggested the marks on them had a significance she didn't want him to discover. "I suppose you need them to find your way to town." Kincade kept his voice light and teasing, but his curiosity was aroused.

"Don't be ridiculous." There was the beginning of anger in her eyes. "I suggest you stop standing around. You have work to do."

Kincade gathered up the reins and stepped onto the bay. He glanced back at Eden. "If you have something you don't want De-Pard to know, I hope you haven't told your brother."

"I don't know what you're talking about." But there was a betraying flicker of unease in her eyes.

"Have it your way." Kincade reined his horse away.

Shortly after seven they arrived at Big Timber, a box canyon formed by the curling finger slopes of a low mountain. They set up camp outside the canyon's mouth. As soon as his tent was pitched and his gear stowed, Kincade went to the mess tent. Wild Jack had a pot of coffee boiled. Kincade helped himself to a cup and took a seat on the wagon tongue to wait for the rest of the crew to finish.

Vince was the last to arrive. "Never knew anybody could take so long stowing their gear away," Al Bender remarked. "What were you doing all that time in your tent anyways?"

"Making sure there weren't any rocks under my bedroll." Vince grinned. "You know me. I like my comfort."

The cow boss, Bob Waters, walked up. "It's time we got the day's work lined out." He crouched down and drew a crude map of the area in the dirt, using his finger. "We'll break this into sections and concentrate on areas near water. That's where we'll find most of the cattle. You'll work in pairs."

Kincade spoke up. "I'll go with Rossiter."

"My thought exactly." Vince gave him a thin smile.

The Paiute glanced from one to the other. "Just remember what you're out there for," he said. "You'll have this east section here, all the way to Butler's Draw." He marked out the area on his map.

Vince and Kincade nodded, then moved toward their horses. They rode east out of camp, traveling at an easy, rocking lope. A mile from camp, they spotted a dozen head of cattle grazing on the next rise. Together they herded the bunch back to the canyon. They worked in silence, their mutual dislike a wall between them.

The next morning, as usual, Vince was the last to arrive at the mess tent. With coffee in hand he joined the others, and Bob Waters started to line out the day's assignments.

"Kincade and I will take the Eagle Gulch section," Vince volunteered. "I know every place a cow can hide in that area."

"You've got it," Waters told him.

The first rose flush of dawn tinted the eastern horizon when the crew made their way to the horses. Kincade swung the saddle onto his horse's back. Off to his right he heard Vince swearing.

"Got a problem?"

"My damned horse is fixing to throw a shoe," he grumbled. "You might as well head out without me."

"You were supposed to check the shoes last night."

"I did. It wasn't loose last night," Vince snapped, then checked his temper. "Make your initial sweep along Eagle Gulch, and I'll swing to the north and hook up with you below Temple Butte."

"Fine. Just don't be long getting there," Kincade told him. "I'd hate to have to come looking for you."

"I'll be there," he replied, a hint of cockiness in his smile.

When Kincade rode out minutes later, Vince was at the bed wagon, pounding the first nail to reset his horse's shoe.

VINCE concealed his lathered horse in some brush behind the knoll, dug his binoculars out of his saddlebag, and scrambled up the slope, settling himself in a dish-shaped hollow at the top. Clumps of sagebrush clung to the sandy bowl, thick enough to obscure his presence, yet thin enough to keep his view unobstructed.

He took off his hat, tugged his bright yellow neckcloth loose, and stuffed it in his hip pocket, then loaded the rifle and levered a cartridge into the chamber. Sweat rolled down his face and stung his eyes. He wiped it away on his sleeve and raised the binoculars to his eyes, making a sweep of the sage flats. He had almost completed the arc when a horse and rider pushing three cows came into view. It was Kincade, less than a mile away. Vince lowered the binoculars, tucked them back in their leather case, and picked up the rifle, nerves tightening. Sweat ran freely now as he brought the rifle up.

BY NINE that morning Kincade had scared up three cows. He drove the red-coated trio ahead of him. A rocky knoll crowned with sagebrush partially blocked his view of Temple Butte, where he was to meet up with Rossiter. Kincade swung his horse out to the left, crowding the cows onto a trail that curved around the foot of the knoll. A long-eared rabbit leaped from beneath the brush at his horse's feet. Startled, the gelding shied and spun to the right. At the same instant Kincade heard the crack of a rifle and felt a puff of wind against his cheek.

Instinct kicked in. Kincade flung up his head, a dozen things registering at once. The loudness of the report meant that it had come from close range, and the knoll's brushy top provided both concealment and a field of fire. Kincade looked up and caught the metal glint of a rifle barrel. Caught in the open, with no cover nearby, he wheeled his horse toward the rocky slope as a second shot tugged at his shirtsleeve. Taking an angle that made him a difficult target, he charged for the top.

A man rose from the brush, trying to get a better shot. Kincade saw at once that it wasn't one of DePard's men. It was Vince. No longer was it strictly instinct that drove Kincade, but rage as well.

Vince got off one more shot before Kincade crested the knoll, but he fired too quickly and missed by a wide margin. Frantically he backed away from the onrushing horse and rider and worked to lever another round into the rifle chamber.

As his horse was nearly abreast of Rossiter, Kincade dove out of the saddle, driving Vince to the ground. Vince landed with a heavy grunt, and the rifle went sailing. Carried by his own momentum, Kincade rolled off. As he scrambled to his feet, his hand touched the smooth metal of the rifle. He grabbed it and pointed it at Vince, who froze in a half crouch, his eyes glued to the rifle. "Dammit, Harris, I had nothing to do with your sister dying."

Harris. The significance of it leaped at Kincade. "You know who I am." The rifle was suddenly a satisfying weight in his hands, lethal and tempting.

"Did you really think I wouldn't figure it out?" Vince challenged, then rushed desperately to his own defense. "But you must believe me. She was alive when I left that motel room."

"And you took every dime she had when you left, didn't you?" Kincade tightened his grip on the rifle, the hatred building. "It was always the money you wanted, wasn't it? It was never Marcie."

"She gave it to me," Vince insisted. "It was her idea. Marcie wanted me to have it."

The sound of Marcie's name coming from his lips and the sight of Vince alive while Marcie was dead combined to break through the last of his restraints. Kincade snapped the rifle to his shoulder and squeezed the trigger. The roar of the rifle blast drowned out Vince's sharp cry as he stumbled backward and fell.

In a blind fury Kincade levered another cartridge into the chamber and fired again and again and again, only dimly aware of the way Rossiter's body jerked with each shot. He kept up the barrage until the hammer finally clicked on an empty chamber, once, twice.

Kincade lowered the rifle, half sickened by the violence that was still within him. For a long moment he stared at the small furrows the bullets had plowed into the ground around Rossiter's tightly curled body. Only when Vince stirred, lowering the hands he had used to cover his face, did Kincade look at the man cowering there, unscathed. The old loathing surged back. "Go on. Get out of here before I change my mind," Kincade warned.

Warily Vince scrambled to his feet, then turned and ran down the slope.

Confused and angry, Kincade looked at the spent shells scattered over the ground. Deep down he had wanted Rossiter to die. But when the moment had come, he hadn't been able to do it.

Why?

A horse snorted somewhere at the base of the rocky knoll. Kincade turned in time to see Vince gallop off across the flats. Scanning the area, he located his own mount some twenty yards from the bottom of the slope. He started after it, then stopped when he heard the drum of hoofbeats approaching from the opposite direction. A rider in a black-and-white cowhide vest halted his horse on the other side of the gully. Kincade recognized him even before he saw the purple birthmark on the man's face.

"What was all that shooting?" Sheehan called to Kincade.

"I saw a snake."

The Diamond D foreman frowned his skepticism. "It took that many shots to kill it?"

"I guess I'm just a lousy shot." Kincade suddenly understood Rossiter's plan—prearrange a meeting with DePard's foreman, kill Kincade from ambush, and lay the blame on Sheehan. "Rossiter won't be keeping his meeting with you, Sheehan," Kincade told him. "You can be glad he won't."

"I don't know what you're talking about." Sheehan put his spurs to his horse, cantering off.

At the bottom of the knoll Kincade caught his horse and mounted. The cattle were long gone. He started back to camp, then saw the dust cloud Vince had raised. Its direction led straight to the ranch house. Vince was running again.

Kincade set out after him, driven by the need to finish what he had started, and grimly aware his heart wasn't in it, not with the same intensity as before. But he couldn't give it up. Not yet.

AFTER a day that had been physically demanding, Eden felt the heaviness of fatigue dragging at every muscle. Visions of a long, hot shower filled her head. As she headed for the stairs, Vince burst through the front door. His face was pinched and pale, something almost frightening in the set of his features. Eden grabbed his arm. "What are you doing here?"

"I'm clearing out, that's what." He jerked his arm free and ran up the stairs.

It was like a body blow. She saw all her plans dissolving before her eyes. She ran after him. Vince was jamming clothes into the open suitcase on his bed when she walked into his room. "You can't leave yet, Vince. We're in the middle of roundup. I need you."

"You'll get along just fine without me." He closed the suitcase with a snap and dragged it off the bed.

"Why are you suddenly in such a hurry to leave?" Eden followed him to the head of the stairs.

"I don't have time to explain, and you wouldn't understand if I did." His spurs clanked as he went quickly down the steps.

She went after him, convinced now that he was in some kind of trouble. It did absolutely no good to tell herself she had enough problems of her own without taking on his. Even with all their differences the bond between them was too strong.

"Vince, what have you done this time?" Eden was right behind him when he yanked open the door of his pickup, threw his suitcase into the cab, and climbed in after it.

"Nothing. Not a thing."

"Just tell me where you're going." Eden ran alongside the truck as he reversed away from the house.

"To Reno. After that . . . I don't know." He shifted out of reverse. "If you need me, leave a message with Axel, like always."

He started to pull away, then leaned out the window and called back, "And don't tell Harris a thing."

"Harris?" She knew no one by that name, but her bewildered response was lost in the accelerating roar of the pickup's engine.

KINCADE rode into the ranch yard at a gallop and wasted no time stripping the gear from his lathered horse. He took a step toward the bunkhouse, then heard a vehicle start up over by the house.

Vince. It had to be, he thought, and broke into a run. He reached the clearing in time to see Rossiter's blue-and-white pickup disappear down the ranch lane. Eden stood in the yard. Kincade hesitated, then took a chance and walked over to her.

"Where is Vince off to this time?" He had to work to make the question sound casual.

"Reno," she replied in an absent murmur, then stiffened and threw him a sharp look. "What are you doing here?"

But Kincade already had more information than he had hoped to get from her. He headed for the bunkhouse, determined not to give Vince a bigger head start than he already had. Moving quickly, Eden blocked his path. "You're supposed to be rounding up cattle."

He looked at her coolly, a hard and relentless cast to his features. "The plans got changed."

"By whose order?"

"Mine," he said, and walked around her.

Turning, Eden watched him cross the yard, his spurs kicking up little snake heads of dust. She threw a glance over her shoulder at the slowly dissipating cloud left by Vince's truck. The connection was easy to make. Too much had gone before that foreshadowed this. Only the reason wasn't clear yet. But now she had to find out.

When she reached the bunkhouse, Kincade was on his way out, duffel bag in hand. "You're going after Vince, aren't you, Mr. Harris?" Because she already knew the answer to that, Eden went on. "That's your real name, isn't it? Harris?"

"It is." He strode away from her toward his truck.

"What do you want with Vince?" Eden demanded. She tried to block him, but he barely slowed down.

"That's my business." He swung the duffel bag into the back end of the truck and dug in his pocket for the keys.

"Vince is my brother. That makes it my business."

"Not this time, Eden." He pinned her with an unyielding look, then climbed into the truck, reversing away from the bunkhouse.

The finality of his words was chilling. Pushed by the strong alarm she felt for her brother, Eden ran to the other side of the truck. She had to help Vince if she could. As the pickup rolled forward, she caught hold of the door handle and pulled the passenger door open. She jumped onto the running board and scrambled inside.

Kincade slammed on the brakes. "What are you doing? Get out!" His glaring look threatened to bodily throw her out.

Undaunted, Eden engaged the passenger-door lock and settled back in the seat. "You're going after Vince. And if you find him, you'll have to go through *me* first, because I'm going with you."

A grimness settled over Kincade's expression. "You're a fool, Eden. Haven't you got enough trouble with DePard without borrowing more from your brother?"

"DePard will wait until I get back." A few days' delay wasn't critical, but the threat to Vince was immediate. She couldn't let him face it alone.

"He wouldn't risk everything to help you."

"That's your opinion."

"No. That's the truth," Kincade fired back. "Your brother thinks only of himself and what he wants. He doesn't care about who he hurts in the process. Not even you."

Her control snapped. "Why? Because you say so? Am I supposed to believe *you*? A total stranger who comes to the ranch looking for work and gives me a phony name? Who lies?"

"I did it for a reason. And for your information my name *is* Kincade. Kincade Harris."

"Is that supposed to justify everything?"

"No." His mouth tightened briefly. "No. I guess not."

"Why do you hate him so much?" Eden demanded.

"I'll let Vince tell you when we catch up with him." He tromped on the accelerator, and the pickup leaped forward, tires spinning.

In record time Eden saw the weathered buildings of Friendly rise out of the sage flats. The truck never slowed until they reached the outskirts of town. Then, unexpectedly, Kincade applied the brakes, and the pickup fishtailed to a stop.

and called out, "Rusty!"

"Yo!" Rusty answered as he plunged a basket of french fries into
the deep-fat fryer.

"Rossiter's on the run. Headed for Reno." Before he finished,
Rusty was tugging off his apron. "We'll use the desk at Harrah's for
messages."

Rusty nodded his understanding. "I'll be right behind you."

That was all Kincade needed to hear.

RENO sprawled across the valley floor, the footslopes of the
rugged Sierra Nevada range rising beyond it. Traffic jammed its
thoroughfares, and more vehicles choked the parking lots of its
opulent hotel casinos—towering monoliths that vied for attention
with sparkling fountains, flashy neon, and showy flowers.

Kincade cruised slowly through another lot, trying to locate
Vince's pickup. Eden had lost track of the number of parking lots
they had already searched. She felt a weariness pulling at her, com-
bining with the tension-filled afternoon to drain her reserves. The
sun had slipped behind the Sierras when she turned to Kincade.
"Maybe he's left town." She hoped he had.

"Maybe. But the way I see it, your brother's been away from the
nightlife for a while. He'll want to sample it before he leaves."

When Eden saw the dazzling display of lights along the Strip, she
had to agree. There were miles of long neon tubing in brilliant
pinks, blues, reds, and white, and acres of lightbulbs. They were all
blinking on and off, racing up, down, and across, shooting into
space and exploding in a cavalcade of more lights. Crowning it all
was the celebrated arch that spanned Virginia Street, spelling out
in lights the town's famous slogan: RENO—THE BIGGEST LITTLE CITY
IN THE WORLD.

Kincade wagged a finger at the blaze of lights. "What do you
think of 'these blessed candles of the night'?"

"I think Shakespeare was referring to the stars."

"Only because he hadn't seen Reno's Glitter Gulch." Kincade pulled the truck into a lot and parked. Together they set out on foot.

The sidewalks were crowded with people wandering from one brightly lit casino to another. Kincade steered Eden toward one of them. A tall blonde in a frothy dress, high heels, and a mink stole was on her way out. "Oops, sorry." The woman executed a graceful side step to avoid Eden.

Eden stiffened under the blonde's assessing glance, painfully conscious of her scruffy cowboy boots, faded jeans, and man's shirt, and two days' worth of dust ground into them. She tugged her hat lower on her head and tilted her chin higher as she responded to the pressure of Kincade's hand on her waist and entered the casino.

The noise assaulted her first—the incessant clatter of slot machines, dinging bells, voices chattering. As they moved deeper into the casino, the people filling the aisles between the slots claimed Eden's attention. A group of cowboys in flashy pearl-snapped shirts, crisp new jeans, and snakeskin boots hooted at a buddy who was swearing at a machine. A young Japanese couple played the slot next to them, whispering and pointing in puzzlement at the winning combinations posted.

An old woman with two scarves tied on her head brushed past Eden. She clutched a plastic tub with a scattering of quarters in the bottom and looked as if she were wearing every article of clothing she owned. The old woman walked up to a quarter slot, carefully put one coin in, and pulled the handle. The reels whirled, then one by one clunked to a stop. Nothing. Expressionless, the woman dropped another coin in the slot and took another chance.

Chance. It was all a game of chance. A fever that got in the blood. Eden felt the contagion of it, the temptation to test her luck. One more roll of the dice. One more pull of the handle. This was where Vince would be, in a casino like this. She understood at last the lure of it. With a new feeling of urgency she scanned the crowd, trying to spot Vince before Kincade did.

They searched casino after casino, going from one to another until they all blurred together. Finally Kincade pushed his way into Harrah's and headed toward the hotel desk.

"Where are you going?" Eden asked.

"To see if there's a message from Rusty."

"Rusty? Who's Rusty?"

"My partner."

"Is he here in Reno, too?"

He nodded. "Somewhere."

Eden made no comment, but he knew it worried her that someone else might be looking for her brother.

At the registration desk Kincade recognized the night manager, a middle-aged man wearing glasses. "Hello, Kirk."

The man broke into a smile. "Mr. Harris. You look like you've had a long drive. I expect you'll want your usual suite."

"No. Not right now at least. Any messages for me?"

"Let me check." He stepped into the back offices.

"You must stay here often," Eden remarked.

"Whenever I'm in Reno." Kincade turned sideways, resting an elbow on the counter.

"I imagine a lot of people do. I wonder if the clerk remembers them." She didn't ask why he remembered Kincade.

"He has a nine-year-old boy who wants to be a cowboy. One year I arranged for his family to have front-row seats at the rodeo."

"That was nice."

"That was easy." Kincade turned back to the counter when he heard the night manager returning.

"Sorry, Mr. Harris. No messages."

"Thanks. Tell Matt I said hello."

"I will," the man promised, then added, "You should see the way he gets around in his new wheelchair. He calls it Dandy, says it's his cutting horse." The man laughed and lifted a hand in parting as Kincade moved toward the casino floor. Eden fell in beside him.

"A wheelchair," she murmured. "You didn't mention the boy was crippled. You have a soft heart after all."

"Not where your brother is concerned," he stated flatly. He slowed to descend the short flight of steps to the casino floor. Eden stumbled on the second tread, pitching forward. Kincade caught her. For an instant she sagged against him, and he felt the soft give of her body. His hold tightened. She immediately pulled back.

A change lady stopped. "Are you all right, miss?"

"I'm fine. Just . . . just tired." Eden pushed his hands away, denying the need for their support. But Kincade saw the exhaustion in her face. "What time is it anyway?" she asked.

The woman glanced at her watch. "A few minutes past two."

"In the morning?" Eden gave her an incredulous look.

"It's hard to tell in here, isn't it?" The woman smiled in understanding and moved off.

Eden pressed a hand to her stomach. "No wonder I'm so hungry."

Kincade took her arm and propelled her toward the restaurant. "Come on. We'll grab something to eat at the coffee shop."

The hostess showed them to a booth. Sliding in, Eden took off her hat, a tired sigh breaking from her. With both hands she pushed the hair back from her face, then flipped open the menu.

Kincade glanced up from his own menu. At that moment her expression revealed little of the tension she was under. But it showed itself in other ways, like the tight curl of her fingers on the menu, the taut muscles in her neck. He thought of all the grief DePard and her brother were causing her. He wondered how much more she could take before she broke under it.

A waitress came by. "Can I bring you something to drink while you look over the menu?"

"Two beers," Kincade said.

"I'd rather have coffee," Eden said, but the waitress had already walked off.

"You're wound tighter than a spring. The beer will relax you."

"I don't need to relax." But that was the only argument she offered.

The waitress came back with the beers, then hurried off. Thirsty, Kincade took a long drink of his beer. Eden did the same, then set the glass down and sagged against the corner of the booth, letting the cushioned sides support her. Her eyes felt dry and gritty from lack of sleep. She decided to close them—just for a little while.

A few minutes later she was sound asleep. She looked small and vulnerable. The sight pulled at Kincade. When the waitress returned to take their order, he nodded at Eden. "I guess she needs sleep more than food. If she wakes up, tell her I'll be back."

"Sure."

But she was still asleep when he returned. "Eden. Eden, come on." He had to shake her awake.

"Wha—" She felt hands lifting her upright. "Where are we going?"

"We're calling it a night." His voice seemed to come from a great distance. She struggled to hear it but missed a few words. ". . . registered for both of us."

"Good." She took a few weaving steps before Kincade scooped her up. "I can walk," she mumbled in a voice thick with sleep.

"Sure you can," he agreed dryly.

By the time he reached the elevator, she was asleep, her head resting in the crook of his neck. He felt a nameless, tender feeling as he carried her into the suite and went unerringly to the second of two bedrooms. Using the point of his elbow, he flipped on a light. A king-size bed filled the room, its covers turned back in precise folds. He carried Eden to the bed and sat her on the edge of it. His hands caught her before she tipped back onto the mattress.

"Come on, sit up, Eden, so I can get your boots off."

She mumbled a vague acknowledgment and spread both arms to prop herself upright. Kincade knelt down and pulled off her boots and socks. She had small feet, as smooth and delicately boned as the rest of her. His fingers trailed over one arch.

As he started to rise, he saw she had her shirt unbuttoned. He felt his blood heating up and a strangling tightness grip his throat. Her hands moved automatically to the snap of her jeans. "I don't remember ever being this tired, Vince," she mumbled, the snap and zipper giving way at the same moment.

She thought he was her brother! Kincade was dangerously close to correcting that impression. Instead he grabbed her pant legs and gave them a yank, tipping her over backward onto the mattress. Two quick tugs, and her dusty jeans were on the floor. He stripped the shirt from her limp arms and tucked her under the covers. She immediately rolled onto her side and snuggled into a pillow.

Kincade walked over to the long plate-glass window and closed the heavy drapes, blacking out the neon glitter of the Strip. He flipped off the light when he walked out the door.

DAWN was breaking when Kincade returned from prowling the casinos. He unlocked the door to the suite and walked in, his duffel bag in one hand and a shopping bag in the other. He glanced at the door to Eden's room, then left the shopping bag in a chair in the sitting room and walked directly to the suite's larger bedroom, his footsteps heavy with fatigue. He really needed a few hours' sleep.

The satin felt cool against his skin when he slipped between the sheets and stretched out. He closed his eyes and tried to forget that Eden was only a room away.

Chapter XI

KINCADE'S eyes snapped open. Sun streamed through the window, framed by the heavy blackout drapes he had deliberately not closed. Thinking the sun had wakened him, he peered at the digital clock on the nightstand. It was a few minutes before ten in the morning.

Kincade swung his legs out of bed. Then he heard it—a muffled cry coming from Eden's room. He realized it hadn't been the sun that woke him. He pulled on a pair of Levi's and went to investigate. When he entered the darkened room, he saw her thrashing about in the bed, strange sounds coming from her throat.

"Eden." When she failed to answer, he moved to the bed and turned on the lamp. She flung her head away from him, her fingers digging into the tangled covers as if she were in pain. It was only when he touched a hand to her damp cheek, checking for a fever, that he realized she was still asleep. "Eden, wake up." He gave her shoulder a gentle shake, then shook it harder when she fought him.

Her eyes opened, round with terror as she cringed back from him. Some instinct kept him from gathering her close, as he wanted to do.

"You had a bad dream," he murmured, and took her hand. For an instant she gripped his fingers hard and held on, then pulled away. "I'll bring you some water."

He left. She took deep breaths, trying to quell the sickening churn of her stomach. Water ran in the bathroom. Then she heard the soft pad of bare feet approaching the bed. She took the glass from him and wrapped both hands around it. She couldn't look at him. Not yet. She just wanted him to go. But when he sat down on the bed, part of her wanted to be gathered close and comforted.

"Talk to me, Eden."

"It is only a dream, just as you said." She kept her gazed fixed on the water glass.

"It's more than that." His fingers brushed her cheek, pushing back a strand of hair. "You need to talk about it. I'll listen."

"I don't need anyone," she insisted stiffly.

"I'm not leaving until you tell me about it."

She took a sip of water. "I dreamed about the night Jeff died. Now, I've told you. You can leave."

Without a word he took the glass from her and set it on the night table, then drew her into his arms. She stiffened, but he ignored her resistance, pressed her head against his shoulder, and stroked her hair. The breath she released fell somewhere between a sigh and a sob. She never talked about it. It was too hard, too painful. Yet with her eyes closed and her head cushioned against his shoulder, the words came.

"I was seventeen. Jeff was older—Vince's age. They were friends. After graduation Jeff went off to college. I saw him a few times when he was home, but I never really knew him. I mean, I was just Vince's kid sister. Jeff never paid much attention to me until that spring." Just talking about it, Eden felt seventeen again, naïve and uncertain. "All the girls were envious that he had noticed me. He was good-looking, a star athlete. On top of that, he was a DePard."

"I wouldn't call being a DePard any recommendation."

Drawing back, Eden saw the smile that lurked at the corners of his mouth before she dipped her head back to rest against his shoulder. There wasn't anything else he could have said that would have made her feel better.

"Back then, it was," she said. "Anyway, one Thursday after school, Vince told me that Jeff wanted to go out with me Saturday night. I reminded Vince that Jed—my grandfather—wouldn't let me go out on dates. Vince said he could sneak me out. He said we would double-date and he would bring Rebecca Saunders. Finally I agreed."

Suddenly Eden needed to move. A restlessness pushed her to the opposite side of the bed. She dragged the sheet with her, wrapping it around her Indian-style as she stood.

"Where did you go?"

Eden walked to the window, freed a hand from the entwining sheet, and lifted the drape to look out. There were cars on the street and people on the sidewalks, but fewer than last night.

"Seven miles south of the ranch, going toward town, there is a series of rock pools fed by a hot spring." She took a long breath and continued, little emotion coming through. "It was arranged for Jeff to pick up Vince's date and meet us at the spring at nine o'clock. Jeff and Rebecca were already there when we arrived. It was a beautiful night. The stars were out, thousands of them. . . ."

WITHOUT the headlight beams on Vince's truck to dim their brilliance, the stars glittered overhead like diamond fragments. Excited and tense, Eden waited for Vince to join her before she approached the pair waiting by the small fire.

"Ready?" Vince flashed her a smile.

She nodded and ran exploring fingers over one side of her hair to make sure no tendrils had escaped. "Do I look all right?" She had pulled her hair back from her face and anchored it with combs in an effort to appear older and more experienced. She didn't want Jeff to suspect she had never been on a date before.

"You'll knock him dead, sis," Vince promised with a wink.

Taking her arm, he guided her over the rocky ground to the ledge of smooth stone that extended out to form the upper rock pool. Yellow flames blazed cheerily near the center of the ledge, the flickering light revealing two blankets that had been spread over the flat stone. A red-and-white cooler sat between them, a portable radio and tape deck on top of it, surrounded by cassettes.

Eden saw it all, looking anywhere but at the tall, broad-shouldered man backlit by the fire. She could feel Jeff's gaze, moving over her like a pair of invisible hands. It was unnerving, but exciting, too. She glanced at the woman next to him, her sun-streaked hair tousled in deliberate disarray. Older than Eden by two years, Rebecca Saunders had worked in Reno for nearly a year before her father became ill, after which she returned home to look after him. The black jeans she had on were so snug, Eden knew she could never climb on a horse in them. Her T-shirt was equally tight, and the baggy vest she wore over it did little to conceal the lack of a bra.

"Hi," Vince said. "Hope you haven't been waiting long."

"Just long enough to get the fire started," Jeff replied, the low and lazy pitch of his voice turning Eden's nerves all jittery.

"That's right," Rebecca chimed in. "Jeff picked me up early, and we stopped to eat. We were having such a good time, we were almost late ourselves."

Jeff's glance went to Eden. "Hello, Eden."

"Jeff." She sounded a little breathless; she was a little breathless.

"Yes, hello, Eden." Rebecca echoed his greeting and sent her a smile that was pure poison. Confused, Eden wondered what she had done to make Rebecca dislike her.

"You look wonderful tonight," Jeff murmured.

"Thank you." She touched a hand a little proudly to the wide eyelet collar of her white blouse. It lay in soft ripples, creating a ruffle effect around the V neckline. It was her best blouse, plain enough to satisfy her grandfather, yet feminine enough to suit her.

Jeff held out a hand. Eden hesitated, then placed hers in it. He drew Eden closer to the fire. "There's beer in the cooler, Vince. Help yourself." He glanced at Eden. "Want one?"

She shook her head. "Not right now. Thanks."

"You don't mind if I have one?" He was already moving toward the cooler.

"Of course not." Eden sank onto the blanket, adjusting her skirt over her legs. Jeff came back and sat next to her.

"Let's have some music." Rebecca popped a cassette in the tape player. A slow, sentimental ballad came over the twin speakers. "I feel like dancing." She looked pointedly at Jeff. When he didn't move, she pulled Vince up to dance with her.

Jeff reached down for Eden's hand. Self-consciously she let him pull her to her feet. "I'm not a very good dancer," she warned.

"There's nothing to it." His hand slid around her waist, drawing her close. "Just relax and let your body sway with the music."

Eden had begun to do just that when he released her hand and fingered the ruffle of her blouse. "I like your blouse." He ran his fingers down it, the back of his hand brushing over her breast. "What do you call this material?"

"Eyelet." She somehow managed to get the word out.

"Eyelet." He explored the embroidery around one of the holes. "I like it. Especially on you." His glance lifted to her face.

Eden lowered her chin to conceal any blush. Almost immediately she felt his cheek against her hair.

"You smell good."

"It's my perfume. Vince gave it to me for Christmas."

"Did you put some behind your ears?" His head dipped down to discover the answer for himself, the warmth of his breath feathering over her ear and neck. She closed her eyes.

"What's the name of it?" His lips repeatedly touched her neck as he formed the words.

Eden could barely breathe, let alone think. "Emeraude," she whispered, finally remembering the name on the bottle.

"It does things to a man." He rubbed his mouth along her cheek. "It makes him want to find out if you taste as good as you smell."

His mouth was at the corner of her lips. Aroused yet unsure, Eden turned her head just that fraction necessary to make contact. He wasted no time claiming her lips.

It wasn't her first kiss. When she was fifteen, Buddy D'Angelo used to walk her from class to class. One time he stopped her in an empty stairwell and kissed her. But it hadn't been like this, all hot and moist, scary and thrilling at the same time.

The song ended, and another took its place, propelled by a fierce, driving beat. Jeff gave an angry mutter and pulled away, striding to the cassette player and switching it off. Rebecca laughed, soft and husky. "Lord, nothing destroys a mood quicker than the wrong music," she declared in a voice still rich with amusement.

Without Jeff's body against hers, Eden felt the coolness of the night air. She shivered and hugged her arms together.

Jeff glanced at her. "Cold?"

"A little."

"Better come over by the fire and warm up." He took her hand and pulled her down beside him on the blanket. With a forefinger he traced the curve of her jaw, circling the point of her chin, then moving up to her mouth. Her lips parted with the pressure of his finger. She didn't understand the sudden darkening of his eyes or the near groan that came from his throat. He moved his hand away and brought his mouth down, grinding it against her lips.

There was pain in the kiss and a crude kind of pleasure that she wasn't sure she liked. On and on it went, his lips devouring her with wet, open-mouthed kisses. His hands ran over her back and shoulders, down her waist and hips, rough and demanding sometimes, soft and stimulating at others.

Embarrassed, she pulled away and darted an anxious glance in Vince's direction. Jeff caught her chin and turned it back. "Don't worry about him. Your brother is too busy to notice us."

But Eden was too self-conscious to respond to Jeff's next kiss with the same ardor. When the pressure of his mouth became insistent, she twisted away from it.

Just then Vince wandered over to the fire. "It's getting a bit chilly. Come here, Rebecca, and warm me up. Would you like another beer?"

"None for me. I need to get home and make sure Dad's all right. Ready, Jeff?" She faced him, her stance challenging.

"Hey, what is this?" Vince frowned. "If you have to go, I'll take you home."

"You don't need to. Our place is right on Jeff's way."

"Vince can take you," Jeff spoke up. "Eden and I will load things up, put out the fire. I'll take her back to the ranch."

"Let's go." Vince turned Rebecca toward the truck. She hurled an angry look at Jeff and Eden, then moved stiffly off.

After the pickup had disappeared down the rough track, Jeff rose and took another beer from the cooler. "Are you sure you don't want a beer? Your brother's gone now."

"No. I really don't want one." Eden felt his eyes on her, unnerving in their steadiness. She was suddenly very uncomfortable. She wished Vince hadn't left. She had felt safer when he was there. Which was ridiculous, she told herself. She was perfectly safe now. Just the same, she stood up. "I'll take the tape deck to your truck."

"Why?"

"I thought you wanted to load up before you took me home."

"What's the hurry? I'll put on some music so we can dance." He slipped a cassette into the tape player. Within seconds a slow song drifted from the speakers.

With an odd reluctance Eden let him draw her into his arms. His mouth traveled over her hair to her cheek. She could smell the beer on his breath. She had noticed it before, but now it bothered her. A dozen times and more, his demanding mouth sought hers. It was good, and yet it wasn't. She wanted this, and yet she didn't. What was wrong with her? She pressed closer to him, conscious of one song fading into another and another.

He pulled her down onto the blanket. She wanted to object, but the words wouldn't come. She was out of her depth and knew it. When his mouth closed on hers, she tried to push him away, but his weight was already pressing her down. The first seeds of fear took root. "Jeff—" She began a choked protest, but her resistance inflamed him further. The weight of his body grew heavier, crushing the air from her lungs.

Then his mouth rolled off hers, and he shifted slightly, giving her space. She gulped in a quick breath, swallowing back a sob, and rolled sideways to get out from beneath him

The suddenness of it took him by surprise. She almost made it. But his hand caught hold of her blouse. When she tried to wrench loose, she heard the fabric rip. "My blouse!" Anger trembled in her voice. "You tore it." It was the nicest one she owned.

"You don't need it." Too late she discovered his fingers at the buttons. "Take it off." The first two were already free, and he was at work on the third when she brought her hands up to interfere.

"No!" The refusal was quick and hot.

In reply he drove her back flat on the blanket again, hooking a leg over her to hold her. Frantic, she grabbed his hair and tugged. He caught her arms and forced them high above her head, trapping her wrists in the vise grip of one hand. "Don't pretend you don't want it." He pushed his face closer to hers, an ugliness in his expression. "I remember the way you pushed against me."

"No, no, no." It was the word Eden repeated over and over again as she twisted under him, her body arching and bucking, trying to throw him off. Blood pounded in her ears, and her breath came in swift, panic-shallow sobs. Through a veil of hot tears she saw his arm, the one that held her wrists pinned above her head. Raising her head, she twisted to reach it. The instant she felt it, she sank her teeth into the fleshy part and bit down hard.

There was a yowl of pain from him, and her arms were loose. "You bit me, you little animal."

An exploding agony spread across her jaw, the force of Jeff's backhanded blow splitting her lip and snapping her head to the side, banging it on the blanket-covered rock. She tasted blood on her tongue—her own blood. He hit her again and again, brutal in his intent to subdue, his voice filtering through, hurling obscenities.

One moment he was hitting her; the next, his hand was tugging at her skirt, pulling it up, his nails scraping her flesh.

"No!" The word came out in a throaty shriek of fear. Eden struck out at this degradation, this awful helplessness.

Her first blows landed harmlessly on his shoulders. Swearing, Jeff tried to capture her wildly swinging fists, but one got through and slammed into his nose. He grabbed it, his eyes closing against the sharp pain. With added strength coming with a surge of adrenaline, Eden tumbled him off her and struggled to her feet. She saw Jeff rising up, blood gushing from his nose.

"When I get my hands on you, I'll kill you."

She believed him. Catching back a sob, she broke into a run. If she could make it to Jeff's pickup, she had a chance.

KINCADE remained on the edge of the bed, his body angled toward Eden. She stood at the window, her body stiff, her fingers gripping the heavy drape.

"It was like a nightmare," she murmured. "Jeff was gaining on me. Yet the harder I ran, the slower my legs seemed to move. When I reached the pickup, I was so scared and shaky, I fumbled with the handle and just barely got in and locked the door before Jeff was yanking on the handle. I scooted over to lock the passenger side, then started looking for the key. Suddenly Jeff tapped on the window. I looked out and saw him laughing and dangling the keys."

Kincade saw a shudder quiver through her. He felt a stir of anger rising and fought it down.

"When he put the key in the door lock, I threw myself at the passenger door. I knew if I could get out the other side before he got the door open— But he grabbed my leg. He dragged me across the seat, telling me all the vile and filthy things he was going to do to me. That's when—" She stopped and closed her eyes to shut out the memory of what happened next.

Kincade waited, giving her time to collect herself. But even after she opened her eyes, the silence continued. Kincade prompted her with a question. "Jeff had a rifle in his truck, didn't he?"

Eden looked at him for a moment, then turned back to the window. "Yes," she replied at last. "He had two hanging on the rack in his back window."

She released the drape. When she spoke again, there was a rehearsed quality to her words. "I don't remember grabbing it. I don't remember pulling the trigger. I only remember the way Jeff laughed when he saw it, then the explosion and the look of shock on his face."

"You had no choice, Eden."

"No," she agreed with a small troubled shake of her head. "The bullet struck him in the chest. He wasn't dead, but he needed help. I tried to stop the bleeding." Eden looked down at her hands, remembering the warm, wet feel of his blood on them, the distinctive odor of it. She dragged in a long breath. "Somehow I managed to get Jeff into the truck. It was too far to town, but Spur was only seven miles away. It was the longest seven miles I ever drove. . . ."

THE house loomed as a solid black shape just beyond the stab of the headlight beams. Gulping back a sob of relief, Eden laid on the horn, sending out one long blast. Lights blinked on as she came to a stop near the front porch. She cast an anxious glance at Jeff, lying on the seat, then pushed out of the truck and ran for the house. As she reached the porch steps, her grandfather came out, hurriedly pulling his suspenders over his undershirt. He frowned when he saw Eden. "What are you doing out here? I thought you were in your room asleep."

She shook off his questions. "You've got to get a doctor, an ambulance. He's been shot."

"Who's been shot? Vince?" He bulled his way past her and headed straight for the truck.

"It isn't Vince." Eden ran after him. He opened the passenger door and peered in, the dome light clearly illuminating Jeff's deathly pale face and the bloodstains all over his shirt. "It's—" She stopped.

"The DePard boy. Duke's little brother." He shot Eden a quick look, the thick brush of his heavy eyebrows drawing together to form a solid line. Then he climbed in the cab.

"He's bleeding bad," Eden said. "I tried to stop it, but . . ."

Jed backed out of the truck and turned, a stunned and hopeless look on his face. "He's dead."

"No." Numbly Eden shook her head. "You're wrong." She tried to push past him into the cab, but her grandfather caught her.

"He's dead, Eden," he repeated.

"I WENT A LITTLE CRAZY THEN," Eden admitted. "I started crying and screaming. Jed slapped me a couple of times. I was hysterical," she said in defense of her grandfather's actions.

"And someone saw your grandfather strike you." Kincade shook his head. "That's where the idea came that he had roughed you up to make it look like Jeff had assaulted you."

"Yes. Jed asked me what happened, and I told him that Jeff had tried to rape me. . . . That's when Vince came out of the house. Jed told him to take me inside."

"Then Vince was already home."

She hesitated, then nodded. "Yes. He got there a few minutes before I did. He and Rebecca had quarreled, so he had taken her straight home and come back. Later the sheriff arrived—and the ambulance. Lot Williams started questioning me."

"You didn't have an attorney present? Did he read you your rights?"

"He did, yes. But I didn't think I needed a lawyer. It wasn't murder, and I didn't know how he could say that it was."

"But he did."

"Everyone did. Duke DePard made sure of that."

"Not everyone. The jury believed you."

"True." Her smile was full of irony.

"It's over, Eden."

"No." She sighed. "DePard won't let it be over." She rubbed a hand along her arm, her skin crawling with the memory of Jeff's hands on her. "I need a shower." She walked to the adjoining bath.

Kincade watched the door close behind her. He sensed there was more to the story than Eden had told him, but it could wait. He went to the window and threw open the drapes, staring at the traffic below. Vince was out there somewhere, but for the first time in a long, long while, Vince didn't dominate his thoughts. Eden did. He told himself he shouldn't care what happened to her, but it was too late. He already did. With a restless swing he turned from the window and headed for the door.

Ten minutes later, fully clothed now, Kincade rolled a cigar between his lips. The plush carpet absorbed the tread of his boots as he made a slow circle of the suite's sitting room.

The jingling of the telephone pulled him around. In two strides he was at the writing desk, the receiver in his hand. "Hey, Kincade, it's me," Rusty's voice came over the line. "Any luck?"

"None. You?" He laid his cigar in an ashtray.

"In a way. I figured if our boy was a regular in town, somebody had to know him. Sure enough, I was right."

Kincade searched for some sense of elation. It wasn't there. "Who is it? Where can we find him?"

"He's a blackjack dealer at the Nugget, works the evening shift. His first name is Max or something like that. His hair is dark, parted in the middle. He has a long handlebar mustache. The cocktail waitress said we can't miss him. I plan to be at the Nugget when the evening shift comes on, in case Vince shows up with this Max guy."

"I'll meet you there."

"I wouldn't if I were you. Vince will be watching for you, but he won't be looking for me. If he doesn't show up at the Nugget, maybe I can get his friend to give me a line on where he might be."

Kincade was forced to concede, "That's probably the best way to handle it."

"I think so. Just stick close to the hotel so I can get word to you in a hurry if I turn up something."

"All right." Kincade hung up.

"That was your partner, wasn't it?"

He turned. Eden stood in the doorway to her room, her hair wet from the shower, a terry-cloth robe provided by the hotel tied around her and a scrubbed-clean glow to her face. "Did he find Vince?" She was motionless, tension in every line.

"Not yet." He gave her a long, considering look. "Does the name Max mean anything to you?"

"Max?"

"That's right. Max."

"No. Is Vince supposed to know him?"

Kincade smiled. "I would hate to play poker with you, Eden. Sometimes you don't let your expression give anything away."

"I don't know what you're talking about."

"No?" He lifted an eyebrow, amused.

"No. I—"

There was a knock at the door. "Room service," came the muffled announcement.

"I ordered breakfast. I thought you might be hungry." Kincade crossed to the door.

A white-jacketed waiter wheeled the serving cart into the suite. "Afternoon, Mr. Harris. Good to have you back." He flashed Eden a smile. "Afternoon ma'am." She nodded and slid a hand up the front of her robe, clutching it together near her throat.

The waiter pushed the cart near the writing desk, snapped the table leaves up, arranged the place settings, and retrieved the hot food from the warming ovens below. Delicious aromas of freshly brewed coffee and yeasty breads filled the sitting room.

Kincade signed the check, and the waiter headed for the door. Kincade locked the door behind him and turned back. Eden still stood in the bedroom doorway. "Better come eat before it gets cold." He pulled a chair out and sat down.

Eden walked over and took a seat. She unfolded a mauve napkin and laid it across her lap, then cut into her omelette. Spicy odors steamed up.

"How is it?" Kincade asked after she had taken a bite.

"Very good. And you were right—I am hungry."

"I figured you would be. I knew I was." When she made no reply, Kincade let the silence stretch for a time and concentrated on his breakfast. "Want to tell me the rest of what happened?"

"The rest?" Startled by his question, Eden looked up.

"Given what you told me, there wasn't sufficient evidence to charge you with murder. There had to be something more." He spread strawberry jam on a slice of bread and handed it to her.

"Rebecca Saunders," she said. "She told the sheriff that she had a date with Jeff that night, not Vince. She made up a story about how Vince and I had barged in on them and how jealous I was because Jeff was with her. She claimed that Jeff had insisted she let Vince take her home so he could cool me down."

"And when Vince said differently, the sheriff decided he was lying to protect you," Kincade guessed.

"Rebecca was very convincing." Eden broke off a piece of toast.

"So what happened? Did Rebecca eventually change her story?"

"Are you kidding?" Eden showed the first trace of real bitterness. "She found out how beneficial it was not to."

Kincade frowned. "What do you mean by that?"

"I mean that within a month after Jeff died, Rebecca's father had the bypass operation he'd been needing, paid for by DePard. A little later their house was painted and Rebecca had a big new car. She had discovered her own silver lode, and she mined it for every dime she could get." Eden poked at her eggs with a fork. "If she had testified against me at the trial, I would probably be in prison now."

"She didn't?"

"No. She was killed in a car accident two months before my case went to court."

"What happened when you met privately with DePard?"

Her fork slipped from her fingers and clattered onto the plate. "How did you know about that?"

"It stands to reason." Kincade poured coffee for them. "If I were DePard and you were accused of killing my brother and the sheriff was my cousin, I would demand to meet you face to face."

"He did," Eden admitted. "That morning right after Jeff died, while I was still in jail. I could see the pain in his face, and I could feel his hatred for me. . . ."

CONSCIOUS of DePard's grief, Eden felt she had to say something. "I'm . . . I'm so sorry," she began.

"Not as sorry as you're going to be," Duke snapped. A grief-born fury rumbled up from deep inside him. "Sheriff Williams has given me your sensationalized account of last night's events, but I have learned, Miss Rossiter, that you are not telling the truth."

Panic clawed at her throat. "What do you mean?"

"The sheriff spoke with Rebecca Saunders. She was the one who had a date with Jeff last night, not you."

"No. It's true Jeff picked her up, but—"

"Please. She has no reason to lie, while you most certainly do. That's why you made up this lurid story claiming my brother attempted to force himself on you."

"He did," Eden insisted. "He hit me and held me down and—"

"That's a damned lie." Duke vibrated with anger. "Everybody knows that any number of women would have willingly spread their legs for him. He would never resort to rape."

"But he did." Eden battled to hold back the sobs rising in her throat. "I never wanted him to die. I tried to get help."

"But you failed. Jeff is dead," DePard stated, blunt and hard. "If you are truly sorry for what you've done, you will not destroy his name with these lies."

"They aren't lies!"

"They are, and I can prove it. If you persist with this vicious story, you will be ruined. Do you understand?"

Eden was stunned into silence.

"Fortunately," DePard continued, "no one other than Sheriff Williams and myself knows about this account of yours. There is still time to retract it."

"Retract it?" Eden wiped at the wet tear tracks on her face, accidentally rubbing the bruised flesh where Jeff had hit her.

"Exactly. Everyone knows Jeff was a gun buff. He loved to hunt and target-shoot. It would be very likely that last night he showed you his new rifle. Maybe he let you try it, and at some point something went wrong. Perhaps you thought the rifle wasn't loaded or that the safety was on when the gun *accidentally* discharged."

Eden looked at him. "You want me to say the shooting was an accident?"

DePard nodded. "A terrible, tragic mishap. No charges will be filed against you."

"What about Rebecca and the things she said?"

"Rebecca Saunders can be persuaded to cooperate," DePard stated. "Are you going to change your story or not?"

"I . . . I don't know."

When she hesitated, DePard took an angry step toward her. "It's money, isn't it? How much do you want? Ten thousand? Twenty?"

"I don't want any money from you," Eden protested.

"Fifty thousand, and that is my final offer," DePard threatened. "You take it and you change your story, or I swear by everything that's holy, you'll regret it."

EDEN broke off her sightless stare into the past and looked at Kincade, then dropped her glance. "His voice kept getting louder. The accusations, the threats . . . After all I'd been through, they became too much. I started yelling back, telling him that just because he was wealthy and powerful didn't mean he could buy me off. I was seventeen and scared—and horribly idealistic, I suppose.

I thought the truth would vindicate me. Looking back, I know I should have accepted the deal. If I had, I would have been free to live my life without being constantly harried by DePard."

"I have a feeling that deep down you aren't really sorry."

"I suppose not. Lies aren't easy to live with either." Eden placed her napkin on the table. "Breakfast was good. If you'll excuse me, I need to dry my hair and get dressed."

Kincade rose. When she disappeared inside her bedroom, he walked over to a chair and picked up the shopping bag he had left there, then headed for her door. She opened it just as he got there.

"Where are my clothes?"

"I sent them out to be cleaned. They'll be back tonight. In the meantime you can wear these." He handed her the shopping bag. "I had to guess at the sizes, but I think they'll work."

"You bought me clothes?" She looked surprised.

"I didn't think you would want to sit around all afternoon in that robe," he replied with a teasing smile. "Go ahead. Try them on."

Fifteen minutes later Eden emerged, all woman and looking it. The dress Kincade had chosen was a simple royal-blue cotton knit, belted at the waist, with push-up sleeves and a wide, flaring skirt.

"How does it look?" She stood before him.

Kincade ran an admiring eye over the result. "The dress looks fine, and *you* look beautiful." He gathered up his hat. "Ready?"

"I take it we're off to the casinos again, looking for Vince."

"Rusty's handling that. I thought we'd get some fresh air."

Chapter XII

SIDE by side they left the hotel and walked straight into a swirling wind. It whipped at the hem of Eden's dress, lifting the material and threatening to send it flying up about her face. She battled the billowing skirt down. She shot a glance at Kincade and saw the lazy, wicked gleam in his eyes. "Things like that don't happen when I wear jeans," she said in criticism of his clothes choice.

"More's the pity," he drawled, and opened the pickup's passenger door for her. She laughed, startling herself. She hadn't expected to be this relaxed with Kincade.

He drove to a city park a short distance from downtown Reno and went straight to an area that had kiddie rides. With tickets in hand he guided Eden to the carousel. It was a measure of the progress he'd made that she raised no objections when he lifted her onto the back of a prancing steed. Round and round they went, taped calliope music filling the air with its happy sound.

They ate cotton candy and laughed at the stickiness the pink clouds of spun sugar left on their hands and faces. Later, armed with bags of popcorn, they wandered to the pond to feed the ducks. Kincade watched Eden as she tossed her popcorn, making sure the more timid ducks in the back received their share of bounty and crouching down to feed the bolder ones from her hand.

He studied the smile on her lips and the carefree look she wore. He had put those there. A whole host of feelings swelled inside him—pride, tenderness, and desire among them.

When she straightened from her crouched position by the pond, the heel of her sandaled pump sank into the soft ground, tipping her off-balance. Before she could recover on her own, his hands had caught her and pulled her to him.

Gripping his shoulders for support, Eden glanced up, and the laughing comment died on her lips at the look in his eyes. She could feel the sudden thump of her heart in her chest. His mouth feathered over a corner of her lips as his hands slid onto her back. Need rolled inside her with a pang that came as much from fear as desire.

"You taste of cotton candy." He skimmed his lips to her ear.

She forced herself to look at him. It had always been her way to face things, not run away from them.

His hand traveled up her spine. "I won't hurt you."

He smiled, and she was lost, heart racing, breath trapped as he slanted his mouth over hers. She could taste sugar and smoke and heat as he coaxed her lips apart.

Kincade kept his passions tightly chained. She needed something more than desire, and he needed to give something more. But his control could only be stretched so far, and he drew back, nerves scraped raw by the glaze of heat in her eyes.

"Ready to go?"

She blinked in surprise. "What?"

"I wondered if you were ready to leave—head somewhere else."

"Oh." It was like being released from the effect of a drug, Eden thought. The addictive kind. "Yes, if you are."

"Good." He dropped a quick kiss on her lips, then lightly gripped her hand to lead her back to the truck.

With the sun slowly sliding toward Peavine Mountain, Kincade followed a winding back road to another park, on the outskirts of town, with a stunning view of the city. Leaving the pickup in a parking lot, they walked a few feet down a slope. Kincade shook out an Indian blanket he kept behind his truck seat. He helped Eden onto the blanket, then stretched out beside her, plucking a seedstalk and chewing on the end of it.

"What a view." Eden gazed at the city sprawl of high-rises and homes.

"Reno at your feet."

For a moment Eden took advantage of the silence to study him. He sat propped on an elbow, his long legs sprawled in front of him, gazing at the city below with quiet intensity. She found herself wanting to know more about him. "Where are you from, Kincade?"

"Texas."

She smiled at his noninformative answer. "Where in Texas?"

"A half-dozen different places. My dad worked for various ranchers. He'd leave one job to get better pay, then leave it for better hours or better benefits. Once we hit high school, though, he stayed in one place. Mostly for Marcie's sake."

"Marcie was your sister," Eden guessed. "I'll bet she was a barrel-racer. Did she go on the rodeo circuit with you?"

"Marcie never liked horses." Kincade pulled the seedstalk from his mouth and sat up, bending his knees and resting his arms on them. "She was afraid of horses. Especially after—" He clamped his mouth shut, grimness pulling at the corners.

"After what?"

He tossed the grass stem away. "She took a bad fall when she was eight, and wound up with a crippled left leg. It was my fault."

"What happened?"

He was a long time answering. "We were living outside Big Springs. It was one of those hot September days in Texas. After school Marcie and I went to the creek about two miles from our house to cool off. She rode her bike, and I took a bay gelding named Rocky. Anyway, we got to fooling around and lost track of time. Suddenly the sun was going down. We were supposed to be home before dark, a rule our parents strictly enforced. You never saw two kids move as fast as we did, pulling on our shoes, grabbing up our clothes. That's when we discovered her bike had a flat tire. She wanted to push it home, and I wanted her to ride double with me. We started arguing. I called her a scaredy-cat for being afraid of horses. I finally talked her into riding with me, but she said I had to promise not to go fast.

"Promise not to go fast." Kincade repeated the phrase in a voice bitter with regret. "Those words were like a dare." His mouth twisted in a humorless line. "I only wanted to scare her a little. When she started screaming for me to stop, I made Rocky go faster. I never thought she would have the guts to let go of the saddle horn and grab at the reins. Unfortunately, she only got hold of one, but she pulled that horse's head around so hard that we were going down almost before I realized what she'd done. I bailed off before we hit the ground, but Marcie went down with the horse."

"That's when she hurt her leg?"

"Smashed it to pieces. Literally." He looked up at the sky, a sheen of moisture in his eyes. "Before that day I didn't know what it was to be scared—not deep-down, sick-in-the-gut, shaking-all-over scared. I took one look at Marcie's leg and threw up. Some tough guy, huh?" he said in self-scorn.

"Kincade." She laid a hand on his arm, wanting to comfort, to take some of the pain.

"She needed help, but I couldn't leave her. I was scratched in a couple of places. So I took my handkerchief and smeared blood on it, then tied it to the saddle horn and gave Rocky a slap for home."

"That was clever."

Kincade dismissed it with a shrug. "It was dark before they found us. I don't know how much longer it was before the ambulance came. Or how many operations Marcie ended up having. They said she was lucky to come out of it with only a bad limp."

"You were a boy."

"Right, and that excuses everything." Kincade rolled to his feet and held out a hand to her. "What do you say we have dinner? That cotton candy wasn't exactly filling."

The unspoken message was clear—his sister was a closed subject, not to be reopened. Now or later.

IN AN atmosphere redolent of old San Francisco, with heavy woods, gleaming chandeliers, and secluded tables, Eden and Kincade dined on steaks while a harpist played songs of love and longing. They talked about everything and nothing, staying clear of potentially touchy topics, like Vince.

The plates were cleared, and the waiter returned, picking up the nearly empty wine bottle and turning to Eden.

"No more for me, thank you." She placed her fingers over her wineglass, still half-full of ruby-red wine.

The waiter topped off Kincade's glass, emptying the bottle, and retreated.

Kincade looked at Eden, aware of the building silence. The candlelight flickered over her face, accenting the faint hollows of her cheeks. She held the wineglass in both hands, staring into it in a preoccupied fashion.

"Something wrong?" Kincade asked.

She looked up and shook her head. "Just thinking."

"About what?"

"I was supposed to join the crew at Big Timber Canyon yesterday. They'll be wondering what happened to me." Not to mention Vince and Kincade, but Eden deliberately didn't mention that. "I was wishing I could get word to them that everything is fine."

"You figured out a way to get around DePard, didn't you?"

"I don't know what you mean." She stiffened a little.

He smiled. "I think you do. You weren't carrying those maps in your back pocket for no reason. Come on, what's your idea?" When she hesitated, he guessed the reason for her wariness. "Don't worry about me saying anything to DePard, Eden. It's your brother who doesn't want you to get those cattle to market, not me. He thinks if you don't, you'll be forced to sell. And if that's what Vince wants, I intend to make sure he doesn't get it."

"I see." She hesitated a moment longer, then admitted, "I *had* a plan." She stressed the past tense. "But with you and Vince gone, I'm not going to be able to pull it off."

"What was the plan?" He was curious now.

She ran a finger around the rim of her wineglass and smiled. "Take the cattle to market myself."

"Where would you rent the trucks to haul them?"

"I wasn't going to use trucks." She leaned forward, and the candlelight caught in her eyes. "I was going to drive them to the sale pens across the border in Oregon."

"The maps. You were checking the route."

"Water was the critical factor. I had to make certain it would be available at the end of each day's drive. It is."

"How long will the drive take?" Kincade asked when the waiter came with the check.

"Ten days, give or take."

"DePard might get suspicious when neither you or any of your crew are around for that long." He slipped some bills into the leather folder with the dinner tab.

"That's the beauty of the plan. During fall roundup we're usually out for six weeks," Eden explained. "This time I planned to scour the areas with the highest concentration of cattle and skip the rest." She stood and accepted the guiding pressure of Kincade's hand at her back to steer her toward the exit. "If it went as planned, we'd be back before DePard even knew we left. I wish I could see the look on his face when he found out."

"Revenge is sweet, right?" Kincade smiled down at her.

Eden shook her head. "How can revenge be sweet when it turns to stone the heart of the man who commits it?"

He arched her a questioning look. "Shakespeare?"

"No. Eden Rossiter." She expected a smile or some amused comment. Instead she was met with silence. There was only one explanation for that—Vince.

DURING the drive back to the hotel, Kincade amused her with accounts of his rodeo days. The moment in the restaurant when he had turned silent might never have happened. Eden was relaxed again when Kincade unlocked the door to the suite. Walking in, she felt regret that this innocent time with him was winding to an end, that soon they would be at odds again over Vince.

A pair of wire hangers holding her freshly laundered shirt and blue jeans hung on the doorknob to her bedroom. Seeing them,

Eden fingered the soft knit of the dress he had bought her. She turned back when he closed the door. "I enjoyed dinner, and the afternoon." She smiled her pleasure in it.

He tossed the key on a table and faced her. "I'm glad, because I did, too." Before she could step out of his reach, he laid his hands on her shoulders, then ran them down her arms with unnerving gentleness. Very naturally he linked his fingers with hers. He raised one hand, kissed it, then lifted the other. Like a rocket, the heat tore up her arm. Eden found it was one thing to ignore what she had convinced herself she never needed and another thing entirely to resist what she discovered she did. When he cupped the back of her neck and his mouth whispered over hers, her heart leaped into her throat. But she knew it was no good and turned from it.

"I'm not like other women, Kincade."

"No, you definitely aren't." Instinctively he trailed his finger along her neck, soothing and reassuring even while his mouth played havoc with her senses.

"I can't give you what you want," she said.

"Then I'll only take what you can give me."

When he deepened the kiss, Eden sighed. There was a mixture of despair and wonder in the sound. For an instant, and only an instant, she gave in to it, pressing her body against him, her lips parting. Then she was pulling back. "I can't. It won't work."

"Because of Jeff?" Again Kincade curved his hands on her shoulders. "There's nothing I can say that will erase the memory for you, Eden. Or ease the fear it left in you. But it doesn't have to be that way between a man and a woman."

He smoothed a hand over her face and cupped her cheek. Eden closed her eyes and absorbed the sensation of his fingers on her skin. "I'm afraid," she admitted.

"So am I."

Her eyes snapped open. "Why should you be afraid?"

"Because you are important." He slid his fingers into her hair. "Because this is important." Gathering her close again, he kept his touch gentle. "I think this was inevitable from the first moment I saw you on the street." His mouth brushed her lips in a mere whisper of a kiss, lightly rubbed and retreated, again and again. Kincade saw the confusion in her expression and the hunger building as he teased her lips. But he wasn't driven by the need to possess. Not this time. Not with Eden. Tonight demanded all the skill and patience he possessed.

He made good use of it. When he finally touched her, she seemed ready. Her hands moved cautiously over his shoulders and back, sliding under the tail of his shirt and onto his bare skin.

Eden heard the sharp breath he drew at the contact. His kiss became heated. He murmured something, but she was past hearing. She felt his muscles tremble when he scooped her up in his arms and carried her to his bedroom.

MUCH later, as they lay in a sated tangle of arms and legs, Kincade felt a completeness holding her close to him, a feeling that warmed him like the golden glow of a lamp in the window on a stormy night. He hadn't been looking for it. He hadn't been aware that he even wanted it. But he knew he didn't want it to end.

"I've been with more than my share of women, Eden." He stroked her hair. "But you need to know it was never like this for me. Not with any of them."

"You don't have to say that." She lay very still in his arms.

"I know I don't, sweetheart. I want to. I don't want you to think this was just another good time in a whole string of good times for me."

"Is this what's known as letting a girl down gently?" Eden mocked, wishing he hadn't said anything. It would have been easier if he hadn't brought feelings into it.

In the next breath she was flipped on her back, her arms pinned to the mattress, and Kincade loomed above her, anger and impatience darkening his face. "Dammit, I'm serious!"

The telephone rang, and he swore again. Releasing her, he rolled away, swinging his legs out of bed and sitting up. Even before he picked it up, he knew this was the call he had been dreading.

So did Eden.

"Wait a minute," Kincade said into the phone, and flipped on the bedlamp. "Let me find something to write on." Eden slipped off the other side of the bed and padded to the bathroom. "Okay. Go ahead."

After a quick wash she donned the bathrobe hanging on the door hook and walked out. She felt his eyes on her as she returned to her own room. Her heart ached for things that couldn't be.

Collecting her clothes, Eden dressed quickly. As she tugged on her boots, she heard Kincade moving about in the other bedroom. She pushed her tousled hair into some semblance of order, jammed her hat on, and walked back into the suite's sitting room. Fighting the urge to pace, she waited for Kincade to emerge from his room.

He came out, giving his shirt a final tuck inside the waistband of his Levi's. His glance traveled over her white shirt and creased jeans with a thoroughness that reminded Eden he had touched every inch of skin they covered. "You know where Vince is, don't you?" She held his gaze, daring him to deny it.

His features were hard; there was no warmth anywhere in his face. "Yes." He gave her a long, measuring look. "Does the name Axel Gray mean anything to you?"

"Yes." A blackjack dealer at the Nugget, Axel Gray was only a voice on the phone to Eden. Vince had met him shortly after their grandfather had died. Since then Axel's place had been their message center whenever Vince went on one of his extended trips. Vince called Axel his good-luck charm, insisting nothing bad would happen as long as he stayed in touch with Axel.

Kincade exploded. "Why didn't you tell me about him, Eden? You could have saved us both a—" He broke off and swung away from her.

Saved what? Eden thought. A lot of heartache? But she agreed those words were better left unsaid.

"Vince is my brother, Kincade."

He shot her a glaring look. "Do you think I'm not sorry about that?" He snatched up his hat and started for the door.

Eden pulled at his arm. "Don't go after him, Kincade."

"I have to." He steeled himself against the silent appeal in her eyes. Just as she had a loyalty to her brother, he had one to his sister. He owed this to Marcie.

"No, you don't," Eden argued. "You can forget whatever it is he's done to you and walk away."

"No."

The one-word answer stung more than all his angry shouting. "If what we just shared really meant something to you, you'd let him go."

"Is that why you did it?" he challenged hotly. "So you would have something to hold over my head?"

She slapped him, and the crack of her hand across his face rang through the room like a verbal declaration of war. Seething, her eyes smarting with tears, Eden wheeled away.

"No." Kincade grabbed her arm and spun her back. "What happened between us was special, Eden," he said in a voice still thick with anger. "Nothing can destroy that." He relaxed his grip. "But it doesn't change anything else. I have to find your brother. And you feel you have to protect him. Don't try to stop me, and I won't try to stop you." He released her and held out his hand. "Deal?"

Eden hesitated. "I'm coming with you."

"I won't stop you."

"Deal." She shook his hand, but she didn't return his smile.

When Kincade turned to leave, she followed him. The bargain wouldn't last. Eden was convinced of that. A clash was inevitable, and when it came, all of Kincade's high words and allusions to love would go up in smoke.

Eden reminded herself of that and ignored the achiness in her throat as Kincade drove along the Reno streets. When they passed into the city limits of Sparks, Kincade checked the directions he had written on hotel notepaper. Two blocks farther he turned onto a side street and followed it to an apartment complex. He spotted Vince's truck in the parking lot. Rusty's pickup was next to it. Kincade pulled into the space beside it and climbed out of the cab.

Rusty moved out of the shadows to meet him. "The apartment's on the top floor, third window from the left. He's up there. I saw him at the window."

Eden came around the back of the truck. Rusty gave her a startled look of recognition, then turned to Kincade for an explanation. Kincade offered none.

"Eden, this is Rusty Walker, a friend of mine. Eden Rossiter." Kincade identified her with a lift of his hand.

"Ma'am." Rusty briefly gripped the point of his hat brim just as the apartment light went out.

Kincade had been watching. "Looks like Rossiter is coming to us. Let's meet him." He looked at Eden. "Are you coming?"

"Of course." She fell in step with him, her mind searching for a way to warn Vince. A pair of lantern-style lights were mounted on the brick wall flanking the building's glass door, illuminating the area immediately in front. The paved walkway to the parking lot lay in shadows. Eden had a clear view of Vince coming toward them. She made a break for the door, but Kincade caught her and pulled her back into the shadows. He called to Rusty to take the other side.

"I thought you weren't going to stop me." Eden twisted her arm, trying to break his hold on her wrist.

"From protecting him, no. But I can't let you warn him."

Raging, Eden turned back as Vince came sauntering out, whistling a tuneless air. "Vince, look out!" she shouted.

He stopped with a jerk.

"Going somewhere, Rossiter?" Kincade stepped out of the shadows, drawing Eden with him. Rusty slipped from behind a shrub and stepped between Vince and the apartment entrance.

Vince wheeled back for the door, saw the way blocked, and spun around to glare at Eden. "You told him where to find me?"

"I didn't—"

Kincade broke in. "She didn't tell us anything, Rossiter. You weren't hard to find."

Vince went on the attack. "What are you doing with my sister? I swear, if you hurt her, I'll kill you."

"You tried that once, remember?"

"What do you mean?" Eden saw at once she wasn't going to get an answer from Kincade. "Vince, what is he talking about?"

"Nothing. He's just trying to act tough," Vince jeered. "All right, you've found me. Now what, big man?"

"Now we're going for a little ride."

"Where?"

"Why, to your favorite place, of course." Kincade's smile was thin and cold. "I know how much you love it back at the ranch." Kincade ignored Eden's surprised look.

"The ranch?" Vince scoffed. "You're kidding. I despise that hellhole. . . . Ahh, that's your game, is it?" He nodded slowly. "You plan on making my life miserable."

"I haven't begun to make your life miserable, Rossiter. Your sister is determined to keep the ranch, and you're going to sweat blood to help her. You got me?"

"I got you," Vince grumbled.

"Rusty." Kincade never took his eyes off Vince.

"Yo."

"I could use another pair of eyes to keep track of Slippery Sam here. Feel like working some cattle?"

"Why not? I haven't got anything better to do."

"Any objections to hiring Rusty?" Kincade spared Eden one quick glance.

"No." But she still wasn't sure what to make of any of this.

"Good." Kincade dug in his pocket. "Do you think you can find your way back to the hotel?"

"I think so." Eden frowned. "Why?"

"Take my truck and go get our things." He handed her the keys.

"What are you going to do?"

"Rusty and I are going to help your brother pack." When she made no move toward the pickup, Kincade added, "Don't worry. There won't be any rough stuff unless your brother gets cute."

"How can I be sure you'll be here when I get back?"

"You've got my truck."

Eden looked at the keys in her hand. After a second's hesitation she turned and went to Kincade's pickup.

Kincade, Vince, and Rusty were waiting for her by Vince's truck when Eden drove into the parking lot. "Your things are in the back," she told Kincade.

"Good." He looked at Vince. "You'll follow me, but don't get any ideas. Rusty will be on your tail all the way back to the ranch."

"Wait," Vince protested. "How come she's riding with you?"

"Because I said so."

Twenty minutes later the trio of pickups was headed east on the interstate. Eden hadn't exchanged a word with Kincade since they left the apartment. "Why are you doing this?" she finally asked.

"Doing what?"

"Taking Vince back to the ranch," she replied.

"You heard him—he hates the place. It's a prison sentence to him."

"Is that all?"

"I wish that was all," Kincade muttered in self-directed anger. "I wish I could say you didn't enter into it. But you did. I can't let your brother get away with what he did, but I don't want to hurt you either." That was the problem. He couldn't summon up that fierce hate anymore. Now when he looked at Vince, he thought of Eden, not Marcie. A fact that weighted him with guilt. "It's a hell of a mess, isn't it?" He sighed. Without thinking, he reached over and took her hand, linking their fingers.

Chapter XIII

SHORTLY before noon the next day, the four of them rode into the camp at Big Timber Canyon. Wild Jack trotted out to meet them, long gray hair bouncing against his shoulders. He held the reins to Eden's horse while she swung out of the saddle. "It's about time you got here. Everybody thought this time you weren't coming back, that maybe DePard had run you off."

"That will happen when cows fly."

"I've seen cows fly. Four of them," Wild Jack stated.

"Yeah, and how drunk were you?" Vince mocked.

The cook puffed up indignantly. "I wasn't drunk. I was sober as a Baptist preacher the day they loaded four prize heifers in the airplane. I saw the plane take off. Those four cows flew."

"He's got you there, Rossiter." Rusty grinned.

"The hell he does. The plane flew, not those cows."

"The plane flew. The cows were in it. The cows flew." Wild Jack gave a wide grin, then looked at Rusty and frowned. "Who are you?"

"This is Rusty Walker. He just signed on." Eden took back the reins. "This is our cook. Everybody calls him Wild Jack."

"Hello." Rusty touched his hat to him.

Just then Bob Waters rode in. "Where have you been?" he asked Eden.

"Sorry, but there wasn't any way to get word to you. I hired a new man—Rusty Walker." She indicated Rusty with a nod. "This is my cow boss, Bob Waters. You'll take orders from him."

"Does he know the situation with DePard?" Bob asked.

Eden replied with a nod. "We were about to grab a cup of coffee before we hit the saddle. You might as well join us and fill us in on areas that still need to be covered."

She was back to being boss again, in capital letters, Kincade noticed. The woman who had laughed and made love with him was locked back inside.

In thirty minutes they were out scouring the hills for cattle. The unvarying pattern of their days was established. Rousted from their beds while the sky was still glittering with stars, they trudged to the chuck wagon for that all-important first cup of coffee. All day they searched for cattle, herding their catch back to camp by late afternoon. There the day's catch was sorted, the calves branded, the injured doctored. They were dragging by the time they reached the mess tent. Most nights if there hadn't been a meal waiting for them, they would have been too tired to fix their own. The only change in the routine came when they moved camp every three or four days.

The only complaints were from Vince, and he kept his grumbling to a minimum, especially around Kincade. Not that Kincade particularly cared. As the days wore on, he thought less and less about Vince and more and more about Eden.

She did more than give orders; she led by example. She was the first one up every morning, the last to turn in at night. Kincade had seen her stumble in exhaustion, catch herself, shake off the effects, and push on to the next task. He might have admired that if he hadn't been growing steadily more irritated with the way she acted toward him. There was nothing in her attitude to suggest he was— or had ever been—anything other than a ranch hand. She treated him exactly as she treated everyone else. He told himself that under the circumstances, it was probably best. Yet the longer it went on, the more it grated. After the second week he'd had enough.

With dawn's flush chasing back the darkness, Kincade swung aboard his sorrel and walked the horse over to Eden, who was already mounted. "I'll be riding with you today," he told her.

He appeared primed for an argument, but she wasn't about to give him one.

"All right. If you're ready, let's go." She wheeled her horse toward the open country and nudged it into a shuffling trot. Kincade rode alongside her.

"There's a natural tank in the canyon at the base of Cobbler's

Peak," she said after they'd traveled some distance. "We'll check that area first."

"Fine by me," Kincade replied, and let the silence build again. "So what are you going to do about it?"

"About what?"

"Us."

"There is no *us*." She sounded amazingly calm.

"Really? I suppose the time we spent in Reno never happened."

"Of course it happened," Eden said, striving for lightness. "It was a pleasant interlude. Now it's over."

"An interlude. Is that what you've decided to call it?"

"That's what it was." She silently congratulated herself for handling the discussion so well. "Are you disappointed that I'm not mooning over you? Would it help if I apologized?"

"Don't bother. I should have realized you're a coward."

She reined in. "I am not."

He swung his horse around and rode back to her. When he pulled up, their knees brushed and his hand closed on her saddle horn, catching up her rein in his grip.

"You are a scared, pitiful little coward."

Eden denied that hotly. "That's an outright lie! I simply have no desire to become involved with you or any man. Is that what offends you? That I was the one to end it, not you?"

"No." He leaned closer. "What offends me is the way you reduced what happened between us to a cheap one-night stand."

"What does it matter if it was one night, two, or a dozen?" Eden stormed to hide the shame that came with hearing the truth.

"Damn you." He was out of the saddle and jerking her to the ground before she could mount a defense.

Both horses shied away from the struggling pair as Eden fought to pull free of his crushing hold. The point of her boot connected with his shin, drawing a curse from him. In the next second they were tumbling to the ground. Before she could roll free, he was on top of her, pinning her arms to the side.

"It was more than a one-night stand, and you know it." He was breathing as hard as she was. "It wasn't just sex, it wasn't rape, and I'm not Jeff." She went still and turned her head to the side, scraping her cheek against the soil beneath. "But it isn't just Jeff, is it?"

he said. "It's every man in your life. From a father you hardly saw to a worthless brother who only shows up when he needs money to a bunch of cowhands who work for a few months, then drift on." His face was close to hers. He could see the tension, the denial, and the pain. "Hate them if you like, Eden. You sure have the right. But I'll be damned if you'll measure me by them or anyone else."

"Not even DePard?"

Kincade went grim. "Vince—he was your out. You decided you didn't have to try to make things work between us, because my quarrel with Vince would eventually end it anyway."

"Well, won't it?" she challenged, battling back tears.

"Only if we let it."

"You're a fool."

"And you're a coward. You're afraid to find out whether I'm right or not."

"No!" She made the mistake of turning to look at him.

"Prove it." His mouth came down on hers, not with gentleness or with the heat he had shown her before, but with a raw demand edged with hunger. Eden stayed limp, determined to give him nothing and to take nothing for herself. But her resolve weakened under the heady assault. Her breathing quickened and her lips opened.

In the bright sunshine of morning there was darkness, a black velvet swirl of it. The air was thick and heavy. Between hot and hungry kisses they shed their clothes and used them as a bed to lie on. The scent of passion rose, sharp and pungent and arousing, like the stray bits of crushed sage beneath them.

SHE stirred against him, and his arm automatically tightened to keep her beside him, but Eden made no move to get away. Her fingers curled into the springy golden hairs on his chest.

"I think I'm onto your game," she murmured.

"Oh? And what's that?"

"You like to 'commit the oldest sins the newest kind of ways.' "

Kincade chuckled. "I've used that line from *Henry IV* before. It always worked. But there was another one I used a lot, too."

"Which one was that?"

" 'Let me take you a button-hole lower.' " He waggled his eyebrows in mock lechery.

Eden laughed, delighting in the line. "Which play is that from?"

"*Love's Labour's Lost.*"

"You're kidding," she said, and laughed again.

"I've missed that." He rubbed his hand up and down her arm.

"What?"

"Hearing you laugh."

Eden sobered at the comment, reality stealing in. "If we lay here much longer in this sun, we'll get burned." She sat up and tugged at the shirt trapped beneath him.

As they dressed, Kincade was conscious of her silence. He watched as she tucked her shirt inside her Levi's and glanced at the horses grazing a few yards away. An innocent action on the surface, but he knew she was building up the wall he had just battered down. He picked up her neckcloth and handed it to her.

"Thanks." Her glance bounced off him as she took it from him and wrapped it around her neck.

"Eden—" he began.

"Don't." She took a long breath before she looked at him. There was pain in her eyes but also determination. "I don't need this kind of complication in my life right now."

"That's progress of sorts, I suppose. At least now you regard me as a complication."

"Don't make jokes. I'm serious. I've got a fight on my hands with DePard. I have to concentrate all my energies on that."

"You don't have to wage the fight alone, Eden."

She shook her head in disagreement. "You don't understand."

"I understand better than you think. The key word here is trust."

"Have you forgotten Vince?" She couldn't keep that touch of bitterness out of her voice.

"No, and I'm not about to," he replied. "Why don't we take this as it comes? A day at a time, a step at a time."

Eden scooped her hat off the ground and batted the dust from it, releasing some of her frustrations. "You aren't going to let up until I agree. I don't have time to fight with you." And she couldn't tell him to leave, because she needed his help. Kincade knew that, too. "We'll try it your way for a while," she said.

"That's my girl." Kincade smiled as she turned toward the horses. She spun back, furious. "I am not your girl. And let's get something else straight. Around the crew you aren't to come near me."

"You mean I can't visit your tent?" The grooves around his mouth deepened with his effort to hold back a smile.

"No!"

"We can't go for moonlight strolls?"

"No."

"I can't blow you kisses across the campfire?"

Pivoting, she threw up her hands and stalked after the horses. Chuckling, Kincade followed.

A ghost of that smile still haunted the corners of his mouth when they rode into camp. Eden immediately peeled off to find her cow boss. Kincade watched her as Rusty rode up.

Kincade glanced at him. "Did Vince give you any trouble?"

"He's too tired to even think about it. Can't say the same about you, though," Rusty said, looking him over. "You look downright pleased with yourself."

"Do I?" Kincade smiled and glanced at Eden.

Rusty followed the direction of his look. His eyes widened briefly in surprise. "So that's the way the wind blows." He scratched his head. "Well, what d'ya know? Kincade Harris is in love." Then he saw the problem. "What are you going to do about Vince?"

"Exactly what I set out to do."

"You'll lose her."

"Not if I can help it," Kincade stated, but his smile left him.

Chapter XIV

YEARS ago Sayer's Well had been the site of a prospector's cabin. Only the well that had been dug to provide a water supply remained. It was here, with Black Rock Desert stretching just beyond the rocky finger of a mountain, that the final sort was made and the cattle bound for market were bedded down for the night.

With the evening meal finished, Eden wandered over to the crackling fire, where the weary crew had gathered. An old stump sat on the outer edge of the circle. She sat on it and took off her hat, shaking her hair loose in a tired gesture. Kincade sat across the fire from her. She felt his glance touch her and move away. She had learned in the last week how much could be communicated by just a simple glance.

Bob Waters poked at the burning logs with a stick, the firelight reflecting on the round lenses of his glasses. "It took us just over three weeks to complete the roundup. That's pretty fast time."

"I should shout it is," Al declared.

"But we missed a lot." Bob felt obligated to remind Eden of it.

"We'll hit them in the spring," she said.

"Fall, spring—I don't see what difference it makes," Vince stated. "I mean, what good is it to gather up these cattle when you haven't any way of getting them to market?"

Kincade's glance came back to Eden expectantly, but she offered no defense of her actions, and the silence around the fire grew loud. Finally Kincade rose to his feet. "What we need is a little music." He glanced at his friend. "You still got that harmonica, Rusty?"

"It's like my bank card." He grinned. "I never leave home without it."

"Well, warm it up. I feel like doing a little two-stepping." Kincade walked over to Eden and pulled her to her feet. "You can be my partner. I don't like to two-step alone."

"Too bad. I don't know how," she stated.

"Do you know how to walk?"

"Of course, but—"

"Then you can learn to two-step. It's simple."

"I don't think so." She pulled back.

"Come on, boss, you can do it," Bob Waters chimed in.

"I—" Eden shook her head.

"Just try it," Kincade coaxed. "All you have to do is take two slow steps and two quick ones."

More calls of encouragement followed, and Eden sensed it wasn't authority the crew wanted her to show now, but some humanness. "All right, I'll try."

"Stand beside me." Kincade maneuvered her into position. "Starting with the right foot, we'll take one slow step, then another slow one, then two quick ones. Got it?"

"I think so."

Around and around they went as the harmonica's lively notes filled the air. Gradually the slow-slow, quick-quick pattern came naturally to Eden, and she stopped concentrating on her feet and gave herself over to the enjoyment of the moment. "I've got it, haven't I?" She looked up at Kincade and basked in the beam of approval and something else in his eyes.

"You've got it. Want to try a circle turn?"

"Why not?" At that moment she was game for anything.

"Attagirl." He grinned. "All right, when we come to the quick-quick part, you'll do the turn. Okay?" At her uncertain nod he smiled. "Here we go. Slow-slow, pivot."

His hand pushed her into the start of a turn, but she was half a beat slow in responding. In her haste to catch up, Eden got her feet tangled and stumbled into Kincade. Both of them staggered side-ways. When he started laughing, Eden joined him. She looked up, and their eyes locked with an almost audible click. His face was close, and his mouth . . . She dug her fingers into his shirt, wanting him, needing him. His head dipped closer—and someone coughed.

The silence hit her. There was no music, only the snap of burning logs. Self-consciously Eden pulled back and glanced at the grinning faces around the campfire. All except Vince. He glowered at them, his hands clenched into fists at his sides.

"That's enough for me." She forced a lightness into her voice, try-ing to pretend nothing had happened. "I think I'll call it a night."

She hadn't taken two steps toward her tent before Vince was at her side, gripping her elbow. "I'll walk with you." She could feel the barely restrained fury in his fingers. Well away from the others, he stopped her. "Stay away from that guy." It wasn't well-intentioned brotherly advice. It was an order.

"What?"

"Don't play innocent with me. He was making a move on you, and you were going for it." Vince looked at her, his face twisted with anger and regret. "He's been working on you all along, hasn't he? I should have guessed he would do that."

"What are you talking about?"

"He doesn't care about you, sis. He's just using you. He wants you to fall for him so he can get back at me."

"What?" She felt a squeezing in her chest, intense and painful.

"He's been sympathetic, hasn't he?" Vince challenged. "Pre-tended to believe your story." His gaze narrowed on her. "How did he handle the situation with me? Did he say his problem with me had nothing to do with you?"

"Why are you saying this? Why would he do that?"

"As far as he's concerned, it's poetic justice."

"Why? What did you do, Vince?"

"Nothing. I told you that."

"You had to do something, or he wouldn't be so determined to get even with you. Why would hurting me be poetic justice?"

"Because his sister killed herself. Okay?" he snapped.

She stepped back, reeling inwardly from his answer. "Marcie," she whispered, feeling suddenly sick. She looked at Vince. "Why? It had something to do with you, didn't it?" He looked away, but not before Eden caught the flicker of guilt in his eyes. "Oh, no." Her breath caught on a sob. She pivoted, turning her back on him.

"Sis. Sis, it isn't what you think. I just dated her a few times when I was in Oklahoma."

His hands curved onto her shoulders. Eden shrugged them off. "Don't lie, Vince."

"All right, I went out with her a lot."

"Why?" She spun around. "She was a cripple. Hardly your style." Pain made her harsh.

"How did you know that?" He looked at her in surprise.

"Never mind. Just answer my question. Why?"

"The horses were racing at Remington Park. I had some tips that didn't pan out, and I got in deep with a couple of bookies. One of them threatened to get rough when I didn't pay up. She was there."

"She gave you the money to pay him, didn't she?"

"I never asked her for it."

"No, you never do. You just hint around until it's volunteered." Eden hated to remember how many times he had used the same ploy on her.

"But even when she offered it, I didn't take it. I thought we could just skip town. I didn't know the guy had a tail on me. Suddenly there were these two thugs pounding on the motel-room door. She had the money with her and gave it to them."

"If you were trying to skip town, why did you take her with you? Why didn't you just leave?"

"She wanted to come. I never made her any promises."

"And that makes it all right?" Eden mocked. "Vince, don't you see she wanted you to love her? She thought if she paid the money, you would really care about her."

"Dammit, everything was fine when I left. She said she understood. She was alive. How was I supposed to know she was going to take those pills?" he demanded angrily.

"No, you couldn't know. But it doesn't change anything, does it? She's still dead." Numbly Eden moved toward her tent.

"Sis . . ." He took a step after her.

"Good night, Vince." Eden crawled into her tent and stretched out on the blankets, letting the tears come. She cried for Marcie, for Kincade, for Vince—and for herself.

WITH the roundup over, everyone slept until first light. Eden waited for the crew to gather for breakfast, then announced they would be driving the cattle to market. "We'll rest up today," she stated, ignoring the stunned looks on every face except Kincade's. "Tonight we'll pull out and cross Black Rock Desert. With a little luck we'll be in Oregon the first of next week. Ike Bedford has a place just over the mountains. He's agreed to sell my cattle."

Her decision wasn't open to discussion. To make that point, Eden took her coffee and walked away, telling herself her action had nothing to do with the fact that she wasn't ready to face Kincade. Not with what she knew now. It was all too fresh, the ache too raw.

It was Vince who came after her. "You aren't serious about this, are you?" he demanded, incredulous.

"I'm dead serious."

"But you can't go traipsing across other people's property with a bunch of cattle," he protested. "It's illegal. You need permits."

"Probably. I didn't bother to check. This way I can honestly say I didn't know I was breaking the law if it turns out we are."

"That's stupid."

"No. It's desperate. DePard has too many friends. One question to someone in authority would tip my hand. If I get slapped with a fine, I'll pay it. But first I have to get the cattle to market."

"Don't be a fool. He'll find out what you're doing."

"Not from you." Kincade joined them.

Vince reddened, then stiffened and turned an accusing look on

Eden. "He knew about the drive before this morning, didn't he?"

Kincade's smile was cool and sardonic. "I told you that you were going to help Eden keep the ranch."

Vince clamped his mouth shut and stalked off, leaving Eden alone with Kincade. Something she didn't want. She shifted away from him. "You'll have to excuse me. I've got a lot to do." She ducked inside her tent and drew in a deep breath to calm her shaky nerves.

THE barren expanse of Black Rock Desert stretched into the darkness—a vast white shimmer under the moon's spotlight. Summer's heat had sucked all the moisture from the broad mud plain and baked it until it had hardened into a pale marblelike surface. The night rang with the clatter of hooves on the hardpan, the confused lowing of cattle, and the creaking of saddle leather.

Eden rode alongside the herd, strung out in a dark red stream of beef. Now and then the cow dog darted close when a head turned toward the open desert with a notion of bolting.

Kincade rode beside her. "It's begun," he said. "Nervous?"

"A little." But the tension she was feeling had nothing to do with the start of the drive. She said bluntly, "I know about Marcie."

After long seconds of silence Kincade said skeptically, "Do you really?"

"She gave Vince money to pay off his gambling debts. When he left her anyway, she couldn't stand it and took her own life. And you blame Vince for that."

"He took more than her money. He took her will to live." The words were pushed through clenched teeth.

She heard the anger he used to cover his pain. "Now you're using me to punish Vince for what he did to your sister."

His head jerked around. An instant later his hand closed around her reins, pulling her horse to a halt. "I told you not to judge me by the men you've known. I don't use women."

"That's very convincing, but you don't expect me to believe you, do you?"

"Dammit, it's the truth!"

"It doesn't matter." She breathed in, trying to ease the tightness in her chest. "What Vince did was wrong, but that doesn't make him responsible for your sister's death. It was her decision. You can't blame him for it."

"The hell I can't."

She released a sad and silent laugh. "You're just like DePard. He holds me responsible for Jeff's death, as if I'm to blame for the fact that Jeff assaulted me, that I somehow invited it. Vince never gave your sister those pills. She acted on her own. But you can't accept that. You have to hurt someone. You think it will somehow wipe out what she did."

"You don't know what you're talking about," he snapped almost savagely.

"Don't I?" Eden flared. "Maybe you need to ask yourself just who you are trying to punish. Vince? Or yourself? Isn't it your own guilt you can't live with? You have to shove the blame on someone else. That way you can feel noble."

"That's not true."

"Isn't it? Marcie was crippled in an accident. She probably forgave you for your part in it long ago. But you never forgave yourself. Now you're going to make Vince pay for it. That isn't noble. That's twisted." She kicked her horse into a lope, riding away from Kincade. Tears burned the back of her eyes.

Rusty rode over to Kincade. "It's amazing how far sound carries in this desert country," he remarked, smiling. "She gave you a real tongue-lashing."

"She doesn't know what she's talking about." Kincade's response was curt and irritated.

"I don't know." Rusty tipped his head to one side. "I don't think Marcie could have said it better." He rode off, leaving Kincade to chew on that.

The next night Kincade cornered Eden as she approached camp lugging her saddle. He faced her, his hard features set in cold, uncompromising lines. "I'll see your cattle to market," he told her. "After that all bets are off."

"As far as I'm concerned, they were never on," Eden replied, just as cold and hard as he was.

Chapter XV

AFTER six days on the trail they were almost a full day ahead of schedule. Shortly after one o'clock they pulled out of their noon camp, as always leaving Wild Jack behind to stow the last of the gear in the chuck wagon and hitch the team.

An hour later Bob Waters swung in alongside Kincade, who was riding drag. "The boss wondered if you'd seen any sign of Wild Jack." He turned in the saddle to scan their back trail.

"No." Kincade looked back as well. "He should have caught up with us by now."

"I'd better see what's keeping him."

"I'll go with you," Kincade said, and called to Rusty. "We're going back to look for the chuck wagon. Keep an eye on Rossiter." Rusty signaled his understanding with a wave.

Kincade and the cow boss were nearly to the noon camp when they saw the chuck wagon with only one horse hitched to it. The other was gone. So was the cook. Bob Waters studied the tracks Wild Jack had left. "I don't profess to be a great tracker, but it looks like he unhitched the horse and headed west."

"I think I've found the reason." Kincade stared at the broken bottles of vanilla extract scattered over the ground behind the wagon. A small cupboard door hung open in the back of the wagon. "It looks like the latch broke and his supply of vanilla spilled out when he was coming up this incline."

"Ten to one he's headed for the bar in Gerlach. Old Dandy is strong"—Waters waved a hand at the horse still standing in the traces—"but he isn't strong enough to pull this wagon by himself. We'll have to leave it and take what food we can carry."

"The packsaddle is still in back," Kincade remembered. "In two days we'll be in Oregon. We'll load the horse with enough supplies to get us by until we get there."

That night Rusty was assigned to the cooking duties. But he didn't have the luxury of the chuck wagon's propane stove. He had to use an open fire.

"What the hell do you call this?" Vince held up a biscuit in disgust, showing the charred bottom and the doughy center. "This food isn't fit to eat."

A beleaguered Rusty instantly bristled. "If you think you can do better, go ahead."

Grumbling to himself, Vince scooped up a spoonful of beans. Like the biscuits, they tasted scorched and half cooked. No one went back for seconds.

LATE the next morning they reached the highway on the northern edge of the state. Scouting ahead, Eden looked in both directions. The only thing visible was the canopied roof of a combination gas station and convenience store nearly a mile down the road.

Bob Waters reined in next to her. She wasted no time issuing instructions. "It's all clear. We'll station two riders on the highway, one on each side of the herd, in case a car comes. About a mile north there's a big hollow. We'll noon there."

"Done." Waters rode back to issue instructions of his own. "We're taking them across now. The boss has the point. She'll lead them over. Al . . . Kincade, I want you to push the leaders. As soon as they're across, take up a position on the highway. The rest of us will bring up the rear. Any questions?" When none were offered, he nodded. "Okay, let's move out."

The lead yearlings eyed the pavement suspiciously, then trotted across it. Kincade took up his post, watching as the cattle streamed across. The sun came straight down, setting up a heat fog that distorted Al Bender's shape on the other side of the herd.

Vince reined his horse close to Al. "Al, have you got some cash?"

"Some. Why?" Al eyed him warily.

"That convenience store down the road—they make pizza. After eating those leather weights Walker called flapjacks this morning, I want something decent at noon. You want to chip in?"

Al dug in his pocket and came up with a couple of wadded bills. He handed them over to Vince. "No peppers. They give me gas."

"Thanks." Vince spurred his horse into a run.

On the opposite side of the herd, Kincade spied Vince taking off. "Where's Rossiter going?" he shouted to Al.

"After pizza," Al yelled back.

Kincade swore and checked the impulse to go after him. He

scanned the trailing riders. When he finally spotted Rusty, he shouted and waved his arm until Rusty lifted a hand in response. "Rossiter," he yelled, and pointed to the rider galloping toward the convenience store. "Go after him!" Rusty immediately swung his horse into a run after Rossiter. The last of the cattle trotted across the highway, and Kincade swung in behind them, trusting that Rusty wouldn't let Rossiter get away.

At the noon camp the crew came together in a grassy basin. Kincade watched the lip of the hollow, tension bunching his muscles with each passing minute. Then he heard the drum of hooves. An instant later Vince crested the rise, holding aloft four cartons of pizza tied together with a string. Rusty came behind him, balancing a Styrofoam cooler on the saddle in front of him.

"Pizza and cold beer." Vince stepped out of the saddle. "This is what I call good eating."

Deke came up to take the cooler from Rusty and wasted no time in hauling out a six-pack from its bed of ice cubes.

"Any problems?" Kincade asked Rusty the first chance he had to see him alone.

"None. He was right inside the store when I rode up."

Kincade lifted his hat and ran a hand through his hair, his glance straying to Rossiter. Instinct said not to trust the man. "Do you think he made any phone calls?"

"He already had the pizzas ordered when I got there. He might have had time to make a call, but it would have been a fast one." Rusty looked at Kincade. "You're thinking he could have phoned DePard and told him where we are?"

"It's the way his mind works," Kincade concluded grimly. "He'd do it now just to spite me."

"What do you think we should do?"

"Not much we can do." He slapped a hand on Rusty's shoulder. "Come on, let's get some of that pizza and beer before it's all gone."

A GOLD Cadillac sped across the sage flats, clouds of dust trailing like a banner behind it. DePard was bent over the wheel, his gaze fixed on the catch pens ahead of him. He slowed as he neared them, and laid a hand on the horn, the loud blast carrying above the din of bawling cattle.

Sheehan sat atop his big bay horse, one leg hooked over the saddle as he watched the work in the pens. When he saw the Cadillac, he instantly straddled the saddle, walking the gelding forward to meet the car when it stopped.

DePard rolled down the window. "Starr just called." Frustration and anger edged his voice. "Eden Rossiter is driving her cattle to market. She's nearly to the Oregon border now."

Sheehan stiffened, then swung out of the saddle. "Frazier, take care of my horse," he ordered one of the workers in the pens, then climbed into the car and slammed the door.

DePard reversed the Cadillac and pointed it back toward the Diamond D headquarters. "Get Pete on the radio," he said. "Tell him to fuel the plane, have the engine running. We'll be there in"— he checked his watch—"twenty minutes."

SPOOKED by the low-flying aircraft, the herd threatened to scatter. It took better than twenty minutes to get them settled down. Eden joined the two riders on the near side of the herd. Too late she saw Kincade on the other side of Rusty Walker and her brother.

"That was DePard in the plane." Vince gave her a hard you-should-have-listened-to-me look.

"I know." The Diamond D insignia on the plane's tail had been impossible to miss.

"I wonder how he knew where to find us," Kincade mused, sliding a look at Vince. "It couldn't be that you made a quick phone call to him back at that convenience store?"

Indignant, Vince straightened from his slouched position in the saddle. "I never called DePard."

"Are we splitting hairs now?" Kincade taunted.

Eden broke up the argument. "It doesn't matter how DePard found out. He knows, and now we have to deal with that."

"How?" Vince scoffed.

Eden had thought about that. In truth, she had thought of little else since she recognized the twin-engine plane. On the other side of the mountain Ike Bedford was waiting to sell her cattle. She had planned to take them through the pass in the morning and be at Bedford's by late in the day. Now she could not wait. She knew DePard would try to get to Bedford. She had to get there first.

"We're going through the pass tonight," she said.

Vince stared at her. "You're crazy."

"The way I see it, it's the only chance. You and Kincade give Deke a hand with the cavvy." She nodded to the horse remuda still stirring restlessly a quarter mile from the herd.

"You heard the boss," Kincade prompted when Vince showed reluctance. Vince threw him a glare and reined his horse away, lifting it into a trot. Kincade followed.

A near smile deepened the corners of Rusty's mouth. "You got rid of everybody else. I guess that makes me next."

His observation was a little too accurate. She tried to pretend it wasn't true. "I don't know what gave you that idea."

"Kincade tells me I get crazy notions now and then." He watched the line of her mouth tighten. "You don't like me mentioning him, do you?" Before she could deny it, he went on. "I was hoping you might have squared things between you."

"I don't know what you're talking about."

"Oh, I think you do." He smiled. "You've been good for him, you know. When Marcie died, it was like her death had killed all the warm and good feelings inside him. But I've seen them back in his eyes when he looks at you."

"You knew his sister?"

"I was in love with Marcie since high school. But she never looked at me that way. To her I was like another brother."

Eden listened for bitterness but heard only regret. "Then you must hate Vince, too. As much as Kincade does."

"No. I tried to. I almost made it a time or two," Rusty admitted. "But Marcie was so happy with him. How can you hate a man who can make a woman that happy?" He smiled at the memory.

"But"—Eden was confused—"look how much he hurt her when he left."

"I know." Rusty nodded. "I also know if Marcie were alive, she'd be hurting bad, but she wouldn't hate him for that."

"You seem very sure of that."

"I am. I know Marcie." Rusty looked off into the distance. "She was timid. She didn't make friends easily even before she got her leg hurt. Then afterward . . . I guess Kincade and I were both guilty of protecting her a little too much."

"That's understandable."

"When she met your brother, she blossomed like a rose in the full sun. Love took her too high. Losing pushed her too low. I would have been there for her." He looked at Eden, his eyes bleak with grief. "If she only had reached out, I would have been there. I guess that's what I'm most sorry about. She'd been hurt, so hurt that she was afraid to reach out to someone else. And that's when you need to do it the most. Remember that, Miss Rossiter. Marcie didn't."

He bent his head down and reined his horse away to slowly circle the herd. Hurting inside, Eden watched him.

THE cattle were a moving tide of black shapes traveling up the barren mountain slope. With only a quarter moon hanging in the sky, the night was dark, and the breeze tunneling through the pass ahead of them had the nip of winter's breath in it.

Eden rode near the front of the herd. Farther ahead, at the point, Bob Waters was nearly to the summit of the pass. The ground began to level out beneath Eden's horse, and the cattle nearest her broke into a trot, as if knowing the long climb was nearly over.

Suddenly Bob Waters wheeled his horse around and threw up an arm, shouting, "Look out!"

Startled, Eden checked her horse as a deafening boom shook the ground. The side of the pass erupted in a black shower of flying rock. Her horse reared straight up, twisting from the blast. The ground vibrated with another series of explosions. Frantic, Eden clung to the horse's back, fighting to keep her balance when it lunged into the air again. Fleeing cattle blocked its path of flight.

On the other side of the herd, Kincade had a glimpse of Eden's pale face as her horse skyed again, then came down and vanished behind a swarm of black shapes. Her horse was down. Eden was down. Fear leaped into his throat. He whipped his own mount into the maelstrom of frightened cattle, his eyes glued to the spot where Eden had disappeared. Halfway across, he saw her horse trot off riderless. He never noticed that the explosions had stopped, that the only sound was the loud and eerie rumble of hooves and rubbing hides.

A rider streaked into Kincade's view, taking a high path along the curving wall of the pass. He plunged his horse down the path and bailed out of the saddle before the horse came to a full stop. Eden lay motionless on the ground. Kincade reached her a full second after the other rider knelt beside her. He piled out of the saddle at a run, his heart pounding with dread. "Eden."

Before Kincade could drop to his knees beside her, Vince stopped him with a savage glare. "Stay away!" He gathered her up, carefully cradling her upper body in his arms.

"Is she . . ." Kincade couldn't say the words.

"Dead?" Vince hurled it at him. "No." The answer came out in an ugly snarl. Then Vince looked at Eden, his expression and voice softening. "She's just unconscious." He glanced at the blood on the hand cupping the back of her head, then looked at Kincade again. "You did this to her," he accused. "You encouraged her to make this drive. If you hadn't been around, I could have talked her out of it. I knew DePard would never let her get away with it. That was him up there." He jerked his head toward the summit of the pass. "Him and his men. Throwing dynamite. That's how crazy he is."

Bob Waters rode up, saw Eden, and immediately swung out of the saddle. "The boss—is she okay?"

"She will be." Vince scooped her legs up and stood. "I need to get her to a doctor. Catch my horse."

"Take mine." Bob Waters led his horse to Vince and helped Vince lift Eden onto the saddle.

"Let me—" Kincade took a half step toward them.

"No," Vince snapped, warning him off again. "You stay with the cattle, deliver them to the pens—if you can."

Kincade watched him ride off with Eden in his arms.

Chapter XVI

MORNING sunlight bounced off the glass doors to the emergency medical clinic, throwing its blinding glare back into Kincade's face as he approached the entrance. Steeled against this moment, he pushed through the doors. Rusty followed.

The plump rosy-cheeked nurse behind the counter glanced up when he walked in. "May I help you?"

"I'm Kincade Harris. I came to see Eden Rossiter."

"You're the mysterious Kincade," she said with a twinkle in her eyes. "She mumbled your name a few times when she was coming around. Her brother didn't seem to know who you were."

"Is she all right?"

"Oh my, yes." The nurse laughed softly. "Other than a nasty bump on the head, a mild concussion, and some bruises. The doctor's checking her over. Why don't you come with me?"

She came out from behind the counter and walked briskly down a wide corridor to one of the rooms at the end. She pushed the door ajar and peered in. Over the top of her head Kincade could see a doctor in a white lab coat, but he couldn't see Eden.

". . . have a dandy headache for a few days," the doctor was saying. "The prescription I've given you will help that. Just try to take it easy. Otherwise you're fine."

"Excuse me, Doctor," the nurse interrupted. "Your patient has visitors."

He pivoted to face the door, smiling. "She's not my patient anymore. She's on her own now." He walked out of the room as Kincade walked in. Eden sat on the edge of the bed, and the sight of her was like a wild wind spinning through him. She looked strong and vital despite the smudges of fatigue under her eyes.

Unsteadied by the rip of longings, Kincade halted. His glance flicked briefly at Vince. Exhaustion had made hollows of Rossiter's eyes. He was haggard and drawn, going on nerve alone.

"Did you get the cattle penned?" Eden broke the silence when Kincade didn't.

"No. DePard got to the owner first."

"I told you," Vince jeered.

Kincade ignored him. "Bedford refuses to let any cattle owned by you pass through his sale barn." He reached inside his denim jacket and pulled a set of papers from his shirt pocket. "I'm buying your cattle. Here's a check and a bill of sale for you to sign."

Eden took the papers from him.

"You aren't going to be stupid enough to sign that, are you?" Vince demanded. "How do you know his check is good?"

"She can call the bank." Kincade held her gaze when she finally looked up. "I came away from the rodeo with more than broken bones to show for my time."

"I'll need a pen," she said.

"Right here." Rusty stepped forward with one.

"You aren't really going to sign that?" Vince protested.

"There comes a time, Vince, when you simply have to take some things on trust." She clicked the pen and signed her name, then handed the bill of sale back to Kincade.

Hesitant to read too much into her words, he slipped the document back in his pocket.

"This isn't going to work, you know," Vince challenged.

"It will work. Eden doesn't own the cattle anymore. I do. Bedford has no reason to refuse. Even DePard would agree."

"DePard." Distracted by the mention of his name, Vince turned away. "Every time I think about that dynamite going off and your horse going down— He could have killed you."

"But he didn't," Eden reminded him. "I'm fine, Vince."

"This time," he said grimly, and started for the door.

"Where are you going?"

He stopped at the door and looked back, his eyes haunted with pain and guilt. "I've got to talk to him." He charged out the door.

"No." Eden stood up too quickly. Pain slammed through her head, and the room swayed. She grabbed Kincade's arm.

"Take it easy." He steadied her, his hands at her waist.

She resisted him. "I have to go after Vince. I have to stop him."

"He's a grown man, Eden. He knows what he's doing."

"You don't understand." Her glance raced to the door, then just as swiftly to Kincade's face. "How did you get to the clinic?"

"I borrowed a pickup from Bedford. Why?"

"Let me have the keys." She held out a hand.

"No."

"I have to go after Vince."

"You're in no shape to drive."

"Then you drive me. I don't care."

Kincade tried to calm her. "Look, you're upset."

"Yes, I'm upset. I'm afraid—" Eden cut off the thought.

"What is there to be afraid of? DePard isn't after your brother. And Vince certainly doesn't need you to protect him."

"If you won't help me, then get out of my way."

Kincade's temper was on a short fuse, and she just lit it. "Eden, your brother has twisted us both up in knots—me with the way he used Marcie, and you with his gambling debts and lies. Yes, he loves you in his own peculiar way, but that doesn't change what he is."

"And it doesn't change the fact that he is my brother. I can't take the risk that he might—" She broke off the sentence.

"He might what? Get hurt? Let him. It's time he got hurt after the way he's hurt so many others. Are you so blind that—" This time it was Kincade who stopped, pieces suddenly fitting together. "Or has everyone else been blind, including me?"

"I don't know what you mean," Eden murmured warily.

"Just what is it you're afraid your brother might do? Kill De-Pard? Why would you think he might do that?"

"He wouldn't."

"Wouldn't he?" Kincade remembered too well Vince's ambush of him. Taking Eden by the shoulders, he shoved her into Rusty's keeping and pulled the bill of sale from his pocket. "Take care of this." He handed it to him, then pointed to Eden. "And keep her here."

He was striding down the corridor by the time Eden managed to recover and pull away from Rusty. He blocked her path to the door. "I'm going after them," she said. "Either with you or without you."

"I already figured that out, so calm down. I'll do the driving, but first we've got to find ourselves some wheels."

DUST churned up by Vince's vehicle hung in the air when Kincade drove into the town of Friendly. He spotted a gold Cadillac parked next to a Diamond D Ranch pickup, and slammed on the brakes.

Even before he opened the door to Starr's, Kincade recognized Rossiter's voice, raised in anger. He stepped inside. Roy was behind the bar, managing to look less bored than usual. Starr stood close to the action. DePard sat at a center table. Sheehan stood to his right, his chair pushed back from the table. "You said yourself she'll be all right, Vince," DePard said calmly. "I don't understand what you're upset about."

"Dammit, she's my sister," Vince raged. "I won't let you go on hurting her." His back was to the door. He didn't see Kincade walk in.

"If you really want to protect Eden, why don't you tell DePard who really shot Jeff?" Kincade challenged.

Vince whirled, his face going as white as the shirt DePard was wearing. His reaction confirmed Kincade's suspicions.

"I don't know what you're talking about," Vince insisted. "I wasn't even there."

"Is that why you look sick? Turn around so DePard can see your face."

Vince's tongue flicked out, wetting dry lips. He threw a quick glance at DePard and tried to laugh. "This is ridiculous. The man doesn't know what he's talking about."

"Don't I?" Kincade said. "What happened that night, Vince? Did you get scared when you found out Jeff had died? Did you decide that Eden would have a better chance of getting off than you?"

"Shut up. Dammit, shut up." Vince swung a fist.

Kincade saw it coming, dodged it, and threw a quick jab to the ribs. Vince staggered sideways, recovered his balance, and came back at Kincade like a wild man.

Intent on the brawling pair, no one noticed when Rusty and Eden walked in. A hard right to the jaw sent Vince crashing against the bar. His hat flew off, landing at Starr's feet. Eden gave a little cry and started forward. Rusty stopped her.

Kincade grabbed Vince by the shirtfront and hauled him into a chair. He leaned down, a hand gripping each armrest as he brought his face close to Vince's. "You ready to talk, Vince?" Kincade was breathing hard from the brief but violent fight. Blood trickled from a corner of his mouth. "It was you that night, wasn't it? You went back to the spring after you dropped Rebecca off, didn't you?"

"Yes." It was barely more than a whisper.

"Louder, Vince," Kincade ordered. "DePard can't hear you."

"Yes, dammit. Yes!" Vince shouted the words in belated defiance. Kincade pushed back from the chair and straightened to stand erect. "Jeff dragged Eden out of his truck," Vince hurried to explain. "Her blouse was torn. She was trying to get away from him. He was forcing her back to the blanket. I yelled at him, told him to let her go. But . . . he just laughed. That's when I saw the rifles in his truck. I only meant to scare him," Vince insisted. "I thought when he saw I had a rifle, he'd let Eden go. Instead he started coming toward me, taunting, laughing."

Kincade turned away, and Vince saw DePard. He leaned forward, lifting a hand in a beseeching gesture. "I never meant to shoot Jeff, DePard. One minute he was jeering. Then he lunged for the barrel. I don't even remember squeezing the trigger. The rifle went off. It just went off. You've got to believe me. It was an accident."

"You bastard." DePard took a step toward him.

Kincade held up a hand, checking the movement. "When did you decide Eden should take the blame?"

"I never thought about it until the old man—Jed—took it for granted that she had shot Jeff. That's when I got the idea." He looked down at the floor. "I didn't want to go to prison."

"So you sentenced your sister to one," Kincade said in disgust. "With DePard for a warden."

Vince hung his head lower. "I knew it would be hard for her at first, but I thought it would all blow over."

"It didn't, though, did it? It only got worse."

Vince nodded, then looked up. "How did you know about Jeff? No one else ever guessed."

Kincade sighed a humorless laugh. "Maybe I recognized the signs of a guilty conscience. I don't know."

"What will happen now?" Vince glanced around uncertainly.

"That's up to DePard." Kincade turned and saw Eden. He walked over to slide a hand on her shoulder and draw her forward. "I guess it depends on whether DePard has a conscience or not. Eden was never anything but a victim." He looked straight at De-Pard. "First a victim of your brother, then of you and everyone around here. It's hard to admit when you're wrong. But if Vince hadn't shown up that night, your brother would have been guilty of rape. To me that would have been a lot harder to live with. That's why you've been doing your best to cover it up, isn't it? But the louder you shouted his innocence, the guiltier you were."

Sheehan stepped up. "You have no right to talk to him like that."

"Let him be," DePard ordered.

Kincade studied him. "I have a feeling you'll let Vince walk rather than see this thing splashed across the headlines again."

DePard glared at him, then looked away, recognizing there was nothing to be gained.

Vince rose cautiously from the chair, his glance darting around the group as if he wasn't sure he would be allowed to leave un-

harmed. As he took a step toward the door, Starr picked up his hat
and moved to intercept him.

"You're not coming back this time, are you?" Her voice was
pitched low, intended for his hearing only.

"No." He took the hat from her. "The kid needs a father he can
be proud of. I'm a loser, Starr. I always have been." He walked
swiftly toward the door, his head down. When he reached Eden, he
paused. "I'm sorry, sis. I've got to go."

"I know." She realized he couldn't bring himself to face the
stares, the talk, the censure that would follow this.

"You'll be okay," he said to assure himself.

"Of course."

He threw one last hurried glance over his shoulder and walked
out the door. With his departure the attention shifted to DePard.
Feeling it, DePard cast a challenging glance at the watching faces.
His mouth tightened beneath his heavy mustache. "Let's get the hell
out of here," he muttered, and strode stiffly toward the door, certain Sheehan would follow. He did.

But DePard's steps slowed when he drew level with Eden. He
stopped, his chin lifting a fraction, his expression cool and harshly
proud. "It seems a mistake was made." It was clear from his tone
how difficult it was for him to say those words, how much he
resented the necessity of saying them.

"It was," Eden agreed with an equal amount of pride. "But don't
bother to apologize. I wouldn't want you to choke on it."

DePard stiffened. "That attitude is unnecessary."

"Probably. Right now you want to offer an apology only for appearance' sake. If you are ever truly sorry, I'll accept it."

Resentment darkened DePard's eyes. He stared at Eden and
trembled on the verge of temper, then walked out.

Eden sighed, her shoulders slumping a little. She lifted a hand
and pressed her fingers against the throbbing in her temple.

Rusty immediately led her to a chair. "You better sit down." He
eyed Kincade. "Do you want me to follow Vince?"

Kincade shook his head. "Let him go. It's over." He glanced at
Eden. "Why did you do it, Eden? Why did you say you shot Jeff?"

"I don't know." She lifted her shoulders in a light shrug. "Vince
had killed a man to protect me. Taking the blame seemed a small

thing to do for him. Neither one of us thought any of this would happen."

"No, I suppose not." Kincade studied her, watching for some sign that would give him an insight into her feelings, but she avoided his eyes. "With Vince gone, there isn't any reason for me to stay—except you."

She lifted her head, her expression guarded. "What am I supposed to say to that?"

"You could say you want me to stay, if you mean it."

"There's always plenty of work at the ranch."

"That isn't what I meant, and you know it. If I stay, I'll look at you whenever I want. Put my arms around you, steal a kiss, and I won't care who's watching. There won't be any 'Yes, boss,' 'No, boss.' "

Eden wrapped her hands together, trying to keep control over that sudden surge of joy inside. "I'm not used to someone fighting my battles for me."

"Like today, you mean," Kincade guessed. "I wasn't fighting that battle *for* you. I was fighting it *with* you. There's a difference. Do you want me to stay?"

She looked at him. "I don't want you to go."

"That's good enough for now." Kincade smiled, watching the pleasure come into her eyes and feeling his own chest swell with the fierceness of it.

Rusty beamed at the two of them. "Wasn't it Shakespeare that said 'All's well that ends well'?"

Eden looked at Kincade, mirth sparkling in her eyes, and they both started laughing. Rusty glanced from one to the other and frowned in bewilderment as they laughed some more.

"What did I say that was so funny? Come on, what'd I say?"

They just laughed.

JANET DAILEY

I t's obvious that Janet Dailey has not let her incredible success spoil her. Although her accomplishments are many—more than 100 million books sold, flourishing business ventures, a long and happy marriage—she prefers to talk about values. Values, she believes, are the secret of her success. "I think my themes tend to touch something we all hold common," she says, adding that her books focus on "the things that are most important: the family, the hard-work ethic, honesty, the desire to do the right thing. And the land. There's always the tie to the land."

Dailey traces her own tie to the land to her midwestern childhood, when she often visited her grandparents' farm. Later she and her husband, Bill, spent six years on the road, crisscrossing the continent, with only a trailer as their home. Travel gave Dailey the inspiration to write, as well as a wealth of material for her books. But at the end of their journey she and Bill were happy to settle down on their own land, near Branson, Missouri, which she describes as a small town of "good, honest, hardworkin' people." Just like the ones in her books.

Snow Wolf.

It's the most explosive operation the CIA has ever attempted.

Its success could avert a war.

Its failure could start one.

THE PRESENT

Chapter One

Moscow. I had come to bury the dead and resurrect ghosts, and so it seemed somehow appropriate that the truth and the lies of the past should begin in a graveyard.

It was raining that morning in Novodevichy Cemetery, and I was burying my father for the second time.

It isn't often that a man gets to be buried twice. As I stood alone under the dripping chestnut trees, I could see a black Mercedes come in through the cemetery gates and brake gently to a halt near the grave. Two men stepped out, one of them middle-aged and gray-haired, the other a bearded Orthodox priest.

It's a tradition in Russia to open the coffin before it's buried, a chance for friends and relatives to kiss their dead and say their last good-byes. But there would be no such tradition observed this wet day in June for a man who had died over forty years before, just a simple ceremony to finally acknowledge his passing.

As I stood there in the pouring rain, I saw the gray-haired man from the Mercedes put up his umbrella, then come toward me, smiling warmly. He offered his hand. "Brad Taylor, U.S. embassy. You must be Massey?"

The handshake was firm. As I let go, I said, "For a while there I was afraid you wouldn't make it."

"Sorry I'm late. I got held up at the embassy." He took a pack of cigarettes from his pocket and offered me one. "Smoke?"

"Thanks. I don't mind if I do."

He lit both our cigarettes. "Bob Vitali tells me you're a journalist. Have you ever been to Moscow before, Mr. Massey?"

"Once, five years ago. What else did Bob tell you?"

"He said you were a friend of his from way back, when you were at boarding school together. And he said to make sure everything went smoothly for you while you're in Moscow."

Taylor hesitated and looked over at the priest standing a short distance away. He was making himself ready, arranging his white vestments under his black raincoat and lighting a censer of incense.

Taylor said, "I guess we're almost ready to begin."

Someone had left a fresh marble slab against one of the trees and I could make out the simple chiseled inscription in Cyrillic letters:

JAKOB MASSEY
BORN: 3 JANUARY 1912
DIED: 1 MARCH 1953

Nearby was an old unmarked slab that had been uprooted from the grave. There was another one still lying on the ground, marking a second grave beside my father's, looking just as old.

I realized how suddenly everything had come together. A week ago and over five thousand miles away in Washington I had received a phone call from Langley, telling me they had arranged the funeral and that Anna Khorev would meet me in Moscow.

The Orthodox priest stepped forward and shook my hand and said in perfect English, "Shall I begin now?"

"Thank you."

He stepped toward the grave and started to pray, chanting the prayers for the dead in Russian.

When it was all over, the priest withdrew and went back to the car. Two gravediggers began to set the fresh headstone in place.

Taylor said, "Your lady friend, Anna Khorev, arrived this morning from Tel Aviv. The place she's at is in the Swallow Hills, outside Moscow. Belongs to the Israeli embassy." He handed me a slip of paper. "That's the address. They're expecting you at three this afternoon." He hesitated. "You mind if I ask you a question?"

"Ask away."

He nodded at the grave. "Bob told me your father died forty years ago. How come you're having this service here today?"

"All I can tell you is my father worked for the American government. He died in Moscow in 1953."

Taylor said, "I thought Moscow was out of bounds to Americans during the cold war. How did your father die?"

"That's what I'm here to find out."

Taylor looked puzzled. "Well, I'd like to stay and talk, but duty beckons. Can I give you a lift someplace?"

"No need. I'll find a taxi. I'd like to stay awhile."

"Whatever you say." Taylor smiled. "Good luck, Massey. I hope you find whatever it is you're looking for."

THIS is what I remember.

A cold, windy evening in March 1953. I was ten and at boarding school in Richmond, Virginia, when I was told that my father had died. I was never told where exactly he had died, only that it was somewhere in Europe and that it had been suicide. The body had been in water for weeks and it wasn't a pretty sight for a young boy, so I wasn't allowed to see it. There was a funeral, but no explanations or answers to my questions, because no one bothers to tell a child such things, but years later those questions always came back. Why? Where? It was to take a long time to learn the truth.

Ten days ago, when my mother died, I went back to the small apartment on New York's Upper East Side where she had lived, and I embarked on the ritual of going through her things. There were no tears, because I had never really known her. My parents divorced soon after I was born, and my mother had gone her own way, leaving my father to bring me up.

I remember the place was in disarray. An untidy single bed, some empty gin bottles, and letters from old boyfriends and from my father, kept in an old tin box under her bed.

I found the letter from my father. It was dated January 24, 1953.

Dear Rose,

Just a line to let you know William is well and doing fine at school. I'm going to be away for a time, and if anything should happen to me, I want you to know (as usual) there's enough money in my account to see you both through.

One more thing should anything happen to me: I'd be obliged

if you'd check the house, and if you find any papers lying around
in the study or in the usual place in the cellar, do me a favor and
pass them on to the office in Washington. Will you do that for me?

Jake

I thought about that line about papers. The house that had been
my father's was now mine, an old clapboard place he had bought
when he and my mother first moved to Washington. The day I got
back from sorting my mother's affairs, I went down to the cellar. It
was a place I hardly ever went, filled with long-forgotten bric-a-brac
and boxes of stuff I'd kept over the years. I shifted the cardboard
and wooden boxes around and checked the concrete floors.

I found nothing.

Then I started on the walls. It took me quite a while before I
found the two loose red bricks high above the cellar door.

My heart was pounding a little, wondering whether I would find
anything, as I reached up and pulled out the bricks. There was a
deep recess inside, and I saw a large yellowed legal pad lying there
between the covers of a faded manila file.

I took the old pad upstairs. Two pages had been written on, in
blue ink, in my father's handwriting. Four names. Some dates. Some
sketchy notes, as if he was trying to work something out, none of it
making much sense. And a code name: Operation Snow Wolf.

My father had worked for the CIA. He had been a military man
all his life and had worked in the Office of Strategic Services (OSS)
during the war, operating behind German lines. That much I knew,
but not much else, until I found that old yellow pad.

For a long time I sat there trying to figure it all out; then I saw
the date on one of the pages, and it finally clicked.

I drove to Arlington Cemetery. For a long time I looked at my
father's grave, looked at the inscription.

JAKOB MASSEY
BORN: 3 JANUARY 1912
DIED: 20 JANUARY 1953

I looked at those words until my eyes were on fire from looking.
Then I went to make photocopies of the written pages I'd found
and delivered the originals in a sealed envelope to my lawyer. I

made a call to Bob Vitali. He worked for the CIA in Langley. I told him what I had found, but not the contents.

"So what?" Vitali said. "You found some forgotten papers of your old man's. Sure, he worked for the CIA, but that was over forty years ago. Do yourself a favor and burn them."

"I really think someone should come and look at them."

Vitali sighed, and I could picture him looking at his watch at the other end. "Okay, what's in there? Give me something I can work with, and I'll ask around, see if what you found is important."

"Operation Snow Wolf."

"Never heard of it," Vitali said impatiently. "Bill, I'll tell you what. I'll ask some of the old-timers here and see what I can come up with. See if this Snow Wolf thing rings a bell. Listen, I've got a call coming in. I'll talk to you soon." The line clicked dead.

I went into the kitchen and made coffee. It must have been about an hour later when I heard the screech of car tires outside. I looked out the window and saw two black limousines pull up and half a dozen men step out briskly, Bob Vitali among them.

When I went to the door, he said urgently, "We need to talk."

The others waited outside on the porch while Vitali came into the room with just one other man. Vitali said, "Bill, I guess you figured this is about those papers you found—"

The other man interrupted sharply. "Mr. Massey, my name is Donahue. I'm a section head with the CIA. May I see the papers?"

I handed him the papers. "These are copies. The originals are in a safe place."

He looked white as he slowly read through the photocopies. Finally he sat down with a worried look. "Mr. Massey, the papers you hold are still classified top secret. The operation referred to in the file was a highly secret and sensitive one. I can't stress both words enough. The original papers, please."

"I'll make a deal with you."

"No deals, Massey. The papers, please," Donahue demanded.

I was determined not to be bulldozed. "My father died over forty years ago. I never knew where or when or how. Now I want answers. I want to know exactly what this Operation Snow Wolf was."

"Out of the question, I'm afraid."

"I'm a journalist. I can have the papers published, write an article, investigate, see if anyone who worked for the CIA back then remembers something. You might be surprised what turns up."

Donahue paled again. "I can assure you that not a paper in the land will publish anything you may care to write on the matter we're discussing. The CIA would not allow it."

"So much for democracy," I said. "Maybe I couldn't publish here, but there are newspapers abroad you can't control."

Donahue fell silent. "What do you want, Massey?"

"I want to know the truth. And I want to meet the people involved with my father on that mission—whoever's still alive."

"That's quite impossible. They're all dead."

"There must be someone. I want to speak with one of those names on the pad who knew my father and knew the operation and knows how he really died. And," I said firmly, "I want to know what happened to his body."

This time Donahue really did turn terribly pale. "Your father was buried in Washington."

"That's a lie. Look at the copies, Donahue. There's a date written on the last page—22 January 1953—in my father's handwriting. The date on his tombstone is 20 January. Now I may be dumb, but dead men don't write notes. The CIA said my father died abroad, but he was *here* in this house on that day. You know something? I don't think you buried my father. I don't think you had a body. That's why you people gave me all that crap about him being in the water too long. I was a kid; I wouldn't question not being allowed to see the body. But I'm questioning it now. My father didn't commit suicide. He died on this Snow Wolf operation, didn't he?"

Donahue gave a weak smile. "Mr. Massey, I think you're being highly speculative and really over the top here."

"Then let's not speculate any longer. I went to see my lawyer. I'm having the body exhumed. And when that coffin's opened, if I don't find my father inside, I'll have you and your superiors dragged into a public court to explain."

Donahue stood up, looking as if he wanted to hit me. "You do that, Massey, and you'll find yourself in a whole lot of trouble."

I adopted a more conciliatory approach. "If you tell me what really happened to my father, I'll return the papers. And I'll agree to sign whatever you want, pledging my silence afterward."

Donahue sighed. "I think I should tell you that this matter is no longer within my control. I'm going to make a phone call, Mr. Massey. The person I speak to will have to call someone else. Both these people will have to agree before your demands can be met."

I looked at him. "Who are you going to call?"

"The President of the United States."

It was my turn to react. "And who's he going to call?"

"The President of Russia."

THE rain had stopped as I walked back to the cemetery gates, found a taxi, and was driven to Swallow Hills, where flowers bloomed in the gardens of big houses overlooking the Moscow River.

The taxi dropped me at the gate of a rambling villa. There were two men in plain clothes, Israeli guards, standing beside a security hut. They checked my passport, then telephoned the villa before they opened the gate for me, and I walked up to the front.

A tall, dark-haired young woman opened the door when I rang the bell. She said in English, "Mr. Massey, please come in," and led me out to the back of the villa. The gardens were dazzling with color in the bright sunshine. As I followed the girl across the patio, I saw an elderly woman waiting at a table.

Anna Khorev would have been in her late sixties; although her hair was completely gray, she looked like a woman ten years younger. She wore a simple black dress that hugged her slim figure, dark glasses, and a white scarf tied round her neck.

She smiled and offered her hand. "Mr. Massey, it's good to meet you. Would you like something to drink? A coffee? Some Russian brandy? Or is that too strong for you Americans?"

"Not at all. That sounds fine."

The girl poured me a drink from a tray and handed it across.

Anna said, "Thank you, Rachel. You may leave us now." When the young woman had gone, she said, "My granddaughter. She traveled with me to Moscow." She offered me a cigarette from a pack on the table, and I accepted. She took one herself and said, "So tell me what you know about me."

"Over forty years ago you escaped from a Soviet prison camp. You're the only survivor of a top secret CIA mission code-named Snow Wolf."

"I can see your friends in Langley have filled you in."

"They've told me hardly anything. I think they're leaving that to you. Except they did tell me my father wasn't buried in Washington but in an unmarked grave here in Moscow. He died on active service for his country, and you were with him when it happened."

She nodded at me to continue.

"I found some old papers of his. Four names were written on the pages. Yours and three others—Alex Slanski, Henri Lebel, and Irena Dezov. There was also written on one of the pages, 'If they're caught, may God help us all.' I was hoping you could help me there."

For a long time she said nothing, just looked at me through her dark glasses. Then she removed them, and I saw her eyes. They were big and dark brown and very beautiful.

"So when you read this, you realized there was more to your father's death than you had been told, and you went looking for answers?"

"That's when I was offered a deal. If I agreed to hand over the papers, I'd be present when my father was given a proper burial service. But the matter was still highly secret, and I had to sign a declaration promising to uphold that secrecy. I was told that it was all up to you whether you'd tell me what I wanted to know."

"Which is?"

"The truth about my father's death. The truth about Snow Wolf and how my father ended up in a grave in Moscow."

She didn't reply, just looked at me thoughtfully.

I said, "I have another question. The second grave, the one beside my father's— It too had the same unmarked headstone. Whom does that grave belong to?"

A look of sadness passed across Anna Khorev's face, and she said, "Someone very brave. Someone quite remarkable indeed."

She looked out at the view of the city, toward the red walls of the Kremlin, trying to make up her mind, and then she finally turned back to look at me. "You know, you look very much like your father. He was a good man, a very good man." She paused. "Tell me, what do you know about Joseph Stalin, Mr. Massey?"

I shrugged. "Not much. He was one of the great despots of this century. They say he was responsible for as many deaths as Hitler."

Anna Khorev shook her head fiercely. "More. Twenty-three million deaths. Not including those who died in the last war because of his stupidity. Twenty-three million men, women, children. Slaughtered. Shot or sent to die in camps worse than the Nazis imagined."

I sat back, surprised by the sudden ferocity in her voice. "I don't understand. What has this got to do with what we're discussing?"

"It has everything to do with it." Anna Khorev's face looked deadly serious. She said, "The story I'm going to tell you goes back a long time, to when it first began in Switzerland."

THE PAST

Chapter Two

Lucerne, Switzerland, December 11, 1952. The three bodies were found in the woods.

The hunter who found them threw up when he saw the child's body. Even the hardened policemen of the Lucerne KriminalAmt thought it one of the most brutal murder scenes they had ever witnessed. There was always something pitiful and particularly brutal about the body of a murdered child.

The forensic examination determined that the girl was between ten and twelve years old. There was bruising on her legs, arms, and chest, which suggested she had been beaten before being shot. The same with the man's corpse lying next to hers.

The only corpse that could be identified was that of a bakery worker, Manfred Kass. In his wallet was a driver's license and a shotgun permit. The police learned that he had gone hunting after his Friday night shift, and they deduced that he had stumbled on the slaughter of the man and the child and had paid for it with his life.

But of the murderer, or his identity, there was no trace at all. There was no evidence that linked the two unknown corpses to missing persons. Both had no personal identification and had been wearing clothes that could be bought in any large clothing store in Europe. The only clue was a faded minute tattoo on the man's right arm. It was of a small white dove, centimeters above his wrist.

Washington, D.C., December 12. It was a little after eight in the evening when the DC-6 carrying President-elect Dwight D. Eisenhower from Tokyo landed at Andrews Air Force Base.

Although he was not to take over the reins of power until January, Eisenhower had flown to Seoul a month after his election to assess personally the war situation in the Far East.

His meeting with President Harry Truman the next day was unofficial, and after the brief welcome Truman suggested they take a walk in the White House gardens. The two men seemed a strange pair: the small, bespectacled President with the bow tie and walking cane and the tall, erect military man.

They reached one of the oak benches, and Truman gestured for them to sit. He lit up a Havana cigar, puffed out smoke, and said seriously, "Tell me, Ike, what's your opinion of Stalin?"

Eisenhower shrugged. "The man's a despot and a dictator. You could say he's the cause of almost all our present problems."

Truman leaned forward, his voice firm. "Ike, he is the whole damned problem. The way the Russians are moving with their nuclear research, they're going to be way ahead of us militarily. They've got some pretty good technical minds working for them. The top ex-Nazi scientists. We've exploded a hydrogen device, but they're working on the actual bomb. And they'll make it, Ike, you mark my words. Our intelligence people say six months. Maybe sooner. The word is, Stalin has authorized unlimited funds."

Truman put down his cigar and spoke again. "There's something else you ought to know. I was sent a highly classified report by our special Soviet Department near the Potomac. I want you to read it. The source is a highly placed contact we have who has links to the Kremlin. The report has me scared. More scared than I've been in a long time . . ." Truman broke off and shook his head.

There was a look of surprise on Eisenhower's face. "You mean the source of the report is a Russian? Who is he?"

"Ike, even I can't tell you that. That's a matter for the CIA. But you'll know the first day you're sitting in the Oval Office."

"Then why let me read this report now?"

Truman took a deep breath. "Because, Ike, I'd like you to be prepared before you come into office. The contents of that report are going to determine not only your presidency but the future course of this country—maybe even the future course of the whole world."

Truman sat quietly, his hands resting on his cane, while Eisenhower read from the manila file, the cover and each page marked in red lettering FOR THE PRESIDENT'S EYES ONLY.

Finally Eisenhower placed the report on the seat beside him. He stood and paced restlessly, hands behind his back. In another five weeks he would inherit the President's chair, but suddenly the prospect held less appeal for him. Truman's voice brought him back.

"Well, what do you think?" Truman stared at Ike.

Eisenhower shook his head. "I don't know what to think." He paused. "You trust the source of the report?"

Truman nodded firmly. "I do."

Eisenhower took a deep breath. "Then with respect, sir, the day I become President, I'm walking into a minefield."

"I guess you are, Ike," Truman replied matter-of-factly. He stood. There were dark rings under his eyes, and his soft face looked troubled, as if the strain of eight years in office was finally taking its toll. "To tell the truth, I'm glad it's going to be a former five-star general sitting in that President's chair and not me."

Soviet–Finnish border, October 23, 1952. Just after midnight the snow stopped, and she lay in the cottony silence of the Russian woods, listening to her heart beating in her ears.

She was cold. Her clothes were soaked through, and her hair was damp, and she was aware of the icy sweat on her face. She was more tired than she had ever been, and suddenly she wanted it to be over.

For the past hour now she had watched the sentry hut beside the narrow metal bridge that ran across the frozen river. Her uniform coat was covered in frost and snow, and as she lay in the narrow gully behind a bank of fir trees, she tried not to think of the past, only the future that lay beyond the narrow bridge.

She could see the two guards on the Russian side, standing by the small wooden sentry hut. One of them had a rifle slung over his shoulder, the other a machine pistol draped across his chest.

There was a guardhouse to the left, a bank of fir trees beside it. She knew that was where the other guards would be resting, off duty. On the bridge electric light blazed from arc lamps in the trees, and the red-and-white barrier poles were down at both ends.

There was a flood of light on the Finnish side of the border also, and more guards, but in the gray overcoats and uniforms of Finland.

She saw a sudden movement on the Russian side. The guard with the rifle stepped into the sentry hut, while the other moved into the trees, unbuttoning his fly to relieve himself. She rolled over in the snow, and her gloved hand found the cold butt of the Nagant revolver in its leather holster.

She rolled back and looked at the guard urinating. She knew this was her moment, and she took a deep breath. She stood, and her legs trembled with fear. As she came out from behind the cover of the trees, she slipped the weapon into her overcoat pocket.

The guard with the machine pistol buttoned his trousers and turned. He stared at her, in her captain's overcoat with green epaulettes, as if she were a ghost. Then he said, "I'm sorry, Captain, but this is a restricted area. Your papers, comrade."

As the guard unslung his machine gun, he stared suspiciously at the young woman's face, but he didn't see the Nagant revolver, and that was his mistake. It exploded twice, hitting him in the chest, sending him flying backward. The air came alive with the noise, and the second guard came running out of the sentry hut.

The woman fired, hitting him in the shoulder, spinning him around, and then she started to run toward the bridge.

There was mayhem behind her on the Russian side, sirens going off and voices raised, as the soldiers came rushing out of the guardhouse. She was barely aware of a voice behind her, screaming for her to stop, as she ran toward the Finnish barrier fifty yards away, her breath rising in panting bursts, her lungs on fire. Up ahead Finnish guards were unslinging their rifles. She didn't see the Russian guard behind her take aim, but she heard the crack of a weapon and saw the frosty cloud explode in the snow off to her right.

And then another rifle cracked, and she was punched forward, losing her balance, a terrible pain blossoming in her side. But she kept running until she collapsed in front of the Finnish barrier, crying out in agony. Strong hands grasped her, and a young officer barked orders while his men carried her toward the guardhouse.

There were sirens going off now, but she was aware only of the flood of pain in her side and a terrible feeling of tiredness, as if a dam had burst inside her head and all the pent-up fear and exhaustion had come spilling out.

The young officer was looking down at her. She heard the urgency in his voice as he screamed at one of his men to fetch a doctor.

She closed her eyes. All she remembered after that was darkness.

Helsinki, October 25. A man with cropped gray hair sat beside Anna Khorev's bed. His face was rugged, and his mouth was set in a grim impression of aggression. It was a face that had seen a lot of unpleasant things in life—cautious and wary and full of secrets—but the gray eyes were not without feeling. One of the Finnish intelligence officers, who had already interviewed her, had told her the American was coming and that he wanted to talk with her.

He looked in his early forties as he sat back in the chair. His Russian was fluent and his voice soft as he said, "My name is Jake Massey. They tell me you're going to make a full recovery."

When she didn't reply, the man leaned forward and said, "I'm here to try and fill in some of the gaps in your story. You are a Soviet citizen, and your name is Anna Khorev. Is that right?"

"Yes."

He said, "I realize you've been through a difficult time, Anna, but you must understand one thing. Finland gets a considerable number of people escaping over the Russian border." He smiled gently. "Not all so dramatically as you did, perhaps. Some of them are genuinely trying to flee Russia. But sometimes your countrymen send people over here to spy. I need to make certain you're not one of those people. Do you feel well enough to talk?"

She nodded. "Yes."

He hesitated. "Why did you shoot the guards at the bridge?"

"To escape."

"Escape what exactly?"

"From the gulag at Nicochka."

"The Soviet embassy in Helsinki says you murdered an officer at the camp. Is that true?"

She hesitated, then nodded.

"Why did you kill the man, Anna?"

She opened her mouth to speak, but somehow the words wouldn't come. Massey looked at her. "Anna, I think I had better be completely honest and tell you the situation. I work for the American embassy. Your people are making all kinds of diplomatic noises to have you sent back to face trial for murder. Under the terms of the Soviet-Finnish treaty, there are grounds sufficient for your return to Russia on that charge. The only way the Finns can avoid that is to hand you over to the American embassy and say that you have requested political asylum in America. They want to help you. Russia is not exactly their best friend. That's why I was asked to talk with you and decide if my embassy can be of help." Massey paused. "If I know the full story of your background, my embassy can judge if you're a suitable case for political asylum."

"What is it you want to know?"

Massey said gently, "Everything you can tell me. About your background. The camp. Why you killed the officer."

Suddenly a terrible grief flooded her mind, as if to remember was too painful. She closed her eyes and turned away. The man said softly, "Take your time, Anna. Just start at the beginning."

WHEN the German army panzers swept into the Baltic States in 1941, there were many inhabitants who were pleased to see them.

On Stalin's orders only a year before, the Red Army had swiftly and brutally annexed each of the tiny independent Baltic countries of Estonia, Latvia, and Lithuania. Thousands were tortured, executed, or shipped off to labor camps by the invading Russians. And so the German troops were seen as an army of liberation. People lined the streets to welcome the Wehrmacht soldiers while every road north and east was clogged with a defeated Soviet army retreating from the mighty German blitzkrieg.

But not all Soviet commanders chose to flee the might of the Third Reich. Some chose to stay behind and fight. One of these Russian officers was Brigadier Yegor Grenko.

At forty-two he was already a divisional commander, with a wife and a fifteen-year-old daughter named Anna. The initial battle orders from Stalin after the German invasion had been to engage in the minimum of conflict. Still foolishly believing that Hitler would not push deep inside Russia, Stalin had hoped to lessen the conflict by not angering the Germans with a savage counterattack.

Yegor Grenko saw it differently. He didn't believe the Germans would hold back at the Russian border. Convinced that within a week the battle orders would be changed to an offensive, Grenko decided to fight a rearguard action and ignored cables from the Moscow military command ordering him to retreat. Finally, though, when he could ignore the cables no more, he and his men boarded a troop train near Narva and headed back to Moscow.

When the train pulled into Riga Station, Yegor Grenko was arrested. When his wife tried to intervene, she was brushed aside and told bluntly that his arrest was none of her business.

Grenko was tried by a military tribunal and found guilty of disobeying orders. The following day he was executed.

A day later fresh battle orders from Stalin were made public: Every citizen was to repel the invading Germans with every means, even to death, and no Soviet soldier was to retreat.

For Yegor Grenko the order had come a day too late.

After his death the family home in Moscow was confiscated. Anna's mother never recovered from the injustice of her husband's execution. In the second month of the siege of Moscow, Anna came home to find her mother's corpse hanging from a water pipe.

For two days after they had cut down the body, Anna lay in her bed, not eating and barely sleeping.

On the third day she packed what meager belongings she had into one small suitcase and moved out of the apartment into a squalid, tiny room on the eastern side of the Moscow River.

The German army was six miles away, but Anna Grenko was too young to fight. She was sent to work in an aircraft factory. On her seventeenth birthday she was called up for military service, given three weeks' basic training, and shipped south to the front and General Chuikov's Sixty-second Army at Stalingrad.

And it was at Stalingrad that she was to learn the real meaning of survival: fighting from street to street, holding out against the Germans in a siege that was to last for over six months, crossing enemy lines at night in the mud and snow, the fighting so savage and close she was often near enough to the enemy that she could hear their whispered voices in nearby trenches. Twice Anna was wounded, and twice she was decorated. On the fifth incursion behind German lines she was captured by a detachment of Ukrainian SS. After interrogation she was brutally raped and left for dead in a bomb crater. She was found by her own troops the next day when the lines were overrun.

The war ended, but it was to be five more years before Anna Grenko was to find any sort of personal happiness.

After the war Anna found secretarial work in a Moscow factory, and with time on her hands she went to night school at the Moscow Language Institute. One of the young lecturers was Ivan Khorev.

He was only twenty-four—a slim, pale, sensitive young man, already an admired and popular poet—and his work had been published in several respected literary magazines.

One night after class he asked Anna out for a drink.

They went to a café on the banks of the Moscow River. They ate zakuski and drank Georgian wine, and Ivan talked about poetry. When he recited a poem by Pasternak, she thought it the most beautiful thing she had ever heard. He listened quietly and attentively to her opinions. And he liked to laugh.

A band was playing on the terrace, a soft, sad waltz from before the war, and he asked her to dance. He didn't try to touch or kiss her. Afterward he walked her home, but instead of a good-night peck, he formally shook her hand.

She fell in love, and they married a month after she graduated. When their first child was born a year later, Anna found her life complete. It was a daughter, and they called her Sasha. They were allotted a small apartment off Lenin Prospect, and she and Ivan often took their baby for walks in nearby Gorky Park.

She never forgot the first walk they took together as a family. A man with a camera had taken their photograph for fifty kopecks— the three of them together, she and Ivan smiling, Sasha wrapped in a woolen cap and a white blanket, her face fat and pink and healthy. Anna kept the photograph on the mantelpiece, and every day she looked at it, as if to remind herself that her happiness was real.

In that first warm summer of complete joy she could never have imagined the pain that was to come.

The pounding on the apartment door came one morning at two. Three men burst into the apartment, and Ivan was dragged outside to a waiting car. He was accused of writing and publishing a poem in a dissident magazine. For that crime he was banished to a penal colony at Norylsk in Siberia for twenty-five years.

A week later the men from the secret police came back. Anna Khorev cried and screamed and kicked. When they took her child, she almost killed the men who dragged her to the car waiting to take her to Lefortovo Prison, but it did no good.

For her association with Ivan she was sentenced to twenty years in Nicochka Penal Camp. Sasha was removed to a state orphanage, where she would be brought up to be a good Communist.

After she had been in prison six months, Anna received a letter from the penal camp information service informing her that her husband had died of natural causes in Norylsk.

She cried that night until her heart felt as if it were going to explode with grief. She didn't eat her meager rations of black bread and cabbage soup, and within a week she was suffering the effects of severe malnutrition. When she finally collapsed on her work detail, she was marched to the camp commandant.

The commandant gave her a stern lecture, but she knew by the man's tone that he didn't care if she lived or died.

The telephone rang in another room, and when he was called outside, Anna Khorev noticed a map on the wall. It was of the surrounding area—the terrain and border posts, the roads and military bases and civilian prison camps. She moved closer and stared at it intently for almost five minutes, burning every detail into her mind.

After the commandant dismissed her, she went back to her barrack hut and ate her first meal in eight days. That night she made up her mind. She wasn't going to die a prisoner in the Arctic Circle.

The border toward Finland was a tortuous landscape of thick forest and hills teeming with wolves and bears, glacial ravines and wide frozen rivers. The most accessible crossings were guarded, but one of those was her best chance, even if it was dangerous.

There was a camp officer she had noticed—a rough and lustful man who took the risk of bedding the female prisoners, trading extra food for sex. She let it be known that she was available.

The officer came to her after dark. They met in a woodshed at the rear of the camp. She waited until he had undressed her, and when he had taken off his coat and tunic, she drove a six-inch metal blade into his back. It had taken her three weeks, in the hours of darkness, to make the weapon, but only moments to use it.

Ten minutes later she unlocked the side gate with the man's keys and walked through into the freezing, snowy night, wearing his uniform and coat and fur hat, carrying his pistol.

Within four hours, frozen and exhausted, Anna had finally reached the border with Finland.

SHE spoke with Massey for almost an hour. When she finished, he looked at her with compassion, and she knew he believed she was telling him the truth and would do his best to help her.

He said for now she was to rest and try to build up her strength.

She watched him go, and then she was left alone in the small white room. Off in the distance she could hear a radio playing cheerful dance music, and it made her think of the first night Ivan Khorev had taken her dancing on the banks of the Moscow River. She felt the grief suddenly flood in on her like a tidal wave.

THE next evening two men met for dinner at Helsinki's Savoy Restaurant, a favorite haunt of embassy staff and diplomats.

Doug Canning's title at the American embassy was political counselor, but his real function was as a CIA senior officer.

Canning had made the initial report on Anna Khorev to the American ambassador, and once a decision had been made to call in expert help to interrogate and assess the woman, Jake Massey, head of the CIA's Soviet Operations Division in Munich, had been put on a plane for Helsinki. After Massey had delivered his assessment, he got a phone call to join Canning for dinner.

Doug Canning was a tall, lean Texan with blond thinning hair and tanned good looks. He wielded considerable influence with the U.S. ambassador, the man who would ultimately decide Anna Khorev's suitability for political asylum.

Canning had ordered a bottle of Bordeaux. He sipped his wine appreciatively and smiled across the table.

"It sounds from the report as though the girl had a pretty rough time. But is she telling you anything we could find useful, Jake?"

Massey shook his head. "There's nothing much she *can* tell us. It's been eight years since she was discharged from the Red Army, so any information in that regard would be pretty much out of date by now. But whether or not she can help us with intelligence information, on humane grounds alone I think she has a case."

Canning hesitated, then wiped his mouth with his napkin. "Jake, let me give it to you straight. Some pretty strong noises are being made by Moscow about this one. They say she's a common criminal and in order not to further damage the already delicate relationship between our two countries, we ought to send her back."

"So what do you think's going to happen?"

Canning looked concerned. "We don't need the kind of diplomatic trouble this can bring, Jake. So my guess is that the ambassador will send her back. And there's something else you ought to know. Russia has a right to interview any border crossers convicted of serious crimes. The Soviet embassy has already made it clear it wants to do that. It gives them a chance to get the escapee to return with promises of leniency. There's a senior official in town right now who's handling it. Some guy called Romulka, from Moscow."

"Doug, if we send the girl back, the ambassador will be signing her death warrant. He may as well pull the damned trigger himself."

As MASSEY and Anna sat in the interview room in the city police station, two Russians in civilian suits stepped in, past the policeman who opened the door. The older of the two was in his early forties, tall and broad. Cold blue eyes were set in a brutal-looking face that was pockmarked with acne scars. He curtly introduced himself as Nikita Romulka, a senior official from Moscow.

The second Russian, a young embassy aide, sat beside him and handed him a file. Romulka flicked it open and, without looking up, said, "You are Anna Khorev." The man barely looked at her as he spoke.

Massey nodded to Anna, and she answered, "Yes."

When the man looked up, he stared at her coldly. "I am here to offer you a chance to redeem yourself by facing the serious crimes you have committed on Soviet soil. Should you return to Moscow, your entire case will be reviewed and you will be accorded the utmost leniency that is due to every Soviet citizen. Do you understand me?"

Anna hesitated. "I don't want to go back."

Romulka said firmly, "I'm giving you the opportunity to return of your own free will and have your case reviewed. If I were you, I would give such a proposal serious thought."

"I don't want to go back. I was imprisoned for no wrong, I committed no crime before I was sent to the gulag. And it's the people who sent me to a prison camp who ought to be tried."

Romulka's face suddenly twisted in anger. "Listen to me. Imagine how unpleasant we could make things for your child. Come back, and you may see her again. Don't, and I swear to you the rest of her life in that orphanage can be made very unpleasant indeed."

Massey tried hard to control the urge to hit the man, and then he saw the emotion welling in Anna's eyes, the pain growing on her face until suddenly all the anguish flooded out. She lunged across the table, and her nails dug into Romulka's face.

"No! You won't hurt my daughter like that. . . . You won't!"

Massey and the aide stepped in between them. Then a policeman appeared at the door, and Massey ushered Anna from the room.

As Romulka removed a handkerchief from his pocket and dabbed blood from his face, he glared at Massey. "You haven't heard the last of this! Your embassy will learn of this outrage!"

Massey stared angrily at the Russian. "Tell who you like. But she's made her decision." He jabbed a finger hard in Romulka's chest. "Now get out of here before I hit you myself."

For a moment it seemed as if Romulka would rise to the threat as he glared back at Massey, but suddenly he stormed out of the room.

MASSEY returned to the hospital that evening and suggested they go for a walk outside. Anna said, "What I did today didn't help, did it? Has your ambassador decided what's going to happen to me?"

She looked at Massey uncertainly, but he smiled. "After he heard about Romulka's threat, he agreed to grant you asylum. We're going to help you start a new life in America, Anna. Give you a new identity and help you settle down and find a job. You won't be given citizenship straightaway. You'll have to be a resident for five years, just like any other legal immigrant. But if you don't do anything crazy, it shouldn't be a problem."

Massey saw her close her eyes, then open them again slowly. There was a look of relief on her face. "Thank you."

Massey smiled. "Don't thank me. Thank the ambassador. Or maybe you should thank Romulka."

For a long time Anna Khorev said nothing. Finally she said, "Do you think I'll be happy in America?"

Massey saw that it was only now she realized the enormity of what had happened and the uncertainty that lay ahead.

"It's a good country to make a fresh start in. You've been badly hurt. You'll probably feel confused and lost for a while. But you'll heal with time. I know you will."

"You know something, Massey? I hope I see you again. I think you're one of the nicest men I've ever met."

Massey smiled. "Thanks for the compliment. But I guess you haven't known many men, Anna. I'm just an ordinary guy, believe me." Some instinct made him touch her shoulder gently. "You'll be okay. I know you will. Time will heal your heart."

"I wish I could believe that."

Massey smiled. "Trust me."

Chapter Three

Washington, D.C., January 22, 1953. The collection of wooden buildings on the bank of the Potomac River looked like dismal, run-down barracks. The walls inside were pockmarked with holes, and the plaster ceilings were smudged with damp stains.

Originally a World War I army barracks, the ramshackle huts had later housed the offices of the OSS—the Office of Strategic Services, the organization responsible for America's wartime foreign intelligence. Transformed in function four years after World War II, the buildings now housed the Central Intelligence Agency.

The barracks complex was divided into sections with alphabetic titles. The Q building was where highly sensitive and secret operations were planned and executed against the Soviet Union.

The office at the end of a long corridor on the second floor of the building had no name on the door. Inside, it was pretty much like all the other offices, with the same green desk and filing cabinet.

At fifty-six Karl Branigan was a blubbery but muscular man, with a tightly cropped GI haircut and a fleshy, ruddy face. Despite the army haircut, Branigan had never seen frontline action, but had been a deskbound intelligence officer most of his working life.

It was almost two o'clock that cold January afternoon when his secretary rang to say that Jake Massey had arrived.

Jake Massey and Karl Branigan had known each other for almost twelve years. Both were capable and hardened men, and both were dangerous to cross. Massey had just been recalled from the CIA's Soviet Operations Division in Germany to CIA headquarters in Washington. He eased himself into the chair opposite Branigan. "So Max Simon and his daughter are dead," he said after the usual greetings. "Tell me how it happened."

Branigan hesitated. "You and Max were friends a long time?"

"Thirty years. I was Nina's godfather. Max was one of the best people we had." Massey flushed angrily. "Damn it, Branigan, why were they killed? The girl was only ten years old. Who did it?"

"We'll come to that later. I'm sure you realize that it was an execution, pure and simple. They were both shot in the head at close range. I assume the girl was killed because she saw whoever shot her father, or they meant her death as a further warning."

"They?"

"Moscow, of course."

"What do you mean, a warning?"

"Max was gathering some pretty sensitive information for us before he was killed. We didn't know about the deaths until a routine Interpol report reached our office in Paris. We had the bodies identified and shipped back." Branigan hesitated. "Max arrived in Lucerne from Paris on the eighth of last month after traveling from Washington. He took his daughter with him for the trip. She'd been ill recently, and he wanted her to see a Swiss doctor."

"Is that the reason he was in Switzerland?"

"No, it wasn't. He was there to arrange a meeting with a highly placed contact from the Soviet embassy in Berne. They were to meet in Lucerne, but Max never made the meeting. We think Max and his girl were abducted from their hotel."

"Have you any idea who murdered them?" Massey asked.

"Why? You got revenge on your mind?"

"A year ago Max was moved out of my operation in Munich to work for Washington. Now he's dead, and I'd like to know why."

"Who did it I can tell you with certainty. A man named Kurt Braun. Braun's not his real name. He uses a lot of aliases."

"Who is he?"

"A hired killer the Soviets use. Operates all over the place. East

German national, speaks English and Russian fluently. We've got at least three murders put down to him. But I'd get revenge out of your mind. We've got other plans for you."

"What plans?"

Branigan smiled. "All in good time."

Massey said, "Then tell me what it was Max was doing for you that cost his life and his daughter's."

Branigan shrugged. "He'd been buying information from a Soviet embassy official. Only, someone in Moscow got to hear about it, and the official was called back home. What happened to him, you can guess. And we know what happened to Max and his kid."

"What sort of information? Is this why I was recalled?"

Branigan shifted his heavy bulk in the chair. "There's something I want you to see. It'll explain everything." He unlocked his desk drawer and slid out a buff-colored file with FOR THE PRESIDENT'S EYES ONLY stamped along the top in red letters. "Needless to say, the classification says it all. But it seems you're a special case."

He slipped his jacket from the back of the chair and pulled it on. "I'm going to leave you alone for, say, fifteen minutes. That ought to be enough time to read what's inside and prime you for what you're going to hear later from the assistant director. It's all in the file. You'll find the reason why Max and his kid were murdered."

THE white house in Georgetown looked as imposing as any in the select neighborhood that housed Washington's elite. The three-story colonial sat in a walled private garden of cherry and pear trees, and although it was winter, the three men sat out on the back patio in wrought-iron garden seats. The assistant director, William G. Wallace, was silver-haired and in his late fifties.

When the small talk was over, the assistant director looked over at Massey, smiled faintly, and said, "You read the file, Jake?"

"I read it." Massey nodded.

"Have you any questions?"

"One. Who knows about this?"

"Besides us? Only the President and the director."

Branigan said, "Maybe I better fill in the gaps, sir?"

The assistant director nodded. "I guess you better, Karl. I want Jake to be crystal-clear about what he's read."

Branigan looked at Massey. "Jake, what you saw back in the office was a confidential report written by Joseph Stalin's private physicians. We received it from Max a month before he was murdered. You know the contents, but I'll go over it again to clear up any points. Number one: Stalin has had two strokes in the last six months, and as a result his speech and movement are impaired.

"Number two: The medical people agree that he's become mentally unstable. He's displaying signs of paranoid schizophrenia.

"Now we already know he's certifiable, but this report confirms it and puts it in perspective. Something else you ought to know. The Kremlin doctors who wrote the medical report were arrested on a charge of trying to poison Stalin and have been taken to the Lubyanka prison. We've no information on their fate, but I'd guess it ain't rosy. Most of the doctors were Jews. Stalin's made no secret of the fact he hates the Jews. Our intelligence people have confirmed that he's building concentration camps in Siberia and the Urals. He clearly intends to finish what the Nazis started."

Massey stared at Branigan. "What exactly are you saying—"

The assistant director interrupted. "Jake, let me put it simply. Stalin is a danger. And I don't mean only to America but to the whole damned world. Everybody from Congress to the man in the street believes there's another war on the horizon. And this one won't be like the last—but it may well be the last. The potential for worldwide destruction is enormous. Stalin has set his sights on completing his hydrogen bomb program before we do, and we think it's going to happen. And that's a mighty dangerous scenario."

Massey looked impatiently from Branigan to the assistant director. "Will someone kindly tell me just what all this is leading to?"

"Jake, the President believes Stalin's going to use that bomb just as soon as it's ready. Now we either sit and wait for the worst to happen or we come up with a solution to remove the problem—a solution that's much better for everyone in the circumstances. It calls for a pretty special operation. And I want you to head it."

Massey said, "And what solution is that?"

It was Branigan who answered. "We kill Stalin."

THE silence went on for several long moments. The assistant director looked at the bare winter trees, then back at Massey.

"You don't look happy, Jake. I thought you'd be impressed."

Massey pushed himself up from the chair. "Sir, what you're suggesting is impossible. It would be suicide for whoever goes in."

"And that's exactly why it would work. Moscow would never expect it," the assistant director said. "Naturally, it's a solution not without its risks. That's why the mission will be limited to a small number of personnel operating externally. The operation would be yours and yours alone."

"Why me?"

The assistant director smiled. "Easy. I can't think of anyone more qualified or experienced."

Massey crossed to the end of the patio. "It's a crazy idea. For one, Stalin's quarters in the Kremlin are impregnable. Walls twenty-four feet high and five feet thick. There're over five hundred guards stationed in the Kremlin Armory, all handpicked, all fanatically loyal. You both know that at Stalin's villa at Kuntsevo his personal security is impossible to breach. A twelve-foot-high fence. Guards with dogs stationed all around the perimeter. You come within a mile of the place without a special pass, and you're dead."

Branigan interrupted. "Jake, every suit of armor has its chink. It's a matter of finding the right chink. You know that."

Massey shook his head. "With Stalin there are no chinks."

The assistant director sat forward. "Jake, what if I told you we have a plan—ways to get close enough to Stalin to kill him."

"Then I'd like to hear it. Especially who you'd send to Moscow."

Branigan smiled. "We all know there's only one man capable of pulling this off. Alex Slanski. He can play a Russian to the hilt, and he'd have no hesitation in putting a bullet in Stalin's head."

Massey said, "You're right about Slanski. But sending him into Moscow alone would be suicide. He's an American—born in Russia, but he hasn't been in Moscow since he was a kid."

The assistant director smiled. "He'll need help. Someone to act as his wife on the journey, until he reaches Moscow, and help him get his bearings. There's a Russian woman named Anna Khorev. Border crosser. You met her in Helsinki. She knows Moscow."

Massey frowned, doubt clouding his face. "Why should she help you? She's already been to hell and back."

"So I read. I guess we'll have to give her a motive."

"What motive?"

The assistant director turned to Branigan. "Karl, why don't you go get us all a drink while I explain to Jake. I think we're going to need one after this."

IT WAS two hours later when Massey reached his house east of Georgetown. He called the boarding school in Richmond and made arrangements to see his son the next day. He was looking forward to seeing the boy. He knew he had been less of a father than he should, but he felt that somehow the boy understood.

Then he went into the bathroom and ran the cold-water tap and splashed the icy liquid on his face.

He seldom looked at himself in the mirror, but that evening he was aware that he looked older than his forty-one years. He had known and respected Max Simon for many years. They had grown up together, joined OSS together, been friends all their lives.

Jake had arrived with his widowed father from Russia in 1919, when he was only seven years old. They had settled in the area of Brooklyn called Brighton Beach.

Massey looked down as he rolled up his sleeve. There was a small tattoo of a white dove on his wrist. Two urchin kids up in Coney Island for a day's fun and chasing girls, and Max had wanted the tattoos to cement their friendship. He had been a gentle soul, Max, who lost his father to the Reds and had made it to America on a tough winter crossing, like Massey and his father. He had only wanted to do his best for his adopted country, and the little girl had been the only family he had. Massey felt the anger rise inside him again. He toweled his face dry and went into his study.

He took a pad and pen and went over the plan again, looking for flaws. Even though Anna Khorev's background was ideal for the mission, he wondered if she would be up to it, barely three months after her escape. He also knew he was sending her to certain death if the mission failed. And something worried him about sending her in with Slanski. He could be quite merciless.

Alex Slanski was Russian-born, a naturalized American citizen, age thirty-five. He and Massey had worked together during the war, when Slanski was one of a group of highly trained assassins OSS dropped into occupied France and Yugoslavia to help the resistance operating against the Germans. Slanski had worked under the code name Wolf and was one of Massey's top agents.

As a boy, Alex Slanski had escaped from a state orphanage in Moscow. He managed to get aboard a train for Leningrad and eventually stowed away on a frigate bound for Boston. When the American authorities were landed with him, they didn't know what to do with the obviously disturbed twelve-year-old. He was withdrawn and rebellious and behaved like a wildcat. He told them virtually nothing about his past, despite the best efforts of the psychologists.

Eventually someone had the idea to send him to stay with a Russian-speaking émigré living in New Hampshire—a trapper and hunter—who agreed to take the boy for a time. The forests up near the Canadian border had once teemed with Russian immigrants. It was remote, wild territory.

Somehow the boy settled in, and the authorities gladly washed their hands of the matter. There he remained until he joined OSS in 1941.

No one ever learned what had happened to his family, but everyone who worked with Slanski in OSS guessed it was something pretty bad. One look into his cold blue eyes told you that.

He spoke fluent German and Russian and could kill ruthlessly and in cold blood. Branigan and Wallace had been right; there was no one Massey could think of more suitable to carry out the mission.

Massey slid his pad into a manila folder. He had a seven a.m. start, and it was a long drive to Kingdom Lake, New Hampshire.

He went down to the basement. Two loose red bricks were above the cellar door—a safe hiding place he used whenever he was working at home rather than leave any notes or files lying around or in locked drawers or a safe that could be broken into. He placed the manila folder and the pad inside the recess and replaced the bricks.

It was just after five p.m. on Thursday, January 22, 1953, two days after Dwight D. Eisenhower became President of the United States.

New Hampshire, January 23. The New England towns with their brightly painted clapboard houses looked pretty in the light dusting of snow. There was hardly any traffic on the road and by late afternoon Jake Massey was driving down a thickly forested track that led to a two-story cabin at Kingdom Lake. He saw the snowcapped mountains in the distance, and a sign at the track entrance proclaimed TRESPASSERS KEEP OUT!

Massey switched off the engine and climbed out of his Buick, taking his briefcase with him. There was a narrow wooden veranda at the front of the cabin, and he went up the steps. The front door was unlocked, and the room he stepped into was empty.

It looked neat but could have done with a woman's touch. It was barely furnished, with a scratched pinewood table and two chairs set in the center and several pairs of deer antlers on the walls. A rifle storage rack stood in a corner, two weapons missing from it.

Massey guessed Slanski and the old man had probably gone hunting. He decided to walk down to the lake.

The water was choppy, and rain clouds were gathering overhead. A razor-sharp icy wind suddenly whipped across the lake. Massey said aloud, "Good Lord, that's cold—"

He heard the barely audible click of a weapon behind him.

"You'll be a damned sight colder if you don't take those hands out of your pockets. Keep them in the air and turn around slowly."

Massey turned and saw the man. There was a thin, crazy smile on his unshaven face, and he looked thoroughly dangerous and unpredictable. He was of medium height and blond. He wore a heavily padded windbreaker, and his corduroy trousers were tucked into knee-length Russian boots. He held the butt of a Browning shotgun lightly against his waist, the barrel pointed at Massey.

His face creased in a grin. "Jake Massey. For a second I thought you were a trespasser. You almost got yourself peppered."

"I guess I got here earlier than expected, Alex." Massey smiled.

The man lowered the shotgun as he stepped forward and shook Massey's hand. "Good to see you, Jake. No problem finding us?"

"No. I saw the sign at the entrance road."

Suddenly it started to rain, a heavy, drenching downpour.

Slanski smiled. "How about we go up to the house? I've got a bottle of bourbon that'll warm that old Russian heart of yours."

THEY sat at the pinewood table, and Slanski opened the bottle and poured bourbon into two shot glasses.

He raised his glass. *"Na zdorovye."*

"Za tvoyo zdorovye." Massey sipped his drink. "Where's Vassily?"

"He's in the woods someplace. Don't worry about him."

Massey swallowed the bourbon and pushed forward the glass. As Slanski refilled it, Massey said, "What did Branigan tell you?"

"Enough to get me interested. But seeing as you're running the show, I want to hear it from the horse's mouth."

Massey undid the security lock on his briefcase, removed the file marked FOR THE PRESIDENT'S EYES ONLY, and handed it across.

"Inside you'll see two reports. One is the result of highly secret intelligence work carried out for the CIA by the Moscow contacts of some of the anti-Stalinist émigré groups. It gives details of the old czarist escape tunnels in the Kremlin that date back hundreds of years. One tunnel in particular is interesting. It's a secret underground train line that runs from the Kremlin to Stalin's dacha at Kuntsevo, just outside Moscow. We discovered it can be easily breached two blocks from the Kremlin. The tunnel is checked at weekly intervals but not normally guarded except at the entrance and exit."

Massey outlined more details of the operation, and when he had finished, Slanski looked through the file and said, "I'm impressed, Jake. But why the sudden need to kill Stalin?"

"Look at the file again. There's a second report at the back. It ought to explain."

Slanski took the file and read. When he finished, he looked up and smiled. "Interesting. But I don't need a report to tell me Stalin is crazy. He should have been put in a rubber room long ago."

"Maybe, but this time we're in deep enough trouble to have to put the man down for the dangerous beast that he is. Do you remember Max Simon?"

"Sure. He's a friend of yours, as I recall."

Massey explained about the deaths of Max and his daughter and why they'd been killed. A look of distaste crossed Slanski's face.

"Okay, let's assume I do the job. The KGB is going to be swarming all over Moscow afterward. There are five hundred Kremlin guards behind those red walls. That's a lot of angry comrades."

"You leave the Kremlin or the dacha the same way you enter. After that you lie low in a safe house I'll set up in Moscow. A week later, if things work out the way I intend, I take you out."

"How?"

Massey smiled. "I'm working on it. But either way you don't go in without the safe house and exit being in place."

"Branigan said there's going to be a woman?"

"She'll be with you as far as Moscow; then we take her out."

Slanski shook his head. "You know I always operate alone, Jake. Taking a woman along will only slow things up."

"It's for your own good. Traveling alone to Moscow might make you a target for suspicion. She'll accompany you, acting as your wife, but for obvious security reasons she won't know the target."

"You'd better tell me about her," Slanski said.

Massey spread his hands on the table. "Her name's Anna Khorev. Age twenty-six. She escaped from a Soviet gulag near the Finnish border three months ago, and we gave her asylum."

"Jake, you must be crazy picking someone with that background."

"She wasn't my choice. And if I had my way, I'd leave her out of it. But she's the best we're going to get at short notice."

"Can she handle herself?"

"She can use a gun if that's what you mean. But all she's really got to do is play the part of being your wife and make your cover seem plausible until you reach Moscow. We can use Popov for a week or so to put you both through your paces."

Dimitri Popov was a CIA weapons and self-defense instructor, one of the best. As an émigré Ukrainian, he hated the Russians, having fought against them with a Ukrainian SS regiment during the war.

Slanski frowned. "Why has she agreed to go back into Russia?"

"She hasn't agreed to anything yet, because I haven't told her. But her reasons will be personal and nothing to do with you."

"This isn't going to be a walk in the woods, Jake. You think it's fair that she doesn't know how deep and dangerous she's getting in?"

"Maybe it's best. If she knew, she probably wouldn't go."

Slanski thought a moment. "Where had you in mind for training?"

Massey nodded over toward the window. "Maybe here. The terrain is similar to what you'll be crossing. If that's okay with you."

"I guess Vassily won't object. He'll keep out of the way."

"Any more questions?"

"Just tell me the odds on the plan working."

Massey shook his head. "I can't answer that. Nobody can. At best you succeed; at worst you die."

He saw a sudden look of doubt on Slanski's face and said, "You're still in?"

Slanski was silent for several moments. He said, "On one condition. I have the final say on whether the woman's in. You let me meet her as soon as she's made up her mind."

"Let's cross that bridge when we come to it." Massey picked up the file. "We've got a code name for the operation—Snow Wolf. But I keep the file, I'm afraid. No one but you, me, and the folks at the top get to see it. We'll go through the details again later so there won't be any mistakes, but the file stays with me."

He replaced it in his briefcase, then removed another. "In the meantime, you'd better read this. It gives you everything we know about Joseph Stalin—his background, his personality, his weaknesses, his strengths, his present security arrangements. Destroy it when you've memorized everything you need to."

Slanski half smiled. "Then all things being equal, I guess there's really only one more question. When do I go in?"

"A month from now."

New York, January 26. The apartment was on the top floor, and she came to the door as soon as Massey knocked.

"Hello, Anna."

She hesitated, then a smile lit up her face. "Massey!"

"You look surprised."

"I thought I'd never see you again."

She took him by the hand, led him inside, and closed the door. The apartment was a studio, with a single bed, a table, and two rickety chairs. She had done her best to make the place pretty. There were no family photographs on the walls, and it made Massey feel sad, knowing how lonely she must feel.

He handed her a brown-wrapped parcel. "For you."

She smiled and opened the brown paper. The surprise lit up her face. It was a box of Kuntz's chocolates.

Massey said in Russian, "My way of saying hello again. One Russian to another. How have you been, Anna?"

"Good. And even better now I've seen you again. Thank you for the present, Jake."

"It's nothing." He looked at her figure. "Don't get angry when I say this, but you've put on weight since Helsinki, and it suits you."

She laughed. "I'll take it as a compliment."

"It's good to see you smile, Anna. I guess last time we met, you didn't have much to smile about. I hear you have a job?"

"In a garment factory owned by a Polish American. It's a crazy place, but I like it," she said. "I'm glad you came to see me, Jake."

"Actually, it's unofficial business, not pleasure. But it's good to see you too." For several moments Massey didn't say anything. When he finally spoke, his voice was quiet and serious. "Anna, will you do something for me? Will you just listen to what I have to say? Then we can talk some more. But for now, just listen."

Anna hesitated, then nodded.

Massey ran a hand through his hair. "First, I want you to understand that what I have to tell you is strictly confidential. If you speak about it to anyone, your right to remain in this country will be revoked." He saw the look of fear on her face and said, "I'm sorry for being so blunt, Anna, but you'll understand why when I've finished. I want to put a proposition to you. If you say no, then I walk away from here and you never see me again. If you say yes, then we talk some more. Is that clear?"

She nodded slowly. "I understand."

"Good." He took his time before he began. "Anna, the people I work for need a woman to be part of a mission. A very sensitive mission. They plan to send a man—an American—into Russia. Moscow to be precise. They need a woman to accompany him. This woman would act as the man's wife. It would be dangerous, and there's no guarantee she'd come back."

"I don't understand. What has this got to do with me?"

"The people I spoke about want you to be that woman."

Massey studied her face. She looked totally confused.

"I don't understand. You're asking me to go to Moscow?"

"I know it sounds crazy. What you escaped from doesn't bear thinking about. To ask you to go back again is like asking you to return to hell. But not for nothing, Anna. There's something these people can do for you in return."

She looked at Massey, dumbstruck; then she said, "What?"

"Get you your daughter back."

It was as if a painful, terrible wound had opened. Her face

drained of color, and she stared at him. "You can really do that? You can bring Sasha to America?"

"I believe it can be done, Anna. You'll just have to trust me. Do you want a little time to think about what I've said? If you like, I can take a walk and come back in an hour."

"No. I want to hear what you have to say."

She listened intently. When Massey finished, she asked, "How long would I be in Russia?"

"At the outside, ten days. We'll do our best to keep it brief."

"What is this man going to do in Moscow?"

"Kill someone."

Massey said the words so matter-of-factly he thought she would be shocked, but she didn't react, her face blank. "Who?"

"That's not something you need to know." He paused. "Anna, I'll be honest with you. It's a very difficult and dangerous operation. And like I said, you may not come back. But that's a risk you're going to have to take to get your daughter back."

She hesitated a moment. "How will you find her?"

He shook his head. "I can't tell you right now. But if you go along with what I've proposed, you'll have my word the deal will be kept. I'll arrange new identities for you and Sasha and whatever you'll need materially to start a new life together afresh."

He stood up slowly. "Maybe things are moving a little too fast for you right now and you need to be alone to think this through." He wrote down a phone number on a slip of paper. "I'm staying at the Carlton. There's someone at the hotel I want you to meet. He'll have the final decision whether you go to Moscow or not. But call me tonight one way or the other."

As Massey left the note on the table, Anna shook her head. "That's not necessary. I've already thought about it. The answer is yes."

SLANSKI sat in the room on the eighth floor of the hotel off Lexington Avenue sipping a Scotch. He heard footsteps outside; then the door opened, and he saw Massey standing in the doorway. Beside him was a very beautiful woman, with high Slavic cheekbones and dark hair, wearing a simple, inexpensive black dress.

Her face held him. Something in those dark Slavic eyes suggested a curious mixture of strength and remorse.

Massey said, "Alex, meet Anna Khorev."

Anna saw his eyes take her in. It seemed as if he was trying to make up his mind about something.

Then Slanski glanced at Massey, and as he looked back at Anna, he smiled broadly and said, "I guess it's welcome to the club."

THE two men sitting in the black Packard across the street from the hotel had followed the yellow cab to Manhattan's East Side. As Massey and Anna had climbed out, the man in the passenger seat had rolled down the window and steadied the Leica.

The man got two shots of the couple as they got out of the cab, another three as they went up the steps into the hotel.

Chapter Four

January 27. The man who called himself Kurt Braun was sitting in a dingy bar on Manhattan's Lower East Side docks.

The private club Carlo Lombardi ran as a sideline was doing good business. It was only eight, but the place was buzzing already.

He looked at a girl serving drinks. "Do me a favor and tell Vince that Kurt Braun is here."

"Sure." She walked away.

Five minutes later Vince, Lombardi's bodyguard, came to Braun's table. Broad and well built, he had a nose that looked as if it had been flattened into his face with a sledgehammer.

"Carlo is upstairs," Vince said. "He said to go right on up."

THE sign in scratched gold lettering on the door said LONG-SHOREMAN'S UNION, C. LOMBARDI—DISTRICT CHIEF.

Carlo Lombardi was a small, fat Sicilian in his middle forties, with a thin mustache. As his title suggested, he ran the Manhattan Lower East Side dockland as if it were his private territory.

He heard the knock as Vince opened the door to admit Braun.

"Mr. Braun to see you, Mr. Lombardi."

"Leave us, Vince."

The door closed, and when Lombardi had shaken the man's hand, he said gruffly, "You want the story on the broad?"

"That's why I'm here."

Lombardi sighed and reached toward a drawer and pulled out a large brown envelope. He handed it across. "It's all written up the way you wanted it. Nothing new, except the girl had a visitor."

"Who?"

"A guy. Stayed one night at the Carlton. Name of Massey. Took the girl there too. She left after a couple of hours." Lombardi nodded to the envelope. "It's all in there. Including the pics."

Braun opened the envelope and examined the contents briefly, looking at the photographs, then closed it again and put his hand in his inside pocket, took out another envelope, and handed it across.

"For you."

"Amigo, I thank you from the bottom of my black heart."

IT WAS almost ten when Braun arrived back at his one-bedroom apartment in Brooklyn. He let himself in, leaving the lights off as he closed the door. He saw a man sitting in the shadows by the window. He wore an overcoat and hat and smoked a cigarette.

The man said, "Working late, Kurt?"

Braun let his breath out and said, "I wish you wouldn't do that, Arkashin."

The man named Arkashin laughed and stood up. He was short and stocky. His fleshy cheeks were limp and sagging, small eyes hard in a weathered face. At forty-eight he was an attaché with the Soviet mission to the United Nations in New York. In reality, he held the rank of major in the KGB.

"You have the report on the woman?" Arkashin asked.

Braun told him, and Arkashin raised his eyebrows. "Interesting. You trust Lombardi?"

"I'd sooner trust the devil himself. Moscow may secretly contribute to his union, but he has his fat fingers in a lot of pies, most of them illegal. And that's dangerous."

Arkashin shrugged. "We have no choice but to use him. If the Americans discovered us mounting our own surveillance operation, there would be hell to pay. Besides, Lombardi owes us. Without our help he'd still be a union steward."

"So who do you think this man Massey might be?"

Arkashin said, "Who knows? The photographs are not the best

quality—amateurish, really—but I'll have our people check and see if any of our station officers recognize him. In the meantime, you tell Lombardi you want the woman watched more closely. A twenty-four-hour operation. And tell him you may have a job for him soon that will pay well."

"What sort of job?"

Arkashin looked across and smiled. "You know Moscow doesn't like it when the Americans slight us, Kurt. We need to let them know they can't make fools of us."

"So what does Lombardi have to do?"

Arkashin said, "We're going to take the girl back to Moscow. We'll need Lombardi to kidnap her. You think he'll do it?"

"He'll do anything you tell him, for money. But taking her back to Moscow is going to be difficult."

"I agree. But Lombardi controls the docks. Getting her on board a Soviet vessel shouldn't be difficult."

New Hampshire, February 1. She saw the lake and the wooden house as they came around the bend on the narrow private road. There was snow on the mountains in the distance, and the forested scenery below looked remarkably wild and beautiful.

When Slanski halted the car, Massey opened the door for her and took her suitcase. Slanski took them inside and showed Anna to a small upstairs bedroom. "This is your room. When you've finished unpacking, I'll be downstairs."

His eyes lingered on her face a moment, and then he left. There was a single bed and a chair. Fresh towels were beside an enamel water jug and basin on a stand, and the window overlooked the lake. When she had unpacked, she went back downstairs and found Massey and Slanski sitting at the pinewood table drinking coffee.

Slanski said, "Sit down, Anna."

She sat, and Slanski poured her coffee. Then he looked at her. "There are some ground rules I want you to understand. You don't talk to anyone about the mission apart from us here. We'll be doing some preparation together for the journey, but in ten days a man called Popov arrives. He'll put us through some training in Soviet weapons and self-defense. On no account do you talk to Popov about our intentions or our plans. Is that understood?"

She glanced briefly at Massey. He was staring at her. "Anna, while you're here, Alex is in charge. You do as he says."

She looked back at Slanski. "Very well. I agree."

"Good. Another rule. You work hard and do your utmost to absorb everything you're going to learn. I want to be sure of who I'm going in with. I want to be sure I can depend on you."

"You can."

Slanski stood up slowly. "Okay. Concerning the mission itself, when the time comes, we'll be going into Russia through one of the Baltic States, landing by parachute. Tallinn, Estonia, to be precise. At all times during the mission we behave as man and wife. We'll make our way to Moscow via Leningrad, using regular transport— trains and buses. We'll have a predetermined route and enough contacts to help us as we need. Once we reach Moscow, you'll be passed on to another contact to be taken back to America."

Anna said, "I've never parachuted before."

Slanski said, "Don't worry; we'll sort it out." He checked his watch before saying to Massey, "I've got to pick up some supplies in town. You want to show Anna around? Vassily should be back soon. He's taken the boat out on the lake to do some fishing."

Massey nodded. Slanski crossed to the door and went out. Anna heard his jeep start up moments later and drive off.

Massey looked at Anna's face. "What's wrong?"

"Something I saw in his eyes. Either he doesn't like me or he doesn't trust me."

"Alex is always blunt when it comes to tactical business. He's also a difficult man to get to know. But don't worry; you'll be fine."

"I'm not worried, Jake."

"Good." Massey smiled. "Come on, let's see if we can find Vassily. I think you're going to like him."

As they reached the lake minutes later, a small boat was coming in to the shore. An old man sat in the bow, and when he saw Massey, he waved. He wore a deerskin jacket and an old woolen deer-stalker cap. As he climbed out of the boat and tied up, he studied Anna's face briefly before he shook Massey's hand.

He spoke in heavily accented English. "Massey. Welcome."

"Vassily, I'd like you to meet Anna. Anna, this is Vassily."

Anna offered her hand. There was something warm about the old man's face, a kindness in his eyes that she found endearing. When he shook her hand, she said instinctively, "*Zdravstvuite.*"

He smiled and replied in Russian. "Welcome, Anna. Welcome to my house. Alexei never said you were Russian."

"From Moscow. And you?"

"Kuzomen."

Now she recognized the old man's features, the dark Laplander looks of those who inhabited Russia's northern tundra. "You're a long way from home."

A big smile creased the man's brown face. "A very long way and too far to go back. But this place is just like home." He looked at Massey. "Did Alexei offer our guest bread and salt?"

It was an old Russian tradition with visitors, and Massey smiled and said, "Just coffee, I'm afraid."

The old man removed his hat and shook his head. "Typical. Like all the young, he forgets tradition. Come, let me do the honors, Anna. Give me your arm."

Vassily held out his arm to her, and Anna slipped her hand through his. She winked at Massey as he stood there amused, and let the old man lead them up to the house.

MASSEY was standing at the window smoking a cigarette twenty minutes later when he saw the jeep pull up outside.

Slanski climbed out and carried two cardboard boxes of supplies up to the house. Massey opened the door for him.

"Where's the girl?" Slanski asked.

"Vassily's giving her a tour of the place. He's taken quite a shine to her."

"It's just been a long time since he's smelled perfume. But suddenly I'm not so sure about her, Jake."

"You've got doubts already?"

"I don't think she fully realizes what she's getting herself into here," Slanski said. "Once she's with me, I think she'll be okay. But if we part company, I'm not sure she'll make it on her own."

"You ought to give her more credit, Alex. She's spent almost a year in the gulag. Anyone who can survive that and do what she did to escape isn't going to give in easily. And she'll be fine once Popov puts her through her paces."

"Maybe," Slanski said. "So what do you want me to do with the girl in the meantime?"

"Start to get her and yourself into shape. Daily runs and exercises. Another thing. Seeing as you'll both be parachuting in and Anna hasn't dropped before, you'll have to cover the basics."

"What will you be doing while we're sweating it out here?"

"Me?" Massey smiled. "I'll be in Paris, enjoying myself."

WHEN the Red Army rolled over the plains of Poland on its way to crush Berlin and the German Reich, Henri Lebel had been liberated from the Auschwitz concentration camp. There had been two long months spent in a Russian field hospital to build up his strength before he was allowed to return to his native Paris.

Lebel had survived the war, but it was a war that had cost him his wife—gassed, then burned in the ovens of Auschwitz not only because she was Jewish but because Lebel had been a member of the French communist resistance.

For the last eight years he had resumed the furrier trade his father, an émigré Russian Jew, had begun in Paris. Henri Lebel had gradually built it up into a flourishing business. There were frequent trips to Moscow, where his resistance connections had gone down well with the Soviet authorities, and as a result, Lebel was soon outfitting the Parisian rich with the best of Russian sable and fur, turning himself into a wealthy man, with a suite at the Ritz Hotel.

Life, it seemed, despite its horrors, had turned out reasonably well for Henri Lebel. But unknown to his business contacts in Moscow, he had a dark secret he kept hidden from them.

HE HAD first met Irena Dezov while he was at Auschwitz.

She was a young Red Army driver in her late twenties who had been captured and sent there along with a ragged convoy of Russian prisoners. Lebel had hardly exchanged a word with her until the day he found out that his wife had been gassed.

He went to his filthy bunk and lay there, curled up in a ball, weeping. The grief and anguish flooding his body were unbearable.

It was Irena who came to see Lebel and comforted him. She suggested they say *Kaddish* over his wife.

And so in the midst of all the pain and death around him, Lebel had knelt with the young Russian woman and said the ancient prayer for the dead. Afterward he had cried again, and Irena had hugged him. Then she offered him her body.

Not for sex but for solace. Despite the filthy barrack surroundings, there was a beauty and a touching kindness to the lovemaking that somehow reaffirmed Lebel's belief in humanity.

After that day Henri Lebel and Irena Dezov became friends as well as lovers. They endured the humiliations of camp life, laughed together when they could, and shared what scraps of food they managed to scavenge to supplement their meager rations.

The last time Lebel saw Irena there was three days after the Russians finally liberated the camp. She was being helped onto the back of a truck to take her behind Russian lines, her frail legs barely able to stand. They kissed, embraced, and promised they would write.

In the five years after the war Lebel tried to forget his past, but somehow Irena Dezov never left his mind.

A year later he had to visit Moscow on business. As he came out of the Moscow Hotel, he saw a woman across the street, and he froze, rooted to the spot with shock. She looked like Irena. She climbed on board a tram, and in panic, Lebel did something he had never done before. He evaded his KGB chaperon and followed the woman to an apartment off Lenin Prospect.

When she saw him, she went white, and when the shock subsided, her eyes were wet as she led him inside the two-room apartment.

For a long time they embraced and kissed and cried. There were two things Lebel learned that day: One, that he still loved Irena Dezov, and two, that she was married—or rather had been when they had their affair in the camp. The husband, a much older, stern-faced army colonel, had later died in the final battle for Berlin.

But Irena wasn't sad about it. She confessed that the day she learned of his death, she opened a bottle of vodka and got quietly drunk with joy. The man was a brute, and the only good he had done was leave her a pension and a dacha on the outskirts of Moscow.

They made love that day with an intensity Lebel had never known, and every time afterward that they could get to Irena's dacha.

But Lebel knew Irena would never be allowed out of Russia. Nobody was allowed out of Stalin's Russia. Dissidents were shot, committed to asylums, or imprisoned for life, not given exit visas. Each time he and Irena met at the dacha—four, six times a year, more if possible—he had to take care he wasn't followed.

It wasn't perfect, and it wasn't safe, and every time he saw her, he feared their relationship would be exposed and, worse, stopped.

Paris, February 3. The penthouse suite Henri Lebel lived in was on the fifth floor of the Ritz and had one of the most pleasant views in Paris, overlooking the magnificent cobbled Place Vendôme.

Lebel's offices and warehouses were in the suburb of Clichy, but he seldom used them to conduct business. His suite in the Ritz was far more private.

As he stepped into the study that afternoon, he saw Massey standing by the window. Lebel smiled. "Jake, good to see you."

"Hello, Henri. I hope I didn't disrupt your afternoon."

Lebel took a cigar from a humidor on the lacquered table, lit it, and blew out a cloud of smoke. "So what brings you to Paris, Jake?"

Massey looked at the chubby Frenchman. His pencil-thin mustache was neatly clipped, and the gold Rolex watch and diamond cuff links gave him an air of affluence.

"Just a brief visit to have a chat, Henri. How is business?"

"One can't complain. In fact, it's very good. Since the war ended, your rich Americans have no shortage of cash. They like the best, and they particularly like my sables and ermine. I grossed five million francs from America alone last year."

Massey's eyebrows rose. "That's good, Henri. You still see any of the boys from the resistance?"

"Once a year we meet and crack open a couple of bottles. You should come next time. They still remember you fondly. Killing Germans was the highlight of their lives. Now they raise chickens or kids and live boring lives. How could life ever be the same?"

"You're not doing too badly." Massey looked around the elegant room. "Being in the resistance has been good to you, Henri."

Lebel shrugged. "It had its price, but of course I don't deny it. It helped with my Moscow business contacts after the war."

"That's partly why I'm here. I need a favor, Henri."

Lebel smiled. "Is it something highly dangerous or simply illegal?"

"Both. Right now you're the biggest Russian-fur dealer in Europe.

You're one of the few people allowed to visit Moscow almost at will. I guess that makes you kind of special."

Lebel nodded. "That's true. But Jake, get to the point."

Massey said, "I need you to take three people out of Moscow for me on one of your private goods trains."

Lebel's mouth opened. "You want *me* to smuggle people out of Russia?" He laughed, a derisory snort. "Have you lost your mind?"

"I'm not asking you to do it for nothing. It would be a business arrangement, pure and simple. You'll be well rewarded."

"Correction, *mon ami*. It would be suicide, pure and simple. God himself couldn't persuade me to take such a risk."

Massey stood. "Hear me out, Henri. How many trainloads of furs do you take out of Russia each year?"

"Four, maybe six in a good year. It depends on demand."

"Do the Russians check you both sides of the border—going in and coming out?"

Lebel smiled. "The border guards check all the wagons with sniffer dogs, Jake. Believe me, nothing goes in or out of that country without Moscow knowing about it."

"You mean *almost* nothing." Massey took an envelope from his jacket and handed it to Lebel. Lebel opened the envelope. Inside was a single page. He read the page and his face dropped.

"What's the meaning of this?" he demanded angrily.

"As you can see, it's a report on the last three consignments you exported from Russia. You've been a naughty boy, Henri. You had a hundred and twenty more sable pelts than you claimed in the customs declaration, all hidden in a secret compartment under the train. The Finnish customs found the compartment when they had a discreet look at your train in Helsinki Station after it came back from Moscow two trips ago. Naturally, they reported it to us, just in case Moscow was up to something. But now I know they're not. It's your operation, isn't it? Who else knows about this, Henri?"

"The train driver," admitted Lebel. "In fact, the method was his idea. He saw it done during the war. Jake, you've no idea what the Finns charge me in import taxes."

"So naturally, when your friend found a way around it, you jumped in."

Lebel gestured with his cigar at the report in Massey's hand.

"Until you showed me that, I thought I'd done the clever thing, but now I know I was foolish. Okay, Jake, what's the story? You get the gendarmes to slap the bracelets on me and haul me away?"

"The American embassy in Helsinki advised the Finns to hold their fire for the moment." Massey smiled briefly. "But I've a feeling things might get pretty difficult for your company if the Finns prosecute."

"Don't tell me, but you can save me from all that?"

Massey smiled. "If you were willing to cooperate."

Lebel sat back with a sigh. "I was waiting for that."

"First tell me how you got around the Soviets. Who else is in on this?"

"Certain greedy associates I deal with in Russia—bureaucrats and railway officials. They make sure the Russian guards turn a blind eye when the train passes through the border checkpoint."

"Did you ever take out *people* for Moscow?"

Lebel shook his head fiercely. "To take people would be impossible, believe me, and the train driver would never agree. Furs are one thing, people quite another. He'd be shot if he was caught."

"What if the plan was foolproof?"

"No plan is foolproof, especially where Russians are concerned."

"Foolproof. Worth half a million Swiss francs. And there's a cherry on the cake."

Lebel frowned with curiosity. "What's the cherry?"

"The Finns throw away their file on you so long as you promise not to be a bad boy again."

For a long time Lebel was silent; then he spoke. "What if I said I would help you, but not for money?"

"It depends on what you have in mind instead."

"An extra passenger."

Massey's eyes widened. "You'd better explain."

Lebel told him about Irena.

Massey said, "She's Jewish?"

Lebel nodded. "Another reason why I'd feel safer if she got out of Moscow. Many times I've thought of trying to get Irena out, but the risks are too great. If the Finnish authorities found her on board the train, they might send her back to Russia and me to prison. But you could make sure that wouldn't happen, couldn't you, Jake?"

"You're a dark horse, Henri. This dacha Irena owns outside Moscow. Is it safe?"

"Of course. That's why we use it. Why?"

"I'll explain later. I think we can do a deal."

New Hampshire, February 11. Anna was standing at the window when she saw the old black Ford pull up outside the house.

The man who climbed out was big and powerfully built. His beard and greasy black hair gave him the appearance of a wild-looking mountain man. When he and Slanski came up on the veranda and stepped inside the cabin, the big man saw her and grinned.

"So this is the woman," he said to Slanski.

Slanski said, "Popov, this is Anna."

The man held out a huge bearlike paw. Anna didn't offer to shake it but said to Slanski, "When you want me, I'll be outside." She walked past the Ukrainian and down the steps of the veranda.

Popov watched her retreating figure appreciatively as she walked toward the woods. "Did I say something wrong?"

"I don't think former Ukrainian SS are her favorite types."

Popov grunted. "Massey said she was Russian. Russians and Ukrainians have always fought like cats and dogs." A brief smile flashed on his face. "Still, I'd call a truce as far as that one's concerned."

"Let's go down to the lake. I want to talk."

As they walked down to the water, Slanski said, "You think you can cover everything in ten days?"

"You, I know about. The girl, I don't. It depends on her."

New York, February 19. In the tenth-floor office of the Soviet mission in the United Nations building, Feliks Arkashin stood hunched over the half-dozen black-and-white photographs.

He turned to the man standing beside him and said, "You're certain about this, Yegeni?"

Yegeni Oramov was small and thin and wore thick black spectacles and had wild tufts of wiry black hair.

"Certain as we can be. I had the photos checked with our people here and in Europe. It looks like the man named Massey."

"Tell me about him."

"He runs the Munich CIA Soviet Operations office. Apparently he's been a thorn in our side for a long time. The question is, what do we do about it?"

Arkashin shook his head. "The question is, surely, what's he doing with the woman, Anna Khorev?"

Oramov smiled. "I had copies of these photographs sent to our station in Helsinki. We think Massey was present when our people interviewed her. Colonel Romulka's aide remembers him, and the description would seem to fit."

"What about the second man?"

"We're pretty certain it's a man named Alex Slanski."

Arkashin said, "*The* Alex Slanski? The one they call the Wolf?"

Oramov nodded. "The same. We've wanted him for a long time."

For several moments Arkashin stood deep in thought. Then he turned to his visitor. "You can go now, Yegeni. Well done."

The man left. Yegeni Oramov had supplied Arkashin with the confirmation he needed of Braun's report. He picked up the telephone and dialed his superior's office. The line clicked. "Leonid? Arkashin here. Can I come up? I'd like your opinion on something."

LEONID Kislov was a stout man in his late fifties. As senior KGB station officer in the New York mission, with the rank of colonel, he had a lot of worries. That morning he was in a foul mood, and as he gestured for Arkashin to sit, he said, "Make it quick, Feliks."

Arkashin explained about the photographs and the woman as he laid the shots on the table and Kislov examined them.

"We're as sure as can be that the two men in the shots are Massey and Slanski," Arkashin said.

Kislov leaned forward. "Interesting."

"That's what I thought. As you know, Colonel Romulka has taken a personal interest in the woman's case." Arkashin smiled faintly. "Apparently she made quite an impression when she met him in Helsinki. And the Wolf's been a scourge for quite some time."

"You'd better fill me in on what's been happening."

"We're using Lombardi to watch the woman, but Braun's acting as the link."

"Braun? That animal?"

"Even an animal has its uses."

"I'm aware of that. So what do you propose?"

"Something tells me Massey is up to something. And with this Slanski in the picture it might suggest Massey has an agent drop in mind. Maybe even using the girl. She knows our country."

Kislov shrugged. "Possible, but speculative. So why come to me?"

"We have three choices. One, take out the woman, as we intended. Two, take her out and kill Massey and Slanski in the process as a bonus. Or three, we keep tailing them and see what they're up to. If it's a drop Massey intends, we could find out where and when and get them when they land on Soviet soil."

Kislov sat back in his chair and thought for a moment. Finally he shook his head. "The second option is not the best way to go, and the third is risky. We may not be able to discover when or where they're going to drop, if that's what's happening. The first seems the best choice. Besides, it's what Moscow ordered." He frowned. "You never told me how you know where these people are."

Arkashin smiled. "Simple, really. Lombardi had a couple of his men follow Massey and the woman when they took a train to Boston. They were met there by this man—Slanski." Arkashin pointed to a grainy photograph taken at the Boston railway station of Massey shaking hands with Slanski, Anna Khorev beside them.

"The woman had a suitcase with her," Arkashin went on. "Lombardi's men followed the three of them out of the station but lost them after they drove off. They got the license number—a New Hampshire registration—and had it checked out. It's registered to an Alex Slanski in Kingdom Lake, New Hampshire."

Kislov nodded. "Anything else?"

Arkashin half smiled. "There's a Soviet cargo ship due into New York in five days. I'll need you to authorize a dollar payment for Lombardi if we're to go ahead with the woman's abduction."

"Can Lombardi be trusted with such a delicate matter as this?"

"He's as shifty as a sewer rat but a true capitalist who'll do anything for money. Besides, he's not averse to killing."

Kislov thought a moment. "Could Braun and Lombardi make the deaths of Massey and Slanski look like accidents?"

"It could be arranged, I'm certain."

Kislov grinned slightly. "Then perhaps your second option was best after all. There could be promotion in this for both of us."

Arkashin smiled back. "That's what I thought."

Chapter Five

New Hampshire. The days following Dimitri Popov's arrival had
been spent on self-defense and weapons training. Anna had begun
to feel fit. Every morning she and Slanski ran for five miles through
the woods. The excruciating exercises they did toned her body, and
Anna felt more alive than she had in a long time. Slanski covered
the rudiments of parachuting, and he and Popov rigged up a basic
training drop to teach her how to land properly. The entire regimen
gave her little time to be alone and think.

It was snowing on the last day of training, and when they finished
supper, Anna left the cabin and walked down to the lake.

She heard a voice behind her minutes later and turned. Slanski
stood there in the shadows, smoking a cigarette. He looked over at
her. "Are you okay?"

Anna nodded.

Slanski smiled. He flicked away his cigarette. "Tomorrow I'll take
you into Concord. There's a hotel. It's not much, but the cooking's
better than Vassily's. And there's a dance during dinner."

She looked at him, surprised. "Why should you take me there?"

"No reason, except maybe you deserve it after all your hard
work. And maybe it's time we started to act like man and wife.
Massey's going to be back tomorrow night to go over some final
things, so we haven't much more time to get to know one another."

She hesitated. "Why are you doing this, Alex? Going into Russia.
What's your motive?"

"Why do you want to know?"

"I think maybe you volunteered. And happy men don't volunteer."

Slanski looked up at the night sky, then back at her. "None of
your business, I'm afraid. Just as your motives are none of mine."

He turned without another word and walked back to the cabin.

AS HE sat in his bedroom, Slanski heard Anna come in ten minutes later and climb the stairs. He heard her wash and undress and
get into bed. The house went silent again.

He crossed to the corner of the bedroom. Hunching down near

the window, he took out his penknife, slipped the blade between two short wooden floorboards, and prized. The wood gave easily. He put his hand into the recess and removed an old rusting biscuit tin and, beneath it, the manila file Massey had given him to study.

The file contained no details of the mission—only information about Stalin's habits, his health, his personal security arrangements, and particulars of his elite bodyguard.

Before the drop, Slanski would commit the file's every word and detail to memory. When he finished studying it, he replaced it in the recess under the floor. He picked up the biscuit tin, opened it, and removed the contents—two locks of hair and a small photograph album, its black lacquered cover cracked and worn.

He remembered how he had clutched them after his escape, during the long, cold journey across the tossing Atlantic swells, hidden in the hold of the stinking boat, hunger in his stomach like a pain, but not as bad as the terrible pain in his heart. What was in that box was his only tangible reminder of his family.

He looked down at the locks of hair. He had loved them both, Petya and Katya, had always wanted to protect them. He remembered a night a storm came and little Petya had been so afraid. Lying in his bedroom in the darkness, Slanski heard him crying.

"Don't be afraid, Petya. Come, sleep beside me."

Petya had snuggled in beside him, a mass of dark curls and puppy fat, still sobbing as Slanski hugged him close.

"Don't cry, Petya. I'll always keep you safe. And if anyone or anything ever tries to hurt you, I'll kill them. You understand, Petya? And when Mama has her baby, I'll keep baby safe too."

He had held Petya close all night, warm and safe.

But he hadn't kept him safe afterward. Nor Katya.

SLANSKI parked the pickup in the town's main street. In the evening darkness he and Anna walked to the hotel. There was a dance band playing on a rostrum, and a waiter showed them to a table set with fresh flowers and a red candle.

When their meal came, Slanski said, "It's not exactly New York, but this is where the locals come for their night out."

"It's the first time I've been to a place like this in America. Is this where you come to find girlfriends?"

He smiled and shook his head. "Hardly. It's only my second time." He looked across and said, "Tell me about yourself, Anna."

"No," she said. "First you tell me about yourself. How did you come to live in America?"

He toyed with his glass, as if he seemed to be wondering how much to tell her. "My family lived in a village near Smolensk. When my parents died, my younger brother, sister, and myself were sent to an orphanage in Moscow. I was twelve. I hated the place. So I made up my mind for us to escape. A relative lived in Leningrad, and I thought he'd take us in. The night we planned to escape, we were caught. But I managed to get away alone. When I reached Leningrad, the relative wasn't very pleased and wanted to hand me back. I wandered the streets until I found myself at the docks, looking at a ship. I didn't know where it was going, but I knew that ship was destiny waiting for me. So I stowed away on board. Two weeks later I was on the Boston waterfront, cold and very hungry."

"For a boy of twelve what you did was remarkable. And your brother and sister, what happened to them?"

He didn't reply, and as Anna looked at him, she realized it was the first time she had seen any real sign of emotion in his face. There was a flash of pain, but then he suppressed it.

"Now it's your turn," he said. "Were you ever married, Anna?"

She said, "Do we have to talk about it now?"

"Not if you don't want to." He looked at her, then stood and held out his hand. "Come on, let's dance," he said. "This is getting too serious."

He led her onto the floor, and they danced two sets. She was aware of Slanski holding her tight and of how comforting it felt. It had been a long time since she had danced with a man.

Later that night, when they walked back to the truck, Slanski draped his coat around her shoulders to keep out the cold. As they climbed into his pickup, neither of them noticed the blue Ford sedan parked across the street, the two men inside watching them.

MASSEY'S car was parked outside the house when they got back. He was sitting at the table drinking coffee with Vassily when they went in, and when Massey saw Anna, he smiled.

"It looks like you two have been enjoying yourselves."

211

Slanski said, "All part of the training, Jake. Where's Popov?"

"Gone to bed. He's starting early back to Boston tomorrow."

They sat and talked for ten minutes, and then Vassily went to bed. Anna said good night shortly thereafter. Massey waited until she had gone upstairs, then said, "So how's she shaping up?"

"Better than I thought." Slanski told Massey about the training, then asked, "How was Paris?"

Massey told him about his meeting with Lebel. "We'll use Lebel's girlfriend's dacha when you two get to Moscow."

"You think it's right getting Lebel's friend involved?"

"She won't be. If things go according to plan, as soon as both of you arrive in Moscow, she and Anna will leave on Lebel's train."

Massey went over the details, and then Slanski looked across at him. "You look like you've got something on your mind, Jake."

Massey stood. "Remember what I told you about Max Simon and his little girl? I think I've found out who did it. A man who uses the name Kurt Braun. One of Moscow's hired killers."

"So what are you going to do?"

Massey crossed to the window and looked back, a look of anger on his face. "Branigan wants me to forget about him."

"But you have other plans, right?"

"I checked with immigration. Braun arrived in New York, using a West German passport, three months ago. I've got his address in Brooklyn. I want to pay him a visit and settle the score."

"What about Branigan?"

"He needn't ever know if we do it properly."

"We?"

Massey said hopefully, "I was kind of expecting you'd come along for the ride. I'll need someone watching my back."

Slanski said, "When?"

"Tomorrow."

February 22. Dimitri Popov rose early and left at six to drive to Boston. Ten minutes later he saw a Packard with New York plates overtake him at speed. He saw the same Packard five minutes later parked off the road, the driver kicking the front wheel in anger.

The man waved him down, and Popov pulled over and rolled down the window. "What's the problem?"

"I hit a pothole in the snow." The man held up a wheel jack. "The tire's warped as a bent nickel, and my jack's broken. You got one I could borrow?"

Popov grunted and stepped out of the car. The little fat man looked useless, all blubber, with a New York accent. Popov found the jack in the trunk and said, "Here, let me."

"Hey, thanks, mister, you're an angel."

The tire looked undamaged. As Popov bent down to examine it, he felt a crushing blow on the back of his skull. He keeled over. Then he heard a rush of feet from out of nowhere and the fat man's voice saying, "Get the hick into the car."

Then something sharp jabbed into Popov's arm, and he went under.

New York. As Feliks Arkashin turned away from the bedroom window of Braun's apartment, he looked at Popov slumped in the chair. Lombardi's two men had delivered him, and the ropes around the big man were tied securely, but Arkashin knew there was no need. Barely conscious, the man was hardly capable of moving.

Arkashin stared down at Popov's bruised face; then his hand reached over and lifted the man's chin.

"You're really making this very difficult. Don't you think it would be a lot easier if you told me what Massey is up to at the lake?"

Popov grunted, and his eyes flickered; then his head rolled in Arkashin's hand and slumped to one side. Arkashin sighed. He and Braun had spent an hour trying to make the man talk, and he had barely uttered a word.

His wallet lay on the table. His name was Dimitri Popov, which told Arkashin nothing except that he was Russian or Ukrainian. There was a hypodermic syringe on the table and a vial of scopolamine, the truth drug—Arkashin's last resort. As he reached for them, he heard a knock on the door and turned, slightly alarmed.

He crossed to the living room and was reaching for the Walther pistol on the coffee table when he heard a voice.

"I really wouldn't, not unless you want to lose your fingers."

The man who stood behind him held a Tokarev pistol in his hand. The window that led to the fire escape was open, the curtain blowing in the breeze. Arkashin paled when he recognized Slanski.

"Just drop the gun on the table, then open the front door."

Arkashin did as he was told.

As Massey came in, Slanski said quietly, "Jake, I think you'd better take a look at who our friend's got in the bedroom."

MASSEY sat in the chair opposite Arkashin and said, "You'd better tell me what's going on here, and fast." He held up the gun and clicked back the hammer. "Five seconds, and I'm counting."

Arkashin smiled nervously. "I could very well ask the same. But I ought to tell you, I'm an accredited diplomat with the U.N. Soviet mission and, as such, immune from law."

Just then Slanski came back into the room, supporting a dazed-looking Popov. When the big Ukrainian saw Arkashin, his eyes blazed. "If you don't pull the trigger, Jake, I will."

Massey said to him, "Tell me what happened."

Popov wiped a trickle of blood from his mouth and pointed to Arkashin. "Our friend here's after the woman. They've been tailing her. After I left the cabin, some of his men fooled me into stopping my car and knocked me unconscious. Then they took me here and tried to get me to talk. His name's Arkashin."

Slanski tossed a handful of photographs on the table. "These were in the bedroom. It looks like Arkashin's got a keen interest in us."

Massey looked at the photographs. Some of them were of Anna alone; others were of him and Anna together at the Carlton, and still others with Slanski at the Boston railway station. There were also maps of New Hampshire, and he noticed that the lake was circled.

Massey looked at Arkashin. "Where's your friend Braun?"

Arkashin said gruffly, "I don't have to answer your questions."

Massey crossed to him and put the gun against his forehead and said, "I don't give a damn about your immunity, Arkashin. So talk before I lose my patience and this thing goes off."

Arkashin sighed and spread his hands in a gesture of helplessness. "You understand, we couldn't let the woman get away just like that. We've been following her since she arrived in this country."

Massey was silent; then he said, "Why? She's a nobody."

"Where people like you and me are concerned, ours is not to reason why, Massey. We simply do what our masters tell us."

Massey's face flushed angrily. "Where's Braun?"

Arkashin hesitated. "Gone to get the woman."

"What's he going to do with her?"

"Put her on a Soviet boat in New York harbor."

"How long has Braun been gone?"

Arkashin said, "He left for Boston two hours ago by train."

Slanski said to Popov, "Take him inside and tie him up. Good and tight. So he can't move or talk."

"With pleasure. And then I'm going to beat him to a pulp."

Arkashin turned noticeably pale. As Popov went toward him, Arkashin grabbed for the Walther on the table. When Popov reached to wrench it from him, he was too slow, and the gun went off, hitting the Ukrainian in the face. As Popov was flung back, Slanski fired once, hitting Arkashin in the heart.

Massey turned white. He felt Popov's pulse. "He's dead."

Slanski came back from Arkashin's body, which was sprawled on the floor. "This one too. Jake, this is getting muddier by the minute. What now?"

"We get out of here fast. I'll figure out what to do later."

Slanski said softly, "We'll never get to the lake in time. It's six hours away by car, and Arkashin's people have a head start."

"Then let's get going."

As Massey moved toward the fire escape, Slanski gripped his arm and said, "Wait!" He crossed to the table and picked up one of the maps. "There may be a quicker way. But it's just a chance."

New Hampshire. Carlo Lombardi hated the countryside. He was used to the smell of gas fumes and smog—chirping birds and trees weren't really his thing. He wrinkled his nose as Vince rolled down the Packard's window.

"Put that thing up. What you trying to do? Kill me?"

Vince did as he was told, as Braun sat silently in the back. They had come off the highway ten minutes ago, Lombardi doing the driving after picking up Braun from the Boston station.

When Lombardi saw the sign on the road—TRESPASSERS KEEP OUT!—he turned the Packard onto the snowed-under dirt track.

Fifty yards farther along, they saw the lake in the distance. Lombardi pulled over, and Vince and Braun were already climbing out as he switched off the engine. Braun nodded down toward the cabin and looked at Lombardi. "That's it?"

"That's it. Uncle Tom's cabin. Ready when you are."

Braun said, "I'll take the back way; you two take the front."

VASSILY saw the two men come up the track as he stood at the kitchen window of the cabin. They were fifty yards away, and one carried a shotgun and the other an M-1 carbine. He picked up his Winchester rifle, stepped onto the veranda, and said to the men, "You're on private property. Turn around and go back the way you came."

The fatter of the two strangers, the one with the thin mustache, appeared to be in charge. He went to move closer. "Hey, take it easy," he said. "We got lost. Maybe you can help us."

Vassily raised the Winchester and said, "No closer, or I'll help you to the cemetery. I said you're on private property."

The fat man said boldly, "Put down the rifle, old man. All we want is a friendly talk with the woman. Where is she?"

Vassily turned pale and cocked the Winchester's hammer with his thumb. "You step any closer, fat man, and I kill you."

Lombardi cursed. The shotgun in his hands came up and exploded. The shot hit Vassily in the shoulder, and he was flung back against the wall. As he fell onto the veranda, the men were already moving toward him. When he grabbed for the Winchester, one of them kicked it away, and he saw the flash of a knife blade as the fat man knelt over him. "Too slow, old man. Where's the woman? Where is she, or I cut your heart out."

IN THE woods, looking for kindling for the stove, Anna heard the gunshot, and her heart skipped. As she turned, she saw a man off to her right. He held a shotgun in his hands, and at first she thought he was a hunter. Then he raised the weapon at her.

"Stay where you are."

Anna halted, confused, and the man came toward her.

"Nice and easy now. We're going back the way you came."

THE small harbor in the broad inlet sixty miles south of Boston known as Buzzards Bay was deserted. The man who walked to the waterside hangar with Massey and Slanski was tall and thin.

"What's the big rush to get up to the lake, Mr. Slanski?"

"An emergency."

Abe Barton looked out doubtfully at the sea. "Well, I ain't too keen about taking off in those waves and coming back in darkness, but I guess on account of it's an emergency, I can oblige."

It had taken Slanski and Massey almost three hours to drive north to the bay, and the tension on both their faces showed.

The hangar was at the far end of the seawall. There was a skid ramp for launching the flying boat into the water.

The flying boat worked out of the bay, taking hunting and fishing parties up to northern New England in season, and Abe Barton was the pilot, mechanic, and caretaker. He unlocked the padlock to the hangar and rolled back the doors to reveal a bulbous-nosed Seebee single-engine flying boat inside.

They winched the Seebee into the water. Then Barton climbed into the cockpit and started the engine. It throbbed into life.

Fifteen minutes out from Buzzards Bay the clear air became turbulent, and Barton had to increase altitude to five thousand feet to avoid the worst of it.

It was growing dark in the cockpit, and they could see the vast speckle of lights that was Boston off to the right. Barton turned and said above the engine noise, "Another ten minutes and we'll be over New Hampshire. I'll try to get as close to the cabin as I can, but I can't promise, mind."

Slanski said, "Forget the cabin. I want you to land a mile up the shore. And leave off the landing lights on the way in."

Barton looked puzzled. "I thought this was an emergency."

"It is."

"Well, I need those lights to see what the water's like," Barton protested. "If I hit whitecaps too hard, they can crack the prow."

Slanski put a hand on Barton's shoulder. "Just do as I ask, Abe."

BRAUN went through the cabin's upstairs rooms one by one while Lombardi and Vince stood watch over the woman and the old man, who was tied to a chair. Even though Braun believed the house was empty, he moved cautiously, the shotgun ready in his hands.

He found the woman's room first and searched through her clothes and a suitcase under the bed. There was nothing of interest.

The other rooms were bare and functional. The old man's had nothing much besides clothes and a couple of Russian books.

When he found Slanski's bedroom, he went through it with much more care. He searched through the clothes in the wardrobe. He turned over the mattress and looked underneath, but found nothing.

In frustration, Braun kicked over the bedside locker. He went to the window, and as he stood there, something made him look down. The locker had rattled the floorboards under the window, and one of them felt loose as he stepped on it. He knelt and prized it with his nail. He saw the biscuit tin in the recess and opened it. After examining the contents, he flung them away. Then he saw the file. There were four pages inside the folder, and he read them quickly.

For several moments he stood there; then he smiled to himself. Moscow would pay for what he had just found, no question. He folded the file and tucked it carefully down his trousers. When he had finished checking the other rooms, he went back downstairs.

It was growing dark outside, and Lombardi was lighting an oil lamp. He looked over at Braun. "What did you find?"

"Nothing," Braun lied.

Lombardi said, "So what next?"

"We leave and take the woman with us."

"I thought we were going to wait for the broad's friends?"

"There isn't time." Braun crossed to the table and picked up the oil lamp and said to Lombardi, "Untie the ropes on the old man."

"Why? What you got in mind?"

Braun removed the glass cowl on the oil lamp.

Lombardi frowned. "You going to set the place on fire?"

"As a lesson to our absent friends. The nearest town is five miles away. With this terrain no one will see the flames."

Lombardi frowned. "What about the old man?"

"He's seen our faces. Kill him."

THE Seebee had landed north of the cabin. A mile into the woods and Massey was out of breath.

He saw Slanski racing ahead of him in the dusk, running like a man possessed. Massey had trouble keeping up.

Five minutes later he saw Slanski slow and look back, pointing to tell him he was going on ahead, and Massey waved back. He saw Slanski give a burst of speed, and then he disappeared.

A hundred yards farther Massey had to slow down to catch his breath. Suddenly he heard the roar of an engine and then another sound—one gunshot, then another.

LOMBARDI undid the ropes around Vassily. Braun lit a cigarette from the naked flame of the oil lamp and said, "Move back."

Lombardi stepped back, and Braun tossed the lamp into a corner of the room. The fuel spread on the wooden floor and ignited.

As the flames started to lick the corner walls, Braun said to Lombardi, "I'll take the woman to the car. Finish the old man."

Braun led Anna outside. Moments later Lombardi handed Vince his shotgun and took out his pistol. As he went toward Vassily, he sensed a presence behind him. Lombardi looked around as an angry voice said, "Touch him and I kill you."

A blond man stood there in the kitchen door with a pistol.

Lombardi said, "What the hell?"

The pistol in Lombardi's hand came up, and Slanski shot him. He screamed, and as Lombardi was punched back out the door, the second man fired both barrels of his shotgun. The shots went wide and hit Vassily in the chest and flung him into the flames.

Slanski screamed, "No!" He fired, hitting the second man again and again, a terrible rage in him.

The flames rose and spread in the cabin, and smoke filled the room, choking the air. As Slanski tried to move toward Vassily's limp and bloodied body engulfed in flames, he already knew there was nothing he could do.

BRAUN was fifty yards from the cabin when he heard the shots and the scream. He looked back and saw the flames inside the cabin, but no sign of Vince or Lombardi. The woman tried to struggle free, but Braun dragged her on toward the car.

He had gone another twenty yards when he looked back and saw a blond man dragging a body out of the burning cabin. Then the man looked up, saw Braun, and broke into a run toward him. Braun fired off two quick shots in his direction, then pulled the woman against him as a shield and shouted, "Come any closer and I kill her!"

The man slowed but kept coming, and then Braun saw the gun in his hand. He flicked an anxious look back at the Packard. It was thirty yards away along the narrow track. Close enough to get to.

He moved backward smartly, still holding the woman in front of him. Braun pressed the gun hard into the woman's head and roared, "Another step and I kill her!"

Slanski halted thirty yards away, as Braun reached the car. He yanked open the driver's door and shoved Anna inside. He fumbled for the keys in the ignition. They were gone.

"Kurt Braun?"

Braun spun around in his seat. Another man sat behind him, in the back, rage in his eyes and a .38 in his hand.

"I asked, are you Kurt Braun?"

Before Braun could reply, Massey squeezed the trigger.

THE cabin was still in flames as Slanski held a storm lamp over the bodies laid out a distance away. There was a terrible look of grief on his face as he gazed at Vassily's corpse. It was the first time Massey had ever seen him so anguished.

"This is my fault. I'm sorry, Alex."

Slanski was white with anger. "It's no one's fault but the people who did it. Someone's going to pay for this, Jake. Someone's going to pay dearly, so help me . . ."

"Leave that to me, Alex. But right this minute, all bets are off. We're canceling the operation."

"You do that, and I go in alone. I mean it, Jake."

"We can't do it, Alex. Branigan would never go along, not when he hears what's happened to Arkashin. And what's happened here only makes it worse. It's a security risk."

"When they find Arkashin, no one will know who did it. And Arkashin couldn't have known what we intend. Besides, he's dead."

Massey shook his head. "Maybe, but Popov's body is in Braun's apartment. And Branigan will put two and two together."

Slanski looked over at Anna and said to Massey, "Either way it's going to take time before Branigan finds out. Anna can stay if you're worried. But me, I'm going in."

Anna looked at him and said quietly, "If you go, I go too."

Massey sighed and said, "Okay, Alex, we do it your way. We'll have to bury the bodies in the woods in case anyone comes by. I'll worry about Branigan later." Suddenly he seemed at a loss for words. "I'll help you bury Vassily."

Grief flooded Slanski's face again. He said, "Not in the woods with those vermin who killed him. Down by the lake."

Massey said quietly, "There's a shovel in the jeep. I'll get it."

As Massey moved toward the jeep, Slanski grabbed his arm and said in a hard voice, "Just tell me, when do we go in?"

"There's a flight to London from Boston tonight, with a connection on to Helsinki," Massey said. "We can make it if we hurry."

Chapter Six

New Hampshire, February 23. It was almost nine a.m. when a man named Collins drove up to Boston's airport from New York. Collins met a group off a Canadian Airlines flight from Ottawa—two women and a man, younger than himself—and by the time they had hired the camping trailer and equipment in Boston and applied for hunting permits in New Hampshire, it was almost noon.

Collins was in his early forties, and his eyes had the steely, detached look of someone who has seen death and even dispensed it. The younger man wore glasses, and his dark hair was cropped short.

The two women were in their late twenties, both pretty and vivacious, but Collins—otherwise known as Major Grigori Galushko, KGB, First Directorate—knew they would be as capable as he was with any kind of weapon, even their hands. For the purpose of the mission they were friends who had met on a camping holiday the previous summer at Lake Ontario, renewing their acquaintance.

They turned onto the road that led down to Kingdom Lake just after one that afternoon. They parked the trailer a mile from the cabin. After changing into their hunting clothes, they started to stroll toward the cabin. They joked and laughed as they walked, acting like friends out for a winter shooting holiday, but their eyes were everywhere, watching any movement, hearing every sound.

A hundred yards from the lakeside cabin they stopped for a cigarette. Galushko's eyes flicked nervously about the landscape. He saw the boat tied up at the promontory and the burned-out cabin, smoke still curling from its embers, but no sign of life.

They skirted the cabin and walked back into the woods. It took them another half hour to determine that the area was deserted, circling carefully until they finally came back to the charred remains of the cabin. They saw no sign of a disturbance at first, but then Galushko's practiced eyes saw the bloodstains on the ground. After that they moved more quickly.

An hour later they had still found nothing, and Galushko was frustrated. They were about to go back to the trailer when one of the women went off to relieve herself in the woods.

The others had almost reached the trailer when she came running after them breathlessly. Then she was beside Galushko, saying, "I think you'd better come back and have a look."

Finland. The SAS Constellation landed at Helsinki's Malmi Airport a little after five that afternoon. Ten minutes after the aircraft touched down, Massey, Slanski, and Anna came through arrivals.

A blond-haired man wearing a worn leather flying jacket came out of the waiting crowd and shook Massey's hand. He had a cheerful face, and his straw-blond hair was unmistakably Nordic.

"Good to see you, Jake. So this must be the cargo?"

Massey turned to Anna and Slanski. "I'd like you to meet Janne Saarinen, your pilot. One of Finland's best."

Saarinen smiled as he shook their hands. "Don't pay any attention to Jake," he said. "He's an old flatterer. You must be exhausted after the flight. I've got a car outside, so let's get you to our base."

It was very cold and eerily dark outside, just a faint trace of watery light on the Arctic horizon. Saarinen climbed in the front of a small, muddy green Volvo. Massey slid in beside him, Slanski in the back with Anna, and they drove out of the airport.

"WELCOME to Bylandet Island," said Saarinen.

They rattled over a bridge and came to a small cove with a couple of buildings, a stretch of frozen beach in front of them, and a thick forest behind. Saarinen drove toward a big two-story wooden house and halted in front. Wood fuel was piled against one wall, and a clump of frozen netting hung from a hook.

"The place used to belong to a local fisherman," Saarinen told them.

The house was all bright-colored pine inside, and freezing cold. Saarinen lit a couple of oil lamps and showed them around. A large room downstairs served as the kitchen and living-room area. There was a wood-burning stove in the corner, and when Saarinen lit it, he showed them their rooms upstairs.

When they went downstairs ten minutes later, Saarinen had got the electric generator going and made coffee. A couple of maps were spread out on the kitchen table, showing the southern coast of Finland and the western coasts of Russia and the Baltic countries. On one Saarinen had marked their flight route with a red pen.

He smiled. "Tomorrow night's crossing shouldn't take more than thirty-five minutes." He pointed to the map and the red curved line he had drawn that ran from Bylandet Island to a point across the Baltic Sea, just outside Tallinn, Estonia. "From the island here to the drop point near Tallinn, it's exactly seventy-five miles. A pinch, really, if things go according to plan."

Anna looked at him. "Where's the runway on the island?"

Saarinen shook his head and grinned. "There isn't one. The aircraft is fitted with skis so we can take off from the ice."

Massey said, "You think the weather will be a problem?"

"According to the Helsinki meteorological office, it couldn't be better for a covert drop. Strong winds tonight, followed by a heavy cold front with a threat of some cumulonimbus cloud across parts of the Gulf of Finland. That kind of cloud can give snow, hail, and even thunderstorms. We'll have to try and avoid the worst of it."

"Surely the Soviets scan the area with radar," said Slanski.

Saarinen tapped a finger at a point on the map near Tallinn. "There's a Soviet air base right here, equipped with MiG-15P all-weather interceptors, with onboard radar that's only just been introduced. It operates a Baltic air patrol for a full twenty-four-hour shift. If any aircraft comes into Soviet airspace, they blast it out of the skies without asking questions. But the way I understand it, in really bad snow the MiG pilots keep above the cloud because they're not yet fully used to operating the new onboard radar."

He smiled. "On a clear day they can pick up the buzz of a wasp. But on a bad one, with snow and hail, the Soviet radar units often can't discriminate between a target and the clutter produced on their screens by the weather. That's where really bad conditions help us. But I'll stay as low as I can within the cloud to avoid being picked up on their screens. There's a chance we'll be noticed by their radar once we come out of the cloud for the drop zone. That's why I've got to find the target quickly and drop you."

Saarinen sat on the edge of the table. "Any more questions?" No one spoke, and Saarinen smiled broadly. "Good. That must mean you trust me."

Washington, D.C., February 24. It was just before two a.m. and raining hard as the unmarked black Ford sedan drew up outside the rear entrance to the White House. As the three passengers climbed out, Secret Service men led them briskly through to the Oval Office.

President Eisenhower was already seated behind his desk, wearing a dressing gown, his face looking tired and drawn. He stood briefly as the three men were ushered into the room. "Take a seat."

Allen Welsh Dulles, the acting director of the CIA, took the chair next to Eisenhower. Appointed only six weeks previously and not to be sworn into office for another four days, the sixty-year-old Dulles was to be the CIA's first professional director.

The other two men were the assistant director of the Soviet Operations Division, William G. Wallace, and Karl Branigan, the special operations chief. Both men sat facing Eisenhower's desk.

Eisenhower opened the meeting. "You had better begin, Allen. It's bad enough being woken at one thirty, so let's not waste any more time. I presume this isn't going to be good news?"

Dulles cleared his throat. "Sir, I believe we have a major problem. Mr. President, as of this morning we believe Moscow may be aware of our intention in regard to Operation Snow Wolf."

At once Eisenhower reacted. "You're certain about this?"

"As certain as we can be."

Anger showed instantly on Eisenhower's face. "You mind telling me how one of the most sensitive top-secret operations your department's ever handled has been blown? What's gone wrong?"

Dulles shakily began. "At exactly ten thirty last night a diplomatic attaché named Leonid Kislov, from the Soviet U.N. mission in New York, boarded a plane for London, with onward connections to Moscow. As you might expect, Kislov is no attaché—he's a KGB station head. He had with him a diplomatic bag. We believe it contained information from a copy of a secret file we had given Massey on Stalin's personal security and habits."

Eisenhower frowned. "And what makes you assume that?"

Dulles explained about the bodies found in the Brooklyn apartment. One had been identified as Dimitri Popov, who worked for the CIA. The body of the second man was Feliks Arkashin, a Soviet attaché and KGB major. Karl Branigan knew Popov had been seconded to Massey for agent training, so he had decided to have the house in New Hampshire visited for the sake of security.

Dulles went on worriedly, "The cabin had been burned to the ground, and Massey and his people had vanished. Branigan called in one of our teams to check the property. As of an hour ago four bodies have been found—three in the woods, another near the lake. One body is of a killer named Braun, who worked for the Soviets, and the body had a file hidden on it—the file I referred to. Massey had been supplied with a copy for Slanski to study. It contained details on Stalin's background, his personality, his weaknesses."

"Did the file contain any details about Snow Wolf?"

"No, sir, it did not."

Eisenhower said impatiently, "Then just how do you suppose the Soviets could have deduced what we intend?"

Dulles hesitated. "I think maybe the assistant director can better answer that question, sir." Dulles nodded to William Wallace.

The assistant director looked uncomfortable. "Our people believe Braun's body had already been disturbed before we found it. We also now suspect Moscow had been watching the woman and sent Braun to kill or abduct her. Braun must have found the file in the cabin before he was killed, most obviously by Massey or one of his people. We concluded that when Braun and his team didn't return, the KGB sent someone to check. We think Kislov flew to Moscow because whoever was sent to find out what had happened to Braun also found the file. They examined it but left it on the body. Kislov was informed and realized what the information might suggest."

Eisenhower said quickly, "Has our team gone yet?"

"No, sir," said Dulles.

Eisenhower sighed. "The obvious answer is for us to abort the whole operation. It's a damn pity. The way things are going with Moscow, I had hoped your people stood a chance, however slim." He shook his head resignedly. "So where's Massey?"

The assistant director looked uncomfortable. "Sir, despite what's developed, we know he's flown to Helsinki for the final stage of the mission, but we don't know exactly where in Finland he is."

Eisenhower stared over at Dulles. "I thought you said the operation hadn't started yet."

"We can really only assume that. As you know, the operation was entirely run on Massey's discretion. He was to send a signal when he was ready to drop his two people, to give us a chance to cancel the operation if we so wished. So far that hasn't happened."

"This gets worse by the minute. Is the man dumb or crazy? I thought you said he was one of the best we had."

"He is the best, sir," the assistant director said. "Mr. Dulles worked with him in Europe during the war and can attest to that."

Eisenhower stood up. He was angry. "If those two people make it onto Soviet soil and they're captured, there's only one outcome for us. I think we all know how the Russians would respond." Eisenhower looked around. "We're not just talking about a cause for a war, gentlemen. We're talking about *the* war. We're talking about a Soviet response that could put us back twenty years. They can march into West Berlin on the pretense that it's now a question of security or retaliation. We're talking about the greatest disaster that could ever hit this country and our allies."

Dulles looked at Eisenhower. "Mr. President, we're doing everything we can to locate Massey. Branigan here has already assembled a team, and they'll soon be on their way to Finland."

"Mr. President, we can still stop them," said Branigan.

"How?"

"Most operations into Russia and the Baltic are weather dependent," Branigan explained. "If the weather's good, the CIA never drops by air, because the Russian radar can easily track our aircraft. The report Massey was shown recommends an airdrop into the Baltic area, and I'm certain that's the way he'll do it. He'll need a local pilot, someone with experience of flying in Russian airspace. We've checked the weather report for the region. It suggests a bad snowstorm moving in at eight p.m. Helsinki time. That's around the most likely time Massey's people would go. With enough manpower we could find them before that happens. And with the cooperation of the Finnish air force we could make it impossible for Massey's team to make the crossing. With enough aircraft patrolling the area, they could make sure the plane doesn't get near its destination."

"You mean blow it out of the sky?"

"If necessary."

Eisenhower looked at the three men. "Then I don't care how, but I want it done. I want Massey and the others found. Found or stopped any way you can, even if it means their deaths. An unpleasant thought, considering they're brave people, but the consequences are far too threatening otherwise. You understand that?"

The three visitors nodded in turn.

Finland, February 23. Slanski and Anna spent that evening going over their weapons and forged papers with Massey in the kitchen.

He gave them each a Tokarev 7.62 pistol. He also produced a Nagant 7.62 revolver, which he handed to Slanski.

Slanski had three sets of papers: one for an Estonian worker, another for a Red Army captain, and the third in the name of a KGB major. Anna had another three sets in the same family names, posing as his wife in each case.

Then Massey took a miniature tin box from his pocket and opened the lid. It contained two black capsules. Massey picked up one of the pills. "This is only to be used in a dire emergency."

"What is it?" Anna asked.

"Cyanide. It kills you in seconds."

IT WAS almost midnight, and Slanski lay in the dark listening to the wind rage outside. He heard the door open, and Anna stood there in a cotton nightgown.

She said softly, "Can I come in? I can't sleep."

"Come in. Close the door."

She came to sit at the end of the bed. He noticed she was trembling, and he said, "Are you cold?"

She shook her head. "Just frightened. Maybe I've suddenly realized everything about this is deadly serious. Especially when Massey gave us that pill. Now it's not a game anymore." She bit her lip. "Will you do something for me?"

"What?"

"Just hold me. Hold me tightly."

He saw it in her face then, a real and terrible fear. He realized she was more afraid than he had ever imagined. His hand touched her cheek as he looked into her eyes. He said, "My poor Anna."

Her arms went around his neck, and she held him close. Then suddenly she was crying and kissing him fiercely.

"Make love to me."

When he hesitated, she kissed him again, her tongue finding his, and he felt himself reacting. After that they were in a frenzy, their bodies in the grip of some kind of urgent desperation, until finally they spent themselves. And then Anna started to cry again.

"What's wrong, Anna?"

She didn't reply, and then, her eyes full of tears, she said, "Do you want to know why I'm going back to Russia with you?"

"Only if you want to tell me."

She told him, told him everything, and she was still crying when she finished.

Slanski held her close and whispered, "Anna. It's all right, Anna."

It was a long time before her tears stopped.

February 24. The wheels of the U.S. Air Force B-47 Stratojet bit the icy runway with a squeal as they touched down at Helsinki's Malmi Airport at exactly six p.m. Karl Branigan was exhausted after the long and turbulent flight from Washington, a journey of almost ten hours.

Twenty minutes later his car drove up to the front entrance of the American embassy, and Branigan stepped out, turning up his coat collar against the cold. A tall, lean man came out.

"Mr. Branigan? I'm Douglas Canning," the man said. "If you'll come this way, I'll take you to our temporary operations room."

The dimly lit room in a back office of the embassy was thick with sweaty men, cigarette smoke, and the babble of voices. The Finn who stood beside Branigan was tall but chubby-faced.

Henry Stenlund was the deputy director of SUPO, Finnish counterintelligence, which was composed of ten men, three clapped-out Volkswagens, and half a dozen rusty Raleigh bicycles. He had received a call from the U.S. embassy just as he was leaving his office and had brought the files to the embassy that Branigan requested. He and Branigan went through a list of names. All were mercenary pilots who risked their lives flying into Soviet airspace from the

Baltic on covert Finnish military and CIA agent-dropping missions.

Stenlund said, "There are fifteen men who operate freelance with their own aircraft for either our people or yours. We can eliminate most, however, by assuming the people you're looking for will want to cross the Baltic in the quickest possible time. The pilot would need a base within close proximity to Soviet soil."

Branigan nodded. "So who are the likely suspects?"

"Two possibilities. A man named Hakala, who lives in a small fishing village near Spjutsund. The second is a man named Saarinen."

"How far is the first?"

"Spjutsund? About fifteen miles east of Helsinki. An hour there and back by car. The other guy, Janne Saarinen, uses a place at Bylandet Island, twenty miles west of here. Both are pretty much the same distance from Tallinn as the crow flies."

Branigan hesitated, the tension in the small room stifling. "Okay, we try Hakala first, then this guy Saarinen. I'll organize a car."

"As you wish."

SLANSKI and Massey were sitting at the table when Anna came down the stairs. She wore a heavy woolen skirt and a white blouse, a woolen scarf and an overcoat, and she carried a suitcase.

"Nervous?" Slanski asked.

She looked at him, and said, "I'm shaking."

Slanski smiled. "Don't worry; it'll be all over before you know it."

Massey nodded to the corner of the room to where the parachutes, canvas jumpsuits, helmets, goggles, and gloves waited.

"You can leave those until Janne's ready to go. If you somehow separate from each other after you jump, or your contact who's to meet you at the drop doesn't make it, the rendezvous will be the main railway station in Tallinn, the waiting room, nine tomorrow morning. If no one shows, go the next day an hour later. If there's no show on the third day, you're each on your own, I'm afraid."

The door opened then with a blast of freezing air, and Saarinen appeared carrying a heavy-duty flashlight. He wore a yellow oilskin and a scarf over his flying suit and a pair of thick woolen gloves.

"What a night," he said, closing the door. He checked his watch and looked at Anna and Slanski. "Ten more minutes, I reckon. You'd better get into those jumpsuits."

As Anna and Slanski went to put on their suits, Massey crossed to the Finn. "How's the weather turning out?"

"It seems a bit rough, but don't worry; I've seen worse."

Massey nodded. Slanski and Anna dressed in the green canvas suits and helmets and goggles, but left the gloves until last.

Massey could feel the growing tension in the room. He looked over at Anna and Slanski, then Saarinen. "Are we ready?"

Saarinen nodded and smiled. "Onward and upward."

He picked up the flashlight and his parachute, and they followed him out the door to the hangar.

THE tiny office for the Finnish air force liaison unit at Helsinki's Malmi Airport was bitterly cold, despite a stove going full blast in the corner. The wing commander had been summoned from a dinner party, and his pinched face showed his irritation as he looked up at the warrant officer standing in front of his desk.

"I wouldn't send up a balloon in weather like this. They can't be serious, Matti."

"I'm afraid they are, sir. It's priority one. If the aircraft manages to get airborne, it's to be stopped before it reaches Russian airspace."

"What's going on?"

The warrant officer shrugged. "I wish I knew, sir. But the orders were quite specific. The aircraft is to be stopped at all costs."

The wing commander stood and crossed to the window. He sighed. "Well, I suppose we'd better do as we're told. Okay, Matti, give the order to crank up. We'd better warn the boys to be extra careful. It's going to be pretty rough up there."

DARKNESS had swallowed up the sea, and the sky was pitch-black. They all helped to slide Saarinen's plane, a Norseman, out of the hangar and onto the ice. It slid for a couple of yards, then came to a halt. Saarinen told them to move back before he started the engine. He opened the door and hauled himself into the cockpit.

Moments later the Norseman's engine erupted into life. As Saarinen went through his preflight check, Massey looked up at the sky. The storm was obviously getting worse. Flakes of snow began to fly around them in gusts. Anna and Slanski hauled on their parachutes, looking a little absurd in their jumpsuits, helmets, and goggles, with the worn suitcases beside them. Saarinen shouted above the engine noise, "Whenever you're ready."

Massey said to Slanski and Anna, "Well, I guess this is it." He shook Slanski's hand, then Anna's. "Good luck."

There was nothing else to say. Anna hesitated; then she leaned forward and kissed Massey on the lips. "*Do svidaniya,* Jake."

For a long time Massey looked at her frozen face, but before he could reply, she climbed into the Norseman, Slanski after her, closing the cockpit door as Massey stood back.

There was a crunching sound as the skis started to move out slowly across the ice to the right of a string of yellow lights that glowed brilliantly and marked out the runway. Saarinen eased the throttle forward, and then the Norseman started to move rapidly.

It took only seconds for the speed to build up, and then the little aircraft was skimming fast over the uneven surface of the frozen sea. The sound of the engine faded in the wind, and the plane disappeared into the swirl of snow and blackness.

JANNE Saarinen had smelled trouble for some time now. It was twenty minutes after takeoff, and the Norseman was rocking violently. The aircraft plowed through a thick cloud of blinding whiteness at fifteen hundred feet, tossing about like a balloon in a hurricane.

Janne Saarinen turned to glance at his passengers. The girl's face was a mask of white. The American seemed calm enough, but he was gripping the seat hard to stop himself from being thrown about.

Saarinen pushed the stick forward and eased off on the throttle, and the Norseman nosed down to avoid the worst of the weather. They broke into clear air at twelve hundred feet, and the rocking subsided. Saarinen pointed to a faint haze of lights on the left. "That's Tallinn. The drop's eight minutes east of here."

There was a sudden swish of violent air, and Saarinen looked up as a flash of gray rocketed past on their port side.

"What was that?" shouted Anna.

Before Saarinen could reply, they saw a burst of tracer fire off to the right, and another flash of gray roared past out of nowhere.

"We've got company. Let's see what we can do about it."

He quickly applied power and pulled back on the stick. The

Norseman rose back into the turbulent cloud, shuddering as it was sucked up into the air, and the buffeting resumed as before.

"What's up?" Slanski asked.

"You tell me," said Saarinen. "Those were Focke-Wulfs from the Finnish air force. I don't understand it. Those guys are in Soviet airspace. We must have been picked up on Helsinki military radar and the air force decided to investigate. They probably think we're a Russian reconnaissance plane making the most of a bad night."

"What do we do?"

"The only thing we can. Stay in the cloud. Uncomfortable, but safer than having my own countrymen shoot us out of the sky."

Saarinen checked his instruments. The panel was shaking fiercely with the turbulence. After a few minutes he eased back on the throttle and pushed the stick forward again. They broke cloud at twelve hundred feet into almost completely still air. Saarinen had his earphones on and was fiddling with a knob on the radio receiver.

He suddenly tensed as he concentrated on the earphones. He adjusted an instrument knob on the panel, then turned back and shouted, "Drop's coming up in twenty seconds. Open the door!"

Slanski pushed open the door. A blast of freezing air raged into the cabin. He gripped Anna's arm and indicated that she go first.

She moved to the door, and then Saarinen roared, "Go! Go! Go!"

For a second she seemed to hesitate; then Slanski pushed her out, counted to three, lunged after her, and was swallowed up by the rush of freezing air and darkness.

In the cockpit Saarinen held on to the stick with one hand, reached back, and released the catch, and the door slammed shut with a thunderclap. He let out a sigh of relief, then banked the plane around. He just hoped those Focke-Wulfs were not still lurking out there somewhere, because if they were, he might be in trouble.

MASSEY stood over the stove. His hands, numb from the chill outside, shook as he tried to warm them. He pulled up a chair beside the stove. Suddenly figures stormed into the room out of the darkness and crashed into him. He was winded and fell back onto the floor, knocking over a chair.

"What the—"

As Massey struggled to his feet, something hard hit his skull.

AT FIFTEEN THOUSAND FEET, skimming above the clouds in darkness, Lieutenant Arcady Barsenko, age twenty-one, watched the rush of winking stars against the cockpit glass of the Soviet air force MiG-15P. The scene almost put him to sleep. He yawned and rubbed his nose tiredly with his fur-lined leather glove.

He could have done with being back in the mess in Tallinn, toasting his feet at the stove. A crazy night to be out, with the storm below, but the commander of the air base had insisted that all patrols go ahead, and had warned the crews to be extra vigilant.

Barsenko ran his gloved fingertips lightly over the panel instruments and grinned. She was a beautiful machine, the latest model MiG. His leather-clad thumb playfully rubbed the smooth red cap at the tip of the control stick. Underneath the cap were the red buttons that fired the twin 23-mm and single 37-mm cannons.

The MiG bumped fast in sudden turbulence, then settled. Barsenko checked his instruments. He had the new onboard radar switched on, and he idly twiddled the knobs until the antenna inside the MiG's nose cowl pointed down into the gray mass of cloud below. He glanced at the green illuminated glass. Nothing but clutter.

Suddenly he saw a bright white blip twenty miles ahead and below. Then another. And another. Three blips. They vanished.

Barsenko came wide-awake and rubbed his eyes. Had he really seen something? Snow sometimes gave you ghost images. Or else the radar was acting up.

But three strong blips? Three fast aircraft out there in the blinding swirl of the storm—still in Finnish airspace but coming his way? What was going on? It was probably clutter.

Still, no harm in having a look below. The cloud was broken in places, and maybe he'd see something. He eased back on the throttle, and the nose of the MiG dipped into a gentle dive.

Ten seconds later, as he broke cloud into a sudden clear pocket of air, Barsenko's jaw dropped and his eyes opened wide in horror.

He saw a little light aircraft dead ahead, approaching on a direct collision course. He banked frantically to starboard.

IF THERE was a hell, then this was it, Janne Saarinen decided.

He had been in bad weather before, but nothing as bad as this. Besides, if you saw storm cloud, you avoided it if at all possible.

This time it wasn't possible. As he scanned his instruments, a sudden downdraft dropped him out of the cloud. Instinct made him look up sharply. He saw the MiG as it roared toward him.

"No!"

The MiG crashed into Saarinen's left wing, tore it off with a terrible juddering bang. Then came a grating sound of shearing metal, and the MiG exploded in a burst of violent, intense light.

Another explosion came a split second later, tearing through Saarinen's cockpit like a roll of thunder as his own fuel tank ignited. There was a brief, intense feeling of searing hot pain, and then he was consumed by a ball of orange flame.

SLANSKI sank through the freezing air, vicious cold cutting into his bones, icy wind rushing in his ears. A sparkle of lights that was Tallinn glowed off to his left, and to his right he saw fields of white and a ribbon of road. What appeared to be the lights of a convoy of military vehicles snaked along it. He craned his neck and swung in the harness, trying to see Anna's parachute. Nothing.

When he looked down again, the snowy fields were coming up rapidly to meet him. He braced himself; then he let his body tension go, hitting the ground hard and rolling right.

He tore off his harness and gathered up his chute. Behind him lay a tall, thick line of birch trees on top of a raised bank of earth. In front of him he could make out the frosty Baltic in the distance.

But where was Anna?

It took him several minutes to remove the jumpsuit and bury the parachute, digging a hole near some undergrowth. Then he started to move up toward the bank of trees, carrying his shabby case.

As he came down the other side of the bank, he saw a narrow road below, then froze when he saw a Zis army truck parked by the side. As he reached for the Tokarev, he heard the click of a weapon.

A beam of light flashed in his face from somewhere in the trees, blinding him, and a voice said in Russian, "Don't move or I shoot!"

Slanski blinked. The beam of light moved slowly off his face and traced down his body. Behind it he could make out two men in uniform, another figure between them. One of the men, a young KGB captain, was armed with a pistol, and the other held a flashlight.

"Come forward. Slowly."

As Slanski moved closer, his heart sank. Anna stood between the two men, her hair tossed, her jumpsuit torn.

The captain with the gun looked over at him and grinned.

"Welcome to Estonia, comrade."

Chapter Seven

Moscow, February 25. The black Zis glided silently to a halt outside the Kremlin Armory courtyard at three minutes to midnight.

Major Yuri Lukin of the KGB Second Directorate stepped out of the car into thickly falling snow. He was thirty-two, of medium build, a handsome man with dark hair and a calm, pleasant face. His left hand from the forearm down was missing, and in its place was an artificial limb sheathed in a black leather glove. A young captain was waiting at the bottom of the courtyard steps. He stepped forward and said, "This way, Major. Please follow me."

The captain climbed a flight of stone steps up to an archway, and Lukin followed. He wondered what was going on. This summons to the Kremlin at so late an hour could only spell trouble.

The call to his apartment had come half an hour ago. He was to be ready within ten minutes for an urgent appointment at the Kremlin. The sleek black Zis pulled up on the street outside even as he spoke on the telephone, and three minutes later he had dressed in his best uniform and kissed his pregnant wife, Nadia, good-bye before he went down the stairs to the waiting car.

At the top of the steps two massive doors were set in the archway. Two uniformed guards snapped off salutes before the captain opened one of the doors. Lukin entered a long, ornate hallway.

When they reached the end of the corridor, they entered a large, plush outer office of red carpet and magnificent czarist tapestries and Bokhara rugs. A faint sound of music came from behind a pair of oak doors directly opposite.

A fat, pasty-faced colonel sat at a mahogany desk flicking idly through some papers, his double chins spilling over his collar. The captain showed him his signed pass, saluted, and left.

The colonel smiled at Lukin. "Major, please take a seat."

"Am I permitted to know why I've been brought here, comrade?"

The colonel grinned. "Relax. You'll know soon enough."

Lukin sat and tried to relax, but it was impossible. Off in the distance he heard the Kremlin clock tower chime midnight, and at that precise moment one of the oak doors burst open.

A colonel in a KGB uniform stood half in, half out of the room, blue light flickering in the darkness behind him. He looked like a man of powerful energy, tall and broad. Cold blue eyes were set in a brutal-looking face pockmarked with acne scars. The rugged colonel stared at Lukin. Then he wagged a finger and said curtly, "This way." Lukin stood and stepped toward the door.

There was a blaze of colored light and music and a strong smell of tobacco smoke. Lukin saw he was in a large private cinema. Several rows of plush red seats faced the front, heads jutting from the darkness in the front row. A color film flickered on the screen as Lukin looked up. He had never seen the actors or actresses before, but he guessed it was an American film.

"In there, Lukin. And keep quiet." The colonel pointed to one of the seats at the very back. "The show isn't over yet."

Lukin sank into a deep red leather seat, and the big colonel slipped into the seat beside him. It took several moments for Lukin to accustom his eyes to the semidarkness. There were perhaps half a dozen men in the front row. A blur of cigarette smoke curled to the ceiling, and a table was set against the far right wall. Silver trays of vodka, brandy, and mineral water were laid out neatly.

Ten minutes later the film reeled to a close and the lights came on. Lukin blinked. There was an outburst of coughing as fat, weary bodies pushed themselves slowly out of their plush seats.

Lukin froze in shock.

The figure of Joseph Stalin rose from one of the seats in the front row—the bushy gray eyebrows and hair, the heavy mustache unmistakable. He wore a simple gray tunic and looked frail, but he was smiling as he lit his pipe and went to stand among a group of well-fed men. They were laughing, as if someone had made a joke.

Lukin recognized the other faces instantly: Nikolai Bulganin, the former defense minister, and Georgi Malenkov, the senior member of the Communist Party Presidium. One other figure stood out—a bald, heavyset man. Behind his wire-rimmed glasses, dark eyes looked full of menace. Lavrenty Beria, head of State Security.

Lukin sat rigid in his seat in a cold sweat. What was going on? Why had he been summoned here? The colonel next to him stood. "Wait here." And then he was gone toward the front row.

The room started to empty. Lukin felt his pulse race. He was unsure if Stalin was smiling or glaring at him, but the man was definitely looking his way. Uncomfortably, Lukin went to rise from his seat, but just then Stalin turned and went out a door to the right. Now only the colonel who had led him in and Beria remained.

Suddenly the colonel beckoned for Lukin to join them. Lukin stood and moved down to the front row.

The colonel said bluntly, "Major Lukin, Comrade Beria."

Beria was standing. From behind his glasses, reptilian, olive-black eyes bored into Lukin, and a silky voice said, "So this is Major Lukin. The pleasure is all mine, I'm sure."

"Comrade Beria."

Beria didn't offer a hand, but slumped into a leather chair. He snapped his fingers at the colonel opposite. "The file, Romulka."

The colonel stepped forward and handed over a file. Beria flicked it open idly. "I've been reading your background, Lukin. An interesting story." He grinned crookedly and glanced at Lukin's left arm. "Were it not for your little error in '44, doubtless you'd be a full colonel by now and still have your hand. By all accounts you were one of the best counterintelligence officers we had during the war. You had a particular talent for hunting down enemy agents."

"That was a long time ago, Comrade Beria. Those days are behind me. The war's over, and now I'm just a simple policeman."

"Don't demean your position, Lukin. You're far from simple, and the KGB doesn't recruit fools."

"I meant—"

"Forget what you meant," Beria said abruptly. "What if I told you there was a threat to our glorious Comrade Stalin's life?"

Lukin stared at Beria. "I'm not sure I understand."

Beria gestured to the KGB colonel. "This is Colonel Romulka, one of my personal staff. Tell Lukin the present situation."

Romulka stood with his hands behind his back. "Two hours ago one of our MiG fighters on patrol in the Gulf of Finland disappeared from radar control in Tallinn. We believe the pilot had detected an intruder in Soviet airspace. We sent three other MiGs to where the aircraft disappeared. The wreckage of the missing MiG was spotted on the ice in the Baltic Sea. There also appears to be the wreckage of a light aircraft it collided with. A foot patrol is on its way across the ice to examine the crash site."

Beria took over. "According to our intelligence sources, the Americans intend infiltrating two agents, a man and a woman, into Moscow with the purpose of killing Comrade Stalin. We believe a parachute drop of these people may already have taken place near Tallinn and the light aircraft was their transport. Lukin, I want you to find the man and woman and bring them to me."

Lukin looked stunned. "I don't understand."

"It's simple, Lukin. I'm giving you a chance to redeem yourself. As of this moment, you're in charge of this case."

Beria handed a file across. "Take that and study it. Inside you'll find everything we have on the woman and man we believe the Americans have sent. There are photographs that should be of some help. You will have absolute authority to do as you see fit to apprehend these criminals."

Beria produced a letter from his pocket and handed it across with a flourish. "Should anyone doubt your authority, that states you are working directly for me, and all assistance demanded by you will be given without question. Choose any personnel you need from among your own staff. Colonel Romulka here will act as my personal representative in the case. He's of superior rank, but you will be in command. You look shocked, Lukin."

"I don't know what to say, comrade."

"Then say nothing. A MiG is standing by at Vnukovo to fly you to Tallinn as soon as the weather clears. The local KGB and military have already mounted patrols to find the couple and will be expecting you. Colonel Romulka will join you later."

Beria's eyes flashed dark and dangerous. "These are high stakes, Lukin. So don't fail me. I'd hate to think of you someday in front of a firing squad. Find the man and woman and bring them to me. The moment you do, Stalin himself has promised to make you a full colonel. Fail me, and I will be unforgiving. You are excused."

Bylandet Island. Masscy came awake with a splitting headache. Slowly the pain and fog washed away. He was in one of the bedrooms of the island house, the blankets tossed carelessly around him on the bed. He remembered dark figures bursting in through the front door and the blow across the back of the neck, but after that, nothing. He got to his feet. Who was it who had struck him?

Suddenly he heard footsteps on the stairs, and the door opened. Branigan stood there, grim-faced. "So you're back in the land of the living."

Massey said, "What the hell's going on? You almost killed me."

"I could ask you the same question."

Massey went to brush past him, but Branigan moved to block his way. "If you're thinking about your friend Saarinen, forget it."

"What do you mean?"

"He's dead."

Massey turned white. "How do you know that?"

"The Finnish air force tried to stop him at our request. They picked up the crash on their radar when Saarinen was on the homeward leg. It looks as if he bumped into a patrolling MiG."

"Why did you try to stop him, for heaven's sake?"

"I should have thought that's obvious," Branigan said angrily. "You really messed up, didn't you, Jake? I'm talking about the bodies in the woods. I'm talking about Braun—and Arkashin."

Massey was quite pale. He said quietly, "How did you know?"

"After we learned about Arkashin and Popov, we decided to pay the cabin a visit." Branigan paused. "You should have contacted me as soon as you had problems. Why didn't you?"

"The men at the cabin came looking for trouble. But I figured they only wanted Anna. After it was over, we buried the bodies. Slanski still wanted to go through with the mission. Nothing was going to stop him after Vassily was killed. I went along with him. I figured how could it really matter if we went ahead?"

Branigan leaned closer. "It matters all right. You want to know how much?" He explained about the Stalin file found on Braun's body and the suspicion that a Soviet team had visited the cabin.

Massey was deathly silent; then he said, "Slanski thought the file had been destroyed in the fire."

"Well, it wasn't. And if your two friends landed safely, my guess is they've walked into big trouble. That MiG that bumped into Saarinen's plane wasn't a coincidence—every damned Soviet border post and naval and air base is on alert. And you know what's going to happen if Moscow captures them alive? World War Three."

"Slanski would never let himself be taken alive."

"You can't guarantee that, Massey. No one can. That's why we've got to stop this thing. I want to know exactly how this plan of yours works. I want names, safe houses, routes. Every last detail. Because we're going to abort this mission. No matter what it takes."

Tallinn, Estonia. The Zis army truck jerked to a halt, and Slanski peered out beyond the canvas flap. Anna sat beside him.

They had halted in an alley beside an ancient inn. Beyond lay a deserted cobbled square. Brightly painted medieval houses ringed the square. Slanski guessed they were in the old town of Tallinn.

A moment later the KGB captain tore back the canvas flap and grinned up at them. "Right, bring your things and follow me."

Slanski jumped down and helped Anna from the truck. They followed the officer to a door at the side of the inn. He knocked on the door. A big, stoutly built man with a bushy red beard appeared.

The officer smiled and said in Russian, "Your guests arrived on time, Toomas. Got a bit of a shock when they saw our uniforms. Good job we found the two of them before the army did. Those bastards are swarming all over the place."

The innkeeper wiped his hands on his smock. "You'd better not hang about, Erik. Get that truck back to the barracks sharpish."

The officer nodded and was gone, and the innkeeper ushered Slanski and Anna into a hallway. When he had closed and locked the door, he shook their hands. "My name is Toomas Gorev. Welcome to Estonia. I take it everything went well with the drop?"

Slanski said, "Apart from the shock of having the KGB waiting for us, reasonably good."

The innkeeper grinned. "Some Russian general put the army on maneuvers at the last minute. The area you landed in was smack in the middle of their route. Using the army truck was the only way our resistance could pick you up. But don't worry; you're safe now."

AN EMKA staff car turned into the main square of Tondy barracks in Tallinn just after three a.m. and ground to a halt.

As Lukin climbed out tiredly, he looked around him and shivered.

The snow had lightened, but the early morning air was ice-cold. An army captain waited for him at a barrack door. He saluted. "Captain Oleg Kaman at your service, sir."

"Carry on."

The captain led Lukin up a stone stairwell to a sparsely furnished office on the third floor. A map of the Baltic States and Estonia hung on the wall. When the captain had taken Lukin's overcoat, he said, "Tea or coffee, Major?"

Lukin shook his head. "Perhaps later." He sat in the chair. "You have a progress report for me?"

"Yes, sir," the captain said. "So far, what we know is that at approximately nine p.m. a MiG-15P all-weather fighter on coastal patrol disappeared."

He pointed to an area of sea on the map. "We think the MiG vanished here. When the alarm went up, three other MiGs were sent to scour the area. They spotted two areas of wreckage on the ice. One was the MiG. The other appeared to be a light plane."

Lukin said, "You're certain about the second aircraft?"

"Absolutely. That's what the pilots reported. They suggest a mid-air collision occurred. We've sent a foot patrol out onto the ice, but it may be dangerous to go too close to the wreckage, since the crash will have weakened the ice nearby."

Lukin asked, "You think the light aircraft managed to drop these people before it crashed?"

"Sir, it's likely." Kaman pointed at the map. "The radar picked up several blips west of Tallinn along this route here. Assuming that one was the light aircraft, its heading suggests the drop had already been made and it was turning back, possibly toward Finland. So we must assume the man and woman are now on Russian soil."

Lukin stood. The file Beria had given him contained background details and a photograph of the woman, Anna Khorev. The woman's past made unpleasant reading. She was the daughter of a disgraced army officer, her husband had died in a camp, and her child was in the care of a Moscow orphanage.

The man's file didn't go into much detail. There were a couple of pages missing. Alexander Slanski, known as the Wolf, was a Russian-born naturalized American citizen. There was a fuzzy photograph taken from a distance. Lukin read the brief character sketch, but there was no information concerning Slanski's childhood in Russia, and Lukin wondered about that. Such information might help him.

"A question, Captain. If you were an enemy agent parachuted onto Russian soil with your destination being Moscow, and your enemy knew of your arrival, how would you proceed?"

The captain thought for a moment. "Lie low for a couple of days. Then take an indirect route, using public transport. But in disguise. I would try to behave like a local so as not to arouse suspicion."

Lukin nodded. "Good. Though these people would hardly know that the aircraft has crashed and we're looking for them. Still, I want checkpoints placed on every major and minor road, every railway and bus station, and the airport. Use every available man. Inform the local militia that if anyone is spotted acting questionably or if parachutes or any suspicious equipment are found, I want to know about it. If that turns up nothing, we start sector searches. Area by area, house by house."

"Very good, sir." The captain gestured to a door. "I've taken the liberty of having a bed made up for you in the next room."

"Thank you, Captain. Carry on."

Kaman saluted and left. Lukin lit a cigarette and stood at the window. The meeting with Beria had disturbed him. Of one thing Lukin was certain—he couldn't fail. He could imagine the outcome if he did. The way Beria played the game, Lukin would forfeit his own life and perhaps even his wife Nadia's.

Lukin remembered a spring day in a forest near Kursk during the war and the young German girl he had cornered, no more than eighteen. She had parachuted in on a reconnaissance mission behind Russian lines by the Abwehr in a last-ditch German offensive.

He and two of his men had tracked her down to an abandoned house in some woods. She was wounded, helpless, and frightened. Lukin had gone in by the back door with his gun drawn, but when he saw her huddled in a corner with a coat thrown over her, her young face frozen white with fear, something had made him drop his guard. But the indecision had proved almost fatal. The ragged burst from the machine pistol hidden under the girl's coat had nearly torn off Lukin's arm. One of the other men had to shoot the girl. After he recovered, Lukin was transferred back to Moscow.

His heart wasn't in it anymore.

But now was different. Now it was find this man and woman or die. With the descriptions and information he had and the swiftness of Moscow's response, he imagined it would be over quickly. By dawn, hopefully. Estonia was a small country, Tallinn a small town, the places the couple could run to or hide in limited.

THE kitchen at the back of the inn was warm and cozy and a table was set with plates of cold meat and oily salted fish, goat's cheese, and dark bread. Gorev poured vodka into three tumblers.

"Eat. The fish are called salty manyards. They go well with the vodka. It's about all they go with. The alcohol kills the taste."

He dug a hand into the plate of tiny salted fish and scooped out half a dozen, swallowing them heads and all.

Slanski drank the vodka, but he and Anna ignored the food.

"Where did your friends get the truck and uniforms?"

Gorev laughed. "The truck came from the Red Army supply depot in Tallinn. The Estonian resistance supplied the KGB uniform. Erik, the officer who brought you here, is a Red Army conscript, but he is also in the resistance. He told the quartermaster he wanted a truck to travel to Pärnu to meet his girlfriend. For a crate of good Estonian beer the quartermaster obliged." He looked over at them. "You'd better tell me who you're supposed to be."

"I'm your niece from Leningrad," Anna said, "on honeymoon with my new husband."

Gorev lit a cigarette and blew out smoke. "It's believable enough, I suppose. We get a lot of Russian visitors to the old town. Tomorrow night I plan to put you both on the train to Leningrad. You'd better show me your papers so I'll get the names right if I'm asked."

Slanski and Anna handed Gorev their papers, and as he examined them, there was a rumbling noise of vehicles outside. "Russian army trucks heading toward the coast," Gorev explained. "Those damned maneuvers will keep half the town awake."

He saw the look of alarm on Anna's face. "Don't worry, girl. Not even Beria's KGB friends will bother you here."

"What makes you so certain?" Anna asked.

"Because I've got two KGB officers staying at the inn. Here for a few days of drinking and carousing. Having the KGB as guests is always an advantage. That way the militia doesn't harass me."

"Who are the officers?" Slanski asked.

"A colonel and a young captain. Old customers paying a visit to a couple of local tarts they met while stationed here a while ago." He handed back their papers. "Let's get you settled in."

Gorev led them up a flight of creaking stairs to the second floor. He opened a door and flicked on a light. Inside was a small, shabby oak-beamed bedroom.

"It isn't the height of luxury, but it's warm and comfortable." He grinned. "I've left clean sheets. Breakfast is at eight in the dining room. I expect to see you there, playing the newlyweds."

"Thanks, Toomas."

"My pleasure. Sleep well." He bade them good night and closed the door.

Slanski looked at Anna as she made the bed. He sat on a chair and studied her face as he lit a cigarette.

"What are you looking at?"

"You. Has anyone ever told you how beautiful you are, Anna?"

She couldn't resist a smile. "You sound like a very bad actor reading an even worse script. Aren't you going to sleep?"

"I'd rather sit and watch you."

She looked at him, her voice suddenly firm. "Understand something. What happened last night is not going to happen again. I was vulnerable, that's all."

Slanski put his cigarette in the ashtray, then stood up and pulled her toward him. She could feel his strength, but she resisted, and then his mouth was on hers, kissing her fiercely.

She pulled back and said, "Alex, don't. Let's get some sleep." As Anna switched off the light, he reached for her hand.

"I said no!"

But he held her while his other hand undid the buttons of her blouse. She tried to stop him, but there was a determined look in his eyes. Part of her wanted to protest; another part of her wanted to feel close to him, to be held and protected again. He looked into her eyes. "Anna, what happened between us—I want you to know it was good. Maybe the closest I've ever felt to a woman."

She looked up at his face, and she knew that he meant it. Something stirred inside her. She felt a surge of passion overcome her, and she kissed him fiercely on the mouth in the darkness.

THE TWO KGB OFFICERS WERE already seated in the dining room beside the bar when Slanski and Anna came down to breakfast. Both stood up politely when they saw Anna enter the room, their eyes red from a late night and too much alcohol.

The older was middle-aged, with a ruddy face, a large stomach, and a bushy mustache. He introduced himself as Colonel Zinov.

The second man was a young captain. His eyes took in Anna's body as he offered his hand. "Captain Bukarin at your service. Your uncle just told us about your arrival. This must be your husband." He shook Slanski's hand, and then it was the colonel's turn.

"Pleasure to meet you both. I do hope your honeymoon will be pleasant. Will you be staying long in Tallinn?"

"A couple of days, just enough time to visit relatives and see the old town," Slanski replied.

The captain smiled over at Anna. "Perhaps you'd both care to join us for drinks tonight?"

"I'm afraid we've already made plans, but thank you for the offer."

Bukarin smiled charmingly and clicked his heels. "Of course. Another time, perhaps. Enjoy your breakfast."

Slanski led Anna to a table by the window. Gorev came in moments later, carrying a jug of coffee. He chatted with the two officers a moment before they finished their breakfast and left the room.

He came over. "Looks like you both passed with flying colors." He winked at Anna. "And the young one, Bukarin, has definitely taken a fancy to you. I can see that."

"I'm supposed to be a married woman."

"That hasn't stopped either of them before."

Slanski stood up and went to the window. An Emka was parked outside. They saw the officers step into the car. It rattled off noisily over the cobbles. Slanski said, "Where have your two guests gone?"

Gorev poured coffee and said scornfully, "Off to pick up their girlfriends for more drinking and carousing."

When Gorev fell silent, Slanski said, "What's the matter?"

Gorev wiped his hands on his apron. "A deliveryman who came this morning said there were plainclothes militia at the railway station, checking papers. They seemed quite thorough. I'll contact Erik and find out what's happening, but it may take a couple of hours. In the meantime, I suggest you remain here at the inn."

LUKIN CAME AWAKE A LITTLE after eight, his head aching and his mouth dry. He had slept for only three hours.

As he dressed, there was a knock on the door, and Kaman entered. "Sorry to disturb you, Major. Some news just came in. The foot patrol managed to get within twenty yards of the wreckage sites. One's definitely the missing MiG. The other is a light plane, make unknown but definitely not one of ours."

"Any bodies?"

"Two. The MiG pilot and the pilot in the light aircraft."

Lukin crossed to the wall map. "Have the checkpoints turned up anything yet?"

"Nothing except a half-dozen deserters and a black marketeer. One of the deserters was shot and wounded trying to escape."

"Excellent. At least we've done some good for the state."

"Sir?"

"A joke, Kaman. Tell me, if you wanted to hide a couple of enemy agents in Tallinn, where would you put them?"

Kaman scratched his chin. "Lots of places. Parts of the old town go back to the fourteenth century. There are underground passageways—cellars and tunnels we don't even know about."

Lukin thought a moment. "And the outskirts of the town?"

Kaman hesitated, then shook his head. "Too few people. And countryfolk would spot a stranger a mile off."

Lukin nodded. "Very well, forget about the rural areas for now. Concentrate on the city and the old town. I want checkpoints and roadblocks on all the main roads and the old entrance gates of the citadel. Anyone fitting the ages or descriptions of the agents is to be stopped and their papers checked thoroughly."

"Yes, Comrade Major."

"I'll be inspecting the checkpoints personally at intervals."

LATER that day Gorev, his face pale, looked from Slanski to Anna as they sat in their bedroom.

"Bad news. I had a visit from the local militia sergeant."

Slanski said worriedly, "What did he want?"

"To see the inn's guest register. Luckily, I hadn't written in your names. We're in the clear for now, but it doesn't look good.

"According to Erik, the army and militia are setting up roadblocks everywhere," Gorev continued. "They're watching the bus and railway stations and the airport. It seems almost everyone's papers are being checked. Apparently some KGB major arrived here from Moscow last night to take charge of the operation. His name's Lukin. He's looking for two agents who parachuted in last night."

Slanski went white. "How could this Lukin know about us?"

"Search me. Maybe some yokel found your buried parachutes. But he does, and that spells trouble for all of us," Gorev said. "My intention was to put you on a train for Leningrad, but that's out of the question now with the station being watched."

Anna said anxiously, "What can we do?"

Gorev stroked his beard nervously. "Normally our resistance people in the forests would hide you. But getting you through the roadblocks would be too difficult, and their camp is too far."

Slanski slammed a fist on the table in frustration. "Damn it! We have to move. We haven't a chance staying here."

"But how can we get out of Tallinn?" Anna asked.

Gorev said, "You could try the sewers under the old town, but you'd be asphyxiated by the fumes before you got ten yards."

"Where do the sewers lead?"

"To the edge of the town. But after that where would you go?"

They all heard a screech of tires on the cobbled street below, and they looked out the window anxiously.

The Emka had drawn up, and the two KGB officers, Zinov and Bukarin, stepped out, two young women accompanying them. They all looked the worse for drink. Gorev's face screwed up in disapproval. "Drunken bastards. Back for more drinks at the bar and a roll in the hay with those tarts from the town."

Slanski thought for a moment, then said, "When do they leave?"

"Zinov drives back to Leningrad tomorrow morning. Bukarin, the younger one, is staying another couple of days. Why?"

"Maybe there's another way out of this rattrap." Slanski smiled. "You think you could find me an army captain's uniform?"

ZINOV was sitting at the bar when Slanski went in. One of the women, a blonde, sat next to the colonel, nibbling his ear. A bottle of champagne was in front of them, two glasses poured.

Zinov said, "Ah, you're just in time for some champagne."

The colonel's eyes were glazed from alcohol, and as Slanski sat down, he said, "Your wife isn't joining you?"

"Tired, I'm afraid. She decided to have a lie-down."

Zinov grinned crookedly. "My captain friend and his lady had the same problem. Shame. This Crimean champagne is really excellent. Don't just stand there with a dry mouth. Have a drink."

Zinov poured a glass of champagne for Slanski and another for himself. Slanski said, "Actually, sir, I came to ask you a favor."

"Oh, and what's that?"

"I received an urgent call to report back to Leningrad. My unit is setting out for winter training maneuvers tomorrow night."

"Funny. I thought you had a slight look of the army about you. What's your rank and division?"

"Captain. The Seventeenth Armored. I brought my uniform with me, half expecting a call, but not so soon."

"What a shame. Rather upset your honeymoon plans. You want me to try and twist a few ears so you can stay on?"

"Thank you, sir, but I'm anxious to get back. I was really hoping you might be able to oblige us with a lift. Toomas mentioned you were traveling to Leningrad, and I wondered if you had any empty seats in the Emka. But forgive me if I'm speaking out of turn."

Zinov smiled. "Nonsense. A pleasure, and I'd be glad of the company. I have an early start, mind. Seven a.m. Does that suit?"

"Perfectly." Slanski finished his champagne and put down the glass. "My thanks for the drink, Comrade Colonel. Good night."

February 26. It was pitch-dark and freezing as the Emka rattled down the narrow cobbled roads of the old town. Like most small Russian cars, the Emka had no heater, so Zinov had suggested that Anna and Slanski sit in the back seat and use the heavy woolen blanket he kept for passengers to cover their legs.

When he turned left, they all saw the checkpoint ahead.

A group of plainclothes men and uniformed militia manned a temporary red barrier placed across the road between two oil barrels. There were two vehicles in front—a private car and a delivery truck—waiting to be allowed to pass. The militiamen finished searching the first, and it drove through when the barrier was removed.

Zinov eased on the brakes and pulled in behind the truck. He tapped the steering wheel impatiently with his fingers. "I suppose there's not much we can do but wait our turn."

At that moment they heard a vehicle rattle on the cobbles. Slanski saw a green army Zis drive up to the checkpoint from the opposite direction. The car braked to a halt, and a man stepped out. He wore a KGB uniform and a heavy overcoat. Slanski noticed he wore only one leather glove, on his left hand. The KGB man crossed to a uniformed officer at the checkpoint and spoke heatedly with him. The officer barked an order, and the militiamen manning the checkpoint started to work more smartly.

Slanski felt Anna's hand grip his tightly as they watched the scene. He counted twelve militia and army personnel plus the KGB man with the leather glove and his driver. Five agonizing minutes passed, and the truck showed no sign of being allowed through.

Zinov slammed his fist on the steering wheel. "Damn it! At this rate we'll be lucky to make Leningrad by midnight."

Slanski leaned across to Anna. "Get ready to move if we have to run for it," he whispered. "Try to make it back to the inn."

Zinov glanced around suddenly. "You said something?"

Slanski smiled. "Perhaps we should've taken the train, Colonel."

But suddenly it was their turn as the truck was waved through. The barrier came down again as Zinov advanced the Emka, halted, and rolled down his window. A militiaman ran forward.

"Get out of the car and have your papers ready."

Zinov flushed red at the man's bluntness. He flashed his ID. "You're talking to a colonel in the KGB. Watch your manners." He waved at the barrier. "Allow us to pass and be quick about it."

The militiaman looked at Zinov's ID and shook his head. "Everyone's got to be checked and their vehicles searched. So just do as you're told, and we'll get this over with as quickly as possible."

Zinov could hardly contain his anger at the man's impertinence. "Who's in charge here? I want to see him. Now!"

"It won't make any difference, comrade. His name's Major Lukin, KGB Moscow. So in the meantime, step out of the car."

The man named Lukin strode over. "Is there a problem?"

"Look here," said Zinov. "My friends and I are in a hurry. We've got important business in Leningrad."

"I'm afraid no one passes without being checked. There is a

search for enemy agents in progress. Would you all please step out of the car and have your papers ready."

Zinov flushed a deep red, then stepped out and slammed the door after him. As Slanski and Anna slid out from the rear, Lukin showed a sudden interest. "Papers, please, Captain."

Slanski handed them across. For a long time the major looked at Slanski's face, then examined the papers. "And who is this lady?"

"My wife, Major. We've been staying in Tallinn on a short visit."

"And the purpose of your visit to Tallinn, Captain Petrovsky?"

Slanski nodded at Anna. "Our honeymoon, comrade."

"Where were you staying?"

"With a relative of my wife's. Is there a problem, Major?"

"Yes, there is. We're looking for a man and a woman—enemy agents." Lukin looked at Anna. "So you say this lady is your wife?"

Slanski said proudly, "Indeed she is, comrade. We were married three days ago. I can assure you, Major, she is not an enemy agent."

There was a laugh from one of the militiamen standing nearby, but Lukin's expression didn't change. He said evenly, "My congratulations to both of you. May I see your papers also, madam?"

"Of course."

Anna fumbled in her handbag and handed them over. Lukin examined the documents thoroughly. He didn't hand them back, but looked at Slanski and said, "Your destination, Captain Petrovsky?"

"Leningrad. I'm joining my division."

"And which division is that?"

"The Fourteenth Armored."

The major glanced at Slanski's uniform. "Would you mind if we searched your luggage?"

Slanski shrugged. "Of course not."

Zinov came over. "Look, Major, is that really necessary? We're in a hurry. This officer is known personally to me. And also the young lady. I happen to stay frequently with her uncle here in Tallinn."

"Quite. But this won't take long."

A militiaman removed the bags from the car, and Lukin examined both suitcases externally first, running his fingers along the joints. The major looked up. "Open the cases please, Captain."

Slanski did as he was ordered. Lukin knelt and shone a flashlight through the belongings. He examined the clothing and felt the material of each garment. Finally he stood up and studied Slanski again. "You look familiar, Captain. Have we met before?"

"I can't say we have, Major."

"Did you serve during the war?"

"With the Fifth Kursk Infantry."

"Really? You knew Colonel Kinyatin?"

Slanski shook his head. "I was only with the Kursk for three months before I was transferred. I'm afraid I never heard of him."

Zinov interrupted again. "Really, Major, the poor fellow and his wife have had their honeymoon plans upset as it is. You can see he's a genuine officer. Are you going to make a fool of yourself and arrest him or are we all to just stand here and freeze to death?"

Lukin hesitated for a long time, then slowly handed back the two sets of papers. "My apologies for the delay. You may proceed."

They all climbed back into the car. The Emka moved off, rattling over the cobbles, Zinov muttering angrily to himself.

IT WAS just before nine a.m. when Lukin returned to the Tondy barracks. Kaman was waiting with a sheaf of papers. "Some more reports for you, Major. Still definitely no sign of the man and woman, I'm afraid. You think at this stage we're wasting our time?"

Lukin fixed him with a stare. "On the contrary. I want the operation continued and expanded. Every house, inn, and shop in the town is to be thoroughly searched."

"Yes, Major." Kaman saluted and left, closing the door.

Lukin ran his hand through his hair in exasperation. The roadblocks and checkpoints and the checking of the hotel registers should have yielded something.

He thought of the captain and his wife at the checkpoint. He was sure he had seen the man's face somewhere before. But where?

The captain's wife was attractive but hardly beautiful. Her makeup had spoiled her face. A little too heavy. Maybe it was deliberate? The man had said they were on their honeymoon. She should have been happy. She didn't look happy, just anxious.

He should've checked their story. He picked up the photographs of the woman and the man known as the Wolf. He looked down at them for a long time. The Wolf's picture was really too blurred to be useful and had been taken from too great a distance. Another thing kept bothering Lukin—the fact that there were two pages missing from the man's file. Perhaps Beria had his reasons for withholding the pages, but Lukin felt somehow less than trusted.

He picked up the phone and quickly dialed Kaman's extension.

"Lukin here. I want a Captain Oleg Petrovsky checked out. See if he's with the Fourteenth Armored at Leningrad. I want details from his personal file. Background, marriage, and so on."

Kaman said, "Who is he?"

"Never mind that for now; just do it. And phone the local air force commander and have a helicopter stand by in case I need it."

Chapter Eight

THEY took the main highway to Kivioli. Once past the town, they followed the coast road to Leningrad. It was clogged with military traffic, and Zinov had to drive slowly.

"Good to see Stalin still likes to let the Balts know that we're in business," he commented, then said casually, "I must say, that major back in Tallinn seemed very uncertain about you."

Slanski smiled. "I must have a suspicious face, Colonel."

Zinov laughed. "Well, if you're enemy agents you've certainly picked the wrong traveling companion in a KGB colonel."

After another hour the traffic cleared, and Zinov made up for lost time. When they passed the town of Narva, he suggested they stop and stretch their legs before they continued on to Leningrad.

Slanski glanced at Anna. The major at the checkpoint had made them uneasy. He said to Zinov, "Perhaps we ought to press on?"

"Nonsense. We've plenty of time. We'll be in Leningrad in under two hours. There's a perfect spot ahead."

The winter morning was still dark as Zinov turned off the highway and drove along a forest road. After a hundred yards they dipped over a rise and came out in a clearing beside a frozen lake. The view was really rather beautiful, the birch trees along the shoreline sugared prettily with snow.

Zinov climbed out and said to Slanski, "Splendid, isn't it? Get the vodka and food, man; it's in the trunk. There's some smoked eel and bread I bought in Tallinn. I'm sure your wife's hungry."

Slanski went around to the trunk and removed a picnic basket. As he turned back, he heard a small cry from Anna and saw Zinov grab her savagely by the hair, his pistol pointed at her head.

"Put your hands in the air," he ordered Slanski. "Undo your pistol belt very slowly. And I mean slowly. Then throw it over here."

"What's going on? Is this some kind of joke?"

Zinov's eyes narrowed suspiciously. "Something's not right with you two. That major in Tallinn was right. You're enemy agents."

"Colonel, this is nonsense," Slanski said reasonably. "Our papers were in order. Put the gun away. You're making my wife nervous."

Zinov said sharply, "Shut up. Last night you told me you were with the Seventeenth Armored. But you told the major at the checkpoint you were with the Fourteenth. Perhaps you'd care to explain?"

"A mistake. I don't know what I was thinking of." Slanski shifted his stance, ready to move, but he was standing well back, too far to get closer to the colonel.

Zinov aimed the pistol at Slanski. "Now, you're going to tell me who you really are, or I pull this trigger."

"I'm Captain Oleg Petrovsky, Fourteenth Armored Division."

There was a brief look of uncertainty on Zinov's face, and then he said, "You're trying my patience."

Anna said, "Colonel, I think you ought to know the truth."

Slanski went to speak, but Anna interrupted. "No. I have to tell him." She looked at Zinov steadily. "We're not married to each other. My husband is an army officer in Leningrad. This man is who he says he is. But we went to Tallinn to be alone together."

Zinov grinned. "Lovers. You'll have to do better than that."

"In my bag you'll find a photograph of my husband and me."

Zinov hesitated, suddenly unsure. "Get it for me."

Anna moved to the car and found the handbag.

Zinov stepped closer to her and said, "Toss it here."

She threw the bag, and as it landed, Zinov bent to pick it up.

Slanski was already racing across the ground. His foot kicked the gun from the colonel's hand, and his fist smashed into his jaw. Zinov fell back in the snow, blood streaming from his mouth.

Slanski grabbed the weapon and shot the colonel between the eyes. He turned to Anna. "Help me bury the body. Quickly."

It took them five minutes to bury Zinov's body in a shallow grave, digging in the snow with their hands. When they finished, they were soaking wet and their clothes were covered in blood.

Slanski said, "We'd better change. I'll get the suitcases."

She started to strip, and Slanski fetched the suitcases from the trunk. He put on a corduroy suit and cap. When Anna was dressed, he crossed to some bushes and buried their soiled clothes.

"Let's go."

When they reached the car, Slanski looked at her face. It was pale and drawn, and he could see real fear in her eyes. "Anna, what I did was necessary, you know that."

"Yes, I know." She shivered.

"We can be in Leningrad in less than two hours. With luck, no one's going to know Zinov's missing for some time. Come on, let's go. The quicker we're away from here, the better."

He stowed the suitcases in the trunk, and they climbed into the car. He turned on the headlights and lit up the track that led through the woods back to the highway.

A sudden dull chopping noise filled the air high above them, and a powerful beam of light swept through the forest behind, the sound growing louder until it became a deafening thunder.

Suddenly a helicopter reared above the trees, the light from under its fuselage dazzling as it caught them in its beam. A shot rang out, and the Emka's passenger window shattered.

"Hold on!" Slanski frantically started the Emka. It gave a roar, and then it shot forward down the forest track.

LUKIN sat in the freezing dome of the Mil helicopter as his eyes swept the ribbon of highway that snaked below.

They had taken off in the morning darkness from the Tondy barracks an hour before, flying at barely fifty yards above the main Leningrad road. Acres of birch forest ran on either side, coated white.

The news had come back from Leningrad ten minutes after Kaman had made the call. There was no Captain Oleg Petrovsky with the 14th. Lukin's instinct had been right.

By his own calculations the Emka had to be somewhere close ahead. Even traveling at fifty miles an hour, the maximum distance the car could have traveled was a hundred and twenty-five miles.

He looked down at the highway again. Empty. He shouted to the pilot. "Check the minor roads, those that lead into the forest. The car could have pulled in somewhere."

The pilot pointed at the sky and shook his head. "There's going to be snow soon. Besides, there are high-voltage cables off the main highway. In this poor light we could clip one. It's too dangerous."

"Do as I tell you," Lukin commanded.

They were over forest now, and the helicopter's searchlight was on. They had been sweeping along the road for almost ten minutes when the searchlight passed over a narrow road in the forest, and Lukin suddenly picked out the tire tracks of a car.

"Over there!" He pointed, and the pilot saw the marks. As they came sweeping over the lakeshore, Lukin saw the black Emka and his heart skipped. He saw the couple's surprised faces through the car's windshield, frozen in the searchlight—the same couple from the checkpoint. He tore open the small window at the side of the helicopter, aimed his pistol at the car, and fired.

He saw glass shatter on the passenger side, and then suddenly the car lurched forward and sped through the forest.

"After them!" Lukin roared. "Go lower!"

"Major, if we get too close to those treetops—"

"Do it, man!"

The pilot shook his head in exasperation but obeyed the order. The clatter of the blades was deafening. The Mil followed the Emka as it twisted and turned and snaked through the woods.

Lukin's eyes were on the car. He had his Tokarev pointing out the side window, trying to get a clear shot at the driver, but it was impossible. He told the pilot, "Try to keep this thing steady."

"I'm doing my best!"

The Emka slowed, and they overtook it. As the Mil swung around and the pilot tried to settle the searchlight on the car, there was the sound of gunfire, and three holes cracked in the glass above their heads. The Mil lifted, and the Emka started to move again.

They were fifty yards from the highway when Lukin suddenly felt a frightening shuddering.

The pilot screamed, "Oh, my God!"

In horror, Lukin saw an electricity pylon almost dead ahead. The pilot tried to veer away at the last moment, but the blades clipped the electric cables, and there was a powerful blinding flash.

The Mil yawed into the massive pylon. The noise of the blades died abruptly, and the helicopter sank in a burst of flame.

Leningrad. The tram halted on Nevsky Prospect, and Anna and Slanski climbed down. It was early afternoon, and traffic clogged Leningrad's broad main street. Slanski took Anna's hand as they walked along the crowded avenue. It had started to snow.

They had abandoned the Emka in a suburb six miles away, taking a bus to the edge of the city and then one of the yellow city trams the rest of the way. Within half an hour they were in the center of Leningrad. When they reached the corner opposite the main railway station, Slanski found a telephone box and dialed a number.

THE thin-faced man placed three tumblers of vodka on the shabby table. "Drink up. You're going to need it."

Vladimir Rykov was a Ukrainian nationalist. He had met the couple near the Winter Palace an hour after they phoned him and brought them back to his home, a filthy two-room tenement.

"What's the problem?" asked Slanski.

"Everything you've told me suggests a problem," Vladimir said. "Number one, both the KGB and the militia are going to be looking for you. Number two, whatever route you take is going to be difficult."

"We have to get to Moscow somehow," Slanski said.

"Easier said than done. By rail there's the overnight express between Leningrad and Moscow, but the railway station will probably be watched. Flying's the quickest way, but you'd have to wait a couple of days to get tickets, and that's if you're lucky. No doubt the KGB and militia will be watching the airport too."

"What about traveling by bus?"

Vladimir shook his head. "There's a bus service, of course, but no direct one to Moscow. The journey could take days."

Anna said to Vladimir, "There must be some other way."

Vladimir grinned. "Maybe." He thought a moment, then looked at them. "I've got an idea. It may work. Come, I'll show you."

Rykov headed toward the door, and Slanski and Anna followed him outside to a storage room at the end of a courtyard. The room was packed with ancient rotting furniture. In a corner stood a German army BMW dispatch rider's motorcycle. The bike's gray paint-work had been repainted dark green, and the tires were broad and deeply grooved. Rykov ran a hand lovingly over the leather saddle.

"I could say a lot against the Germans, but the bastards still made the best motorcycles." He wheeled the BMW out into the center of the room and said to Slanski, "You've ridden before?"

"Never. But I could learn quickly."

"On Russian roads? You may as well put a gun to your head and pull the trigger. Here, you'd better start it and try it for size."

Slanski climbed onto the machine. He found the kick starter, flicked it out, gave it a blow with his foot, and the machine started the first time. A steady reassuring throb filled the storeroom.

Rykov smiled. "Well, what do you think?"

"Considering we don't have many options, it's worth a try."

Estonia. Lukin woke, shivering in the poor light. There was frost on his clothes and face. Cold bit into his flesh and bones like fire.

As he lay there in the snow, he became aware of a strong smell of kerosene fuel mixed with an acrid, sugary stench. Burning human flesh. He craned his neck to look around and felt a pain shoot down his left arm. He looked down on his body. He saw that his false hand had been sheared off, and that he was propped up against a fallen tree trunk.

There was a tangle of hissing metal nearby, steam rising from the wreckage of the Mil. The forest had not caught fire, but there was a small blaze in what remained of the cockpit. He saw the charred body of the pilot lying half in and half out of the wreckage.

Lukin winced. The man was dead, and it was his fault. He had been too intent on stopping Slanski and the woman from escaping. But they had escaped. So close. He had been so close.

He heard a sound, like an animal cry.

He had heard that cry before, in childhood. He and his brother as small boys playing in a field near their father's house one winter's evening. His father off in the distance by the house, chopping wood, looking up, waving at them.

And then the noise had startled them. When they looked around, they saw two pairs of piercing yellow eyes staring at them from the trees. Two white wolves. Snow wolves.

Lukin had screamed in fright and run back to his father as the man raced toward him. He swept him up in his arms.

"Wolves, Papa!" Lukin had screamed.

"Bah! He's afraid of everything," his brother, Mischa, protested.

His father said, "Wolves don't kill humans. Not unless they're threatened. Remember that. Now, come, Mama has supper ready."

And what had happened afterward? He tried to think, but a fog rolled in. He remembered so little of that time before Mischa died. Proud and brave Mischa. He blinked and pushed the fleeting memories from his mind. Now was important, not the past.

He focused on the wreckage and the half-burned corpse of the pilot. Maybe the wolves had smelled the human flesh.

He tried to push that prospect from his mind. The fire was still dying, the embers smoldering. If he could get closer to the fire for heat, maybe he could thaw out his bones. Slowly he dragged himself over to the fire. The heat from the embers was like a balm.

The shock had gone now, replaced by anger. Somehow he had to get down to the highway. If he could alert the militia in the nearest town, he could still catch the man and woman.

He felt his legs start to warm. He hauled himself up, ignoring the pain burning through his arm. He looked toward the highway. Headlights flickered through the trees as a convoy trundled past.

He stumbled through the forest, his lungs on fire with the effort. It took him over ten minutes to reach the edge of the highway.

It was deserted. Lukin swore, breathless.

Suddenly a pair of headlights appeared up ahead as a truck came around a bend and loomed at him. Lukin stumbled into the middle of the road and waved.

Leningrad. It was after five p.m. and dark outside when Slanski climbed on the BMW in the middle of the storeroom. He pulled on the helmet and goggles and heavy winter coat that Vladimir had given him. Anna wore two sets of clothes under her coat to keep out the cold, and their small suitcases were strapped to the carrier at the rear. She climbed on and put her arms around Slanski's waist.

He nodded to Vladimir, who stood by the door. "Ready when you are." Slanski kicked the starter arm, and the BMW came to life, the engine purring solidly under them.

Vladimir opened the door and went into the street, looking left and right to check that there were no militia about, before signaling for them to move out. He slapped Anna on the shoulder. "Go. And may the devil ride with you both."

The BMW roared off into the night. Slanski had ridden around the yard for half an hour that afternoon to get the feel of the machine. With Vladimir's instructions he learned how to change gears and operate the various switches on the handlebars.

Vladimir had suggested they avoid the main roads out of the city. There were many minor roads through hilly uninhabited forest they could take. With luck they would be in Moscow in twelve hours.

A FEMALE doctor dressed Lukin's arm.

They were in a large room on the second floor of the red brick building that housed KGB headquarters in Leningrad.

The doctor gave him a mild shot of morphine. Then she basted a green ointment onto his stump to ease the pain, and after dressing the wound, she pinned back the sleeve of his tunic.

Suddenly the door burst open and Colonel Romulka appeared, wearing an overcoat slung loosely over his shoulders, a swagger cane in his leather-gloved hand. "There you are, Lukin. The adjutant told me I'd find you here. Still alive after your mishap, I see." He jerked his thumb at the doctor and said, "You—get out."

The woman took one look at Romulka's frightening presence in the black uniform, packed up her black bag, and scurried out.

Romulka pulled up a chair and sat. "I've spoken with a colonel here at headquarters. The militia just found the couple's car in Udelnay." He glanced at Lukin's arm. "Tell me what happened."

Lukin told him. When he had finished, Romulka grinned maliciously. "Not a very promising start, was it, Lukin? You let the couple slip from your grasp. Comrade Beria won't like that."

Lukin said shortly, "Why are you here?"

"This case is my responsibility too, or had you forgotten?" Romulka stood, towering above Lukin. "I have a personal interest in this case. The woman especially." He tapped Lukin's chest with his stick. "As soon as she's caught, I want to interrogate her."

"And in case you've forgotten, I'm in charge. If she's caught alive, I decide who interrogates her."

Romulka's eyes narrowed in an icy glare. "I suggest you don't cross me, Lukin. Life wouldn't be worth living."

Lukin nodded toward the door. "I'm busy, Romulka. Is there anything else you wish to say before you leave?"

Romulka grinned. "Actually there is. Another aspect to the investigation you ought to know about. Unfortunately, I won't be remaining in Leningrad. I have other pressing matters to attend to."

"What matters?"

"It struck me the Americans will need someone in Moscow to help them. Possibly to aid their escape once the deed is done."

Romulka removed a sheet of paper from his pocket and handed it across. "This is a list of foreigners who because of important business interests vital to the state are allowed to come and go in Moscow virtually unchecked. One name on the list particularly interests me. A man named Henri Lebel. A French fur dealer. During the war he was a member of the communist resistance in Paris and had connections to the man named Massey, who was involved in organizing the American mission."

"What do you intend?"

Romulka smirked. "To question him—discreetly."

Lukin thought for a moment and nodded. "Very well. But I suggest you proceed with this cautiously. No doubt Lebel has important connections in Moscow, and we don't want any embarrassment."

Romulka took the list and slipped it back into his pocket. "Whether you agree or not, Lukin, the matter of this Frenchman is my responsibility. It's already been agreed to by Beria. Besides, I have a feeling about Lebel. I assure you I won't be proven wrong."

Romulka turned toward the door. "One more thing, Lukin. I meant what I said about the woman. Do keep up the good work."

He laughed as he went through the doorway just as the adjutant came in, almost knocking the young officer over.

The startled adjutant said to Lukin, "A friend of yours, sir?"

"Hardly. Well, have you any news?"

"Nothing from any of the checkpoints. We're scouring the neighborhood where the car was found, but so far no one has seen anything. Our patrol recovered the body of the pilot in the woods, also the missing colonel. He was buried nearby."

Lukin sighed. "What about the hotels?"

"Most have been checked. So far no persons remotely resembling the ones we're looking for have been found."

Lukin crossed to a map on the wall. The adjutant followed.

"We've also drafted in another two thousand men, Major. The pins on the map indicate where we've set up checkpoints. Now all we have to do is wait until something turns up."

AS THEY came around a bend in the road, Slanski saw a string of red taillights up ahead. Two covered jeeps stood in their path. An army sergeant with a Kalashnikov and a militiaman wielding a rifle stood next to one of the jeeps. Another militiaman, sitting in the front seat, was manning a portable radio, his rifle resting across his knees. The officer in charge was nearby, casually smoking a cigarette.

As Slanski brought the BMW to a halt, the officer came forward and flashed a light in their faces. "Well, what have we got here? Two lovers out for a ride in the country?"

The men and the sergeant laughed, but Slanski said calmly, "What's the problem, comrade?"

The officer looked at the motorcycle, then Anna.

He said to Slanski, "Papers, both of you."

They handed over their papers. The officer shone the flashlight from the papers to their faces. "Your destination?" he said.

"Novgorod," replied Slanski.

"That's a long drive on a cold night like this. Your purpose?"

Slanski jerked a thumb back at Anna. "My wife's mother is unwell. They don't think the old woman is going to make it through the night. My wife needs to see her before it's too late."

"Where have you come from?"

"Leningrad. What's going on tonight? This is the second time we've been stopped on this road."

The officer handed back the papers. Slanski's reply seemed to ease his tension, but then he stepped closer and said to Anna, "Where was the last checkpoint where you and your husband were stopped?"

The question hung in the air like a threat. Anna hesitated. "Two miles back. There was a car and two militiamen."

The officer's eyebrows rose. "We drove that way not half an hour ago. There wasn't a checkpoint." He turned to the militiaman manning the radio in the jeep. "Kashinsky, call up central exchange. Ask them if they have a checkpoint where the woman says. If there's a checkpoint there, then we're wasting our time hanging about here."

The militiaman in the jeep was talking on the radio, but Slanski couldn't hear the words, just a babble of static and crackle.

Finally the man in the jeep climbed out with his rifle. "She's lying! There's no checkpoint on that part of the road!"

It happened quickly. As the officer went for his pistol and the other men raised their weapons, Slanski flicked the switch on the handlebar and the headlight blazed into the darkness, blinding the men for an instant. He wrenched the Tokarev from his coat and shot the officer in the chest, then fired twice at the sergeant.

He fired two quick shots at the two young militiamen as they scurried for cover behind the jeep; then he screamed back at Anna, "Hold on tight!"

He kicked the starter, and the BMW revved wildly and roared forward. He tore between a narrow gap in the jeeps.

LUKIN was sitting at a table in the staff canteen, eating a plateful of cabbage and pickled beef and potatoes, when the adjutant burst in through the swing door and strode over, carrying a map.

"Some news just in. A militia mobile patrol stopped a man and woman on a BMW, who resembled the ones we're looking for. When the couple were challenged, the man produced a gun and killed two officers. The other two militiamen managed to raise the alarm. Right now they're pursuing the culprits in a jeep."

Lukin grabbed the map and spread it on the table. "Show me where."

The adjutant pointed to a spot on the map. "Here. By car maybe half an hour away. I've alerted six patrols in the area."

Lukin jumped to his feet. "Get a car, and have two motorcycle outriders ready."

SLANSKI was doing sixty, taking corners as fast as he dared, skidding dangerously each time he tore around bends.

Anna shouted, "Slow down, or you'll kill us both!"

"Those two militia are going to radio in what happened," Slanski roared back. "We have to get away from here fast."

At the next bend he looked back and saw a blaze of headlights approaching at speed behind them on the road. Across the road, twenty yards away, was an open gate leading into a field covered in snow. It led down a long slope into darkness.

The convoy was almost on top of them as Slanski drove toward the gate. Suddenly there were blasts of gunfire and bullets kicking up snow as voices barked orders and vehicles screeched to a halt.

Slanski revved the engine, and they tore through the gate into the field and down the slope.

THE siren screamed into the night as the Zis ate up the road.

They had already covered twenty miles in twenty minutes, the two militia motorbike riders on either side of the car racing ahead every now and then to clear traffic in the way.

Suddenly Lukin saw headlights up ahead, half a dozen vehicles cramming the narrow road, uniformed men milling about.

Lukin's car halted. He climbed out and ran up to a captain who looked in charge.

The captain saluted. "They got away, sir. The crazy bastards drove into a forest down below. I've sent a dozen men down after them, but we haven't got suitable transport to pursue."

Lukin noticed that a gate into a field was open, a single tire mark cutting down the starched white slope. He saw figures at the bottom with flashlights. Lukin turned back to the captain. "Make sure all roads leading out of there are blocked off. And inform any patrols going into the area that I'm on my way down." Lukin ran back to the two motorcycle riders, who had dismounted. He grabbed one of the machines, climbed on and kicked it into life.

As the startled rider protested, Lukin roared, "Out of my way!"

The captain looked at Lukin doubtfully as he sat on the machine with only one good hand. "Sir, it might be better if you waited. Going after those two alone is only begging for trouble. Besides—"

"Besides what? I'm a cripple? The advantage of one good arm, Captain, is that it soon gains the strength of two. Out of my way!"

The machine roared, and the captain jumped back as Lukin drove through the gate and down the slope.

SLANSKI was lost. The forest was a maze of narrow paths, and in the darkness it was impossible to guess which led where. Suddenly the road widened, and a wooden sign before a bend up ahead said CAUTION—EXIT TO KOLIMKA ROAD. TRAFFIC AHEAD.

As he came around the bend, he braked hard and skidded to a halt. Half a dozen jeeps and a line of soldiers stood across the road. A voice called out, "Halt and throw down your weapons!"

As Slanski tore back the way they had come, there was a terrible volley of fire that exploded through the forest, lead zinging through the air and cracking all around them.

IT WAS almost impossible. Lukin had to use his feet for balance, finding it hard to control the machine with one hand. He halted on the bumpy lane that led through the woods.

He had followed the tire marks through the forest, but now he switched off the engine, listening for the sound of another vehicle. All he heard was his own heart, thumping in his ears.

And then—a thunderous volley of gunfire erupted somewhere close. He started the motorbike and drove toward the noise. He had gone only fifty yards when he saw a single headlight flashing through the trees, coming toward him. He pulled off the road.

The BMW roared past, and he saw the man and woman.

He shifted into gear and drove after them.

He was twenty yards behind the BMW when the woman looked back. Lukin saw her face in the beam from his headlight, her mouth open in fear and surprise. The BMW suddenly picked up speed, racing dangerously fast over the rough path.

As it rounded a corner in the forest, Lukin saw a line of head-lights—army trucks and jeeps straddling the road a hundred yards ahead as another roadblock obstructed the way.

The BMW swung a hard right to avoid it, roaring up a bank lead-ing into trees. Its rider put on a burst of power and growled up the rise, but just before he reached the top, the BMW seemed to stall, bucking like a horse unwilling to jump the final fence.

The woman was thrown off, hit the earth hard, and rolled back down. Lukin stopped his machine and raced toward her.

Up on the top of the rise he saw the driver fighting hard to con-trol the machine, until it nosed down and the tires gripped, and then it was safely at the top. The driver looked back down in hor-ror as the woman's body rolled to a halt at the bottom of the bank.

There was a moment of indecision, then a scream of despair. "Anna!"

Soldiers ran forward, climbing the rise after the BMW and firing, but the man turned and sped away into the darkness.

The woman was trying to put something into her mouth. Lukin lunged at her, landing on her so hard she cried out in pain. He shoved his fingers into her throat.

Chapter Nine

Paris. It was just before ten that same evening when a sleek black Citroën pulled up on the Boulevard Montmartre and Henri Lebel climbed out. "You can go now, Charles," Lebel said. "Pick me up from Maxim's at midnight."

"Very good, sir."

Lebel watched the Citroën disappear before he crossed the boulevard and turned down a narrow alleyway. At the end of the lane he came to a blue door on the right. Lebel knocked.

A grille opened, and a man's face appeared. "*Oui?*"

"I'm expected."

There was a rattle of bolts, and the man admitted the visitor.

Lebel went down a winding metal staircase to a packed, smoky room, the tables occupied by tough-looking workingmen drinking beer and cheap wine. He walked through a curtain behind the bar, then went to a door at the end of a shabby hallway and knocked.

"Come in if you're good-looking," a voice said.

Lebel opened the door and stepped into a tiny room with a single lightbulb dangling low in the center; the rest of the room was in shadows. A small, wiry man in his middle thirties sat at a table. He gestured to a chair. "Henri, always good to see you."

Lebel sat. "Unfortunately, Bastien, I wish I could say the same."

"As always, the diplomat." Pierre Bastien smiled. "You're looking well, Henri. Business is good?"

"I presume you didn't ask me here to discuss such a repulsive subject as my moneymaking, so perhaps you'd better get to the point. What is it this time? Another contribution to the party?"

Bastien said, "Actually, just a friendly talk, Lebel. There's someone I'd like you to meet. You can come in now, Colonel."

A door opened somewhere in the shadows, and a man appeared. Bastien said, "Colonel Romulka, KGB Moscow, meet Henri Lebel. Colonel Romulka here tells me you were due to travel to Moscow in two days' time. He wants to get you there a little earlier."

Lebel said palely, "What's going on here?"

Romulka snapped his fingers, and two men appeared from behind the door. They grabbed Lebel and rolled up one of his sleeves, and Romulka came forward and jabbed a hypodermic into his arm.

Washington, D.C. Rain streaked against the Oval Office French windows, and a flash of lightning lit up the black evening sky.

Eisenhower sighed as he sat down heavily at his desk and looked at the three other men in the room. "Let me get this straight. You're telling me now it's impossible to stop this thing?"

Allen Dulles, the head of the CIA, sat near the President; Karl Branigan and Jake Massey were in front of the walnut desk.

Branigan sat forward in his chair. "I'm afraid it looks bad, Mr. President. As Massey explained, the only way we could get word to Slanski in Moscow was through Lebel. We had our Paris desk try to contact him, but he couldn't be found. Lebel's chauffeur claims he was to pick him up from Maxim's club at midnight Paris time. Our men were waiting for him at the club, but Lebel never turned up. Our Paris desk monitored an unscheduled Soviet diplomatic flight leaving from Le Bourget airport with a flight plan for Moscow. There were several passengers bundled on board just before take-off, one of them on a stretcher and accompanied by a doctor. According to the French, the Soviets claimed he was a member of their embassy staff being taken to Moscow for urgent medical treatment. However, we now suspect the man on the stretcher may have been Lebel. Which leads me to believe Moscow has figured out his connection to Massey, and they want to interrogate him."

Eisenhower rubbed his eyes. "It gets worse by the hour."

"Mr. President, taking Lebel to Moscow suggests he hasn't already cooperated. But no matter what we order Slanski to do at this stage, I'm convinced he'd ignore our command."

Eisenhower looked up. "Even a direct command from me?"

"Even a direct command from you, sir, if it were possible to relay one to him."

Eisenhower sighed again and turned in his chair. "Mr. Massey, what's your opinion about this Lebel? Do you think he'll break easily under interrogation?"

"Lebel was in a concentration camp during the war, so he's been through the ordeal before. He'll hold out as long as he can, but I wouldn't expect that to be more than a couple of days."

Allen Dulles said, "It strikes me that if Lebel can be counted on to hold out, that gives us time and maybe a way out of this mess."

"How?" asked Eisenhower.

"We kill Slanski and Khorev. Callous as it sounds, it's about the only solution I can think of."

There was silence in the room. Massey said with feeling, "We're talking about two people risking their lives for us. Two people who had the guts to carry out this operation, and you want to kill them?"

Dulles fixed Massey with a stare. "This isn't a perfect world, Jake. It's the only solution I can think of, and maybe the only shot we've got left." He looked at the President. "Branigan and I have been doing a little homework, trying to figure this thing out. We have two agents in Moscow we think could help. Former Ukrainian SS."

"So what are you proposing?" Eisenhower asked.

"We're due to send a message to these men tomorrow night. We could tell them about the man and woman we want located. Massey has told us about Lebel's lady friend in Moscow. She's got a dacha Slanski's going to use as a safe house. If Slanski and the woman show up there, well, I think you can guess the rest. But we'll need someone in place in Moscow to make sure the plan is carried out."

"But how do we get someone to Moscow?"

Dulles said, "We're working on it, Mr. President. Mossad, the Israeli intelligence service, seems the most likely bet. They've got contacts in Russia and Eastern Europe, and they have a number of agents in Moscow in the KGB and the Soviet military."

"You really think it could work?" said the President.

Dulles said, "It's going to be risky and difficult, sir. And it needs to be done with great speed but also with great care. Me, I think it's a chance we've got to take. But I believe Jake's the one to answer that question. He sent each of these people in."

All faces turned to Massey. He thought for a moment, then said flatly, "I don't want any part of this."

Eisenhower flared. "The question I asked was, can it work? And let's not forget why we're here, Massey. You're partly responsible for what's happened. Answer the question."

Massey sighed. "Maybe. But it's only an outside chance. Slanski's the best man we ever trained. Killing him won't be easy."

"But even if there's just a slim chance, we've got to take it. There's only one man who can identify Slanski and the woman and stop them. And that's you. I know you don't want to kill them, but you and I both know why you have to. Make no mistake. If we fail to stop this thing, there will be war. Don't save two lives when you may lose millions." Eisenhower looked into Massey's eyes. "I'm asking you, Jake, don't let your country or me down on this one."

Dzerzhinsky Square, Moscow, February 27. When Anna opened her eyes, she was slumped on a chair in a room with black steel bars on the window. She guessed she was in a prison, but she had no idea where or how she had got there.

The room was bare and functional. Green walls and a wooden table and two chairs facing each other. The metal door in the far wall had a small grille and a tiny peephole.

Anna felt sick with fear, and when she tried to move her arm, she felt a sharp pain stab through her shoulder. Maybe it had been dislocated when the KGB major threw himself on top of her in the forest.

She pushed herself painfully from the chair and went to the window. There was a large cobbled courtyard below. She counted seven floors on the opposite side of the building, and there were bars on all the windows. Her heart sank. As she turned away from the window, the door opened suddenly.

The KGB major stood there with a manila file under his arm. He put the folder on the table.

"How are you feeling?"

His voice was soft, inquiring, and when she didn't reply, he pulled up the chair opposite and sat. "Please, sit down. Cigarette?"

Again Anna didn't reply. He lit a cigarette for himself and glanced at her shoulder. "My fault, I'm afraid. You've got a nasty dislocation a physician had to reset. It's going to take a couple of days before the pain goes away. Sit down, please."

She sat facing him.

"My name is Major Yuri Lukin. I'm sorry you were hurt. Can I get you something? Tea? Coffee? Water? Some food?"

"I'm not hungry or thirsty."

"That's impossible. You haven't eaten or drunk anything in almost twelve hours. If you think accepting my offer would seem like a sign of weakness, you're being foolish, I assure you."

When she didn't reply, Lukin sighed and stood up. "I know what you're feeling, Anna. Fear. Anxiety. Confusion." He took the cyanide pill from his breast pocket and held it up. "I managed to stop you crushing it just in time."

She turned her face away. "How long have I been here?"

"You were flown in late last night by military transport." He opened the file on the table and flicked through the pages. "I've been studying your file. You've had quite a life, Anna Khorev. A lot of pain. A lot of grief. So many tragedies."

Anna looked at Lukin in amazement. "How—how do you know who I am?"

"We've known you were involved in this for a long time. Even before you landed on Soviet soil. You and Slanski both. Anna, if you tell me everything you know, it will be easier on both of us."

She looked at him steadily. "I have nothing to tell you."

"Anna, there are people here who could make you talk. People who would take pleasure in hurting you. Take pleasure in hearing your screams. I am not one of those people. But if you don't talk to me, they will make you talk. Please believe that."

Anna didn't reply.

Lukin said, "I know Slanski came to kill Stalin."

She looked up at Lukin suddenly, her face deathly white.

Lukin looked at her. "I believe you were simply used by the Americans to help him get to Moscow—to pretend to be his wife to avoid arousing suspicion. But Slanski's mission has already failed. Last night he escaped, but he can't have gone far. One of our patrols will hunt him down. In the meantime, you may as well help me by telling me who your contacts were in Estonia. Who were meant to be your contacts in Moscow. Answer these questions, and I can help you by pleading for mercy when your case comes to trial."

There was a look of resignation on her face, and she didn't reply.

Lukin said quietly, "Anna, you're being very brave or very obstinate." He picked up the folder. "I'm going to give you a little time to reconsider. For your sake I hope you will talk to me rather than the others."

He crossed the room and went to the door. It clanged shut. Only when she heard his footsteps fade beyond the door did she bury her face in her hands.

AT TWO o'clock Lukin drove through the main gates of the Kremlin and parked in the Armory courtyard. Five minutes later he was ushered into Beria's sumptuous office by a guards captain. Beria sat behind his desk, and he looked up as Lukin entered.

"Major, sit down. I believe congratulations of a sort are in order."

"Thank you, comrade." Lukin pulled up a chair.

Beria frowned. "But you let the man slip from your grasp. Not good at all. You disappoint me, Lukin. Has the woman talked?"

"Not yet, comrade. It will take a little time. She was injured, as my report explains—"

"I read the report," Beria interrupted sharply. "You failed to capture the American not once, not twice, but three times. I expected more from you, Lukin."

"I can assure you, I'll find him, Comrade Beria."

"To do that, you must have some idea where he is. Do you?"

Lukin hesitated. "I believe he's still in the forest, hiding out. There are over a thousand men searching the area as we speak. I've also requested roadblocks on all roads in the area. It's only a matter of time before the Wolf turns up, dead or alive."

"I hope that's so, Lukin. For your sake." Beria fingered a pen on his desk, the slim fingers playing with it a moment. Then he said, "But so far you haven't exactly inspired confidence. Perhaps I should interrogate the woman myself? I think it's time to take off the gloves, don't you? A little violence to soften her."

Lukin looked at him. "With respect, I don't believe simple torture is going to work in her case. I don't believe she'll respond to it. I need just a little time to gain her trust and confidence. The best way to do that is to deal with her alone. Just me and her."

Beria sighed. "Very well. I'll give you forty-eight hours to make her talk and to find the man. After that, if you haven't succeeded, Romulka will deal with her. That is all. You're dismissed."

When Lukin hesitated, Beria stared at him. "What's the matter?"

"I have a request to make."

"And what request is that?"

"I couldn't fail to notice there were two pages missing from the Wolf's file. I'm certain Comrade Beria had good reason not to include those pages in my copy. However, it strikes me that all information concerning the Wolf should be made available to me. It may help me apprehend him."

Beria half smiled. "You're quite right about the pages, Lukin. But believe me, you have all the information relevant to your mission. Your request is denied. You may leave."

IRENA Dezov's dacha was in the Ramenki District, five miles from Moscow. Slanski got off the bus two stops early and walked the last five minutes down a secluded birch-lined road until he found the address. Disheveled and unshaven and covered in grime, he still wore the coat Vladimir Rykov had given him. But he had abandoned the motorbike in a remote woods outside the suburb of Tatarovo, buried Anna's and his own suitcase, then walked half a mile to the nearest train station. The fear of what might have happened to Anna depressed him. Was she still alive? Had Lukin caught her? He hoped for her sake she had bitten the pill, even though that thought made him more despondent.

The dacha was big, two story, and painted green. It was set in its own large grounds. There were several other dachas nearby, but judging by the shuttered windows, they were deserted.

He watched the place for five minutes. Because of everything that had happened, he was two days early, and he wondered if the woman was at home. He decided to risk knocking on the front door.

He walked up the narrow pathway and knocked hard. Moments later the door opened and a woman appeared. "Madame Dezov?"

She looked at him cautiously. "Yes."

"I'm a friend of Henri's. You were expecting me."

The woman went visibly pale. "Come inside."

She led him into a large kitchen at the back. "You're early. And there were supposed to be two of you, a man and a woman."

"I'm afraid there was a problem. My friend didn't make it."

The woman said hesitantly, "What happened?"

Slanski told her, but didn't go into details. He saw the fear on her face and said, "Don't worry; she knew nothing about you."

He looked at the woman and noticed the concentration camp numbers tattooed in blue ink on her wrist. Then he saw a framed photograph on the wall. It showed a man in a colonel's uniform.

"Who's that?"

"My husband, Viktor. He was killed during the war."

"I'm sorry."

The woman laughed. "Don't be. The man was a pig. I only keep his picture there to remind myself how lucky I am without him. Are you hungry?"

"Starving."

"Sit down. I'll make you something."

She cut several thick slices of bread and goat's cheese. As Slanski ate ravenously, she poured them each a glass of vodka.

"You look like you've been to hell and back."

"I guess that's close enough."

"Eat and drink some more. Then I'll heat some water for you to wash and shave. You smell worse than a cattle train. There's some old things of Viktor's somewhere that should fit you."

"If the KGB took my friend to Moscow, where would they have taken her?"

The woman shrugged at the question. "Most likely the Lubyanka prison, because it's part of KGB headquarters. Why?"

Slanski didn't reply. Instead, he said, "You're certain I'm safe here? What about the neighbors?"

"Perfectly safe. Most of the dachas around here are never used in winter. They're owned by army officers and party officials."

"I'll need transport."

"There's an old Skoda under a tarpaulin in the shed," the woman said. "Viktor brought it back from Poland in '41. The car still works perfectly well, and the tank's full."

"Can you show me around Moscow?"

"Will it be dangerous?"

"I doubt it. Just a nice leisurely drive to help me get my bearings."

THE small park off Marx Prospect was empty that afternoon. With its ponds and landscaped gardens and wooden pavilions, the park had once been a favorite haunt of Czar Nicholas. But then the KGB had decided to acquire it for their own private use. Tall birch trees protected it from the eyes of passersby, and the wrought-iron gate was constantly guarded by an armed militiaman.

Lukin was sitting in the BMW in front of the gate when he saw the Emka pull up. Two plainclothes KGB men climbed out of the back. Anna Khorev was handcuffed to one of them.

Lukin climbed out of the BMW and crossed to the men. "You can take off the handcuffs. That'll be all."

When the handcuffs had been removed, the two men left. Lukin nodded to the militiaman to open the gate, then looked at Anna. "Come, let's walk."

Silver birch trees lined the narrow walks, and the place was peaceful apart from the faint hum of traffic.

"Why have I been brought here?" she asked.

"Anna, my job is to find Slanski dead or alive. You're the only one who can help me find him. I told you I'd give you time to consider your situation. But I have to tell you, my superiors are becoming impatient. They want answers, and they want them fast. If I can't get you to talk, then they'll use someone who will."

"You're wasting your time. I told you already. I can't help you."

"You know what will happen to you if you refuse to talk. But there may be a future for you if you help me."

"You know I won't be set free."

"True, but any alternative to death is a welcome one. If you help me, I'll ask the court prosecutor to consider penal servitude in the gulag instead of a death sentence."

Anna asked, "Have you ever been in the gulag, Major Lukin?"

"No."

"Then you've never seen what goes on there. I think if you did, you'd know that death is a better alternative. I can't tell you what you want to know, because I really don't know where Slanski might be. As for those who helped us, they too knew nothing of Slanski's plans. To tell you their names wouldn't help you find Slanski, but simply expose them to suffering and death."

Lukin saw the angry defiance on her face. "I'm sorry it's come to this. I admire your bravery, but I think you're being foolish. Yet whatever your decision, I want you to have this moment."

She frowned. "What do you mean?"

Lukin nodded to the militiaman at the gate. A moment later a little girl appeared, clutching his hand. She was very pretty. She wore a red coat and a woolen hat and gloves and tiny brown boots. Anna Khorev's cry shattered the silence of the park. "*Sasha!*"

The little girl started at the sound of her name. She stared over at her mother uncertainly; then her lips trembled, and she began to cry.

Anna ran to her daughter and swept her up. She smothered her in kisses, touched her face and stroked her hair, washed away all the confusion the child felt, until finally the little girl had stopped crying and held her mother tightly.

Lukin stood there watching until he could bear it no longer. He looked at Anna. "You have an hour. Then we talk again."

SLANSKI stared out beyond the Skoda's windshield as Irena drove. Moscow's broad boulevards were jammed with yellow trolley buses and covered trucks. Droves of small Emka taxis whizzed by, and a few shiny black official limousines.

"Now," Irena said, "what do you want me to do?"

"Drop me off at KGB headquarters on Dzerzhinsky Square."

Irena looked at him in disbelief. "Are you crazy?"

"Pick me up outside the Bolshoi Theater in an hour."

Irena shook her head in horror. "The KGB are looking for you, and you want me to leave you outside their front door?"

"That's the last place they'll expect me."

A car honked as Irena cut across its path, and then Slanski saw the red walls of the Kremlin. Irena turned into a series of narrow streets and finally came out onto a massive square. A giant metal fountain stood in its center, the water turned off in the icy temperature. Directly across the square stood a huge seven-story building.

Irena pointed to it. "KGB headquarters. The entrance to the Lubyanka prison is around the back. There's a pair of big black metal gates, and security is tight—no one's ever escaped; anyone in Moscow will tell you that." She looked at Slanski's face as he studied the building. "You're wasting your time if you think you can rescue your friend. You'd be committing suicide even to try."

"Let me out over there." He pointed to an archway on the left side of the square. A sign above the archway said LUBYANSKY

ARCADE. Irena drove over and pulled in, but kept the engine running as Slanski opened the passenger door. He climbed out, slammed the door, and moved out onto the crowded sidewalk.

LUKIN looked at Anna Khorev's face as they sat on the park bench. She looked miserable, and her eyes were red from crying. The little girl had been taken back to the orphanage. Lukin had seen the grief on Anna's face when she refused to let go of her daughter. She had clung to the child as if her life depended on her. The militiaman at the gate had to help Lukin hold her mother down while the child was taken to the car.

Tears had racked Anna Khorev's body as she saw the car drive away. Then she slumped onto the bench, inconsolable.

Lukin felt overcome by guilt. He had put her through a terrible trauma; she had not seen her daughter in well over a year.

She spoke, pain in her voice. "Why have you done this to me?"

"I thought you'd want to see Sasha again."

"Because I'm going to die?"

"I told you the alternative. And if you help me, I'll do all I can to make sure that you be allowed to take your daughter with you."

"And what sort of life would that be for her? Living in the hell of a camp in some frozen wasteland. You think she'd survive that?"

"At least you'd be together."

"She'd survive the orphanage. In a camp she'd be dead within a year."

Lukin sighed. "Anna, if you don't talk, it's not only you who'll die. Sasha may die with you."

He saw her face turn white as she stared at him. "No. . . . You couldn't do that. She's—she's only a child."

Lukin stood. "It's not up to me, Anna. But I know Beria. And I know Romulka, the man who will interrogate you if I fail. They'd do it if they can't make you talk." He looked down into her wet eyes. "Help me, Anna. For Sasha's sake, help me find Slanski."

SLANSKI walked past the tiny drab shops of the Lubyansky Arcade. When he came out of the arcade at the far end, he was in a narrow cobbled street opposite the side entrance of the west wing of KGB headquarters. He saw a pair of massive black gates and

guessed it was the entrance to the Lubyanka prison. Two uniformed guards stood beside a sentry hut, rifles slung over their shoulders.

As Slanski stood there, one of the guards on the gate noticed him. Slanski turned around and walked back to the square. One side of it consisted of dingy cafés and restaurants. As he passed the window of a café, he saw men in dark blue uniforms sitting inside. He guessed that they were guards from the prison on their break.

He looked back at the KGB building across the street and saw an olive-green BMW halt at a set of traffic lights. He could hardly believe his eyes. Lukin sat in the driver's seat, Anna beside him. The light turned green, and the BMW started to move toward the Lubyanka entrance. Slanski broke into a run. He was hardly aware of the passersby staring at him: He was like a man possessed.

The BMW was halted in the middle of the road, waiting for a break in the oncoming traffic so that it could turn into the cobbled street that led to the prison. Slanski kept running, his eyes on the car. Thirty yards. Twenty. Ten. Five. Close enough to get a shot.

He wrenched the Tokarev from his inside pocket. He could see Lukin's face clearly. Slanski cocked and aimed the Tokarev.

Suddenly a truck coming in the opposite direction screeched to a halt. Slanski saw the driver stare in disbelief at the gun.

Thinking that the truck had stopped for him, Lukin applied a burst of power, and the BMW swung toward the black gates of the prison. They opened, and the car disappeared inside.

Slanski swore as he quickly put the gun away. Too late. The gates of hell had opened and closed and swallowed Anna up.

LUKIN stood at his apartment window.

Across the river he saw the lights of the late evening traffic moving across Kalinin Bridge. He had arrived home an hour ago, needing to get away from headquarters and from the grip of hopelessness he felt crushing him. And he needed to see Nadia.

She had made supper for them both—soup and cold sausage and a half liter of Georgian wine. The wine had lifted his spirits just a little, but now its effect had worn off, and he felt wretched again.

To make matters worse, he had hardly spoken to Nadia during the meal. He saw her reflection in the window as she cleared away the supper plates. She looked over at him, then went into the kitchen. When she came out again, he was still standing at the window. She said, "You hardly touched your food, Yuri."

Lukin smiled weakly. "The soup was good. I just wasn't hungry."

He felt desperate, totally lost. Anna Khorev still hadn't talked. Now there was nothing he could do to save her. The roadblocks to find the Wolf had turned up nothing. Lukin felt certain he was in Moscow. But how did you scour a city of five million souls?

Nadia's voice brought him back. "Sit beside me, Yuri."

Lukin sat next to her on the couch. She touched his arm. "This is the first time I've seen you in four days. But you're not really here in spirit, Yuri. Is there anything you need to talk about?"

Lukin never talked to his wife about his work, but right now he had a powerful urge to tell her everything.

"I'm sorry, my love. It's not something I can talk about."

"I understand. But you worry me, Yuri. I've never seen you like this. Distracted. Lost. Dejected. You're like a different man."

He let out a deep sigh of frustration.

She gently touched his face. "The baby is kicking. Can you feel it?"

He laid his hand on his wife's belly and felt a sudden sharp jolt. He put his head on Nadia's stomach and kissed her bump.

As he lay there silently, Nadia's hand stroking his hair, he thought of Anna Khorev in the park. Her screams when they took her daughter away. The memory played over and over in his mind.

Nadia whispered, "Tell me, Yuri. For heaven's sake, tell me what's troubling you before it breaks your heart."

He said, "I can't. Please, don't ask me."

He heard the anguish in his own voice, and then something seemed to break. His whole body shook, and he heard himself crying—for Anna, for Nadia, for his unborn child, for himself.

SLANSKI sat in the kitchen at the back of the dacha. Irena sat facing him. She had returned from Moscow in the Skoda minutes before, carrying a large shopping bag.

Slanski said, "Okay, tell me what you got."

She searched in her pocket and placed a slip of paper on the table. "The most important thing first. Have a look at that."

He took the slip of paper, read what was written on it, and smiled. "Did you have any problems?"

"There were over a dozen Yuri Lukins listed in the city telephone directory in the post office in Gorky Street. I rang them all, but when I got to the last, I was pretty sure I had got the right one."

"How?"

"A woman answered. I said I was with the army pensions office and I was trying to trace a Major Yuri Lukin who had served with the Third Guards Division of cavalry during the war. She said it couldn't have been her husband; he was certainly a major, but he hadn't served with the army. I apologized for calling the wrong number and put down the phone."

"What happened then?"

"I went to the address given in the phone book. It's an apartment off Kutuzov Prospect. I spoke to one of the neighbors' children. It must be the same Lukin. He drives a green BMW, and he's married, with no kids. The apartment's on the second floor."

"Good. Did you get everything I asked for?"

She opened the bag and spread the contents on the table. "It wasn't easy. But you can get anything you want on the black market once you have the money."

He examined everything carefully. There were several thin ropes, an army penknife, a hypodermic syringe, and two small glass bottles, one of clear glass and the other opaque brown. He picked up both. One contained Adrenalin, and the other ether.

"You did better than I hoped, Irena." Slanski smiled. "What about the rest of the things?"

"I've taken in Viktor's old uniform, so it should fit. Considering what you're going to do with it, Viktor is probably turning in his grave right now. It serves him right."

"The man didn't deserve you. Thanks, Irena."

"I must be mad to go along with this."

He had explained everything to Irena that afternoon, because he needed her help. He had lost his chance to rescue Anna, but now he had a plan. A simple plan.

Irena had hesitated, doubt on her face. It had taken Slanski half an hour to convince her and to go over the details of the plan, but even though she didn't like it, in the end she reluctantly agreed.

Now he glanced at his watch and looked at Irena. "You'd better get some sleep. We've got a busy day tomorrow."

February 28. Major Lukin arrived at Dzerzhinsky Square the next morning at six. While he drank his first coffee of the morning, he laid several sheets of paper on his desk. If the Wolf was in Moscow as he suspected, people had to be helping him.

The sheets of paper in front of him were lists of names of dissidents. Eight pages that contained three hundred and twelve names and addresses. It was a mammoth task to check them all, but it had to be done. The hotels in the city still had to be checked, though he doubted that Slanski would be so foolish as to stay in a hotel.

As he reached for the telephone to call the rostering office, the door opened and Lieutenant Pasha Kokunko came in. Kokunko was a squat Mongolian in his late thirties who had worked with Lukin for several years. His yellow face and muscular bowlegged body gave the impression of a man who would have looked at home sitting on a horse on the Mongolian steppes.

Lukin put down the phone. "Any news?"

Pasha shook his head. "Not a whisper. It's been as quiet as the grave. Apart from a visit from Romulka, that is."

Lukin sat up. "What happened?"

"He turned up last night. Said to tell you he had a Frenchman named Lebel in custody. He also said he wanted to see the woman."

"And?"

"And I wouldn't let him. I told him he'd have to see you first."

"Thanks, Pasha. How is she?"

"Like someone switched the lights off inside her heart. She just sits there saying nothing and staring at the walls." Pasha sighed. "You really think she'll talk?"

"Somehow I doubt it. And I get the feeling she may not know where Slanski is, as she claims. The problem is, that means we're going to have to hand her over to Beria soon. It wouldn't be beyond him to harm the child to make her talk."

Pasha stood. "Whatever happens, either way the woman's dead. You know that, Yuri. Beria won't send her to a camp. He'll kill her."

"I know," Lukin said solemnly, and then told Pasha about the missing pages in the Wolf's file. "If we could see the original," he said, "maybe there's something that could help us—relatives he had in Moscow, friends he might be tempted to approach if he's desperate. I already asked Beria, but he said no."

Pasha grinned. "There are other ways to crack a nut."

"How? The archives office is out of bounds without a permit."

"The chief of archives is a Mongol. He drinks like a camel after a month without water. I could get him drunk and borrow his keys and have a look for the original."

"Forget it, Pasha. It's too risky."

Pasha shrugged. "If you say so."

IT WAS seven that morning when the Skoda pulled up on Kutuzov Prospect. Dressed in the dead Viktor Dezov's uniform, Slanski climbed out and said to Irena, "I'll be as quick as I can."

"Good luck."

He watched as Irena drove off, and then he walked along the street. Number 27 looked much like its neighbors. It was a big old four-story residence from the czar's time that had been converted into apartments. There was no sign of the olive-green BMW.

Slanski walked up the front garden path. Inside the porch, he saw the names and numbers of the occupants written on small white cards above recessed letter boxes. Apartment 14 showed the name Lukin. The entrance door was open, and he stepped into a long dark hallway and climbed the stairs up to the second floor. At number 14 he put his ear to the door but heard no sound from inside. He guessed Lukin's wife was still sleeping.

He went down the stairs again and walked around to the rear of the apartment block. The side path had been freshly swept of snow. There was a communal garden at the back, with a wooden door set in a crumbling granite wall that he guessed led to an alleyway.

As he walked back around to the front of the building, a voice behind him said, "Can I help you, comrade?"

Slanski turned. An old man stood just inside the porch. He wore a greasy black peasant's cap and a patched overcoat, and he had a garden broom in his hands. Slanski guessed the man was the janitor.

He smiled. "I'm looking for an old friend of mine. Major Lukin. I believe he's in apartment fourteen."

"He's a friend of yours, is he?" the old man said suspiciously.

"From the war, comrade. I haven't seen him in years. I'm on leave in Moscow. Just got in from Kiev this morning on the overnight train. Is the major at home?"

"He left early, I'd say. His car's not here. You ought to find him at Dzerzhinsky Square. But his wife ought to be back soon. She usually goes to the vegetable market early on Saturday mornings."

"Of course, Yuri's wife. I'm afraid I can't remember her name."

The old man gave a cackled laugh as he leaned on his broom handle. "Nadia. A redhead. Good-looker."

Slanski smiled back. "That's her. I'll call back later."

Slanski crossed over to the other side of the street. A café stood fifty yards beyond. He went inside to get a glass of tea and found a free table by the window, where he had a good view of the apartment block across the street.

Fifteen minutes later he saw the woman. He didn't notice her red hair at first because she wore a fur hat, but when she turned onto the path he spotted the flame-red color at the nape of her neck. She carried a shopping basket. He watched her go in the front door.

He sat in the café for another five minutes, then stood up and crossed the street briskly. Irena, he knew, was waiting with the car in the alley at the back of the apartment block. Slanski walked to the front of number 27 and climbed the stairs to the second floor.

He took the bottle of ether out of his pocket, doused a handkerchief with a splash of the liquid, and knocked on the door.

The red-haired woman appeared almost at once. When she opened the door, she frowned slightly at the sight of the uniform.

Slanski glanced over her shoulder. The narrow hallway behind her was empty. "Madame Lukin? Nadia Lukin?"

"Yes."

Slanski pushed in the door and lunged at the woman. Before she could scream, his hand went over her mouth, and he kicked the door shut behind him.

LUKIN was standing at the office window smoking a cigarette when he saw the courtyard gates below swing open and two Zis trucks drive in and brake to a halt. Plainclothes KGB men jumped down and forced a crowd of civilian prisoners from the trucks.

As he stood watching, there was a knock on the door. "Enter."

Pasha came in and joined him at the window. "More work for the bullyboys in the cellars. They're the people on the dissident lists being brought in for questioning. The rest are still being rounded up.

We should have everyone covered by tonight. The men are working flat-out."

Lukin sighed. "Hardly quick enough." He nodded down at the courtyard. "Tell whoever's in charge to go easy on the prisoners, Pasha. They're citizens, not cattle for the slaughter."

"As you say." Pasha nodded and left.

The telephone jangled. Lukin picked it up.

A man's voice said, "Major Lukin?"

"Yes, this is Lukin."

There was a pause; then the man said, "Major, we need to talk."

Chapter Ten

LUKIN saw the white plaster walls of Novodevichy Convent in the wash of the BMW headlights. He braked, switched off the engine, doused the lights, and stepped out.

The gilded onion domes of the deserted convent rose up into the twilight. A frozen river lay at the rear of the building, and he walked toward it. He found the bench near the edge of the bank and sat.

"Novodevichy Convent," the man had said. "Be at the east wall, the second bench by the river, at three o'clock. Come alone and unarmed or you don't see your wife alive again."

"Who is this?" he had asked.

"An acquaintance of yours from Tallinn, Major Lukin."

And then the line clicked dead.

At first Lukin had been confused, and then a terrible realization dawned, and he felt an icy chill go through him—it was Slanski. It had to be. He felt a surge of fear and cold rage.

If Slanski had harmed Nadia . . .

He had left the office in a daze. Ten minutes later he was bounding up the steps to his apartment. When he unlocked the door, there was a pungent smell in the hallway. A handkerchief lay tossed on the floor. He called out Nadia's name and got no answer. He put the handkerchief to his nose and sniffed. Ether.

Lukin checked the bedroom—empty—then moved into the kitchen. He sat at the table for almost an hour wondering what to do next. Nothing. He could do nothing until he met Slanski.

He imagined Nadia hurt, Nadia ill, Nadia frightened and locked up somewhere. Why had she been taken?

And then he understood. Slanski wanted to trade—Nadia for Anna Khorev.

It was so obvious that in his turmoil he hadn't seen it.

It was two hours later when Lukin left the apartment. Slanski had chosen his meeting place well. Novodevichy Convent was deserted, the nuns long ago shot or deported to the penal camps.

He heard a rustle behind him and turned. A man stepped out of the shadows, his face visible in the twilight—Slanski. He wore a long dark overcoat and held a Tokarev pistol in his right hand.

"Stay where you are. Don't move and don't talk."

Slanski reached over, and his free hand searched Lukin's body. When he had finished, he stepped back and said, "I want Anna Khorev. And I want her tonight."

Lukin shook his head. "That's impossible. I can't release her. I don't have the authority. You must know that."

"Impossible or not, you bring her here tonight. Eight o'clock. Just you and her. You come unarmed and tell no one what you're doing. My people will be watching you. Fail me or try anything foolish and you won't see your wife again. Is that understood?"

Lukin was numb with shock. Slanski had him watched. In the middle of Moscow this American had *him* watched. He felt anger flare inside him. "I have a condition. You bring my wife here tonight. I get her back when I hand over the prisoner."

"I'll think about it."

"No thinking. You agree or you don't. I don't trust you."

"Very well. But remember the rules. You do anything foolish, you get no second chances."

"And you understand. When this is over, I'm going to kill you."

Slanski grinned. "But you'll have to catch me first." He pointed the Tokarev in Lukin's face. "Close your eyes tight. Count to twenty. Nice and slow."

Lukin shut his eyes. Silence. Cold. He counted to twenty.

When he snapped open his eyes, the Wolf was gone.

THE Lenin Hills were covered with snow as Lukin parked the BMW on the rise of a hill and climbed out. He ran to the top of the hill. In the valley below, Moscow was a million winking lights. When he reached the top, he knelt and smashed his fist into the snow. Whichever way he looked at it, he was dead. By releasing Anna, he was signing his own death warrant. Perhaps Nadia's also.

How could he explain to Beria? The man would never listen.

Lukin tried to think, but his head felt like a block of ice.

Think.

Think.

A wind raged across the hill, its icy chill gouging at his eyes. His mind was racing now as a plan started to form in his head. It was dangerous, but it was his only hope. If it went wrong, he and Nadia were dead. They were dead anyway if he released the woman. This way, at least they stood some chance. He had to risk it.

THE guard unlocked the cell door, and Lukin stepped inside.

Anna Khorev barely acknowledged him as she sat on the edge of the bed. Her eyes were red from crying, her face drawn and pale.

As the door clanged shut behind him, Lukin said, "Anna, I want you to listen to what I have to say. I'm releasing you."

He told her what had happened to his wife. He saw the shocked reaction on her face, but she didn't reply.

"I'm exchanging your life for hers. That's what Slanski wants."

When she still looked unconvinced, he said, "Anna, this is no elaborate trick. As far as the chief warden is concerned, you're being transferred to Lefortovo Prison. But I need your cooperation. Please don't do anything rash when we leave the building. And when we meet Slanski, I want you to do something for me."

"What?"

"Persuade him not to harm my wife. She's pregnant. Whatever's between Slanski and me doesn't concern her. Will you do as I ask?"

Anna Khorev continued to look at him as if she didn't believe what was happening. After a while she nodded.

"Thank you." Lukin moved toward the door. "We'd better go."

"What will happen to you?"

"Does it matter? Ultimately we're all dead. You and Slanski because I doubt you'll get out of Moscow alive after Beria learns about this. And my wife and I for what I've allowed to happen."

"What will happen to my daughter?"

Lukin saw the utter misery in her eyes. He shook his head. "I can't answer that, Anna. I honestly can't."

He saw the grief flood her face, and it almost broke his heart.

LUKIN switched off the engine and doused the headlights. As he stepped out of the car, he said to Anna, "Please wait here."

He started to walk toward the deserted convent. Halfway there he looked back at the BMW. Anna Khorev was still sitting in the passenger seat. He heard an owl hoot.

There was an arched entrance in front that led into the convent. A rusted trellis gate was padlocked with a heavy chain. He heard a voice behind him. "Turn around slowly."

Lukin turned, his pulse racing. Slanski stepped toward him, the Tokarev in his hand. "Up against the wall and spread your feet."

Lukin did as he was told. When he had finished searching him, Slanski said, "Where's Anna?"

"In the car."

"You came alone?"

"Only with the woman. Where's my wife, Slanski?"

"How do you know my name?"

Lukin felt the gun barrel in his neck. "We knew all about you and the woman before you parachuted onto Soviet soil."

"What else do you know?"

"You're here to kill Stalin."

There was a silence; then Lukin again felt the gun press into his neck. "Walk toward the car. Try anything and I drop you."

"You're either a brave man or a complete fool. After tonight you won't stand a chance of getting near Stalin. The entire army will be searching for you. You're throwing your life away. And Anna's."

He felt a sharp blow on the back of his skull, and the bolt of pain jolted him.

"Why don't you shut up and keep walking."

They reached the BMW, and Slanski shone a flashlight in Anna's face. "Are you alone?"

"Yes."

"Were you followed?"

"I—I didn't see anyone."

Slanski flashed the light inside the car. "Okay, step out slowly."

When Anna had stepped out, Slanski said to her, "At the back of the convent there's a road by the river. You'll see a car parked. Someone's waiting in the driver's seat. Get going, fast."

Anna didn't move. "What about Lukin's wife?"

"Get going. Leave this to me."

"Not until you release his wife and promise me you won't harm them."

Slanski stared at her in disbelief. "Whose side are you on? Move!"

Anna didn't flinch. "I mean it. I'm not going until I know his wife's safe and you won't harm him."

Slanski had a wild look on his face, and for a moment Anna thought he would kill both her and Lukin. Slanski said angrily, "Go to the car. The wife's inside. Bring her here. Quickly."

She ran toward the convent. Slanski gestured to Lukin with the gun. "Get down on your knees. Then lie flat on your stomach."

Lukin did as he was told. "If you're going to kill me, do it now. Do it before my wife comes. I don't want her to see this."

Slanski put the tip of the barrel against the back of Lukin's skull. For a long time he hesitated; then he said, "It's tempting, but not this time, Lukin. Your life's just been saved. I can't think why. But let me tell you this. If I see you again after tonight, you're dead."

Slanski heard a noise and turned. Anna raced out of the shadows of the convent wall clutching Lukin's wife by the arm. Slanski shouted, "That's far enough! She comes the rest of the way alone."

Anna let go of the woman's arm. Slanski was already moving back toward the convent, the Tokarev still aimed at Lukin. He passed Lukin's wife and shouted at Anna, "Get back to the car."

For a second she hesitated, wanting to be certain that Lukin and his wife were safe; then she turned and ran. Slanski followed her.

When he was twenty yards away, Lukin pushed himself up from the snow and grabbed Nadia. "Get in the car. Drive to the end of the street and wait there."

He saw the naked fear on his wife's face as he pushed her into the BMW. Already he was reaching under the left-front fender of the car. He worked feverishly, fumbling until he found a knotted cord and tugged. A Tokarev slipped free as the knot released. He placed the weapon on the hood and felt under the fender again, tugged at a second cord, and a Negev flare gun plopped into the snow.

When he looked back through the windshield he saw Nadia's face stare in horror at the weapons. "Quickly, woman. Go!"

For a moment she seemed to hesitate; then the car started to move. Lukin looked back at the convent. He could still see Slanski moving toward the river in the shadows of the wall, sixty yards away. He cocked the Negev flare gun and squeezed the trigger.

A deafening crack erupted as a burst of brilliant orange light exploded in the darkness, and the flare turned night into day.

Lukin saw Slanski halt. Already he was turning, reacting, when a black Emka came roaring out of nowhere and skidded to a halt. Pasha burst out of the driver's door clutching a machine pistol.

Lukin dropped the flare gun and grabbed the Tokarev. In one swift movement he knelt and cocked and aimed the revolver. He caught Slanski clearly in his sights and squeezed the trigger.

The shot missed and ricocheted off the convent wall. Then Pasha opened up with the machine pistol. What happened next Lukin could hardly believe. Slanski calmly knelt, aimed, and fired twice.

The first shot kicked up snow, but the second hit Pasha. He screamed and rolled over. Before Lukin could aim again, the orange light flickered. The flare extinguished, and light plunged into gloom.

He clambered to his feet, running forward like a man possessed, ignoring Pasha's body writhing in the snow. When he reached the road by the river, he was just in time to hear a car roar away.

THE Skoda pulled up outside the dacha, and Slanski, Anna, and Irena climbed out. Irena led them inside, and when she had lit the woodstove and oil lamps, she went into the kitchen and came back with a bottle of vodka and three glasses. She poured them each a drink with trembling hands and swallowed her own quickly.

Her face was white with anger as she stared over at Slanski. "We all could have been killed tonight."

Slanski put a hand on her shoulder. "Take it easy, Irena. It's all over, and you're safe."

"Safe? When I saw the sky light up and heard the shooting, I thought I was dead for sure. We're lucky we didn't have half the army on our backs after what happened." She put her glass down and touched Anna's arm. "What about you? Are you all right?"

"Yes."

"You don't look it. You look like death. Take a drink; it'll calm your nerves. You're going to need a bath and a change of clothes. I've got some in the room at the back. I'll get them."

When Irena went out, Slanski said to Anna, "Drink. Irena's right—you look as if you need it."

Anna ignored the vodka. As she stood there, Slanski saw a lifeless look in her eyes and said, "Tell me what's wrong."

"Lukin told me you came to Moscow to kill Stalin."

Slanski didn't reply.

She said, "If that's true, you're insane."

"No, it's Stalin who's insane. And yes, I'm here to kill him."

"It's impossible. You could never do it."

"Best let me be the judge of that," Slanski said. "You know, you almost got us killed tonight. You should have let me shoot Lukin."

"He didn't deserve to die like that."

"The man tries to kill us, and you're defending him."

"Lukin took me to see Sasha."

He saw the pain in her face and put down his glass. "Tell me."

She told him everything that had happened since he lost her in the woods. When she finished, Slanski said, "So that's why you were with him in the car? Listen, Anna. There's only one reason Lukin would have allowed you to see your daughter, and that's to make you talk."

He saw her struggle to hold back her tears. His hand reached out and touched her face. "Anna, I'm sorry. If there was something I could do to get Sasha back, I would, but it's too dangerous. I can't take the risk of trying to rescue her, even if I knew where she was. It would only jeopardize what I came here to do."

Anna looked at him. "You're being reckless. You know what you plan is impossible. Stop before it's too late."

He smiled. "Definitely too late for that, Anna. Irena will drive you to a railway station outside Moscow before it's light. There's a goods train leaving for Finland, and you'll both be on it. A man named Lebel will look after you. I'm truly sorry about Sasha."

Anna said, "You know you're dead if you stay in Moscow."

"I mean to finish what I started. No one's going to stop me now."

IT WAS almost ten that evening when a Tupolev 4 military transporter arriving from Vienna touched down on the snowy runway at

Moscow's Vnukovo airfield. Among the military-only passengers was a bulky man in his early forties with cropped gray hair. He wore a Soviet air force major's uniform and had hardly spoken throughout the bumpy four-hour flight, pretending to sleep in his seat while the other military passengers drank and played cards.

Now, as he carried his kit bag down the metal steps, an imposing black Zis drew up alongside the Tupolev, and a young air force lieutenant introduced himself and led him to the waiting car.

It took almost ten minutes to exit the airport—the papers the lieutenant produced being checked thoroughly at the special gate reserved for military traffic before the Zis was waved through.

Half an hour later the car pulled up on a dark country road on the outskirts of Moscow. The young officer looked around and smiled. "This is where I was told to drop you, sir."

Massey climbed out silently, dragging his kit bag after him. Mossad had actually managed to get him into Moscow.

NADIA came out of the kitchen with a bottle of vodka and two glasses. Her hands were trembling.

Lukin said, "You really think you ought to drink?"

"I need it. So do you."

There was a firmness in her voice Lukin hadn't heard before. She poured two glasses and came to join him on the couch.

What had happened was a nightmare. They had left Pasha at the office of a Mongol doctor he knew. A bullet had chipped his shoulder bone, but the wound wasn't life-threatening. Now, as Lukin sat on the couch, Nadia handed him the glass of vodka.

"You'd better tell me everything, Yuri. Because if you don't, I'm packing my things and leaving. My life's been put in danger. And the life of our child."

He shook his head. "Nadia, regulations don't permit me—"

"I mean it, Yuri. After tonight you owe it to me to tell me everything. What if that madman hadn't released me when he did?"

"Pasha would have tried to follow him."

"That was still putting my life in danger. Tell me the whole truth, Yuri. Who was that man?"

Lukin put his glass down very slowly, took a deep breath, let it out, and told her everything. When he had finished, his wife stood up, a look of anguish on her face. "I don't believe this is happening."

"Nadia, I want you to leave Moscow, go somewhere far away. The Urals. The Caucasus. Once Beria learns I've released the woman, he'll have me arrested and shot. He'll see you as an accomplice who should be punished. This way at least you stand a chance."

"I'm not leaving you here alone. I won't go without you."

"You have to, if only for our child's sake."

Nadia seemed to crack then, and Lukin saw the flood of tears.

Seeing her like this was killing him. "Tell me what happened this morning. What did Slanski do to you?"

Nadia wiped her eyes. "He came to the door and forced himself in. He put something over my mouth, and I blacked out. When I came to, he said he'd kill us both if I didn't do as he said."

"Tell me what happened after he took you outside."

She told him, and Lukin said, "When Slanski took you to the car, was he alone?"

"No. There was someone waiting in the driver's seat."

"Who?"

"I couldn't see. As soon as I got in, he blindfolded me."

"Do you remember what type of car?"

"I—I'm not sure. It might have been a Skoda."

"Do you remember the color?"

"Gray, maybe. Or green. I can't be certain."

Lukin sighed. "Do you remember anything about the driver?"

"I could smell something . . ."

"What?"

"A clean smell, like perfume . . . but I'm not sure."

"Could the driver have been a woman?"

Nadia shook her head. "I don't know. I suppose."

"Tell me about the room you were kept in."

"I told you, I was blindfolded. There was no sound of traffic. I heard birds outside, but it was very quiet and still. It seemed like somewhere in the country, but it was Moscow, I'm sure of it."

"Why are you sure?"

"When I was taken to the convent, I was still blindfolded, but I couldn't have been in the car for more than half an hour."

Lukin stood up. He pulled Nadia close and held her tightly. "Come into the bedroom. Try and sleep."

"Where are you going?"

"Nadia, I have to try to find Slanski."

"Yuri, please be careful."

He kissed her forehead. "Of course. Now try and rest."

He watched as she crossed to the bedroom door. She looked back at him, a frightened look that almost broke his heart. Nadia's information hadn't been much. Maybe a green or gray Skoda. Maybe a house on the outskirts of Moscow. A dacha, perhaps. Maybe a woman involved. It was nothing much to go on.

THE house in the Degunino District north of Moscow had been the home of a wealthy czarist officer, but now it was converted into flats. Massey sat in the front room of a shabby second-floor apartment.

He had changed out of the air force uniform and now wore a cloth cap and a coarse, frayed suit. On the table in front of him was a bowl of cabbage soup and some fresh bread, but he ignored the food. The man seated opposite, big and red-haired and powerfully built, was a former Ukrainian SS captain. He said gruffly in Russian, "You want to tell me what's going on, *Amerikanets?*"

Massey said flatly, "You got the message with your instructions."

"It said to give you total assistance. That it was top priority."

"Then that's all you need to know. Tell me about the dacha."

"Sergei's there now, covering the place. So far it seems the occupants haven't moved."

Massey said, "How far is it from here?"

"By taxi, over half an hour. But I suggest we take public transport." The man hesitated. "You still haven't told me why we're watching these people."

Massey stood and crossed to where he'd left his kit bag. Inside it were two Tokarev pistols with silencers and spare magazines. There was also a Kalashnikov AK-47 automatic assault rifle.

The Ukrainian looked at the weapons. "We're to kill them?"

"Yes."

"You don't look too happy about it."

Massey ignored the remark and slipped a Tokarev with a spare magazine into his overcoat pocket. "We ought to have this over and done with in a couple of hours. Any trouble with the militia showing up, and we still finish the job, no matter what it takes."

The Ukrainian grinned. "This could turn out to be interesting."
Massey didn't reply. He just stood there grimly, then picked up
the other Tokarev, silencer, and magazine and handed them across.
"For your friend. Let's not waste any more time."

THE phone rang on Lukin's desk. He picked it up.
It was Pasha's voice. "We need to talk, Yuri."
"I thought I told you to rest."
"It's important," Pasha said. "It's about the Wolf. Meet me in the
Sandunov bathhouse in ten minutes."
The line clicked dead.

THE faded wooden sign above the blackened granite building
said SANDUNOV PUBLIC BATHS.
The double doors were closed, but Lukin saw a splinter of light
showing at the bottom. He opened the door and stepped into a
warm tiled hallway.
Lukin went down a couple of stone steps and entered a dressing
room lined with metal lockers. Off to the left, a glass-fronted door
fogged with steam led to one of the sweat rooms.
Lukin could feel a wave of heat from the next room, pleasant
after the icy air in the freezing street outside. He undressed and laid
his clothes neatly on one of the benches. Then he opened the glass
door and stepped into the scented mist.
Pasha lay naked on a damp stone bench, looking terribly pale, a
white cotton towel around his shoulders, a patch of blood on his
bandaged wound. When he saw Lukin, he raised his body painfully
from the stone bench. "Sit down, Yuri."
There was something odd in his tone. Lukin sat on a bench opposite him. The steam room was hot. He said, "How do you feel?"
"It could be worse. The morphine the doctor gave me to ease the
pain is wearing off, but this place helps me to relax."
"Tell me what this is about. Tell me what's so important."
Pasha stood and nodded toward the dressing room. "Come, let's
go inside. There's something I have to show you."
When they stepped into the dressing room, Pasha crossed to a
bench and undid the straps on his briefcase. He removed a file.
"Did anything about the Wolf strike you as strange?"

Lukin frowned. "What do you mean, strange?"

"For one, we know there were several pages missing from the copy of his file. It's usual that an investigator be given access to *all* information for the case he's working on."

"Look, what's this about, Pasha?"

He said, "I found out why Beria picked you for this case. You're a good man, Yuri Lukin. And a good investigator. However, they've fooled you."

"Who have?"

"Stalin and Beria." Lukin frowned in confusion as Pasha handed the file over. "I want you to see this. It came from Alex Slanski's original file."

"Pasha, you fool."

"Don't lecture me, Yuri. We're desperate. We're down a dead end, so I went to the archives office and stole a key and had a look for the original file." Pasha hesitated. "Yuri, there's something in the file you were deliberately not allowed to see. And there's more, but first you should examine what I've given you."

Lukin opened the file. There was a single photograph and a single faded flimsy page inside. Lukin looked at the photograph first. It was old and yellowed. It showed a man and a woman. The man was handsome and clean-shaven. The woman was blond and quite beautiful. They looked happy and very much in love.

From their clothes Lukin guessed the photograph had been taken in the late '20s or early '30s. There was something familiar about their features, and he guessed they were Slanski's parents. He had the odd feeling he had seen their faces somewhere before. They could have been well-known party members.

The single page gave brief details of Slanski's family background. His family name was Stefanovitch, his father a rural doctor living in Smolensk. The report stated that the OGPU, a precursor to the KGB, had called to arrest him and his family.

According to the report, the doctor had resisted arrest and had been killed trying to escape. His wife had tried to assist his escape and was shot also. The three children were arrested. The death warrant for the doctor had been authorized personally by Stalin.

Lukin read the file carefully. The tragedy made him better understand Slanski's powerful motive of revenge, but little else.

There was nothing there that could really help his investigation. He looked up. Pasha was studying Lukin's face. "Did you find nothing familiar in what you just read and saw?"

Lukin shook his head, confused. "What happened to Slanski's father and mother happened to many children during the purges."

Pasha shook his head. "That's not what I meant, Yuri. There's a reason you were chosen to find and kill this American, a reason why the page and photograph were missing from the Wolf's file."

"Why?"

"Stalin probably told Beria not to let you see them. Because once you did, you'd see through his sick joke. It was no doubt Stalin's idea to pick you to hunt down and kill Slanski. He had a perverted reason that amused him. Think back, Yuri. Like me, you were an orphan. What happened to my parents could have happened to Slanski's. Think back to your own life, before you were sent to the orphanage. Think back to your family."

"I—I can't remember."

"You can. But you don't want to. You've tried to blot everything about your past from your mind, just like me."

He handed another photograph over to Lukin. "That was also in Slanski's file. It's a photograph of the couple's children." He held up another flimsy page. "So was this. It says the children were sent to an orphanage in Moscow. Two of them, a boy and a girl, were later given different names. Study it closely."

Lukin looked at the photograph. It was of two small boys and a very young girl with blond hair. The oldest, the one in the middle, was obviously Slanski as a child. He had his arms around the smaller children protectively. Suddenly the two other faces in the photograph jolted Lukin. The girl was no more than four or five. And the second boy—his face was suddenly and frighteningly familiar.

Pasha said, "The little girl's name was Katya. She was your sister. The boy on the right is you, Petya Stefanovitch, before you were given the name Yuri Lukin. You were seven years old."

Lukin turned white, his body numbed with shock.

Pasha said, "Alex Slanski is your brother."

LUKIN signed in at the entrance hall of the officers club on Dzerzhinsky Square and climbed the marble staircase to the second floor. The room he entered looked like a palace, with columns, gilded chandeliers, and red-carpeted floors. The air was thick with cigarette smoke and a babble of voices. Lukin pushed his way through the crowd to the bar and ordered a large vodka, but as the orderly poured, he said, "I've changed my mind. Give me the bottle."

He took the bottle and glass to an empty table by the window. He filled the glass to the brim and swallowed. He had emptied three glasses and poured a fourth before he noticed he was shaking.

Suddenly he felt tears welling up, and distress overcame him. He could hardly believe what Pasha had told him. The man and woman in the photograph were his parents.

The little girl was his sister, Katya.

Alex Slanski was his brother, Mischa.

Lukin's own name was Petya Stefanovitch.

A wave of anger rose and almost smothered him. His mind fogged. Then cleared. He racked his brains for memories from his past. Racked his brains until his head hurt. Once, he had always tried to forget; now he could do nothing but remember.

He had a vague recollection of his father, but a stronger memory of his mother. Lukin was a small boy. She was walking with him in a woods. It was summer. One of her hands held his; another held his brother's. At last he saw his brother's face clearly, as if a curtain had lifted inside his head. The same face as Slanski's.

He *knew* there was something oddly familiar about the face at the checkpoint in Tallinn.

A fog rolled away. He remembered the day the wolves came and he had run to his father's arms. "Wolves, Papa!"

"Bah! He's afraid of everything." Mischa laughed.

His father carried them into the warm house, and his mother fussed over them. And afterward, that same night, lying in his bed, the storm came, and he heard the wolves again, howling in the woods, and Mischa's voice saying across the darkened room, "Don't be afraid. Mischa will protect you. Come, sleep beside me."

He had snuggled in beside his brother, still crying, and Mischa's arms went around him and hugged him close.

"Don't cry, Petya. Mischa will always protect you. And if anyone tries to hurt you, I'll kill them. You understand, little brother?"

And all through the night Mischa had held him. *Mischa—*

"I'm surprised you find time to relax, Lukin."

He started at the voice behind him and turned. Romulka stood there, a mocking grin on his face, a glass of brandy in his hand.

Lukin turned away. "Go to hell."

Romulka smirked. "What's wrong, Lukin? Worried what might happen to you and your wife when Beria learns you've failed him? I just thought you'd like to know the Frenchman, Lebel, still hasn't talked yet. He's holding out remarkably well." He held up his glass and grinned. "It's thirsty work, and I needed a little refreshment. But I have something in store for him that's certain to loosen his tongue. That can only mean one thing. Once I find the American, you'll be finished and the woman will be my responsibility. Only, something bothers me. I hear you had her transferred to Lefortovo this evening, but the prison has no record of receiving her. Where is she, Lukin? Where is she?"

As Lukin stared up at the man's face, he felt a terrible overpowering rage. "You want to know where the woman is? Here's your answer." He threw his drink in Romulka's face. Then he turned and strode out the door.

WHEN Henri Lebel came around, a blinding light blazed in the ceiling and his body was drenched in sweat. As he struggled to sit up in the filthy cell, he found he couldn't. He was lying on a metal table and was tied down with leather straps. The pain was unbearable.

Suddenly a bucket of water was splashed in his face, and Romulka's voice roared, "Wake up, Jew! Wake up!"

Lebel spluttered as Romulka leaned over the table. He looked pale and in a savage mood.

"You're being stupid, Lebel, don't you think? A simple question is all you have to answer. Who in Moscow is helping your friends? You tell me how I find them, and I release you."

Water ran down Lebel's face. He mumbled incoherently.

"You have something to say?"

"You bastard. . . . You're . . . making . . . a mistake."

There was a murderous look on Romulka's face. "Have it your way." He shouted to one of his assistants, "Get the scopolamine."

The man came over with a syringe filled with yellow liquid, and Romulka said, "The truth drug. You're going to talk, Lebel."

IT WAS ELEVEN THIRTY WHEN they reached the street. There was no street lighting, and Massey had to strain his eyes to see the van parked at the end of the road. The glass was iced, but patches had been scraped away so that the driver could see out. The Ukrainian tapped on the window. "Open up, Sergei. It's me."

The driver's door opened, and a young man peered out, his breath fogging the air. "About time, *Kapitan*."

Massey and the Ukrainian slid into the freezing cab.

Massey said, "What's the situation?"

"They're still in there. They haven't moved so far as I can tell. The dacha's the third on the left."

Massey rubbed a patch in the icy window. He saw the dark outline of the house across the street. He turned to the driver and explained everything he had told his companion. Massey would go in alone first. If he wasn't out in half an hour or the men heard shooting, they were to enter the house, back and front, and finish the job.

As the driver checked the action of his weapon and screwed on the silencer, Massey said, "I want you to cover the rear."

The young man grinned. "No problem."

Massey looked at the red-haired man. "You stay out front and keep undercover in the front garden. If anyone other than me comes out, you both know what to do."

The red-haired man grinned. "Whatever you say, *Amerikanets*."

They synchronized their watches, and Massey said, "Okay, let's go."

The three of them climbed from the van.

LUKIN sat in the operations room leafing through lists of car registrations. He had been stupid to do what he did to Romulka. But his rage had been so overpowering, he couldn't help himself. He tried to concentrate on the papers in front of him.

By law all vehicles in the Soviet Union were registered with the militia and the KGB. He had gone to the registrations office and showed the officer in charge his letter from Beria. Ten minutes later the man had given him a ten-page list of Skoda owners for Moscow.

It had taken Lukin another fifteen minutes to find a couple of likely suspects. There were a dozen Skodas registered to women owners. One was named Olga Prinatin. Lukin knew she was a famous ballerina with the Bolshoi.

Another woman, Irena Dezov, had a gray Skoda registered in her name. Her address was in the Ramenki District, southwest of Moscow. It was a place where many senior army officers had weekend dachas. The kind of place Nadia could have been held.

As he scrambled to his feet, the door opened. Pasha came in. He saw the papers in Lukin's hand. "What have you got there?"

When Lukin explained about the woman, Pasha smiled. "You think Alex Slanski could be using her place as a safe house?"

"It's all I've got, Pasha."

"There's something you ought to know. I just saw Romulka getting into a Zis out in the courtyard. He seemed in a hurry, and there was another car following behind with some nasty-looking heavies. I phoned the cellars. Apparently, the Frenchman's in a bad state, and the prison doctor had to give him a shot of morphine."

Lukin whitened.

Pasha said, "Looks like Lebel's been drugged up to the eyeballs with scopolamine to make him talk. What are you going to do?"

Lukin reached for his holster belt and hurriedly buckled it on. "Follow them and see what direction they're going in. If it's toward Ramenki, as I suspect, we can try and get to the woman's address before Romulka does."

Pasha hesitated. "What do we do if we find Slanski?"

"Heaven only knows."

"If Romulka gets his hands on him and the woman, Anna, they're finished. So are we."

Lukin said, "I've a better idea. Where's Lebel now?"

"In the prison surgery. The doctor's patching him up."

"Get Lebel and bring him up to the courtyard. We're taking him with us. Let's see if he can tell us what he's told Romulka."

Chapter Eleven

IT TOOK Massey five minutes to thread his way through the woods to the rear of the dacha.

The shutters on the dacha's windows were open, but all the windows were closed, and no light showed behind the curtains. He could make out an open shed off to the left, with a car parked in it.

He moved forward, staying in the shadows, and made his way to a small stone-flagged patio at the rear. He tried the back door. It was unlocked. He pushed. The door creaked a little, then opened.

The room inside was pitch-dark. Massey stood there for several moments listening for any sound within the house.

Nothing. The silence rang like thunder in his ears.

He flicked on his flashlight. The room was large and basic—a kitchen table and chairs and some pots and utensils. He saw a hallway ahead. A yellow crack of light spilled out under a door halfway down. He moved carefully toward the light.

When he reached the door, he hesitated and listened again. Silence. He cocked the Tokarev, took a deep breath, then pushed in the door and stepped smartly into the room.

As he sought a target, he felt the cold tip of a gun against his neck. Behind him Slanski's voice said, "I wouldn't, Jake. Now how about you drop the gun. I think we need to talk."

MASSEY sat in a chair, the Tokarev pointed at him. He looked at Slanski steadily. "It's over, Alex. Lebel's been taken by the KGB, and it can't be long before he talks. And that can only mean one thing—the boys in black are going to pay this place a visit."

"If you think I'm giving up now, Jake, you're crazy."

Massey shook his head. "You're throwing away your life and the lives of Anna and Irena."

"Washington didn't send you all this way just to have a talk. You came here to put a bullet in me, didn't you, Jake?"

Massey was silent, but Slanski saw the reaction on his face. "Could you do that, Jake? Kill Anna and me?"

"If I have to," Massey said flatly. "There's a bigger picture at stake. Moscow will want you both alive. And once they have their evidence, they'll have enough reason to start a war."

Slanski said, "You know damn well I'd never let them take me alive. Besides, do you think Moscow would tell the world that someone got close enough to kill Stalin? It'd be the biggest loss of face the Kremlin's ever had. They'd keep their mouths shut and pretend nothing had happened."

Massey went to stand.

Slanski said, "Stay right where you are."

"Then you mind if I smoke?"

"Go right ahead. But move nice and slowly." Slanski sat down. "I never thought it would come to this, Jake. You and me. Like *High Noon*."

"It doesn't have to be that way. You give me your word you'll stop this now, and I'll take you and the women back with me. It's against my orders, but I'm prepared to take that risk."

"And if I don't agree?"

"You won't get out of here alive. You, Anna, or Irena."

"Why not take Anna and Irena and leave me to finish this?"

Massey shook his head. "No deal, Alex. It's all of you or nothing. So I guess Anna's life's in your hands. What's it to be?"

Slanski smiled faintly. "What a terrible world we live in, Jake. We were friends, and now you're ready to kill me. Anna too. It makes my heart bleed, but there you have it."

Massey said, "Something tells me I'm wasting my time here."

As he reached over to crush out his cigarette, his hand came up to grab the silenced pistol. But Slanski was too quick. He fired once, the pistol spat, and the bullet nicked Massey's wrist.

Massey fell back in pain, gripping the wound.

"You're getting slow, Jake. Maybe I should just kill you."

He took a handkerchief from his pocket and tossed it over to Massey, who put the cloth on the wound. "Alex, you're making a big mistake. . . . Listen to me . . . for Anna's sake."

There was a sudden hard edge to Slanski's voice. "What do you care about Anna? Sorry, Massey, I'm past listening. Get up."

As Massey struggled to move, there was noise on the stairs, and then Anna appeared in the doorway. When she saw Massey, there was a look of utter shock on her face.

LUKIN was headed toward the Ramenki District in his BMW.

Lebel was in the back seat, out of it, his eyes closed. Lukin had put handcuffs on him when he collected him from the Lubyanka, but the man was going nowhere, still drowsy after the drugs. According to the prison doctor, the combination of scopolamine and morphine acted as a strong painkiller but caused drowsiness, and Lukin wondered if taking Lebel along had been a waste of time.

The traffic out to the country was thin, and the roads were cov-

ered in snow. When they reached the intersection with Lomonosov
Prospect, Lukin saw the taillights of another vehicle a hundred yards
in front. It was a black Zis, and there was another Zis ahead of it.

Pasha said, "I think we're in luck."

The two cars up ahead were moving fast over the hard-packed
snow, but Lukin had snow chains, and the BMW had a powerful
engine. He put his foot down and pulled out to get a better look.
The engine roared as Lukin swung the steering wheel left. He overtook the rear car and came up alongside the lead Zis.

He glanced right and caught a glimpse of the driver, then of Romulka sitting in the passenger's seat. The driver and Romulka
glanced over just as Lukin overtook them. There was a look of
astonishment when Romulka saw Lukin's car. Then his twisted,
angry face was gone from view as the BMW raced ahead.

Lukin felt the sweat drip from his brow as he said to Pasha,
"How much farther?"

"I reckon another three miles."

SLANSKI blew out the oil lamp and the room was plunged into
darkness. He flicked on the flashlight and held the Tokarev in his
other hand. He shone the beam into a corner of the room.

Massey was sitting on the floor, his hands tied behind his back.
Anna and Irena sat huddled beside him.

Massey saw that Anna was staring at him, hurt on her face. Slanski had told her why Massey had come, and he had seen the disbelief in her reaction.

Massey said suddenly, "Anna, I'm sorry. This isn't my doing. If
Alex goes ahead with this, we're all dead."

There was a look of hopelessness on her face as she turned away.
"I don't think it matters now, does it, Jake? Nothing matters."

"Tell him to stop, because it's the only way we all walk away from
this alive. . . . You've nowhere left to run to."

Before Anna could reply, Slanski said, "Shut up, Massey. Make
another sound and it'll be your last."

He flicked off the flashlight and moved to the window. He pulled
back the curtain and peered out. The front garden looked quiet in
the moonlight. He thought he saw a figure, and then it was gone.
He switched on the flashlight again and shone it at Massey.

"How many people have you got outside?"

Massey didn't reply. Slanski aimed the Tokarev at Massey's head. "You hesitate again and I take your head off. How many?"

"Two men."

"You'd better not be lying to me." He tossed Massey's weapon to Anna. "He moves, you shoot him. If you don't, he'll kill you."

He handed the flashlight to Irena.

"Switch it off until I get back. Give me the keys to the car."

Irena fumbled for the keys, handed them to Slanski, then turned off the flashlight. The room was plunged into darkness again.

They heard the door creak faintly, and Slanski was gone.

THE kitchen was in darkness and freezing cold. Slanski saw that the door that led outside was ajar. He crossed the room silently and peered out into the courtyard.

He didn't know if Massey was telling the truth. There could be more than two men out there, but there was only one way to find out. He lay flat on his stomach and crawled out the door. Moments later he was slithering across the stone courtyard until he reached the shed. He waited for any movement or sound, and when none came, he stood and unlocked the car door.

Then he heard a faint click behind him, and a voice said, "Drop your weapon and turn around slowly."

He let the Tokarev clatter to the ground, turned, and saw a young man standing in the shadows ten feet away. He was heavily built and held a pistol in his hand. "I'll say this for you, you move pretty silently, but not silently enough. Where's my American friend?"

"Back in the house. There were supposed to be two of you. Where's your comrade?"

"You'll soon find out. Turn around and move toward the dacha."

"Whatever you say. Except there's something you forgot."

"Oh? And what's that?"

"This." Slanski's silenced Nagant came up and spat once. The man had no chance. The single shot hit him square, and he fell back against the car and slid to the ground.

"TURN on the flashlight."

Irena flicked it on, and Slanski stood there looking down at Massey. "Looks like maybe you were right about the numbers, Jake. But now you're one down. Tell me about the man out front."

"His name's Boris Koval. A former Ukrainian SS captain."

"Weapons?"

"A Kalashnikov."

Slanski gave a low whistle. "Then I guess we're in trouble." He turned to Irena and Anna. "We're going out the back way. Massey too. When I give the word, you pile into the back of the car and keep your heads down. Leave the rest to me."

PASHA checked the street map as Lukin drove.

Lukin said, "How much farther?"

"Take the next left, and we're there."

Lukin entered a long, wide, treelined road with dachas on either side. The homes looked dark and deserted. He halted at a junction.

Pasha grabbed a machine pistol from the back seat and laid it ready on his lap. "So what's the drill?" he said.

Lukin doused the lights. The road looked eerily quiet. "If Slanski's here, I need to talk to him alone. I want you to wait outside."

"What are you going to do? Knock on the door and say you've called by for a visit? He'll blow your head off."

Suddenly in the rearview mirror Lukin saw a blaze of headlights sweep into view behind them at the far end of the road.

Pasha looked back and said, "The bastards are here already."

Lukin said, "You think you could hold them off a little longer?"

"You mean fire on Romulka?"

"In the darkness they're not going to know who's shooting. Just blow the tires—that'll slow them—then meet me at the dacha."

"Presuming you're still alive. Okay, let's do it."

Pasha slipped from the car and disappeared around the corner, clutching the machine pistol. The Frenchman, Lebel, still lay slumped on the back seat.

Lukin shifted into gear and swung the BMW into the street. He counted off the numbers as he drove, and then he saw the dacha.

The lights were out. He drove another fifty yards to the next dacha on the same side of the street. The place looked deserted. He slowed, then backed up quickly into the driveway.

Lukin stepped out of the car. What exactly he was going to do, he still didn't know. But whatever it was, he had to do it fast. Any second now Romulka would come and Pasha would start firing. If Slanski heard the shooting, that wasn't going to help.

The file Pasha had stolen was tucked into Lukin's tunic. He lifted the flap on his holster and released the safety on his pistol. He didn't intend to use it, but he wasn't taking a chance.

Suddenly he heard a blaze of gunfire followed by a screech of tires from the far end of the street. A split second later another volley of shots came. Pasha had opened up on Romulka's convoy, and by the sound of it Romulka and his men were firing back.

Sweat pumping from every pore, Lukin ran toward the dacha.

AT THE kitchen door Slanski peered out into the moonlit back garden. Behind him Anna and Irena waited expectantly. Massey was in front, Slanski's gun pressed into the base of his skull.

"You first, Massey," Slanski whispered. "We're going to move out to the car nice and smartly. Keep it quiet."

Half expecting gunfire, he pushed Massey out into the courtyard. When none came, they hurried to the shed and the Skoda. Slanski opened the rear door and pushed Massey inside; then Anna slid in beside him. Irena was already in the passenger seat.

Slanski jumped into the driver's seat and turned the key in the ignition. The engine spluttered and died. Slanski's heart sank.

At that moment all hell broke loose. A crackle of gunfire erupted like fireworks in the darkness, followed by a screech of tires and brakes. There was another burst of gunfire. Slanski turned the ignition key again, and this time the engine exploded into life.

AS LUKIN approached the dacha, the sound of gunfire still raged in the distance. When he jogged toward the driveway, he saw a figure moving out of the bushes at the front of the garden.

A big man, ruggedly built. He had a Kalashnikov in his hands.

Lukin froze. The man was partly in shadow, and he couldn't make out if it was Slanski.

Before he could react, an engine erupted and a car roared out of the darkness and down the driveway. The man in the garden spun around and fired off a rapid burst as the Skoda shot past.

Lukin flung himself down as the weapon chattered. A volley of fire answered from the driver's window. The Skoda shot onto the street, and the man with the Kalashnikov ran after it, firing wildly.

Windows shattered as the car swung out into the middle of the street. As it swung, a rear door flew open with the sudden force of the turn and a man came hurtling out onto the snow.

Lukin watched in disbelief as the man with the Kalashnikov kept firing at the Skoda, and then suddenly he caught a glimpse of Slanski at the steering wheel.

The man with the Kalashnikov had emptied his magazine, and he tore another from his pocket and hastily reloaded the weapon.

Lukin wrenched out his pistol just as the man turned. Lukin got off two shots, hitting him in the chest and punching him back in the snow. He ran out into the street and saw the Skoda disappear.

There was a groan of pain. Turning, Lukin saw the figure from the car writhing in the snow. He was wounded in the chest, and his face was twisted in agony. "Help me. . . ." The man spoke in English.

Lukin stood in total confusion. Then he heard shouts and saw a knot of men coming down the street, Romulka leading the way.

Where was Pasha? Lukin knelt and gripped the wounded man by the collar and dragged him back to the BMW.

He glanced back. Romulka and his men were less than fifty yards away. "Halt! Stay where you are!" Romulka shouted.

Lukin kept going, the man's weight like lead. When he reached the driveway, he flung open the passenger door of the BMW and lifted the man inside, then climbed into the driver's seat.

As he drove out onto the street, two men ran up, firing pistols at the car. Lukin heard shots puncture metal and glass, and the rear window shattered. As he glanced back, Lebel suddenly became conscious, and Lukin heard a moan.

"Keep down!" He didn't wait to see if Lebel obeyed. He hit the accelerator, and the car roared forward.

Lukin sweated as he drove. What he had done was crazy, but he knew he had to follow Slanski. All he saw up ahead now, though, was night and empty white streets.

The Skoda had a head start of maybe only a minute, but the BMW was faster, so it couldn't get far ahead.

The Frenchman was conscious now in the back, the drug wearing off. When he saw the wounded man in the front seat, he came alive. A bewildered look was on his face as he spoke. "Jake . . ."

Lukin didn't know what the word meant or if it was French or English. The man beside him was barely conscious. His head was slumped on his chest, and he was coughing up blood.

The Frenchman leaned over shakily and felt the passenger's pulse and said in confusion, "What's going on? Can't you see he's dying?"

There was something in his tone and action that suggested Lebel knew the man. Lukin said urgently, "You know him?"

Lebel looked at him. "Who are you? How did I get here?"

"Major Lukin, KGB. I released you from the Lubyanka."

The Frenchman fell silent. Before Lukin could speak again, he noticed the red taillights of a car a hundred yards ahead. He had almost reached the Moscow River, and a bridge ahead led across to Novodevichy. When the car in front trundled over the bridge, Lukin realized the vehicle was headed toward the old convent.

It had to be Slanski.

Lukin saw the beginning of the convent walls on the left-hand side of the road. He felt his heart thumping against his ribs as he saw the car slow and then turn left toward the convent entrance.

As he came toward the left turn, Lukin drove straight on past. He turned to look and saw the Skoda drive in through the archway and disappear. He eased on the brakes and switched off the engine.

"Listen to me, Lebel, and listen well," Lukin said. "I mean you no harm. If you do as I say, you go free. Do you want to go free?"

Lebel stared in disbelief as Lukin unlocked the handcuffs.

"Who's your friend?" Lukin asked.

Lebel hesitated. "An American. His name's Jake Massey. And if you want to know any more, ask your comrade Colonel Romulka."

"Time for explanations later. And Romulka's no friend, I can assure you. But right now I want you to deliver a message to the convent." He saw the puzzled look on Lebel's face. "Your friends from the dacha just drove in there. There's a man named Slanski with them. Tell him I want to talk and that I mean him no harm. Here, give him this." He removed the file from his tunic and handed it over. "When he's read it, I need to talk."

Lebel frowned uncertainly.

Lukin said, "*Please.* Trust me and do as I ask. I mean none of you any harm. Take my gun if you don't believe me."

He removed the Tokarev from his holster and handed it to Lebel. When the Frenchman didn't take the weapon, he grabbed his hand and forced the gun into his palm and closed his fingers around it.

"*Take it.* Take my car and drive into the convent," Lukin said. "Tell Slanski I'll be waiting by the river. Take your friend with you. The others may be able to help him."

He climbed out of the car and helped Lebel out of the back and into the driver's seat, the Frenchman wincing in pain.

Lukin said, "Go, please. Quickly. And remember what I told you."

Lebel drove unsteadily toward the convent gate, and Lukin watched him disappear into the dark courtyard beyond.

He walked on down to the river and found a bench and sat.

THE buildings around the convent courtyard had been allowed to go to ruin, and the vestry at the back of the church was no different. It had no electricity, and the plaster walls were peeling.

Anna held a flashlight while Irena, in shock from seeing him again, supported Lebel and Slanski carried Massey inside. Blood streamed through his clothes from his wounds, and his face was deathly white.

Once they were inside the room, Slanski put Massey down and said to Irena, "Take off his coat, quick as you can."

Irena went to do as he said. Slanski was feeling Massey's pulse. "Irena, see if you can find some water." She hurriedly left the room.

Lebel said to Slanski, "I was told to give you these." He held out the file and the Tokarev. "Compliments of a Major Lukin."

Slanski went very still, and his face tightened.

Lebel said, "Lukin drove Jake and me here. He was alone, and he told me to tell you he means you no harm." He saw the look of confusion on Slanski's face and said, "Take it from me, whoever's side the major is on, it's not the KGB's. He just rescued me. And by the way, that's Lukin's gun you're holding—he's unarmed."

"Where's Lukin now?"

"Outside by the river, waiting for you to join him. But he says you're to read those papers first."

Slanski switched on his flashlight and opened the folder.

Massey groaned, and Anna turned to him. He was losing blood fast. She put a hand on his fevered brow, leaned closer, and whispered, "Don't die on me, Jake."

Massey's eyelids flickered. "Anna. Anna . . . forgive me. . . ."

"Don't move or talk, Jake. Take it easy."

Massey's eyes closed, and his head slumped to one side. There were tears in Anna's eyes as she turned to Slanski. "For God's sake, can't you do something?"

But he wasn't listening. He stood there holding the file, an odd look on his face, which was dazed and suddenly very pale. He held a photograph in his hand, and he stared at it silently.

Anna screamed at Lebel, "Do something!"

Lebel moved closer and felt Massey's pulse just as Irena came in carrying a battered zinc bucket slopping with water.

Lebel looked up and let Massey's limp wrist fall.

"I'm afraid we're wasting our time. He's dead."

SNOW started to drift down, and the icy river looked ghostly white in the darkness. Beyond the silver birch trees on the far bank Lukin could see the lights of Moscow.

Slanski sat beside him. He had made his way down to the riverbank, warily at first, until he had seen the trauma on Lukin's face when their eyes met, a look that told him he had nothing to fear. For a long time the two men sat there, neither speaking. Then Lukin said, "Your friend. Will he make it?"

"He's dead."

"I'm sorry."

"It comes to us all. Nothing could be done."

Lukin looked at Slanski. "You read the file?"

"Yes."

"Who would have imagined it? Now you know why I was picked to track you down and kill you. A sick joke of Stalin's. Pit brother against brother. Blood against blood." Lukin sucked in a deep breath and blew a cloud of steam into the air. "I still can't believe it."

"Tell me what happened the night I left the orphanage," Slanski said. "Tell me what happened afterward."

"Do I have to?" There were tears at the edges of Lukin's eyes, and his voice was thick with emotion. "So much of what happened in my past I've locked away. It seemed such a terrible nightmare. Until I read the file, I thought I'd managed to bury it all."

"You have to tell me."

Lukin was overcome with emotion. Slanski put his hand gently on his brother's shoulder and said, "Take it easy, Petya."

They sat there for several moments, not speaking; then Slanski said, "When I left you and Katya behind that night at the orphanage, it felt like I'd lost everything. I never knew what had happened to you both. And afterward that pain seemed worse than knowing you were dead. It was like someone cut my heart out and there was a hollow where both of you used to be. I need to know."

Lukin looked away. "The night you escaped, Katya and I watched you from the window. It was like losing Mama and Papa again. The same grief, the same pain. Katya was inconsolable.

"When one of the wardens discovered you were gone, she raised the alarm and put us both in one of the basement cells. Two men came from the secret police. They demanded we tell them where you had gone. They threatened to kill us if we didn't. Katya was five years old, but they beat her, tormented her, just as they did me.

"After three or four days they told us you were never coming back. Your body had been found on a railway track near Kiev Station, crushed by a train. Something happened to Katya after that. It was like a light went out inside her. She wouldn't eat or drink.

"The next day they sent me to a correction school. From that institution the secret police often picked their recruits. Katya they sent to an orphanage in Minsk, and I never saw her again." He looked up. "Only it wasn't an orphanage. It was a special hospital, a home for the retarded. Katya had become so withdrawn they locked her in a cell. But there was nothing really wrong with her except her heart was broken." Lukin paused. "When the war came, Stalin ordered that the inmates of all special hospitals be liquidated to conserve food supplies. They took the patients out into the woods and shot them. Katya was one of them."

Slanski stood and closed his eyes tightly, as if the pain was too much to bear. After a time he looked down. "Tell me how you learned the truth. How your people knew about my mission."

Lukin told him. Slanski just stood there listening, not speaking.

Finally Lukin said, "You must know now it's impossible to kill Stalin. He has moved to his dacha at Kuntsevo because of the threat to his life. And it's more tightly guarded than the Kremlin."

Slanski half smiled. "When the cards are stacked against you, reshuffle the deck. There's an alternative plan. A secret underground train line runs from the Kremlin to the Kuntsevo villa. It can be breached near the Kremlin and leads right under the villa."

"I know about the train, but you can be sure the line is heavily guarded. You'd be dead before you got anywhere near Stalin's villa."

"It's a chance I'm going to have to take."

Lukin thought for a moment. "Maybe there's another way into the dacha that stands some chance. Only there's a price to pay."

"What price?"

"Both our lives."

Slanski hesitated, then shook his head. "Me, I figured on dying anyway. But this isn't your battle."

"It's as much mine as yours. We can both repay everything that happened to us. Stalin has an appointment with death. It's an appointment long overdue. We can make sure he keeps it."

"What about your wife? The child she's carrying?"

"You can't do what I have in mind without me. Your friends might still make it to the border with Lebel. The colonel I told you about, Romulka, may suspect that Lebel's train will be used, but if things go the way I plan, the entire Moscow KGB will be in chaos and your friends just may get away in the confusion. It's the only chance they have. Nadia can go with them. Staying in Russia, she stands no chance. Going with Lebel, she may make it over the border."

Slanski looked at him intently. "You're sure about this?"

"I've never been more certain about anything in my life." Lukin paused. "But there's something else I want to do before the train leaves. Something important."

"What?"

Lukin told him. Slanski's forehead creased in thought as he sat there in the cold night, as if trying to take it all in. "You know, I never thought I'd be glad I didn't kill you when I had the chance."

Lukin smiled, a sad smile. "Maybe it was fate."

Suddenly Slanski seemed to crumple, and his shoulders sagged, a lifetime of hardened anguish peeled away, as if his soul was exposed. He said, "God, Petya . . . it's good to see you again."

Lukin put a hand on his shoulder, then embraced him.

As they sat together, the snow started to fall more heavily, drifting against the silver birch trees.

Chapter Twelve

SLANSKI stood on the platform of the deserted railway station, Lebel beside him. A train stood waiting on the tracks. The two men watched the train driver slide open the door of one of the goods wagons. He stepped inside, carrying a steel crowbar.

The driver had been reluctant to take the two extra passengers— a woman and a child. But a bonus of ten thousand rubles had finally persuaded him.

Lebel said, "It shouldn't take him long to loosen the floorboards. He's already vented the wood so they won't suffocate. Your friends will be able to come out once we have a clear run to the border, but they'll have to go back in hiding before we cross the checkpoint."

Lebel looked over at the group huddled on the platform beside the open carriage. Lukin was embracing his wife, who was looking bewildered and upset. Next to them, Anna Khorev was holding her daughter tightly in her arms as Irena fussed over the child.

Lebel said, "Your lady friend I know about, but who's the child?"

"Her daughter," Slanski said. "The child was in a KGB orphanage. Major Lukin just forged Beria's signature to release her."

Lebel said palely, "Good Lord, this gets worse by the minute."

"After what happened tonight, it's hardly going to matter much. You did the favor I asked?"

Lebel took out a set of car keys and handed them to Slanski. "All I could manage was a blue Emka van. One of my contacts from the Trade Ministry who owed me a favor left it parked where you said. He won't report it stolen until tomorrow morning."

"Thanks. What about the train? Can you manage that too?"

"Slightly more risky. We halt at a station named Klin, an hour out from Moscow, to hook on a cargo of coal. That shouldn't take more than an hour. The train driver ought to be able to stretch it to two, taking on water for the engine and attending to some imaginary repairs, but he won't be able to wait much longer than that. So if you're going to join us, I suggest you don't delay." Lebel nodded toward the train. "It seems you have a farewell in store, my friend. I'd better see what's keeping the driver."

As Anna handed her daughter to Irena and came toward them, Lebel shuffled to the train. Then Anna's arms were around Slanski's neck, and she pulled him to her tightly. "What Lukin did—I don't know how to thank him."

"Look after his wife. That'll be thanks enough."

She looked into his face. "Please. Come with us. It's not too late to change your mind."

"Far too late, I'm afraid."

And then her lips were on his, and he heard her sobbing. Finally he broke away. For a long time he looked at her. "Take care, Anna Khorev. I wish you a long life and happiness with Sasha."

The train suddenly whistled, and Lebel appeared. "The driver's ready to go. Let's move, my friends. This isn't the Gare du Nord."

Slanski took Anna's hand and pulled her toward the train. Lukin helped Lebel up beside the driver, then got the others on board. A final look passed between them all—Slanski and Anna, Lukin and Nadia—and then Irena slid the carriage door shut.

Slanski saw the terrible look of anguish on Lukin's face as the train started to move off. Slanski said, "You said your good-bye?"

"As best I could under the circumstances."

"How did Nadia take it?"

Lukin said grimly, "I don't think she believed me when I told her I'd see her again. But she knows what she's doing is for the best. And for our child. On my way to pick up Anna's daughter I called at Leningrad Station. I showed Beria's letter to the duty official in charge of the railway lines to Helsinki and told him to keep the lines clear for Lebel's train. Let's hope he does what I tell him. All we can do is hope by some miracle they all survive."

"It's still not too late for you to change your mind," Slanski said. Lukin shook his head. "This is for Katya. For our parents. For us." Slanski touched his arm. "Let's go. There isn't much time."

IT WAS still snowing as Lukin pulled up across the street from KGB headquarters. As he switched off the engine, he turned to Slanski and said, "Give me fifteen minutes. I need to know if Pasha's safe. If I haven't showed up by then, get away from here as fast as you can. Ditch the car and go to the nearest Metro. After that I'm afraid you'll have to make your own way to Kuntsevo."

Slanski nodded. "Good luck."

Lukin climbed out of the car, crossed the street, and went in through the side doors. A guard checked his papers before Lukin stepped into a lift. The fourth-floor hallway was empty.

Lukin stepped into his office. Romulka stood by the window, a Tokarev in his hand. Two brutal-faced KGB men stood in front of Pasha's desk. They held rubber truncheons. Pasha was tied down in a chair, his face bloodied almost beyond recognition.

Lukin's heart sank. "What's the meaning of this?"

Romulka stepped forward. "Remove your pistol and place it on the desk. Nice and easy. Or I'll be tempted to take your head off."

Lukin removed his Tokarev and placed it on the desk.

Romulka crooked a finger. "Come closer, away from the door."

As Lukin stepped forward, Romulka slammed a fist into his jaw. He fell back against the wall. Romulka yanked him savagely by the hair and hauled him into a chair.

"Did you expect to get away with what you did tonight? Preventing me from catching the American? Releasing the woman and taking the child from the orphanage? You must think I'm a fool."

He stared into Lukin's face. "You know what I don't understand, Lukin? Motive. There must be an explanation. And you're going to give it to me." He put the barrel of Lukin's pistol against Pasha's temple. "Either you talk, or I blow his brains out."

Pasha seemed barely conscious, his eyes unable to focus. Then suddenly a gurgling sound came from his throat, and with a burst of rage he came to life. "Tell him nothing, Yuri—"

Romulka's face erupted in rage. The Tokarev was pressed into Pasha's temple, the hammer clicked, and the gun exploded.

Pasha's head snapped sideways, his body suddenly limp.

Lukin roared, "No!"

As he tried to struggle from the chair, the two men held him down. Romulka turned to him. "Now it's your turn, Lukin. You're going to talk if it's the last thing you do." He produced what looked like a pair of pliers from his pocket. "On the desk with him."

As the two men dragged Lukin onto the desk, a voice said, "I really wouldn't do that."

Romulka and the men turned at once. Slanski stood in the open doorway, the silenced Nagant in his hand.

One of Romulka's men went to reach for his pistol, and Slanski shot him in the neck. As the man spun, the second man lunged forward, and Slanski fired twice, hitting him in the throat and chest.

Meanwhile, Lukin grabbed Romulka's gun, pushed him back against the wall, and managed to kill him. Afterward he turned to Slanski in disbelief. "How did you get in here?"

"As soon as you stepped into the lift, the guard on the desk couldn't wait to reach for the phone. So I decided to keep you company. It's lucky the building's almost empty at this time of night."

"Thanks, Mischa."

Slanski nodded at Pasha. "But too late to help your friend."

Lukin stared at the corpse, grief etched on his face. For several moments he didn't speak. "He was a good man." It took time for him to compose himself. "What happened to the guard?"

"Dead in one of the offices. Did you make the call?"

"There wasn't time."

"Then make it now."

It took Lukin less than a minute to make the call, and when he replaced the receiver, he looked at Slanski and said, "It's done."

"Then let's get out of here before someone raises the alarm. Don't forget the uniform."

Lukin crossed to his locker in the corner and took out his spare uniform, gloves, boots, and cap. He took a long, painful look at Pasha's bloodied face, then followed Slanski out of the room.

THEY reached the Kuntsevo road ten minutes later. There was hardly any traffic. Slanski looked ahead through the falling snow. On the left side of the road stood a flat-roofed derelict building.

He pointed through the windshield. "What's that?"

"A bomb shelter from the war."

"Pull in beside it. Let's go over the plan again."

Lukin swung the wheel and pulled over in front of the shelter. Steps led down beyond the dark mouth of the entrance.

As Lukin switched off the engine, he saw the silenced Nagant appear in Slanski's hand, pointed at him.

Alarmed, Lukin said, "What's going on?"

"Listen to me, Petya. I can do this alone. You have a wife and child to think of. There's no need for you to throw away your life."

Lukin saw it then. Saw everything. His face drained of color. "You never intended for us to do this together, did you?"

"I guess not."

"Mischa . . . please. You'll never get inside the villa alone."

"That's where you're wrong. You made the call, and you're expected. I can get in with your identity card."

Lukin shook his head fiercely. "Mischa, this is crazy. Together we stand some chance. Alone you have none."

"It's a better chance than having you explain I'm a fellow officer. With tight security they may not even let me inside." He shook his head. "I don't want you to die. If you come with me, he'll have killed all of us in the end. I won't let him destroy us all."

He removed a set of keys from his pocket. "I'm going to leave you here. Lebel's waiting with the train at a station called Klin, northwest of Moscow. There's a parked blue Emka van half a mile back down the road. Here are the keys." He stuffed them into Lukin's pocket. "Live your life, brother. Live for all the family."

"Mischa, no!"

"Good-bye, brother." Slanski's fingers came up quickly and closed around Lukin's neck like a vise, the thumb pressing hard into the point below his ear. Lukin fought back, but Slanski was stronger.

It was only a matter of seconds before Lukin blacked out. Slanski stepped out of the car into the freezing night, carried Lukin down the steps into the shelter, and propped him against a wall.

It took him another five minutes to do everything he had to do. Moving quickly, he pried the interior mirror from the car and used it as he applied engine oil to his hair. When he finished, he pulled on his brother's single leather uniform glove. He found the identity card with the photograph in Lukin's breast pocket.

After he checked himself in the mirror, he shone the flashlight at the unconscious figure propped against the shelter wall. He wouldn't be out more than another five minutes. For a long time Slanski stared at Lukin's face, almost overcome with emotion; then he knelt down and kissed him hard on the cheek.

As he climbed back into the BMW, he glanced over his shoulder at the dead body lying on the back seat. "Well, I guess you got to see it through to the end after all, Jake. If there's a heaven, and you're already there, wish us both luck. We're going to need it."

THE GUARDS HEARD THE CAR long before they saw it. One of them pulled back a shutter in the metal gate and peered out into the falling snow. When the BMW drew up, searchlights in the watchtower above the gate sprang on, flooding the area with white light.

The man approached the car. "Papers," he demanded.

The uniformed KGB major rolled down the window and smiled as he handed them over. "Major Lukin. I'm expected."

The guard examined the identity card. Moments later he shone a flashlight inside the car. When he saw the body lying across the back seat, he recoiled in horror. "What the hell!"

The major grinned. "I think if you check with the duty watch officer, you'll find everything is in order." He glanced back at the corpse with obvious disgust. "An American enemy agent. Comrade Stalin wishes to see the body personally."

The shaken guard regained his composure. "Wait here."

He stepped back inside the gate, and Slanski heard the jangle of a field telephone. Moments later the guard reappeared.

"Looks like you're in business, Comrade Major. Follow the road for half a mile until you reach the dacha."

As the guard stepped back, the gates yawned open. Half a dozen elite Kremlin guards with blue bands on their caps stood inside the entrance fingering their weapons.

Slanski shifted into gear, and released the clutch, sweat rising on his forehead. The car rolled forward along the narrow road.

As he drew up outside the dacha entrance, two Kremlin guards stepped out from behind the double doors. Slanski switched off the engine and climbed out of the BMW. Between the two guards appeared a massive guards colonel, immaculately dressed.

"Major Lukin, I believe?"

Slanski saluted, and the colonel returned the salute smartly. "Colonel Zinyatin, head of security. Your papers, Major."

Slanski handed over the papers. The colonel examined them thoroughly. Then he handed them back and peered into the car.

Slanski said, "An American agent. He proved to be quite an adversary. Unfortunately, I was unable to capture him alive."

"So I heard."

"Then you know Comrade Stalin wishes to see the body."

The colonel stared down at the corpse before turning back. "I'm certain it won't be necessary to take the corpse inside. Comrade Stalin will take my word for it that the American's dead." The colonel smiled without humor.

"One more thing. Your side arm. Procedure forbids visitors to Kuntsevo to carry weapons." The colonel thrust out his hand. Slanski unholstered the Tokarev and handed it over.

"Now, if you'll follow me, Comrade Stalin is expecting you."

The polished double oak doors opened silently on their hinges, and Slanski followed the colonel into a dazzling room. A log fire blazed in one corner, and a long walnut table stood in the center, a dozen or more chairs set around it. An ornate crystal chandelier hung overhead, its light flooding the entire room. Bokhara rugs were set around the floor, and rich tapestries draped the walls.

Joseph Stalin stood at the end of the table. He smoked a pipe and held a glass in his hand. A half-full bottle of vodka was on the drinks trolley beside him. He was dressed in a simple gray smock tunic, and his thick graying hair was swept back off a pockmarked face, his mouth half hidden under a bushy gray mustache.

The colonel crossed the room and whispered something into his ear. Stalin put down his pipe and glass and crooked a finger. "Comrade Major Lukin, come here."

As Slanski stepped forward, Stalin turned to the colonel. "Leave us." The colonel saluted and left.

Suddenly Stalin kissed Slanski on both cheeks. "So you brought me the American's body."

"Yes, Comrade Stalin."

"And what about the woman?"

"Under lock and key in Lefortovo Prison."

Stalin's gray eyes smiled coldly. "You have surpassed my expectations, Lukin. My congratulations. You will have a drink."

The old man shuffled to the drinks trolley and poured vodka into a tumbler. He handed it to Slanski and raised his own glass.

"I drink to your success, Comrade Lukin. And to your promotion. As of now, you are a full colonel."

"I don't know what to say, Comrade Stalin." Slanski raised his glass and sipped, while Stalin swallowed his vodka in one gulp.

He looked over at Slanski suspiciously. "But you know, something bothers me. You didn't see fit to follow protocol and inform

Comrade Beria of your visit here. I've just been on the phone to him. He's as surprised as I am by your success. According to him, you've been deliberately obstructing one of his officers, Colonel Romulka, in his duty. Your behavior has been somewhat unusual and unorthodox, Comrade Beria thinks. And I agree. He claims you have kept the woman from him. Why is that, Lukin? Did you want all the glory for yourself? Or are you keeping a secret?"

Slanski put his glass down carefully on the table. "There is a matter I needed to discuss in private. It concerns the American plot."

The bushy eyebrows rose. "And what matter is that?"

Slanski slipped off the black leather glove and the small Nagant appeared in his hand. There was the softest of clicks as he cocked the hammer and aimed the weapon at Stalin's head.

Horror shone in the old man's eyes as Slanski leaned in closer and whispered, "Not something you're going to enjoy. But you'll listen or I'll take your head off. Sit down. The chair to your right."

Stalin lowered himself shakily into the chair. Slanski removed his officer's cap. Stalin stared at the face, then at the ungloved hand. "You—you're not Lukin. Who are you? What do you want?"

"I'm sure the answer to the first question should be obvious by now. As for the last, I want you." Slanski smiled chillingly. "But first, comrade, I'm going to tell you a story."

LUKIN opened his eyes in the freezing blackness of the air-raid shelter. His brain throbbed. He shook his head, and a million stars exploded inside his skull. He sat groggily for several moments, rubbing his neck, before he found the strength to get to his feet. Then he staggered out the door and up the steps of the shelter.

He realized where he was and what had happened.

Then his heart raced wildly. How long had he been unconscious? He looked at his watch and tried to focus in the poor light.

One twenty. He must have been out cold for over five minutes.

He remembered the van. Half a mile away. Five minutes if he ran. He could still make it to Stalin's villa.

"MY FATHER'S name was Illia Stefanovitch," Slanski said. "Do you remember him?"

Stalin shook his head. "No. I don't remember him."

Slanski pressed the Nagant hard into his temple. "Think again."

"I—I don't know who you're talking about."

"Yuri Lukin is my brother. Illia Stefanovitch was our father. You killed him. You killed his wife. And his daughter. Our sister. You killed them all. Our family. And you haven't stopped trying to kill us. You pitted my brother against me."

"No. You're mistaken. Who told you this? Who told you I was responsible? Lies!"

"Then let me remind you of the lies you speak of. My father was a village doctor near Smolensk. One day the secret police came to our village. They demanded the summer harvest. There was a famine raging. A famine deliberately caused by you. The villagers barely had enough to feed their children. So they refused. Half the men in the village were shot in reprisal and their grain stolen. There was nothing to eat. Women and children starved. My father was spared, but he couldn't believe Comrade Stalin would allow such a thing to happen to his village. So he decided to do something. He wrote to you about what had happened and expressed his revulsion. You read the letter, but the reply wasn't what my father expected.

"You sentenced him to death as a traitor. The secret police came to his surgery. They thought they'd make this troublesome doctor's death a little more interesting than merely shooting him. So they made his wife watch while they held him down and injected him with a lethal dose of one of his drugs, Adrenalin. Do you know the effect such an amount of Adrenalin has on a body? The heart races, the body trembles, the lungs swell. A fatal dosage causes the blood vessels in the brain to burst, but death still comes slowly.

"They made my mother watch every moment. Until one of them had the pity to put a bullet in her head. Only it didn't kill her. They left her lying there, bleeding to death, slowly, for hours. I heard it happen, because one of the men held me in the next room."

Slanski leaned in close. "You say you don't remember my father, but you will. Illia Stefanovitch. Remember that name. It's the last name you're going to hear before you go screaming to hell."

Slanski placed the Nagant on the table and removed a hypodermic from his pocket. He flipped off the metal sheath and exposed the needle. The glass was full of clear liquid. "Pure Adrenalin. And now I'm going to kill you the way you killed my father."

As Slanski moved in, the old man rose and lunged at him like a bull. "No!"

Slanski grabbed at the Nagant, and the weapon exploded. As the shot rang around the room, everything seemed to happen at once.

The dacha went mad, screams and voices everywhere.

The doors burst open, and the big colonel was the first in, crashing into the room like an enraged animal.

Slanski stabbed the needle into Stalin's neck, and the plunger sank. "For my father."

Then the Nagant came up smartly and pressed against Stalin's temple. "And this for my mother . . . and sister."

The Nagant exploded, and Stalin's head was flung back.

As the colonel frantically wrenched out his weapon, he watched in disbelief as Slanski turned the Nagant toward himself, slipping the barrel into his mouth. The weapon exploded again.

THE Emka's wipers brushed away the snow, but it was ceaseless.

A hundred yards from the dacha Lukin heard the sirens going off, and his heart jolted. Dogs barked; voices screamed orders.

Lukin slowed the Emka. There was a rutted lane off to the right and he pulled in and switched off the engine. His body was shaking violently, and his heart was racing.

He was too late.

He stumbled out of the car and fell to his knees, no longer hearing the sirens and the noises in the forest, only his own sobbing.

It seemed as if a dam burst inside his head, and when the scream finally came, it came from deep inside him. *"Mischa!"*

The scream seemed to go on forever in the white darkness.

THE PRESENT

Chapter Thirteen

IT HAD started to rain again, and we moved indoors.

Anna Khorev stood at the window and stared toward the distant red walls of the Kremlin. When she finally turned back, she smiled, a brief sad smile. "And there you have your story, Mr. Massey."

"It's a remarkable story."

She lit a cigarette. "Not only remarkable, but true. You're one of the few people to know what happened that night at Kuntsevo. It took almost four days for Stalin to die, but die he did. The drug caused him to have a hemorrhage; the bullet made sure he'd die. And there was nothing his doctors could do to save him."

"So the official version of how Stalin died was a lie."

"The Kremlin claimed he died naturally of a cerebral hemorrhage. But you'll also read in some history books that the bodies of two men were taken from the dacha grounds the night Stalin fell fatally ill. It's not a widely known fact, but it's the one small grain of truth that hints at something unusual happening that night. The bodies were those of Alex and your father."

"What about afterward?" I said a moment later. "What happened after you escaped from Moscow?"

She sat down. "Russia was in chaos for days. With Romulka dead, our escape wasn't that difficult. We made it to Finland, but there were problems. The CIA, naturally, thought I and the others might be an embarrassment if the mission were ever leaked or discovered. And Henri Lebel was fearful for his life when he realized he had been in a small way party to Stalin's death. But Henri had been rather clever. After your father first struck a deal with him in Paris, he transcribed all the details and sent them in a sealed envelope to his lawyer, with instructions that the contents be made public if he or Irena were ever harmed. That way he was insuring himself against the CIA trying to blackmail him into working for them again or double-crossing him. So the CIA kept your father's promise. They arranged through Mossad for myself and Sasha, along with Henri and Irena, to live in Tel Aviv under new identities. They thought we'd all be safer there and out of harm's way if the KGB ever wanted to exact revenge on us, but thankfully that never happened."

"Why did the CIA claim my father committed suicide?"

"Your father's death was a problem for Washington. They had to cover it up without any of his colleagues becoming suspicious. The official explanation was that he had committed suicide while traveling in Europe. They claimed he was depressed and unstable. The date they gave for his death was before our mission began so that no one might ever connect him to what subsequently happened. It wasn't fair on the character of your father, but it had to be done for security. And, of course, no body was buried, just a coffin full of stones."

"What happened to Lebel and Irena?"

Anna Khorev smiled. "Henri opened a clothing business in Tel Aviv, and they married and lived happily together until Henri died ten years ago. Irena followed him soon after."

"And Yuri Lukin?"

"He made it to the train that night, much to the relief of his wife, but he was distraught, as you can imagine. He had found his brother after all those years and then lost him again. When we arrived in Helsinki, we were all debriefed for several days by Branigan. I never saw Yuri Lukin again after that. I would have liked to very much. He was a remarkable man, Mr. Massey."

"Do you know what became of him?"

"I can only tell you what I heard from the CIA. After Helsinki he and his wife were flown to America. They were given new identities and settled in California, where his wife gave birth to a son. Three months later, they told me, Yuri was killed in a car accident."

"You think the KGB had him killed?"

"No, I don't believe they did. It was definitely a freak accident. And I'm certain the CIA didn't kill him. In many ways, had it not been for him, the mission wouldn't have been so successful. But I suppose his death was convenient for both the Kremlin and Washington. There was one less person alive who knew the truth."

I sat there for several moments taking it all in. Beyond the glass the rain had stopped. The sun appeared from behind the sullen Moscow clouds, glinting off the Kremlin's golden domes.

I looked back. "Did you ever remarry?"

She laughed gently. "What an odd question. But the answer is no. Sasha eventually married a nice Russian émigré in Israel. They have a son and a daughter, Rachel, whom you met when you arrived." She smiled. "I loved two remarkable men in my life, Mr. Massey. My husband and Alex. And that's really been quite enough."

Anna Khorev stood. "So there you have it, Mr. Massey. I've told you everything I can. I'm afraid you must excuse me. Rachel and I have a flight to Israel to catch. I hope you understand."

"May I ask one more question?"

"And what's that?"

"Do you think my father would have killed you and Alex?"

She thought for several moments. "No, I don't believe he would have. Your father came to Moscow because he was ordered to. But I think if it had come down to it, he wouldn't have killed us. He was a fine man, Mr. Massey. He was a father you would have been proud of. And to be honest, maybe I was a little in love with him too." She glanced at her watch. "We have some time, so why don't you ride with us in the car? We can drop you at your hotel on the way to the airport. And if you don't mind I'd like to pay a visit to Novodevichy on the way."

WE WALKED together to the graves. Rachel waited in the car, and as the sunlight washed down through the chestnut trees, the grave-yard hardly seemed like the same place. The sky was clear and blue, and the dry heat of the afternoon lingered under the trees.

When we came to the two gravestones, I stood back to let Anna Khorev say her final prayer. She wasn't crying, but I saw the pain in her eyes when she turned back.

"I decided a long time ago that this will be my final resting place when my day comes, Mr. Massey. I know Ivan, my husband, would have understood." There was a faraway look in her brown eyes.

"I'm certain he would have."

She half smiled. "Are you ready, Mr. Massey? I'm afraid grave-yards are not one of my favorite places."

I nodded and took her arm, and we walked back to the car.

I HEARD six months later that Anna Khorev died.

Bob Vitali rang from Langley and said she had passed away in the Sharet Hospital in Jerusalem. She had suffered from lung cancer. The funeral was to be in Moscow four days later.

I organized the tickets from Washington, for some reason wanting to be part of the end of things.

The funeral at Novodevichy had already started when I arrived. A half-dozen or more Israeli embassy staff huddled around the open grave as an Orthodox priest chanted his prayers for the dead.

I saw Anna Khorev's granddaughter holding on to the arm of a handsome woman in her forties whom I guessed was Sasha, both their faces pale with grief.

Something remarkable happened then.

As I stood watching the gravediggers lower the coffin into the frozen ground, I noticed an old couple standing arm in arm among the mourners. The woman's face was deeply wrinkled, but under the head scarf she wore, I could see a tint of red in her graying hair. The man was very old, his body almost bent double with age.

He wore a black leather glove on his stiff left hand.

The couple waited until the coffin had been lowered into the ground before the old man came forward and placed a bunch of winter roses in the open grave. When he stepped back, he stood there for several moments; then I saw his eyes look over at Alex Slanski's headstone. He stood there, as if lost in thought, until the woman took his arm and kissed his cheek and led him away.

As they shuffled past me, my mind was on fire with excitement. I touched his shoulder. "Major Lukin? Major Yuri Lukin?"

The old man started, and his watery eyes looked up to study my face. For a time he seemed undecided about something, before replying, "I'm sorry, sir. You're mistaken. My name is Stefanovitch."

The couple walked on. I went to say something then, remembering the name—Slanski's family name—but I was struck dumb. I saw the couple step into one of the black cars parked nearby and drive off down the narrow cemetery track.

Was it Yuri Lukin?

I like to think he hadn't really died as Anna Khorev had said.

But it was all such a long time ago. I had found my own truth. I had resurrected my ghosts, and now it was time to bury them.

I took one last look at the three graves, then turned and walked back toward the cemetery gates.

GLENN MEADE

"My family always thought I should have worked for the CIA," says Glenn Meade, an author who has long been interested in modern history's most perplexing questions. One event, in particular, intrigued him: the death of Joseph Stalin. Was the Soviet despot murdered, as his family believed? Or did he die naturally?

Looking for answers, the author read Dwight D. Eisenhower's presidential diaries. "I knew he and Stalin were tremendous enemies. It struck me as strange that at the time of Stalin's death, Eisenhower made virtually no mention of the Russian dictator," Meade says. "I realized that his death at the hands of the CIA was quite feasible, considering the historical events of the period."

The author knew he had a great idea for a novel. To prepare himself, he spent a month in Russia, absorbing the atmosphere, traveling the route followed by his characters, and talking with former KGB agents. "Some of the KGB people I spoke with had, let's say, reputations as hard men," Meade says. He remembers asking himself, "Am I a lunatic for doing this? Maybe I've gone in a little too deep." Then he adds, "But once you get into researching a story and get caught up in it, caution is thrown to the wind."

Meade has worked as both a journalist and an engineer. He is now a flight-simulator instructor and lives in Dublin, Ireland.

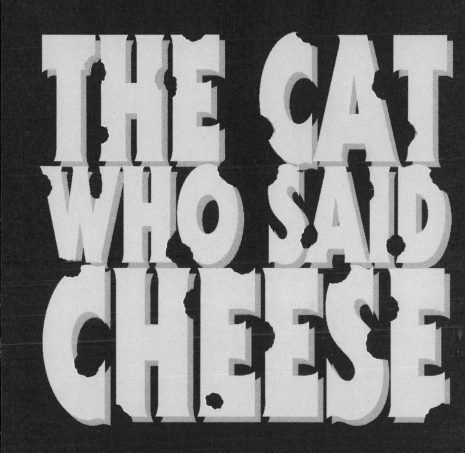

THE CAT WHO SAID CHEESE

LILIAN JACKSON BRAUN

Something's rotten in the town of Pickax!

And it isn't the cheese for the Great Food Explo, the gastronomic event being held in Stables Row.

A lethal bomb, a brawl over the Cornish pasties, a turkey with deadly stuffing—why, it's enough to give reporter Jim Qwilleran a bad case of indigestion. And to send those feline sleuths, Koko and Yum Yum, sniffing for clues.

Chapter One

AUTUMN, in that year of surprises, was particularly delicious in Moose County, four hundred miles north of everywhere. Not only had most of the summer vacationers gone home, but civic-awareness groups and enthusiastic foodies were cooking up a savory kettle of stew called the Great Food Explo. Then, to add spice to the season, a mystery woman registered at the hotel in Pickax City, the county seat. She was not beautiful. She was not exactly young. She avoided people. And she always wore black.

The townsfolk of Pickax—population three thousand—were fascinated by her presence. "Have you seen her?" they asked each other. "She's been here over a week. Who do you think she is?"

The hotel desk clerk refused to divulge her name, saying it was prohibited by law. That convinced everyone that the mystery woman had bribed him for nefarious reasons of her own, since Lenny Inchpot was not the town's most law-abiding citizen.

So they went on commenting about her olive complexion, sultry brown eyes, and lush mop of dark hair that half covered the left side of her face. Yet the burning question remained, Why is she staying at that firetrap of a flophouse? That attitude was unfair. The New Pickax Hotel, though gloomy, was respectable and painfully clean, and there was a fire escape in the rear. Nevertheless, no one had been known to lodge there for more than a single night—or two at the most—and travel agents around the country were influenced by an entry in their directory of lodgings:

NEW PICKAX HOTEL, 18 miles from Moose County Airport; 20 rooms, some with private bath; presidential suite with telephone and TV; bridal suite with round bed. Three-story building with one elevator, frequently out of order. Prisonlike exterior and bleak interior, circa 1935. Public areas unusually quiet, with Depression-era furnishings. Cramped lobby and dining room; no bar; small unattractive ballroom in basement. Sleeping rooms plain but clean; mattresses fairly new; lighting dim. Fire escape in rear. Dining room offers breakfast buffet, luncheon specials, undistinguished dinner menu, beer and wine. No liquor. No room service. No desk clerk on duty after 11:00 p.m. Rates: low to moderate. Hospital nearby.

Business travelers or out-of-towners arriving to attend a funeral checked into the hotel because no other lodgings were available in town. In the hushed dining room the business travelers read technical manuals while waiting for the chopped sirloin and boiled carrots, and the out-of-town mourners silently counted the peas in the chicken potpie. And now, in addition, there was a woman in black who sat in a far corner, toying with a glass of wine.

One resident of Pickax who wondered about her was a journalist—a tall, good-looking man with romantically graying hair, brooding eyes, and a luxuriant pepper-and-salt mustache. His name was Jim Qwilleran; friends called him Qwill, and townsfolk called him Mr. Q. with affection and respect. He wrote a twice-weekly column for the *Moose County Something,* but he had been a prizewinning crime reporter Down Below—local parlance for metropolitan areas to the south. An unexpected inheritance had brought the Chicago native north and introduced him to small-town life.

Wealth did not interest him; he enjoyed working for a living, cashing a weekly paycheck, and practicing economies. When the Klingenschoen billion descended on him, he considered it a burden and an embarrassment and turned the vast holdings over to a foundation. He drove a small car, walked around town, and pedaled a bike in the country. He had many friends, and the fact that he lived alone—in a barn, with two cats—was a foible they had learned to accept.

Qwilleran's housemates were no ordinary cats, and his residence was no ordinary barn. Octagonal in shape, it was a hundred-year-old apple storage facility, four stories high, and topped with a cupola.

The interior, open to the roof, had three balconies connected by a spiraling ramp. On the ground floor the main living areas surrounded a giant white fireplace cube, with great stacks rising to the roof.

As for the cats, they were elegant Siamese whose seal-brown points were in striking contrast to their pale fawn bodies. The male, Kao K'o Kung, answered to the name of Koko. He was long and muscular, and his fathomless blue eyes brimmed with intelligence. His female companion, Yum Yum, was small and delicate, with violet-blue eyes that could be heart melting when she wanted to sit on a lap, yet that dainty creature could utter a piercing shriek when dinner was behind schedule.

One morning in September, Qwilleran was closeted in his first-balcony studio, the only area in the barn totally off-limits to cats, trying to write his Friday column, Straight from the Qwill Pen.

> Emily Dickinson, we need you!
> "I'm nobody. Who are you?" said this prolific American poet.
> I say, "God give us nobodies! What this country needs is fewer celebrities and more nobodies who live ordinary lives, cope bravely, do a little good in the world, and *never* get their names in the newspaper or their faces on TV."

"Yow!" came a baritone complaint outside the door.

It was followed by a soprano shriek. "N-n-now!"

Qwilleran consulted his watch. It was twelve noon, time for their midday treat. He yanked open his studio door, and the two determined petitioners hightailed it down the ramp to the kitchen. Although he took the shortcut via a spiral metal staircase, they reached the food station first. He dropped some crunchy morsels on their plates, then stood to watch their enjoyment.

"Is it okay with you two autocrats if I go back to work now?"

Qwilleran muttered. Satisfied with their repast, they ignored him completely and busied themselves with washing masks and ears. He returned to his studio and wrote another paragraph

The phone interrupted his writing. The caller was Junior Goodwinter, young managing editor of the *Moose County Something.* "Hey, Qwill, we'd like you to attend a meeting this afternoon."

Qwilleran avoided meetings whenever possible. "What about?"

"Dwight Somers is going to brief us on the Great Food Explo. He's been in Chicago with the masterminds of the K Fund, and he'll be flying back on the three-fifteen shuttle."

Qwilleran mellowed somewhat. The K Fund was the local nickname for the Klingenschoen Foundation that he had established to dispense his inherited billion. Dwight Somers was a local public relations man with credentials Down Below. "Okay. I'll be there."

"By the way, how's Polly?"

"Improving. She's now allowed to walk up and down stairs—a thrill she equates with winning the Nobel Prize." Polly Duncan was a charming woman of his own age, currently on medical leave from the Pickax Public Library, where she was chief administrator.

"Tell her Jody and I were asking about her. Tell her Jody's mother had a bypass last year and she feels great!"

"Thanks. She'll be happy to hear that."

Qwilleran pounded out another few sentences on his typewriter; then the telephone rang again. Qwilleran answered gruffly but changed his tune when he heard the musical voice of Polly Duncan. "How are you?" he asked anxiously. "I phoned earlier, but there was no answer."

"Lynette drove me to the cardiac clinic in Lockmaster," she said with animation, "and the doctor is astonished at my speedy recovery. He says it's because I've always lived right, except for insufficient exercise. I must start walking every day."

"Good. We'll walk together," he said, but he thought, That's what I've been telling her for years; she wouldn't take my advice. "I'll see you tonight, Polly. Anything you need?"

"All I need is some good conversation—just the two of us. Lynette is going out. *A bientôt,* dear."

"*A bientôt.*"

He remembered her late-night call for help, her frightened eyes as the paramedics strapped her onto a stretcher, his own uneasy moments while she was in surgery and intensive care. Now she was convalescing at the home of her sister-in-law.

He finished his column in time for the meeting, then said goodbye to the Siamese, telling them where he was going and when he would return. The more one talks to cats, he believed, the smarter they become. His two Mensa candidates responded, however, by raising groggy heads from their afternoon nap and giving him a brief glassy stare before falling asleep again.

He walked downtown to Lois's Luncheonette for a piece of apple pie and arrived at the newspaper conference in good humor.

The *Moose County Something* was published five days a week. Originally subsidized by the K Fund, it was now operating in the black. The office building was new. The printing plant was state of the art. The staff always seemed to be having a good time.

The meeting was held in the plain, wood-paneled conference room. Staffers sat around a large teak table, drinking coffee from mugs imprinted with newspaper wit: IF YOU CAN'T EAT IT, DON'T PRINT IT . . . DEADLINES ARE MADE TO BE MISSED . . . A LITTLE MALICE AFORETHOUGHT IS FUN.

"Come on in, Qwill," said Junior Goodwinter. He was not only the managing editor but a direct descendant of the founders of Pickax City. In a community four hundred miles north of everywhere, that mattered a great deal. "Dwight isn't here yet. Since we hate to waste time, we're inventing rumors about the mystery woman."

Among those present were Arch Riker, publisher, editor in chief, and Qwilleran's fellow journalist from Down Below, now realizing his dream of running a small-town newspaper; Hixie Rice, in charge of advertising and promotion, another refugee from Down Below; and Mildred Hanstable Riker, food writer and wife of the publisher, recently retired from teaching fine and domestic arts in the schools.

Qwilleran nodded pleasantly to each in turn and took a chair.

Riker cleared his throat. "While we're waiting for the late Mr. Somers, let us resume our deliberations. Who is the mystery woman and what is she doing here?"

Mildred said, "She always wears black. I think she's in mourning, having suffered a great loss. She's come to this quiet town to deal with her grief."

Qwilleran stroked his mustache, a sign of purposeful interest. "Does she ever venture out of the hotel?"

"Sure," Junior said. "She's been seen driving a rental car—a dark blue two-door with an airport sticker."

"And," Hixie added, "one day when I was getting an ad contract signed at the Black Bear Café, I saw her in the hotel lobby with a man! He was wearing a business suit and carrying a briefcase."

"The plot thickens," Riker said.

Qwilleran said, "Is she good-looking? Young? Glamorous?"

"Why don't you have dinner at the hotel and see for yourself?"

"No thanks. Last time I went there, a chicken breast squirted butter all over my new sport coat. I considered it a hostile attack."

"Perhaps she's a government undercover operator, casing the area as a possible site for a toxic waste dump," Riker suggested.

"Or a visitor from outer space," Mildred said merrily. "We had a lot of UFO sightings this summer."

"You're all off-base," Hixie declared. "I say the man with a brief-case is her attorney, and she's Gustav Limburger's secret girlfriend, now suing him for patrimony."

Laughter exploded from all. Gustav Limburger was the mean-spirited eighty-year-old Scrooge who owned the Pickax Hotel.

There was a knock on the door, and Dwight Somers walked in. The PR man had looked better before he shaved off his beard, but what he lacked in handsome features he made up in enthusiasm and personality. "Sorry, gang. The plane was late."

"No problem," Riker said. "Was this your first visit to Klingen-schoen headquarters, Dwight? I hear it's impressive."

"Man, it's staggering," Dwight said, taking a chair. "They have specialists in investments, real estate, economic development, and philanthropy. Their thrust is to make Moose County a great place to live and work without turning it into a megalopolis. They're for sav-ing the beaches and forests, keeping the air and water clean, creat-ing businesses that do more good than harm, and zoning that discourages high-density development. If it works, it'll be a proto-type for rural communities throughout the country."

Someone asked about business opportunities.

"Now we come to the point," Dwight said. "The county's already known for fisheries, sheep ranches, and potato farms. Now the K

Fund is backing enterprises such as a turkey farm, ethnic restaurants, and food-specialty shops. The Great Food Explo will be a festival of food-related happenings." He opened his briefcase and handed out fact sheets. "It opens a week from tomorrow."

Someone said, "It sounds like it could be fun."

"The trend is to food as entertainment," Dwight said. "There are a lot of foodies out there! People are dining out more often, buying cookbooks, taking culinary classes, joining gourmet clubs."

Dwight closed his briefcase. "I hope you'll jump on the bandwagon, and call me if I can help."

"It's an appetizing prospect," Riker said.

Chapter Two

QWILLERAN needed no coaxing to participate in the Great Food Explo. He hoped it would open up new sources of material for his Qwill Pen column. Finding topics for the twice-weekly space was not easy, considering the boundaries of the county and the number of years he had been Qwill-penning.

From the newspaper he walked to Toodle's Market to buy food for his fussy felines. Toodle's dated back to the days when grocers butchered their own hogs and sold a penny's worth of tea. Now the market had the size and parking space of a big-city supermarket and was run by Mrs. Toodle, with the assistance of sons, daughters, in-laws, and grandchildren. Qwilleran bought a few cans of red salmon, crabmeat, cocktail shrimp, and minced clams.

He walked home along Main Street, around Park Circle, through the theater parking lot, then along a wooded trail to the apple barn. The theater, a magnificent fieldstone building, had once been the Klingenschoen mansion, and its carriage house was now a four-car garage with an apartment upstairs. The tenant was unloading groceries from her car as Qwilleran crossed the parking lot.

"Need any help?" he called out.

"No thanks. Need any macaroni and cheese?" Celia Robinson replied with a hearty laugh. She was a jolly gray-haired grandmother who supplied him with home-cooked dishes.

"I never say no to macaroni and cheese," he said.

"I've been meaning to ask you, Mr. Q. What do you think about

the mystery woman at the hotel? I think you should investigate."
Mrs. Robinson was an avid reader of spy fiction, and twice she had
acted as his confidential assistant when he was snooping into situations that he considered suspicious.

"Not this time, Celia. No crime has been committed, and the gossip about the woman is absurd. . . . And how about you? Are you
still in the Pals for Patients program?"

"Still doing my bit. They've started a Junior Pal Brigade, and I'm
training them—college students who want to earn a little money.
Nice kids. They're good at cheering up housebound patients."

As Qwilleran approached the barn through the dense evergreens
that screened it from the heavy traffic of Park Circle, he was aware
of two pairs of eyes watching him from an upper window. By the
time he unlocked the door, the cats were downstairs to meet him.
Before feeding them, however, he consulted the Black Creek section
of the phone book and called a number.

A crotchety, cracked voice shouted, "Who's this?"

"Are you Mr. Limburger?" The old man mentioned at the meeting was a genuine character, and Qwilleran appreciated characters;
they made good copy.

"If that's who you called, that's who you got. Whaddaya want?"

"I'm Jim Qwilleran from the *Moose County Something.*"

"Don't wanna take the paper. Costs too much."

"That's not why I'm calling, sir. Are you the owner of the New
Pickax Hotel?"

"None o' yer business."

"I'd like to write a history of the famous hotel," Qwilleran per-
sisted. "It's a landmark. I'd like to visit you and ask some questions."

"When?" the old man demanded in a hostile tone.

"How about tomorrow morning around eleven o'clock?"

"Iffen I'm here. I'm eighty-two. I could kick the bucket any
time."

"I'll take a chance," Qwilleran said pleasantly.

"N-n-now!" came a cry not far from the mouthpiece of the
phone.

"Whazzat?"

"Just a low-flying plane. See you tomorrow, Mr. Limburger." He
chuckled and opened a can of minced clams for the Siamese.

BEFORE GOING TO SEE POLLY, Qwilleran read the fact sheet about the Great Food Explo. Opening festivities would center around a complex called Stables Row, a block-long stone building on a Pickax back street. In horse-and-buggy days it had been a ten-cent barn: all-day stabling and a bucket of oats for a dime. Now it was embarking on a bright new life. Large and small spaces had been re-modeled to accommodate a pasty parlor, soup bar, bakery, wine-and-cheese shop, kitchen boutique, old-fashioned soda fountain, and health food store. Special events during the Explo would include a pasty bake-off, a celebrity dinner-date auction, and a cooking course for men only.

"Okay, you guys, I'm going to visit your cousin Bootsie," Qwilleran informed the cats before driving to Pleasant Street. Nicknamed Gingerbread Alley, it was a neighborhood of Victorian frame houses built by affluent Pickaxians when carpenters first discovered the jigsaw. Here Polly's unmarried sister-in-law, the last Duncan-by-blood, had inherited the ancestral home, and here Polly was recuperating. On arrival, Qwilleran turned a knob in the front door, which jangled a bell in the entrance hall, and Polly arrived wearing a filmy blue caftan he had given her as a get-well gift.

"Polly, you're looking wonderful!" he exclaimed.

"All it takes is a good medical report plus blush and eye shadow," she said gaily. They clung together in a voluptuous embrace, then went into the parlor, which several generations of Duncans had maintained in the spirit of the nineteenth century, with velvet draperies, fringed lampshades, pictures in ornate frames, and rugs on top of rugs. A round lamp table was skirted down to the floor, and as Qwilleran entered the room, a fifteen-pound missile shot out from under the skirt and crashed into his legs. It was Bootsie, Polly's adored male Siamese, with whom Qwilleran—a competitor for her affection—had never been friendly.

"Naughty, naughty," Polly scolded with more love than rebuke. To Qwilleran she explained, "He was only playing games."

Oh, sure, he thought.

Polly offered him tea and dietetic cookies. "Elaine Fetter visited me today and brought some gourmet mushroom soup," she said.

"Do I know her?"

"You should. She zealously volunteers at the hospital, the historical museum, and the library. But she's a snob and not well liked."

"How was the soup?"

"Delicious, but too rich for my new diet—heavy on butter and cream. Elaine grows her own mushrooms—shiitake, no less."

Qwilleran's interest was alerted. Here was a subject for the Qwill Pen. There was something mysterious about mushrooms.

"Would she agree to an interview?"

"Would she! Elaine loves having her name in the paper."

"Did you have any other visitors today?" he asked, thinking about Dr. Prelligate. The president of the new college was being much too attentive to Polly, in Qwilleran's estimation.

"Mrs. Alstock, my assistant, brought some papers from the library for me to sign. She's doing an excellent job in my absence."

"I hope she filled you in on the latest gossip."

"Well," Polly said, "the mystery woman came into the library and checked out books on a temporary card."

"So the library has her name and address on file." Qwilleran smoothed his mustache in contemplation and looked at Polly conspiratorially under hooded eyelids.

She recognized the humor in his melodramatic performance and retorted sweetly, "You're plotting a dirty trick! The Pickax plumbers will break into the library after hours and burglarize the files, and we'll have a Bibliogate scandal."

Before he could think of a witty comeback, there were footsteps in the hall and Lynette joined them. Qwilleran reflected that while Lynette was a decent person—pleasant, helpful, generous—it never occurred to her that he and Polly might like a little privacy.

He made an excuse to leave, and Bootsie escorted him to the front door, as if to speed the parting guest.

AT THE apple barn his own Siamese were glad to see him. They had been neglected most of the day.

"Okay, we'll have a read," he announced. "Book! Book!"

One side of the fireplace cube held shelves for Qwilleran's books, grouped according to category: fiction, biography, drama, history, and so forth. In between the collections were spaces large enough for Koko to curl up and sleep. He also liked to knock a volume off a shelf occasionally and peer over the edge to see where it landed.

In fact, whenever Qwilleran shouted "Book! Book!" that was Koko's cue to dislodge a title. It was a game. Whatever the cat chose, the man was obliged to read aloud.

On this occasion the selection was *Stalking the Wild Asparagus* by Euell Gibbons. The chapter Quill chose to read was all about wild honeybees, and he entertained his listeners with sound effects: *bzzzzzzz.* The Siamese were fascinated. Yum Yum lounged on his lap, and Koko sat on the arm of the chair, watching the reader's mustache.

Chapter Three

FRIDAY started with a whisper and ended with a bang. First Qwilleran fed the cats. He watched in fascination as they groomed themselves from whisker to tail tip. The female was dainty in her movements; the male, brisk and businesslike.

Later, while Yum Yum lounged contentedly, Koko crouched behind her, lashing his tail in slow motion. Body close to the floor, he moved nearer, wriggling his hindquarters. She seemed oblivious of his curious pantomime. Suddenly Koko pounced, but before he landed, Yum Yum was whizzing up the ramp with Koko in pursuit.

BEFORE going to Black Creek for his interview with Gustav Limburger, Qwilleran had breakfast at Lois's Luncheonette. The proprietor—a buxom woman with a host of devoted customers—was at that hour waitress, cook, and cashier. "The same?" she mumbled in his direction. In a few minutes she banged down a plate of pancakes and sausages and sat down across the table with a cup of coffee.

"I hear your son won the silver in the Labor Day bike race," he said.

"It ain't real silver," she said, jerking her head toward the silverish medal displayed behind the cash register. "He's in college now, and he's tellin' me all I been doin' wrong for the last thirty years. I bet those professors don't teach 'em about all the headaches in the hash-slingin' business. I should be teachin' at the college."

"Will he take over this place when he finishes his course?"

"Nah. His ambition is to be manager of the New Pickax Hotel. That fleabag! He's outa his bleepin' mind."

"Do you know the old gentleman who owns it?" Qwilleran asked.

"Gentleman? Hah!" Lois made a spitting gesture. "He'd come in here for breakfast and leave a nine-cent tip. Talk about cheap! One day he had the nerve to ask if I'd like to marry him and run his mansion like a boardinghouse. I told him he was too old, too tight, and too smelly. He stomped out without payin' and never come back."

THE town of Black Creek, not far from Mooseville, had been a boomtown when the river was the lifeline of the county, and was now a ghost town. All that remained of downtown was a bar, an auto graveyard, and a weekend flea market in the old railroad depot. In the former residential area all the frame houses had burned down or been stripped for firewood, leaving only the red brick Limburger mansion rising grotesquely from acres of weeds. Victorian in style—with tall, narrow windows, a veranda, and a turret—it had been a landmark in its day. The Limburgers had spared no expense, even importing old-world craftsmen to lay imported brick in artful patterns. Now one of the stately windows was boarded up, and paint was peeling from the wood trim and carved entrance door.

When Qwilleran drove up, an old man was sitting on the veranda in a weathered rocking chair, smoking a cigar.

"Are you Mr. Limburger?" Qwilleran called out as he mounted the crumbling brick steps. "I'm Jim Qwilleran from the *Moose County Something.* May I sit down?"

He lowered himself cautiously into a splintery rocking chair with a woven seat that was partly unwoven. A dozen stones as big as baseballs were lined up on the railing. "This is an impressive house. Do you know when it was built, Mr. Limburger?"

The old man rubbed his nose with a fist as if to relieve an itch. "My grandfader built it. My fader was born here, and I was born here. My grandfader came from the old country."

"Is he the one who built the Pickax Hotel?"

"Yah."

"Then it's been in the family for generations. How long have you been the sole owner?"

"Long time."

"How large a family do you have now?"

"All kicked the bucket 'cept me. I'm still here."

"Did you ever marry?"

"None o' yer business."

A blue pickup drove onto the property and disappeared around the back of the house. A truck door slammed, but no one made an appearance.

Qwilleran said diplomatically, "Lately I've noticed a fine-looking woman at the hotel, dressed in black. Is she your new manager?"

"Don't know 'er." Limburger rubbed his nose again.

"Do you mind if I ask a personal question? Who will get the hotel and this house when you kick the bucket, as you say?"

"None o' yer business."

Qwilleran had trouble concealing his amusement. As he turned away to compose his facial expression, he saw a large reddish brown dog coming up the brick walk. "Is that your dog?" he asked.

For answer the old man shouted in his cracked voice, "Get outa here!" He reached for a stone on the railing and hurled it at the animal. "Mis'rable mutt." He seized a stick that lay at his feet and struggled to stand up. Brandishing the stick in his hand, he started down the steps, yelling, "Get outa here! Filthy beast." Halfway down, he stumbled and fell to the brick walk.

Qwilleran rushed to his side. "Are you hurt? I'll call for help."

The man was groaning and flailing his arms. "Get the man. Get the man!" He was waving feebly toward the front door.

Qwilleran bounded to the veranda in two leaps, shouting, "Help!"

Almost immediately the door was opened by a big man in work clothes, looking surprised, but not concerned.

"Call 911! He's hurt!" Qwilleran shouted.

An ambulance responded promptly and took the old man away. Qwilleran turned to the big man. "Are you a relative?"

The answer came in a high-pitched, somewhat squeaky voice that seemed incongruous in a man of that size. Also incongruous was his hair: long and prematurely white. The journalist's eye registered other details: age, about thirty; soft, pudgy face; slow-moving; unnaturally calm, as if in a daze.

"I'm not a relative. I just kinda keep an eye on the old man. Nobody else does. I go to the store and buy things he wants. He don't drive no more. He's got a bad temper, but he don't get mad at me. He gets mad at the dog. Comes and dirties the walk. I told him he'd fall down them steps if they wasn't fixed. I could fix 'em if he'd spend some money on mortar and a few bricks."

With rapt attention Qwilleran listened to the rush of words that answered his simple question. Then he held out his hand. "I'm Jim Qwilleran from the *Moose County Something*. I was interviewing Mr. Limburger about the hotel."

The fellow wiped his hand on his pants before shaking Qwilleran's. His eyes were riveted on the famous mustache. "I seen your picture in the paper. I read it at Lois's when I go there for breakfast. Do you eat at Lois's? Her flapjacks are almost as good as my mom's. D'you know my mom?"

Qwilleran said, "I don't even know you. What's your name?"

"Aubrey Scotten. You know the Scotten Fisheries? My granddad started the business, and my four brothers run it now. My mom lives on the Scotten farm on Sandpit Road. She grows flowers to sell."

"Aubrey is a good Scottish name."

"I don't like it. My brothers got pretty good names—Ross, Skye, Douglas, and Blaire. I asked my mom why she give me such a dumb name. In school the kids called me Big Boy. That's not so bad."

"Do you work with your brothers?" Qwilleran asked.

"Nah. I don't do that kinda work no more. I got me some honeybees, and I sell honey. I'm startin' at the new turkey farm next week. A real job—maintenance engineer they call it. I don't hafta be there all the time. I can take care of my bees. D'you like bees? They're very friendly if you treat 'em right. I talk to 'em, and they give me a lot of honey. I requeened the hives this summer."

Qwilleran had no idea what the man was talking about, but he recognized possibilities for the Qwill Pen. "This is very interesting, and I'd like to hear more about your friendly bees. How about tomorrow? I'd like to write about it in the paper."

The garrulous beekeeper was stunned into silence.

ON THE way back to Pickax, Qwilleran rejoiced in his discoveries: two more characters for the book he would someday find time to write. It was easy to imagine a comic dialogue between the talkative, good-hearted young man and the grumpy oldster who was stingy with words as well as money. It was less easy, however, to imagine Aubrey Scotten as a maintenance engineer.

Qwilleran knew about the new Cold Turkey Farm, underwritten by the K Fund. His friend, Nick Bamba, had been hired to manage it, with option to buy in two years. The farm would raise the birds, fast freeze them, and ship to markets Down Below.

Nick's wife, Lori, had had an idea accepted by the K Fund: a restaurant in Stables Row called the Spoonery. She would serve only food that could be eaten with a spoon—like soups and stews.

Qwilleran admired the energy and ambition of the young couple in tackling new challenges, but questioned Nick's choice of maintenance engineer. When he returned to the barn, he phoned his friend. After a few pleasantries Qwilleran said, "Nick, I just met a man who says he's been hired as your maintenance engineer."

"Aubrey Scotten? Yeah. He's a genius at repairing things. Refrigeration, machinery—anything! He has a God-given talent."

"Well," Qwilleran said, "I'm surprised, to say the least."

"It's a long story. I'll tell you when I see you," Nick said.

Koko was antsy that afternoon. He drove Yum Yum crazy, pouncing on her and chasing her up to the rafters. When he started rattling the handle of the broom closet, Qwilleran got the message. He opened the door, and Koko bounded inside and sat on the cat carrier.

"You rascal!" Qwilleran said. "You want to roll on the concrete."

During the summer he had often taken the Siamese to his beach cabin, where their chief pleasure was rolling on the concrete floor of the screened porch. They writhed and squirmed and flipped from side to side in catly bliss that Qwilleran failed to understand. Yet he indulged their whims. Soon they were driving the thirty miles to the cabin he had inherited from the Klingenschoen estate.

At the sign of a letter K on a post, a relic of the Klingenschoen era, they turned into a narrow dirt lane that wound through woods and up and down sand dunes. Koko became excited, bumping the sides of the carrier and making noises that alarmed his partner.

Qwilleran recognized the performance: The cat was sensitive to abnormal situations; something unusual lay ahead. He noticed recent tire tracks and was annoyed to find a trespasser's car parked in the clearing adjoining the cabin. When he parked behind the car, he saw that it was a dark blue two-door with an airport rental car sticker in its back window, and his reaction was a gradual buildup of disbelief, amazement, and triumph. He was about to come face to face with *that woman*. And he had her trapped!

Chapter Four

QWILLERAN walked to the edge of the high sand dune on which his cabin perched. At the foot of the weathered wooden steps leading down to the beach, he saw a large straw hat. Under it, back turned to him, a figure dressed in black sat in an aluminum folding chair.

He started down the steps, calling out, "Hello, down there."

The straw hat flew off, and a dark-haired woman turned to look up at him.

"Beautiful day, isn't it?" he said in a comradely voice.

She jumped to her feet, clutching a book. "My apology. I not know someone live here." Her accent was charming.

"That's all right. I live in Pickax and just came by to check for damage. There was a severe storm a few days ago. What are you reading?" That was always a disarming question, he had learned.

"Cookbook." She held it up for proof. "I go away now."

"Don't rush off. Perhaps you'd have a glass of cider on the porch. By the way, I'm Jim Qwilleran of the *Moose County Something.*"

"You are too kind," she said.

"Not at all. Let me carry your chair." He ran down the few remaining steps. "And what is your name?"

She hesitated. "Call me Onoosh."

"In that case, call me Qwill," he said jovially.

She smiled for the first time, and although she was not a beauty by Hollywood standards, her olive complexion glowed and her face was radiant. A gust of wind blew her hair away from her left cheek, revealing a long scar in front of her ear. She stuffed her belongings into a tote bag.

Qwilleran reached for it. "Allow me."

He ushered her to a chair on the screened porch. "Excuse me for a moment while I unload the car. Do you like cats?"

"All animals I adore." Her face again glowed with happiness. She

could be in her thirties, he guessed as he went to the car; could be from the Middle East. She may have lived in France. Her black pantsuit had a Parisian smartness.

He served the cider and asked, "Are you vacationing up here?"

"Yes, but no," she replied cryptically. "I look for place to live. I like to cook in restaurant."

"Where are you staying?

"Hotel in Pickax."

"Have you been there long?"

"Two weeks. Desk clerk very nice. Give me big room in front."

"How did you come to Moose County? It's off the beaten path."

Shyly she explained. "My honeymoon I spend here—long ago."

"So your husband is no longer with you?" He considered that a good way of putting a prying question.

She shook her head, and her face clouded, but it soon brightened. The Siamese, who had been rolling and squirming on the concrete of the back porch, had arrived. "Be-yoo-ti-ful!" she said.

"They are especially fond of people who read cookbooks."

"Ah! Cooking I learn very young, but something more is always to learn."

"What do you think of the food in our local restaurants?"

She looked at him from behind her curtain of hair. "Is not good."

"I agree with you, but we're trying to improve the situation."

"Mediterranean restaurant—very good here, I think."

"You mean stuffed grape leaves and all that? When I lived Down Below, I haunted Middle Eastern restaurants. We used to ask for meatballs in little green kimonos."

"Very good," she said. "I make meatballs in little green kimonos." She waved a hand toward a tangle of foliage on the dune. "Wild grape leaves you have. You have kitchen? I stuff for you."

Qwilleran's taste buds were alerted. "I'll buy what you need in town."

"Is too much trouble," she protested.

"Not so. Tell me what to buy."

"Ground lamb, rice, onion, lemon, fresh mint," she recited. "I pick leaves—boil five minutes—ready when you come back."

Before leaving, Qwilleran checked out the Siamese. They were asleep on the guest bed. If Koko had wanted so badly to drive to the cabin, why had he spent five minutes rolling on the concrete and the rest of the afternoon in sleep? Cats were unfathomable.

Qwilleran drove back to Pickax. At Toodle's he bought the lamb, lemon, onions, and mint.

At the rice shelf he was puzzled. There was long grain, short grain, white, brown, precooked, preseasoned.

"Having a problem, Mr. Q.?" asked another customer. "Perhaps I can help. I'm Elaine Fetter. We met at the library, where I volunteer."

"Of course," he said emphatically, as if it were true. She was a woman with an air of authority and surely some opinions about rice. "What kind of rice do you suggest for, uh, meatballs?"

"I believe you'd be safe with white, short grain," she said.

At that moment they were both startled by a loud boom.

"What was that?" she exclaimed. "It sounded so close!"

"I'd better check it out," he said. "Thanks for the advice." He snatched a package of white, short grain and paid for his purchases.

As he pulled out of the parking lot, the flashing lights of emergency vehicles could be seen coming from the hospital and the firehall. Main Street traffic was being detoured. He parked where he could and ran toward the center of town.

A procession of pedestrians was hurrying to the scene, and the shout went up: "It's the hotel! The hotel blew up!"

A cordon of yellow crime-scene tape kept onlookers away from the shattered glass and debris that covered the sidewalk and pavement in front of the hotel. Stretcher-bearers hurried up the front steps. The medical examiner arrived with his ominous black bag and was escorted into the building by the police.

"Somebody's killed," the watchers said.

On the far side of the yellow tape was a gathering of persons Qwilleran knew from Amanda's Design Studio. One of the studio's plate-glass windows was cracked, and the staff was out looking up at the second floor of the hotel.

The windows of all three floors of the solidly built stone building were shattered. Fragments of draperies and clothing hung from projections on the outside of the building. The arm of an upholstered chair lay on the sidewalk.

"Hi, Qwill," said Fran Brodie, Amanda's attractive young assistant. "Are you covering this for the paper or just nosing around?"

She was not only a good designer; she was the daughter of the police chief. She said, "Dad always complains that nothing big ever happens on his turf. This should keep him quiet for a while."

The chief was swaggering about the scene.

"Does anyone know what happened?" Qwilleran asked.

In a confidential tone Fran said, "They think it was a homemade bomb. They say room two oh three is really trashed. Everyone's wondering about the mystery woman."

Qwilleran thought of Onoosh; hadn't the desk clerk given her a big room at the front? "Any injuries?" he asked.

"Lenny Inchpot came out with a bandage on his head and was hustled away in a police car—to the hospital, no doubt."

Outside the yellow tape a reporter was maneuvering to get camera shots; a WPKX newswoman was thrusting a microphone in front of officials and eyewitnesses. Then the coroner came out, followed by medics carrying a body bag on a stretcher. A sorrowful moan arose from onlookers, and the question was asked, Who was it? Guest or employee? No one knew.

"I can't hang around," Qwilleran told the designer. "I'll tune in my car radio to hear the rest."

He wanted to break the news to Onoosh gently and observe her reaction. It would reveal whether she was really a cook looking for a job in a restaurant or the intended victim of a murderous plot.

As he drove back to the cabin, he heard a news bulletin on the radio. "An explosion in downtown Pickax this afternoon claimed the life of one victim, injured others, and caused extensive property damage. Thought to be caused by a homemade bomb, the blast wrecked several front rooms of the New Pickax Hotel. A member of the staff was killed. Others were thrown to the floor and injured by falling debris. All windows facing Main Street were shattered. Police have not released the name of the victim, pending notification of relatives, nor the name of the guest registered in the room that received the brunt of the blast. Stay tuned for further details."

Qwilleran stepped on the accelerator. A quarter mile from the letter K on the post, he saw a car leave his driveway in a cloud of dust. It turned onto the highway without stopping, heading west.

He thought, The mystery woman was involved in the bombing and sent me to buy lamb so she could escape. She was headed to the airport. He felt his face flushing. He was embarrassed to have fallen for her ruse.

He jumped from his car when he reached the clearing, and rushed indoors. She had left her beach hat, the folding chair, and three books from the public library—all cookbooks.

In the kitchen a paper towel was spread with damp grape leaves, and the saucepan in which they had been boiled was draining in the sink. The chopping board and knife were standing ready. The countertop radio was blaring country music. He turned it off irritably.

Only then did he realize that Onoosh had been working in the kitchen and listening to the radio when the bulletin was broadcast. She had dropped everything and headed for the airport because she knew the bomb was intended for her. He searched for a note, but all he found was a number on the telephone pad. He called the number and was connected with the airport terminal.

"Do you remember a woman in a black pantsuit boarding the five-thirty shuttle?" he asked.

"Yes sir," said the attendant, who sold tickets, rented cars, and even carried luggage in the small terminal. "She turned in a rental and ran to the plane. Didn't even have any luggage. Lucky we had a seat for her. On Friday nights we're usually sold out."

Now Qwilleran thought he understood. Whether or not she was a cook, she was a fugitive—in hiding—fearing for her life.

Chapter Five

QWILLERAN sat glumly on the porch organizing his reactions. He grieved over the senseless death of the hotel employee. Further, he regretted the wanton destruction of the building, no matter how substandard its rating or how disliked its owner. And he was disappointed by the sudden departure of the fascinating woman who had said, "Call me Onoosh." All of these considerations added up to a determination to solve the who and why of the bombing.

He returned to the apple barn, fed the cats a can of red salmon, then went to Lois's for the Friday dinner special, fish and chips. Lois was waiting on tables and venting her rage about the bombing.

"Did you hear the six-o'clock news? D'you know who was killed? Anna Marie Toms—Lenny's girlfriend. Sweet girl. . . . Sit anywhere."

She was gonna be a nurse. Lenny and her were goin' to college together. She worked part-time as a housekeeper at the hotel. . . . How many pieces, hon? Cole slaw? . . . Lenny just called. He heard it on the radio. He's bein' very brave, but he's hurtin' bad inside. He got her the job. That makes it twice as bad. . . . Coffee, anybody?"

QWILLERAN put through a call to the police chief at home. "The explosion—was it pretty bad, Andy?"

"Everything in a certain radius was blown to bits. That poor girl never knew what hit her."

Qwilleran asked, "Am I correct in thinking room two oh three was registered to the mystery woman?"

"Right, and she hasn't been seen since."

Qwilleran said, "I spent the afternoon with her."

"What! How come? How'd you meet her? What do you know?"

"Why don't you come over for a Scotch?"

In five minutes the police chief drove into the yard. Tall and husky, he was an impressive figure, especially when he wore full Scottish kit and played the bagpipes at weddings and funerals. He walked into the barn with a piper's swagger.

Qwilleran had a tray ready with Scotch and cheese, and Squunk water for himself. As the two men settled into big chairs, the Siamese walked into view with a swagger of their own. Coming close to the coffee table, they sat down, noses level with the cheese platter. As the guest raised his glass, the two noses edged closer.

"No!" Qwilleran thundered. They backed off a quarter inch.

"Try this cheese, Andy. It's from the new Sip 'n' Nibble shop in Stables Row. It's run by two guys from Down Below. They like to be called Jerry Sip and Jack Nibble. Jerry's the wine expert, and Jack knows everything about cheese."

"Gimme a slice. Then tell me how you met that woman."

"It was weird. This afternoon I drove to the cabin on a routine inspection, and the woman was sitting on my beach."

Andy Brodie grunted at intervals as Qwilleran told the whole story. "So she offered to make some stuffed grape leaves if I'd buy the ingredients, and that's what I was doing when the bomb went off."

The chief chuckled. "She wanted to get your car out of the drive so she could make a getaway."

"That was my first thought. Then I realized that she'd probably heard the radio bulletin and knew the bomb was intended for her. I called the airport, and they said she'd boarded the shuttle."

Brodie said, "She might have decamped in a hurry because she was a conspirator in the bomb plot. She was conveniently out of the building, hiding out on your property when the bomb exploded."

Qwilleran drew a heavy hand over his mustache, as he always did when he was getting a major hunch. A tingle on his upper lip was a signal that he was on the right track. "I maintain, Andy, that she's a fugitive trying to go underground. When the wind blew her hair away from her face, I saw a long scar in front of her ear."

"Could be the result of an auto accident," Brodie suggested. "What name did she give you?"

"Only her first name: Onoosh."

"Onoosh? On the hotel register she signed Ona Dolman."

A dark brown paw stole slowly over the edge of the coffee table.

"No!" Qwilleran bellowed, and the paw was quickly withdrawn.

"Well, I guess we'll never see Ona Dolman again," said the chief. "The hell of it is the murder of that innocent girl."

"Do you know exactly how it happened, Andy?"

"I'll fill you in—off the record." Brodie had gradually accepted Qwilleran as trustworthy and useful. The journalist's prior experience as a crime reporter had given him insights into investigative processes, and his natural instinct for snooping often unearthed facts of value. In pursuing his private passion, Qwilleran was satisfied to tip off the authorities and take no public credit.

"About four o'clock this afternoon an unidentified white male— about forty, medium build, clean-shaven—came in the front door of the hotel with a gift package and flowers for Ona Dolman. Lenny, on duty at the desk, said she wasn't in but he'd send them up to her room. The suspect said the gift was handblown glass, very fragile, and he'd feel more comfortable taking it up himself. He asked for a piece of paper and wrote 'Open with care, honey.' So Lenny told him to ask Anna Marie to let him into two oh three. The suspect came back down and went out the back door. The porter saw a blue pickup drive down the back street and pick up a man in a blue jacket."

Qwilleran asked about witnesses on the second floor.

"The manager's office is up there. She didn't see the suspect, but

Anna Marie took the vacuum into two oh three, telling the manager that the flowers had made a mess on the rug. When she plugged in the cord or pushed the machine around, she probably tripped the bomb."

"Can Lenny describe the suspect?"

"Both Lenny and the florist who sold him the flowers got a close look at him. The SBI—State Bureau of Investigation—computer is making a composite sketch from their descriptions."

Qwilleran poured another Scotch for Brodie and asked how he liked the cheese.

"Good stuff. What d'you call it?"

"Gruyère. It's from Switzerland."

"Yow!" came a loud demand from the floor, and Qwilleran gave each cat a tiny crumb of cheese, which they gobbled and masticated and savored at great length as if it were a whole wedge.

Brodie asked, "Did Ona Dolman say anything at all that might finger the bomber?"

"No. I'm afraid I missed the boat. I intended to ask some leading questions while we were eating our grape leaves."

"Well, now that we know she left on a plane, we can start a search. If she was in hiding, she falsified information, but there'll be prints on the car if they haven't cleaned it." He called the airport; the car had been thoroughly cleaned when it was returned. Qwilleran said there would be prints on the kitchen sink at the cabin, and he turned over the key to Brodie, along with the folding chair, cookbooks, and straw hat that she had left behind.

"We'll need your prints, too, Qwill. Stop at the station tomorrow. . . . What did you call that cheese?"

"Gruyère."

"Yow!" said Koko.

Brodie stood. "Better go home, or my wife'll call the police."

Just then a low rumble came from under the coffee table. As the two men turned to look, Koko came slinking out, making a guttural noise, waving his tail, sneaking up behind Yum Yum.

"Watch this," Qwilleran whispered.

Pow! Koko pounced. *Whoosh!* Yum Yum got away, and they were off on a wild chase up the ramp.

"They're just showing off," Qwilleran said.

Chapter Six

ON SATURDAY morning Qwilleran fed the cats, policed their commode, and brushed their coats. Koko had pushed a book off the library shelf. "Later," Qwilleran said, as he replaced the playscript of *A Taste of Honey*. Then he thought, Wait a minute. Does that cat sense that I'm going to interview a beekeeper?

He went to the police station to be fingerprinted and then to the library for a book on beekeeping. While there, he heard the clerks greeting Homer Tibbitt, who arrived each day with a brown paper bag, even though a sign specified NO FOOD OR BEVERAGES. Homer was in his late nineties, and allowances were made. With a jerky but sprightly gait he walked to the reading room to do research.

Qwilleran followed. "Morning, Homer. What's today's subject?"

"The Goodwinter clan. Amanda found some family papers in an old trunk and gave them to the library—racy stuff, some of it."

"Do you know anything about the Limburgers?" Qwilleran asked.

"Yes, indeed. I wrote a monograph on them a few years ago. As I recall, the first Limburger came over from Austria in the mid-nineteenth century. He was a carpenter, and the mining companies hired him to build cottages for the workers. But he was a go-getter, ended up building on his own, and got rich."

"What happened to his housing empire?"

"One by one the buildings burned down or were pulled down. The Hotel Booze is the only one still standing. The family itself— second generation—was wiped out in the flu epidemic of 1918. There was only one survivor, and he's still living."

"You mean Gustav?" Qwilleran asked.

"Haven't seen him for years, but I remember him as a young boy. Pardon me while I refresh my memory." The old gentleman struggled to his feet and went to the rest room, carrying his paper bag. It was no secret that it contained a thermos of coffee laced with brandy. When he returned, he had recalled everything.

"Yes, I remember young Gustav. I was a fledgling teacher in a one-room school, and I felt sorry for him. He'd lost his folks, and he was sent to live with a German-speaking family. His English was poor, and, to make matters worse, there was a lot of anti-German sentiment after World War One. It's no wonder he ran away a couple of times and finally dropped out."

"Didn't he inherit the family fortune?"

"That's another story. Some said his legal guardians mismanaged his money. Some said he went to Germany to sow his wild oats and lost it all. I know he sold the Hotel Booze to the Pratts and kept the Pickax Hotel. I hear it was wrecked by a bomb yesterday."

"Apparently Gustav never married," Qwilleran remarked.

"Not to anyone's knowledge. But who knows what he did in Germany? When I was writing the Limburger history, I tried to get him to talk, but he shut up like a clam."

EN ROUTE to Black Creek, Qwilleran detoured through the town of Brrr, so named because it was the coldest spot in the county. He wanted to chat with Gary Pratt, owner of the Hotel Booze and chummy host at the Black Bear Café. Gary was a big bear of a man himself, having a shaggy black beard and a lumbering gait. He was behind the bar when Qwilleran slipped onto a barstool.

"The usual?" he asked, plunking a mug on the bar and reaching for the coffee server.

"And a bearburger—with everything," Qwilleran said.

Gary leaned on the bar. "What are they jawboning about in Pickax today?"

"The bombing. What else?"

"Same here."

"Any brilliant theories as to motive?"

"Well, folks think it has to do with that foreign woman. She'd come in here for lunch, and I'd try to get her into conversation. No dice. Last Saturday she had dinner with one of our guests—a man."

"What kind of guy?"

"Looked like a businessman—clean-cut, wore a suit and tie. Checked in about five thirty, which looks like he came on the shuttle. She drove him here, and they had dinner in a corner booth."

"Was he swarthy like her?" Qwilleran asked.

"No. He had light skin, reddish hair. They were together the next day, too, and then I think she drove him to catch the Sunday night shuttle. He checked out around four thirty—paid his bill with cash. Makes you wonder what he had in his briefcase."

The bearburger arrived, and Gary changed the subject to the Labor Day bike race. "I didn't finish—didn't expect to—but it was fun. Now the Pedal Club's sponsoring a bike-athon to benefit the hot meal program for shut-ins. Sponsors can pledge anywhere from a dime to a dollar per mile. I figure I'm good for thirty miles."

"I'll sponsor you." Qwilleran signed a green pledge card for a dollar a mile. Then he said, "Do you know Aubrey Scotten?"

"Sure. I know all the Scotten brothers."

"I'm supposed to interview him about beekeeping this afternoon. Can you fill me in on a few things?"

"Such as . . ."

"Is he a reliable authority on beekeeping? Is his honey considered good? Was his hair always snow-white?"

Gary looked uncertain, and then decided it was all right to talk. "Well . . . about the hair. It happened while he was in the navy. He had an accident, and his hair turned white overnight."

"What kind of accident?"

"Something aboard ship, never really explained. He got dumped in the ocean and nearly drowned. In fact, he was a goner when they hauled him out, but he came back to life. Changed his personality."

"In what way?"

"For one thing, he'd been a bully in high school, and now he's a kindhearted guy who won't swat a fly. For another, he used to work in the Scotten fishing fleet; now he's terrified of boats and water. The navy gave him a medical discharge and sent him home." Gary poured Qwilleran another cup of coffee. "But there was a plus. Aubrey turned into some kind of genius. He can repair anything—*anything*. He was never that way before."

Qwilleran's blood pressure was rising; a near death experience would be more newsworthy than the honeybee business.

Then Gary said, "Aubrey won't talk about his accident, and neither will his family—especially not to the media."

For the second time in two days Qwilleran had seen a good lead turn out to be no story, so . . . back to the honeybees.

THE Limburger mansion loomed like a haunted house. Still, Qwilleran thought as he parked at the curb, it could be renovated to make a striking country inn, given a little imagination and a few million dollars. The exterior brickwork—horizontal, vertical, diagonal, and herringbone—was unique. The tall, stately windows had stained-glass transoms or inserts of etched and beveled glass.

Qwilleran rang the doorbell. When there was no answer, he walked around the side of the house. "Hello! Hello? Is anyone here?" he shouted in the direction of the weathered shed. A bulky white-haired figure materialized from the interior gloom.

Qwilleran said, "I was here yesterday when Mr. Limburger fell down the steps. I'm Jim Qwilleran, remember? I told you I'd return to ask you all about beekeeping."

"I di'n't think you'd come back," the young man said. "Folks say they'll come back, and they don't. A man ordered twelve jars of honey, and I packed 'em all up. He never showed. It's not friendly."

"Some people don't have consideration for others," Qwilleran said with sympathy. "How is Mr. Limburger? Do you know?"

"I just come from the hospital. He was in bed and yellin' his head off about the food."

Qwilleran pointed to the shed. "Part of your honey operation?"

"That's where I draw the honey off."

"Do you have any for sale? I'd like to buy a couple of jars."

Aubrey disappeared into the dark shed and returned with two oval jars containing a clear, thick amber fluid.

"Why are honey jars always flat?" Qwilleran asked.

"Flat makes the honey look lighter. Most people want light honey. I don't know why. The dark has lotsa taste. This is wildflower honey. I took some to Lois, and she give me a big breakfast."

They sat on the porch, and Qwilleran turned on the tape recorder. "Let's talk about bees. Do you ever get stung?"

Aubrey shook his head gravely. "My bees ain't never stung me. They trust me. I talk to 'em. I give 'em sugar water in winter."

"Would they sting me?"

"If you frighten 'em or act unfriendly or wear a wool cap. They don't like wool. I don't know why."

Piecemeal, the interview filled the reel of tape: A beehive was like a little honey factory. Every bee had a job. The workers built honeycombs. The queen laid eggs. The fieldworkers collected nectar and pollen from flowers. They brought it back to the hive to make honey. The doorkeepers guarded the hives against robbers. The drones didn't make honey—they just took care of the queen. If the hive got crowded, the drones were thrown out to die.

Qwilleran asked, "How do they get the nectar back to the hive?"

"In their bellies. They carry pollen in little bags on their legs. Wanna see the hives?"

They walked down a rutted trail to the river, where all was quiet except for the rushing of the rapids and the cawing of crows. On the bank stood a shabby cabin.

Aubrey said, "My family had six cabins they rented to bass fishermen. Two burned down. Three blew away in a storm. I live in this one. The walls were fulla wild bees, and I hadda smoke 'em out and take off the siding, and underneath, the walls were fulla honey."

On the south side of the building, protected from the north wind, were the hives—wooden boxes elevated on platforms. Aubrey said, "The bees do all the work. I take the honeycombs up to the shed and draw the honey off and put it in jars."

"What do the bees do in winter?" the journalist asked.

"They cluster together in the hives and keep each other warm."

It was a fantastic story, if true, Qwilleran thought. He would check it against the library's bee book. He paid for his honey and left with a new respect for the thick amber fluid.

Chapter Seven

QWILLERAN drove to Toodle's and bought some corned beef—enough for the cats' dinner and a late-night snack for himself—then drove downtown to buy flowers for Polly.

Downtown Pickax was a three-block stretch of stone buildings: large, small, impressive, quaint, ornate, and primitive—relics of the era when the county was famous for its quarries. To Qwilleran, Main Street was Information Highway; friends and acquaintances stopped him to report the latest scandal, rumor, or joke.

Qwilleran stopped first at Exbridge & Cobb, Fine Antiques. Susan Exbridge was a handsome match for her upscale establishment. She collected Georgian silver, won bridge tournaments at the country club, and bought her clothes in Chicago.

Susan opened the door. "Come in and see my new collection."

The premises always gleamed with polished mahogany and

shining brass, but now a space was filled with antiques of a dusty, weathered, folksy sort.

"Do you recognize any of those primitives?" she asked. "They were in Iris Cobb's personal collection."

The late Iris Cobb had been an expert on antiques, a wonderful cook, and a warmhearted friend to Qwilleran. "What is that?" he asked, pointing to a weathered wood chest with iron hardware.

"An old sea chest," Susan recited glibly, "found in an attic in Brrr. It had been washed up on the beach following an 1892 shipwreck and was thought to belong to a Scottish sailor."

"Uh-huh," Qwilleran said skeptically. "How much?"

"Because you're an old friend of Iris," she said, "I'll give you a ten percent discount. We'll deliver it to the barn for you."

Qwilleran grunted. Iris would have given him twenty percent. He said, "I don't suppose her personal cookbook turned up, did it? It was left to me in her will, you may recall—a joke, I presume, because she knew I was no cook and never would be."

"I wish it had! Some of my customers would mortgage their homes to buy it. She kept it in that old school desk, but by the time I was appointed to appraise the estate, it was gone."

Qwilleran went next door to the florist. "Hello, Mr. Q.," said a young clerk with long, silky hair and large blue eyes. "Daisies again? Or would you like mums for a change?"

"Mrs. Duncan has an overriding passion for daisies and unmitigated scorn for mums," he said sternly. "Why are you pushing mums? Did your boss buy too many?"

She giggled. "Oh, Mr. Q., you're so funny. Most people like mums because they last longer, and we have a new color." She showed him a bouquet of dark red. "It's called vintage burgundy."

"Just give me the daisies—without any of that wispy stuff, no ribbon, no balloons." Then, having asserted himself, he said in a genial tone, "You had some excitement across the street yesterday."

She rolled her expressive blue eyes. "I thought it was an earthquake." She added in a whisper, "The police were here, asking questions. The man that planted the bomb bought some flowers from us."

"Did you see him?"

"No. I was in the back room. Mr. Pickett waited on him. He bought mums in that new color."

"Well, tell your boss to stock up on vintage burgundy. There'll be a run on it when the public discovers it was the bomber's choice."

SOMEWHAT behind schedule because of his stops on Main Street, Qwilleran hastily chopped corned beef for the Siamese. He was driving to Gingerbread Alley for a turn around the block with Polly, then meeting Dwight Somers at Tipsy's Tavern for dinner. But meanwhile, he had time to read some more Aristophanes to the felines. "Do you realize," he said to them, "that you're two of the few cats in the Western world who are getting a classical education?" They liked *The Birds,* especially the part about Cloud-Cuckoo-Land, where the birds built a city in the sky. He embellished the text with birdcalls. Yum Yum purred, and Koko became quite excited.

TIPSY'S Tavern was a roadhouse in a sprawling log cabin—with rustic furnishings and a reputation for good steaks. Dwight ordered a glass of red wine. Qwilleran had his usual Squunk water.

They talked about the plans for the Explo. The bombing had hurt morale downtown, but Dwight had jacked up the hype, and merchants were rallying around. That was the commercial aspect of Explo. There was more. "The K Fund, frankly, is afraid of being perceived as a year-round Santa Claus, so they're encouraging community fund-raising for charity. They're matching, dollar for dollar, all the money raised by the celebrity auction, bike-athon, pasty bake-off, et cetera. All proceeds will go to feed the needy this winter."

"Who are the celebrities to be auctioned?" Qwilleran asked.

"The idea is to have five bachelors and five single women. In some cases the dinner-date package will include a gift. Everything is being donated. The public will pay an admission fee—and that'll add a couple of thousand to the take."

"Who's the auctioneer?"

"Foxy Fred. Who else? He's donating his services, and you know how good he is. People will have lots of fun. Here's a list of the packages being offered." He handed Qwilleran a printout.

Qwilleran read the list, nodding at the choices and chuckling a couple of times. "Everything else looks good, but you have only nine packages on this list."

"Precisely why I'm buying your dinner tonight," Dwight said

slyly. "Check this for number ten: A complete makeup and hair styling at Brenda's Salon, prior to dinner at the Old Stone Mill with popular newspaper columnist Qwill Qwilleran."

The popular columnist hemmed and hawed.

"You're an icon in these parts, Qwill—what with your talent, money, and mustache. Women will bid high to get you."

When the steaks arrived, Qwilleran had had time to consider. The adventure would be material for the Qwill Pen. "But I hope we don't have to stand up in front of the audience like suspects in a police lineup," he said.

"Nothing like that," Dwight assured him. "We've booked the high school auditorium, and there's a greenroom where the celebrities can sit and hear the proceedings on the PA. Onstage there'll be an enlarged photo of each celebrity, courtesy of John Bushland—Bushy, as he likes to be called. After each package is knocked down, the winner and celebrity will meet onstage and shake hands—amid applause, cheers, and screams."

"I'm glad you explained all this, Dwight. It gives me time to disappear in the Peruvian mountains before auction night."

Chapter Eight

ON SUNDAY morning the church bells rang on Park Circle—the sonorous chimes of the Old Stone Church and the metallic echo of the Little Stone Church.

Earlier in the morning Qwilleran had received a phone call from Carol Lanspeak, who lived in fashionable West Middle Hummock. She and Larry drove into town every Sunday to the older, grander of the two places of worship. This time they were bringing a new couple to church, recently arrived from Down Below: J. Willard Carmichael and his wife, Danielle. "He's the new president of Pickax People's Bank, a distinguished-looking man and a real live wire," Carol said. "His wife is much younger and a trifle, well, flashy. But she's nice, and they're both dying to see your barn. Would you mind if we stopped by after the service—for just a few minutes?"

Qwilleran couldn't say no. The Lanspeaks were a likable pair—not only owners of the department store but enthusiastic supporters of every civic endeavor. "I'll have coffee waiting," he said.

To the Siamese, he said, "I want you guys to be on your best behavior. Some city dudes are coming to visit." They listened soberly,
Koko looking aristocratic and Yum Yum incapable of crime.

When the Lanspeaks' car pulled into the parking area, Qwilleran
gave the visitors a few minutes to admire the barn's exterior before
going out to greet them. The newcomers were introduced as
Willard and Danielle from Grosse Pointe, Michigan.

Carol Lanspeak said, "We've brought you some flowers from our
garden." It was a pot of mums, blooming profusely.

"Thank you," Qwilleran said. "Unusual color."

"Vintage burgundy," her husband, Larry, said.

Indoors, there were the usual gasps as the newcomers viewed the
balconies, lofty rafters, ramps, and giant white fireplace cube from
which the Siamese looked down with bemused whiskers.

As Qwilleran served the coffee, he was thinking that Danielle was
hardly Moose County's idea of a banker's wife—everything about
her was studiously seductive: her style, her glances, her semi-drawl.

The sharp edge of her voice was disturbing the Siamese. Koko
stood up and stretched in a tall hairpin curve, then swooped
down onto the Moroccan rug
that defined the lounge area.
Yum Yum followed, and while
she checked the banker's
shoelaces, Koko walked slowly
toward Danielle with subtle

intent. She was sitting with her attractive knees crossed, and Koko started sniffing her high-heeled pumps as if she had stepped in something unpleasant. He wrinkled his nose and bared his fangs.

"Excuse me a moment," Qwilleran said, and grabbed both cats, banishing them to the broom closet.

When he returned to the group, Larry said, "We have something to discuss with you, Qwill. The recent financial disaster in Sawdust City is going to leave hundreds of families with no hope of a Christmas. We're planning a benefit, a cheese tasting. Sip 'n' Nibble will supply cheese and punch at cost, and sort of cater the affair."

A yowl came from the closet as Koko heard a familiar word.

Larry said, "We were planning to hold the event at the community hall, but we could charge more for tickets if we held the cheese tasting in a really glamorous place. There are people in the county who'd pay a hundred dollars a ticket to see this barn—especially in the evening when the lights are on. It's enchanting."

It crossed Qwilleran's mind that the K Fund could write a check to finance all the Christmas charities, but it was healthier for the community to be involved. He said, "Why not charge two hundred dollars and limit the number of guests? The higher the price and the smaller the guestlist, the more exclusive the event becomes." And, he mused, the less wear and tear on the white rugs.

"In that case," said Willard, "why not make it black-tie and increase the price to three hundred dollars?"

There were sounds of thumping and banging in the broom closet and an attention-getting crash. "We'd better say good-bye," Carol said, "so the delinquents can get out of jail."

Larry pulled Quill aside as they walked to the parking area and said, "The chamber of commerce has formed an ad hoc committee to inquire into the future of the hotel. We can't afford to have a major downtown building looking like a slum. Not only that, but the city needs decent lodging. The owner is in the hospital, possibly on his deathbed. The committee will go to Chicago to petition the K Fund to buy the hotel. I hope you approve."

"Excellent idea!" Qwilleran said.

They drove off, and Qwilleran released two poised animals from a closet cluttered with plastic bottles, brushes, and other cleaning equipment knocked off hooks and shelves. Cats, he reflected, were the inventors of civil disobedience. As for Koko's impudent charade with Danielle's shoe, it might be one of his practical jokes, or it might signify a personality clash.

Chapter Nine

THE electronic chimes of the Little Stone Church clanged their somber summons on Monday morning as hundreds of mourners flocked to the memorial service for Anna Marie Toms. The crowd overflowed the church, clustered on adjoining lawns, and filled the circular park that divided Main Street. Photographers from the *Moose County Something* and the *Lockmaster Ledger* were busy. The afternoon papers would carry their first coverage of the Friday bombing, and they would go all out.

Qwilleran walked to the newspaper office and handed in his Tuesday copy. He said to Junior Goodwinter, "I saw Roger and Bushy at the memorial service. The *Ledger* was covering it, too."

"Yeah, we're giving it the works. Police releases are minimal, as usual, but we've got man-on-the-street stuff, photos, and the SBI's computer sketch of the suspect based on witnesses' descriptions. Then we've got a sidebar on the history of the hotel, courtesy of Homer. Roger went to the hospital, hoping to get an interview with Gustav Limburger, but the old crab threw a bedpan at him."

"What about the mystery woman? Wasn't her room the target?"

"Yeah. Ona Dolman, her name is. At least, that's the way she registered, and the name she used at the car rental and the library and on traveler's checks. There's no evidence that she used a credit card or personal checks anywhere. . . . So we've been busy."

AFTER talking with Junior, Qwilleran made the rounds. He wanted to have words with Arch Riker, but the publisher was just back from lunch, so he stopped to pick up his fan mail from the office manager. He knew her only as Sarah, a small woman with steel-gray hair and thick glasses, who had never married. Junior called her Qwill's number one fan. She memorized chunks of the Qwill Pen and quoted them in the office; she knew the names of his cats; she crocheted catnip toys for them. For his part Qwilleran treated

Sarah with exaggerated courtesy and suffered good-natured ribbing in the city room about his "office romance."

"Would you like me to slit the envelopes for you, Mr. Q.? There are quite a few today." She kept a record of his columns according to topic, plus a tally of the letters generated by each one. She was able to say that cats and baseball were his most popular topics.

"Yes, I'd appreciate it if you would," Qwilleran said, and went into the publisher's office. "Were you having another power lunch?" he asked Archie. "Or was it a three-Scotch goof-off?"

Riker rebuked him with a frown. "I was having an important luncheon with the editor in chief of the *Lockmaster Ledger.* We both think the bombing is a two-county story. We're sharing sources. By the way, how about taking on an extra assignment?"

Qwilleran was wary. "Like what?"

"Wednesday night's the opening of Mildred's cooking course for men, and it's a sellout. We should have a reporter there."

"What's the matter with Roger?" Roger MacGillivray was a general assignment reporter married to Mildred's daughter, Sharon.

"Sharon is assistant demonstrator for the course, so Roger has to stay home and baby-sit," Riker explained. Then his usually bland expression changed to a roguish one. "However, Roger could cover the story, and you could baby-sit. Or Sharon could stay home with the kids, and you could help Mildred with the demonstration."

Gruffly Qwilleran said, "What time is the class? And where?"

"Seven thirty at the high school. Take a camera."

"Okay, Arch, I'll do it," Qwilleran said, "but you owe me one."

On the way out of the building Qwilleran picked up a paper from a bundle that had just come from the printing plant. The headline read SEARCH TWO COUNTIES FOR BOMB MURDERER. He planned to read it with his lunch at Lois's.

"IS THAT today's paper?" Lois asked. "Is Lenny's picture in it?"

Qwilleran scanned the paper. "Doesn't look like it," he said. "How's he doing?"

"He's down in the dumps. What'll it be for you today?"

He ordered a Reuben sandwich, coffee, and apple pie—one of Lois's specialties. While waiting, he perused the paper. There were photos of the shattered interior of room 203; the fallen chandelier lying on the reservation desk; the hotel exterior, windowless and draped with debris. There was also a photo of Anna Marie.

Of unusual interest was the computer composite of the suspect's probable likeness, this being the first time such a technical advance had appeared in the local paper. It would also be running in the *Lockmaster Ledger,* and the good folk of two counties would carry it around and peer suspiciously into every passing face.

QWILLERAN finished his lunch and went to Amanda's Design Studio to speak with Fran Brodie. The designer was cloistered in the consultation booth with an indecisive client. Fran saw him and made a grimace of desperation, but Qwilleran signaled no-hurry and ambled about the shop.

When Fran finally appeared at his elbow, she said, "Hey, you made a big hit with the new banker's wife. She came in this morning, and all she could talk about was you and your barn. She thinks you're charming. Don't let Polly hear about Danielle; she'll have a relapse. . . . Is that today's paper you're carrying?"

"Take it. There's nothing new," he said to the police chief's daughter. "You probably know more than the newspaper."

"I know they've run a check on Ona Dolman. Her driver's license is valid, but there's no such address as the one she gave the hotel. The suspect was described as wearing a blue nylon jacket and a black baseball cap with a 'fancy' letter D on the front. He got into a blue pickup behind the hotel."

Qwilleran thought, Nine out of ten males in Moose County drive pickups and wear blue jackets; but they wear high-crowned farm caps advertising fertilizer or tractors. . . . Baseball caps are worn chiefly by sportfishermen from Down Below. The suspect's black one sounds like a Detroit Tigers cap.

He bought a small gift for Polly and asked to have it delivered.

Chapter Ten

AS QWILLERAN fed the cats on Tuesday morning, questions unreeled in front of his brain's eye: Who had bombed the hotel—and why? Would he strike again? Would the hotel be restored? Was this the beginning of the end for downtown Pickax?

Qwilleran found himself yearning for other times, other places—when Iris Cobb was his housekeeper. Would her cookbook ever be found? he wondered.

He went to breakfast at Lois's. It was raining, so he drove his car.

He sat in his favorite booth and ordered pancakes. Lois's son, Lenny, was serving. The large bandage on his forehead indicated that he had looked up when the bomb exploded and the chandelier dropped.

"Will you be able to ride in the bike-athon Sunday?" Qwilleran asked him.

"I don't much feel like it, but everybody tells me I should." Lenny Inchpot had the lean and hungry look of a bike racer and the stunned look of a young man facing tragedy for the first time.

"If you bike, I'll sponsor you at a dollar a mile."

"Take it!" Lois shouted from the cash register. "Give him a green card."

Qwilleran asked Lenny, "What's the best place for pictures?"

"About a mile south of Kennebeck, where the road runs between two patches of woods. We're just starting out—no dropouts, no stragglers. It's some sight! A hundred bikers coming over the hill."

As they talked, Qwilleran felt someone staring at them from a nearby table. It proved to be Aubrey, eating pancakes.

"Good morning," Qwilleran said. "How are your flapjacks?"

"They're almost as good as my mom's. Lois always gives me a double stack and extra butter. I bring my own honey. D'you like honey on flapjacks? Try it." The beekeeper leaned across the table, offering Qwilleran a plastic squeeze bottle shaped like a bear cub.

"Thank you very much. How is Mr. Limburger?"

"He wants to come home. The doctor says, 'No way!' "

Qwilleran dribbled honey on his pancakes and staged a lip-smacking demonstration of enjoyment. "Delicious." He noticed Monday's newspaper on Aubrey's table. "What do you think of the bombing?"

"Somebody got killed!" the beekeeper said in horror. He stared at his plate briefly, went to the cash register, and left the lunchroom.

"Wash his table good," Lois told her son. "It's all sticky. How'd you like the flapjacks, Mr. Q.?"

"Great! Especially with honey. By the way, could I scrounge a little something for the cats?"

"I always have a handout for those two spoiled brats. Ham okay?"

WITH the ham tidbits in the trunk of his car Qwilleran drove to the library for a conference with Homer Tibbitt, but the aged historian was not to be found. One of the clerks explained that he stayed home in rainy weather.

A phone call to the nonagenarian's home produced an invitation. "Come on over, and bring the file on the Plensdorfs." At ninety-five-plus, Homer Tibbitt had no intention of wasting a morning.

When Qwilleran arrived, Rhoda Tibbitt served tea while he explained his mission. "I want to know about Moose County's foremost regional specialty."

The Tibbitts said in unison, "Pasties!"

"If you write about them," Homer said, "tell the greenhorns from Down Below that they rhyme with nasty, not hasty. You probably know that Cornish miners came here from Britain in the mid-nineteenth century. Their wives made big meat-and-potato turnovers for their lunch, and they carried them down the mine shaft in their pockets. They're very filling. Takes two hands to eat one."

Rhoda said, "There's disagreement about the recipe, but the secret of the authentic pasty dough is lard and suet, and the authentic filling is diced or cubed beef or pork. *Ground meat is a no-no.* The filling is mixed with diced potatoes and rutabagas, chopped onion, salt and pepper, and a big lump of butter. You put the filling on a circle of dough and fold it over. Some cooks omit the rutabagas."

HAVING been briefed in pasty correctness, Qwilleran went to Stables Row to check out the Pasty Parlor, not yet open for business. He knocked, identified himself, and was admitted by the owners, a bright young couple in paint-spattered grubbies.

"Are you natives of Moose County?" he asked.

"No. But we've traveled up here on vacations and eaten a lot of pasties, and we decided you people need to expand your horizons," the young man said. "We made a proposal to the K Fund in Chicago and were accepted."

"What was your proposal?"

"Designer pasty! Choice of four crusts: plain, cheese, herb, or cornmeal. Choice of four fillings: ground beef, ham, turkey, or sausage meat. Choice of four veggies: green pepper, broccoli, mushroom, or carrot—besides the traditional potato and onion, of course. Plus your choice of tomato, olive, or hot chili garnish."

"It boggles the mind," Qwilleran said with a straight face. "I'll be back when you're open for business. Good luck."

From there he hurried through the rain to Lori Bamba's brainchild: the Spoonery. The energetic entrepreneur was lettering signs. "Are you serious about serving only spoon food?" he asked.

"Absolutely! I have dozens of recipes for wonderful soups: mulligatawny, Scotch broth, Portuguese black bean, eggplant and garlic, and lots more. Soup doesn't have to be boring. . . . How are Koko and Yum Yum? I haven't seen them for a while."

"Busy as usual, inventing new ways to complicate my life."

Lori said with her usual exuberance, "Do you know what I read? Cats have twenty-four whiskers, which may account for their ESP."

"Does that include the eyebrows?" Qwilleran asked.

"I don't know. They didn't specify."

"Are there twenty-four whiskers on each side, or is that the total?"

"I don't know. You journalists are such fusspots!"

"Well, I'll go home and count," Qwilleran said. "And good luck, Lori. I'll drop in for lunch when you open."

IT WAS still raining. He went home to give the Siamese the ham he had begged from Lois, and he found Koko doing his grasshopper act. The cat jumped in exaggerated arcs from floor to desktop to chair to bookshelf. It meant that there was a message on the answering machine. The faster he jumped, it appeared, the more urgent the call. How did the cat know the content of the message? Perhaps Lori was right, Qwilleran thought. Cats have ESP whiskers.

The message was from Sarah, the office manager, who had never phoned him at the barn before. "Sorry to bother you at home," said the deferential voice, "but an express letter came for you."

He got her on the phone immediately. "Sarah, this is Qwill. About the express letter, what's the return address?"

"It's hotel stationery. No one's name. It's from Salt Lake City."

"I'll pick it up right away. Thanks." Qwilleran felt a tingling on his upper lip; he had a hunch who was writing to him. He drove to the newspaper via the back road to make better time. Sarah handed him the letter, and he tore it open. The handwriting was hard to decipher; she spoke English better than she wrote it.

Dear Mr. Qwill—
I sorry I leave and not say thank you—I hear it on radio about hotel bomb—I panick—he is threttan me many time—he want to kill me—I think it good I go long way away so he not find me—how he find me in Pickacks is not to know—now I afraid again—I leave this hotel now—I sign my right name—
Onoosh Dolmathakia

When Qwilleran read the letter again, beads of perspiration soaked his forehead—not at the thought of Onoosh being terrorized by a stalker, but at the realization that Koko had been feeding him this information ever since the bombing, and even before. Koko had been stalking Yum Yum boldly and repeatedly, in a purposeful campaign.

Qwilleran telephoned the police station. "Stay there!" he barked at Brodie. "I have some curious information." A few minutes later he walked into the chief's office.

"What've you got?" Brodie demanded gruffly.

"A letter from Onoosh Dolmathakia, a.k.a. Ona Dolman. She addressed it to me at the paper."

Brodie read it, then threw it down on the desk. "Why the hell didn't she tell us his name—and how to find him?"

"Panic," Qwilleran protested. "She's not thinking straight."

"We can assume he lives Down Below. That means he transported explosives across a state line—a federal offense. The FBI will get into the act now. Did the guy fly up here with a bomb on his lap?"

Qwilleran said, "Dolman is obviously an Americanization of Dolmathakia and not the name of her ex-husband. All we know about him is that he might be a fan of the Detroit Tigers, judging by the description of his cap."

"There's gotta be a local connection. How would he know she was here? Who drove the getaway vehicle? Did the same blue truck pick him up at the airport?"

"Well, the ball's in your court, Andy. I have unfinished business at home."

QWILLERAN WENT HOME AND counted whiskers. He counted Koko's first and then Yum Yum's. It was just as he had surmised. He telephoned Polly immediately.

"I want you to count Bootsie's whiskers and call me back," he said. "Include the eyebrows."

"Is this a joke?"

"Not at all. It's a scientific study. I plan to introduce it in the Qwill Pen after the Food Explo. Cats all over the county will be having their whiskers counted."

"I still think you're being facetious," she said, "but I'll do it."

In a few minutes she called back. "Bootsie has twenty-four on each side. Is that good or bad?"

"That means he's normal," Qwilleran said. "Yum Yum has twenty-four also. Koko has thirty!"

Chapter Eleven

THE Great Food Explo was about to blast off, with Mildred Riker's cooking class lighting the fuse Wednesday evening.

At lunchtime Qwilleran went to Lois's. Her Wednesday luncheon special was always turkey, and he always took home a doggie bag. Lois's Luncheonette was on Pine Street, not far from Stables Row, and as he approached, he saw a crowd—men in work clothes and business suits, women office workers and shoppers—gathered on the sidewalk. He quickened his step.

Qwilleran asked loudly, "What goes on here?" No one answered, but there was a general hubbub of indignation and complaint. Then he saw the crayoned sign in the window: CLOSED FOR GOOD.

"Where'll we get ham and eggs? There's no place for breakfast."

"Where'll we get lunch?"

"Who'll have apple pie that's any good?"

Qwilleran asked some of the quieter protesters, "Why did she close? Does anybody know?"

"If you ask me," said a salesman from the men's store, "she's teed off because Stables Row got all slicked up by the K Fund. If she wanted to fix up her place, her customers had to pitch in and do it."

Indeed, Qwilleran himself had often dropped a twenty into a

pickle jar near the cash register, to help defray the cost of shingles or paint. Labor was willingly donated on weekends by a confraternity of loyal customers. To work on Lois's beloved lunchroom was the Pickax equivalent of knighthood in the court of King Arthur. There was, in fact, a large round table where the in-group met for coffee and conversation. And now Lois was leaving the food business. It was a calamity. First the hotel bombing—and now this!

THE cooking class was scheduled for seven thirty, but Qwilleran arrived early, hoping to glean some quotes from the eleven participants, who had assorted reasons for attending:

Mechanic from Gippel's Garage: "My wife went back to work, and she says I've gotta do some of the housework."

Hardware salesman: "I'm a single parent with two kids."

Derek Cuttlebrink, the excessively tall waiter from the Old Stone Mill: "My girlfriend gave me the course for a birthday present."

There was an unmistakable aroma of Thanksgiving dinner in the room. At seven thirty Mildred appeared, her ample figure filling out a white bib apron. A floppy white hat topped her graying hair.

After a few words of welcome she began: "Thanksgiving is not far off, so tonight we'll take the mystery out of roasting the big bird. This will be a two-bird demonstration, because roasting takes several hours. Bird number one has been in the oven since four and will be ready for carving and sampling at the end of the session."

Qwilleran's interest in the class increased as he visualized take-homes for the Siamese. He clicked his camera as Sharon Hanstable entered the arena with the uncooked bird number two on a tray. In bib apron and floppy hat, she was a younger, thinner version of her mother, Mildred. Smiling happily, she handed out notepads, pencils, and brochures containing roasting charts and stuffing recipes.

Mildred said, "This handsome gobbler arrived in a frozen state from the new Cold Turkey Farm and has been defrosting for two days in the refrigerator. Please repeat after me: *I will never . . . thaw a frozen turkey . . . at room temperature.*"

A chorus of assorted male voices obediently took the oath.

"Now for step one: Preset the oven at three hundred and twenty-five degrees. Step two: Release the legs that are tucked under a strip of skin, but do not cut the skin."

Eleven pencils and Qwilleran's ballpoint were taking notes.

"Step three: Explore the breast and body cavities and remove the plastic bags containing the neck and giblets. These are to be used in making gravy. Step four: Rinse the bird and drain it thoroughly."

Qwilleran thought, I could do this. What's the big deal?

"Meanwhile, Sharon has been mixing the stuffing. It's called rice-and-nice in your brochure. It consists of cooked brown rice, mushrooms, water chestnuts and other flavorful veggies. So . . . ready for step five: Stuff the cavities lightly with the rice mixture."

Mildred tucked in the legs, placed the bird breast-up on a rack in the roasting pan, brushed it with oil, inserted a thermometer, and explained the basting process. By the time bird two was ready to go into the oven, bird one was ready to come out—plump-breasted and golden brown. Mildred demonstrated carving and the making of giblet gravy. Then the men were invited to help themselves.

"Good show," Qwilleran said to Mildred.

"Stick around," she said in a whisper as he filled his paper plate again. "You can have the leftovers for Koko and Yum Yum."

FRIDAY was the big day in Pickax. A yellow ribbon a block long was tied across the front of Stables Row and its seven new business enterprises subsidized by the K Fund.

The block was closed to traffic, and as noon approached, it began to be crowded with downtown workers, shoppers, mothers with preschoolers in tow, and members of the chamber of commerce.

Dwight Somers dashed around and talked on his cellular phone. "The school bus just arrived with the band. Alert the mayor to leave city hall in five minutes."

When a police siren signaled the approach of the mayor's car, the band crashed into "The Washington Post" march with the confidence of young musicians who know most of the notes. A police officer cleared the way for the mayor. Gregory Blythe was a middle-aged, well-dressed stockbroker, handsome in a dissipated way, and insufferably conceited. Yet he was always reelected; after all, his mother was a Goodwinter.

Dwight Somers led the applause as Blythe mounted a small podium and spoke into the microphone. "On this festive occasion I want to say a few words about the future of Pickax."

"Make it short!" someone yelled from the crowd.

"Excellent advice," Blythe replied, with a smile in the heckler's direction. Then he proceeded to speak too long despite murmurs in the audience and the lack of attention.

Finally a child's shrill voice cried out, "Where's the balloons?"

"Let there be balloons," the mayor decreed.

Two photographers rushed forward. The ribbon was snipped. Then as the band struck up "The Stars and Stripes Forever," multicolor balloons rose from behind Stables Row and the crowd converged on the new shops.

Qwilleran caught sight of a husky, heavily bearded young man lumbering about. "Gary!" he shouted. "What brings you to town?"

"Just checking on my competition," said the proprietor of the Black Bear Café.

"What do you think of the Stables?"

"The building's neat. The Spoonery's a good idea. But the Pasty Parlor is off the wall. The owners don't know a pasty from a pizza."

Qwilleran observed the crowds for a while and then went into the Kitchen Boutique, managed by Sharon Hanstable.

He glanced around at the gadgets so foreign to his lifestyle: garlic presses, nutmeg grinders, pastry brushes. "What are those knives with odd blades?"

"Cheese knives," Sharon said. "The wide blade is for crumbly cheese; the pointed one for hard varieties; the narrow, squarish one is for soft and semisoft."

"I'll take a set. Since Sip 'n' Nibble opened, I'm becoming a cheese connoisseur. So are the cats."

WHEN he returned to the barn, he found a mess in the lounge area. Someone had uprooted the Lanspeaks' vintage burgundy mums and scattered them all over the white Moroccan rug.

Koko was sitting on the fireplace awaiting Qwilleran's reaction.

"You, sir, are a *bad cat!*" was the stern rebuke.

Koko flicked a long pink tongue over his black nose.

Then Qwilleran relented. "I didn't think much of them myself. They look like dried blood. Sorry, old boy."

He stayed home for the rest of the day. When the sea chest arrived from Exbridge & Cobb, he had it placed outside the back door to receive packages. Finding a wood shingle in the toolshed, he made a crude sign for it: DELIVERIES HERE. For dinner he hacked enough meat for two cats and one man from the carcass of bird number one. Later he read to the Siamese. Koko chose *Poor Richard's Almanack,* which provided such pithy tidbits as "A cat in gloves catches no mice."

As the evening wore on, Qwilleran frequently tamped his mustache and consulted his watch. Koko was nervous, too. He prowled incessantly after the reading. Did he sense the forthcoming fireworks as he did the approach of a storm? The merchants on Main Street would serve cookies and punch until nine o'clock; then the crowd would move to the Stables block for the sky show.

When the fireworks began, Yum Yum hid under the sofa, but Koko was agitated. He growled; he raced around erratically. Qwilleran could hear the crackling, thudding, and whining of the rockets. At one juncture Koko howled as if in protest.

The radio was tuned in to WPKX, broadcasting live from a van on the Stables block. Qwilleran was in the kitchen, scooping up a dish of ice cream, when an announcer broke in with a bulletin.

"The Food Explo festivities in Pickax tonight were marred by the killing of a downtown merchant in the course of an armed robbery. Police have not released the victim's name, pending notification of family. The shooting took place while crowds were watching the fireworks. Further information will be broadcast when available."

Chapter Twelve

THE WPKX bulletin reporting a homicide in downtown Pickax struck Qwilleran like the bomb that wrecked the hotel. His mind raced through a roster of his friends who were merchants on Main Street: the Lanspeaks, Fran Brodie, Susan Exbridge, and more. He knew virtually everyone in the central business district.

He phoned the police chief's home. "Andy isn't here," Mrs. Brodie said. "He got a phone call and took right off. There's been a murder. Isn't that terrible?"

"Did he say who was killed?"

"Only that it wasn't our daughter, thank the Lord. I don't know when he'll be back. If he calls, I'll tell him you phoned."

Around midnight the phone rang. It was Brodie. "Did you hear the news?" the chief barked. "They took out one of our witnesses."

"No! Which one?"

"I'll stop by the barn on my way home if you're gonna be up."

Within a few minutes headlights could be seen bobbing through the woods. Qwilleran went out to meet his friend.

"They got Franklin Pickett," were Brodie's first words. "Poor guy died with flowers clutched in his hand."

Qwilleran poured a Scotch and a glass of Squunk water, and they sat at the bar, within reach of a cheese platter.

"The cash drawer was rifled," Brodie went on, "but the robbery was a red herring. The real motive was obviously to silence a witness. Notice the timing! Everybody was at Stables Row gawking at the fireworks. You could have shot a cannon down Main Street."

"Who discovered the crime?"

"Danny, on patrol. Main Street stores were supposed to be locked up by then, but Pickett's lights were full on. Danny found the door unlocked—no answer to his shout. He saw the cash register open and found Pickett facedown in front of the flower cooler."

Qwilleran said, "If the killer had bought flowers on the day of the bombing, shouldn't Pickett have recognized him?"

"He could've worn a disguise, or it could have been his local accomplice on a mopping-up mission. We already decided there was a local connection. That would account for the timing. Somebody around here would know the schedule of events and when to hit."

"What kind of flowers was the victim clutching?" Qwilleran asked with grim curiosity.

"Something dark red."

"Have some cheese, Andy."

"Is it the good stuff you gave me last time?"

"Yes. Gruyère."

"Yow!" came a startlingly loud comment from under the bar. Koko knew by experience where to wait for crumbs.

Qwilleran said, "If it's witnesses they're after, what about Lenny Inchpot? He's riding in the bike-athon Sunday. The paper printed his name and shirt number in today's edition—also the route."

"We're trying to find him. His mother's visiting her sister in Duluth, and you can bet Lenny's crashing with his bike buddies. We may have to nab him at the starting gate and ship him off to Duluth."

"Has the SBI come up with any leads on the bombing suspect?"

"Well, with no name, car license, or fingerprints, they're working against odds, but the homicide tonight may be the thin edge of the wedge." Brodie downed his Scotch and said it was time to go, adding, "Why doesn't your smart cat come up with some clues?" It was half in jest and half in wonder at Koko's past performances.

"He's working on it, Andy." Qwilleran was thinking about the cat's frenzy during the fireworks, his trashing of the dark red mums, his ominous howl at one particular moment. Were his psychic senses registering a gunshot on Main Street?

Now Lenny Inchpot was in danger.

Qwilleran checked his green pledge cards for the bike-athon. He'd left them on the telephone desk, under the brass paperweight, but Lenny's was missing. A search turned it up in the foyer—on the floor—well chewed. Neither cat was in sight.

SATURDAY was the day of the pasty bake-off, and Qwilleran would join Mildred Riker and the chef of the Old Stone Mill in the judging. At one thirty he reported to the fairgrounds, identified himself as a judge, and was directed to a room at the rear of the exhibition hall where local cooks were exhibiting and selling homemade baked goods, preserves, and canned garden produce.

In the judges' chamber Mildred welcomed Qwilleran with a hug and a judge's badge. "Now," he said, "tell me how many hundred pasties I have to sample today."

"I hate to disappoint you," she said cheerfully, "but the preliminaries have narrowed the field down to fifteen. The crust judges eliminated about a third of the entries. Other judges checked ingredients and correct prep of the filling—no ground meat, no disallowed vegetables. We'll do the final testing for flavor and texture."

"How many judges have been nibbling at the fifteen pasties before we get them?" he asked.

Before she could reply, a tall gangling youth shuffled into the room. He threw his arms wide and announced, "Guess what! You got me instead of chef-baby."

"Derek! What happened to Sigmund?" Mildred cried in disappointment and some annoyance.

"He slipped on a sun-dried tomato and sprained his ankle."

"Well, I'm sure you're a connoisseur of anything edible," she said dryly. "Let's all sit down at the table and discuss procedure. First, the guidelines. The purpose of the competition is to preserve and encourage a cultural tradition, thus forging a spiritual link with the past and celebrating an eating experience that is unique to this region of the United States."

"I don't even know what that means," Derek said.

"Never mind. Just taste the pasties," she said sharply. She went on. "Entries are limited to twelve inches in length, with traditional crust and ingredients."

"Okay, let's get this show on the road," Derek said impatiently.

Mildred opened the door and gave the signal, whereupon the pasties were brought into the room. Reduced by the preliminaries to half their size, they were cut into chunks and served to the judges, whose comments were brief and emphatic: "Too much onion." "Rather dry." "Needs seasoning."

One pasty in particular was praised by the two male judges, but Mildred tasted it and said indignantly, "This is dark meat of turkey! It's disqualified. How did it slip past the other judges?"

Qwilleran said, "But it deserves some kind of recognition. I wonder who baked it."

"Well, we can't accept it," Mildred said firmly. "Rules are rules when you're judging a contest."

"You can't convince me," Qwilleran said, "that the early settlers didn't make pasties with wild turkey—or venison or rabbit or anything else they could shoot or trap."

"That may be so, but if we break the rules, future competitions will lose significance and we'll have a controversy on our hands."

After some retasting, number eighty-seven was named the winner. They left the judges' chamber and handed the winning number to the chairperson of the bake-off.

"Attention, please," he announced on the public address system. "The blue-ribbon winner in the pasty bake-off has been selected by our esteemed judges, and will receive a prize of one hundred dollars, but we have a slight foul-up. In order to preserve the anonymity of contestants during the judging, their names were deposited in the safe at our accountant's office, and since the office is closed until

Monday, we cannot identify the winner at this time. The winner will be notified, however, on Monday morning, and the name will be announced on WPKX and in the *Moose County Something*."

As the judges left the exhibit building, Mildred said to Qwilleran, "Weren't you shocked by last night's murder? We've never had anything like that in Moose County."

Qwilleran knew more than he wanted to disclose to the publisher's wife. He said, "The SBI is on the case, and we can assume it's a criminal element from Down Below that's responsible—not some bad boy from around here."

FOR Qwilleran, one more Explo commitment remained: the celebrity auction. He dressed for the event with care. His sartorial mentor, the owner of Scottie's Men's Store, had recommended a bronze silk-blend sport coat, olive-green trousers, and a silk shirt in olive, to be worn open at the neck.

The crowd that gathered for the auction had paid plenty for their tickets and were convinced they were going to have a good time. The auctioneer, Foxy Fred, circulated in his western hat and red jacket, whipping up their enthusiasm. His spotters, also in red jackets, handed out numbered flash cards to those intending to bid. The celebrities were assembled in the greenroom backstage, where they would be able to hear the proceedings on the PA system.

Qwilleran said, "I expect Foxy Fred to hawk me as 'a gen-u-wine old newshound in fair condition, with the patina of age and interesting distress marks.' Then the bidding will start at five dollars."

Fran Brodie muttered to Qwilleran, "If I were in the audience, I'd bid a month's commissions on you. Danielle Carmichael was in the studio yesterday looking at wallpaper. They're both here tonight. Willard is going to bid on me, and she's going to bid on you, although he won't let her go over a thousand."

At that point Pender Wilmot of the Boosters Club arrived in the greenroom to brief the somewhat nervous celebrities. "Packages will be auctioned in the order that appears in the printed program. When your package is knocked down, the winner will come to the platform and you'll walk out to meet your dinner date. Relax and have fun. It's all for a good cause."

Foxy Fred banged the gavel, and bidding commenced. The

mayor's package—dinner at the Purple Point Boat Club—was knocked down for seven hundred and fifty dollars to Elaine Fetter.

Fran whispered, "She's been running after the mayor ever since she lost her husband. I did her house. It has a fabulous kitchen."

Her own package—dinner at the Palomino Paddock—brought one thousand dollars from Dr. Prelligate. After meeting him on-stage, she said breathlessly to Qwilleran, "He's not at all like a college president; he's quite sexy. I wonder what I should wear for the dinner."

Qwilleran's package was the last to go on the block. While other packages had been greeted with murmurs of interest and a few youthful shrieks, this one brought a storm of clapping and cheering.

Foxy Fred shouted, "Who wants to have dinner with a famous journalist? Shall we start with five hundred? Who'll give me five hundred? I hear four hundred. . . . Who'll make it four fifty?"

"Hep!" shouted a spotter, pointing at a flash card.

"Four fifty I've got. Make it five fifty."

"Hep!"

"That's the ticket. Now we're rollin'. Who'll bid six fifty? Waddala waddala bidda waddala . . . Six fifty I've got. Make it seven!"

"Hep!"

"Make it eight. Chance of a lifetime, folks. . . . I see eight in the back row. . . . Nine I've got over there at the left. Make it a thou! Dinner date you'll never forget. . . . A thousand I've got! Who'll bid twelve hundred? Twelve I've got from the lady in the back row! Fourteen is bid. Make it fifteen! Where's that card in the back row?"

Qwilleran and Fran exchanged glances. Had Danielle exceeded her thousand-dollar cap? He passed a hand over his warm face.

"Do I hear fifteen? Don't lose him now! Make it fifteen!"

"Hep!"

"Fifteen is bid! Who'll go sixteen? Sixteen? Sixteen? Fifteen once, fifteen twice!" The gavel banged down. "Sold for fifteen hundred to the lady back there with number one thirty-four."

Qwilleran said, "Who can it be?" A list flashed into his mind: women who had been pestering him for the last five years—women who could afford fifteen hundred dollars, women he liked, women he didn't like. If only Polly could have been in the audience. They could have rigged it: She'd bid; he'd pay.

The crowd in the auditorium was going wild. Derek and Bushy pulled him to his feet and pushed him toward the stage. Foxy Fred shouted, "Come on out, Mr. Q. Don't be bashful!"

Suspense was building. The auctioneer bawled, "Here's the lucky lady! Come right up, sister. Feeling a little weak in the knees?"

Qwilleran tidied his mustache, took a deep breath, squared his shoulders, and walked onstage. The sight of the famous mustache increased the uproar. He looked across the stage to see a red-jacketed spotter assisting a little gray-haired woman up the steps.

"Sarah!" he shouted in astonishment.

Chapter Thirteen

AT THE newspaper everyone called her Sarah. Now she gave her name as Sarah Plensdorf. Qwilleran walked across the stage toward the nervous little woman, extending two reassuring hands. Tears of excitement or triumph were streaming down her face. His own reaction was: How could she—why would she—spend that kind of money on a dinner date with *anyone?* It must be a practical joke, he decided, financed by Riker, Hixie, and Junior. It was the kind of trick they would play—expensive, but tax-deductible. Well, he would spoil their fun; he would put on a good show. He grasped Ms. Plensdorf's trembling hands, bowing over them courteously. Then he brought down the house by giving her a bear hug.

An attendant ushered the two of them to a table in the wings, where Pender Wilmot invited them to set a date for their dinner.

"Would Monday evening be too soon?" Ms. Plensdorf asked.

"Monday will be perfect," Qwilleran said. "I'll reserve the best table at the Mill and pick you up at seven o'clock." She lived, he now learned, in Indian Village, an upscale complex of apartments and condominiums outside of town.

Back at the barn, he wasted no time in phoning Polly to report the news.

"Sarah Plensdorf. What a surprise!" she exclaimed. "Well, I'm glad she won you, Qwill. She's a very sweet person."

"I know her only as office manager at the paper. What I wonder is, Can she afford fifteen hundred dollars?"

"I'm sure she can. She donates generously to the library. The

Plensdorfs made their fortune in lumbering in the early days, and I imagine she inherited a handsome amount."

"I see," Qwilleran said.

ON SUNDAY morning Qwilleran left the barn at seven thirty and drove toward Kennebeck. The wooded hill south of town was lined with cars, vans, and pickups on both shoulders. Early arrivals were having tailgate breakfasts.

A sheriff's car came slowly over the crest of the hill and started down the long, gentle slope, followed by more than a hundred lightweight cycles with helmeted riders crouched over the handlebars. Lenny was nowhere in sight; the police department had successfully grounded him.

Later, when Qwilleran returned to the barn, he glanced into the sea chest before unlocking the back door. To his surprise there was a carton labeled PRODUCT OF COLD TURKEY FARM. WEIGHT, 12 POUNDS.

Payola, Qwilleran thought, but then he remembered that in the country neighbors accepted neighborly expressions of gratitude with good grace. The question was, What to do with the bird? Actually, as he remembered Mildred's demonstration, prepping a turkey was not a staggering problem, and the oven did the rest. He opened the carton and put the plastic-wrapped turkey into the refrigerator on a tray to defrost.

On the hour he tuned in WPKX, expecting to hear a report on the bike-athon. Instead, he heard a startling news bulletin.

"A fisherman was found dead this morning as a result of multiple beestings, according to the medical examiner. The body was found in a cabin belonging to Scotten Fisheries, on the bank of Black Creek. No further details are available at this time."

Qwilleran had a sudden urge to visit Aubrey Scotten.

IT WAS a nice day—sunny, just cool enough for a sweater. He drove into the side yard of the Limburger mansion and tooted the horn. The door of the honey shed was open, and after a second blast of the horn a dejected figure appeared in the doorway. His whole frame drooped, and his pudgy face sagged.

Qwilleran jumped out of his car and went toward him, saying, "Remember me? Jim Qwilleran. I came to buy some honey."

Without a word Aubrey disappeared into the shed and returned with two jars. The transaction was made in silence.

"How's Mr. Limburger?" Qwilleran asked.

"Same, I guess," Aubrey said in his squeaky voice.

"Did you hear that Lois has closed her restaurant?"

The beekeeper nodded in a daze.

"How do you like your new job at the turkey farm?"

The man shrugged. "It's . . . okay."

"Look here, Aubrey. Are you all right?"

Two tears ran down the soft face.

Qwilleran slipped into his big-brother role. "Come on, Big Boy. Let's talk." He steered the young man to a weather-beaten bench outside the honey shed. They sat in silence for a moment. "I was sorry to hear about the accident at your cabin. Did you know the man?"

Aubrey sighed heavily. "He was my friend."

"Is that so? How long had you known him?"

"Long time."

"Had he ever been up here before?"

There was more weary nodding.

"Where were you when it happened?"

"In the house." He jerked his head toward the brick mansion.

"He evidently did something that frightened or upset the bees."

Aubrey shrugged shoulders that seemed weighted by a heavy burden.

"I wish I could think of something to say that would help you, Aubrey. It takes time to recover from a shock like this. Keep busy. Face one day at a time." While he was babbling platitudes, he was thinking about a recent morning at Lois's when the bombing was mentioned and the sensitive young man said, "Somebody got killed!" Then he rushed from the restaurant without finishing his pancakes. Now a friend had been killed—and by his own bees, compounding the anguish. "Aubrey," Qwilleran said, "think of me as a friend, and call me if I can help. Here's my phone number."

Aubrey took the card, then surprised Qwilleran by following him to his car. "The police were here," he said anxiously.

"What did they say?"

"They kept asking about the bees. Could they arrest me for what my bees did?"

"Of course not. Cops always ask a lot of questions. They may come back and ask some more. Just answer them truthfully. If they give you a hard time, let me know."

On the way home Qwilleran frequently tamped his mustache with his fist. Instinct told him there was more to this story than appeared on the surface. Furthermore, Koko had been agitated all weekend, a sure sign that he was trying to communicate. For one thing, he kept knocking *A Taste of Honey* off the bookshelf.

FROM the desolation of blighted Black Creek, Qwilleran drove to West Middle Hummock, where fine estates nestled among rolling hills and winding roads. Elaine Fetter had suggested Sunday afternoon for the mushroom interview because her weekdays were consumed by volunteer work.

In preparation he had consulted the encyclopedia and had learned that the edible fungus is a sporophore consisting largely of water and having a curious reproductive system—what they called the sexuality of the mushroom. Although he was no gardener, he knew that one could plant a radish and get a radish, but there was something murkily mysterious about the propagation of mushrooms. Mrs. Fetter specialized in shiitake, which she pronounced shee-tock-ee.

The Fetter residence was an old farmhouse on which money had been lavished. "Do come in and have a cup of tea in the keeping room," Elaine Fetter said. She led the way through spacious rooms furnished with antique pine and cherry—to a large kitchen with a six-burner range, a bank of ovens, and shelves filled with cookbooks. Separated from the cooking center by an iron railing was an area with a fireplace and Windsor chairs around a trestle table.

"I call this the nerve center of the house. I spend my mornings here, testing recipes and experimenting with new dishes. I'm writing a cookbook, you see."

He set up his tape recorder, then asked, "Could you describe briefly the procedure in growing shiitake?"

"Of course. First you find a young healthy oak tree and cut it down before it leafs out in spring. It should be four to six inches in diameter, with just the right thickness of bark. After cutting your bed logs in four-foot lengths, you drill holes in them and inoculate them with commercial spawn. Then you seal the holes, after which they incubate for three months."

"Do you ignore them during the incubation?"

"Not at all! You must maintain the humidity by occasional deep soaking or frequent watering with a gentle spray. An electric gauge measures the interior moisture of the logs." She explained the process like a lesson memorized from a textbook. "After inoculation you can expect fruiting in six to nine months."

"And what do you do with your crop?"

"Sell them to restaurants and markets in Lockmaster. Local grocers consider them too expensive, although shiitake are more delicious and nutritious than ordinary mushrooms. I'll sauté some for you later—with parsley, garlic, and freshly ground black pepper."

From the kitchen they stepped through sliding glass doors to a patio, then along a path to a wooded area on the bank of a stream. In partial shade the bed logs were sprouting little buttons. "Just beginning to fruit," she said. "And over there is a flush, ready to crop." She pointed to logs ringed with ruffles of large mushrooms, the caps as big as saucers and furrowed in a pattern of brown and white.

On the way back to the kitchen he said, "This shiitake project sounds like a lot of work, considering all your other activities."

"Oh, I have a little help," she said nonchalantly.

While she sautéed shiitake, Qwilleran perused her large collection of food-related books: Larousse, Escoffier, and Brillat-Savarin, as well as ethnic cookbooks and recipe collections of all kinds. Before he had a chance to examine the books, she called him to the table and he tasted the best mushrooms he'd ever eaten.

Later he reported the entire incident to Polly as they took their walk. "What did you think of Elaine?" she asked.

"Well, I'm impressed by her expertise and her collection of cookbooks, but"—he patted his mustache—"I have a sneaky feeling she wasn't telling the whole story."

"Did she mention her son?"

"No. What about her son?"

"Donald lives with her. He was driving the car when it crashed and killed her husband, and he's confined to a wheelchair. Growing shiitake is his therapy. It gives him a reason for living."

"Hmmm. That puts a different slant on the story," Qwilleran

said. "And actually it's a better story—one that could be rather inspirational. The question is, Why did she withhold that aspect of the enterprise? Does Donald avoid publicity because of his physical condition? Or does his mother want the publicity for herself?"

"An astute observation," Polly said. "What will you do about it?"

"Put the column on hold, but I'd scheduled it for this week, and now I'll have to find another topic." He didn't mention it, but there was more than the shiitake situation that bothered him.

Chapter Fourteen

BACK at the barn Qwilleran called Celia Robinson.

"Hi, Chief!" she hailed him in her usual cheerful manner. "What a beautiful day. Did you do something special?"

"No. I'm just a working stiff," he said. "I did an interview out in West Middle Hummock. That's why I'm calling. Do you happen to know a Donald Fetter?"

"Sure. He's a subscriber to Pals for Patients. Why?"

"It's too long a story for the phone. Why don't you drive down here? I have some new cheese for you to try, and I may have a new assignment for you."

"Whoops!" she cried in her youthful way. "I'll be right there."

Qwilleran hung up and turned to the Siamese. "Our neighbor is coming for a conference, and I want you two heathens to behave like civilized human beings. Or, at least, civilized beings," he corrected himself. He arranged a cheeseboard for his guest and gave the cats a crumble or two: Havarti for Yum Yum, feta for Koko.

Celia arrived in a flush of smiles. "What's that box outside?"

Qwilleran replied, "It's a historic sea chest to be used for deliveries of macaroni and cheese if I'm not home."

As she went to the lounge area with her large handbag, the Siamese followed. They knew that handbag sometimes contained a treat. "What's the new cheese?" she asked.

"Goat cheese from Split Rail Farm. It's feta—quite salty."

"Yow!" said Koko.

"When my husband was alive," she said, "we kept goats and sold milk to folks who had trouble with cow's milk." She gazed into space. "Seems a long time ago." Then she snapped back to the present. "How was the autumn color in West Middle Hummock?"

"Spectacular. I went out there to interview Elaine Fetter about her mushrooms."

"*Her* mushrooms? It was Donald's idea! He was very depressed until he heard about growing— What do you call them?"

"Shee-tock-ee. They're a Japanese mushroom."

"Well, it gave him something to live for. We send Junior Pals out there, and they help with the heavy work—those big logs, you know. Did you see that kitchen? What's his mother like? I only met her once. Donald doesn't get along with her too good."

"She's a prominent clubwoman and volunteer, a gourmet cook— and she's writing a cookbook."

"I never saw so many cookbooks as she has in her kitchen."

"That, madame, is precisely why you are here," Qwilleran said. "First a little background information: Have you heard of Iris Cobb? She died before you moved up here. She contributed greatly to the community, but she's chiefly remembered for her cooking. Her collection of personal cooking secrets was left to me in her will, but it disappeared before I could put my hands on it."

"You don't cook, Chief. What good would it do?"

"I think it was supposed to be a joke, but I planned to publish it and donate the proceeds to charity, in her name."

"Any notion what happened to it?"

"There are three possibilities: It was in a piece of furniture that was sold to an out-of-state dealer when her estate was liquidated. Or it was thrown out as junk, being a greasy, scuffed notebook with a broken spine and loose pages. Or it was simply stolen. A request for its return, no questions asked, produced no results."

"Sounds like something I wouldn't mind reading," Celia said.

"You may get a chance. When I was in Mrs. Fetter's kitchen, I noticed a battered black book among all the slick new ones. I didn't think too much about it at the time. Later I remembered that the spine of the black book had been repaired with tape, and my suspicions arose." He touched his mustache tentatively. "The next time you go to see Donald, could you manage to sneak a peek?"

"Could I! You know me, Chief. Is there anything special I should look for, besides grease spots?"

"I don't imagine Iris ever put her name on it, but look first for almost illegible handwriting. Next look for certain recipes that made her a legend in her time, like butter pecan gingersnaps and lemon coconut squares. She also had a secret way with meat loaf."

"Oh, this will be fun." She gathered up her large handbag and struggled to rise from the deep cushions of the sofa.

Qwilleran escorted her to her car. When he returned, Yum Yum was doing extravagant stretching exercises and Koko was sitting in front of the refrigerator, staring at the door handle. Inside, the frozen turkey was still hard as a rock.

THE next morning a delegation arrived to discuss arrangements for the cheese tasting: the two men from Sip 'n' Nibble, who were catering the event; Hixie Rice as volunteer publicist; Carol Lanspeak and Susan Exbridge, representing the Country Club.

Jerry Sip and Jack Nibble were overwhelmed by the barn's size and rustic magnificence. "This is some place," Jack said. "We can handle a hundred people here without a hitch. We'll have the punch bowls on the dining table and set up two eight-foot folding tables on either side—for the cheese service."

"And," Susan added, "I'm bringing two very tall silver candelabra and a silver bowl for an arrangement of fall flowers."

"Don't worry about cars. Guests will park in the theater lot," Carol explained, "and jitneys from County Transport will deliver them to the party. The whole evening is going to be gala."

"Do you think I should lock up the cats?" Qwilleran asked.

"No. Let them mingle with the guests. They're a delightful addition to a party—so elegant, so well behaved."

He uttered a grunt of doubt. "We're talking cheese bandits here."

"Yow!" came a loud comment from the kitchen.

"Everything will run smoothly," said Jack. "Trust me."

And Carol added, "Everyone will have a perfectly fabulous time." Then, as the delegation was leaving, she said to Qwilleran, "Your dinner date was at the store when we opened this morning. She bought a rust-colored silk with a Chanel jacket piped in black."

As they left, Hixie handed him an advance copy of the cheese-tasting program.

Having said good-bye to the group, Qwilleran found Koko sitting in front of the refrigerator in rapt concentration, as if willing the door to fly open and the turkey to fly out. "Sorry, old boy," he said. "You'll have to wait a couple of days. How about a read instead?" He waved the program.

With mumbles of appreciation the Siamese ran to their positions: Koko jumping on the arm of Qwilleran's favorite chair and Yum Yum waiting patiently for his lap to become available. First he read the preface aloud. It said that the night's event would feature cheese from nine countries. It said that those selected could be considered the Bach, Beethoven, and Brahms of the cheese world.

At each mention of cheese Koko responded with a yowl.

"I appreciate your interest," Qwilleran complained, "but your comments get boring after a while." It occurred to him that Koko might confuse "cheese" with "treat," or even "read." He wondered if a cat's ear is tuned to vowels and not consonants. As a test, he tried using the French word for cheese.

"If Roquefort is considered the king of *fromages,* cheddar must surely be the Houses of Parliament. The centerpiece on each *fromage* table is a large wheel of cheddar, one from Great Britain and one from Canada. Even so, be sure to sample all twenty *fromages* in this unique adventure in tasting."

Koko yowled at every mention of *fromage,* leading Qwilleran to conclude that the cat was not comprehending words; he was reading minds, and the extra whiskers were probably responsible.

The program then listed the twenty cheeses with country of origin. As Qwilleran read the list aloud, Yum Yum fell asleep on his lap, with a foreleg over her ears, but Koko listened attentively. Three times he yowled—at Brie, Gruyère, and feta. Because they're salty, Qwilleran reasoned, but so is Roquefort. Yet Koko was unimpressed by the king of cheeses.

At midday Qwilleran walked to the newspaper office and picked up his mail. Sarah was not there. The office boy said with a grin, "She took the day off to get her hair and face done. Whoo-ee!"

For lunch Qwilleran went to the Spoonery, where the day's specials were New Orleans gumbo, Viennese goulash, oxtail, and turkey-barley. He had a bowl of the oxtail and pronounced it sensational. He also asked Lori if the turkey-barley soup really had any turkey in it.

"It's loaded! Big chunks. Want a bowl?"

He ordered a quart to take out, planning to fish out the turkey for the Siamese. That should satisfy them until the bird in the refrigerator was ready to fly.

Before he left the Spoonery, several copies of the Monday paper were delivered and Qwilleran grabbed one. The weekend had been an editor's delight, with the celebrity auction, the pasty bake-off, and the bike-athon. The pasty winner, whose name had been locked in a safe, was identified as Lenore Bassett of Trawnto Beach.

Mrs. Bassett was out of town, but the paper quoted her husband, Robert: "Me and the kids always said Mom makes the best goldanged pasties anywhere."

Another story caught Qwilleran's attention, although it was buried on page four and notable for its brevity.

BIZARRE INCIDENT IN BLACK CREEK

The body of a tourist from Ohio was found in a riverbank cabin Sunday morning. Victor Greer, 39, renting the cabin for a weekend of fishing, had been stung to death by bees, according to the medical examiner. The incident was reported by the beekeeper, Aubrey Scotten. The cabin is owned by Scotten Fisheries.

Use of the word bizarre in the headline was a mistake in Qwilleran's opinion. The wire services would pick that up, and news crews would fly up to cover the "death cottage" where "killer bees" attacked an innocent fisherman from Down Below. They would fluster the poor beekeeper and trick him into saying something that would sound suspicious, and the cameras would zoom in on the buzzing bees and make them look like monsters.

Qwilleran sensed the need to steer Aubrey out of harm's way. His motive was not entirely altruistic; as a journalist, he was drawn to a newsworthy character with an exclusive story to tell.

He walked home briskly to pick up his car keys. The turkey soup he put in the refrigerator, closing the door as quietly as possible. Then he left the barn without disturbing the sleeping cats.

Arriving at the Limburger house, he parked in the side yard and rang the doorbell. No response. He banged on the door without results. He rang again and peered through the etched glass. A shadowy figure was shambling toward the front door. "Aubrey, it's your friend from Pickax!" Qwilleran yelled. "I need some more honey." Purposely he used two buzzwords: friend and honey.

The door opened slowly, and Aubrey said in his squeaky voice, "Threw it all out. I'm gonna let my bees go wild."

"Have the police been talking to you again?"

Aubrey shook his mop of long white hair. "They come back, but I hid in the cellar."

"Well, let me give you some friendly advice. You should get away from here. Strangers will be coming from Down Below, and they're worse than the police. Go and stay with your family for a while. I'll drive you. Do you want to pack a bag?"

"I don't need nothin'." Then, as Qwilleran steered him toward his car, Aubrey added, "I wanna go to my mom's."

"That's fine. Tell me where to go."

The Scotten homestead, between Black Creek and Mooseville, had a well-kept lawn and what seemed like acres of mums in bloom, some of them the color of dried blood. A woman was digging up clumps of mums and transferring them to pots. When the car pulled up, she stuck the spade in the ground and came forward. A tall woman, she wore denims, with kneepads buckled on her legs.

"You look terrible!" she said, throwing her arms around her big son. "You need something to eat." She looked at Qwilleran's mustache. "You must be the man who wrote about the bees."

"I'm also a customer of Aubrey's. I stopped at the house to buy honey and thought he looked in need of some home cooking."

"Poor boy. I'll make you a big stack of flapjacks," she said.

Qwilleran caught her eye and mumbled, "I want to speak to you."

"Aubrey, go and wash up. I'll be right there."

Qwilleran said, "All sorts of people will want to pester him—for various reasons. Don't let anyone know he's here, not even your sons, till this blows over."

Chapter Fifteen

QWILLERAN went home to feed the cats and dress for his dinner date with Sarah Plensdorf. He showered, shaved, and dressed in his navy-blue suit with white shirt and red paisley tie.

When he arrived at her apartment, she was ready and waiting—somewhat breathlessly, he thought. In her new dress with Chanel jacket she looked quite smart, and Brenda's Salon had given her a flattering hairdo and natural makeup that gave her a certain glow.

Gallantly he said, "I've been looking forward to this, Sarah."

"So have I," she said. "Would you care for an apéritif?"

"I'd like that, but we have a reservation for seven thirty, and I think we should be on our way."

While she went to pick up her handbag, Qwilleran appraised the interior: large rooms—evidently two apartments made into one—antique furniture, old oil paintings, good Orientals. He was surprised to see a dog. Dogs were not permitted in apartments in the Village. This one was a basset hound. Strangely, it was standing on hind legs with forepaws on a library table.

Sarah returned. "That's Sir Cedric," she said. "A Victorian piece, carved wood. Realistic, isn't it?"

"I must say it's unique," Qwilleran said. The table was dark pine with ordinary carved legs at one end, while the other end was supported by the dog. "Clever! Very clever."

As they drove away, he asked his passenger, "How do you like working at the newspaper?"

"It's most enjoyable. It's the first job I've ever had."

"Is that so?" he asked in surprise. "You handle it with great aplomb."

"Thank you. I attended an eastern college and could have had a fine position in Boston, but my parents wanted me at home. I was an only child, you see, and we had a lovely family relationship. I went to Europe with my mother and on business trips with my father. Then there was community service. My one regret is that I never had a career. I think I would have been quite successful."

"I'm sure of that," he said. Then, to introduce a light note to the conversation, he added, "*My* only regret is that I was born too late to see Babe Ruth at bat or Ty Cobb in center field."

"That's right. You're a baseball fan. My father started taking me to the World Series when I was seven. My mother didn't care for spectator sports, so he and I flew all over the country, and I learned to keep a detailed scorecard and figure batting averages."

Qwilleran glanced at her with admiration. He said, "Do you still follow the sport?"

"No," she said sadly. "Not since Father died."

When the two baseball fans arrived at the Old Stone Mill, they were shown to the best table and there was applause from other diners. Everyone in Pickax knew about the fifteen-hundred-dollar dinner date. Sarah blushed, and Qwilleran bowed to the smiling faces at other tables.

The waiter served them one dry vermouth and one Squunk water, and Sarah said, "When you write about Koko and Yum Yum in your column, Qwill, you show a wonderful understanding of cats. Have you always been a cat fancier?"

"No. I was quite ignorant of feline culture when I adopted them, but they soon taught me everything I needed to know—"

He was interrupted by the forceful presence of Derek Cuttlebrink, presenting the menus and reciting the specials: "Chicken breast in curried sauce with stir-fried veggies . . . roast rack of lamb with green-peppercorn sauce . . . and shrimp in a saffron cream with sun-dried tomatoes and basil, served on spinach fettucine."

Sarah said, "I developed a taste for curry when we traveled in India, so that would be my immediate choice."

Derek asked Qwilleran, "You want a sixteen-ounce steak and a doggie bag?"

"You don't happen to have any turkey, do you?"

"Come back on Thanksgiving Day."

When the waiter had left the table, Sarah said, "He's rather outspoken, isn't he. But he's refreshing."

Qwilleran agreed. "Now, where were we? Speaking of cats, I assume you like animals."

"Very much. I wash dogs at the animal shelter on Saturdays."

"Small ones, I hope," Qwilleran said.

"All sizes. Every dog gets a bath when he arrives at the shelter. None has ever given me trouble. They seem to know we're doing something nice for them. Last Saturday I bathed a Great Dane."

"Apparently you're accustomed to dogs."

"Yes. We always had them at home. Now all I have is Sir Cedric. When I go home at the end of the day, he greets me and we have some conversation—rather one-sided, I'm afraid. I wouldn't tell this to anyone else, Qwill."

"I understand exactly how you feel," he said with sincerity.

The meal ended with crème brûlée for her and apple pie with cheese for him. She declared it the most delightful dining experience of her entire life. As he drove her home, the conversation turned to the food.

Sarah said, "Did you know I was one of the preliminary judges for the pasty contest Saturday?"

"No. Filling or crust?"

"Filling. And now I must confide in you: There was one pasty that was extraordinary. To me it tasted as good as Iris Cobb's! It was made with turkey, which was disallowed, but the other judges and I were mischievous enough to pass it through to the finals." Her comment on the extraordinary pasty, by raising the ghost of Iris Cobb, supported Qwill's growing suspicions.

They were turning into the gates of Indian Village. Shyly, Sarah said, "Would you care to come in?"

"Thank you, but I have some scheduled phone calls to make. Another time, perhaps," he said, "but I'll see you safely indoors and say good night to Sir Cedric."

The animal holding up the library table looked eerily alive. There was the shading of the brown and white coat, with the delineation of every hair, and there was the sad hound-dog expression in the eyes. Qwilleran patted his head. "Good dog."

As soon as he arrived home, he made some phone calls. It was late, but not too late for certain night owls of his acquaintance.

At the Riker residence, Mildred answered. "How was your date?"

"Read about it in the Qwill Pen," he replied briskly. "Right now I'm interested in who baked that super-pasty."

"If I tell you, will you promise you won't even tell Polly?"

He promised.

"Okay. It was Elaine Fetter. What's this all about?"

"Tell you tomorrow. I'm in a hurry."

He hung up and called Celia Robinson. There had been lights in the carriage house when he drove in, and he knew she would be sitting up reading the latest espionage thriller. In an undercover voice he asked, "Any luck?"

"You were right. I found what you wanted." She spoke in a hushed voice with abstract references. "There wasn't any name on it, but I checked what you mentioned. It's the real McCoy, all right."

"Good going," he said. "Talk to you later."

And now, he wondered, how do we get our hands on it without

embarrassing anyone? He sprawled in a lounge chair with his feet on an ottoman and cudgeled his brain. The Siamese sat quietly nearby, sensing that he was doing some concentrated thinking.

Suddenly he swung his feet off the ottoman and went to the telephone desk. He called Hixie Rice at her apartment.

"What's on your mind, Qwill?"

"I want to run an ad in tomorrow's paper, if it's not too late, but I must not be identified with it in any way. Can you handle that?"

"How big an ad?"

"Whatever it takes to be seen across the room: bold headline, sparse copy, plenty of white space."

"What's the message? Can you give it to me on the phone?"

He dictated about twenty words.

"Hmmm . . . interesting," she said. "Do you expect results?"

"I don't need results," he told her. "This is a bluff. Stay tuned."

Chapter Sixteen

THE cheese tasting was scheduled for Tuesday evening. That morning Qwilleran had breakfast at the Scottish Bakery: scones, clotted cream, and currant jam served by a bonnie lassie wearing a plaid apron.

Later he walked over to the chamber of commerce. He found them making plans for a Lois Inchpot Day in an effort to lure her into reopening her lunchroom. Loyal customers were painting the walls and ceiling, water-stained from the last roof leak.

After that, he visited the Kitchen Boutique to buy a thermometer, basting syringe, and roaster with a rack. He was going to roast that blasted bird if it was the last thing he ever did in his life.

By that time, the paper was on the street, and he read his ad. Within a few hours the entire county would be talking about it:

$10,000 REWARD
for information leading to the recovery of the late Iris Cobb's personal recipe book, missing since her death. Confidentiality guaranteed. Write to PO Box 1362, Pickax City.

He returned to the barn and tested the progress of the thawing turkey, but before he could close the door, Koko executed a grand jeté over the bar and landed in the refrigerator with the bird.

"Out!" Qwilleran yelled, dragging him from the refrigerator and slamming it shut. The cat howled as if his tail had been caught in the door, and he went slinking away, his feline ego wounded.

QWILLERAN dressed for the cheese tasting in dinner jacket and black tie, with a rare set of black studs in his shirtfront. They were from India, inlaid with silver and gold—a gift from Polly. Appraising himself in the full-length mirror, he had to admit that he looked good in evening clothes.

It was dark when the jitneys started delivering the well-dressed guests, and the exterior lights transformed the barn into an enchanted castle. Indoors, illumination from hidden sources dramatized the balconies and overhead beams, the white fireplace cube and its soaring white stacks, the contemporary tapestries, and the clean-cut modern furniture. Add to that the glamour of beaded dinner dresses, the courtliness of men in evening wear, and the bonhomie of such an occasion; it had all the ingredients of a magical evening.

Bushy, a professional photographer, was on hand with a camcorder, the idea being to sell videos of the festivities and raise an extra thousand or two for a good cause.

Among those present were the Rikers, Lanspeaks, and Wilmots; the mayor in his red paisley cummerbund; and the new banker with the flashy Danielle. If one wanted to count, there were three attorneys, four doctors, two accountants, one judge—and five public officials coming up for reelection.

The focus of attention was the dinner table with its silver punch bowls and lighted candles. Flanking it were the two white-skirted buffets, each with eight cheese platters and a large wheel of cheddar. Jerry Sip and Jack Nibble presided at the buffets, assisted by college students in white duck coats.

Jack Nibble was heard to say, "We have three blues on the cheese table. Try all three and compare. The one from France is crumbly; the Italian is spreadable; the one from England slices well."

Jerry Sip said, "If you like a rich, creamy cheese with superb flavor, try the double-cream Brie."

"Yow!" came an endorsement from the floor.

Pender Wilmot, who had cats of his own, said, "They all know the word cream when they hear it."

Not all the conversation was about cats and cheese. There were speculations about the bombing, the murder, and the ten-thousand-dollar reward. Arch Riker pulled Qwilleran aside and demanded, "Did you run that ad? You're crazy! Who's going to pay off?"

"Don't worry. No one will claim it, but it's large enough to put a lot of sleuths on the trail. I bet that the guilty person will mail the cookbook anonymously to the PO box, rather than be exposed."

The evening wore on, with much consumption of cheese and punch. Voices grew louder. Suddenly there was a commotion in the kitchen—a thumping and growling, followed by a shattering crash. Conversation stopped abruptly, and Qwilleran rushed to the scene. Koko was racing around the kitchen in a frenzy, flinging himself at the refrigerator. When Qwilleran tried to intervene, the cat crashed into a lamp, sending the shade and the base flying in opposite directions. Women screamed and men yelled as Koko zipped around the fireplace cube and headed for the cheese tables.

"Stop him!" Qwilleran shouted as the cat skidded through the cheese platters and scattered crumbs of Roquefort, cubes of cheddar, slices of Gouda, and gobs of runny Brie before leaping to the punch table and knocking over the lighted candles.

"Fire!" someone shouted.

Qwilleran dashed to a closet for a fire extinguisher, at the same time bellowing, "Grab him! Grab him!"

Three men tore after the mad cat as he streaked around the fireplace cube with fur flying. Around and around they went.

"Somebody go the other way!"

Somebody did, but the trapped animal only sailed to the top of the cube and looked down on his pursuers.

"We've got him!"

A moment later Koko swooped over their heads and pelted up the ramp, not stopping until he reached the roof, where he perched on a beam and licked his fur.

Qwilleran was embarrassed. "My apologies. The cat went berserk. I don't know why." Truthfully, Koko wanted everyone to go home, Qwilleran suspected, leaving him unlimited access to the cheese tables.

The guests were understanding, and made a joke of it. It was a merry crowd that boarded the jitneys to ride back to the parking lot, and the students cleaning up the mess grinned. It was the best thing that would happen all semester.

The Sip 'n' Nibble partners were philosophical. Jerry said, "There's nothing like a minor catastrophe to make a party a success, Qwill. They'll talk about this for the rest of the century."

"That's what I'm afraid of."

Carol Lanspeak said, "It was really funny to see three adult males chasing a little cat in a cloud of flying fur. Better than a car chase. Aren't we lucky that Bushy got it on tape! We'll sell loads of videos."

When everyone had gone, Qwilleran changed into a jumpsuit and went into the kitchen. Koko was ahead of him, trying to claw his way into the refrigerator.

"You rascal," Qwilleran said. "So that's why you wanted everyone to go home! If you'll just cool it, we'll prep the turkey tonight and cook it in the morning. Stand back." He opened the refrigerator door cautiously, expecting a flank attack, but Koko knew when the battle was won. He watched calmly as the prepping began.

Qwilleran remembered Mildred's instructions: Release the legs without cutting the skin; explore the two cavities. He put his hand gingerly into the breast cavity and withdrew a plastic bag containing the neck. Then he turned the bird around and, with more confidence, explored the body cavity. Koko was watching with ears back and whiskers bristled. Qwilleran groped for the plastic bag. Instead, he found something hard and very very cold. He threw everything back into the tray and shoved the

naked bird into the refrigerator. Then he called Nick Bamba at home. "Hope I'm not calling too late, Nick. Just wanted to thank you for the cold turkey. But I have a question: Was there anything *special* about the bird you delivered to me? . . . No. There's nothing wrong with it." He tamped his mustache. "Thanks again, Nick. I'll let you know how it turns out."

Next Qwilleran punched out the number of the police chief. When the gruff voice answered, he said, "We had the cheese tasting here tonight, you know, and Jerry and Jack left a variety of cheeses. Why don't you run over for a nibble—and a sip? Also, I have something peculiar to report—very peculiar."

Brodie arrived in a matter of minutes. They sat at the bar, with a plate of leftover cheeses.

"Where's the one I like so much?"

"Gruyère. Everyone liked the Gruyère."

"Yow!"

When Brodie had finished his first Scotch, Qwilleran said, "I'd like you to look at a gift I received Sunday." Keeping one eye on Koko, he brought the turkey from the refrigerator and pushed the tray toward the chief. "What would you say this is?"

"Are you pullin' my leg? It's a turkey."

"Put your hand in the body cavity and see what you find."

With a glowering glance at his friend, Brodie thrust his hand into the bird. Immediately, an expression that was a mixture of shock and disbelief spread across his face. "What the hell!" He drew forth a small handgun. "Who gave you this bird?"

"Nick Bamba. It was frozen solid when it arrived—probably part of a shipment going Down Below. It's been thawing in the fridge for two days. Do you want a plastic bag for the evidence?"

"Gimme a trash bag," Andy said. "I'm taking the whole bird."

"THERE goes your turkey," Qwilleran said to Koko. To his surprise the cat seemed unconcerned, sitting on his haunches in his kangaroo pose and grooming a small patch of fur on his chest. Could it be that Koko sensed there was something not quite right about that turkey? Certainly there was something not quite right at the Cold Turkey Farm. Did one of Nick's employees shoot the florist and hide the gun in a turkey to be shipped Down Below?

Chapter Seventeen

THE morning after the cheese tasting, the Country Club sent a crew to remove the folding tables and silver punch bowls and to return the furniture to its normal arrangement. In the afternoon Qwilleran went for a long bike ride, hoping to clarify his thinking. As he pedaled, he thought about Iris's cookbook. Did Elaine pilfer the book? How will she react to the advertised reward? If she takes the book to the post office to be weighed for postage, the postal clerks will notice that it's going to box 1362, with no return address. They'll recognize her. Even if she mails it from Lockmaster, it's risky. The *Ledger* picked up the story of the reward. So maybe she won't mail it. She could burn it—after copying a few of the recipes.

Too bad I didn't take the book myself when I was there. I was lawfully on the premises, and the book is lawfully mine. No crime. And she couldn't accuse me without incriminating herself. I could have Celia sneak it out of the kitchen, but that's burglary. It's not her property. I can't involve her.

After a breather Qwilleran biked home, arriving just before dusk. In the sea chest he found two deliveries: a department store bag and a foil-wrapped brick, slightly warm. The Siamese knew what it was and gave him a clamoring welcome.

"Okay, okay. Later," he said, tossing the brick into the refrigerator for security reasons. Then he turned his attention to the bag. In it was a thick, black, scuffed, greasy notebook with loose pages.

"It's Iris's cookbook," he said aloud. He rushed to the phone.

It was Celia. "Did you find my meat loaf?"

"That's not all!"

"Were you surprised?"

"That's putting it mildly. I didn't expect you to . . . help yourself to the evidence."

"I didn't!" she cried defensively. "Donald saw me reading it and said, 'Why don't you take that something-something piece of something home and keep it? Mom's not supposed to have it anyway.'"

"Celia, I'm promoting you to senior executive assistant in charge of sensitive investigations."

Her laughter rang out as he said good night.

He examined the book. Its black cover was gray with decades of spilled flour; Iris had always boasted of being a sloppy cook. It bulged with loose pages and yellowed newspaper clippings smeared with olive oil, chocolate, coffee, juice. Splashes of liquid had blotted some of the writing, which was virtually indecipherable even at its best. He went to his studio and typed a release for the *Moose County Something* and *Lockmaster Ledger:*

> A missing cookbook, originally owned by Iris Cobb, has been anonymously returned to its rightful owners, the Klingenschoen Foundation, which intends to publish it. The announcement of a $10,000 reward for information leading to its recovery produced no tips or clues, according to a spokesperson for the K Fund. The return of the book was voluntary, and no inquiries will be made.

It was while he was giving the Siamese a couple of slices of meat loaf that the phone rang. His hello brought only labored breathing. "Hello?" he repeated with a questioning inflection.

Then he heard a high pitched voice say, "I'm gonna kill myself."

"What? Is this Aubrey? Are you at your mother's?"

"I come home. I come home to get a gun and shoot myself."

Qwilleran had heard suicide threats before. Aubrey needed to talk to someone. "Now wait a minute, Big Boy. I'm your friend. I want to know what's troubling you."

"I got the old man's gun. I'm gonna put it under my chin and pull the trigger."

"Okay, but don't do anything until I get there. I'm leaving right away. I'll be there in ten minutes. Turn the outside lights on."

Qwilleran rushed out to his car. Gunning the motor, he made a tire-screeching turn onto Park Circle. Traffic was light at that hour, and he could speed. Reaching Black Creek, he saw the yard lights of the Limburger house in the distance. It meant that Aubrey had been listening; he was obeying orders.

Qwilleran parked at the curb and hurried to the lighted veranda. As he climbed the steps, the front door opened and a ghost of a man stood there, his shoulders drooping, his face almost as white as his hair, his eyes unfocused.

Qwilleran followed him into the front hall. A single dim lightbulb burned in the branched chandelier. The door to the gun cabinet was open. "Look here, Big Boy," he said. "Let's get away from this gloomy place. Let's go. Turn out the lights. Lock the door."

Aubrey did as he was told, moving slowly, as if in a trance. Qwilleran piloted him down the steps and into the car, where he sat slumped in a stupor as they drove to Pickax. They turned off Park Circle, crossed the theater parking lot, and plunged into the woods. As they emerged from the dark stand of evergreens in front of the barn, Qwilleran hit the remote control, and instantaneous flood-lights turned the towering barn into something unreal. Aubrey sat up and stared.

"An old apple barn," Qwilleran told him. "Built more than a hundred years ago. Wait till you see the inside."

As they walked through the kitchen door, the two cats, who had been sleeping on the sofa, rose, arched their backs, stretched, and jumped down to inspect the visitor. They circled him inquisitively, sniffing his field boots and finding them quite fascinating.

"What are they?" Aubrey asked.

"Siamese cats. Very friendly. You can see they know you like animals. Talk to them. Tell them your name."

"Aubrey," the man said hesitantly.

"Yow!" Koko replied in his piercing Siamese baritone.

Qwilleran said, "See? He's pleased to meet you. Take off your jacket and sit down. Would you like coffee? Beer?"

"Beer," Aubrey said as he sank into a deep-cushioned chair. He could not take his eyes from the cats, who were striking poses, gazing at him, doing all the right things, as if they had been assigned to patient therapy.

Yum Yum jumped into Aubrey's lap, kneading in the crook of his elbow, purring loudly, and looking up at him with soulful eyes.

Qwilleran thought, She's a witch.

"Big eyes," Aubrey said. "Why's she lookin' at me like that?"

"She wants to play Blink. She stares at you; you stare at her. And the first one who blinks loses the game."

Koko jumped to the arm of the chair and sniffed Aubrey's sleeve. Then the cold wet nose traveled up his sleeve and sniffed his ear.

"It tickles," he said, almost smiling. It was as though some healing flow of energy was passing from the cats to the man. "I used to have a dog. When he was killed, I di'n't want another one. I joined the navy. I was gonna learn electronics. But I had an accident. I hadda come home."

With all the kindliness he could muster, Qwilleran asked, "What kind of accident?"

"I come near drownin'. When I come to, I thought I was dead. I felt different. But I wasn't dead. I was in sick bay. The medics said I owed my life to my buddy. Vic, his name was. He jumped in after me. They said there was sharks all around."

"Frightening experience."

"When somebody saves your life, you owe 'im one."

"Do you still keep in touch with . . . Vic?"

Aubrey turned a horrified face to Qwilleran. "That was him in the cabin!" He broke down in a fit of sobbing, covering his large face with his hands. When the sobbing finally subsided, Qwilleran said, "Perhaps you're ready for something to eat now?"

"Yeah. I'm hungry."

After devouring two meat loaf sandwiches and three cans of beer, Aubrey wanted to talk. Qwilleran listened attentively. Suddenly he said, "I'll be right back," and went up to his studio to call Brodie.

"Andy, I think you should haul your bagpipe over here on the double. It's important. I want you to meet someone."

"What the hell kind of invitation is that?" the chief demanded.

"Trust me. You won't be sorry."

"Business or pleasure?"

"Tomorrow it may be police business. Tonight you're off duty. Tonight it's off the record, off the cuff, and off the wall."

"Get out the Scotch. I'll be right there," Brodie said.

Chapter Eighteen

QWILLERAN and his guest were in the lounge area with mugs of coffee when a weird noise came from outside. Andy Brodie approached the kitchen door, skirling a Scottish tune on his bagpipes.

"Is this the place where they give free drinks to pipers?" he called out as Qwilleran went to meet him.

"Depends on how good you are," Qwilleran said.

Brodie dropped his bagpipes in the kitchen. He swaggered into the lounge area, where Aubrey was sitting with one cat on his lap and another on his shoulder. "Aubrey! What are you doing here?" he barked.

"Hi, Andy. I had a big sandwich and a coupla beers, and now I'm talkin' to the cats. They're friendly. We play Blink."

Qwilleran said, "You guys seem to know each other."

"I've known Aubrey since he was in high school. His mother grows the best flowers in the county. How's she doin', Aubrey?"

"Mom's got arthritis, but she's doin' all right. She still makes flapjacks better'n Lois's. D'you know Lois's lunchroom is closed?"

"Don't worry. She'll be back in business again. She's always threatening to close. Who are your two friends?"

"This one's Yum Yum, and this one's Koko. He wants to tickle my ears with his whiskers."

Qwilleran said to Brodie, "Make yourself comfortable. Aubrey was telling me an interesting story you ought to hear."

Turning to the young man, the off-duty chief said, "Aren't you the one that reported the body down by the river?"

"Yeah. I found him in my cabin. That's where I live."

"How come this fisherman was in your cabin?"

"I knew him a long time. He liked to come up and fish for bass sometimes. I always let him use my cabin, and the old man would let me sleep in the big house."

"Aubrey, didn't you say your friend spent his honeymoon in your cabin, some years back?" Qwilleran prodded.

"Yeah. He married a nice lady, but she di'n't like fly-fishin', so she never come up again. He always come alone."

"Tell Andy how you met this guy," Qwilleran said.

Aubrey repeated the story of his near drowning. "Vic always said I owed him for saving my life. That's why I always let him use my cabin. His name was Victor, but I called him Vic. He'd call up from Down Below and say, 'How's about usin' your shanty for a coupla days, Big Boy?' He'd fly up, and I'd pick him up at the airport. He'd fish, I'd do my chores, and we'd eat his catch for supper."

Brodie interrupted. "What did Vic do for a living?"

"Electronics. I wanted to do that, but I hadda come home."

"Tell us about seeing Vic's wife at the Black Bear Café a couple of weeks ago," Qwilleran said.

"Yeah. They weren't married anymore. She got a divorce. I don't know why. She was a nice lady. I saw her at the Black Bear with some man. She di'n't see me. When Vic called me next time, I told him. Coupla days after, he called me again. I like gettin' long-distance calls, don't you?" He looked at his two listeners, who nodded. "He told me to meet him at the airport."

"But at Lockmaster, not Mooseville," Qwilleran said with a significant glance at Brodie.

"Yeah. Lockmaster. He was kinda quiet when I picked him up. He said he wanted to make up with his wife. He had a birthday present for her—all wrapped in silver paper and fancy ribbons."

"Go on, Aubrey," Qwilleran encouraged.

"Next day he borrowed my truck. Put a lotta miles on it. I hadda buy gas. Come afternoon, I drove him to the hotel so he could leave the birthday present and a bunch of flowers he bought. Then I drove him back to Lockmaster."

Brodie asked, "When did you find out the present was a bomb?"

"Goin' to the airport. . . . I asked him why. He said he loved her and di'n't want nobody else to get her. He told me to keep my mouth shut or I'd be arrested. He said I hadda buy a paper and send him what they printed about it. I di'n't feel good about it, but I owed him one." Aubrey jumped up. "I hafta go outside a minute."

Brodie said, "I hope he's not gonna go fugitive."

"He'll be back. He's accustomed to outdoor plumbing."

"Can we believe this story?"

"Wait till you hear the rest of it, Andy. It fits together like a jigsaw puzzle: mystery woman in room two oh three . . . battered wife with scarred face . . . divorced and trying to escape a stalking ex-husband . . . coming to this remote town for refuge, never thinking she'd be recognized. That's where she made her mistake."

"And he made his mistake by buying flowers; he killed the wrong woman," Brodie said grimly.

When Aubrey returned, Qwilleran offered him more coffee and said, "Tell us how Vic came up again the next weekend."

"Yeah. I picked him up in Lockmaster again. He said two people described him to the police—that's what he read in the paper. He wanted to know if I could get at the old man's guns."

"How did he know about them?"

"He seen 'em the week before."

"Okay," Qwilleran said. "Tell us about the handgun."

"Yeah. Vic took one and loaded it. He wanted to go to the flower shop on Main Street. I drove him. Wasn't nobody around. They was all at the fireworks. When he come out, I wanted to stay and watch the fireworks, but he wanted to get outa there. That's when he told me I hadda get rid of the gun or I'd be arrested."

"Whose idea was it to hide it in a turkey?"

"We talked about it. I hadda go to work at midnight. They hadda get a shipment ready for Down Below. Vic said it'd be funny if somebody bought a turkey and found a gun in it."

"Very funny," Brodie growled.

"When I come home from work, Vic said we hadda get the hotel clerk—Lenny. We hadda hide in the woods and pick him off with a rifle when the bikers went by. The paper printed Lenny's number. He said it was my turn to do it. He was drinkin', and I thought he di'n't mean it, but he did. I said I couldn't kill anybody, and he said I hadda do it."

"Because you owed him one."

"Yeah. I di'n't know what to do, so I went down and talked to my bees. When I come back, the whiskey bottle was empty and he was dead-drunk. I hadda lug him to the cabin and dump him in the bed. There was a quilt that my mom made—red stars and green circles—but he had the shakes, so I got him the old man's heavy German blanket. He won't need it no more. He's gonna kick the bucket."

"Did the blanket help?" Qwilleran asked, urging him on.

"I dunno. He'd been sick, and the cabin stunk. I opened a window and got outa there."

"And the next morning?"

"He di'n't come up for cornflakes, so I went to the cabin, and he was dead. His hands and face was all swelled up. I ran outa the cabin and cried. I cried because I wouldn't hafta shoot Lenny."

Brodie said, "If you had shot Lenny, you'd be the next victim. Nobody but you knew Vic was here, and *why* he was here. You can thank your bees for what they did."

"They're gone," Aubrey said. "I smoked 'em out."

When Qwilleran accompanied Brodie outside, the chief said, "That kid's sure got himself in a pickle."

"He'll never be charged—under the circumstances," Qwilleran predicted. "It's a clear-cut case of exploitation and coercion. I'm calling George Barter in the morning. He's handled other sensitive legal matters for me. Thanks for coming over, Andy."

"Glad to see this nasty business come to a head." Brodie stepped into his car and then rolled down the window. "Say, how much was your smart cat involved in this case?"

"Well . . ." Qwilleran said. "More than I thought."

Indoors, Aubrey was on his hands and knees, frolicking with both cats on the Moroccan rug. The big man rolled on his back, and they climbed all over him. They had never paid so much attention to a stranger.

Qwilleran thought, Do they sense that he needs friends?

HE LET Aubrey give them their bedtime snack, then sent him up to the guest room on the second balcony. With the Siamese locked up in their apartment above, Qwilleran settled down to read. He was just beginning to feel drowsy when the phone rang. It was the night editor of the *Something*. "Sorry to call so late, Qwill, but there's a long-distance call for you on the other line—from California. It's a woman. She doesn't realize the difference in time zones."

"What's her name?"

"It's a tricky one. I'll spell it. O-n-o-o-s-h."

"Get her number and tell her I'll call her back immediately."

Within minutes he was talking with Onoosh Dolmathakia.

"Oh, Mr. Qwill," she said breathlessly; "I see little thing in *USA Today*—man stung to death. He was marry to me. Is too bad I not feel sad. Now I go back to Pickax and start new restaurant."

"Get in touch with me as soon as you arrive." He gave her his phone number and hung up with a sense of satisfaction. Now he would get his stuffed grape leaves.

IN THE morning Qwilleran went to wake Aubrey. The guest room door was open, and the guest had gone, but there were sounds of hilarity on the third balcony. Aubrey and the Siamese were having a ball.

Qwilleran phoned the attorney. The first thing Aubrey said to George Barter when he arrived was, "I'm gonna get me a cat."

Chapter Nineteen

IN ALL, Aubrey Scotten told his story five times: first to Qwilleran, again to Brodie, next to the attorney, then to the prosecutor, and finally to a sympathetic judge at an open court hearing. No charges were brought against the beekeeper, who was entrusted to the guardianship of his mother.

The "old man" in the case did not appear in court. Gustav Limburger had died, leaving a will in the hands of his Lockmaster attorney. To the surprise and consternation of the locals, his entire estate was bequeathed to a daughter in Germany.

Meanwhile, Moose County was experiencing a glorious Indian summer, and Polly was preparing to return to the workplace. "Are you still reading Aristophanes to the cats?" she asked Qwilleran after an afternoon spent walking the beach at Trawnto.

"Yes. We're reading *The Frogs*. Their favorite line is 'Brekekekex ko-ax ko-ax.' "

"I imagine you read it with amphibian authority," she said.

"I did the play in college and still remember some of my lines."

"Did you ever find out who surrendered Iris Cobb's cookbook?" she asked.

"No one has confessed," he replied truthfully but evasively, protecting Elaine Fetter's reputation as well as Celia's cover.

"It surprised me that Aubrey Scotten's statement to the court was printed in the *Something*. Why did the bees attack the man? Was it the foul odor?"

"Who knows?" Qwilleran said with a shrug. "Bees are sensitive and intuitive creatures—and even more mysterious than cats."

"Everyone hopes Aubrey will go back into the honey business."

"He will," Qwilleran said. "His hives have been moved to his mother's farm, and he's found a new swarm of wild honeybees. He'll continue to work at the turkey farm. Aubrey will be all right."

"What will Limburger's daughter do with the hotel?"

"The K Fund is negotiating with the estate for the purchase of the hotel and the house, which will make a good country inn. If the Scottens agree to sell the cabin, the inn property will extend to the river, where the bass fishing is said to be the best around."

"By the way, I saw the video of the cheese party, and the cat chase is hilarious! What caused Koko's catfit?"

"Your guess is as good as mine." He wanted to tell her about the handgun in the turkey but held his tongue. She discouraged him from getting involved in police business. Neither could he reveal Koko's uncanny ability to sense wrongdoing and sniff out wrongdoers. The practical librarian would look at him askance.

"Lisa Compton is spearheading a program to help battered women," she said. "Apparently there is a great deal of abuse going unreported in Moose County. Remember the wild rumors circulating about the mystery woman? No one dreamed she was a victim, being stalked and threatened by an ex-husband."

Qwilleran huffed into his mustache. Her statement was not true. Koko had sensed the situation. He had tried in his catly way to communicate. He started stalking Yum Yum and had a sudden interest in *Stalking the Wild Asparagus.* Wild coincidence? And was it coincidence that Koko lost interest in Euell Gibbons and stopped stalking Yum Yum after Onoosh revealed her plight in a frantic letter? Was it coincidence that Koko howled at the moment Franklin Pickett was shot? Or that he chewed up Lenny's pledge card when the biker was in danger? Or that he campaigned for a ride to the beach on the afternoon that the mystery woman was there? And how about the times he pushed *A Taste of Honey* off the shelf?

THAT evening Qwilleran settled down in the library with a mug of coffee and some cheese and crackers.

"Gruyère, anyone?" he asked, expecting a yowl from Koko. When there was no response, he said, "How about some double-cream Brie?" Still no reaction. Qwilleran reeled off a list of the world's great cheeses, including feta. Koko was silent.

What did it mean? He never did anything without a reason. Abnormal behavior on his part always signified an attempt to communicate information. Now the case was closed, and Qwilleran realized, in retrospect, the meaning of Koko's messages.

The cat had sensed that the evildoer could be identified by a sound like Gruyère, and Brie suggested the unwitting accomplice. To a cat's ear Gruyère, Brie, Greer, and Aubrey would be merely sounds, like "treat" or "book." To Koko's ear they had significance.

Then he slapped his forehead as another possibility occurred to him. "Oh, no," he said aloud. "Feta . . . Fetter . . . cookbook . . . Iris Cobb . . . meat loaf!" The cats had been fond of their former housekeeper, and they missed her meat loaf, the secret of which—

Qwilleran's ruminations were interrupted by a low rumble in Koko's chest, followed by a leap to the bookshelves.

"Okay, we'll have a read. 'Brekekekex ko-ax ko-ax.' " With Koko on the arm of his chair and Yum Yum on his lap, he continued his reading of *The Frogs*.

He reached his favorite line. "Who knows whether living is dying . . . and breathing is eating . . . and sleeping is a wool blanket?"

"Yow!" said Koko with equal seriousness.

Qwilleran felt a tingle on his upper lip as he guessed the answer to a puzzling question: Why did the bees attack Victor Greer? It was the old man's heavy woolen blanket! Did Aubrey realize what he was doing? Did he know the blanket was wool? Did he forget that bees were antagonized by wool? Or did Aubrey purposely take the wool blanket to the cabin? Later, when he found the body, he wept because, as he said, he would not have to shoot Lenny.

"How about that, Koko? Do you have an opinion?"

The cat was sitting in a tall, stately pose on the arm of the chair. He swayed slightly. His blue eyes were large and fathomless.

"Okay, we'll play a game. If Aubrey purposely caused Victor Greer's death, blink."

Qwilleran stared into Koko's eyes. Koko stared back, eyeball to eyeball. The trancelike impasse went on and on. Qwilleran forgot to breathe. With all thought and feeling suspended, he was crossing over into hypnosis; he had to blink.

Koko had won. Aubrey was absolved. But then, Koko always won.

LILIAN JACKSON BRAUN

PHOTO: PATRICIA BECK

Foul play. "That's how it all started," says Lilian Jackson Braun about her phenomenally successful The Cat Who . . . mystery series. The writer's first Siamese was killed in a fall from a tenth-floor window. Braun's neighbors suspected foul play, and to get the tragedy out of her system, she wrote a short story of crime and retribution in which the murdered cat was avenged. That was three Kokos, three Yum Yums, and eighteen novels ago.

When Braun began writing her first novel, she was working for the Detroit *Free Press,* so it was only natural that she make the two-legged hero of her books a newspaperman. Besides, Braun says, she likes Qwilleran's profession as a reporter because it gives him the opportunity to investigate lots of different subjects, such as growing shiitake mushrooms, raising turkeys, and delving into the origins of Cornish pasties, all of which he does in *The Cat Who Said Cheese.*

Braun credits part of the popularity of her series to the fact that while "not all mystery fans like cats, all cat-fanciers seem to like mysteries. That makes for a large audience, since twenty-six percent of American households own 53.9 million cats." And you can bet that a good many are Koko and Yum Yum look-alikes.

GE

**SOHEIR
KHASHOGGI**

She'd lied about her past so many times that the lies had become a kind of truth. But she was always looking over her shoulder, always afraid someone was watching her.

Maybe it was that man at the newsstand.

Or him, the one in the car behind hers.

Someone.

Waiting.

To take her back to hell.

Prologue

Boston. The Present

THE studio in which Barry Manning taped his radio show—a show that Jenna Sorrel disliked on principle but on which she was to be the guest in an hour—was in a renovated warehouse on Commercial Street, overlooking the Boston Harbor.

As Jenna got out of the taxi, she was so taken with the proudly refurbished loveliness of the old buildings that she hardly noticed the blue car slowly passing—or the red-haired man in it looking disinterestedly at her, then turning away.

She'd taken three steps before she realized that she had seen the man before—that morning, near her favorite bookstore on Newbury Street—and that he had given her the same casual glance then.

Her first instinct was to run. She turned back to the cab, opened the door, stopped.

"You forget something, lady?" the cabbie asked.

"No, no. I thought I had." She sounded foolish even to herself. The blue car moved steadily down the street.

There had been a time when the fear of being followed was as much a part of Jenna's life as eating or sleeping. But the years had passed and nothing had happened, and now she could not remember the last time she had worried about the man who seemed always to be at the bus stop or the car that seemed always to be in the rearview mirror. Until just now.

She was sure it was the man she had seen near the bookstore. Almost sure. But what if he was? Boston wasn't such a large place. It was possible for a person to be on Newbury Street in the morning and on Commercial Street in the afternoon. But still . . .

Far down the street the blue car turned right and disappeared. Jenna took a deep breath. Forget it, she told herself; it's nothing. She went into the building. A security guard sat at a mahogany desk. She signed the in-out register. "I'm here for the Barry Manning show. Has a Mr. Pierce arrived?"

The guard scanned the register. "Pierce? No. Don't see him."

Damn. Jenna had hoped that Brad would be there to help her through her stage fright—the butterflies were already beginning to flutter their cold little wings—but apparently he was still angry. Or perhaps he wanted to remind her what it was like to be alone.

The offices of the Manning organization were surprisingly small, and the few people all looked to be caught up in crises. Finally a woman with earphones dangling around her neck noticed Jenna and introduced herself as Courteney Cornmeyer, the show's producer. "We're very happy to have you," she said sincerely, and propelled Jenna to the station's greenroom. "You can do your makeup here," she said, indicating a mirrored vanity table, "unless you want to use Angela. She's awfully good."

"No! Thank you," Jenna added hastily, realizing how inappropriately vehement she'd sounded. Jenna didn't want a stranger studying her face, noticing things she'd hidden for so many years.

"Suit yourself," Ms. Cornmeyer said agreeably.

After closing the door behind her, Jenna sank into a chair, took the cosmetic case from her bag, and leaned toward the three-way mirror. First she brushed her thick chestnut hair. Roots already? It seemed that she was having to go to the colorist every other week.

Pretending to be someone else was hard work, she thought for perhaps the thousandth time. A constant effort. The hair, the green contact lenses covering her own brown eyes. And the lies.

As she'd been instructed to do, Jenna laid on the foundation with a heavy hand—the Manning radio show had a studio audience and harsh studio lights. Her fingers traced a delicate scar above her left brow and another at the hairline. The surgery to repair her face had been expert, but traces of it lingered, along with the memory of the man who had tried to destroy her beauty—and her life.

Jenna applied a matte finish, blusher, and eye shadow. She was lucky in her looks, she knew. Her next birthday would be her fortieth, but with just a few minutes of deft contouring and highlighting, she looked a young thirty. And gorgeous.

She folded and unfolded her hands as she waited. Her throat was dry, her stomach clenched. Was it just stage fright? The fight with Brad? The strange feeling of being followed? Jenna got up and wandered out into the hall. She almost collided with Courteney, who had in tow a short, round-faced man.

"Dr. Sorrel, I presume? Barry Manning." He extended a hand.

"Five minutes to air," said Courteney. "I'll be in the booth."

"So what happens now?" Jenna asked Manning. The butterflies were now in full flutter. "I've never been on the radio."

"There's nothing to it. C.C. will give us a countdown; the red light will come on. I'll introduce you, ask you about your book. You'll tell me about it, we'll take some questions, you'll answer, I'll make some comments, and it'll be over before you know it."

Jenna breathed deeply. "All right, let's go."

"Whoa! We've got four minutes—an eternity in this business. Let me ask you something. What's a nice girl like you doing in a place like this? I mean, why my show?" Manning smiled, no doubt aware that he had a reputation for skewering guests.

Yet Jenna felt that he was not playing a role, but seriously wanted an answer. "You know the saying, Preaching to the converted?" she asked. "Lately I've begun to think that's what I've been doing in my work. I spoke at a symposium at Harvard yesterday—psychiatrists, psychologists, psychiatric social workers—and every one of them knew what I was going to say and agreed with it in advance. But many of your listeners are conservative. They haven't heard what I have to say, and many of them won't agree with me when they do hear it."

Manning looked at her with unexpectedly quiet appraisal. "I love your voice," he said. "What's that little touch of an accent?"

"I was born in Egypt but grew up in France. I married there and was widowed young." All lies, but repeated so often they had taken on their own kind of truth. "I came here fifteen years ago." Truth.

"One minute to air," Courteney warned from a wall speaker.

Suddenly Barry Manning was animated again. "Come on, Doc," he said. "Let's go change the world."

The whole setup was disorienting. There was a glass booth in which she and Manning would sit at a desk with three computer terminals. The studio audience sat in rows of folding chairs at an angle to the booth. Jenna looked for Brad. He wasn't there. Someone clipped a tiny microphone on her lapel. The funky blues instrumental that Barry Manning used as his theme welled up. The audience clapped fiercely as Manning bounced into the booth. After some brief opening remarks he introduced his guest as "Dr. Jenna Sorrel, the renowned psychologist and best-selling author," and held up a copy of her latest book, *Prisons of the Heart: Women in Denial.*

"So what is this book about, Dr. Sorrel? The domination of women by men? The abuse of women by men?"

"To some extent. But *Prisons of the Heart* explores questions I've heard so often, questions which seem to blame the victim: Why don't abused women leave the men who batter them? Why don't they run away? What I've tried to show in my book is that there are no easy answers. What I often hear from battered women is denial. Some cling to that position for years, either out of shame or fear. The fear, I might add, is certainly not invalid—not when we consider the violence perpetrated against women who *have* left their abusers."

When the call-in and audience questions began, it all seemed to shoot by so quickly, so superficially. No one asked about the actual subject of her book. Everyone had his or her own agenda: abortion, gays, Madonna, and what the Bible had to say that might pertain to all of these.

Jenna felt a familiar frustration. It was as if she couldn't bring her listeners quite far enough, couldn't make them feel what she felt. Then, just as the show was ending, there was a question from an intense young woman in the audience. "Dr. Sorrel, have you ever been the victim of the kinds of things you've talked about?"

It was a question she had anticipated. But coming so late, when she was weary and exhilarated and frustrated all at once, it took her by surprise. And she saw the real possibility of shedding the long years' burden of pretending. Why not? she thought. It would be so simple to speak the truth in front of all these witnesses.

It took only a moment for the clouds of long-standing fear to close over again—just long enough to make it seem that Jenna had paused thoughtfully before giving what was in fact her prepared answer: "I'd rather not get into matters that concern my personal history. As a practicing psychologist, I believe the work goes better if the patient doesn't waste time and energy identifying with or rejecting what I have experienced in my own life."

She looked at the young woman who had asked the question, looked at the audience, and knew that it wasn't enough.

"I can tell you this much," she said slowly, quietly. "In some of the richest countries of the world, I've seen things, experienced things that—" She halted. What could she tell them? How it felt to be veiled in black while still a young girl? To lose a mother who could not go on as the lesser wife in her own home? To watch helplessly as a rain of stones snuffed out the sparkling life of a friend?

To her astonishment Jenna felt the hot-to-cold trace of tears down her cheeks. "Well," she said finally, "we've all seen things, terrible things, perhaps in our own lives or in our neighbors' or certainly in the news every night. But if I have one thing to leave you, it's that to see with our eyes is one thing, and to see and know and feel and understand in our hearts is another.

"And I believe that only when we learn to understand in our hearts can we begin to learn the real work of healing."

A long moment of silence followed. Then, just as Barry Manning muttered, "Well said, Doctor," the audience broke into applause.

Jenna let their approval enfold her. She was exhausted. Now Manning was signing off. The theme music came up. The ON AIR light winked dark. It was over.

Outside the booth the whole audience seemed to descend on Jenna and Barry. Several bought Jenna's book on the spot. As Jenna signed books and accepted compliments, she scanned the studio, still hoping. Still no Brad. But there was a small dark man lounging against the doorway. Something about him was oddly familiar, something that made Jenna tense.

As if in response to her scrutiny, the man straightened up and walked out. Had she imagined the way he looked at her?

You're losing it, she told herself. The quarrel with Brad has thrown you off-balance.

When at last the crowd thinned, Barry approached Jenna. They exchanged professional small talk—an invitation to return, promises to keep in touch. Then Jenna was free. But to do what? Up until a year ago she would have hurried home or to her office to lose herself in work. Then Brad had come into her life—and she had someone to share her triumphs, her defeats, someone to hold.

Stop it, she told herself. You're thinking as if he were gone. And he isn't. He can't be. That would be unbearable.

Outside, she looked up and down the street but saw nothing suspicious. Just a sunny day and people going about their business. A cab pulled up in front of her. With a sigh she stepped inside.

JENNA'S Marlborough Street apartment was considered luxurious by the few who'd seen it: a spacious duplex in an old limestone mansion, fireplaces, a skylight, a terrace, simple contemporary furniture mingled with a few Oriental antiques. But to her—a woman who had lived literally in palaces—it was a cozy pied-à-terre.

Not today, though. Not with the remnants of last night's intimacy reminding her of how wrong it had all gone. On the Chinese lacquer bar stood the bottle of Beaujolais that Brad had brought. As he held her, the wine had tasted like sunlight. But after he'd renewed his proposal of marriage and she had given the only answer she could give, the mood broke, and they had parted like strangers.

Now Jenna poured herself a glass of Brad's wine, but it no longer tasted of sunlight. She wished her son, Karim, were home, even with his prickly eighteen-year-old's independence. But he was spending the summer with college friends, sailing the Greek islands—slipping away from her already.

Why couldn't Brad be patient? she thought. Why couldn't he just trust her love? Suddenly she laughed harshly. How could she expect trust when she had none to give? There was a tap at the door.

With a rush of joy she hurried to open it. "Oh, love, I—"

But the man looming in the doorway wasn't Brad. For a moment she didn't recognize him despite the red hair. He was bigger, beefier than he had seemed on Newbury Street or in the blue car. Behind him stood a smaller, darker man.

The big man had ice-blue eyes, and he said two words that froze Jenna's soul. "Amira Badir?"

"There—there must be some mistake." Her hand clutched at the hall table. Without its support she might have fallen.

423

"I doubt it." The man flipped a badge. "INS. Immigration and Naturalization Service. We need to ask you some questions, Ms. Badir. At our office. Get your purse, your coat."

Her mouth dry with fear, Jenna obeyed. She followed the INS men to their car, the blue car. The big man opened the door to the back seat. The two men sat in the front, the small man driving. The familiar streets of Jenna's neighborhood slipped away.

Think, Jenna, think. Think, Amira. A lawyer. I need a lawyer. Brad's company has lawyers. Call Brad. Maybe they can at least keep it out of the papers. Because even in al-Remal, people read *The New York Times*. My husband reads *The New York Times*.

Oblivious to her desperation, the two men chatted in the front seat. Jenna noticed a green sign overhead: LOGAN AIRPORT 1/4 MILE. A terrible suspicion seized her. "Why are we going to the airport?"

The red-haired man turned, a hint of amusement in the cold blue eyes. "We're immigration, lady. We work at the airport."

The car left the main approach to the terminal, took a service road through a gate, rolled onto the tarmac, and pulled up beside an idling Gulfstream with private markings.

"Everybody out," the big man shouted over the engines. "All aboard the pretty bird." He helped her out of the car.

The small man moved up on her other side. Jenna felt close to panic. "Wait a minute. I thought we were going to your office."

"Going to New York," said the red-haired man. "Pay a call on the regional director. You're kind of a big deal, Ms. Badir."

Jenna didn't understand. Was this how the law worked?

She'd call Brad. Maybe they'd let her call from the plane. But once inside the sleek jet, Jenna realized that there would be no call. Something was terribly wrong. The pilot and copilot—she could see them through the open cockpit door—weren't Americans. Were they French? Or— No, it couldn't be.

An older man wearing a steward's uniform materialized beside her. "Some coffee, madam? Or perhaps a soft drink?"

"Yes, all right. A Perrier."

"Yes, madam."

When he brought the bottle, she drained it almost greedily.

The pitch of the engines changed, and she felt motion. Fasten seat belt, she thought. Must fasten seat belt. Her head was very heavy, her eyes leaden. The steward was hovering, watching, concerned.

And suddenly it was clear—so clear she almost laughed at herself for having ever imagined that she could run, that she could have freedom, life, love. As if in a dream, she could picture her husband, Ali, reaching out for her across the years, his arms a billion dollars long, and now they'd caught her, and she was going home to die.

Just before sleep, two faces swam in the darkness before her eyes: Karim and Brad.

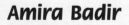

Amira Badir

Al-Remal ("The Sand"), late 1960s

EVEN against the molten noonday sun al-Masagin prison loomed dark and forbidding, its massive iron gates reaching skyward. Thirteen-year-old Amira Badir waited as Um Salih, the village midwife, rang the heavy brass bell in front. It made an oddly melodic sound for so somber a place. A moment later a guard appeared. The gate swung open, revealing a dark maw. The guard beckoned Um Salih to enter. Amira followed close behind. The cheap rayon dress beneath her black *abaya* rubbed coarsely against her skin; the crude leather sandals chafed her feet.

She was accustomed to the finest of fabrics; her shoes were made by an Italian bootmaker. But today she was supposed to be someone else—not the daughter of Omar Badir, one of al-Remal's wealthiest men, but the niece of the village midwife.

Amira had played at masquerades before, gone into the *souk* wearing boy's clothes—white *thobe,* white *ghutra*—with sunglasses for added disguise. But this masquerade was no game. Life and death were the stakes here. If Amira was to be discovered, she knew that even her father's wealth wouldn't protect her from the consequences. As a young child, she'd tried to imagine what the prison might be like, but not even a nightmare could have prepared her for the cold, the dankness, and, worst of all, the stench. The smell of utter despair, impending death.

Ever since her best friend, Laila—the daughter of her father's good friend—had been arrested, Amira had made this trip regularly, disguised as a male servant, bringing food and carrying messages between Laila and Amira's older brother, Malik. But this deception would be the hardest of all. The life of Malik's unborn child depended on it, and perhaps Malik's life as well.

The women's wing was quiet except for the crunching of the guard's boots and the rustle of the two women's garments. A piercing scream bounced off the rough sandstone walls. Amira flinched.

"Stop dragging your feet, laziness," snapped Um Salih. "There's nothing to be afraid of here."

The impertinence, thought Amira—then remembered she was supposed to be a poor girl assisting the midwife. Lowering her eyes, she murmured an apology.

"The girl wants to be a midwife, yet cringes at the cries of a woman in labor," Um Salih complained to the guard.

He stopped in front of a barred wooden door, turned a heavy key in the rusty lock, then pushed the door open.

Laila was half sitting, half lying on a mat of straw, her flowing robe stained with blood and birth fluids. For an instant Amira didn't recognize her. Barely nineteen, Laila looked twice that. Her eyes were glassy with pain, her breath a series of short, ragged gasps.

Um Salih set down her basket and rolled up the sleeves of her dress. Calling out to the waiting guard, she demanded boiling water.

When the guard's footsteps could no longer be heard, Amira removed her veil and put a finger to her lips. "Don't say my name, Laila," she whispered. "I'm supposed to be Um Salih's niece."

"You're really here?" said Laila hoarsely. Something like hope lit her eyes. "Save my baby," she pleaded. "Don't let him be given away. Please. Please. Make sure he has a good life."

"I promise," Amira whispered, gently stroking her friend's forehead. "It's all taken care of. Malik has seen to everything."

From her basket the midwife took a clean linen square. Upon it she placed the tools of her trade—a tube of antibiotic ointment, packets of herbs, a needle and surgical thread, a pair of scissors. Into a glass she emptied the contents of an herb packet, then added some pure drinking water from a large bottle she carried.

"Here," she said, handing the glass to Amira. "Give her a little at a time. Not too much, mind you, or she'll vomit it up."

In spite of the admonition, Laila gulped the herbal mixture greedily, desperate for relief from her suffering. A moment later her back arched. From high inside her throat came a long, keening wail that raised the hairs on Amira's neck. It was the sound of pain and relief and unspeakable sorrow. Amira took her friend's hand. "Squeeze it," she said. "When you feel pain, let me take some of it." With her free hand she wiped Laila's face with a wet cloth.

As the contractions grew stronger, Laila's skin turned ivory.

"Is she going to die, Um Salih?"

"Not tonight, child, not tonight."

No. Not tonight, Amira thought. Tomorrow. Laila would die tomorrow, die by stoning in the dirty little square in front of the prison. All that was keeping her alive was the tiny other life within her body. Once that was taken from her, so would her own life be. For what? For loving Malik? For not loving the cruel and crippled old man who happened to be her husband through no wish of hers? Why?

"Don't cry, child. We have hard work and a long night ahead."

And still the labor went on, Laila's torment worse than anything Amira had ever seen. With the cell's bare bulb dimming and glaring as a generator somewhere outside sputtered, then throbbed to life again, Amira felt that she was caught in a nightmare, that soon she would waken and everything would be the way it was.

For as long as Amira could remember, Laila had been her heroine, more like an admired older sister than a friend. And Amira was
Laila's favorite despite the difference in their ages. They spent more
time with each other than with anyone else. Malik was there, too,
more often than not.

Were Malik and Laila in love even then—not like a grown man
and woman, of course, but in the way the poets describe it, love
written on souls and in the stars? But when Laila was fifteen—with
little time left to waste, in her parents' view—her father arranged
her marriage to one of his close business associates. The man was
fifty-two and noted for his devotion to the Koran, hunting, and
money—although not necessarily in that order.

Two years into their marriage Laila's husband was thrown from
his horse while hunting. The accident crushed a bone in his spine
and left him paralyzed from the waist down. Though Laila publicly
wept and wailed as a good wife should, privately she seemed to
welcome his disability—shocking Amira—because it would mean
the end of some of his husbandly demands. But where previously
he at least had been a vibrant figure, now Laila's husband was
merely an ill-tempered, whining old man who demanded her constant attendance.

The following spring, when Malik came home on holiday from
Victoria College, an exclusive British-style boarding school in
Cairo, Laila used Amira as a go-between to arrange a secret meeting with him. Amira knew that the two should not be alone without the approval of Laila's husband. But how could such a thing be
truly wrong? It was the first of many such meetings.

There came a time when Laila grew subdued, and one morning
when Amira went to visit in hopes of cheering her friend up, a servant turned her away with the icy announcement that Laila's name
was never to be spoken in that house again. Unable to learn anything further, Amira raised the subject that night at dinner.

"Has she died?" she asked timidly.

"She is worse than dead!" her father thundered. "Although she
will certainly die, too. That woman is with child. Not her husband's.
She has shamed herself and dishonored her family. There is only
one rightful end for such a woman."

The punishment for the act Laila had committed was death.

"PUSH," THE MIDWIFE SAID. "A little longer, and it will be over."

"I pray it's a boy," Laila gasped out. "I pray he never suffers like this, that he never endures what a woman must endure."

Amira searched her mind for words of comfort. "Courage," she murmured, "courage, Laila dear." But would *she* have the courage to endure this—a filthy jail cell, abandoned by family and friends? Knowing the child she gave her life for would never know her? Amira blinked back tears.

"Another push," the midwife commanded, her hands pressing on Laila's abdomen. Moments later it was over. A tiny baby girl, wet and slippery, with a thatch of black hair and dark, almond-shaped eyes.

Um Salih cupped her hand over the baby's mouth to keep her from crying, then handed her to Amira. As she'd been instructed to do, Amira slipped a ball of cotton into the tiny mouth. She wrapped the infant in a blanket and placed her in Laila's arms.

Laila held her child, fingers tracing the features of her face—the forehead, the tiny nose, the cleft chin and delicate ears—as if to imprint the image of the baby she would never know.

Then Um Salih gently took the baby back, removed a small bundle from her basket, and put the newborn in its place.

"Save her, Amira. No matter what happens, you must save her." Laila's eyes were feverishly bright, her voice almost inaudible.

"I will," Amira promised. "I will." She held her friend in her arms for the last time. "Good-bye, Laila. Good-bye. God be with you."

"Good-bye, Amira. Don't forget." Closing her eyes, Laila sank back on the straw, exhausted.

Um Salih unwrapped the bundle from her basket. It contained a baby boy, its skin purple-blue, dead since late that morning. It had been born to her niece, and it took only a few small coins to buy its body.

The old woman wet the tiny corpse with water, then smeared it with blood from the afterbirth. Placing the baby beside Laila, she covered it with a white linen square. "Guard!" she called. Footsteps approached. "My work is finished," Um Salih told him. "The child is dead. Allah took him early." She drew away the handkerchief.

The guard looked for only a moment. "Just as well," he said.

Um Salih signaled Amira. "Bring my things, worthless."

"Yes, Aunt."

Leaving the prison, praying that the baby would be able to breathe but would not cry, Amira wanted to run. But Um Salih moved slowly, the picture of an old woman who had no need to hurry. As long as they did nothing to attract attention, no guard would want to look in the basket: unclean things in it, female things. Amira matched the midwife's pace, and the gate clanged shut behind them.

THE hour's walk to Um Salih's village felt like a march of a thousand miles. Night had fallen, and the air was cold. As if to make up for the enforced silence of her first moments of life, Laila's baby began to cry lustily as soon as the cotton was removed from her mouth. Um Salih offered a cloth with sugar to the infant to suck. The sweetness—or perhaps simply the touch of a human hand—seemed to comfort the child. A few minutes later she was asleep.

Just outside the village a silver Porsche shimmered in the moonlight. As the women approached, Malik stepped from beside it. Usually fastidious—Amira often teased him for being vain—he was unshaven and unkempt. His *thobe* looked as if he'd slept in it. He embraced Amira, held her close for a long moment.

"I was so worried," he said. "I was afraid you'd been found out. I never would have forgiven myself if anything happened to you. How is Laila? And the baby? Tell me quickly."

Ignoring the question about Laila, Um Salih lifted the cover of her basket. "A healthy baby girl, sir. She'll be a great beauty."

Malik reached for his daughter, touching her face as her mother had. "I'll call her Laila," he said. "I'll do everything for her. Everything I would have done—should have done—for Laila."

"Don't think of it now, brother," said Amira. "There's nothing you could have done." It was true.

When Laila's crime had come to light, Malik had wanted to step forward. "The sin is mine, too," he said. "Why should I escape when her life is lost? We loved together; it is just that we die together."

But, through Amira, Laila had forbidden him to do so. "Giving up your life won't save mine. It would be a useless sacrifice. Worse, it would make our child an orphan."

All those terrible weeks Laila languished in al-Masagin, Malik paced and roared like a caged animal. He refused to accept what seemed inevitable, hatching one wild scheme after another and trying them out on his cousin and best friend, Farid.

Within the Badir family it was assumed that Farid had inherited the intellectual gifts of his father, Tarik, an eminent mathematician. It was Farid who kept Malik anchored in reality after the trial and the verdict, when all he could think of was an assault on the prison, a rush for the airport, escape in a commandeered private jet.

Farid pointed out that no pilot would risk being shot down by the Royal Remali Air Force for protecting an adulteress.

In the end, it had all come down to this moment in the desert moonlight, pale gold tinkling from Malik's hand into Um Salih's.

"Thank you, sir. A thousand blessings." The old midwife touched her forehead in a gesture of respect.

Malik responded with equal courtesy as he went over the arrangements for his child. "The wet nurse—she's healthy?"

"Oh, yes, sir. My niece, Salima. She gave birth only yesterday; alas, her child—the baby boy we left at the prison—did not survive. But let me assure you this baby will have the best of care."

"I'll come for her as soon as I can. But don't worry, you'll be taken care of, you and your family, for as long as I live."

It was time to leave; Malik's gaze lingered lovingly on his sleeping daughter.

"Would you care to hold her, sir?" The midwife reached into the basket, picked up the baby, and placed her in the crook of Malik's arm. He held her in silence, his dark eyes glistening.

Amira and the midwife were quiet, too, while father and daughter shared their first communion under a sheltering desert sky.

Later, as Malik and Amira drove away, he said, "I mean it, you know. She'll be my sun and moon and stars." Amira studied her brother's face. It seemed older, more rugged, than it had a few short months ago. "It can't be in al-Remal, of course," he continued. "I'll be in exile. I don't know if I'll ever come back."

As they approached the gate to their home, Malik cut the motor. "Go around to the back. The door will be open. I've arranged it with Bahia. She'll have a nightgown waiting. Change and then go to your room. If someone wakes up, say you couldn't sleep."

It sounded so easy, deceiving their parents. And though Amira had never told them a really big lie, she was ready to begin.

As she opened the car door, Malik reached over and took her hand. "I've made a promise, little sister. To myself and to Allah. Now I make it to you: Never again will I be powerless. Never will I be too weak to save someone I love. Remember that."

A short time later Amira was in her own bed. Though the grime of the prison lingered on her skin—she didn't dare risk a shower—her nightgown was clean and crisp, her sheets fragrant with lavender. I'll never be able to sleep, she thought. If I close my eyes, I'll see Laila's face—and that terrible prison cell.

Yet Amira did sleep, deeply, dreamlessly, till the Sudanese servant, Bahia, shook her awake. "I brought you a tray," she said with a conspiratorial smile. On the tray was a steaming pot of tea, some toasted bread, a dish of olives, and a round of white cheese.

"Thank you, Bahia. And thank you for—"

"Hush, child. The less you say, the less I'll have to answer for." Again the conspiratorial smile. "Your brother's with your father now, in the big study. With the door closed."

Amira bolted up in bed. Something important was going on. Ignoring her breakfast, she dressed quickly and ran downstairs.

The study door was indeed closed. Amira put her ear to it, but all she could hear was the rumble of male voices. She turned the knob gently, then pushed. The conversation continued.

"I'm a man now," Malik was saying. "I'm old enough to know what I want in life. I have no interest in studying law—or business. Why should I waste your money at the Sorbonne? I want to make my way in the real world, as you did."

Amira held her breath, waiting for an explosion. It didn't come.

"And exactly what business have you decided to enter, my son?"

"Shipping," Malik replied, as if he had given the matter a great deal of thought. "But I know I can't do much without your help, Father. Will you ask if your friend Onassis can fit me in someplace? I'm willing to work and learn. As you did."

"Ah." Amira was sure her father was smiling. How many times had he told how he had started trading in silk at seventeen, without any formal schooling? Of his success, the whole kingdom knew.

"But that was another time, my son," Omar said, his tone mild.

"Nowadays a college education can be extremely useful for a man."

"You know I'm not a great student, Father." There was a pause. Amira could imagine Malik flashing the grin that few could resist. "Besides," he continued, "aren't you always criticizing your friends' sons who go to European colleges? I've heard you say the only degrees they earn are from the casinos and whorehouses."

Omar laughed. There was the sound of a telephone being dialed, then a conversation in English. When it was over, Omar said, "Onassis has a position for you. Not in Paris . . ." He paused. Was he inviting Malik to protest? "Not even in Athens. In Marseille."

"Whatever it is, I'll take it. Thank you, Father."

Hearing the scraping of chairs against the floor, Amira scampered away.

But as soon as Omar left for his office, she waylaid her brother. Though he had shaved and dressed in a fresh robe, his eyes were bloodshot. "I heard you talking to Father. Why did you tell him you didn't want to go to the Sorbonne? That isn't true."

"It is now, little sister," he said, ruffling her hair. "I have responsibilities, remember? It's a small enough sacrifice. . . ." His voice trailed off, his sentiment a reminder of what was soon to happen.

Malik shut himself in his room. The morning stretched before Amira. She tried to read, she tried to help Bahia—but still, the hours had to be endured.

At one o'clock, after the noon prayers, Laila would die.

Just before eleven Malik burst into Amira's room. "I can't help it, I'm going down there. To be near her."

"Then I'm going with you."

"Absolutely not. This isn't something a kid should see."

"I wasn't too much of a kid to see the inside of al-Masagin prison."

They argued. Malik forbade her to go, and she defied him. "If you don't take me with you, I'll go on my own."

Malik said nothing. Amira took that as consent.

Long before the sun reached its midday position, she stole out of the house, with her boy disguise in a bag. She ran to Malik's car, where she slipped on the white *thobe* and *ghutra*, the sunglasses.

THE barren square was baking with the strongest heat of the day, a thick wooden post planted at its center. Someone had dumped a pile of large, smooth white river stones a few paces from the post.

At first Amira thought the square was empty. Then she saw them—dozens, hundreds, crowding in the shade of doorways and prison walls. She recognized a few friends of her father's or of Malik's, but most of the people seemed to be the poor. Many were women.

Laila, blindfolded, was led out of al-Masagin and tied to the stake. Scarcely a dozen yards away, Laila's family were lined up, rigid as statues. By law they were compelled to be here, the men to share Laila's shame and dishonor, the women to witness what could happen to them if they strayed from the rightful path.

Amira felt as if she might faint, but when she looked up at Malik and saw how terrible he looked—his skin pasty, his face contorted with anticipated pain—she found her courage. Slipping her hand into his, she held it tight. He was whispering something—a prayer. An official read a declaration of the crime and sentence. Then, at some signal Amira missed, Laila's eldest brother stepped forward, a fist-size stone in his hand. Only a few feet from his sister he hurled the rock with all his might straight at her forehead.

This image burned itself into Amira's brain. Did he throw with such strength out of hatred, for the shame Laila had brought her family—or out of love, to kill her instantly and spare her what was to follow?

Whatever his intention, he failed in it. At the last split second, Laila turned her head, and the stone struck a glancing blow. Blood gushed. Laila sagged, straightened, shaking her head as if to clear it. And then came a sound like the snarl of a vicious dog unchained.

The crowd surged forward, fighting to get at the rock pile. Suddenly the stones were flying as thickly as a frightened flock of birds. To Amira's horror the women were the fiercest executioners, screaming curses as they threw, then scurrying to grab another stone.

For a few seconds Laila twisted to avoid her unseen attackers; then she collapsed in her bindings, the rocks thudding into her body, knocking her head loosely, sickeningly, from side to side. It ended as abruptly as a desert thunderstorm, a last stray stone rattling across the baked earth.

A man came out of the prison. He applied a stethoscope to

Laila's battered chest and nodded to a group of guards. Quickly they carried the body back into the prison.

The crowd melted away. Still holding his hand, Amira led Malik away from the square. His eyes were blank; he moved like an automaton. When they reached the car, she released him and vomited into the dust.

Malik seemed not to notice. They got into the car, and staring straight ahead, he turned the key in the ignition; the car lurched forward, then careened into the road. On the drive home he spoke only once, his face sculpted in cold fury. "Never again. I swear it."

Malik

1970

THE plane banked, one wing pointing to pure blue sky, the other to khaki desert. Sky and desert. Al-Remal.

One night in Marseille, in a crowded, smoky café, a business acquaintance of Malik's, a middle-aged American well advanced in drink, had become sentimental and sententious. "You all think you're going to make a pile of money," he informed the group around the table, "and go back home in style. But you can't. You can't go home again. A famous writer said that. I forget who, but truer words were never spoken."

Afterward Malik came to see that the man's words applied to him. He had felt that way ever since the day they killed Laila. Never again. He could not think of Laila without thinking those words, his oath to himself and to God. And he could not think of the Laila he had loved without seeing in his mind the baby Laila he loved now. Would she be walking now? Would she know him? It had been a year. If all went as planned, he told himself, he would never be without her again.

Farid, his trusted friend and cousin, was waiting at the gate and kissed him in greeting. "God's peace be with you, my cousin."

"And with you, cousin. Your father is well?"

"Yes, by the will of God, and your father, too." The formalities satisfied, Farid signaled a Palestinian porter for Malik's luggage. The airport seemed busier than Malik remembered it. As his cousin escorted him past the customs desk with a wave to the official in charge, he could feel pity for the foreign businessmen turning out the contents of their suitcases. Heaven help them, he thought, if they had been so foolhardly—or so ignorant—as to bring in such forbidden items as liquor or *Playboy* magazines.

Farid's car was a Buick, two or three years old—a dream for most Remalis, but not a token of great success for a man of Farid's family. "I'm on the waiting list for a new Lincoln," he explained.

He swung onto Airport Road. "Your flight was good?" he asked Malik. "These jets are very safe, I hear."

The flight had been good, Malik allowed, and by all accounts the new aircraft were very reliable.

"Tell me about France," said Farid.

This was not Europe, Malik reminded himself. It would be unthinkable to broach directly the topic that was on both their minds. He patiently answered Farid's questions about French weather, French food, and, especially, French women.

"And how do you do," asked Farid, "working for the old Greek pirate?"

"Well enough." Malik laughed. It was not the first time he had heard his employer described in those words. "And, God willing, even better someday—but not working for Onassis."

Farid raised an eyebrow. "Better than Onassis, cousin?"

"That's not exactly what I said." Without going into detail, Malik explained that, working in shipping in a place like Marseille, he sometimes met prospective clients who had special needs. "Sensitive cargoes—you understand, cousin?—that Onassis would never handle, because it would be politically dangerous for him. What such a client needs is not an Onassis tanker. What he needs is a tramp steamer registered in, say, Panama."

"Onassis allows this?" Farid asked.

"I spoke with him," Malik said. "He has no objection, if I work on my own and his name is never mentioned."

"Ah, good." Farid squinted up through the windshield. "I wonder if you've had much time to consider the matter of the child."

Only every waking hour, thought Malik. It was why he was in al-Remal at this moment, after all. "I have," he said. Suddenly a panicky thought seized him. "You got my letter, didn't you?"

"Yes, of course. And destroyed it, as you asked."

"Good." Malik relaxed. "What do you think? Will it work?"

Farid pulled the car over and turned to look Malik full in the face. It was all but impossible for a Remali to discuss serious matters when he could not look the person in the eye.

"You may be letting your heart rule your head. As I understand it, your idea is that the child supposedly has some rare illness, that nothing can be done here in al-Remal, but an anonymous benefactor arranges for the child to be treated in France. Do you see how convoluted this is? For one thing, the child eventually must either be cured or die."

"But that's the whole point. After a few months, or a year or two, word comes back that the treatment has failed. The parents grieve for a time, and then the whole thing is forgotten."

Farid grimaced. "In that case, we would be close to telling a direct lie, which I would rather not do. And do you want to send a child into life under the word of death—yet a second time?" Quickly he opened the door and spit on the ground—a sign against the evil eye.

Almost involuntarily Malik did the same. "No," he said softly.

Farid stroked his mustache. "Our plans so far have held to bringing the girl out alone. Wouldn't it be simpler to bring them all?"

"All? Who is all?"

"The foster parents, Mahir Najjar and Salima, along with the child. Surely a man in your position will need servants, and who could serve you better than a good Muslim couple from your own land?"

Malik could only wonder why he hadn't thought of it himself. He was heart over head, as Farid had said.

"Mahir can drive," Farid continued, "and the wife has a certain reputation as a cook. I know the French boast about their cuisine, but when was the last time you had a good *kabsa?*"

Malik raised a hand. "Enough. The stars do not need painting. Your idea is perfect. You have given me hope." Indeed, he felt almost light-headed with relief. "I cannot thank you enough. I wonder if one day—soon, God willing—you will come to work with me in Marseille. We would make a team."

Farid smiled. "I may well do it." With that, they were at Omar Badir's house.

THE home he had grown up in felt somehow smaller than Malik remembered. Even his father seemed shorter, frailer. But the old man still had the look of a falcon, and when the ritual of greeting had been accomplished, the falcon's eyes fastened on Malik's suit.

"Malik was just telling me, Uncle," Farid said mischievously, "that he's the best-dressed man in Marseille."

"Are we in Marseille?" Omar's smile had a knife-edge to it.

"My apologies, Father," Malik said. "I fell asleep on the plane and didn't find time to change. I'll do it now, if you'll excuse me."

"No, no," said Omar, mollified. "Stay as you are for the time being. There is a man I want you to meet." He called for Bahia. The servant appeared with a dark-eyed baby. "Your brother, Yusef," Omar said proudly to Malik.

When Malik had learned in France that he had a half brother, his reaction had been strangely detached. Now, with the child gurgling and smiling before his eyes, a dangerous undertow of emotions pulled at him. Suddenly he had to resist the urge to tell Omar that he was not only a father again but also a grandfather. He felt relief when the old man signaled Bahia to take the baby away.

Omar indicated that it was nearing prayer and the conversation could resume at dinner. "Make yourself at ease," he told Malik—

meaning change into proper garments. "After you've paid your respects to your mother, take a moment to do the same with Um Yusef. And don't neglect your sister. She's been sticking her head out every time the wind blows, thinking it's you arriving."

Malik longed to see his mother and sister. But he feared that paying respects to Um Yusef, his father's second wife, would be awkward. She was only months older than he was and had never appeared to like him. As it turned out, his stepmother was still so overjoyed at having a son of her own—an accomplishment that earned her the right to be called "Um" or "Mother of" Yusef—that she was positively cordial.

With a son, Malik reflected bitterly, she had a security she had not enjoyed before, gained at his own mother's expense.

"But you'll want to say hello to Amira," Um Yusef finally burbled. "I think she's up in her room."

Malik climbed the familiar stairs and, in the Western fashion, knocked at the door. For a moment he didn't recognize the woman who answered. When he'd last seen Amira, she was a tomboyish adolescent, but before him now stood a beauty. "Little sister?"

"Who else, big brother idiot," she said, and threw herself into his arms. She was full of questions. How was he? How was Marseille?

"Has Farid spoken with you?" Malik managed to interject. "About his idea for Laila?" Time was short. It was prayer time.

"Yes. Meet me in the garden after dinner. Then we can talk."

IN THE darkening garden, Malik wandered among oleander, jasmine, and bougainvillea, savoring the fragrance, smiling at the sound of the little fountain. The day's heat had broken and was radiating back to the sky, making the bright early stars shimmer against a background of deepest cerulean.

"Brother?"

"Who else, little sister idiot."

Laughing, Amira stepped from the shadows to take his hand. "I've missed you," she said simply.

"And I you."

"I doubt that you've had time to miss anyone. You must be very busy." Amira looked up at the sky. "Sometimes I think I'd give anything to do what you're doing."

"To work like a slave for Onassis?"

"I don't know. To be in France. To do as I wished."

"And what would that be?"

"To go to school. A real school." She made a gesture of impatience. "A dream," she said. The moon, nearly full, peeked over the garden wall, throwing date palms into silhouette. "I still have Nanny Karin. We study together now. She orders books from London."

"What does Father say about all this?"

"I've convinced him that times are changing and that an education will make me a more valuable wife."

It took Malik a moment to realize what she was saying. "Surely he's not thinking of marriage for you just yet."

"Of course he is. I think he's considered several candidates. He drops little hints now and then—praise of this one, criticism of that one—to see how I'll react."

Malik had the odd sensation that time had slipped. Only yesterday she'd been the vexatious little sister trying to kick the soccer ball he and his cousins were passing—right over there, two date palms for goalposts.

"I don't want to marry," said Amira, "but I must. I want to go to school in Europe, but I can't." In the moonlight, silver bright now, tears glinted on her cheeks. "I won't marry someone I don't want," she said. "I won't be like Laila. I won't!"

"Of course not, little sister," he comforted her, though the mention of Laila cut deep. "God willing, when the time comes, there'll be someone wonderful, and you'll have a wonderful life together." He felt like a fool saying it, but what else was there to say?

Amira was silent for a moment. Then she said, "Farid's plan is a good one. Are you going to do it?"

"I'm going to talk with Mahir Najjar. If he agrees, it shouldn't take me more than a few days to arrange the papers."

They talked in the garden long into the night; there was no certainty when, if ever, they would have an hour alone together again.

WITH Farid as the go-between, Malik arranged a meeting with Mahir Najjar. They agreed to meet in a coffeehouse in a poor section of town. "I will want to see my daughter," Malik said.

Mahir was a small dark-skinned man several years older than

Malik, with perpetually sad eyes. Malik trusted Mahir almost as much as he did Farid. After the necessary courtesies, Malik stated, "A man in my position needs a driver, and I thought of your honorable self before anyone else."

Without mentioning Salima, he added that he would be needing a cook and someone to look after his child, making it clear that Laila would be going to France one way or the other. He would pay well for these services, he said. He named a figure.

When he heard it, Mahir's eyes became sadder. "As always, sir, you are most generous. But I already have an excellent position driving a water truck for the oil Americans."

"Ah. Well then, you are to be congratulated. Naturally, I would not want you to pass up such an opportunity. Nevertheless, I still need a driver and a cook." Malik named a higher figure.

Mahir thanked him. "But France is far away," he pointed out, "and a man has responsibilities to his kin as well as to himself."

"Quite right," Malik agreed—and then named a still higher figure. "And the move to France need not be permanent," he noted.

Not long after that Mahir declared that, water truck be cursed, he had always wanted to see the world—and named a figure of his own.

When the pleasure of bargaining was finally done, Mahir invited Malik to his house "to taste some of the cooking you'll be enjoying and, of course, to see the little one."

At Mahir's small and hot but immaculately clean house, Salima came to her husband's call. In her arms was Laila, her dark, clear eyes gazing into Malik's with what, forever after, he would swear was a look of eternal recognition.

Childhood

1961

THE soccer ball that Malik remembered, Amira remembered, too. She had been no more than five or six when it had come bounding out of the cacophony of the boys' game, stopping an inch from her white sandals. The temptation to kick it was irresistible. But her favorite dress betrayed her; it was ankle-length, of course, with long pants under it, and when she drew back her foot, she stepped on the hem, got tangled, and missed the ball completely. The boys hooted. She lifted the dress and kicked with all her might. The heavy ball stung her toes but sailed like something in a dream—into the fountain. For a moment there was chaos, until her aunt Najla appeared and towed her back to the group of women and younger children.

It was a small memory among countless others that, years later, Amira retrieved with bittersweet nostalgia. Often, while rain fell on chilly Boston or snow piled in its streets, she would think of her father's house with its sunlit garden.

The garden was a place of green growing things, lovingly nurtured with water more precious than oil. Although shielded by high walls, it was like a playground, a bright space always alive with children—cousins, of course, almost every day, but also the children of neighbors and other visitors, and of the servants. Sometimes there were special guests, little royal princes and princesses; less often, the inexpressibly exotic offspring of American oil-company executives or European businessmen.

The garden blended with the house itself, a rambling stucco villa with tall arched windows that could be shuttered against the heat. Women and children shifted perpetually between the outdoors and the rooms of the women's country—the women's section of the house—within.

In the fiercest heat of the day, everyone settled in the shade of the arcade that ran along the main wing, the kitchen fragrance of cardamom or cloves or rosemary spicing the scent of stewing lamb. The women worked at small chores and talked softly, since women's voices heard unrequested in the men's part of the house represented gross misbehavior. The conversation could be fascinating. Amira's mother, aunts, and their friends talked of matters that concerned them deeply—money, sickness, marriage, childbirth, the ways of husband and wife—and little or nothing was censored or softened because children were present.

Looking back across a gulf of lonely time, Amira-in-exile could see that what counted was simply being part of it all. Never since those childhood days had she known such a sense of belonging.

THE first cloud over Amira's young life came from the men's world, a place she rarely saw and in which things happened that were as beyond her control and understanding as the ways of God. Malik, who had been in conference with their father—an event in itself—burst into the kitchen with astonishing news: "Little sister, I'm going to Egypt, God willing! To Victoria College."

"What's that?" Amira was six.

Malik spread some brochures on a table. "Here. Look."

There were large stone buildings and green lawns and, among them, boys in foreign clothes—jackets and ties.

"Who are all these boys?" Amira asked.

"Students, just like I'll be. It's a British boarding school."

Amira contemplated this information. "Can I go?"

"Don't be stupid. You're a girl, silly."

She could see that it was true—there were no girls in the pictures—and she knew it in her heart as well. "I want to go," she said.

Malik tousled her hair. "You can't, little sister."

At that moment Jihan, their mother, walked in.

"Mama, Malik says I can't go to Victoria. Can't I go, too?"

"Well, we'll see, little princess. It's not something you should be worrying about."

Amira knew when "we'll see" meant maybe and when it meant no. This "we'll see" was like a door closing, but she stubbornly chose to interpret it otherwise. When Malik went to Cairo, she clung to the dream that someday she would join him there. She begged Jihan to read his letters over and over so that she could absorb every word. She counted the weeks till his return on holiday or for the long summer break. And when at last he did arrive, she pestered him mercilessly to tell her all about Victoria College.

"Mama, am I going to Victoria this fall?" The second summer both dragged and rushed toward an end. Amira was nearly eight now, and if she was going to Victoria, this was the time.

Jihan sighed sadly. "No, beauty, you're not."

"Why not? Malik gives me his old books. I can do the lessons he did when he first went, almost as well as he could."

Jihan looked at her in wonder. "Are you serious, darling? I didn't know that you were actually studying his books." Then her mouth tightened. "I'm proud of you, Amira. You're a very intelligent girl. But get Victoria College out of your head. You simply can't go."

Amira knew better than to say another word. That night she cried herself to sleep, all her hopes come to nothing.

An evening or two later she overheard her mother and father talking. "As always I bow to your judgment," Jihan said, her tone that peculiar combination of flattery and insistence she used when she wanted something from Omar. "But I know that a man of your position would want his children—both children—to be well prepared for the future. I know you are aware that times are changing. Girls are to be educated now, at least to some extent. I know that if you were not so busy, you would have considered the matter of a proper nanny yourself."

A moment later Amira heard her father's rumble. "I have made a good living all these years, thanks be to God, by being aware of changing times. I dislike what you tell me, but let it be done."

That was how Miss Vanderbeek, Nanny Karin, came into Amira's life.

"WHAT'S she like, your blond nanny?"

Amira had heard the question a hundred times in the years since Miss Vanderbeek had joined the Badir household. No one else had a nanny like her. Amira always tried to find a complaint to make about her—she was too strict, too serious, too foreign—because it was bad luck to praise those you loved.

"Oh, she's all right, I suppose." She shrugged, making a small concession to approval because the person asking was Laila and it was hard to hide the truth from her closest friend. Most of the nannies were from poor countries, like Yemen or Ethiopia. Most had been slaves until, barely a year ago, the king had finally abolished slavery. And most, like the great majority of women in al-Remal, were illiterate.

"Sometimes I don't understand why she stays here," Amira said. "She could be teaching in a university. Do you know I read English almost as well as Malik? And she's teaching me arithmetic."

"What on earth for?" Laila looked genuinely surprised.

"Nanny says that nothing in the Koran says girls should be ignorant. It's like the *gutwah*, the veil. That's not the Koran either."

"She's not the only one who knows things. Did you hear about the village girl who drowned in the well?"

"Of course." It had been on everyone's lips for two days.

Laila lowered her voice. "Well, it wasn't an accident or suicide either. Someone saw her going into a man's house in town. Her brothers found out. They threw her down that well. Everyone in the village heard her screams."

"Laila! How do you know all this?"

"I told you Miss Vanderbeek wasn't the only one who knows things. Would you like to hear more, little sparrow?"

Amira settled back to listen. Learning from Miss Vanderbeek was fun but hard. It was nice to have Laila to talk with about the real world. Someday she would tell Laila her secret wish—that Laila and Malik would marry and they would all live together.

IT WASN'T just a fantasy. It could easily happen. In many ways Laila Sibai was an ideal choice to be Malik's wife. Her father was Omar Badir's lifelong friend and business partner, so the alliance would make sense economically, uniting the two fortunes.

Besides—not that it counted for much in arranging marriages— Laila and Malik liked each other. Amira remembered Laila's mother, Rajiyah, scolding Laila for playing and talking with Malik, a boy who was not *mahram*—that is, a male relative she could not marry.

It probably wouldn't happen, though. The problem was that Malik was still a schoolboy and Laila was a marriageable young woman. Her father could hardly be expected to wait for his old friend's son to grow up; he would be looking for a mature and substantial husband for her—and soon.

"LISTEN, it's them!"

A summer had passed, and another was not far away. Laila and Amira were huddled in Laila's father's library, forbidden territory for females, but Abdullah Sibai was in India buying silk and there were no other men around. Under such circumstances Laila's mother often became inattentive, and Laila and Amira slipped into the library to listen to Abdullah's expensive radio, on which he monitored news and financial developments all over the Middle East.

Laila and Amira put the radio to a different but equally international use: They listened to music from as far away as Istanbul and Cairo. Sometimes they could pick up a Cairo station that played Western music; it was there that they heard a group of musicians that Malik, with British-school snobbery, had mentioned to them as being all the rage in Europe. They were called the Beatles.

"Turn it up," Amira begged.

"No. Mother will hear. Let's dance."

Laila had shown Amira how Western teenagers danced. It was as different from the *beledi* dancing Amira knew—which Miss Vanderbeek said Westerners called belly dancing—as the music was from anything she had ever heard. It was all wild and free.

The song ended on a series of pounding notes on instruments Amira did not recognize, and the station began to fade.

"Just as well," said Laila. "We're tempting fate. Let's go to my room."

Laila's room overlooked the garden from the second floor. Flushed from dancing, they collapsed on the bed.

"Well, I hope you enjoyed that," said Laila, "because I'm sorry to tell you we won't be listening to the radio much anymore."

"Why not?"

"I think my father has chosen a husband for me. I think he'll make his decision known when, God willing, he returns from India."

Amira tried to sound enthusiastic. "Laila, this is wonderful news."

"I hope he's not too old and ugly."

"Oh, he won't be. This is so exciting!"

"Yes," Laila agreed. "Yes, it is. It's like entering a new life. I'll be a real grown-up, and I'll have to act like one. My duty will be to my husband, whoever he might be." Laila was silent for a moment, then said, "I wish that . . . well, never mind." Suddenly she brightened. "Did you know that I've driven a car?"

"What? When?" It was illegal for women to drive in al-Remal.

"With Malik, last summer. I disguised myself as a boy. We went out where they're building the new airport, and Malik showed me."

"But Laila, what could have possessed you?"

"You're right. It was crazy. Anything might have happened. But I'll never forget." Laila reached out to stroke Amira's hair. "You should do it, little sparrow. Get Malik to take you."

"Oh, I couldn't. Never."

Laila smiled and hugged her. "Why not? Do it, sparrow. You'll be married, too, before you know it, and then it'll be too late."

"MY FRIEND Abdullah Sibai has chosen wisely for his daughter," said Amira's father as the Badir family sipped their coffee after the evening meal. "General Mahmoud Sadek is renowned for his piety."

"He has a good appearance," said Jihan agreeably. "But I wonder if he might not be a bit old for Laila. He is, after all, in his fifties."

An old man, Amira thought. Her friend was going to marry an old man. What must she be feeling?

But when Amira questioned her friend, Laila's enthusiasm for her upcoming marriage was unbounded. "He's very rich. And very generous. You should see the gifts he's been sending to the house. A jeweled belt from Beirut. A gold mesh handbag from Tiffany in New York. Something new every day."

"That's wonderful, Laila, but—"

"And he's had a tragic life," Laila continued. "He's lost two wives in childbirth. My mother assures me that if I give Mahmoud a son, he'll treasure me until the day he dies. Isn't that romantic?"

Amira nodded, still not certain in her own mind that this marriage could be described as romantic. "I had a letter from Malik today. He'll be home on Thursday, for a week. Will you come to visit?"

Laila was silent for a long moment. "I don't think so," she said softly, a hint of sadness in her voice. "I don't think that would be proper now that I'm betrothed to Mahmoud."

"Oh."

"Never mind, little sparrow. There's so much to be happy about. Tomorrow I'll begin choosing clothes. Mahmoud has sent sketches from Paris. And we're going to Istanbul. Isn't that glorious? There's so much to do, Amira, I don't know how I'll find the time."

MALIK was as spiritless as Laila was bubbly. One morning Amira found him in the garden, tossing pebbles into the fountain.

"What's the matter, brother? Is it Laila?"

"Laila? What gives you that idea? It's life, little sister. It's passing me by. I have no control over anything."

"It's all in God's control, my brother," she said, feeling the words' ineffectualness as she spoke them. "Will you teach me to drive?"

His eyes snapped angrily toward hers. Then, just as suddenly, his old smile replaced the glare. "She told you about that, did she? Trust a woman with a secret. Well, why not?"

That was how Amira found herself that afternoon behind the wheel of a Mercedes sedan, in the desert beyond the new airport, where the road was little more than a track. She was wearing an old *thobe* of Malik's and had covered her hair with a boy's white *ghutra*. There were no driver's licenses in al-Remal. Any boy who had an adult male's permission could drive.

"All right, put it in first gear. Now let out the clutch and press the accelerator. Easy!"

The car jerked and stalled.

"Try it again."

She tried again and stalled again. And again. Then she managed first gear but stalled when she shifted to second. Then suddenly she got it. She took the Mercedes through to third. The feeling of having the machine in her power was magical. She learned to use the brakes and, at Malik's instruction, switched on the headlights, blinked the turn signals, even ran the windshield wipers.

"All right, little sister, slow it down. Now stop."

She braked to a halt that was only slightly abrupt. Malik came around to take the driver's seat. "You liked that, did you?"

"I loved it!"

"Now you know how to drive. It's something you never forget."

Was that what Laila had meant? Or was it this whole experience— the feeling of power, while dressed like a male, doing something only males were permitted?

LAILA was married in early fall. Malik had already left for Cairo. The wedding was the most elegant Amira ever could imagine. Laila, decked in silk and dripping with gold, looked as beautiful as one of the virgins promised to the faithful in paradise. Her groom, far from elderly, was as handsome as Jihan had said.

Then it was over, and Laila was gone. The couple would honeymoon in Istanbul. For a few days Amira lived on the remembered glory of the wedding. Then a gray loneliness descended on her.

She tried to spend time with her mother, but Jihan seemed to be in her own world these days. Even Miss Vanderbeek was gone, taking her annual vacation in France. On top of it all, Amira's body was changing; things were happening within her that sometimes seemed like torment.

It helped when Laila's letters began to arrive, a new one every day. She raved about the luxuriousness of her honeymoon hotel, the beauty of the Bosporus, the treasures of the Topkapi museum.

> You should see the jewels, Amira, the fabulous diamonds and rubies and sapphires that the sultans gave to their wives. They must have loved them very much. I miss you and wish you were here to share all these wonders with me.

In the third week of Laila's honeymoon came a note in her exuberant hand, warning, "State secret! Hide this away! Aren't they cute?" and a postcard of the Beatles. Amira slipped it between the pages of one of the textbooks Malik had left her. Every night she took it out and wondered what Istanbul was like, and London, and all the other places she might never see.

One midmorning, at an hour when Omar was always in town on business, Amira's loneliness and the urgings of her body made her do a crazy thing. She went into her father's study and turned on the radio. It took her a while to find the Cairo station, but at last there it was, playing a Western rock and roll song. She lifted her skirt and danced, watching her own long legs as she twirled, trying to regain that feeling almost forgotten, that brief sunburst of freedom.

It wouldn't come. The music wasn't the same, there was no Laila, nothing was right. But she was still dancing, mechanically and aimlessly, when her father's voice thundered from the door.

"What are you doing? By God, that I should see this! Are you my daughter?" His face bloodless with anger, Omar dragged her from the room by her hair. In the women's country, there were gasps when he burst in.

"Where is my wife? Where!"

Jihan materialized as the other women vanished in a whisper of cloth and a clatter of sandals. "What is it? What's wrong, my husband?"

"I warned you. It's time and past time. It will be done now!"

Jihan shook her head. "But husband, she's not yet reached her time. She's still a child."

"A child I've just seen flaunting herself like a Cairo whore, in my study, to my radio." Omar spotted Bahia hovering in a corner. "You! You know what's to be done. Go fetch what's needed."

Amira had never known such terror. She had sinned—not just the sin of her shameless dancing but the far worse sin of arousing *ghadab*, rage, in a parent. Children who did that endangered their very souls. Bahia reappeared carrying the *abaya,* the veiling robe.

"This is what God ordains," Omar told Jihan. "See that you do it." He turned and left.

They took her to Jihan's room. Amira wept. Veiling was supposed to be a happy and proud occasion, a passage into womanhood, but she had ruined it beyond hope. "It's too soon," she murmured.

But now it was her mother who was stern. "It's soon enough. Do you dare dispute your father?"

The long black robe came down, covering her face; dulling the colors of the room, of her childhood; shrouding her face from all who might take joy in seeing it—but also hiding her tears.

Jihan

THE desert was bright, the wide sky flawlessly blue. Jihan was standing in a pit in the sand. When she tried to step out, she couldn't. The sand slid beneath her feet, and the pit grew deeper. The harder she climbed, the deeper she sank. Soon the rim was over her head. The hot sand crumbled as she clawed at it. The hole deepened, and the sand choked her. She screamed for help. People appeared above her against the shrinking sky. The pit was as black, the hissing sand as suffocating, as smoke.

Jihan woke up, heart pounding, shivering in sweat.

Like most Remalis, she took great stock in dreams, and she knew exactly when she had first had this one. It was noted in a small diary she kept. "Black Dream," the entry said, a dream of her own death. A few weeks later the same notation, followed after another two weeks by "dream again." Soon Jihan knew with a certainty that terrified her that it would never go away.

The first dream had come exactly three days after the entry "Omar tells me he is taking another wife."

"MOTHER, don't you want to join us outside?"
"I'd rather sit here, child. I'm tired."
"You can sit outside. Come have some tea."
In the end, Jihan let Amira coax her out to the shaded arcade, but the other women's faces, their sudden silence breaking into oversolicitude, told that they all saw the dream on her.

She no longer kept the diary, for the dream came nearly every night now, so that she dreaded sleep. Worse, it haunted her waking hours as well. It was as if the whole familiar world—the house, the garden, the faces she knew—were only a gossamer veil that might lift at any moment to reveal the black sandpit beyond.

She knew that something was wrong with the way she was acting. First and second wives were expected to keep any dissonance between them from intruding on their husband's happiness. Jihan had failed in this, even denying Omar her body for many months now.

But weren't there reasons?

"You'll be the only one, always, the only star in my sky." It was another diary entry, from another time. She had been fourteen when she wrote it, on the morning after her wedding night. Omar, who was eighteen years older, had said it to her. In those days he often spoke to her in words that sounded like poetry. And it was more than words. They had had an understanding, a happy marriage.

"The only one." She shook her head and gave a bitter little laugh.

"Your throat is dry, Um Malik," said Um Yusef, gracefully covering the moment. "Let me bring you some tea." She hurried to the task as a good second wife should. Jihan watched her narrowly, thinking it was well enough for Um Yusef to make a show for the others, but the truth was that this pretty, pretty, young, young woman not only occupied the place of second wife but had usurped that of first wife as well. Ever since Yusef's birth all of Omar's attentions had centered on the baby and its mother. Where was the respect that was due to the first wife, the mother of the firstborn son?

But it was her own fault, Jihan knew, only hers.

IS IT MY FAULT? AMIRA wondered, watching her mother nod as if she was having a conversation with herself. Because I was a bad daughter? Is that why my mother has changed so much, so quickly?

She hardly recognized Jihan these days—the dull eyes that once had sparkled; the pursed mouth that had charmed with its smile, its quick jokes and kisses; the body that had been so full of life yet now lay sunken and motionless for hours in a darkened room.

"I KNOW you have responsibilities there, but if you can possibly come home, even for a few days, please, brother, come soon." Amira signed the letter and gave it to Bahia to mail. She hoped she had conveyed the urgency of the situation without sounding hysterical. It was as if their mother was slipping away a piece at a time.

When had it all started? It was two years ago, just after Omar had announced his intention to take another wife, a few months before the horror of Laila's execution. One morning Amira woke to a sound from her mother's room—a blood-chilling wail. She rushed into the hall. Bahia, appearing out of nowhere, pushed past her and into the room. Jihan was standing by the bed. It was covered with blood. So was the lower half of her nightgown.

"Allah! What is it? Is she cut?"

"No, little miss. Nothing like that. But go and have someone send for the midwife." Bahia had her arms around Jihan, comforting her.

"But what's the matter?"

"She has miscarried. Undoubtedly something was wrong with the fetus. It is God's will."

FOR Jihan the pregnancy had been a miracle and a desperate hope. The conception must have occurred on the last night she and Omar had made love. After their years together he did not come to her bed often, and when he did, the act lacked ardor.

This night had been different. He did not press his desire directly but sat beside her, stroked her hand, and said, "Let us talk for a while, beauty. It seems we never have a moment together these days."

"Is something wrong, Omar?" His words were so unexpected.

"Wrong? I was just thinking. And remembering."

"Thinking and remembering what?"

He smiled—a small, shy smile she had not seen in years that made him look almost boyish behind his graying beard. "The time when your voice was to me like the sound of splashing water to a man burning with thirst. And thinking that it is still that way."

"Why, I hardly know what to say." She laughed with pleasure.

"Listen, it occurs to me, my beauty, that I don't often tell you what you've meant to me—as a wife, as the mother of my children. Perhaps this will help make up for the poverty of my words." He held out a small box of kid leather with gilt trim.

"For me? But, my husband, I've done nothing to deserve a gift."

"Open it."

She did and gasped. It was an emerald necklace—flashing green gems set in gold, with clusters of diamonds around them.

"It's too much. Oh, Omar!"

"Not nearly enough. I love you, Jihan. You will always be my wife."

That night Omar was like a young bridegroom. Three weeks later he informed her that he had decided to take a second wife, the daughter of one of his cousins.

She should have known, Jihan told herself. She should have suspected the shy smile, the sweet words, the ridiculous gift. After a day of tears and hate, she confronted Omar in the hall and demanded a divorce, throwing the necklace in his face. Most men would have summoned a witness and divorced her on the spot, but Omar said with dignity, "I told you that you would always be my wife," and walked away. Only then did she realize the bitter ambiguity of his promise: always his wife, but not his only wife. She ran screaming back to her room.

Bahia retrieved the necklace. "When she is calmer," she told the other women, "I will return it to her jewelry box. The day will come, God willing, when she will wear it proudly."

She replaced the necklace the day her mistress told her she was pregnant. After thirteen futile years it was a miracle.

Jihan locked on to the idea that her pregnancy would change everything. If she could give Omar another child, certainly another son, he would forget his fantasy of taking another wife. She was only waiting for the right moment to tell him the wonderful news.

Then came the morning of blood. Until then the dream had been only a coincidence. Now it came more and more often, until it was a constant torment, like the presence of the new wife herself.

The concept of clinical depression did not exist in al-Remal. There was not a single psychologist in the country. Bahia was sure her mistress was beset by *jinn,* malevolent spirits. When Jihan's affliction became unbearable, she tried folk remedies, but these did not help her.

In the end, at the urging of Najla, Amira, and even Um Yusef, she sent for the doctor. He assured her that all she needed was something to help her sleep. He gave her a large bottle of pills, instructing her to take one just before bed. But she woke feeling as if she were dead. She was certain that she was dying in the dream every night. She put the pills away. From then on, everything was worse. There was no help for her.

"YOU called me, Mother?" Even though she had watched Jihan decline for months, the way her mother looked still shocked Amira: unhealthy complexion with no makeup, hair disheveled, clothes smelling of too long wear.

"Called? Yes, I suppose. Sit, child."

Amira obeyed. For a long time Jihan said nothing, merely stared into space. Then suddenly she blurted, "To fight with a man brings only pain and suffering. Obey your husband and bend to his will. Remember that, and you'll be happier than I have been."

"Yes, Mother. Of course."

Another long silence, then: "Times change, as Omar says. People say they wish they could turn back the clock. I wish I could turn it forward. I wish I were your age. I wish . . . ah, well."

Her mind wanders so, thought Amira. "Let me brush your hair, Mother," she said, noticing Jihan tugging at the tangles.

"What? Yes, that would be nice. Thank you, Najla. I mean, Amira."

Amira brushed out the knots, then neatly braided her mother's hair. "There. Much better. Do you want the mirror?"

"No. I know you did well. Look." Jihan opened her hand. "My father gave it to my mother. I don't know why I've never shown it to you." It was a ring, a star sapphire, almost midnight blue, set in gold.

"Mother, it's beautiful!"

"It's for you. You'd have it anyway, of course."

"Mother, what are you talking about? It's yours. You keep it."

"No. I'm setting the clock forward. It's for you."

Once Amira finally accepted the ring, Jihan became almost cheerful. She bathed, put on fresh clothes, and allowed Amira to do her makeup. "Make me beautiful again," she said with a little laugh.

"You are beautiful, Mother."

That night Amira had hope for the first time in months that her mother had turned a corner. Still, she wished that Malik were here. She woke in the night to find Jihan standing by the bed.

"Mother? Is something wrong?"

"No, dearest. I went to refill my water pitcher and looked in on you to say good night. But you were asleep."

"Asleep? Yes. It's late, isn't it?"

"Is it? I suppose it is. Good night, little princess."

"Good night, Mother."

WHEN she woke again, it was still not light, and she thought for a moment that the woman standing over her was Jihan again. But it was Aunt Najla. "You're awake, child? Oh, my child, a terrible thing has happened. Amira, your mother is dead."

By dawn women were everywhere in the house—aunts, cousins, in-laws, all in black. No one would tell Amira exactly what had happened, but once she heard a voice from the men's section loudly cursing the doctor and his pills.

The women prepared Jihan for burial, which would come that same day, according to custom. They washed the body, wrapped it in white linen. As the cloth was wound, Amira took a last look at her mother's face. In death the sadness and weariness had vanished, and Jihan looked even younger than the young woman she still had been.

Suddenly Amira could not hold back the tears. "Wake up, Mama. You can't leave me alone. Please don't leave me alone!"

"Stop it! Stop it, shameless girl." It was Najla, pulling on Amira's shoulder, dragging her away. "Don't you know that your mother is in paradise? Do you want your tears to torment her there?"

In the hallway, there was a hubbub, and Bahia scurried up. "Little miss, your brother . . ."

Behind Bahia was Malik, shock written on his features. "I got your letter," he said. "I took the first plane. I—"

He stopped. They both knew that there was nothing to say.

"I SHOULD have been here," Malik said, his voice hoarse with sorrow, his eyes brimming. "I could have done something."

Amira wanted to comfort her brother, but how could she when she was without comfort herself? At least Malik had been able to say good-bye to their mother, for it was he who had led the procession of men who buried her. Amira sighed heavily.

As if he heard what was in her heart, Malik said softly, "I marked Mother's grave with a stone so you would know it."

Amira was touched, yet also faintly shocked. The grave of a good Muslim was always unmarked. "What kind of stone?"

"Just a rock I picked up on the beach at St.-Tropez." He shrugged. "When I saw it in the water, I thought for just a heartbeat that it was a ruby. It was that red. I picked it up and saw that it was just a stone, but still, it was pretty. When it dried, of course, it was nothing, but by then I had decided it was lucky. So I kept it."

"You left it there for luck . . . for Mama?" Amira found this paganistic idea disconcerting.

"I don't know. Maybe. Mama didn't have the luck she deserved. Anyway, as long as it's there, you'll know where she is."

SLEEP was fitful as Amira awaited the sun. When daylight at last came, she slipped out of the house. Wrapping her veil tightly around her, she walked the three miles to the mosque.

Where was the marker? Perhaps someone had picked it up or sand had covered it over during the night. Frantically she searched. There, at last, the oxblood-colored stone Malik had described.

Amira dropped to her knees, her lips moving in silent prayer. Surrounded by stillness, she knew she was not alone. She felt her mother's love reaching out to her. She looked to the sky—for so strong a feeling, there should be a sign in the heavens. But there was only the blinding sun. She whispered good-bye, and began the long walk home.

Ali

"WAKE up, laziness. Are you a queen that you sleep until noon?"

Amira rubbed her eyes and stretched, glancing at her bedside clock. "But Auntie Najla, it's only half past eight, and I was up late studying for my examination."

"Only half past eight? Only? Allah, Amira, a good wife could prepare food for an army before nine o'clock—and see to her husband and children as well. Examination indeed. Do you think, my high-and-mighty miss, that the diploma you crave will make you better than the other women of this house?"

Amira bit back a sharp retort. No, she didn't think she was better. But she was different; she felt even more so since Jihan had died. The books she devoured, the home study courses she took, the secret yearnings she harbored—all these set her apart.

"Well then," Najla went on, "hurry up and get dressed. Your father mentioned he would enjoy a good *saleeq,* and if we don't hurry, Allah only knows what will be left in the market."

If she did everything her aunt asked now, perhaps Amira would be left in peace later, so she might study with Miss Vanderbeek, who now acted as her personal tutor. The time they shared was like a magic carpet that transported Amira to other places and other times.

Amira slipped on a favorite cream-colored linen dress, then tried on her new gold earrings, a gift from Um Yusef on Amira's sixteenth birthday. But who of any consequence would see—or care— whether she looked pretty or not? With everyone she loved dead or far away, it seemed as if all the warmth and pleasure had gone from this house. A few minutes later, wrapped in identical black *abaya* and veils, Amira and her aunt climbed into Omar's black Bentley.

Aunt Najla settled into the leather upholstery with a sigh of contentment. Shopping was a highlight of her aunt's day, Amira knew, for she could remember when only men and servants ventured into the market. But with his concessions to modernization Omar allowed the women under his protection to shop outside the home— as long as they were driven by a man, according to law.

"GOOD," Omar said with a contented sigh, "very good indeed." Najla sighed, too, as if a verdict of utmost importance had been rendered. Never mind that it was part of a daily ritual.

"And you, my daughter, did your hand sweeten this delectable dinner?" Omar asked, turning to Amira.

Now, this was a surprise, for since her mother's death Amira's relationship with her father had become distant at best. "Yes, Father," she replied, casting her eyes downward onto her plate.

"Excellent, excellent." Omar smiled benevolently. "Well then," he said, "it's time to share my good news. Today I have spoken with no less a personage than our beloved king."

There were murmurs of appreciation at this news.

"And," Omar continued, "His Royal Majesty has honored my house. It has been decided that his son Prince Ali al-Rashad will be married to Amira."

The women began ululating, a sound of celebration. Omar smiled. "Though I refrained from boasting, His Majesty was favorably impressed with Amira's education. He graciously said that my daughter would be a great asset to his house and to the kingdom."

Amira said nothing. She had known ever since she was a little girl that this day was coming. But now that it was here, she didn't know how she felt. How Laila would have loved this, she thought with a twinge of sadness.

"Well, daughter," said Omar, "to be modest and quiet is admirable. But at a moment like this a smile of happiness would be more than appropriate. And perhaps a prayer of thanks that Allah has provided so well for your future."

"Yes, Father, I do give thanks to Allah. And to you," she added with sincerity, knowing that it was in Omar's power to marry her to anyone. Yet he had chosen for her a prince, well known and well loved. Prince Ali, a pilot and hero, was al-Remal's minister of culture and responsible for its new cultural museum. Life with him would have to be better than at home—wouldn't it?

"THE foreign dressmakers are here," Bahia announced stolidly— as if a visit from the French couturiere Madame Grès were an everyday occurrence. "Your aunts wish you to come down at once."

Amira shut her book and looked imploringly at Miss Vanderbeek. "We'll have to stop now. I don't want to, but . . . well, you know."

"I do know." The Dutch woman smiled. "Now that you have your diploma, French literature just can't compete with French couture."

"But that's not so," Amira protested. Then, realizing she was being teased, she smiled, too. "You do understand."

Miss Vanderbeek nodded. "In truth, you don't really need me anymore, Amira. You're as fluent in French as I am, and your English is quite good, too. If you were going on to university . . ." She trailed off, for she had broached this subject before, urging her pupil to continue her studies, if only by correspondence.

"I want to, but I can't decide that without my husband's consent."

"I know." Miss Vanderbeek sighed. "I know."

There was a long moment of silence.

"I suppose we must be saying good-bye soon."

Amira's eyes filled with tears. For so long the beautiful blond nanny had been her window into the world. "I wish . . . oh, I wish you could come to live with me in the palace." Tears slipped from her eyes.

The Dutch woman and Amira embraced, and Amira thought again that everyone she loved seemed to go away.

DOWNSTAIRS, in the main salon, Amira seated herself on an upholstered armchair; her aunts positioned themselves on either side. Flanked by her personal assistant and two female fitters, Madame Grès stood at the doorway to the dining room, which for the moment was serving as an informal changing room for the three models who'd accompanied her.

Strange, Amira thought as she watched the fashion show that had been created for her alone. Grès was a name she had often read in magazines, a world apart from al-Remal. Now that world had come here to her, and all because she was marrying Ali al-Rashad. Perhaps marriage would be wonderful after all, just as poor Laila had once imagined.

WHERE once Amira's days seemed to drag interminably, they now flew by. The marriage contract, the *katb kitab,* was signed—first by Omar and the king, next by Ali, and last by Amira. But there would be no consummation until the *doukhla,* the party at the palace.

Then it seemed as if all of al-Remal came to call, to offer good wishes, to take a close look at the young woman who would marry the ruler's second son, and to bring gifts.

But the best gift of all came just two days before the *doukhla.* As Amira sat in the garden enjoying the breeze after sunset, a familiar voice called out, "Daydreaming, little sister? I would have thought our aunts would have a million tasks to keep you busy."

"Malik!" She rose and threw herself into his arms. Looking up at him, she saw that the lines of his face were harder, yet his dark eyes were filled with the same love she had always seen there.

"So you are happy, then, Amira?"

"Yes, brother. I'm about to be married. To a prince. Isn't that enough to make any woman happy?"

"You, my dear, are not just any woman. You're my sister, and I will personally skewer any man who fails to—"

Amira squeezed his hand. "I know, but I am all right. Truly."

"I want this marriage to be everything you desire. I need to know that your life is rich with happiness. Enough for both of us."

"But surely you have a good life, Malik. Your daughter must be a source of great joy."

"I adore her," he said fiercely. "More each day." He dug into his pocket and produced a photograph of a chubby little girl laughing.

"She's beautiful," Amira said, longing to see her niece.

"One day soon, little sister, one day I'll find a way for us to be together as a real family should."

IN THE mirror, sun streaming over her shoulder, Amira had looked like a queen. On her hair, she wore her new diamond tiara. From it cascaded a veil of handmade lace that spilled over her shoulders and onto the creamy white richness of her gown.

Now, discreetly covered by a veil of gray silk, she was on her way to the palace. Accompanied by her father and her aunts, she rode in Omar's prize limousine, a vintage Mercedes. Amira waved to the well-wishers who lined the streets, calling out congratulations and prayers for health and happiness. In al-Remal, celebrations for this wedding had begun at dawn, when, by order of the two fathers, hundreds of sheep had been killed and distributed to the poor.

Though Amira had seen the palace many times before, today it was like a fantasy garden drenched in flowers—tens of thousands of blooms flown in from Holland at dawn. Omar escorted his daughter as far as the steps. Kissing her forehead, he murmured, "God be with you." Then he returned to the car, to be driven to the farthest reaches of the palace grounds, where, under brightly striped tents, the men's celebrations had already begun. Amira could hear the sound of male voices raised in song. She could smell the pungent aroma of lambs cooking over open fires, their juices dripping into huge cauldrons of seasoned rice.

Entering the palace, Amira and her aunts were met by a group of young female cousins, who were all dressed in white and carrying tall white candles. When the women had shed their veils, Aunt Najla lit the candles, and the *zaffa,* the procession, began. They made their way down the long marble corridor toward the main reception hall.

As Amira entered the vast room, which was lit by a hundred crystal chandeliers, all the guests, women and children alike, rose to applaud. Amira sat down in a thronelike gilt chair at the head of the room, and the feasting began in earnest: caviar from Iran; foie gras from France; lamb accompanied by rice; grilled pigeons and roast chicken; fish from the Red Sea; desert truffles sautéed in butter and onion; heaping platters of fruit from the four corners of the globe; pastries and ice cream; a giant wedding cake flown in from France.

As the food was served, the Lebanese chanteuse Sabah sang of love—lost, regained, lost again—her husky voice rising and falling, sometimes breaking, her audience calling out their understanding of the feelings she expressed.

As cardamom-flavored coffee and mint tea were served, a half-dozen guests went to the center of the room and began the local circle dance. Arms at their sides, they took tiny skipping steps, moving their heads and shoulders in rhythm to the music.

The audience shouted their appreciation, and as the dancers approached Amira's table, their remarks grew louder and bawdier. Embarrassed as she was to receive this kind of attention, Amira savored every minute of her celebration, and when her aunts said it was time to leave, she did so with genuine regret.

Outside the reception hall, her father was waiting. With a solemnity Amira had rarely seen, he extended his arm and slowly walked her up the marble staircase of the palace that was now her home.

He stopped in front of a richly paneled mahogany door. Though he seemed on the verge of serious words, he settled for an awkward embrace. "May God protect you always, daughter."

Tears flooded her eyes. She kissed her father good-bye and stood for a long moment before her husband's door. What would he be like?

She tapped on the door. It swung open immediately, welcoming her to the most beautiful suite she had ever seen. The furnishings were European antiques, the walls almost hidden by paintings she remembered from books—a Picasso, a Renoir, a Signac.

Prince Ali al-Rashad was as elegant as his surroundings. Wearing a white silk robe over matching pajamas, he was handsome as a film star, not tall, but finely proportioned, with black eyes and silky hair.

For perhaps a full minute he studied Amira. Then he smiled. "May eternity be as beautiful as you are at this moment."

Amira exhaled a sigh of relief. Ali held out his hand. Obediently and with something very much like gratitude—after all, he could have been old and like Laila's husband—she took it.

He led her into the bedroom, which was dominated by a majestic Chinese bed, hand-carved and decorated in gold.

"Champagne?"

She was startled. She knew that people drank in al-Remal despite the laws against it, but she had never tasted alcohol herself.

Ali handed her a crystal tulip filled with bubbling gold. He smiled. "Relax, my dear. It won't hurt you."

Amira sipped. Her mouth tingled, an interesting sensation.

Still smiling pleasantly, Ali said, "Take off your clothes."

Amira froze. This, of course, was expected—but not so suddenly. She knew what she had learned all her life: that no matter what her husband wanted, she must do it, always.

Blushing, Amira retreated to the marble bathroom. She removed her gown, the layers of silk underwear. When she reached the flimsy teddy, she stopped. She didn't want to make her husband angry, but she just couldn't stand naked before him. Timidly she edged back into the bedroom, her feet sinking in the luxurious white carpet.

He didn't seem angry or even annoyed as he admired her once again. "You have a lovely body," he said.

He led her to the bed and began stroking her, as if she were a kitten. Basking in the warmth of his approval, Amira allowed herself the pleasure of his touch. So this is what it was all about, she thought, all the whispering and laughing. This warm fluttering, this weightlessness, this was what had been forbidden.

But when Ali parted her legs with his knee, she stiffened.

He stopped. "Perhaps you require more champagne?"

"Yes, please." She took the glass he offered and drained it.

"Slowly, slowly, Amira. Such pleasures are meant to be savored."

She giggled. Such a lovely feeling, this light-headedness, the cocoon of Ali's bed. He opened his arms and kissed her slowly, deeply.

They fell back on the bed, and she parted her thighs, no longer apprehensive. She felt a liquid heat building inside her. And when she cried out, it was from joy and the thrill of discovery.

She did not notice—nor could she have known—that her husband did not reach a climax. She fell asleep content, thinking that if this was marriage, everything else was pale by comparison.

Marriage

"Why Istanbul?" Ali asked when they were airborne in the king's private jet.

"Because someone very dear to me went there for her honeymoon. She said it was beautiful—and exciting."

Ali smiled indulgently. "Well," he said, "to someone who hasn't seen much of the world, I suppose Istanbul can be impressive. But you, my dear, can expect to see much more. That I can promise."

Amira could scarcely imagine much more. Being served orange juice in crystal goblets at forty thousand feet made her feel as if she were a fairy-tale princess, an impression that lingered long after they landed. A limousine whisked them quickly to the Hilton.

Amira was enchanted. She had never stayed in a hotel before. With its lushly landscaped grounds, crystal-clear pools, and inviting tennis courts, she thought this one even grander than al-Remal's royal palace. And Amira could not take her eyes off the people who crowded the lobby: the fair European men; the beautiful women, unveiled, wearing their fashionable clothes for all to see.

The manager personally escorted them to their quarters. As soon as she and Ali were alone, she dashed from room to room, throwing open the curtains and exclaiming over the dazzling cityscape below.

"Don't be such a bumpkin," Ali said, but with a tender smile that took the sting from his words. "As it is, most Europeans think all Gulf Arabs live in tents and know nothing of indoor plumbing."

"Of course," she said, stopping in her tracks. "You're right." Yet far from upsetting Amira, Ali's words made her feel important, as if she had a purpose outside her own home: to represent her country in a small way, to bring honor to the royal house of al-Remal. She began to walk around the room with a measured pace, imitating the elegant European women she had seen in the lobby.

"Brava," Ali said, clapping. "You look like a queen. Let me show you off to the world right now. And let's leave your veil behind."

"Really?" she asked with some trepidation. "In the street?"

"Yes, of course. We don't want to look as if we've come from some primitive backwater, do we?"

So Amira went sightseeing unveiled. At first she felt quite strange, but her self-consciousness slipped away and she savored the breeze that ruffled her hair, the sunlight that warmed her skin.

At her request their first stop was the Topkapi Palace, once the royal residence of the Ottoman sultans. She wanted to linger, as if perhaps she could feel something of Laila's brief presence at a time when she had been a happy bride. But Ali urged her on, studying various exhibits and making notes. "The king will expect some recommendations for the museum project at home."

Next came the city's great mosques: the magnificent St. Sophia; the Sultan Ahmet, with its sublime blue frescoes; the graceful Suleymaniye, where Suleyman the Magnificent and his wife were buried.

After lunch at a small waterside restaurant, Ali took Amira to the Capali Carsi, the vast and sprawling covered bazaar. The choices laid out before her were legion: carpets woven of richly dyed wools and precious silks; tapestries from the time of the Ottomans; heavy silver jewelry; inlaid furniture set with mother-of-pearl; brass coffeepots and trays and candlesticks; bags and shoes made of kilim carpets. Amira's head was spinning.

Not wanting to appear greedy—or childlike—Amira strolled through the cavernous arcade, admiring a tapestry here, an intricate perfume bottle there. Shopkeepers called out to them, entreating them to stop and look. Ali bestowed a princely smile on all. And when Amira lingered over a silk carpet and later an antique writing desk, he entered into spirited negotiation with the shopkeepers.

"That's all? Are you sure that's all you want?" he asked after the bargaining ritual had been concluded.

She nodded tentatively, wondering if she'd disappointed him.

He laughed. "Perhaps you haven't learned how to manage a man. Else you'd have been taught to be more demanding."

Amira was silent. Was Ali mocking her?

"Don't look so serious, Amira. I was just teasing you. I'm very touched, actually, that you require so little by way of material things. That will make it much easier for me to spoil you."

Instinctively, Amira refrained from saying she had little interest in such things. But later that day, when it was time to dress for dinner, she chose what she felt might please him: one of her more elaborate Paris creations and the sapphire jewelry that had once belonged to her mother. She was rewarded with Ali's murmurs of approval.

They dined at the century-old Pera Palace, the most imposing of Istanbul's grand old hotels. "I thought you might like this place," Ali said as Amira admired the ornate, majestic dining room. "Greta Garbo stayed here. So did Agatha Christie, Mata Hari, and Leon Trotsky. And now you're here, Amira, a royal princess of al-Remal."

Amira laughed. "How wonderful." He was so attentive, she thought. And so elegant as he ordered a sumptuous meal in impeccable French. No one had ever taken such care to please her before.

She wanted to return the favor. So when he asked if she'd like to visit a nightclub, she noted that his eyelids were drooping and thought he might be tired. "Perhaps you'd rather go back to the hotel," she ventured. When he agreed readily, she became quiet and a little shy, in anticipation of the intimacy they would share again.

Yet when they returned to the hotel and entered the elevator, Ali took them to the casino floor. The place was crowded with men and women in evening clothes. Surely Ali's father would not approve of such a place, she thought, but she said nothing.

With a familiarity born of practice, Ali took a seat at the black-jack table with the highest limit and threw down a thick pile of bills for a pile of chips. A moment later a tuxedo-clad waitress appeared at his elbow. "Glenlivet," Ali said. "Bring the bottle."

His movements were languid, almost bored, as he played his hands with careless ease. Within an hour he had almost doubled his pile of chips. Dutifully Amira stood behind his chair, imagining they would soon leave. Yet he continued to gamble, tossing chips on the table as if they had no meaning at all. She was very tired. Finally, at about three in the morning, she said very tentatively, "Perhaps we should go now, Ali. It's late."

A look of molten anger was his reply, so fleeting that Amira wondered if she'd seen it at all. A few minutes later he said, "If you're tired, my dear, perhaps you'd like to retire. I'll be here for a while."

She stood her ground for a while. Was her place here—or would Ali prefer her to go? Fatigue finally made her go.

In their honeymoon suite, the bed had been turned down, her nightgown artfully arranged alongside Ali's silk pajamas. It seemed like a reproach. Why was the appeal of the gambling tables greater than her own? She had no answer.

The remaining days of her honeymoon followed the same pattern: sightseeing, shopping in European-style boutiques, splendid meals at fine restaurants. In the evening, there would be something for Amira—her first ballet, her first opera. Yet they would inevitably finish the evening at the casino, with Ali drinking too much and staying out almost until dawn, while Amira would fall asleep alone, wondering how long it would take to understand her handsome but rather puzzling husband.

LAZY, languid days and long, sleepy nights—these were the rhythms of Amira's life in the palace. And how quickly she adapted to it—as if there had always been a masseuse to pamper and soothe her muscles, a fortune-teller to entertain her with predictions, a hairdresser and a cosmetician to carry out her daily beauty routines.

When Ali went abroad in his role as al-Remal's cultural minister, she went, too, visiting all the legendary places she'd imagined as a young girl. These trips were like a dream come true; yet when she returned to her luxurious cocoon in al-Remal, she often asked herself which was reality and which was the dream.

In the palace she was rarely alone, but often lonely. The king's various wives and concubines, their daughters and daughters-in-law, all these women were like a country within a country. At the heart was the queen, Faiza. It was she who had built the *hammam,* communal bath, where Amira now reclined on a bench of marble. The room was large and airy, with diamond-cut skylights.

As her maid applied the henna that gave Amira's hair reddish highlights and body, the queen entered, wrapped in a saronglike Turkish towel embroidered with silver and silk. "Any news yet, Amira?"

Amira rose to show her respect. "Not yet, Mother."

"Let us hope soon."

Amira returned to her bench, her sense of relaxation gone. She was not pregnant and therefore a disappointment to her mother-in-law. But how could she tell the queen that it was not her fault?

In the weeks and months that followed her marriage, Amira had come to believe that Ali had two faces. Sometimes he was kind and attentive, content to curl up beside her in bed, talking about the changes he envisioned for al-Remal. She loved those quiet moments when it seemed they might be friends and not just husband and wife.

But there were other times when her most innocent actions seemed to anger him, when he came to her bed drunk and brutishly exercised his marital rights as if she were there to serve him, nothing more. Yet since it was those occasions that were likely to give her a child, Amira endured them, as a good wife should.

THE gala to celebrate the opening of the al-Remal Cultural Museum was a glittering but fairly subdued affair. In honor of the Western guests—oil-company executives, foreign diplomats, and their wives—Ali had arranged for a British orchestra. Thanks to his powers of persuasion, the queen and assorted princesses were also present, albeit veiled and segregated from the foreigners.

Ali seemed to be having a good time. Surrounded by reporters from the foreign-language weeklies and the cameras of al-Remal's single television station, he was explaining how important the new museum was. "For us in the so-called developing nations it's important to know that on our land once stood a great civilization. By displaying its artifacts and teaching our children the past, we may yet, *inshallah,* regain our national pride and dignity."

Ali's remarks were well received, and the museum itself, a modern sandstone structure, was enthusiastically applauded by the foreign visitors.

"Did you enjoy yourself, my dear?" Ali asked Amira after the reception. "I thought the evening was a great success."

"I think so, too. I just wish I could be more useful."

"Why not take those college courses you mentioned?" he suggested. "As an educated wife and mother, you can be part of the changes that are coming, that are occurring even now. A few years ago my father never would have allowed a mixed gathering like the one we had at the museum tonight."

AS IF to further prove his point about progress, Ali announced that they would be having a foreign guest to dinner. "Dr. Philippe Rochon. He's come to al-Remal to treat my father."

Amira was impressed. Dr. Rochon was a well-known internist and diagnostician whose brilliant mind and healing skills were in demand not only in his native France but throughout the Middle East.

Normally a dinner like this would be a male-only affair. For Ali to bring him here to their private quarters was indeed progress.

"And you may wear one of those dresses you brought from France," he added. "Without the veil."

Amira was shocked—and pleasantly surprised. Regardless of what she did when she traveled abroad, she had never been unveiled in al-Remal, not since she was a girl.

Philippe Rochon was perhaps forty, pepper-black hair just showing the first sprinkling of salt. Not much taller than Ali, but one of those men who seem to gain stature through their presence.

More than anything else, it was his eyes, Amira thought. Though he greeted her in good Arabic with conventionally elaborate courtesy—"Your Highness, you do your poor servant too great an honor"—his eyes, the changeable, expressive blue of Normandy, spoke far more eloquently.

"It is the guest who honors the house," Amira replied.

"No, no." Ali laughed. "This is not a school for diplomats. Tonight, Doctor, we are doing things *à la mode de l'ouest*. Please call me Ali and my wife Amira."

A Gallic shrug and a smile of helpless acceptance. "Ah, well, then you must not call me Doctor, but Philippe."

Dinner began with foie gras flown in from Strasbourg, followed by quail stuffed with wild rice and a salad of baby greens.

"My compliments on a delectable meal," Philippe said to Amira.

"You are too kind, Philippe." Amira blushed, lowering her eyes.

"Ali tells me you're taking university-level correspondence courses, Amira. Have you found a particular interest yet?"

"No. I'm enrolling in a general program—literature, history, science, philosophy. But I feel as if I'm still shopping. That's what it's like, in a way—like being in some wonderful store where there's so much to buy that you can't make up your mind."

Philippe smiled warmly, his blue eyes crinkling as they looked directly at her. "What a marvelous attitude, Amira. I hope you always feel that way. And as far as a specialty, well, there's plenty of time."

Amira basked in the glow of his approval. No one had ever taken her so seriously before.

"If I had it to do over again," he added, "if I were as young as you, Amira—I believe that I would specialize in psychology."

It was a moment Amira would remember in the years to come, a moment when she glimpsed the future.

She was enjoying herself so much, she wanted the evening to go on and on. But after a second cup of coffee Philippe said, with obvious regret, that he had to leave. "An early flight, alas. But please allow me to return your hospitality. I would be honored if you would visit me in Paris." He kissed Amira's hand, his breath a caress.

Scarcely noticing Ali's searching look, she went to bed reliving that moment, Philippe's touch, his voice, his special glance.

IN THE quiet time before dawn, while she was still fast asleep, Amira felt fingers trailing delicately on her skin. But suddenly the fingers were no longer gentle. They squeezed and pinched and hurt. She cried out in pain and pushed the hand away. A stinging slap jolted her awake. Ali was beside her, his face mottled with anger. "Listen carefully, woman," he said between clenched teeth, "I decide, you understand? I decide what happens in this bed and outside it, and that's how it will be until the day you die."

Amira listened, eyes wide, scarcely breathing. Why was he so angry? Could he possibly know that she had slept with thoughts of another man? She searched Ali's face for answers, but without another word he got up from the bed and left.

Later that day she found a *sura* from the Koran, written on parchment and nailed to the wall of her bedroom. "If you fear that they (your wives) will reject you, admonish them and remove them to another bed; firmly beat them. If they obey you, then worry no more. God is high and great."

And for the first time in her marriage Amira feared her husband.

Motherhood

"ARE you certain, Amira? Absolutely certain?"

"The doctor confirmed it today."

Ali fell to his knees and began kissing her hand. "This is the greatest gift of all, Amira, not only to me but to my father. Now you are truly my queen."

"The king's pleasure and yours are as my own," she said, meaning every word. Now the pressure to conceive was over; now everyone knew she was not deficient in any way. Amira hoped for a boy—because she knew that every man wanted a son—but all that was really expected of her was to deliver a healthy child.

She immersed herself in studies. Inspired by her conversation with Philippe Rochon, she added a course in basic psychology to her correspondence curriculum from Cairo University. Every time she opened a psychology text, she thought of Philippe, remembered the way he'd looked at her, the way he'd kissed her hand.

And even as she daydreamed about another man, she was very much aware that Ali's sexual demands—erratic at best—had stopped altogether. He didn't want to hurt the baby, he said. Yet even as he distanced himself physically, Ali pampered Amira in everything else. To encourage her in her studies, he had her bedroom fitted out with bookcases, a handsome desk, and a custommade chair. He installed a midwife in the palace and had a London specialist flown in every two weeks. "You must have the best of everything," he said. "Anything you need, Amira, just ask."

Yet in spite of the excellent care she received, Amira couldn't help but fear the moment when her child would arrive. The memory of Laila's delivery was still etched in her mind.

"WAKE up, Ali; please wake up," Amira pleaded. She had been wakened moments ago by a mild cramping sensation—and a rush of warm fluid that soaked her nightgown and sheets. It had begun.

"It's time?" Ali asked as his eyes flew open.

"Yes."

Moving with a speed she had never seen, he bundled Amira into a palace limousine and summoned the midwife. Soon they were speeding toward the new al-Remal hospital. The London specialist, who'd been lodged at the Intercontinental Hotel for the past few weeks, was on his way.

In the end, it was far less difficult than she'd imagined. A few hours of discomfort, an hour or so of real pain. A final push and she heard his cry. Her son had been born.

Café au lait skin, a shock of black hair, enormous liquid eyes of deepest lapis. "Beautiful," she whispered when the nurse placed him in her arms. "I love you, my son, more than my own life." And when he gave her a lusty cry, she was sure he had heard and understood.

Ali filled the room with flowers the morning after Karim's birth. And on the following day he presented Amira with a small velvet box. Inside was an antique pendant, an enormous pigeon-blood ruby.

"It belonged to Marie Antoinette," Ali said. "A queen of France."

But such an unhappy one, Amira recalled—and then quickly banished the thought. She thanked her husband graciously.

The ruby was but the first of a shower of gifts. Visitors laden with beautifully wrapped boxes trooped in and out of Amira's room all day long. Malik flew in from Paris with an entire carload of hand-made toys. He was sleeker, more poised, better dressed—and Amira couldn't resist teasing him. "You're looking very prosperous, brother. Have you really become the hardworking and brilliant businessman Father imagines you to be?"

"I am prosperous, *nushkorallah,* thanks be to God. And I do work hard. But as for brilliance, well, Onassis insists that making money takes no particular talent. When I told him I was striking out on my own, he said, 'My young friend, I have just one piece of advice for you. To be successful, you must always have a tan and always pay your hotel bills.' I have tried to follow this advice—though my tan, of course, is permanent."

"Silly," she said, pushing him playfully. Then she lowered her voice. "Tell me. How is Laila?"

The sophistication fell away, and he was a boy again, his eyes sparkling with love. "Wonderful, Amira. Her French is amazing now. Her nanny says she has a great facility with language."

Amira's eyes went to her own son, lying in his cradle.

"They grow faster than you can imagine, Amira," Malik said softly. "And soon you cannot imagine a life without them."

Amira's final visitor arrived on the day she was to return home. Dr. Philippe Rochon. "I've been attending the king this week," he explained, "so I thought I'd look in on you and the baby."

He sat in a chair a full three feet from her bed, yet there was an intimacy to his presence that she had not experienced before.

"The baby is healthy," he went on, "and you, Amira, you . . ."

"Yes?" she asked, holding her breath.

"You're lovelier than ever. If that were possible."

She exhaled slowly. He had crossed a line. A personal compliment. And her husband not present.

"Tell me about your studies," he said, breaking the tension. "Ali tells me you've been very diligent throughout your confinement."

"I'm studying psychology, as you suggested."

Philippe's eyes crinkled with pleasure. "What do you think?"

"It's like learning a new language, a new way of thinking and seeing. I don't pretend to understand it yet, but I will. I know I will."

"I wish I could see it all with you, Amira, through your eyes."

Amira was quiet. Too much had already been said. Philippe got up to go, waiting perhaps to see if she would stop him. She did not. But when he left, the room seemed so very empty. And cold.

FOR a long time after Karim's birth Ali still did not return to their marriage bed. Though he doted on his son, he seemed to have little time for Amira, mumbling excuses about business. She felt shamed by his disinterest. Was something wrong with her? How would she bear another child, another son, if he never touched her? These were troubling questions, but there was no one to talk to.

Desperate to bring her doubts and fears to some conclusion, Amira prepared herself one night as carefully as she had for her wedding. She put on her most provocative French lingerie, and when she heard Ali stirring in his study, she presented herself to him.

"Well, well, what have we here?" He smiled, but did not stop pouring his favorite single-malt Scotch.

Was he teasing her? she wondered. She walked past him, her movements becoming more provocative. He ignored her.

And the Badir pride flared. "As always, my husband, your words have been an enlightenment to your poor servant," she said with sarcastic formality. "But I've interrupted your refreshment too long."

As she turned to stalk away, he was suddenly on her like a madman, knocking her to the floor, ripping away the silk, taking her— raping her, for now she wanted no part of him. "Is that what you want, sow?" he demanded, his voice hoarse with anger. And when he was finished, he pulled his robe around him and left her. Amira gathered up the shreds of her little silken fantasy and went to bed.

The morning light softened the brutality of the night before, made it seem like a bad dream. Amira found a way to blame herself:

throwing herself at Ali when he wasn't in the mood, why wouldn't he be angry? Look at the way Ali treated her outside the bedroom. He never complained when she buried herself in her books. He not only tolerated her work, he encouraged her to do more. Yet even as she tried to catalogue Ali's virtues, she knew instinctively that Philippe would never treat a woman as she had been treated.

From the nursery she heard a beloved cry. Taking her baby to her, she consoled herself with the thought that even if there was nothing else, there would be Karim and her, and that would be enough.

A Man in the Night

WRAPPING her mohair coat around her, Amira stepped out of the George V lobby, and walked toward the Champs-Elysées.

This was the third time Amira had been to the city, and she had come to love it more than any of the other places to which Ali's duties had taken them. She loved walking the broad boulevards and picturesque streets; she adored all the typical tourist pleasures, but more than that, the sense of freedom.

Visiting Paris also meant a visit with Malik, who had established a base of operations here in addition to those in Marseille, Piraeus, Rotterdam. And there would be an opportunity to see Laila, nearly old enough for school now. It was easy to arrange—Ali had claimed an important meeting at the embassy, but Amira knew he had no interest in spending time with Malik.

THE fifteen-room apartment on the Avenue Foch, still smelling of fresh paint, was magnificent. Soaring, elaborately plastered ceilings, marble fireplaces, golden parquet floors, opulent furnishings.

"Who decorated this place?" Amira asked. "I know there's a woman here. I see touches."

Before he could answer, a little girl burst into the room shouting, "Papa! Papa!" Her nanny trailed behind.

Malik scooped his daughter into his arms and held her close, his expression tender. With her dark eyes and elfin face Laila looked like a Parisian gamine dressed in fine clothes.

Amira watched them. Her niece spoke perfect Parisian French—

with an occasional astonishing Marseille obscenity tossed in, at which Malik laughed uproariously.

When she finally turned her attention to Amira, Laila said in rapid succession, "Did you bring me a present today? I still have the pretty dress you brought last time. Do you have any little girls I can play with? Will you come to see Papa again?"

Amira chose her answers cautiously so as not to reveal her relationship to Malik. Though Laila knew Malik was her father—he could not bear for her not to know—she was boarded with her nanny a short distance away. It was not a satisfying situation, but Malik had hinted he might soon arrive at a solution.

Soon the child skipped off with the nanny.

He's been lonely, Amira thought. With a sister's bluntness she asked, "When are you going to settle down, Malik? Laila needs a mother. And if you found a woman to marry, you could find a way to live together openly. As a family."

He paused; then he smiled a shy, melting smile that tugged at her heart. "I don't want to say anything yet. It's too soon. But I have met someone. She's had a hard life, Amira. And she reminds me of Laila. If things work out, I'll have some news for you."

She threw her arms around him. "I'm so happy, Malik."

He laughed, then grew reflective again. "And you? Is marriage treating you well? Is Ali a good husband?"

"He . . . I . . . yes. Everything is fine."

Suddenly Malik was hard-eyed. "Is he mistreating you? Tell me the truth, Amira. If he is, I'll put an end to it. I swear."

"Everything's fine. Ali treats me very well. And he adores our son."

"Well then, good." The moment passed.

Much as Amira wished for harmony between Malik and Ali, they simply did not like one another. Part of it, she thought, was Malik's natural older-brotherly protectiveness. Part was a kind of envy on Ali's part. Though the bad feelings between Ali and her brother caused her some distress, they did give Amira a great deal of freedom. All she had to do was say she was spending the day with Malik, and she was free to do as she pleased.

A FEW hours later she was seated in a sidewalk café. The sky was blue, the sunlight was warm, the day seemed magical. "I wonder what any of us would be like," she said, "without all this money."

"Speak for yourself," Philippe said with a smile, his hand closing over hers. "I'm only a country doctor who makes house calls and has to pay French taxes."

Amira smiled back. She knew very well that the house calls he mentioned often started with a flight to Riyadh or Masqat. But what she was thinking about was what it would be like if she were away from Ali and everything he represented, if she were just a woman on holiday, meeting a man she adored at a sidewalk café.

In the months since they'd first met, Amira had seen Philippe a half-dozen times, a few hours here and there in al-Remal and once at an embassy party in Paris. Yet he'd been with her in dreams and fantasies. Is this what it's like to love a man? Is this what caused Laila to risk her life and then to lose it?

In the burnished gold light of late afternoon they talked fitfully and in murmurs, trying to postpone parting. Then Amira leaned toward Philippe, and suddenly they were kissing, a long, deep, deeply shared kiss that she wanted never to end.

When he drew away, the look in his eyes was almost more than she could bear. "My apartment isn't far from here," he said quietly. "Will you come with me?"

Her body screamed yes, but she looked down and mutely shook her head, a little gesture that might mean almost anything. Eyes closed, she saw Laila's body twitching to the blows of countless stones. Philippe touched her hand. "It's all right. I understand. We're still friends."

"Always." More than friends. Matched souls, Amira imagined, an inseparable pair broken apart long ago in some cosmic accident.

WHEN she first returned to al-Remal, Amira could not stop thinking about Paris and Philippe. Everything in her daily life—everything except her child—seemed stifling. But daily life weaves a strong web, and she could not prevent the time with Philippe from losing its urgent reality. Yet she had changed; she could feel it. This small taste of love was like the scent of food to someone starving. She wanted more—far more.

It was a desire she tried to suppress. Time and again she told herself that even if her husband was almost a stranger to her, her life still was a luxurious one that many women would envy. And whatever Ali's faults, he was generous, she had to admit.

On Karim's first birthday Ali's gift to the mother of his son was a magnificent emerald. Amira took the chance to ask, "Why do you give me such gifts, my husband? Surely I'm undeserving."

"My wife should have fine things," he said, as if it were self-evident.

"But so much . . ." She trailed off. It was not her right to expect some word of love, she told herself. Ali was not that kind of man.

But as the months passed, Ali's indifference gnawed at her. Everything in her upbringing told her that if a man did not love his wife, it was the wife's fault. Perhaps she was being punished for her feelings for another man. Yet sinful though that was, everyone knew of women who had such feelings whose husbands nevertheless worshipped them. No, it must be a deeper failing. Was he seeing other women, draining his passion with them? A man had needs. If his wife was not enough for him, the common wisdom was clear as to who was to blame. Only she. Nothing would change unless she changed it. Then she had an idea.

"Ali, heart," she said, using her best wheedling voice, absorbed from Jihan, "do you know what I'd really like for a present?"

Ali shrugged. "Ask and it's yours." He was on his way out.

"Only you, my husband. Your face has become a stranger's to me. I would like for us to go away for a week or two, love. Just you and me and Karim. Someplace we have never been. Can we do that?"

For a moment he looked at her so uncaringly that she was sure she had angered him. But then he smiled—the handsome, charming Ali. "Of course we can," he said. "And I know just the place."

THE airport was small and had a decidedly bedraggled look. As Amira stepped from the plane into bright sunlight, she braced for the blinding heat she had left in al-Remal but felt only a cool breeze. The temperature could not have been much more than eighty.

A Rolls-Royce waited on the runway. A customs inspector standing beside it merely welcomed them to Alexandria and opened the door. Half an hour later Amira was strolling the grounds of a seaside villa. Red tiles topped a white marble house—a small palace, really. Bougainvillea bloomed profusely, and a lush lawn flowed down to the beach. A long, narrow swimming pool fitted perfectly into the landscape. On both sides of the broad lawn, high walls lined with date palms stretched all the way to the sand.

"You can wear a bathing suit in privacy," Ali pointed out. "Just be sure the male servants are warned away first." He glanced at his watch. "I have a few acquaintances I need to renew in town. I'll probably be rather late getting back, but you'll want to rest anyway, after the flight. We'll see the sights tomorrow."

It wasn't what Amira hoped to hear, but she was too in love with this jewel of a place to be disappointed.

Three days later disappointment had set in with a vengeance. She still had not left the grounds. Ali went out each night and came in late, bleary and smelling of liquor, stumbling off to sleep till noon. Whatever Amira had hoped for this holiday was not happening.

That afternoon she took her stand. "Ali, I want to go home."

"Home? But why? It's beautiful here. Aren't you happy?"

"No. I came here to be with you, but you are never here."

"I'm here right now."

"You know what I mean."

"No. I know that my business in this city is not your business. I know that this trip was your idea. But I don't know what you mean."

A little later she heard the car leaving.

There was nothing she could do. Her idea had failed terribly. Things were worse here than in al-Remal. That night she paced in her room, wondering what was going to happen to her.

Ali wouldn't divorce her. He had said so more than once—not out of love, but out of vindictiveness—when they were arguing. She would be relegated to some back room of the palace to wither while he fathered children by new wives.

She looked at Karim, asleep in his crib. In a few years, he would go off to the men's quarters; then, if she was lucky, he might have lunch with her once or twice a week. She tried to tell herself that it was all God's will, but the words didn't help. She crawled into bed, her hand reaching out in the darkness to touch her sleeping child.

THE moon was high and bright, flooding the room, hurting her eyes. Where was she? Oh, yes: Alexandria. Her head hurt. Something had wakened her. Karim? No. Sleeping peacefully. Voices outside. Ali. Who was he talking to? A servant? He sounded angry.

She slipped from the bed and out onto the balcony. In the moonlight below, by the pool, Ali in his swimming trunks was facing a young man whose clothes testified to poverty.

"Excellency," the man implored, "I mention only your promise. You said you would take care of me."

To Amira's astonishment Ali slapped the man hard. "How dare you come to my home! I warned you never to set foot here."

"Excellency, please listen. My mother is sick. We need money for a doctor, for medicine. I beg you. If I don't please you any longer, let me send my brother. He's only thirteen, very beautiful, very pure."

In the warm Alexandrian night, Amira felt as if she had turned to ice. Suddenly it was all clear: Ali's indifference, his moods and unpredictability. His anger that time when she tried to coax him into making love. Her fingers were tingling, her head light.

"Please, Excellency, just a few pounds."

"Listen, dog, you lose everything by coming here. Get to your kennel!"

But now the young man's cringing attitude changed subtly, a hint of threat in it. "Excellency, I never meant for it to come to this, but I have pictures. Perhaps someone would buy them for just enough to pay the doctor. Please don't force me to do such a thing."

Ali's hands reached for the man's throat. Then he let them drop. "You're lying, of course," he said in his most aristocratic manner, "but I won't waste any more time on this nonsense. Wait here."

He turned and disappeared from view, into the house. The young man's eyes followed him—yes, like a dog's, Amira thought.

Ali reappeared below, holding out a wad of bills in his left hand. Bubbling gratitude, the young man reached for the money. Ali hit him again, this time in the chest. The man grunted, sank to his knees, and sprawled on his back. Only then did Amira see the knife.

"No!" she screamed, the word tiny in the vast night.

Ali turned to find her, his eyes wild. "You're there? One more word, Amira. One word—do you understand?"

There was no need to answer.

Ali clasped the body by the feet and dragged it down the lawn toward the sea. Amira stood shivering. It occurred to her that this was all a nightmare. In the morning it would vanish.

Ali returned, breathing heavily. He splashed water onto the blood beside the pool, then dived into the pool, climbed out, and walked into the house. That was all.

He's a murderer, thought Amira. He'll be caught. But then it came to her that Ali had nothing to fear. Even if the police found him with the knife in his hand and the corpse at his feet, he was a prince of al-Remal and the dead man had been an intruder. Any difficult questions could be answered with money.

All the same, they returned to al-Remal the next day. On the long flight not one word was said between them.

Fear

"YOU'RE a whore, aren't you, a dirty whore. Admit it."

"Ali, please—"

"Say it!" He pulled her head back by the hair.

The pain was bad, but the fear was worse. "All right, yes, I'm a whore. Please." Her scalp felt as if it would tear from her skull.

He moved against her, and she braced for more pain. But nothing happened. He growled in frustration and shoved her face hard into the pillow. She couldn't breathe. Am I going to die now? she wondered.

Suddenly the weight lifted from her head, and she heard Ali lurch from the room. She gulped air as his steps receded unsteadily down the hall. He was going to drink more. Good. He would pass out. But he might take more pills, too—the evil black pills that kept him awake all night. Then he might come back, even more of a madman.

She knew this from hard experience. The two months since Alexandria had been a deepening hell. Ali had never shown the slightest remorse for the killing. Instead, he seethed with anger. The liquor amplified it—the liquor and the pills.

Ironically, he now demanded her body nearly every night. That, too, had become a hell. Before, she had endured occasional cruelty; now there was outright sadism. More and more often, like tonight, he could not become aroused no matter how much he abused and humiliated her.

Maybe he would just give up, go back to his boys. No. That

wouldn't happen. The violence would grow until, sooner or later, he killed her. She was sure of it. Deep in his mind he wanted it. If for no other reason, wasn't she the only witness to his crime?

She was more alone than ever, cut off by the enormity of what Ali had done, was doing. If she told the truth, who would believe her?

She went to the side chamber where Karim slept when Ali made his conjugal visits. She touched his brow, and he murmured in his sleep. Suddenly a thought came to her that made her nearly sick with fear. Her husband's predilections: If she was gone, what might he do with Karim? No, surely, not even Ali.

I've got to get us out of here. But how? She couldn't think tonight. She was too tired, too confused. Tomorrow she would find a way.

Hating her bed, she fell exhausted on it. Everything was quiet. Maybe the liquor had won out over the black pills. She turned out the light and closed her eyes.

Someone was tugging at her, there in the dark. It was Ali. She could smell the liquor. "Ali, what are you doing?"

"Teaching you a lesson."

"Please, Ali!" She tried to push him away, but something held her hands. She was tied.

Ali switched on the light. His pupils were mad pinpoints; the pills had won.

Somehow Amira tore one hand free, then the other. She tried to shield her face as he came for her, but his fist smashed between her hands. She felt the cartilage in her nose snap. She screamed. Surely someone would come. No one did. In his room Karim howled. Amira tried to rush past Ali, but he blocked her into a corner. On her husband's face she saw cold, deadly rage. She saw murder.

A blow to her cheek sent stars dancing through her brain. The room was very bright and distant. Something slammed into her abdomen, driving the breath from her, and she fell.

The last thing she saw was Ali's foot floating toward her in dreamy slow motion, a child's balloon on a string.

COOL pastel colors. A woman in white. A touch on the lips— rough, soft, cold. Ice in a cloth. It hurt, but the dampness was heaven. She was dying of thirst. Her face felt like a melon rotted to bursting. Worse was the burning deep within her. Yet somehow the pain seemed far away. Slowly she understood. Hospital. Nurse. Drugs. She remembered why she was here. She slept.

When she woke, she was in pain. The nurse brought a pill. Amira took it greedily. "My son," she said.

"Your what? Oh, your son. I'm sure he'll be along soon, Highness. But we wouldn't want him to see his mommy in her present condition, would we? But your husband has been here so much that half the patients think he's a doctor."

The nurse gently inserted a thermometer beneath Amira's tongue. "Such a charming man. In case you're wondering, he's not angry about your driving the car. Just look at all the flowers he's brought."

Half a dozen large bouquets crowded the room. Glancing at them, Amira realized that she was seeing with only her right eye. The left wouldn't open. Driving the car.

"No, no, Highness. Mustn't touch the dressings." The nurse rattled on in the maternal tone of her vocation. "You were a naughty girl, Highness—you could have died. But the merciful God was on your side. It's thanks to Him that Dr. Rochon showed up the very day they brought you in. Dr. Konyali asked him to perform the surgery." She removed the thermometer, made a note on the chart.

The painkiller was taking effect. Amira wondered if she was hearing the woman correctly. "Dr. Rochon did surgery on me?"

There was pity in the nurse's eyes. "You had internal injuries, Highness. You were hemorrhaging. They had to operate to save your life. They removed one of your kidneys. And your womb."

How sad, thought Amira. Yet it all seemed so distant, as if it concerned someone else. Thank God for the painkiller. Her womb. How sad.

"At least you have the son, Highness. And you are alive. Rest now. I'll be right here in case you need anything. And the doctors will be checking on you. My name is Rabia, by the way."

Amira was floating out on a tranquil lake. "Can you bring me a mirror?" she heard herself ask.

"I—I'm afraid we don't have one, Highness. Rest now."

"Yes. . . . Philippe."

He was standing behind Dr. Konyali, the other surgeon, concern in every line of his face.

Dr. Konyali cleared his throat. "I'd forgotten you knew Dr. Rochon, Highness." The little courtier would not have forgotten such a thing. He was merely glossing over Amira's impropriety in addressing a man so informally.

She did not care. "Are you well, Philippe? What brings you here?"

"His Majesty had a rather acute episode of his chronic trouble. He asked me to fly down. When I arrived, he had learned of your car accident and sent me directly to assist Dr. Konyali."

Amira caught Philippe's slight emphasis on the word "accident" and his glance at her when he said it. A single thought cut through the fog of pain and medication: He knows!

"We don't want to disturb your rest, Highness," said Konyali. "It's what you need most just now." He shifted uncomfortably. "I gather that Rabia has told you about the procedures we performed."

"Yes."

"It was absolutely necessary, Highness, I'm sorry to say."

"Not your fault. God's will."

Konyali inclined his head. "Your husband is waiting to see you, Highness. I've told him that we can allow him only a few minutes."

Did her fear show? Philippe was studying her. Yes, he knew. "I'll be nearby, Highness," he said. "Nurse Rabia can find me anytime."

Philippe was gone before she could say good-bye. Konyali followed, after giving brief instructions to Rabia. Then suddenly Ali was there. Rabia stood and moved toward the door. "I'll be just down the hall, Highness. Please, Highness sir, only a few minutes."

"Of course."

As the door closed behind Rabia, Ali stepped forward. Amira fought an impulse to scream. Then he did the most astonishing thing: He fell to his knees beside the bed and kissed her fingertips.

"Thank God! Thank God for delivering you. It's my fault. If I'd been a proper husband, you'd never have done such a crazy thing."

"What are you talking about?"

"Why, the accident, of course. You should see the car."

Had he gone mad? Had she? "I wasn't in a car."

He patted her hand. "I shouldn't have come so soon. Rest, my dear. I promise you, things will be very different from now on."

He smiled at her from the door. And there—just there, behind his dark eyes—something flickered, glinting like other eyes entirely, the eyes of an animal in the night. Then it was gone.

FOR TWO DAYS AMIRA HARDLY moved. She was too weak and in too much pain. On the third morning Rabia helped her sit up on the edge of the bed, and late that afternoon she took a few steps, feeling like a very old woman. That same day Dr. Konyali removed most of the bandages from her face, and Rabia finally produced a mirror.

Amira gasped when she saw her reflection. Her face, still swollen, was virtually a single bruise. Adhesive tape still hid her nose. A ladder of stitches crawled down her forehead from the hairline. Her left eye was almost fully open but grotesquely bloodshot.

"There will be a scar here," said Konyali, pointing to the stitches, "and your nose won't have its old shape, but there's no permanent damage."

Philippe had come in and watched somberly while the bandages were cut away. Now he smiled and said, "If you're not happy with your new nose, I can give you the name of a plastic surgeon. He can give you any nose you'd like."

"Thank you, Doctor. How is His Highness, my father-in-law?"

"Much better, I'm happy to say. He really has no further need of me, so as soon as we have you on your feet again, I'm afraid I'll be heading back to Paris." Philippe said it casually, but his eyes were intense with unspoken communication.

"Well," said Amira, "I hope we'll have a chance to talk before you leave. I owe you—and Dr. Konyali—my life."

"I'm sure we'll have that chance, Highness."

But the chance proved hard to find. Although Amira strengthened steadily over the following days, either Rabia or another nurse was always present; Ali had insisted on it. And often Ali was there, so solicitous that she wondered if it was possible he really *had* changed. But no—no, it couldn't be. There was that thing behind his eyes, watching her. No, she would be afraid of him forever.

One afternoon, when Ali had left, Philippe came in to say goodbye. Oddly, at first he seemed less interested in Amira than in chatting with Rabia. "Dr. Konyali tells me you're well traveled."

"I, sir?" Rabia smiled with shy pride. "Well, Pakistan, of course, where I'm from, then Delhi, then England, then here."

"How many languages do you speak?"

"Only my own and a little English and Arabic, sir."

"Not French?"

"No, sir. Not a word, I regret to admit."

"I know a little French," said Amira, catching on, "but it's been ages since I practiced it. Are you going to examine me, Doctor? Ask your questions in French. Tell me where I go wrong."

"Very well." Philippe took out his stethoscope and applied it to her back. "We can't take long," he said in French. "Answer when I ask. Breathe deep. Now exhale. He did it, didn't he?"

"Yes."

"Again. Has he hurt you before?"

"Not like this."

"And again. I believe that you are in great danger."

"I saw him kill a man."

"Once more. You've got to get away. I'll help in any way I can."

"There's nothing you can do."

"Lie back. I need to palpate." His touch was firm, gentle, expert. "Does that hurt?"

"No. If my son and I leave, he'd hunt me down and kill me."

"Cough, please. Good. And if the two of you were to vanish?"

"He'd hunt us down, I tell you. You have no idea."

Philippe leaned close to examine the wound on her forehead. "You've got to get out. I'll try to come up with something."

"Please don't try. You don't understand the danger."

"Oh, but I do. Precisely." He stepped back. "Our patient's doing very well," he told Rabia in Arabic, "and so is her French."

"God is merciful and compassionate."

"Yes. Well, Highness, I leave you in the capable hands of Dr. Konyali. I'll be checking up on you the minute I'm back in al-Remal. His Majesty has invited me to the semicentennial."

Amira's heart leaped. The fiftieth anniversary of the king's ascension to the throne was less than two months away.

"It will be good to see you, Doctor."

Their eyes locked.

"Take care of yourself, Highness. *Au revoir.*"

"He'll be our guest," said Ali. "It's the least I can do. He saved your life, then left without giving me a chance to reward him."

"He might be more comfortable in one of the Western hotels," Amira said, hardly knowing why she said it.

He waved the objection aside. "Every room in the city is taken."

He was right. Most of the dignitaries of the Middle East, and many from Europe and America, were coming for the semicentennial, and al-Remal had only a handful of first-class hotels. Hundreds of guests would necessarily rely on private hospitality. Why was she suddenly uneasy about the prospect of having Philippe as a houseguest? Was it something in Ali's tone?

"In any case, it's done," said Ali. "He's accepted the invitation."

Amira tried to look indifferent. Her husband stepped toward her. She suppressed a flinch, but he merely touched her forehead as if testing for fever. Her skin crawled.

"Are you sure you're strong enough to see to setting up the house? I'll do what I can, but this is a busy time for me."

"I'll be fine."

The house was a large, beautiful place near a small oasis just south of the city. Like many of the younger members of the royal family, Ali and Amira were temporarily vacating the palace to make room for favored visitors.

"I've told some of the servants to begin work this afternoon," said Ali. He glanced at his watch. "Let me know if there's anything you need. The palace will know where to reach me."

He left with a smile. What was its true meaning? she wondered. To all appearances he had become a most considerate husband. It didn't matter. Nothing he did would induce her to trust him. She had forgotten nothing: not the man in the Alexandrian night, not the beating, not her terrible vision of Ali and Karim in a possible future.

With her recovery Amira became an object of pity to the other women. After all, she was now barren, a female without purpose or future, a has-been. Ali would of course take another wife. No one would blame him; in fact, many would fault him if he did not.

Again, it didn't matter. She was waiting for deliverance, nothing else, in whatever form it might take.

FOR three days Amira never had a moment alone with Philippe. The festival swept along, pausing only for prayer or sleep. The palace grounds were thrown open to the public, firepits cut into the lawns, and tents set up in which an army of cooks fed roasted lamb and seasoned rice to all comers until the small hours of the morning.

Everywhere, except in the most liberal private homes, standard segregation of the sexes applied. Even in her own house, what with all the comings and goings, Amira never had a chance to exchange more than a few perfunctory and very public words with Philippe.

It was Ali who finally gave Amira her chance. "Our friend isn't feeling well," he told her on the fourth morning of the festival. "He plans to stay in and rest today."

"I'll tell the servants."

"Good. But we can't leave a guest alone. I'd like for you to stay and keep him company."

"But mightn't there be talk?"

"There's nothing to worry about. It's an unusual situation, after all, and you have my permission. Everything will be fine."

"As you command," said Amira like a good Muslim wife.

After noon prayer she sat down with Philippe to a light lunch of quail, rice, olives, dates, and fresh fruit. She ordered a bottle of white wine from Ali's supply. Philippe seemed pleased by the gesture, although he objected mildly when Amira refused a glass herself.

"It's strange," he said. "To your people, drinking wine is a terrible sin or at best a kind of naughtiness. To mine, wine is a food." For a moment he seemed lost in reflection. "When I was young, I thought nothing in the world did so much evil as religion."

"Let me refill your glass." Amira was uncomfortable. Living in the palace, she had developed a sixth sense about when servants were eavesdropping. There was too much silence behind the doors to the kitchen. Most of the servants were tradition-minded. Their tongues would wag for days about Amira's dining alone with an alcohol-drinking foreign male. Freethinking comments about religion would only make matters worse.

"Well, Amira," said Philippe decisively, "we need to talk."

Instantly she lifted a finger to her lips.

He nodded. "What I need to know," he continued smoothly, "is whether you and Ali have any travel plans. I long to return your hospitality. Will you be in France anytime soon?"

"France? Well, I don't think there are any immediate plans. In the spring we're scheduled to visit Iran—Tehran and Tabriz."

"Tabriz," said Philippe. "Why would you be going there?"

"There's a great old mosque there that was nearly ruined by the earthquake a year or two ago. The shah wants al-Remal to lend its money and moral weight to repairing the building."

He mouthed the question, *"Parle français?"*

Amira shook her head. It would seem suspect.

Philippe took a small notebook and a pen from the pocket of his tweed sports jacket. "Are you sure you're recovered from the accident enough to travel?" he said, writing as he spoke.

"Oh, I'm much better, thanks to you and Dr. Konyali."

"Good." He showed the paper to her. "Are you going to Egyptian Night tomorrow?"

She nodded.

"And yet I worry about my patient," Philippe said, writing again. "It would be dangerous to exert yourself too much."

"I'll be in the garden when you return," the note said. "I'll wait."

"I'll be careful, Doctor," said Amira. "I promise."

FOR the younger women of the Remali elite, Egyptian Night was something new in the last ten years and a keenly anticipated feature of the semicentennial. It was an all-female party at which they could talk without restraint and wear outrageous fashions.

The venue was the ballroom of the Hilton. In her Givenchy gown, with its fitted sequined bodice and flared taffeta skirt, Amira arrived to find what looked like a very large European dinner party—except that there were no drinks and no men.

Three or four hundred women milled and mingled, drinking sweet fruit drinks and munching hors d'oeuvres amid a cacophony of gossip and laughter. A feeling of camaraderie developed: Amira heard complaints about men, laws, and Remali society that would never have been voiced under other circumstances.

At one point she was confronted by a princess she hardly knew, who demanded, "Tell us, Amira. Did you wreck a car or not?"

She was saved from having to answer by an announcement of the main event, a performance by the great *beledi* dancer Sonia Murad.

Sonia was an artist. There was joy, pain, humor, even fear in her dance. It was about being a woman and a human being.

The crowd was hers, clapping and shouting with the music, and when she gestured to one of them, the woman would move toward the stage and begin a dance of her own. Soon a dozen, then two dozen women were dancing. Then Sonia pointed at Amira, and suddenly everyone was urging her to dance.

She did and found herself enjoying a freedom of movement forgotten since the day her father caught her dancing to the radio. But suddenly a sharp pain in her abdomen doubled her; she had not mended enough for this exertion. A face appeared from the crowd around her—the princess who had asked about the car wreck. "It's all right, Amira. We know." What did that mean?

The room was an oven. The dancing women were soaked with sweat, makeup streaming down their faces. Someone had opened the sliding glass doors along one wall to let in the cooling night air.

Suddenly there was a disturbance on the edge of the crowd. Women shouting in outrage, men's angry voices.

"It's the *matawa*," a woman near Amira said.

What were the religious police doing here?

"The music," someone said. "They're angry because they can hear the music outside."

"Females, cover yourselves," a man shouted.

There was near panic. Amira, still in pain, moved with a ministampede to the sliding doors. Then she was out under the cold winter stars. She sat on a low concrete wall, unable to go any farther. A strong hand gripped her arm. Was she under arrest?

"Come with me, Highness. The car is just over there." It was Jabr, the driver.

He half carried her across the street. A green-turbaned member of the *matawa* approached, saw Jabr's scowl, and turned away. Amira sank into the safety of the Rolls.

"There were rumors among the drivers," Jabr told her. "I came early in case something happened."

"Thank you."

Jabr shook his head angrily. "These religious police—what do they have to do with God? Forgive me, Highness."

"There's nothing to forgive, Jabr."

The house was quiet, only a single servant there to greet her. Everyone else was still at the festivities, the girl explained.

"And Dr. Rochon?" said Amira. Only at that moment had she remembered Philippe's promise to meet her in the garden.

"I don't know, Highness. I haven't seen him."

"Go draw me a bath and lay out my nightclothes. Then make some tea."

As soon as the girl was gone, Amira slipped out into the garden.

"Cinderella," said a voice from the shadows, "home from the ball?"

"Philippe! You nearly frightened me to death."

"Ssh. Just act as if I'm not here. We'll talk very quietly."

"All right."

"Amira, I have a plan, but it's a drastic one. Let me ask you this: You're certain that if you just walked away—took Karim and went to France, for example—Ali would pursue you?"

"Yes. He'd take Karim and kill me."

"Then I can see only one possible solution. Suppose that the whole world thought you were dead. Suppose that you and Karim could start a totally new life somewhere. Would you do it?"

"I—I don't know. It's too hard a question." To leave everything she knew behind. "Would Malik know the truth?"

"I don't think he should. Your brother is an impetuous man. He would never tell the secret, but his actions would give it away."

"And you, Philippe? Would I ever see you?"

There was a silence in the shadow.

"Ever is a long time," he replied at last. "Who knows what will happen? Let's get you safe first."

"I can't decide now. I need to think."

"Of course. But the sooner the better. If you decide to go through with this, take all your jewelry when you and Ali go to Iran. I don't have it all worked out yet, but of all the stops on your itinerary, Tabriz is the best choice."

"This sounds dangerous."

"It will be—a little. But not for Karim. Only for you and me."

"You? Why for you?"

"I'll be there, of course. But we've talked enough. Go now, my dear. Think it over. If you decide to do it, let me know by saying something, anything, about Tabriz. Good night, my dear."

Turning to the house, Amira caught a glimpse of movement at a second-floor window. A curtain closing? Perhaps it was just a reflection or her imagination.

"Good night, my love," she whispered into the shadows.

Morning Visitors

THE festival was over, but Ali insisted that Philippe stay for another day or two. "I'm keeping this house for a few days," he said, "so as not to put you to the trouble of moving to the palace or to a hotel. So you see, the plans are already made."

Philippe resisted the invitation, but a call from the palace decided the issue: The nonstop feasting had caused yet another onslaught of the king's gout; Dr. Rochon's services were urgently desired.

Philippe was at the palace all the next day. He returned at dark, looking worn, and went to his room to rest. Ali left for an appointment and later called to say that Amira and Philippe should dine without him. They sat together at the table—again shocking the servants, Amira knew. They exchanged small talk. The word Tabriz hung unspoken in the air. She couldn't say it. Not yet.

THE next morning Amira woke with the vague sense that something was wrong. The house was very quiet, but that was logical: Ali undoubtedly had gone out already. Philippe was probably still asleep. Karim slept peacefully. Yet it was *so* quiet. She dressed quickly and went downstairs. Where were the servants? She called, and got silence for an answer.

Then she saw the little chambermaid, Hanan, dressed in her best clothes, crossing the garden toward the side gate.

"Hanan! Come here. Where is everybody?"

"Why, master sent some of us to the palace to prepare for your return. And some of us he gave the day off—because of our hard work during the festival. I was just on my way to visit my mother."

"When did he order all this?"

"Why, just this morning, Highness, before he left." Hanan looked faintly guilty. "I'm sure those at the palace will be back soon."

"I'm sure you're right. Thank you, Hanan. Enjoy your day off."

In the kitchen, Amira searched for coffee. She was irritated with Ali. Why would he send away all the servants with a guest in the house? It made no sense.

Then suddenly it did. Amira stood stock-still. Under shari'a law a man accusing his wife of adultery had only to demonstrate a pattern of incriminating behavior. To be alone in the house with Philippe was damning in itself. Amira had also dined with him in her husband's absence—and someone, she remembered, had seen them in the garden late at night.

There was no time to waste. She needed to act now. She could leave, she told herself—just walk out. But how would that look? How could she explain it?

She could call the palace, order the servants back. But would they come? What if one or more of them were in on it? Think, Amira.

She went to the telephone and dialed her father's number, praying that someone other than Omar would answer.

"The peace of God." It was Bahia.

"The peace of God, Bahia. It's Amira. Don't ask questions. Just get your daughter and come here now, immediately."

"I'm coming," Bahia said simply, and hung up.

Amira paced in the kitchen. If Philippe came downstairs, she would send him out of the house instantly. Someone—one of Ali's relatives—might be on the way at this very moment, for the exact purpose of finding her alone with the foreign male guest. There was nothing further to do but wait. Why didn't Philippe come down?

Shortly there was a rattle at the servant's gate. Amira let in Bahia and Maryam. "You're both angels from paradise. Come in, come in. I need you to look busy. Make coffee, start putting breakfast together. Look as if you've been here all morning."

As they set to work, she explained about the illustrious houseguest, Dr. Rochon, and the mysterious decampment of the servants. She left out only her fear that Ali was behind it all.

Bahia gave her a long look. "Nothing will come of it, God willing," she said. "But you did well to send for someone."

She had hardly said it when they heard male voices from the front of the house and someone cried out, "Woman, veil yourself."

Bahia and Amira exchanged a glance. Both had noticed the use of "woman," not "women."

Ali's cousin Abdul burst into the kitchen. Three other men followed.

Abdul seemed surprised to see Bahia and Maryam. "Amira, what's going on?"

"What do you mean, Abdul?"

"We come to visit your husband, and the front door is open. Naturally we feared something might be wrong."

"Ali must have left the door open on his way out."

"Your husband isn't here, then?"

"He had an appointment early this morning. But I'm sure he'll be back soon. Please make yourselves at home."

"And your houseguest?" asked Abdul.

"Dr. Rochon? He's asleep, I suppose. I haven't seen him this morning."

"Is that so?"

"Yes, it's so. Abdul, is something the matter?"

"Who are these women? They aren't your regular servants."

"My husband dismissed the regular servants for the day. Bahia and Maryam have been servants of my family all my life, and I asked them for help."

"When did they arrive here?" Abdul pressed.

"They've been here almost all morning."

"*Almost* all morning."

Amira had had enough. "Abdul, you say you came to see my husband. I suggest that you save your questions for him."

"What questions? What's going on here?" It was Ali. He stood in the doorway, face flushed as if with excitement.

"That's what we were wondering, cousin," said Abdul. "We came to see you and found the front door ajar. When we entered, we discovered your wife alone—or, rather, alone except for these women."

Ali glanced at Bahia and Maryam. Was there a trace of anger in his expression? "Well, I know them," he muttered.

"We asked about your distinguished guest," Abdul blundered on. "Your wife claims that he is asleep."

"It's late for anyone to sleep, even a foreigner," said Ali. "I'll check on him myself."

He was gone for longer than it should have taken. In the kitchen no one spoke. The men glared at Amira.

Ali returned. "He isn't there," he said. "Where is he, Amira?"

"I don't know, my husband. I haven't seen him at all."

"Perhaps he left a note or—or something," said Abdul.

"I looked," said Ali irritably. "There was nothing."

"*Bonjour,* my friends. A lovely morning. Am I intruding?" Philippe stood smiling in the doorway. He wore typical European walking clothes, and his pale skin showed a touch of sunburn.

"We—we were just looking for you," said Ali lamely.

"Ah! I've been out. I woke early and saw that it was a beautiful day, so I went for a walk. In fact, I left just behind Your Highness. Then I took an outdoor table at a coffeehouse and watched the world go by."

"What coffeehouse did you visit?" inquired Abdul casually.

"I didn't notice the name. But if you really want to know, you could ask my host's brother Prince Ahmad. He and his entourage passed in the street. He was kind enough to spend an hour with me."

How much did Philippe understand of what was going on? Amira couldn't tell, but the fact that he could call on Ali's brother to account for his whereabouts ended the little inquisition in her kitchen.

That afternoon they drove Philippe to the airport. In the crowded concourse the two men embraced like brothers, exchanging thanks, compliments, and cordial promises of future hospitality. The farewell was interrupted by the public-address system paging Prince Ali Rashad.

"Always something," said Ali. "I'll be right back."

Philippe watched him go. "We have only a minute," he told Amira. "I'm the one who had him paged. I called from the house before we left. Amira, what happened this morning was a frame-up. Just as I said, I woke early and decided to take a walk. While I was dressing, I dropped some coins. One rolled under the bed. When I reached for it, I found a bottle of whiskey, half empty. It wasn't mine—someone had to have put it there. I became worried and searched the room. I found a piece of lingerie tucked into the bed. I imagine it would have fitted you perfectly."

"Oh, no." In al-Remal evidence like that could send a woman to her death.

"I hid the bottle and the lingerie in my pocket—and then threw them away as soon as I got far enough from the house."

"Thank you for that. But what—"

"Amira, you can't wait too long to decide. If it's to be Tabriz, I'll need time to make plans. If not— Well, I fear for you, my dear."

Before she could reply, Ali rejoined them with a joke about confusion in the paging system. "Too many princes named Ali." At that moment Philippe's flight was called.

They walked him to the gate. Passengers were boarding in a line. Philippe said good-bye.

This might be my last minute with him, Amira realized. The words were out before she could think about them. "I almost forgot to ask, Philippe, but haven't you been to Tabriz?"

"Tabriz? Did you say Tabriz?"

"Yes, Tabriz. Ali and I are going there. We've never been. I thought a traveler like you might have been there—to Tabriz."

"Yes," he said, and in his eyes she saw his promise reaffirmed. "They say that it is the unfriendliest city in the Middle East, but I've found good people there. I'm sure your visit will turn out well."

Then he was gone.

Escape

SOMETHING was wrong in Iran. Amira felt it the minute they entered the Tehran airport. They were met by the Iranian minister of culture—a tall, urbane man—but the welcome seemed staged.

Perhaps it was that they were surrounded by hard-looking men in trench coats and sunglasses—SAVAK, the shah's secret police. One of them escorted her, Ali, and Karim to a line of large American cars. The SAVAK man slid into the front seat of one, gave the driver an order, and the limo pulled out in convoy with the others.

Tehran was an unprepossessing large city, an endless agglomeration of concrete structures softened by the backdrop of snow-capped mountains to the north, dimmed by a yellow haze of smog. The line of cars turned in at a large, elaborate gate to the shah's palace. With another speech of welcome, the minister of culture turned them over to a factotum, who led them to their rooms.

There was to be a formal reception that evening, which was Amira's excuse for bringing along every carat of jewelry she owned. She took out the jewel case and poured the brilliant earrings and bracelets and necklaces on the bed. Karim played with them, making little piles and choosing a particular piece to call pretty.

In forty-eight hours she would be in Tabriz. Not long after that, Karim and the jewels might be all she had in the world.

"CAVIAR, Highness?" said the handsome man with graying temples. He was a minister of something that had to do with oil.

"No, thank you," said Amira. The great ceremonial hall on the palace's ground floor was practically buried in caviar. She must have eaten a half pound already, and she didn't even like the stuff.

"This is the only place in Iran where you can find good caviar," said the man, "even though we're famous for it. Almost all of it leaves the country. I bought a few tins in Toronto last week."

It was perhaps the fifth time that Amira had heard about the scarcity of Iranian caviar in the land of its origin—and at least the tenth that someone had alluded to a recent trip to Toronto or New York. She stood looking around the great hall while Ali was engaged with the American ambassador in a discourse about aircraft. Amira, worn from the day's journey, wished she could slip away to sleep.

"Highness," said a familiar voice, "how good to find you here."

"Philippe! What on earth—"

"Highness, Mr. Ambassador," said Philippe to Ali and the American, both of whom greeted him by name.

"Well," said Ali, "what brings you here, my friend?"

"I was about to tell the princess. A colleague asked me to Tehran to consult on . . . on a particularly complicated case."

The ambassador allowed himself a speculative glance across the room at the shrunken, sallow-skinned shah. So, Amira noticed, did Ali. Amira had to force herself to stop staring at Philippe, to play the part of the pleasantly surprised international acquaintance.

"You're here for long?" Philippe asked Ali.

"Only through tomorrow. Then we go to Tabriz."

"Ah, yes. I think you mentioned that the last time I saw you. I leave tomorrow myself."

What did that mean? Amira searched his eyes. She saw nothing except that his pupils seemed dilated and his face was flushed.

"Please excuse me," said Philippe. "I haven't had a chance to eat since this morning."

He wandered away in the direction of the food tables.

"The doctor looks a little unsteady tonight," commented Ali.

"The French," said the ambassador, rolling his eyes. The two men returned to their discussion of the F-14.

"Husband," Amira ventured, "may I bring you something? I'm going to get a little bite for myself."

"I'm glad your appetite has returned," he said. "Nothing for me."

She found Philippe holding a plate of canapés and examining the vast carpet that formed the centerpiece of the ceremonial hall.

"Ah, Princess. Someone told me that this carpet is more than two hundred square meters. I've seen smaller casinos."

"Philippe, it's—"

"Did you know," he interrupted her, "that the Persian weavers always include a flaw in their work? The idea is that only God should be perfect."

He cut his eyes sideways. A few steps away stood a lone man in a tuxedo. Was he studying his drink too intently?

Philippe steered her gently through the crowd. The man in the tuxedo did not follow. Paranoia?

"I didn't expect to see you here," she said.

The noisy chatter of a large group nearby made a good screen for their words. Philippe leaned close to her, smiling as if they were sharing an amusing reminiscence. "Someone will contact you in Tabriz. Do exactly as you are told, and immediately. Do you understand?"

"Of course."

"Have one small bag packed—no more. Two changes of clothes for you and Karim—one traditional, one Western. And your jewels."

"You'll be there?"

"Yes. No more now. It's dangerous. The shah spies on everyone."

"How good to see you again, Doctor. You must promise to visit us when you're in al-Remal."

"With pleasure, Highness. Please convey my regards to your husband again, in case I don't see him." A few words of good-bye, and he disappeared in the crowd.

Amira felt as if she were flying out on the air, the earth rushing to meet her. Only Philippe could save her life.

AMIRA had expected an exotic town of old Persia, narrow streets within ancient walls. In reality, Tabriz was a city of several hundred thousand, as modern and nearly as sprawling as Tehran.

They were greeted by the mayor of Tabriz and the governor of East Azerbaijan Province. After an official lunch, there was an inspection of the Blue Mosque, the structure that Ali's father had agreed to restore.

Then Ali was to meet all afternoon with various officials. Amira and the other wives, accompanied discreetly by the SAVAK man, went to see some of the sights, among them the teeming bazaar and the Arg-Tabriz, the remains of a huge ancient fortress.

Back at the hotel, Amira collapsed on the bed and stared at the ceiling. She was exhausted. In a few minutes she would have Karim brought to her. In a few minutes. Just now she needed rest.

There was a soft knock at the door. A hotel maid entered.

"Highness, I'll be your servant for the night. My name is Darya. Is there anything I can bring you?" She was Amira's age and size and coloring; they could have been taken for sisters.

"No, nothing," said Amira.

"Perhaps your Highness would like some music?" Darya indicated the suite's receiver and tape deck, very new.

"No," said Amira patiently. "Nothing at the moment."

The maid came close and mouthed the word yes. Awareness ran through Amira like an electric shock: This was it, the contact.

"On second thought," she said, "a little music would be nice."

"Thank you, Highness." Darya turned on the radio, raised the volume, and returned to Amira. "Are you ready?" she asked quietly.

"Yes."

"Good. You're going to the celebratory dinner?"

"What? Oh, yes."

"All right. If you can, convince your husband to leave early. Plead sickness, exhaustion, whatever."

"That will be easy enough."

Darya did not smile. "As soon as you are back here, have your son brought to you. Your husband's room is stocked with liquor—a service the hotel offers some guests. Will he drink before going to bed?"

"Yes. I think so."

"Good. There'll be something extra in each bottle. Be ready to go at a moment's notice. When it's time, I'll knock. Bring your things and follow me without a sound."

Amira said nothing. Everything was moving so fast.

KARIM WAS ASLEEP. AMIRA waited in the traveling clothes she had worn from Tehran. From time to time she heard the soft footsteps of the SAVAK man patrolling the hall. What would be done about him?

There was no sound from Ali's suite. Earlier she had heard faintly through the door the familiar tink of bottle against glass, followed after a time by noises of clumsy stumbling. Now nothing.

The single knock seemed as loud as a shot. Surely Ali had heard it. She scrambled for the bag and cradled Karim in her other arm.

Darya opened the door and whispered, "Hurry." Amira followed her to a door at the end of the hallway. Darya used a key to open it. A stairway. Amira's heels echoed loudly in the stairwell. They went down several flights. Another door. They were out in the night, in some kind of alleyway.

"Damn it," said Darya. "Your friend is late."

"Women," said a heavy voice behind them, "what are you doing out in the night?"

They both froze.

The SAVAK man stepped from the shadows. "You'll have to come with me and explain yourselves," he said.

It's over, thought Amira.

Darya flew past her with animal speed and clawed at the man's face. Cursing, he knocked her aside, but suddenly there was movement behind him. Amira heard a slapping thud, then another, and the SAVAK man's legs gave way. Two young men stood over him.

"Are you all right, Darya?" one of them said.

"Yes. Where did he come from?"

"Who knows. What do we do with him?"

"There's only one place to take him," said Darya. She looked down the alley. "Damn it, Princess, where's your friend?"

"I don't know."

"Look, maybe the best thing is— Wait! Who's that?"

A tan vehicle had pulled into the alley.

"That's him, Highness. Go!"

"I want to thank—"

"Go!"

Amira ran to the car, a battered Land Rover. Philippe pushed open the door and pulled her in. "I'm late—sorry," he said. "Let's get out of here."

It must have been around midnight. There was little traffic, but the sidewalks were crowded with men out on the town. Amira felt as if every one of them were staring at her, memorizing her face, as Philippe pulled onto the boulevard and accelerated.

PHILIPPE drove west, through the heart of the city. Karim woke long enough to say, "Hello, Uncle Ph'lipe," then drifted back to sleep in Amira's lap. Around them, cars sped slapdash, threatening to demolish clopping two-horse carriages. Signs for the airport appeared, then slid behind. Amira looked questioningly at Philippe.

"We're not flying," he said. "We're driving out."

"Where are we going?"

"To Turkey, for a start. We ought to reach the border by daybreak if this old Rover is worth half what I paid for it. I bought it in Rezaiyeh, across the big lake. The ferry had engine trouble. That's why I was late." He glanced at Amira. "What happened back there?"

Amira told him about the agent. "What will happen to him?"

"The SAVAK? At best he'll have a very uncomfortable day or two. At worst he'll turn up in the river."

"We're part of that?"

"Indirectly. But you didn't ask him to follow you. Remember that—and what he would have done to you and Darya."

Amira remembered Darya clawing at the agent. She had never seen a woman physically attack a man—not like that. Even more astonishing was that Darya was obviously the commander of the little revolutionary group, the two young men deferring to her.

They were beyond the city now, among mountains in the high desert. The road was dirt. They had been climbing ever since leaving Tabriz. Philippe reached for the black medical bag that he always carried. "Hand me that water bottle, will you, my dear?"

He took two pills from a vial and washed them down. "Methamphetamine," he explained. "Unfortunately, I need it to keep me going. I haven't slept since I arrived in this country."

In the glow from the dash his face was both haggard and surprisingly youthful. Amira thought that she had never seen him so handsome. "How did you do all this?" she asked.

"Money. Old favors. Old friends."

"And why? Why are you doing it?"

"You know why."

"Yes. Thank you."

"Don't thank me. Open that compartment."

There were two French passports, one for her, one for Karim.

"So I'm *femme* Rochon, and this is little Karim Philippe Rochon."

"At least until we're in Turkey. Then you'll be someone else."

There were a hundred questions to ask. Amira let them all evaporate. She should have been exhausted, but instead, a deep elation filled her. She had her child and beside her the man who was the love of her soul, running with her in the desert night from known danger to danger unknown.

Free. The word came to her as if whispered by a secret voice. It was like honey, the first taste demanding the next.

"Whatever happens," Amira told Philippe and the universe, "it was worth it."

DAWN caught them at Maku, a town huddled in a valley hardly wider than the road. Philippe parked the Land Rover and came back in twenty minutes with bread, cheese, kabobs, and a thermos of coffee. There was a cup of honeyed yogurt for Karim.

"I'm going to need another of these to get me to the border." Philippe took out a pill and swallowed it with coffee. "We're only half an hour away. Don't worry. Nothing's going to happen. They may ask me some routine questions, but they rarely question women." He started the Land Rover and winked at her. *"Allons-y."*

As they came out of the valley, a high mountain capped with snow came into view, bright as a bride in the sunrise.

"Ararat," said Philippe. "Noah's ark."

Amira nodded. She was familiar with the story.

At the border the traffic was backed up for a mile. It took more than an hour for them to reach the Iranian guard post. There a harried-looking soldier waved them through after a quick glance. Crossing to the Turkish side, Philippe let out a long breath. "That was the big moment. They haven't heard. The Turks won't know either."

But at the Turkish post, after studying their papers, the guard ordered Philippe to pull aside. Moments later an officer appeared. He motioned Philippe out of the car. The two men exchanged a few words; then Philippe followed the Turk into the building.

Five minutes. Ten. Fifteen. What was wrong? By now someone in Tabriz must have noticed that her room was empty. What if the SAVAK man had escaped from Darya's friends?

Philippe emerged from the building, the officer following. The two were smiling and chatting. When Philippe at length started the Land Rover, the officer saluted.

"What happened?" asked Amira when the border was behind them.

"I don't know. I had the feeling he suspected something. But I played my trump card and ended up having tea with him."

"What trump card?"

"When I was here before, I worked with a young Turkish lieutenant. We became friends. He's a general now. So I asked the captain if he knows my old friend. He does—and fears him, too, I'd say."

Amira laughed. "Philippe, is there any place on earth where you don't know someone?"

"One never regrets kindness," said Philippe. "Always remember that, my love."

"Those pills are turning you into a philosopher."

Now Philippe laughed, too.

They crossed rolling hills under a cloudless sky. Here and there sheep grazed. Every time a flock appeared, Karim pointed happily: "Sheep!" Ararat rose on their right, dominating the horizon.

"Tell me what we're doing," Amira said.

Philippe nodded. "Very soon now your husband will wake with the worst hangover of his life, and soon after that he'll learn that his wife is missing. There will be phone calls to al-Remal and Tehran. Everyone will want to keep the whole thing quiet as long as they can. With luck nothing will become public for a day or two.

"Meanwhile, they'll be looking for you—quietly. Not the regular police. SAVAK. And if Darya was able to complete her task, they'll stumble onto a false trail."

"What do you mean?"

"The plan was for her to take the early flight to Tehran. She should have landed an hour ago. You may have noticed that she looks like you, and she was to specify that a child was traveling with her. Someone will remember when SAVAK comes asking. In Tehran she'll buy tickets at two different airlines, for al-Remal at one and

London at the other. And there the trail will end, because she won't catch either flight. She'll simply disappear in Tehran."

"And what are we going to do while all this is happening?"

"We'll meet a man in a town called Van. He'll get you out of Turkey while I go back to Ararat and lay the second false trail."

It was as if the world had tilted. "You're leaving me?"

He shook his head as if denying it. "I have to, my love. Remember the plan: You and Karim aren't just running away, you're disappearing for good. I'm going back to wreck the car in a river in the mountains. It will look as if the bodies washed away."

"Why can't we go with you?"

"Because three of us could never get away from there unnoticed."

"But what then? Are you going to disappear, too?"

"Yes. Don't worry, my dear. All will be explained later."

"When will I see you again?"

"I don't know, my love. Perhaps not for a very long while."

"I don't like this, Philippe."

"Neither do I, but there's no other way now. Sooner or later SAVAK will check the border posts. When my name comes up, they'll start a covert search in Paris, which is where they'll figure we've gone. But then the wreck will be found, and while they hunt for the bodies, you'll have an open window to slip into Paris."

"I'm going to Paris?"

"Yes. Then to America. As I said, it will all be explained."

"Who is this man? The one we're meeting."

"Brother Peter. He may be the best man I've ever known."

THE air was thin and cold. Sheep and goats grazed among patches of snow, and the mountains were still white. Farmers drove wagons or led heavily burdened donkeys along the muddy rutted road.

Amira stared moodily out the window. Why was Philippe abandoning her and Karim? She had no right to ask such a question, but she couldn't help thinking it. The sweetness of her newfound freedom had vanished, leaving a bitter aftertaste.

"What will I do in America?" she demanded suddenly. She had meant to sound angry, but the question came out merely petulant.

He touched her lightly on her cheek. "Don't be afraid, my love.

America is a country where a person with intelligence and dedication can become whatever he wants. Or she wants. But I've taken the liberty of arranging an opportunity, if it interests you. Would you like to go to Harvard?"

"As a student?"

"What else?"

"But I'm not qualified. And Karim— What about him?"

"You're qualified. And Karim will be fine." He took his hand from her cheek. "This isn't the time for details. You'll get those from a friend of mine in Paris. His name is Maurice Cheverny. He's a lawyer. Call him from the airport. He's expecting you."

A university student. It was something she had wanted almost as long as she could remember. But it was so far away, in so unknown a place. "Come with me, Philippe." There, she had said it.

He smiled sadly. "I wish I could, my love, but I can't. Someday you'll understand. Trust me."

In midafternoon they reached Van, a city of perhaps a hundred thousand people. They registered in a hotel as Monsieur and Madame Rochon.

In the room, Philippe tipped the porter, closed the door, and fainted. Amira gasped, but knew that the pills had worn off. Somehow she lifted him onto the bed. A damp cloth to Philippe's forehead opened his eyes. "Amira, my love, I'm sorry. But I have to sleep, or I won't make it to Ararat. Wake me when it's dark."

"Just sleep."

"At dark. Promise me."

He slept. Karim climbed onto the bed. "I take care of Uncle Ph'lipe." Soon he was asleep, too.

Philippe was dead to the world when night came. Trying to rouse him was like trying to wake Ali when he had drunk too much. After a long effort she got him to a sitting position.

He looked at his watch as if it contained a great mystery, then pushed himself to his feet. "I have to go out and make my presence known. Then we'll have a visitor." He found his medical bag and took a pill. "Two left," he said to himself. "That should do."

"Philippe, you're exhausted. Can't it wait till morning?"

"No. This is the dangerous time. It's possible that they're already looking for us in this country. We have to move fast."

He was gone for an hour. When he returned, he seemed to have regained his energy. "Brother Peter will be here soon. You'll go with him tonight. By morning you'll be in Erzurum." He tore loose the lining of his coat and produced some papers. "Your plane tickets. Erzurum to Ankara, Ankara to Istanbul, Istanbul to Paris. And here is your new passport and some papers for Karim."

She looked at her passport: Jihan Sonnier. Spouse of Dr. Claude Sonnier.

"Not quite two years ago," said Philippe, "an earthquake killed fifty thousand people in the district north of Van. There are many orphans. Karim is one of them. You're here to adopt him and take him home to France. You—you can't have children of your own."

Amira nodded. That much, at least, was true.

"Brother Peter has been closely involved in helping the earthquake victims, especially the children. He can answer any questions that anyone in authority may raise. And he will never betray you."

There was an almost inaudible knock at the door.

The man who entered was small and wiry, with thinning brown hair and faded blue eyes. He and Philippe embraced like long-separated brothers.

"I thank you for this, my friend," said Philippe in English. He introduced Brother Peter to Amira.

Brother Peter said, "I hate to rush things, but we need to get started."

"Ah, yes, of course. Well, how do you want to do it?"

"I don't want Amira—Jihan—or the boy to be seen with me anywhere near Van. Too many people know me. I've made a cubbyhole in back of the mission's panel truck. It won't be comfortable, but it's only for a few hours."

"Good. What else?"

"Go north to Lake Van, toward Agri—slow so I can catch up. I'll leave twenty minutes behind you. If anyone stops you, you're tourists enjoying a lovely moonlight drive along the lake."

"All right."

"Somewhere north of the lake and south of Agri, I'll blink my headlights. Pull over, and we'll make the switch." He looked at both of them. "Well then, are we ready?"

"Why not?" said Philippe.

WITH THE HEADLIGHTS cutting the night, Van was a dream to Amira, Tabriz a distant memory. Karim slept, having been given a spoonful of sweet red liquid from Philippe's bag.

Philippe kept thinking of things to caution her against. "Remember: Call Maurice Cheverny before anything else. And try to be sure no one follows you from Orly. Here's money to get you to Paris."

At two o'clock in the morning Brother Peter blinked his signal. Philippe stopped and opened the door. In the roof light his face was sickly gray.

"Are you all right?"

"What? Yes. A bit worn out. Don't worry."

Brother Peter pulled up alongside and got out. "Well, old frog," he said, "this seems to be it. Be careful."

"And you. Thanks again—for everything."

Philippe turned to Amira. To her surprise tears were streaming down her face. He held her so tightly it hurt. "Good-bye, my love. I wish—I wish it had been different."

"Don't say good-bye, my heart. It's only *au 'voir,* isn't it? We won't lose each other, will we? Promise me?"

"We won't lose each other. We can't. *Au 'voir. Au 'voir,* Amira."

Brother Peter carried Karim to the panel truck. "In here, my lady."

Her eyes met Philippe's one last time as she wedged herself in with Karim. Then Brother Peter rearranged boxes and blankets, shutting out the world. In a moment the truck grumbled to life.

"Next stop, Erzurum," called Brother Peter.

It was pitch-black in Amira's little cave. Time lost its shape.

She woke because they had stopped. A door opened, the blankets flew back, and blinding light flooded in: morning.

"Up front quickly," ordered Brother Peter. "We're nearly to Erzurum. There's a checkpoint ahead. Cover your hair and part of your face. Don't worry: European women often do it out here."

Armed soldiers manned the checkpoint. Brother Peter answered their questions in Turkish. One of the men gave an order. Brother Peter slid over, and a soldier climbed in behind the wheel.

"No fear, Madame Sonnier," said Brother Peter. "Erzurum's a military zone. All foreigners have to be escorted by a soldier."

At the airport, she changed an irritable, half-asleep Karim into fresh clothes. A loudspeaker announced the Ankara flight.

"On time," said Brother Peter. "I've always wanted to witness a real miracle, and here it is. A good sign, Madame Sonnier."

She was in Ankara by noon, in Istanbul by evening. That night she slept seven miles above the earth on a jet bound for Paris.

A New Woman

CUSTOMS at Orly came as a welcome anticlimax; a yawning official barely glanced at her papers before stamping them.

The airport teemed with arriving passengers. Amira towed Karim with one hand, clutching the bag containing all she owned in the other. If they were hunting her, they would be here. Who might be a hunter? A Turkish-looking man scanning the crowd? A blue-jeaned young man lounging on a bench reading a textbook?

She found a telephone and tried to remember which coin was needed. Suddenly someone was beside her. The man in blue jeans.

"Madame Sonnier?" He smiled. "My name is Paul. I work for Maurice Cheverny. You are calling him?"

"Yes." Thank God.

"Go ahead." He inserted a coin for her.

Cheverny's voice was rich and cautiously cordial. "Welcome to Paris, Madame Sonnier. You had a safe journey?"

"Yes."

"Good. We have work to do, but there's no rush now that you're here. Will tomorrow be soon enough? I imagine you need rest."

Paul had a car. As they pulled away from the airport, Amira could not help glancing over her shoulder.

"No one is following," said Paul.

"Where are we going?"

"A hotel that Monsieur Cheverny sometimes uses for clients who require privacy. Small, very discreet, quite nice."

It was more than nice: an elegant jewel north of the Seine.

"Please don't leave the hotel," said Paul after checking the security of her suite. "Call the concierge if you need anything."

When he was gone, Amira kicked off her shoes and luxuriated on the bed. Coffee. She would have coffee. And a real meal. And a long, lazy rest. But before any of that, a long, hot bath.

507

THAT NIGHT SHE DREAMED that she was drinking tea with Philippe in a peasant's mountain hut, snow everywhere around.

Maurice Cheverny called at nine in the morning. Could she meet with him at eleven? Good; he would send Paul.

A maid brought coffee, croissants, and *Le Monde*. As Amira spooned jam onto Karim's plate, a headline caught her eye: FRENCH PHYSICIAN, PHILANTHROPIST, DIES IN EASTERN TURKEY.

She dropped the spoon and ignored her son's outcry.

> Dr. Philippe Rochon died Tuesday in an apparent accident south of Kars, Turkey. . . . body found in a wild mountain river downstream from his wrecked car . . . search efforts under way for a woman and child believed to be traveling with him . . . extremely rugged terrain. Dr. Rochon, in addition to being one of the most esteemed members of his profession, endowed more than 100 scholarships to universities in France and abroad.

It couldn't be true. It had to be a mistake. She called Cheverny.

"I've just seen it myself, madame. Paul is on the way. I've canceled my other appointments."

Maurice Cheverny's office overlooked Paris from one of the city's new skyscrapers. The attorney was a balding, heavyset man in his early sixties.

"I tell you frankly, madame, I am uncomfortable in this situation. I do not know if Jihan Sonnier is your true name—do not tell me—but I believe I can guess. In strict duty I ought to alert the authorities to your presence. But my client's instructions were quite specific."

He unlocked a drawer and brought out a large envelope and a small one. He handed her the large one. "Dr. Rochon left this for you. It is a substantial sum of cash, in American dollars. He also instructed me to put you in touch with a plastic surgeon whose name he gave me. Paul can take you to him. Finally, there is this letter for you." He handed over the smaller envelope.

The letter explained everything. "Pancreatic cancer . . . six months, no more—not good months either. And this way they will believe it." Through her tears Amira read the end of the letter. "I do not believe in an afterlife, but who knows? Perhaps we will meet again after all. Meanwhile, keep me alive in your heart. Be safe and happy with your son. Good-bye, my love."

"He was dying," she told the attorney. "He gave his life to help me and my son escape from . . . from great danger."

"Ah." He removed his glasses. "Philippe Rochon was like a son to me," he said simply. He cleared his throat. "There is one more thing, madame. Philippe— Dr. Rochon asked me to see to your acceptance at an American school, Harvard. I've corresponded with an old friend of mine, an assistant dean. In this and all else, I'll help you in any way I can. Do you want to see this surgeon?"

"Yes. As soon as possible."

IN HIS Paris office a kilometer away, Malik stared at the *Le Monde* article. He couldn't make sense of it. For the dozenth time he went over it. His spies in Ali's entourage had informed him of his sister's escape almost as soon as it occurred. Then he had learned about the dead end in Tehran. And yesterday word had come that Philippe was involved, and the trail led to Turkey.

Malik was sure Philippe would bring Amira to France and fight—if he had to—on home ground. This was no mere affair of the heart. Amira was running not to someone, but from someone. Malik had long had his spies' reports of Ali's idiosyncrasies. What had happened only confirmed his thoughts and fueled his anger.

He had assumed that Amira and Philippe would be in France at any moment and that she would contact him. He was her brother; he was powerful; he could protect her. But now this. Death in some godforsaken mountain gorge in Turkey. It made no sense at all.

"Amira," he said aloud, "little sister"—and in that moment felt the certainty that Amira was alive. He knew it.

Malik already had an agent in Van, where Monsieur and Madame Rochon had stayed briefly in a hotel. The man confirmed Malik's fear that Ali was hunting Amira, too, and his operatives were painting her as a runaway wife. Even if Malik could match the royal billions bribe for bribe, no good Muslim would help him in the face of a husband's rightful demands. And if Ali were to find her first . . .

He summoned an aide and gave orders.

Twelve hours later Malik's agents were crisscrossing eastern Anatolia, as were Ali's men—bribing, cajoling, intimidating airport personnel, cabbies, anyone who might have helped a woman and child leave the area. But even with the full cooperation of the police and the army, nothing concrete led beyond the hotel in Van or the wrecked Land Rover.

Eventually, even Malik had to give up. If not for his inexplicable certainty that his sister was alive, he would have despaired. But surely that feeling was true, he told himself. Surely he would see her again.

ALI'S feelings were simple: rage and fear. Rage at her betrayal—if she turned up alive, he would certainly kill her. Fear that if she was dead, so must be his son.

The more Ali thought about it, the more he was convinced that his brother-in-law was behind it all. He had never liked Malik. The man was a commoner, after all, like his sister. Undoubtedly, the gigolo doctor—who was finished, Ali would make sure of that—was just a pawn. Ali reflected bitterly that the trap he had tried to set in al-Remal had, in a perverse way, sprung on his own hand.

Then came the news from the wilds of eastern Anatolia. At first Ali believed that Amira and Karim must indeed have died with Rochon in the wreck, and his hatred of the woman alternated with grief for his son. But there were many things to doubt in the accounts coming out of Turkey. The men he had sent to investigate soon told him that Malik's men were there.

To Ali that meant two possibilities. The first was that Malik's plan had gone wrong and his men were in Turkey to find out what had happened. The second was that the plan had come off perfectly, leaving the doctor's corpse as a smoke screen. If the first, Amira and Karim were probably dead. If the second, they were alive. In either case, Malik was to blame—and Ali swore he would take vengeance.

AMIRA followed it all in the newspapers and on television. It had taken the press only a few days to connect her with the woman missing in Philippe's accident. She was glad that she was in a place where no reporter could reach her; moreover, any reporter who might would never recognize her. The place was a château in Senlis, a recovery house for women who had had cosmetic surgery.

The surgeon had explained that recognition depended on only two or three key features. Her nose needed repair anyway, after Ali had flattened it. The surgeon would also rearrange the cast of her eyes slightly, and she would wear lenses that changed the brown to a deep green. He would also remove the scar from her forehead.

Three weeks later she had a French passport bearing her new likeness and her new name: Jenna Sorrel. Karim kept his first name; it was Jenna's wish, against the surgeon's advice.

One month from the day she entered France, Amira—Jenna—left on a freighter bound for New Orleans. The mode of transportation represented a last bit of caution: Someone—probably Philippe— had decided that it offered the least likelihood of scrutiny.

At New Orleans, she filled out papers for status as a foreign student. She found a hotel that had childcare facilities, then went out to find a jeweler.

She passed a shop on Royal Street three times before going in. The jeweler rose to greet her, his loupe perched above his right eye.

"I want to sell some jewels." She emptied her case on the counter.

The old man looked for a moment, then said, "This is quality. This is beauty." He lowered the loupe and inspected the jewels. Now and then he sighed with pleasure. At length he said, "I will buy these, even though I'll have to borrow to do it."

He named a figure. It seemed terribly low to Amira, but something about the man made her trust him. "Very well. I'll take it."

"Come back tomorrow morning. I'll have a cashier's check." He looked at the jewels for a moment. "You must know that I'm offering only a fraction of what these are worth. That's because there are certain risks involved. But this one, no." He pushed the pigeon-blood ruby toward her. "That's not part of the price. I recognize it, and so would any other fine jeweler in the world. Keep it."

The next afternoon she caught a plane to Boston, where, after an interview and a special placement test, she was assured of a place at Harvard for the fall term. She would major in psychology.

An All-American Boy

"WHAT happened?" Jenna Sorrel demanded.

Karim's left eye was blackened. A streak of blood had dried under his nose. "I had a fight, okay?"

Jenna heard shame and pride mixed in her son's reply. He was only nine years old, she reminded herself.

"No, it most certainly isn't okay. What happened?"

"Josh Chandler was calling me names."

"What kind of names?"

"Just . . . names."

Jenna remembered the insults thrown at Middle Eastern students during her second year at Harvard, when the hostage crisis had broken out in Iran. Now and then Karim's first name and his complexion had subjected him to similar cruelty from his schoolmates.

"Names are no reason for fighting. You know that, don't you?"

Karim nodded, close to tears.

"Your father always said that most fights happen because someone is afraid not to fight. What takes real courage is to walk away."

Karim nodded again. The father he had never known was his greatest hero. Unfortunately, that father was a lie. Jenna had created him. Physically, the man she invented was smaller than average, as Ali was and Karim himself promised to be. In most other ways he resembled Philippe, except Jacques Sorrel was a ship's captain who had died bringing supplies to an epidemic-stricken port in Africa.

"Come on," she said. "Let's go solve this problem."

She knew the Chandlers slightly from school functions. They lived in elegant Beacon Hill, a brisk walk from Marlborough Street.

A maid answered the door and ushered Jenna and Karim in. Carolyn Chandler appeared, blond, tennis-fit, and smiling graciously, if a bit nervously.

Behind her, big Cameron Chandler loomed up like a cordial but concerned bear. "I understand there was some trouble," he said.

"There was. And I've come to get your assurance that there won't be more."

"But," interjected Carolyn, "I think your son hit ours first."

"If that is so, he was wrong and will apologize. But from what I hear, Josh was attacking Karim's ethnic heritage. And that must stop. I'm sure you agree with that."

Cameron Chandler nodded. "Of course. Josh, come in here."

Josh was inches taller and twenty pounds heavier than Karim. He had a badly split lip.

Cameron took charge. After a few blunt questions elicited what was probably very close to the truth of the episode, he ordered the boys to shake hands and forget the whole thing.

"Want to shoot some baskets?" Josh asked Karim.

"Sure."

The two scurried away. Feeling at loose ends, Jenna gratefully accepted Carolyn's offer of coffee. Cameron joined them with a drink. The Chandlers didn't exactly pry, but Jenna found herself reciting the well-rehearsed fiction of her past. Her hosts seemed to be what everything about them proclaimed them to be: old Boston society. Jenna intuited a certain distance between them, something in their body language. Perhaps they had argued over Josh's behavior.

"So you're a psychologist," said Cameron.

"Yes."

"Of course," said Carolyn, suddenly animated. "*That's* who you are. You have a book out, don't you? I've been meaning to buy it. I saw a very nice review of it somewhere. *Ancient . . .*"

"*Ancient Chains,*" Jenna said with relief. The book had been a sweet surprise. A reworking of her doctoral dissertation, it had received a brief but very positive notice in *The New York Times Book Review,* and it had sold thirty thousand copies.

"What's it about?" asked Cameron.

"It's hard to explain in one sentence. Let's just say it's about the ways women have adapted to various forms of discrimination and abuse."

"A hot topic," said Cameron. "Hot enough to send me back to the liquor cabinet. Get you anything?" He didn't ask Carolyn.

"No, thank you. Actually, I'd better be going."

Carolyn walked her out. Under a backyard goal the boys were playing one on one, to all appearances best friends.

Walking home, Jenna glanced sidelong at her son. Love and sadness welled in her; he was growing up so fast. In those first years, when they were learning a new world together, they had been as close as two people can be. Now—too soon—she could sense the beginnings of distance between them.

She reached out and tousled his hair. He squirmed away but grinned. It was an American moment, she thought. In al-Remal a mother wouldn't treat a male child so familiarly, not at Karim's age. But of course, Karim was an American. She was one herself—or nearly one. She had even become a Red Sox fan. Her English carried just a trace of accent. Karim had an accent, too: pure Boston.

Someday she would tell him the truth, she promised herself. Meanwhile, she had done what she had to, and it was done.

"What do you think, kiddo?" she said, trying to shake off the mood. "Should we see if the bookstore has any new puzzles?" Karim shared her passion for large, difficult jigsaw puzzles.

"Can we order a pizza, too?" Karim asked eagerly.

"Great idea."

And just like that, the distance was gone; he was her little boy again. They were Jenna and Karim, together against the world.

IT WAS four o'clock on Wednesday afternoon. Jenna's final patient had left. Karim would be at soccer practice for another hour. Jenna looked at the pile of forms, bills, and letters that needed doing, and decided on a cup of tea at the Village Greenery instead.

On the way, she bought the *Star* and the *National Enquirer.* The tabloids were the most likely source of news about her brother.

At the coffee shop she settled into the scandal sheets. Disappointingly, she found nothing about Malik. For years now, the stories had identified him as "one of the world's richest men." Lately they had begun dropping "one of" and making it "man." He owned a shipping fleet that would have rivaled that of his old mentor, Onassis. He held investments in enterprises all over the world, and—in the dark speculation of the tabloids—might or might not be earning huge fees on arms sales in the Middle East and elsewhere.

Once in a while the stories mentioned the tragic death of Malik's sister, the Remali princess. Once, there had been a picture of Laila, tall for her age, thin, and looking almost angrily at the camera. There had also been photos of his French wife, Genevieve, a former nightclub singer.

Jenna had never let Malik know that she and Karim were alive. It was the hardest thing in her life, a knife that made a new cut every day. But after seven years she was still afraid. By now, surely, her brother had reconciled himself to her death. So had everyone she had known in her old life. Everyone except Ali.

From the tabloids she knew that her husband had married again and fathered at least one new son. But that wouldn't matter if he discovered that she and Karim were alive. He would be as implacable as a falcon—and as deadly.

"Jenna? May I join you?"

She looked up and recognized Carolyn Chandler. "Of course. What a nice surprise."

Carolyn sat down and looked around. "It really is a small world. I've never been in this place—just popped in on impulse." She ordered a cappuccino. "Have you noticed," she asked when the waitress was gone, "that our sons have become inseparable?"

Jenna smiled. "I *have* heard quite a bit of 'me and Josh' lately."

The late afternoon light warmed Carolyn's tennis tan, accentuating her hazel eyes. She seemed so much friendlier than at their last meeting, thought Jenna. Of course, she had been on the defensive then about Josh.

"Isn't it amazing," Carolyn said, "how little boys can try to beat each other's brains out one minute and be Damon and Pythias the next? Grown men, too. Of course, when a man hits a woman, it's never forgiven, is it?"

"No," said Jenna, although it wasn't that simple. "But even between men it's not the same everywhere. Where I grew up," Jenna said, "if one man struck another, they were enemies for life."

Carolyn shook her head. "How did we get on this depressing subject?" She took a pack of Virginia Slims from her purse.

Jenna checked her watch. "I hate to do it, but I need to run. Karim will be home any minute. It was good to see you."

"Me, too. Listen, we're having a little brunch party Sunday at eleven. We'd love to have you. Bring Karim—Josh will be eternally grateful."

Jenna hesitated. She accepted few social invitations. It was the old fear: In a crowd of new faces, who might at last recognize hers?

"I know it's short notice," said Carolyn.

Jenna decided. "Not at all. It sounds nice. Thank you."

But as she turned in at her door, Jenna already felt uncomfortable about accepting Carolyn's invitation. What had persuaded her to do it? Maybe it was being tired of living like a recluse, she thought. Maybe she was hoping for something good to happen. And why not?

While a stew was simmering nicely, she switched on the evening news. Jenna was half listening, searching for the *TV Guide*, when she became aware of a woman's face on the screen.

"Tragedy today in France," Dan Rather intoned, "where Genevieve Badir, wife of international financial magnate Malik Badir, died in a road accident. Her Mercedes was struck head-on by a truck near St.-Tropez, where the Badirs had one of their many homes."

Jenna clawed for the volume control as the story continued: "Madame Badir, a former singer, was driving alone to a favorite restaurant. A source close to the family told reporters that Malik Badir would normally have been in the car but had been called away unexpectedly on business.

"Badir's name has been linked with intrigue at high levels of the military and government in France and elsewhere, but authorities do not suspect foul play in his wife's death. The truck driver, who was also killed, was said to be, quote, profoundly drunk."

The images of Rather and Genevieve dissolved to a commercial. Jenna stared numbly. "No," she heard herself say. "No, no, no!" She was too shocked for tears. Poor Genevieve. Jenna had never known her sister-in-law, and now she never would.

One thing especially struck her: Malik might easily have been in the car. If so, he would have died believing in her own death. The idea filled her with unbearable guilt. Turning off the television, she found some plain white stationery and wrote:

Dearest brother,

My heart aches for you. I wish I could kiss and comfort you. But I cannot. I beg your forgiveness for causing you sorrow. I can only hope that you understand.

Life has been lonely and hard, but I am well, thank God, and so is Karim. I have established a successful career in work I love. That and my son sustain me. I hope that you, too, can find solace in your daughter's love and in knowing that your sister thinks of you often and wishes with all her heart to see you once more.

She would mail it in the morning. But when morning came, so did doubt and fear. If she simply dropped the letter in the nearest mailbox, the Boston postmark would give her away. She slipped the letter into her shoulder bag. She would mail it, she promised herself, definitely she would. But not just now.

CAROLYN'S brunch turned out to be an anticlimax. The guests all seemed to have gone to college together and to know the same peo-

ple and the same stories. The lone single male, a corporate lawyer—
rather transparently a pairing for Jenna—drank several Bloody
Marys and became sentimental about his ex-wife.

Carolyn called later to apologize. She made several wicked comments at the lawyer's expense. Jenna couldn't help laughing. That
was the real beginning of their friendship.

It was an unusual one. Carolyn, a few years older, tried to be a
mentor, instructing Jenna in subtleties of American tastes. At the
same time, it was obvious that Carolyn badly wanted a confidante,
one from outside her circle. Yet her confidences were slow in coming. They had to do with her husband.

Cameron Chandler was a mystery to Jenna. His demeanor toward
her was at first cordial, then merely indulgent, then almost hostile.
She suspected that he was threatened by her closeness to Carolyn.
But as Jenna's friendship with Carolyn deepened, it became clear
that something was seriously wrong between the Camerons. Little
shades of intonation pointed to a deep lack of respect on both their
parts, as well as to an almost desperate possessiveness.

ONE spring day Jenna and Carolyn were at a soccer game. Josh,
with his long reach, was playing goal. Karim, to even Jenna's surprise, showed every sign of becoming a star striker, fast and sure
with his feet.

The game was an exciting one, but despite several spectacular
saves by Josh, Carolyn hardly stirred from her perch on her old-
fashioned foldout leather seat. It was not stable, and at one point
Carolyn leaned too far and had to brace herself. When she did, she
gasped in pain and fell to her knees.

Jenna was right beside her. "Are you hurt?"

"Just help me to the car," whispered Carolyn between clenched
teeth. In the front seat she began to cry. "That bastard! I think he's
broken my ribs."

"Cameron? He hit you?"

"Yes, he hit me. Where it won't show. That's his little trick."

Jenna couldn't believe it. "You mean he's done it before?"

"Yes."

"Carolyn, listen. You've got to get help—you and Cameron
both."

Carolyn turned on Jenna with something like hatred in her eyes. "I don't need help. I need my husband to be the man I married."

The sense of déjà vu was almost sickening. How many times had Jenna—Amira—thought the same words about Ali?

Carolyn would say no more. By her standards she had gone too far. When Jenna phoned, Carolyn talked about trivia. When Jenna tried to broach the subject of Cameron, Carolyn said with brittle finality, "Everything's fine." The message was unmistakable: Don't mention it again.

After that, Jenna and Carolyn did the old things together—going to soccer games, to the Village Greenery—but gradually the two friends became more distant. Gradually they became hardly friends at all.

Ancient Chains had made Jenna a minor celebrity in academic circles. One result was a stream of invitations to conferences. She usually turned them down, but she decided to accept one: a panel on "Women, History, and Therapy" at a convention in Toronto.

Then, at the airport, there was one of those small chance occurrences that change more lives than wars. Jenna's return flight was delayed, and she went to a coffee shop. Sipping her tea, she couldn't help overhearing two men in the next booth. After some chat about wives and children, one man—he had a British accent—said, "I must tell you I had a bit of a turn in Rome two days back. I'd taken a client to a restaurant. We'd just ordered, when all hell broke loose. Gunfire all over the place, people diving for the floor."

"What was it? Mafia?"

"A kidnapping attempt. Some bloody billionaire was in the place with his daughter. Apparently she was the target. Badir, whatever his name is."

For Jenna everything else in the restaurant vanished.

"Anybody hurt?" the other man asked.

"The two kidnappers shot up rather badly. And I believe two or three patrons were wounded, including this Badir chap."

Jenna whirled around. "Malik was shot?"

"I beg your pardon?"

"Malik Badir—he was wounded?"

"Yes. But not too badly, I believe."

"And Laila—the daughter—is she all right?"

"She wasn't hurt. You talk as if you know these people."

"I'm a family acquaintance."

Her flight was called. As she checked her purse for her ticket, the letter to Malik caught her eye. A bookshop had stamps, and she dropped the letter into a mailbox before second thoughts could take hold. There, she had done it, she thought. But what had she done?

Laila

IN THE weeks that followed, the tabloids were strangely silent on the subject of Malik. Then, two months after the shooting, Jenna read that her brother had acquired an apartment at The Pierre hotel in New York. The brief article noted that Malik was still recuperating from the attack in Rome and that "Badir believes his daughter will be safer in the United States than in Europe." Laila had been enrolled at the Brearley School.

On the Boston–New York shuttle Jenna tried to convince herself that she really did need to keep in touch with colleagues such as her old Adlerian-theory professor, now in private practice in New York, with whom she had a lunch date.

After lunch she took a taxi to the Brearley School, stationed herself outside, and waited. Would she recognize the little girl she had helped deliver on a bed of straw?

She did. Dark hair, almond eyes, the older Laila's heart-shaped face. Something in the set of the girl's shoulders, something brave yet vulnerable, reminded Jenna of Malik a long time ago.

A limousine pulled up. Jenna's heart leaped. She was sure she would see her brother, catch a glimpse of the face she'd missed for so long. But no, the man who stepped out of the car was only a chauffeur, whose thick shoulders and watchful eyes practically shouted bodyguard. A few moments later he and Laila were gone. Jenna stood staring at the space where her niece had been.

Well, now you've seen her, she told herself as she finally forced herself to leave. That will have to be enough.

But it wasn't enough, and a few weeks later she found another pressing reason to go to New York—a bit of library research. Once again she stationed herself outside the school. She had promised herself she would just look.

Then she saw Laila talking with several other girls. Good—her niece had made some friends. No chauffeur this time—good again. The little group walked west. Against all reason Jenna followed.

Kidding and laughing like any teenagers, the girls eventually turned south on Fifth Avenue. They stopped at Bergdorf Goodman, Jenna slipping in behind them. In twenty minutes the little group collectively spent a sum that, Jenna estimated, many of her clients would be happy to earn in a week. Unconsciously she shook her head in disapproval.

The group moved on to Saks. They went in, Jenna behind them. This time they seemed inclined just to look and were soon headed for the door. But wait, what was happening? A man moved quickly, grabbed Laila, and pulled a silk scarf out of her book bag.

Laila began to cry. The other girls had vanished, melting into the

crowd of shoppers. Without a moment's thought Jenna stepped between Laila and the man. "What are you doing, sir?"

"Who are you?"

"I'm this young woman's mother. Who the devil are you?"

"Store security."

The manager appeared. Jenna turned to him, trying to put on a
show of injured innocence. "I asked my daughter to meet me here,
to pick up the scarf this man is holding. It's just like the one I have
at home. I'm sure she was looking for me when he jumped her. Is
that how you treat valued customers?"

The manager looked Jenna over: obviously affluent, the very picture of a valued customer. And the girl hadn't left the store. The
manager yielded. Jenna produced her gold card and paid for the
scarf.

Laila looked bewildered, but didn't make a sound. Once outside
the store Laila whispered, "Thank you." And then, "Who are you?
Why did you do that?"

"I might ask you the same question," Jenna responded. She led
her niece to a coffee shop. Without asking, she ordered two cups
of tea. "I'm Jenna Sorrel. I'm from Boston. I'm a psychologist."

"A psychologist," echoed Laila.

Jenna smiled. "It's okay. I'm off-duty." She couldn't take her eyes
off the girl, drinking her in, seeing the young woman she would
soon become. Jenna had missed her family—the idea of family—for
so long. And here was Malik's baby, her niece, the child she'd
helped deliver.

"You're here for a convention or something?" asked Laila.

"No. Just visiting."

"I'm new here myself. I'm from France."

"Your English is wonderful." It was true. The French accent was
almost imperceptible.

"Well, we've traveled a lot," explained Laila. "And I've had lots
of American friends."

"That's good—to have friends." Careful, Jenna, she warned herself. You have no right to do this. But she couldn't help herself.

"But I don't have any friends at school," said Laila moodily. "I
don't know what I'm doing wrong. I think it's because I'm different.
I mean, my father's from al-Remal, and I . . . look like him."

"There must be other people from different backgrounds in the school, no? More likely it's that you're new. You've seen that in other places, haven't you? Everyone's slow to warm up to the new kid?"

"Maybe it's because Papa is— I won't tell you his name, because you might know it. But he has lots of money. Some of the other kids' parents have money, too, but not as much as Papa. I try to be nice. I buy presents for everyone. They seem to like them. They thank me, but then . . . Today was like a chance, you know, to belong. They said I had to prove myself. I had to steal something." Watching Jenna's face for signs of disapproval, she hastily added, "All the other girls have done it. Nobody ever got caught before."

"I see," said Jenna neutrally. So lonely, she thought. The girl needed someone—her father, obviously. But if not him, who?

"And now I've screwed up," Laila concluded, tears in her eyes.

"Maybe you didn't really want to do it," Jenna offered.

An unhappy shrug.

"Did you ever notice," Jenna said after a sip of tea, "maybe in sports or dancing, that when you try too hard, you screw up? It's the same way with making friends. Sometimes the worst thing you can do is to try too hard."

"But what can I do except try?"

"Just be yourself. And take an interest in other people." Jenna knew the words weren't enough. Before she could think about the wisdom of what she was doing, she blurted out, "Perhaps we could see each other again. Would you like that?"

Laila pulled back, her eyes narrow with suspicion. "Why?"

Of course, Jenna thought, after all that had happened to her, she was bound to question a stranger making overtures. "There's an old proverb that says if you save a person's life, you're responsible for it from that moment on. I didn't exactly save your life, but I think the same principle applies. I just want to know you'll be all right."

Laila cocked her head, then bobbed it. "I guess it's okay if we get together again. The best place to find me is at school. We get out at three. It's the Brearley School. Do you know where it is?"

"Yes."

"So come by sometime. By the way, my name's Laila."

"Jenna."

"See you, Jenna."

And she was gone.

BACK in Boston, in free moments between patients or while doing some mindless household task, Jenna found herself fantasizing about visiting museums and art galleries with her niece, sharing long walks in Greenwich Village and SoHo. She imagined drawing the girl out, listening to her problems, offering help and advice.

She knew she was picturing herself in the role of a parent. Laila needed her. And Jenna was hungry for the family she had left behind.

Then the past stepped in again. On the anniversary of her disappearance, there was an item on a television magazine show, full of speculation that Amira might still be alive. The writer was astute enough to suspect that Prince Ali al-Rashad was not so resigned and disinterested as he wished to appear, and this suspicion was voiced in the story. Jenna felt the old fear as if it had never left her. After all this time, all this disguise, she still wasn't safe.

Her self-deception ended. She couldn't continue to see Laila; it might endanger both of them. She could easily vanish from Laila's life. But Jenna couldn't do that, just couldn't. Feeling a wrenching sense of loss—it wasn't fair, she thought, yet again to have to let go of someone she loved—Jenna again made the trip to New York. They went to a diner—a trendy Upper East Side version—and shared an oversized cheeseburger and a platter of french fries.

"I'm afraid I won't be able to see you often," Jenna began. "I've been neglecting my patients. And I have a book contract that's going to eat up every free moment." None of it was quite true, but it wasn't exactly a lie either.

Laila's eyes reproached her, then turned away. "That's okay," the girl said with forced casualness. "To tell you the truth, I had to lose Ronnie—my chauffeur—today to see you. These last few days, I don't know why, but Papa's become really worried about me. So it won't be easy for me anymore either."

Jenna smiled in spite of herself. Imagine Malik, the old rule breaker, now the rule maker.

"Could I have your phone number?" Laila asked suddenly. "I'd like to talk to you once in a while—if that's okay."

Jenna couldn't resist. "Of course it's okay. Anytime. But will you promise to keep it just between the two of us?"

Laila laughed. "Sure. Besides, it's not like I'm going to run home and tell Papa about the lady who rescued me in Saks."

They shared a chocolate dessert. When the last morsel was gone, there was no avoiding the fact that their time together was ending, too. But Jenna's heart pleaded for a reprieve.

"Shall we walk a bit?" she asked.

"Sure," said Laila.

They strolled down Fifth Avenue. Jenna tried to pretend this wasn't the last time she would see Laila. Maybe it wasn't.

When they reached The Plaza, they hailed two taxis.

"Well . . . *ciao*," Laila said, trying to smile.

Forgetting caution, Jenna threw her arms around her niece and held her tight. "Good-bye," she said. Good-bye, my dearest Laila.

Cameron

THE call came on a cool September night.

"Can you come over, Ms. Sorrel? Like right away?"

"What's the matter, Josh?"

"My dad kind of hurt my mom. He's gone now, and she asked me to call you. I— Can you hurry?"

Jenna did. At the Chandler house, she took one look at Carolyn's face and went to the phone. Apparently Cameron had forgotten his little trick of hitting where it didn't show.

"No." Carolyn pulled the receiver from her and hung it up.

"Carolyn, you may be in danger. Will he be back tonight?"

Carolyn shrugged. "Probably." She didn't appear to be in shock.

Jenna tried to think. "All right, you're spending the night at my place, both of you. In the morning we can deal with this better."

Carolyn simply nodded and said, "Okay. That's not a bad idea."

At her apartment, Jenna doctored her friend's face as best she could. The wounds were mainly bruises and welts.

Carolyn talked about Cameron in an oddly matter-of-fact way that troubled Jenna. "He just needs something that he can control, that he can dominate. Unluckily, that happens to be me."

In the kitchen Josh and Karim sat exchanging a quiet word now and then—almost like grown men already, their closeness expressed more through silence than through speech.

At two in the morning Cameron rang the bell.

"I know my wife's here, Jenna. Let me talk with her."

"Go home, Cameron." She kept the chain on the door.

"Jenna, please. I know I screwed up. Just let me talk with her."

"Cameron, if you don't leave now, I'll call the police."

"Go ahead," he said loudly. "You call the police. I'll call my lawyers. You interfere with my life, you'll regret it."

At that moment Carolyn swept by her with Josh in tow. "Thank you, Jenna, but it's best that you stay out of this."

"Carolyn—"

"Jenna, I appreciate your kindness and your good intentions. But this is between Cameron and me." She fought with the chain, opened the door, and went out into the hallway.

"Oh, babe, I'm so sorry," said Cameron in a wheedling voice. "Are you okay? Are you okay? My love, I'm so sorry."

Josh turned back and looked helplessly at Jenna and Karim, then followed his parents.

Jenna stood silently and watched Carolyn go. There was a wall between them, put in place by Carolyn and never to be breached.

IT WAS a turning point for Jenna. It gave direction to her work. She might have failed her best friend, but if she worked hard enough, perhaps she could help other women facing the same agony.

One morning she woke with the theme and the title of the next book she would write—*Prisons of the Heart: Women in Denial.*

Meanwhile, unknown to her, a man to whom she was truly thankful was about to touch her life again, but with fateful effect.

BROTHER Peter was dying. He had gone to Zaire to explore the possibility of establishing a mission there, but an epidemic of some kind had broken out. Back in Van, he had suddenly developed a blinding headache, followed by nausea, fever, and fierce thirst.

A local doctor loaded Peter with antibiotics, but it was clear that he had no hope for his patient.

The mission was nearly deserted. Another earthquake had struck to the north, and most of the little detachment of brothers had gone there on their work of faith and mercy. The deathwatch over Brother Peter fell mainly to the handyman, Mustafa.

It was ten o'clock at night. For hours Mustafa had watched and listened while Brother Peter slipped in and out of intelligibility. At the moment, the dying man was raving about Joseph, Mary, and Jesus' flight into Egypt.

"Herod sent his men after them. Remember? But Herod was a Jew, and these were Arabs. Remember them? Rich, rich Arabs."

Mustafa listened more closely. He remembered when there had been rich Arabs in Van asking questions.

"Running from them. Mary and Jesus. No more Joseph. Joseph died on Mount Ararat." Brother Peter shook his head fiercely. "Not Joseph. French name. Philippe. Yes, great man."

Mustafa sat very still. The Arabs, he recalled, had offered large amounts of money for information about a woman and child who had been with a man named Philippe.

"So Peter took them in the van. Remember the van we had?"

"Where did you take them?" ventured Mustafa.

"Egypt. Herod's men hot after us."

Mustafa interjected questions, trying to channel Peter's ramblings. It was like conversing with a sleepwalker, but at last he had the bones of the tale. It was Peter who had smuggled the rich man's wife and son out of Van those many years ago, taking them to the airport in Erzurum in the mission's old panel truck. No one around Van would have thought twice about seeing it on the road.

That was all Peter had to tell, now or ever. Toward midnight, with one last shout for Jesus, he fell silent. Then he was gone.

Mustafa went home to search for the card that one of the rich Arabs had given him—"In case you think of anything later," the man had said. Praise God, there it was. The name of a local hotel on one side; on the other, a phone number in al-Remal. The call would cost Mustafa a month's pay. He hoped that what Brother Peter had said was still worth something.

ABDALLAH al-Rashad, head of Remali intelligence and Ali's uncle, closed the folder and waited for his nephew's reaction.

"You believe this peasant, this Turk?" said Ali.

"So far as it can be checked, his story holds up."

"So the sow and my son are alive," said Ali. "Where are they?"

"I've initiated new inquiries. It seems that she and the boy went to Paris. So far, that is where the trail ends."

"Find her."

Abdallah looked aside in embarrassment; Ali's terseness verged on disrespect. "If she makes a mistake, we will," he said quietly. "If not . . . Time is like the sand, nephew. In the end, it covers everything."

"I don't need—" Ali controlled himself with visible effort. "Thank you, Uncle. If anyone can find my son, it's you." Ali rose. "It's been good to see you, Uncle. Unfortunately, I must go."

"Of course. I know how busy your schedule is. But perhaps just one more word while I have the pleasure of your company."

"Certainly." Ali did not sit down. "What is it?"

"Just this, nephew. It is my deepest wish that you be reunited with your son. At the same time, if he and his mother are found, it would reflect badly on al-Remal—and on the royal family itself—if anything untoward happened to her."

"Well, that seems obvious. But what does it have to do with me?" Ali's face was a portrait of surprised innocence.

"Nothing," said Abdallah. "Just a thought that came while we were talking. I've kept you long enough. Peace to you, nephew."

Abdallah saw his nephew to the door. He disliked Ali's temper, his duplicity, and much else of what he knew about him—and he knew a great deal. Yet he did not want Ali for an enemy.

There were many things to think about. Decisions to make. Abdallah opened the safe that contained his most secret files.

He retrieved a tape, put it in the tape deck, and pressed PLAY.

"God's peace be with you, Highness."

"And with you, Tamer. How good to see you again."

The voices were those of Ali and Tamer Sibai, who sounded nervous even in ordinary greetings. Tamer was the brother of Laila Sibai, executed in a famous adultery case. He had thrown the first stone. Abdallah compressed his lips in sympathy and respect for a man who could carry out such a duty.

"You'll do me the honor of having coffee with me?"

"The honor is mine."

Abdallah fast-forwarded through the customary small talk.

"And yet, as great as the pleasure of seeing you again, my friend Tamer, I'm afraid I must spoil it with bad news. I have had the misfortune to learn who dishonored your sister."

"Name him and he dies, even now."

"Ah, you speak like a man. Yet a man like you must not needlessly expose himself—and his country—to the prejudice of the world that does not understand the Remali meaning of honor."

"I thank you for your concern. Who is he?"

"Malik Badir."

A pause on the tape before Tamer spoke again.

"I always thought it was him. Now I know. Again I thank you."

"There's no need to thank me. But I hope you understood what I just said. Badir is a citizen of the world these days. I ask you not to handle the matter in a way that compromises our country."

"I know of only one way. What did you have in mind?"

"I thought that perhaps a third party could be engaged. I know that I'm asking you to forgo a duty that may seem purely personal. But I ask it for al-Remal. And for that reason I will gladly pay any costs that engaging someone might involve."

"That's unnecessary. I can take care of the arrangements myself."

"As you wish. I've learned that at this time of year Badir and his wife vacation at a villa in the south of France, and that twice a week they drive to a bistro in a nearby small town. If there were an accident . . ."

"I understand. A third time I thank you, Ali al-Rashad."

Abdallah stopped the tape. Here was a secret that he and perhaps three other men knew: that Genevieve Badir had died not by accident, but by murder. He had kept the secret because it was in the best interests of al-Remal to do so. But that might soon change. The king was dying, and Ali's brother Ahmad would succeed to the throne.

Ahmad was as practical as Ali was impetuous. Ahmad neither liked nor disliked Malik Badir, but considered him a potentially valuable asset to the kingdom. Perhaps he should be told that his brother's personal enmity had endangered that asset and might do so again. Ahmad would be grateful for the information.

Karim

"AMERICANS have no understanding of the Arab world. Their foreign policy in the Middle East is bankrupt. Their presuming to know what is best for us is hypocritical and destructive."

Good Lord, thought Jenna. She'd never heard such a soapbox speech—not in her own living room, certainly not from a teenage girl.

The speaker was Jacqueline Hamid, daughter of Professor Nasser Hamid, a well-known Egyptian novelist at Boston University. She was a classmate and, it appeared, a special friend of Karim's.

Now he nodded vigorously, eyes shining with admiration. "Exactly. Even you can't disagree with that, can you, Mom?"

How to respond? Jenna not only disagreed but also found Jacqueline insufferable. But to express that opinion would surely alienate her son, who was clearly enthralled by the petite dark-haired beauty with pouting red lips and enormous jet-black eyes.

"I heard your father's lecture on Egyptian feminism," Jenna said, dodging Karim's question. "It was very informative. But I wonder why he's not alarmed by the resurgence of the veil in a city like Cairo."

"Perhaps you don't fully understand the implications of current socioreligious movements in Egypt," Jacqueline said primly. "Karim tells me that you grew up mainly in Europe. You've lost touch with your Egyptian identity."

Jenna was shocked. It hadn't occurred to her that she was being discussed with Jacqueline—and found wanting.

Taking Jenna's silence to mean she had seen the error of her remark, Jacqueline launched into a defense of Arab customs in general and the veil in particular. "In conservative countries—like in al-Remal, for example—women enjoy a level of protection and respect that Western women have never known. All that the feminist movement has done in the West is to turn women into second-class men."

Jenna's blood ran cold. Didn't this girl realize how lucky she was? Didn't she know that she could be punished, perhaps even killed, for saying what she pleased in a conservative Arab country?

"I think life in places like al-Remal isn't nearly as romantic as you imagine it to be," Jenna said evenly. "Would you like some tea, Jacqueline? Or coffee?" It was prudent to forfeit the debate. Jacqueline was not going to be persuaded, and Karim was obviously so infatuated with the girl that he would happily join any *jihad* she wished to declare.

KARIM'S fascination with Jacqueline wasn't the only sign of his struggles at the border of manhood. As his voice had deepened, he had begun to question, argue, sulk, rebel at every turn.

Jenna would become shrill, and Karim would respond with a look of disgust that could have come straight from his father. Once again she would misstep without really knowing how or why, and she would feel an all-too-familiar frustration. It was as if her little boy were disappearing into the body of an argumentative, sneering stranger.

She had tried her hand at some of the popular Egyptian dishes that supposedly had been the food of her childhood, as a way of reaching out to Karim in his newfound interest in all things Arab. For the same reason, she had bought him some cassettes—the old songs of Asmahan and Abdul Wahab—from a small downtown shop.

Her gestures pleased Karim, but she longed for the days when her child believed she could do no wrong.

EVEN Sandra Waters seemed impressed as she strolled, the camera following her, along the decks of the *Jihan*. "She may be the most luxurious private vessel the world has ever seen," Sandra said. "A floating pleasure palace with its own movie theater and film library, a beauty salon, and a helicopter landing pad."

The video showed Sandra entering an extravagant suite. "Here we have electronically operated secret doors. A hot tub. Eight-foot circular bed. And more. It all belongs to this man—Malik Badir."

"Good evening, Sandra," Malik said a bit self-consciously, rising to greet his interviewer. "Welcome aboard the *Jihan*."

To Jenna he looked tired, dark shadows under his eyes.

"You launched the *Jihan* a year ago. I've heard that the christening party lasted a full week. True?"

"Oh, yes. In fact, some of the guests may still be here."

"And your date for the party was—"

"Yes." Everyone watching knew the story of the recently divorced and very famous film star Malik had been seeing at the time.

"Are you two still—"

"Oh, we see each other often. We're friends."

"But there's no one special person in your life?"

"I'm sorry to say, no." He did look genuinely sad. "No one, really, could replace my beloved wife."

The newswoman recounted Genevieve's accident. "Then there was another brush with tragedy," she said to Malik. "You were shot in a kidnap attempt on your daughter. You lost an arm."

Jenna gasped. She hadn't really noticed the way Malik's jacket fell. Now she saw that the left sleeve was simply empty. How could this happen? thought Jenna. Why didn't I know?

"There were complications, infection," her brother was saying. "Nothing to do but lop it off."

"And now there's another difficulty in your life," Waters went on. "Rumors are that you're to be charged with violating French espionage laws for your part in the sale to a third-world nation of Mirage jets that were then resold to the kingdom of al-Remal."

"A misunderstanding," said Malik. "It will soon be cleared up."

Jenna was watching so intently that she hadn't noticed Karim entering the room.

"Do you know him?" he asked. "Malik Badir?"

"Does he seem like someone I'd be likely to know?"

"I don't know. Just asking."

FOR two days Jenna worried about her brother's legal problems. She had to know more. Finally she decided to call Laila, just this once. She had heard from her niece twice since their last meeting, then nothing. Jenna couldn't blame her. And Laila was now a student at Columbia University.

She didn't seem surprised by Jenna's call. "How've you been?"

"Fine, fine. And you? Are you enjoying Columbia?"

"Yeah. A lot."

"And your father," said Jenna as casually as she could. "I don't want to pry, but there have been stories."

"You mean the Sandra Waters thing?"

"Well, yes."

"That's nothing. He has a lot of enemies, you know. They started this whole business. But he'll get it all straightened out."

Jenna could almost hear Malik—confident, even arrogant. A far cry from the young man who'd fled al-Remal to save his life and that of his daughter. And yet, she thought, there was so much his money couldn't buy. Genevieve was dead. And would not Laila have been happier, safer, with a simpler life?

The call ended with mutual promises to be in touch, but Jenna could tell that Laila's thoughts were elsewhere—on a boyfriend, perhaps? She tried to picture Malik's attitude toward his little girl's growing up. Would the aging rebellious son approve of the same tendencies in his daughter? She had to smile at the thought.

THAT winter with Operation Desert Storm was the winter of Karim's greatest discontent. It was not that he favored Iraq, but he believed Egypt had been coerced into the war on the American side.

Jenna could agree with him up to a point. Unfortunately, any word of moderation from her led to torrential idealistic arguments from him. Part of the problem, she was certain, was Karim's continued hero worship of Nasser Hamid, Jacqueline's father. Karim had been reading voraciously about the Middle East, Egypt in particular. He had decided to specialize in the history and politics of the region in college. Perhaps he would become a diplomat.

"Don't diplomats have to see both sides of issues?" she asked.

"Not all diplomats are cowards," he answered.

Like his anger, Karim's plans made Jenna feel guiltier than ever. Her son was building on something that never was.

You've cheated the boy, her conscience told her. You've filled his head with fairy tales when he is, in fact, a royal prince. But it just couldn't be helped.

One evening Jenna put her mind to preparing a grant proposal on behalf of the Sanctuary, the battered-women's shelter where she worked as a volunteer. She labored long and hard on her plea for funds. She considered her work at the shelter as important as anything she'd ever done.

When the doorbell rang, she assumed it was Karim, habitually forgetful of his keys. But it was Laila.

"Hi," the girl—the young woman—said, as if it had been only yesterday that they'd parted in front of The Plaza.

Jenna stared for a long moment, almost overcome by a rush of tenderness. She found her voice, trying to keep her manner light. "Laila! How good to see you. What brings you here?"

"Well, I— Actually, I came to say good-bye. Not forever, but I'm going away. I've transferred to U.C.L.A. I'm going to study filmmaking. It's a really good school for that, you know."

"So I've heard. Come in, Laila. We can talk inside."

Laila took a few steps forward, then stopped. "I can only stay a minute. I have a ride—some friends who dropped me off. They just went to the deli. They'll be back any second."

"You came all the way to Boston to stop by for a minute?" Jenna couldn't make any sense of this.

"I was visiting these friends. From school." Laila looked around the apartment, avoiding Jenna's eyes. She swallowed hard. "I was raped, you know," she said, her voice so low it could hardly be heard. "Four months ago. No, don't look like that. I'm all right. Really."

No, please no, not my beautiful niece. "I'm so sorry," she said, struggling to maintain control. "What happened?"

Laila shrugged, a gesture belied by the pain that showed in her face. "It was someone I knew." She shrugged again. "There's no point in going over it. Talking can't change what happened."

Jenna yearned to comfort her, but everything about Laila said she wanted distance. Not good, Jenna thought, making a professional observation. "Have you seen a therapist?"

"Yeah, sure. She helped some, I guess." Laila studied her shoes. "You know, I thought of coming to you, but it would've been like, I don't know, going to see my mother. That sounds silly, but . . ."

"No, it doesn't." It was all Jenna could do to hold back tears.

"But I'm okay now. It's just one reason I transferred. I wanted to get away."

Though Jenna understood all too well the needs that drove a woman to flee, she wanted to tell Laila that running away wasn't always the answer. "Are you sure—" she began, but at that moment Karim appeared. He looked at Jenna, then at Laila. His expression asked, What's going on?

Not knowing what else to do, Jenna made the introductions.

"Laila Badir?" Karim repeated. "Are you related to Malik Badir?"

"He's my father."

"Wow. I mean . . ."

"I know," Laila said softly. Obviously, it was a reaction she'd seen many times before.

BUT Karim's reaction went deeper than Laila could have suspected. What are you doing here? he wanted to ask, frustrated that his mother had given no explanation. He had the oddest sensation that he knew Laila Badir—not just knew who she was, but knew *her*. I'm staring, he realized. But just as he thought it, she suddenly gave him a small, sweet smile. For a moment it was as if they were the only two people in the room.

"Would you like something to drink?" he asked, feeling awkward. How could his mother have failed to offer any refreshment?

"Actually, I'd like some water, thank you."

Karim hurried to the kitchen, and returned with a Perrier.

"Thank you," Laila repeated. Still standing, she took a few polite sips, then said to Jenna, "I have to go. Really. But it's not goodbye. I'll write, call. I'll probably be in New York now and then."

"Laila, you must call me if you need anything. Anything at all."

"Sure. Well, *au 'voir*."

Suddenly they were hugging each other tight. Karim saw the tears in his mother's eyes. When did she meet this girl? Why did she never tell him? And why had she said she didn't know Malik Badir?

"I'll walk you downstairs," he suddenly said as Laila turned toward the door.

Her ride hadn't come yet. He was glad.

"Where are you from?" he asked for want of a better opener.

"France."

"Your father's from al-Remal, isn't he? Did you ever live there?"

"No. I've never lived anywhere in the Middle East."

"How do you know my mom?"

For a moment he was afraid he had said something wrong. Then Laila shrugged. "I met her in Saks in New York."

"Saks Fifth Avenue? The store?" He couldn't remember his mother taking any shopping trips to New York. In fact, even in Boston she complained that she never had time to go shopping. "You were shopping?" he prompted.

"What? Oh." She looked him in the eyes. Again the feeling of recognition. Did she feel it, too? "Actually, I was shop*lifting*."

Shoplifting? The daughter of the world's richest man? "Why?"

"It's a long story. But she rescued me." She outlined the event.

Nothing about it sounded like his mother. Something was going on here. "Then you're not one of her—"

"One of her patients? No."

A car pulled to a stop.

"My ride," said Laila. "Thanks for waiting with me."

He thought for a moment that she was going to touch him—his arm, perhaps his face. But she didn't.

"I'll send you both my address in California," she said.

Then she was gone.

In the apartment, Jenna had managed something like calm after Laila's unexpected visit. Karim came back in, his expression a mixture of puzzlement and—what? Hope?

"How do you know Laila Badir, Mom?"

"She was a patient. Not for long."

Now his expression was one she had seen on his father a hundred times. Eyes flat, blank, and cold. He shook his head and disappeared into his room.

After a night of broken sleep and a brusque "See you later" from her son on his way out, Jenna was trying to concentrate on her first patient's troubles, when her secretary buzzed.

"Yes?"

"Jenna, there's a police officer out here. She says it's important."

The woman was in plain clothes. "Detective Sue Keller," she said, showing a Boston badge. "You're Dr. Jenna Sorrel?"

"Yes. What's the matter?"

"You know a Mr. and Mrs. Cameron Chandler?"

"Yes." Oh, no. What now? "Tell me what's happened."

"Mrs. Chandler is in Mass General. She's in bad shape. You might want to get over there."

Brad

CAROLYN was in a coma, with massive injuries to her body organs and brain. Cameron was in jail, charged with attempted murder.

In a waiting room, Josh Chandler looked near shock. "I was going to call you," he said distractedly. "I gave the police your name."

"It's okay, Josh. Your mother—have you heard anything?"

"No. I don't know, Ms. Sorrel." He choked back a sob.

"Josh, what happened?"

"Like I told the police, I heard them arguing—fighting—this morning, early. I guess Dad had just come in. It was worse than— I should have done something, but then it quieted down. I went back to sleep. I mean, it's happened before. Not like this, but . . ."

"It's not your fault, Josh. What happened then?"

"Nothing. I mean, I woke up and started to get ready for school. And Mom and Dad's door was open, and I looked in and saw Mom on the floor—" Josh's voice broke. "And I called 911."

"Do you have anyone, Josh? Relatives?"

"Grandmom—my mom's mom. She's on her way from Connecticut. She'll stay at the house until . . . whatever happens."

"That's good. But if you'd like to stay with Karim and me, you're more than welcome. Just pack a bag and come over."

"Thanks. But tonight I want to stay with Mom."

"Okay," said Jenna. "I'm going to see what I can find out."

But all she could learn, even after rather deceptively identifying herself as Dr. Sorrel, was that Carolyn was still in surgery. Only hours later did a nurse finally give her the word: "She's in intensive care now, Doctor. Room two six two three."

Against the crisp white linen of her narrow bed, Carolyn looked frail and utterly fragile, her swollen face the texture and color of rotten fruit. Plastic tubes everywhere. That's how I looked in al-Remal, Jenna thought. Philippe came for me. I was lucky. I lived. God willing, God willing, Carolyn will be lucky, too.

"Dr. Sorrel?" A sallow, weary-looking man in surgeon's green.

"Yes."

"Stan Morgan. You're the primary care?"

"No. Just a friend of the family. What's the prognosis?"

Morgan grimaced. "Not good, I'm afraid, although it's still early. We could lose her. Even if we don't, we may be looking at irreversible coma." Morgan rattled off some technical details of trauma, hemorrhage, oxygen deprivation. What it amounted to was that if Carolyn lived at all, it would be in a vegetative state.

A death sentence, Jenna thought. And all because Carolyn had loved Cameron Chandler.

In the waiting room, Josh had been joined by Carolyn's mother,

Margaret Porter, a petite, delicately lovely china doll of a woman. "She was such a good girl," Mrs. Porter murmured. "Never any trouble."

Don't talk about her that way, Jenna wanted to say. It sounds as if she's already gone. But she simply nodded. "I think they'll let you see her now. Just be prepared. She's very badly hurt. But sometimes these things look worse than they are." Words, empty words.

NIGHT. Visiting hours had ended. Josh and his grandmother were going home; it was clear that they could do nothing more here. Karim had arrived after school and was going with his friend.

Exhausted both mentally and physically, Jenna stopped in the hospital cafeteria for a desperately needed cup of tea. But it did little to soothe her troubled spirit or ease her guilt.

As she rose to leave, she noticed a man nursing a cup of coffee a few tables away. A beautiful patrician face; close-cut dark hair; blue, blue eyes. And the saddest expression she'd ever seen. What was his story? Jenna wondered. Was a loved one upstairs fighting for life?

The following day she stopped by the hospital after her last patient. The prognosis for Carolyn was irreversible coma.

For hours Jenna kept watch beside the empty shell that was once her friend, as if through sheer presence and devotion she could remedy the past. Once again she ended her vigil with a trip to the cafeteria—and again the sad-looking man was there. Impulsively she put her tea on the table next to his. "I hope you don't mind," she said, "but you look as sad as I feel. It might help to talk about it."

The man tried to smile but failed. "My wife's upstairs," he said in a soft, slightly hoarse baritone. "She has cancer."

"I'm so sorry. But this is a good hospital. I hope . . ."

The man shook his head. "No," he said heavily, "I'm afraid not. It's just a matter of waiting. And saying good-bye."

Jenna couldn't bring herself to utter more platitudes. After a few sips of her tea, she left with a murmured good-night.

The following night they had their coffee and tea together. She told him about Carolyn. "And your wife?" she asked. "Any news?"

"It won't be long now." He seemed to drift away. "I'm sorry," he said finally. "I have forgotten my manners. My name is Brad Pierce."

"Jenna Sorrel. Do you work nearby?"

"I own a pharmaceutical company on Route 128."

Though he did not elaborate, Jenna made the connection at once: Pierce Pharmaceuticals was one of the largest in the world.

It was Jenna's turn to tell something about herself. When she mentioned the Sanctuary, she saw a flicker of interest in the blue eyes.

"You might want to get in touch with the Pierce Foundation," Brad said. "We fund a lot of charities and causes."

"Thank you. We depend on donations and grants to keep afloat—but somehow there's never enough to help everyone who needs it."

He nodded, as if he'd heard the story before. "The foundation was really Pat's idea," he explained. "This is the kind of thing she'd support one hundred percent." He sighed. "I need to get back upstairs. It was nice meeting you. I'm serious about contacting the foundation."

"Thanks. It was nice meeting you, too."

The next night, to her disappointment, Brad Pierce was not at his spot in the cafeteria. Odd how she had come to expect him. Something must have happened, she thought, but feeling it would be intrusive to inquire, she simply went home.

THE Boston *Globe* devoted a half page to Patricia Bowman Pierce's obituary. The accompanying photograph showed an attractive woman with a trusting smile. No children, Jenna noted. How sad that must be for Brad.

Though her appointment book was crammed with obligations, Jenna took the time to write him a note. "We don't really know each other, but my thoughts and my sympathy are with you today. If there's anything I can do to ease your pain, please let me know."

In the days that followed, she thought often of Brad, wondering how he was coping with his loss, remembering the tenderness with which he spoke of his wife, the love that was there in his face for all the world to see. When a white vellum envelope from B. Pierce arrived, she was oddly disappointed that it contained only a conventional thank-you note—polite but brief.

Well, what did you expect? she chided herself. Why should he remember a few brief conversations in a hospital cafeteria? This isn't like me, she thought, this feeling of unfinished business with a near stranger who has just lost his wife.

The feeling gradually faded in the turmoil of her own life. There was Karim, who would soon be starting his freshman year at Harvard. And there was the loss of hope for Carolyn. Her mother could not bring herself to request the removal of life-support systems and was moving her to a private facility in Connecticut.

Meanwhile, Jenna sent a proposal to the Pierce Foundation. The women's shelter was running out of room, and an excellent new space was about to come open in the neighborhood. The Sanctuary had taken a ninety-day option. Would the Pierce Foundation help?

In response she received a formal letter from the foundation's executive secretary requesting detailed information on the new space. Jenna sent the documentation, the money came, and construction on the Patricia Bowman Annex began. That was all there was to it.

I could call him, Jenna thought, thank him personally. But wasn't it obvious that he didn't want that kind of contact? She let it go.

Yet when Brad did call—a full five months later—she was so thrown off-balance that she began to babble. "We're all so very grateful. We'll be opening the Bowman Annex in a few weeks—"

"You're entirely welcome," he cut in. "But what I've called about is to ask you if you'd like to have dinner with me Friday evening."

"A date?" she blurted, wishing the moment she heard her own words that she could yank them back out of the phone.

He laughed. "Yes," he said. "I suppose that's what it is."

JENNA ended up in the most expensive boutique on Newbury Street spending an outrageous sum of money on the kind of outfit she hadn't bought in years—a creamy gabardine suit that lightly caressed the contours of her body.

They met at Locke-Ober on Winter Place, with Brad apologizing for not picking her up and Jenna assuring him she didn't mind.

"But I mind. I'm an old-fashioned guy—like this place," he said, indicating the dark-paneled woodwork, the traditional elegance of the private room he'd reserved. "But my meeting ran so long, and I didn't want to just keep you waiting, so . . ."

A tuxedo-clad waiter hovered discreetly at Brad's elbow. "Shall I serve the wine, sir?"

Brad nodded. "I took the liberty of ordering ahead," he said to Jenna, "but if you'd prefer . . ."

"No," she said. "I like surprises."

Deftly the waiter served the meal: consommé, green salad, grilled game hen accompanied by a fine Côte de Beaune.

"I've passed this place dozens of times," Jenna said. "I never realized it was so . . . so quaint."

Brad smiled. "I brought my first important date here."

"Your wife?" Jenna asked.

He nodded. "We met in high school. And there was no more need to look around. I knew it and so did Pat."

"That sounds rather old-countryish."

"I told you—"

"Right." She laughed. "You're an old-fashioned guy." They continued talking over coffee—he reminiscing about his marriage and apologizing for boring her, she enjoying his memories and assuring him she wasn't the slightest bit bored.

"You never had children."

"No."

"And you didn't mind." Despite her years in America, Jenna still reacted as a Remali would, finding it remarkable that a man so desirable continued to love a woman who bore no children.

"We both minded. Very much. But Pat couldn't. Then we talked about all the needy children in the world. That's when we started the foundation. Pat traveled to Africa, to India, wherever kids were starving and in need of medical attention. She established group homes in places where kids were living on the streets."

"She sounds like a remarkable woman."

"Oh, yes." Brad's eyes glistened.

Jenna reached across the table and put her hand over his. The gesture felt right. Strange, she thought, to be drawn to a man *because* he had loved his wife. And yet not so strange; she knew that Brad's devotion to Pat gave testimony to his own capacity to love.

"MAY I kiss you?" he asked at Jenna's door.

"You *are* old-fashioned." But Jenna was charmed.

His lips brushed hers; his hand gently stroked her cheek. An undemanding caress but filled with promise.

SHE DISCOVERED THAT THEY had more in common than loss and loneliness. They loved the North End and the Isabella Gardner Museum, hated diets and much of what passed for modern art. But most important, they discovered they were easy in one another's company. The conversations, the silences they shared, seemed effortless.

Karim, now a Harvard scholar and at the flood stage of his Egyptophilia, showed Brad only a dry-ice politeness. But her son's disapproval no longer upset Jenna. It wasn't that she didn't care what he thought; it was that Jenna felt a rightness about her relationship with Brad.

She pushed aside fear and conscience, ignoring the nagging voice that reminded her that according to the laws of the United States and al-Remal, her rights to a relationship were limited in the first instance and nonexistent in the second.

How did I get along without him? Jenna wondered almost every time she looked into those blue, blue eyes.

"I have a house in Marblehead," he said one night. "Why don't you come up there with me for the weekend?"

"All right," she said, though she knew there was more ahead than a simple summer weekend at the beach.

JENNA marveled at the sprawling oceanfront Victorian with gingerbread woodwork, ornate plaster ceilings, and brass fixtures. "I love this place," she said. "It has a lot of character. Like you."

"I'm flattered. Is that a personal or a professional judgment?"

"Both." It was true. If she had ever been certain about anything, it was that Brad was one of those very rare individuals: a truly good person. Which made her feel miserable about deceiving him. "You seem very much at home here," she observed.

"When I was growing up, we spent every summer here; lots of weekends, too. I always felt that only good things happen here." Brad squeezed her hand. "I thought you might feel that way, too."

I wish, she thought, I wish it were that simple. "Why me?" she asked. "Why not one of those suitable women Boston seems to be full of?"

The blue eyes twinkled. "Because you're a good listener. Because you're beautiful through and through. Because you seemed to care about me when we were just strangers. Because"—he paused—"Pat would have liked you."

They made love that night in a big feather bed, a candle casting flickering shadows on the walls. As Brad caressed her, murmuring endearments and promising to love her forever, she gave herself without fear or hesitation. It was like coming home.

"I WANT to marry you," he said as they snuggled together. "It's going to happen sooner or later, so why waste time?"

Jenna was speechless, joy and dread intermingling. Joy that he loved her. Dread at what she would have to say.

"I've learned how precious life is," he continued. "Losing Pat, realizing how quickly it can all slip away."

"But we don't really know each other well," she protested weakly.

"That's what the next fifty years are for. Because I want to know all about you. I want to know where you go when you get so quiet."

"But I—"

"Hush," he said, gently placing a finger against her lips. "You don't have to explain anything. Not until you're ready. But I want to be with you, Jenna, while you work through whatever it is that stands between us."

Like a parent comforting a child who has nightmares, Brad spoke eloquently and persuasively. But in the end, it didn't matter. His proposal touched her heart—and broke it into a million pieces.

Because Jenna had to say no.

Mirages

THE little room off the main lobby of the al-Remal International Airport was clean and not uncomfortable, but there was no mistaking its function: It was a cell. Waiting for the self-important man with the familiar name to return, Laila, like many prisoners, could hardly believe that this was happening to her.

It had started with a phone call.

David Christiansen was a new force in Laila's life—a force and an anchor. She was beginning to believe that he was the one man, besides her father, she could rely on.

She had been running on the edge for a long time when she met David. Recovering from the shock of rape—the outrage, the self-blame, and finally the psychological numbness—had been like going through a dark tunnel, and when she came out on the other side, it was hard to take anything very seriously. She lived one day and one night at a time. Parties and new faces carried her through to more parties and more new faces.

One day, for no reason that she could think of, she went down to the marina. One boat caught her eye: schooner-rigged, maybe sixty-five feet, lines like a seabird in flight. The *North Star*. While she admired the teak decks and sparkling fittings, a man emerged from a hatch and rummaged through a tool chest. He noticed Laila, gave her a sun-crinkled smile, and turned back to his work.

"She's beautiful," said Laila.

"Thanks. You sail?"

"Some. I'm not Columbus."

"Who is? Come aboard if you'd like. Dave Christiansen."

"Laila Sorrel." It was the name she chose when she didn't want a stranger to know who her father was.

He showed her around the *North Star*. The boat was his—"mine and the bank's, that is." He sailed day cruises and charters. Sailing was his life. "I grew up in Madison, Wisconsin. When I was fourteen, a kid I knew took me out on Lake Mendota in a little Sunfish. From then on, I never thought about doing anything else."

When it was time to go, she thanked him for the tour.

"Listen, I'm doing a group tomorrow, an overnight to Catalina. Want to come? As honorary crew, I mean. No charge."

Why not? "Sure," she said. "Sounds like fun."

They took twenty paying customers out to the beautiful little hill-ringed harbor of Avalon. Laila slept on deck under the stars. The next morning they ran before the wind back to the mainland, where Laila and David toasted a successful voyage with icy bottles of beer.

After that she was on the *North Star* often. David wasn't like the men in her social set. He was as calm, confident, and strong in a storm at sea as when he was holding her close.

On the night he told her he loved her, she told him who she really was.

"You're kidding," was his first reaction. When she convinced him that she wasn't, he laughed. "Well, it's not going to change my feelings any. Hey, I'm no dummy—I know what the whole world will think. But who cares? What matters is what you think."

"I don't think you're after my money, if that's what you mean."

He grinned. "Now there's a declaration of undying love if I ever heard one."

It was a few months later, on a midweek sail out to Santa Rosa, that he asked her to marry him. "You don't have to answer until you're ready," he added. "I just want you to know how I feel."

Two days after that she invented an excuse to go to France. She needed to remember what life had been like without David.

What she discovered was that life without him no longer existed. In the Louvre a seascape reminded her of the *North Star*. Over dinner with friends, she found herself wondering if she could prepare the same meal for David. At a party she wished he was there so that they could laugh later about the people's idiosyncrasies.

Whenever he called, it was a comfortable thing, as if she were just across town. Then, in one conversation, he asked as an afterthought whether she had her birth certificate in California.

"No. Why?"

"I just thought of it. You ought to get it while you're there. Who knows, you might want to get married someday."

She decided that she might as well have the birth certificate. It would be right here in the Paris house—in the wall safe where Malik kept personal papers. He was in Marseille, but she knew the combination from years of watching him open the safe. As she went through the sheaf of papers, some items tugged at her attention.

Photographs of Genevieve brought tears to her eyes. And here was a picture of her father as a boy. Who was the little girl with him? Funny, she looked a little like Jenna Sorrel. An odd letter from someone named Amira, extending condolences about Genevieve and adding that Amira herself was well. Karim was fine, too. Karim? Well, the name was common in the Arab world. Probably this Amira was some old flame of her father's, hoping to slip back into the picture after Genevieve's death.

Another photograph. A striking young woman in Remali dress. Oddly familiar. Where had Laila seen that face? Suddenly a chill ran up her spine. It was like looking in a mirror!

Laila spread the papers on her father's desk. There was no birth certificate, but she found a marriage license for her parents. They had married when she was four years old. And there was a ledger with a record of monthly cash payments to someone in al-Remal— a name Laila didn't recognize, in a town she'd never heard of. The first payment had been made the month she was born.

She looked up from the desk. On the facing wall was an oil portrait of her grandmother, Jihan. Laila had always studied the face, searching for signs of Jihan's tragic fate, but now she noticed the hands—and a ring, a star sapphire set in gold. She had seen that ring before. Jenna Sorrel had been wearing it.

Suddenly it all began to make sense. She wasn't who she thought she was. Her father had lied to her. Her mother, too—if Genevieve was, in fact, her mother. And Jenna—or whatever her real name was.

It was Jenna she decided to call. There was no answer at the apartment in Boston. Laila tried the office. Dr. Sorrel was out of town. No, she couldn't be reached. Laila hung up.

Among the documents in the safe was her Remali passport. As the child of a Remali citizen, she was a citizen herself, and her father had insisted on her having the passport. She was glad of it now. She booked a seat on the first flight to al-Remal.

THE man at the car rental agency looked at her with disgust and anger. Didn't she know it was illegal for a woman to drive here?

She wandered through the terminal. Men stared at her. One said, in heavily accented English, "Cover yourself, woman." She found a taxi and gave the driver the name of the town from the ledger.

"I will take you there," he said, "but not dressed as you are. Dressed as you are, I will take you only to the Hilton."

At the hotel, she instructed the driver to wait, then took a room and sent out for suitable clothes. A maid brought a horrible dark robe. "Show me how to wear this," Laila ordered.

The driver was still waiting. He nodded approvingly at her new garment. The village was an ugly place of poor mud-brick houses baking in the sun. Though Laila's Arabic was serviceable, it took both her efforts and the driver's to find the house that went with the name in the ledger.

Inside were a very old woman and one who appeared merely old.

The room was dark, and Laila instinctively pushed back the obscuring veil. The older woman screamed and rocked back as if about to faint. Then she made a sign against evil and scuttled out the door.

The other woman stared. "Are you who I think you are, young miss?" she asked Laila in Arabic.

"You tell me. Who am I?"

"You are the child I nursed for the first year of her life."

Laila's eyes widened with horror. "My mother?"

The woman seemed shocked.

"Are you the one to whom my father has been paying money?"

"No. That was Um Salih, gone to paradise five years now. Since then the money has gone to another aunt of mine—the woman you just saw."

"Why was she afraid of me?"

"She thought you were your mother come back from the grave."

"Um Salih was my mother?"

"No. So many questions, miss."

"I know I'm rude. I'm sorry. I need to know."

"Then I will tell you." She told the story bluntly and quickly. When it was over, Laila felt nearly as shaken as the old aunt.

"My mother was killed with stones because of me?"

"Because of the law and God's will, miss, not because of you." The old wet nurse had become increasingly anxious to have this sudden guest leave. "Miss, by coming here, you may have killed me. I must go somewhere far. Do you have money for me?"

Laila gave her every rial she had.

"You beware, too, miss. Here is not a good place for you. Not just this poor village, but al-Remal."

A small crowd had gathered outside. Laila drew her veil, and the driver forced their way through. Back at the hotel, Laila used a credit card for more cash and tipped the taximan exorbitantly.

From her room she called California. She needed David's calm voice. The marina manager told her he was on a weeklong cruise.

She reserved a morning flight to Paris, slept fitfully, and was at the airport two hours early. While she waited, two men who were obviously police approached. "Laila Badir?"

"Yes."

"Come with us, please." They took her to the little room, where she met the man with the oddly familiar name: Prince Ali al-Rashad.

"You are Laila Badir, and your father is Malik Badir?" he asked.

"Yes. What's all this about?"

"About violations of our law, Miss Badir." The prince, a short, slight, distinguished man, seemed pleased with himself.

"What violations? What laws?"

"That will become clear later."

After taking her passport, he left her alone in the room.

What had she done? Violated the dress codes? No, they wouldn't send a prince for that. Her visit to the village? But why should that bother anyone? None of it felt right. Laila waited for what seemed like hours. The guard brought her tea, but nothing to eat.

At last Prince Ali swept in again, and he smiled. "Your father's on his way. It's so very like him to come in person."

At last she realized where she had heard his name before. Malik had spoken it with anger and contempt. So this man was an enemy of her father's. "I demand to know why I'm being kept here."

He smiled again. "Let me explain. Long ago a crime was committed in our country—a crime that requires a male and a female. The female was caught and executed. The male was never found. For years I've had my suspicions as to the guilty party, and by your coming here and going where you went, you've allowed me to confirm them. So now we're awaiting the arrival of the second criminal."

So that was it: She was being used as bait to draw in her father.

One of the guards entered. "He's coming in, Highness."

"Good. Come with me, Miss Badir."

They went to an arrival bay with a view of the runways. On the tarmac a dozen plainclothes policemen waited. Laila recognized the flamboyant markings of her father's private 747 as it touched down.

"Always show, always extravagance," said Ali to an aide. "We'll confiscate the plane, of course."

The jet was taxiing toward the terminal. The plainclothesmen spread out in a semicircle.

A truck rolled onto the tarmac and pulled to a stop just as the jet did. Soldiers piled out of the truck and formed a line facing the plainclothesmen.

"What is this?" said Ali.

"I don't know, Highness," said one of his aides.

From behind them a group of military men approached.

"General, what is all this?" Ali demanded of their leader.

"Your Highness, I am ordered by the king to escort this woman to that aircraft."

"The king!" Laila saw the prince's lips tighten with rage.

"This way, mademoiselle," said the general. He led her down a ramp to the waiting 747. An attendant sealed the door behind her. The pilot had never cut the engines, and the plane was moving immediately.

Laila saw Malik coming toward her, his face a sculpture of fatherly concern. As he tried to hold her, she half responded, half pushed him away. "Oh, Papa," she heard herself saying, "I hate you!"

IN THE terminal, Ali was on the secret phone line to the palace. His brother Ahmad—the king since their father's death—answered.

"I demand an explanation, brother," fumed Ali. "I've been humiliated here, and a criminal has been allowed to go free."

Ahmad's tone was dry. "You are too eager in your duty sometimes, brother. Do you remember the Mirages? We wanted those planes badly, and a certain individual helped us to get them. And in a year or two, God willing, he will help us to buy some American F-14s. So I do not wish him to be interfered with."

The phone clicked dead. In the distance Ali could hear the roar of the 747 as it began its takeoff run.

Truth

THE thump of the plane's tires on a runway woke Jenna. The red-haired man sat across the aisle watching her.

"Sleep well, Princess? Get you something? A cup of coffee?"

"No, thank you."

The sunlight was blinding as they stepped from the jet. The surroundings confirmed Jenna's fears: a private airstrip in the desert. A limousine was waiting.

The redhead opened the back door for her, then climbed into the front. "Off we go," he said cheerily. They sped along a two-lane highway. There was something distinctly off-kilter about the whole scene. The desert itself didn't look right—not the sand, nor the scraggly plants. And now ahead, there were big American-style ranch houses. Could al-Remal have changed so much?

She turned to the red-haired man. "What is this? Where are we?"

"Palm Springs, California, Princess."

She felt light-headed. The whole thing had the aura of a dream.

"That's his humble abode straight ahead," said the red-haired man, nodding toward an enormous contemporary wood-and-glass house. They pulled through a gate and up a long drive.

A short, roly-poly man, obviously Remali, hurried down the steps to meet them.

"Oh, this is crazy," said Jenna. "Farid? Is that you, Farid?" She was out of the car, hugging her cousin for all she was worth. "This is too much. Where is Malik?"

"So soon you wish to leave me for your tiresome brother? Very well. This way."

He escorted her into the house. "In there, little cousin. Surprise him—he doesn't know you're here yet." He indicated a large room opening onto a vast patio and swimming pool.

Malik was standing with his back to her at the sliding glass door, looking out, apparently lost in thought. It had to be Malik, even though his black hair had gone to salt and pepper.

"Brother?"

He turned. "Little sister." He rushed to her, and they held each other close. Suddenly she was crying. So was he.

"When I doubt that God is merciful, let me remember this moment," Malik said fervently. "Ah, Amira."

She pushed him away. "But wait, but wait. Why did you drag me here like this? You scared me to death! Until ten minutes ago I thought Ali had caught me."

Malik frowned. "Ryan was supposed to tell you in the air. Maybe I should have given more specific orders. On the other hand, I didn't want him to tell you right away. I meant to teach you a lesson."

"You terrorized me on purpose? I should slap you, brother."

"If I can do this so easily," he said seriously, "others can, too."

She thought it over. "And exactly how did you find me?"

"It wasn't easy. Your letter— Sending it from Toronto was a master stroke. We spent years combing Canada and finding nothing, of course. Then Ryan—he's a private detective, in case you haven't guessed—said maybe we should try the United States."

"But how *did* he find me?"

"We had two main things to go on. One, of course, was that you had a son and that he still had the same name. The other was what you said about 'success in work I love.' I knew it had to be something that called for education—those books you were always reading, even as a kid. So Ryan started with the colleges, alumni publications, yearbooks, stuff like that. It was a massive job. I must have looked at a thousand pictures. No luck. Then he had the idea of finding out what professional conventions were in Toronto when the letter was mailed. There were a dozen, but the psychologists were the ones who seemed most likely. And *voilà!*" He laughed. "We went to Boston, and I spied on you from a distance. I knew it *was* you—something in the way you walk, more than anything else. That was two years ago."

"Two years! Then why did you wait till now?"

"Something told me to wait. She's been hiding for this long, I thought. She must have a reason. But now things have changed."

"What do you mean? What's happened?"

He waved a hand. "Later. Relax now. You must be tired."

"I slept well enough, thanks to your man Ryan." She realized that she was staring at the empty sleeve. "Your poor arm, Malik. I saw the Sandra Waters interview. I felt so . . . I don't know. I just wanted to take care of you."

His dark eyes smiled. "The usual reaction. Don't worry, baby sister, it hasn't cramped my style. Dr. Kissinger was wrong: Power isn't the ultimate aphrodisiac; pity is. The maternal instinct. I was never able to excite it before. Now I can hardly shut it off."

"Idiot," she said hugging him again. "Dear idiot."

"One piece of bad news," he said quietly. "Father died."

"Oh, no!" A terrible wave of guilt swept over Jenna. "Oh, Malik, he never knew that Karim and I were alive."

"Yes, he did. When he was near the end, I told him what I could. Ah, but Amira, how I wish you had come to me for help. Why did you go to the Frenchman instead? And what went wrong?"

She told him as much as she dared. Even now she feared igniting a vendetta against Ali, a fight that Malik could only lose. She described the murder in Alexandria and told the story of Philippe's help and heroism. When she had finished, Malik sat quiet for a moment, reflexively rubbing the empty sleeve.

"This makes a great difference," he said at last. "I had come to hate Philippe. As for Ali, I knew about his preferences, of course. But of this killing—nothing. I'm glad to know of it. It may be useful someday." He leaned forward. "Listen carefully, baby sister. You can't hide much longer. Ali's known for some time that you and Karim are alive. And he's been searching for you. It's only a matter of time until he finds you, just as I did. The question is, what will he do then?"

"I don't know. For years I assumed he'd take Karim and have me killed. Or drag me back to al-Remal to be tried for stealing his son. But to tell the truth, I don't know. It's all gone on for so long."

"All right, then. Let me give you my ideas. First, you and Karim could live with me, under my protection."

"But I have my own life, brother. I wouldn't want to give it up. I don't think Karim would either."

"That leads us to the second option: What if we go public with the story? Our friend Ali has very serious political ambitions. Once the truth comes out, can he afford to let anything happen to you?"

"Malik, we're talking about Ali. Who knows what he might do?"

He grimaced. "Of course nothing's certain. But believe me, Amira—Jenna—you're going to have to make some decisions soon. Just promise me that you won't disappear again."

"Don't worry. I couldn't go through that again."

He nodded, then smiled. "You'd probably like a shower, maybe even a swim. You'll find some fresh clothes in your room."

As he ushered her from the room, she noticed a piece of furniture that took her instantly back to childhood. "Father's chess table."

"Yes."

The table was a masterpiece of inlaid wood in intricate geometric patterns. "It's smaller than I remember it but just as beautiful," she said. As she spoke, she idly opened the table's drawer. Instead of chess pieces, it held a squat black revolver.

She looked at her brother in alarm. He gently pushed the drawer shut. "Unfortunately," he said with his most charming smile, "the games I play these days can be rather dangerous."

AFTER lunch Jenna, Farid, and Malik lounged by the pool. At least Jenna lounged: Farid jumped to answer the poolside phone every few minutes. Sometimes he handed it to Malik; more often he gave orders himself. Obviously, her cousin was her brother's top aide.

She still felt as if she might be dreaming. After the long years on her own, her old life buried deep, how utterly strange, yet familiar, to be with the boys of her childhood.

"I need your advice about Laila," said Malik.

Jenna summoned her courage for a confession. "Did you know that I'd seen her?"

"I found out later. I kid Ryan about it. The great detective is looking all over the continent, and my little girl has already found you."

"I knew I should stay away, not just for my safety but for hers— and yours. But when I saw her, I couldn't help myself."

"Of course, of course." Malik's soft smile seemed to say, How could anyone not love my Laila? Then the smile faded. "You know about what happened to her?"

"I know she was raped."

"Yes. It was not that long after Genevieve was killed. She hasn't really been the same since."

"I should have done something. But when she left New York—"

"It's not your fault. I blame myself. For everything." His hand clenched. "She wasn't even going to tell me. She was afraid I would judge her."

"It's a common reaction to rape. The victim feels that the attack has made her worthless and that others will think so, too."

"I'm sure you're right. I considered bringing charges, but the prosecutor told me how the lawyers would blame Laila. I couldn't expose her to that." Malik was silent for a long moment. "It's interesting," he finally said. "A few months later the boy was caught with four kilos of cocaine and a large amount of unexplained cash. Right now he's serving about the same sentence he would have gotten for what he did to Laila. Justice, wouldn't you agree?"

Jenna wasn't sure what she was hearing. She decided not to ask.

"Not that it helped Laila," Malik continued. "Her eyes—the light was gone from them. That's when she came out here. I built this place"—he waved his arm at the house—"so I could be near her if she needed me.

"Then she became one of these wild California kids. Every night a party, just drifting—I couldn't stop her. But then she met this young man, and everything changed again." He told her about David and how, slowly, love had brought Laila back from the edge.

Jenna had a dreadful feeling that she knew where this was going. "Don't tell me he dumped her."

"What? Oh, no. What happened was that she found out the truth. About me. About you. About her real mother. About herself." He recounted Laila's discoveries in Paris and her journey to al-Remal.

"My God," said Jenna when the reality sank in. The knowledge that one's mother was not one's mother would traumatize anyone.

"Ali will pay for his treatment of my daughter. I swear it," Malik was saying angrily, still caught up in the scene at the airport. He sat silent for a moment, visibly working to calm himself. "When I got her out, we had a terrible scene. Right on the plane. I had to admit the truth about her mother. I thought she'd storm off to her fiancé. But she's cut him off as well, claims he's just another liar like the rest of us. And instead of running away as I feared, she shuts herself in her room like a hermit."

"She's here now? In this house?"

"Oh, yes. She sleeps all day, sits up all night."

Jenna shuddered. This was chillingly reminiscent of Jihan.

"I'm hoping," Malik concluded, "you'll be able to do something."

A deep breath. "What have you told her about me?"

"Just that you are indeed my sister, who vanished long ago and let everyone think she was dead. Which is basically the truth. Of course, to her, you are a liar, too."

"I'll do what I can," Jenna said, "but don't look for a miracle."

THE woman who opened the bedroom door bore little resemblance to the fresh-faced girl Jenna had rescued in Saks. Laila was only in her mid-twenties, but she looked aged, tired—very much like Jihan in her last days.

"Well, look who's here. My secret friend."

The little flare of bitterness encouraged Jenna: Where there were living emotions, even negative ones, there was hope. "Yes, it's me. And I *am* your friend, as well as your aunt. I'm sorry I didn't tell you the last part. I didn't think I could. Maybe someday you'll let me tell you my reasons."

"I don't want to hear them."

A mechanical response, but the choice of words was significant. Jenna would make notes as soon as she could. She had decided to stay, at least until she found a suitable therapist for her niece. "I'll come again tomorrow, Laila. Think about what you'd like to talk about. I'll tell you anything you want to know."

For much of the next day Jenna called patients, rescheduling some, turning others over temporarily to colleagues.

As she punched in the 617 area code, Jenna thought of Brad. Call him? But what could she say? She couldn't tell him the truth.

That afternoon Laila was even deeper in her shell.

"All right," said Jenna, "I'll do the talking. I'll tell you all about Amira Badir." And she did.

The next day she contacted a Los Angeles psychiatrist highly recommended by several colleagues in Boston. She explained the situation and liked the man's analysis of it. They agreed that the best prospect lay in getting Laila's approval for starting therapy.

That afternoon Laila was still uncommunicative but seemed to be waiting for Jenna to begin. Jenna took a chance. "Would you like to hear about the woman who gave you birth? She was my best friend." And she went through it all, including, as gently as possible, the last night and day of the older Laila's life.

When it was over, Laila went into the bathroom and vomited. When she returned, pale and shaking, she said, "Do you know I went there, to al-Remal? I found this woman who had nursed me. A poor woman. Shriveled up early, like so many of the people in that village. And do you know what I was thinking? I was thinking, Is this my real mother? Did my father—" She broke off.

"Maybe you'd like to tell me how you feel," said Jenna.

"A shrink for sure," Laila said, her face contorted. "How do you think I feel? I feel like one of those stupid toys you knock down that bounce back up. 'Your mother's dead, Laila, only she wasn't your real mother—but that one's dead too. Oh, by the way, that woman you met, your so-called friend, she's really your aunt.' Damn you. Damn you all!" She was punching the bed with her fist. "Knock me down. But this time I won't get up."

You're already up, thought Jenna with relief. Now the job is to keep you up.

Over the next few days Laila gradually came out of hiding. One night she appeared at dinner. The next, she put on makeup. She hinted that she would be willing to talk with someone, if Jenna thought it a good idea. There even came a moment when she took the role of therapist: "Are you going to tell your son the truth?"

It was Jenna's turn to be evasive. "I'm not sure the time is right. You know my story. Who I was. Who I'm still married to."

"Tell him now. There has to be a way. He's your son. You can't keep lying to him forever."

Jenna hadn't thought about forever; it was a luxury she had left behind long ago.

HATS. Dozens of hats, one more outrageous than the next. "Pick one," Malik told Jenna and Laila, "and then you can find an outfit to go with it. We're going to the races—opening day at Del Mar."

It was a celebration—a kind of coming-out party for Laila, but also a big day for Malik, who had shipped a number of his top thoroughbreds to the California track for the racing season.

They helicoptered down with Farid and one of Malik's regular bodyguards. The scene at the racecourse was like a California version of Ascot. Women costumed as if for an Easter parade promenaded with men dressed in designer sportswear.

In the fifth race Jenna and Malik sentimentally backed a desperate long shot named Desert Exile, and when the beast romped home ahead of the field, they jumped and hugged like children.

"Telephoto, boss," said the bodyguard. Jenna saw a photographer aiming a long lens at them from down in the stands.

"Don't worry about it," said Malik to the guard. "It's a free country, they tell me." But Jenna lowered the broad brim of her hat.

The next day at breakfast a grinning Malik dropped a popular tabloid on the table. A front-page photo showed Jenna looking fearfully into the camera, tugging furtively at her hat brim, her arm around Malik's neck. The headline read FEMINIST DOC IS MEGABUCKS MALIK'S PALM SPRINGS PLAYMATE in bold type.

She felt violated, yet at the same time had to laugh. After countless excuses for avoiding book-jacket photos and television interviews, this. And what did it matter? If Malik was right, a picture wouldn't make much difference in whether or not Ali found her.

That night she made her habitual call to her answering machine, hoping for word from Karim. To her surprise she heard Brad's voice. The message was brief. "I see that I've misjudged you. Goodbye, Jenna." At first she thought he was referring to her answer to his marriage proposal. Then she realized that he must have seen the tabloid story.

She wanted to catch the first plane home, tear out the answering-machine tape, and throw it into the fireplace—and do the same to Brad. How dare he jump to conclusions like that.

It took hours for her anger to cool, but when it did, the chill went deep. She didn't want to lose him. She called his home. A servant, after asking her name, informed her that Mr. Pierce was unavailable. His receptionist told her the same thing six times the next morning.

Jenna's anger reasserted itself. All right, if that was the way he wanted it, she could live without him. Couldn't she?

SHE needed to go home. Laila was in competent hands. There was little more Jenna could do except be a good aunt. Laila had even asked Jenna's opinion about writing a letter of apology to the banished boyfriend.

"Don't apologize. Explain. Tell him how you felt then and how you feel now. If he's the man you think he is, he'll understand."

Soon, too, Karim would be home from Greece, a new school year beginning.

And there was Brad. Surely she could find a way to make him understand. Her words to Laila echoed in her thoughts.

"For you, cousin," said Farid, bringing a phone.

It had to be Brad. "Hello?"

"Whoa, Mom. Way to go!"

"Karim! Where are you?"

"Athens. You're all over the papers here, Mom. I thought you told me you didn't know Malik Badir."

"It's—it's a long story. I knew him a long time ago but haven't seen him for years. Listen. Don't believe what you read in the papers. Things . . . aren't what they seem."

"Uh-huh." He sounded vaguely disappointed. "Well, he sounds like a pretty impressive guy. I'd like to meet him. Look, Mom, I gotta go. Love you."

How ironic. Her son finally approved of a man in her life—and the man was her brother. It was like a French farce.

FINALLY, after discussing her plans with her brother and Laila, she booked a flight to Boston for the following day.

Malik was on his way to the track. "Come with me," he invited. "We'll make a little good-bye party for your last day."

"No, thanks, brother. I don't want to end up on the front pages again. Go and enjoy yourself. I'll relax by the pool."

He departed with Farid, still inviting her even as the door closed.

She put on a bathing suit, called to the kitchen for a cooler of lemonade and snacks, and found a novel with absolutely no redeeming value. Thus armed, she stretched out in the sun.

It was quiet with Malik gone, Laila upstairs. The house staff wasn't in evidence. Some of the bodyguards would have gone with Malik and Farid, of course. Still, that left half a dozen others. Normally she would have spotted one or more of them checking on her by now.

Ah, there was one of them now, at the sliding door. Squinting in the brilliant sun, she couldn't see just who it was. Coming toward her. Malik must pay his men very well—look at that suit. A new man? She still didn't recognize him. Smaller than the others. Older too, gray at the temples. Oh, no. It couldn't be. Please, God, no.

"Hello, Amira. Don't freeze like a rabbit before a snake."

"What do you want, Ali? You don't belong here. When Malik comes back—"

"I won't be here that long, my dove. And no one else will interrupt our little chat either. I've seen to that. But don't look so frightened. I'm not going to hurt you. Not today. But someday,

Amira—maybe when you're just walking down the street. Think about it. Will you be able to run and hide again?"

"Just go away. Please."

"Ah, beg. I like that. And my son, he'll go with me."

"Don't you dare touch him!"

"I won't have to. Do you think he'll stay with you, whore, after he finds out how you've lied to him?"

"Yes." It was all she could say.

"Do you know how I found out about you? Your picture in that trash paper. Brown hair is black in a black-and-white photo. And green eyes are just dark eyes. And of course, you were with that thieving brother of yours. It all became clear to me in a flash."

Suddenly Malik's voice came from the house, calling to someone. "No. The horse had an inflammation of some kind. Had to scratch him. They got me on the car phone." In a moment he was outside. "Who's this, little sister? You!" He strode straight to Ali and slapped him backhanded. "How dare you enter my house? Out!"

Ali reeled with the blow. Then, with a snarl, he was on Malik like an animal. And suddenly Malik, with only one arm, was down, gasping for breath as Ali's hands clenched his throat.

Even at that moment, and always after, Jenna knew that she could have screamed for help. Someone would have been there in seconds. But pictures were flashing through her mind: Alexandria, the hospital in al-Remal, Ali's sneer just now when he threatened her life.

She didn't scream. She dashed inside, took the revolver from the chess table, pressed the safety lever, walked back to where Ali was choking Malik, aimed at her husband's back, and fired three times.

After that everything was confusion. Malik was holding the gun, and people were swarming: Farid; bodyguards; the chef; and two of Ali's men, who had to be disarmed themselves. And Laila.

Malik, his voice a hoarse croak, was telling everyone, "He tried to kill me. I had to shoot." Then, while someone called the police and a bodyguard hopelessly tried CPR on Ali, Malik took Jenna aside. "I'm going to handle this. No, not a word. Do you remember how I swore to protect those I love? You owe me this chance."

She was too numb to answer. Two questions battled in her mind. What would this do to Laila? And what would she tell Karim?

Retribution

FROM the first, things went badly for Malik. At his arraignment bail was denied on the ground that his resources would make it easy for him to leave the country. Almost daily the media trumpeted some damaging aspect of Malik's past—the espionage case, questions about the circumstances surrounding Genevieve's death. Every story mentioned his vast wealth; the message was that here was a man who considered himself above the law. Well-timed leaks from the office of the district attorney, who was in a close race for re-election, fed the fire.

By contrast Ali was portrayed as a Remali national hero and a friend of America, a royal prince with progressive ideas, who might one day have been king. His grieving widow and children were interviewed. The story of Amira's disappearance and presumed death was retold with sympathy for Ali: He had known tragedy in his foreshortened life.

Malik's defense was straightforward. He had come home unexpectedly and found Ali. They exchanged words, and Ali attacked him. Malik managed to fight his way free. Ali fell to his knees, his back to Malik, but his movements made Malik believe he was reaching for a weapon. Malik drew his gun and began pulling the trigger.

He could offer support for this version of events. First, Ali undeniably was in Malik's home, apparently uninvited. Second, medical evidence showed that Malik had indeed been badly choked. On the other hand, no weapon had been found on Ali. And more damning than anything else, three bullets in the back didn't look like self-defense, even for a one-armed man.

The district attorney, making a great show of fair-mindedness in a televised news conference, announced that he would not seek an indictment for first-degree homicide, only for second-degree. That was the charge the grand jury brought.

People v. *Malik Badir* would not be a long, drawn-out proceeding. Malik not only admitted to the shooting but ordered his two celebrated lawyers to use no delaying tactics. The questioning of witnesses would be brief. In fact, no one claimed to have seen the struggle or the killing. All of Malik's employees had been elsewhere than at the pool. His daughter had been asleep. His houseguest, Dr. Jenna Sorrel, had been in the library, searching for a book, when she heard the shots. She knew nothing else of the matter.

That was the story Malik had whispered to her in the minutes before the police arrived.

"Promise me you'll tell them that, sister. This can't hurt me. An inconvenience. But it could ruin your life—and Karim's."

It was so simple, and she was terrified and in shock. Then, once she had lied the first time, she felt as if there was no going back. Through hours of questioning by detectives, she never wavered.

Now she was wavering. She had killed Ali. And she was at last free of the fear that had haunted her for so many years. Why should Malik risk ruin? Just tell the truth. Let it all out. It was like standing on the edge of a cliff, wondering what it would be like to . . . No, she said to herself. A crazy idea. What about Karim? The truth would send him out into life branded—the man whose mother had killed his father, in a case that would be remembered for decades.

She was a wreck. She had never before taken a tranquilizer, but now she downed Valium regularly. Sleep was a stranger.

She couldn't go back to the Palm Springs house. She would see the bloodstains by the pool, even if they had disappeared. She took a hotel room for the duration of the legal proceedings. The staff were accustomed to patrons who expected privacy, and they kept reporters at a distance. Outside, one of Malik's bodyguards took over.

Her practice had all but disintegrated. Ironically, her remaining patients now sustained her more than she them. One offered to fly out and help in whatever way she could.

Jenna visited Malik daily—he was unfailingly cheerful and optimistic—and Laila, whom Malik had forbidden to come to the courtroom or the jail. She conveyed messages to Farid and the lawyers. During the voir dire she studied prospective jurors closely, and after each session she reported to the lawyers.

They were both superstars: one a tiny, tough New Yorker named Rosalie Silber; the other a tall, tanned, white-maned Texan, J. T. Quarles. Cordially jealous of each other, they nevertheless worked together like a championship doubles team.

Toward Jenna their attitude at first was one of amiable condescension. They had their own experts for juror analysis. But there came a moment when the Texan turned to the New Yorker and said, "You know, Rose, there's a lot in what Dr. Jenna here says. Maybe we should take another look at number fifty-four."

"I concur in both statements," Rosalie replied.

It felt good to contribute. At the same time, Jenna had never felt worse. What did it matter, when with a few words she could set Malik free? It was as if there were two Jennas: one a loving sister and dedicated professional, the other a lying hypocrite.

The first days of the trial did nothing to ease her mind. The forensic evidence was literally sickening. Photos of Ali's body with blood everywhere. Close-ups of the wounds. The shocked looks on the jurors' faces told her how they saw it.

The district attorney, Jordan Chiles, was trying the case himself. It would bring priceless publicity for his reelection campaign. Tanned, athletically trim, he could easily have been one of those slightly over-the-hill actors who turn up at every casting call.

"In your expert experience," he asked a noted Los Angeles homicide detective, "how would you characterize the shooting?"

"Execution-style," the man replied.

No! Jenna wanted to shout. You don't know what you're talking about. Yet, in a way, hadn't it been an execution? She tried to make herself answer that question. She couldn't.

After a few pro forma witnesses, the prosecution rested. The point of the state's presentation was not that Malik had committed the killing, but that he had done so in a way that precluded self-defense.

But now Rosalie Silber of Manhattan and J. T. Quarles of Houston had their turn. They called a few of Malik's employees to establish that Malik had not been expecting Ali and indeed had not expected to be at home that fateful afternoon.

Jenna was not brought to the stand. Malik had ordered Rosalie and J.T. not to call her for the defense, and the district attorney's office had decided that she would only create sympathy for the defendant.

The key witness was Malik himself. He performed impressively. The empty sleeve was eloquent in itself, and when Malik explained the reason for it and why he carried a gun, two jurors nodded in agreement. Later, under cross-examination, Malik never lost control. Yet as good as Malik was at deception, he wasn't good at plain lying. Jenna knew the signs. Could the jury recognize them, too?

Back at the hotel, she opened the vial of Valium, then closed it. She needed to think clearly. Once before, she had saved herself through a deception, and it had cost the life of someone she loved.

She could just stand up in court. But no, they would shut her up, and no one would believe whatever she managed to blurt out. She could call a press conference. *They* wouldn't shut her up. But there was Karim to think about.

Whatever she did or didn't do would be wrong—and she had done so much wrong already.

There was a tap at the door.

"Someone wanting to see you, boss," said the bodyguard. "From Boston. Says you know him. Here's his card."

But Brad was already standing behind him in the hall.

"Yes, it's okay," Jenna heard herself saying. "Yes, it's fine."

The guard closed the door behind Brad, who had never taken his eyes off Jenna.

"I had to see you," he said. "I couldn't leave things the way they were. I don't care what else has happened, Jenna."

"Shut up," she said. "Just hold me. Just hold me."

The world became his arms around her.

"I love you, Jenna. I'll always love you. Always."

"I love you, too."

SHE had dozed but now was wide-awake. What time was it? It had to be long past midnight. She curled close to Brad's strength and warmth. She ran a finger lightly down his chest. He stirred.

"What is it, love?" he whispered.

"I have to tell you something."

"Tell me."

She told him everything.

Now and then he interjected a question, a word of anger or astonishment. "What you've been through," he said when she finished.

She fought down a quick little spasm of sobs. "I've got to do something. What would you do?"

He stroked her hair lightly, thoughtfully. "I don't know what I'd do," said Brad after a moment, "much less what you ought to do. I like to think that I'd tell Karim, then tell the world. But whatever you decide to do, I'm with you. If you want to keep the lid on forever, I'll help you hold it down. If you want to break it open, I'll be beside you all the way."

"You think I should tell, don't you?"

"Yes," he finally said. "For your brother and for yourself."

Again that feeling of standing on a cliff. The thought came to her that it was now or never.

"What time is it in Boston?"

Brad squinted at his watch in the darkness. "A little after six."

She switched on a lamp and reached for the phone. Her hands, she thought distractedly, were freezing. Karim answered on the seventh ring, his voice fuzzy with sleep.

"Mom? Is something wrong?"

"No. Well, yes. Karim, sweetheart, can you come out here? I—I need to tell you something. It's very important."

"So tell me. That's what phones are for."

"All right," she said, "but this isn't going to be easy for either of us." She took a deep breath. "Karim, darling, I'm your mother, but I'm not who you think I am, who other people think I am."

For the second time that night, she told the story.

As it slowly sank in, Karim began to interrupt. His pain and confusion were palpable—and infused with growing anger.

"You're telling me this guy, this prince, this creep that Malik killed was my father? Then what about Jacques?"

"I made him up. Please believe me, I did it for you."

"Believe you? How can I believe you? None of this is real."

"It's real, Karim, and there's more to it." She closed her eyes. "I killed him, son. Not Malik. I did it."

In the next few minutes she learned how her brother had felt on that plane taking Laila out of al-Remal. She would never forget the hatred Karim expressed. And nothing she said got through.

"How could you do this to me? How could you do it? How?"

The phone clicked violently. He was gone.

When the tears finally came, it seemed as if they would never stop. She felt Brad's arm across her shoulders, shrugged it off. No one could help her in this; no one could comfort her. Yet in all the

agony, there was something else—a feeling long forgotten, a mingling of exhilaration and fear that approached pure joy. She had
stepped off the cliff. Was she falling or flying?

MORNING spread colors slowly across the desert. Jenna, eyes still
red from crying, ordered breakfast for two.

"The lawyers say that they'll rest the case today, and the judge
will adjourn until tomorrow. I was thinking of calling a news conference after adjournment." She shivered. "But I don't want them
all screaming at me."

Brad looked at her quizzically, with a glint of amusement. "Are
you joking, Jenna? Maybe you're too close to this thing. You don't
realize how big it is. If you don't want to deal with a crowd of reporters, if you'd rather have a quiet hour with Dan Rather or Di-
ane Sawyer, all you've got to do is pick up the phone."

"I hadn't thought of that. You're sure?"

"I'm sure."

"I've got it. You'll think I'm crazy, but . . ." She went to the
phone and punched a number.

"Mr. Manning's in conference. May I take a message?"

"Tell him it's Jenna Sorrel."

Barry Manning was on the line in four seconds. "Doc, great to
hear from you! You've been a busy little bee since I saw you."

She told him what she wanted.

"Today? Wait a minute, Doc. Aren't you in California?"

"Yes. I want to do it here. Today."

"Yikes! Doc, I gotta ask: This is big, right? I mean, you didn't
just suddenly decide to push a book or something."

"It's big. I'm told it's very big."

"Then you got it." He shouted instructions to someone. "Book
the first flight to LAX. Scratch that. Charter one. Half an hour." He
sounded slightly winded when he came back on. "Don't move a
muscle, Doc. I'll be there."

She hung up and breathed a deep sigh. Then she was laughing.

"What?" said Brad.

"My deep, dark secrets," she said. "I've been hiding them my
whole life, and now suddenly I'm babbling them over and over like
a crazed parrot. Who says God doesn't have a sense of humor?"

THE DEFENSE RESTED AT FIVE minutes to noon, and the court stood adjourned until the following morning. Jenna had a brief moment to spend with Malik before he was escorted back to his cell. For the first time, he seemed deflated.

"I didn't like the way they looked today," he told her, meaning the jury. "I may be in trouble."

"Don't worry, brother. It's going to come out fine."

Three hours later she went on the air with Barry Manning in a rented studio. He had brought video equipment as well as audio.

He introduced her without his accustomed brashness. Clearly he saw this as his graduation to the big time. "Dr. Sorrel tells me that she has something important to talk about, but she hasn't said what. The sensible thing for me to do is get out of the way and let you listen. So here's Jenna Sorrel."

An hour later she and Brad practically had to fight their way out of the studio. At the hotel, police ringed the entrance.

"It's okay," Brad said. "They're here to protect you—for now."

Redemption

THAT night the hotel was a castle under siege. Scores of reporters and hundreds of idly or malevolently curious citizens milled outside. At one point a helicopter hovered, roaring, a few yards from Jenna's window, a cameraman leaning from the door.

Jenna, completely drained, could barely focus on the TV, which was replaying the story in endless detail. From time to time she tried to reach Karim, without success. Brad took charge with an air of quiet command. His first task was to find Jenna a lawyer.

"That little lady's a pistol." J.T. laughed when Brad reached him. "Tell her we're holed up like in the Alamo over here, thanks to her. Tell her we love her, but we just can't represent her. Ever hear of a Boston fella name of Sam Adams Boyle? Hell of a trial lawyer."

Half an hour later Sam Adams Boyle was on retainer.

"He was watching your interview with Barry when I called," Brad told Jenna. "It was too late for the network news back east, but they were running excerpts on a special bulletin."

On the TV, Jordan Chiles was proclaiming the whole thing a desperate stunt and promising to carry forward the murder charge against Malik. Chiles looked a bit desperate himself, with the election barely a week away.

Moments later Malik called from jail. "Amira, why did you do it? Just another day or two. We were winning, I could feel it."

"I'm sorry, brother. I know you were doing it for me. But I just couldn't let you. And I had to stop lying sometime. For myself."

"Who answered the phone?" The protective big brother, even from behind bars.

"Brad Pierce. You'll meet him."

"Ah, baby sister, you've been holding out on me. Bring him to court tomorrow." Jenna could picture his mischievous smile. The man was irrepressible.

A CORDON of police lined the courthouse steps. As Brad hurried Jenna to the building, she was astonished to hear cheers from the crowd. A group of women on the sidewalk lifted signs that read WE'RE WITH JENNA.

Malik was seated with Rosalie and J.T. at the defense table. He turned to smile at Jenna, looked Brad over for a long moment, and nodded. The judge appeared and immediately summoned the defense lawyers and Jordan Chiles into his chambers. When they emerged a half hour later, J.T. was grinning broadly and Chiles was scowling.

The judge explained that at least two jurors had become aware of Jenna's interview with Manning. In his judgment their knowledge would have to be considered prejudicial. Therefore, he was declaring a mistrial. He gave the prosecution seventy-two hours in which to decide whether to file new charges.

Brad and Jenna left the courthouse by a side entrance. They didn't go back to the hotel. After first making sure no one was following, they headed west to the coast road. The house, in Laguna Beach, belonged to a friend of Brad's.

After the desert the chill moisture of the sea air was as refreshing as a waterfall. The timeless crashing of the waves was better than any tranquilizer. Jenna could almost imagine that she and Brad were back at Marblehead and that none of the rest of it had happened.

But her brother was still in jail, and there was the possibility that within a day or two she would be there herself. And there was the constant worry over Karim. She called everyone she could think of who might know where he was. She had called Josh and Jacqueline repeatedly, and was almost certain they were lying when they said they hadn't seen him, but there was little she could do about it.

Sam Adams Boyle arrived on their second day in Laguna Beach. He was a tough, red-faced, silver-haired southie. He was in time to watch Chiles concede that, because "new developments" made it unlikely that a prosecution of Badir could succeed "regardless of its merits," the state would not refile. As for Jenna Sorrel, the investigation was ongoing, and he would not comment on it.

"What does all that mean?" asked Jenna.

"Well, I met Mr. Chiles this morning. He was none too happy to see me, I assure you. I'm certain he means to charge you."

Jenna gripped Brad's hand.

Boyle noticed the gesture. "No fear. He's got as much chance of a conviction as I've got of winning the marathon. But he has to do something or lose his election."

"Let's say he brings charges," said Brad. "What next?"

"We go in and surrender. I'll try to arrange for her immediate release on recognizance or on bail." He frowned. "I'm a bit worried about that. Mr. Chiles will ask that bail be denied on the grounds that Ms. Sorrel's history of traveling on false documents makes her a risk to flee to avoid prosecution. A judge might very well go along."

"That means I'd go to jail?" asked Jenna.

"For a time, at least. It would be an injustice, and I'll do all I can to prevent it, but it may happen."

"For how long? Until the trial?"

"I sincerely doubt it. Mr. Chiles is going to lose his election. And I've taken the precaution of speaking with his opponent. I have the strong impression that she'll be more reasonable."

"And what if it goes to trial?" asked Brad. "What's our defense?"

"I'll know more about that after I've had a long talk with my client. But based on what I've heard, we've got classic self-defense or defense of the life of another. There's also the battered-woman angle." He looked at Jenna. "I don't know if you're aware of it, but you're quite the heroine out there for a lot of people."

That evening at dusk Jenna and Brad walked down to the ocean.

There were so many things to say that they found it hard to speak. The first stars were coming out when Brad finally broke the silence. "Jenna, this will be over soon. When it is, let's go away somewhere. The islands. A cottage in Ireland. You tell me."

"That sounds nice. But it's not over. I don't know what's happened with Karim. And I need to get back to work."

"We could make it a honeymoon. No one could blame us for taking time off for that."

She wanted with all her heart to say yes. She traced a pattern in the sand with her toes. "I love you. It's just—it's just too much right now." How could she explain? It wasn't just Karim or going back to work. It wasn't about marriage. It was about shooting a man to death. She didn't feel guilty, yet she knew she was. She could have screamed, that day at the pool; she could have run for help. But she had done something else entirely. Much of her life's work was devoted to healing the effects of violence. Yet when the choice had been hers, she had chosen violence.

"Whatever you decide," said Brad, hearing what had not been spoken, "just don't give Chiles any more ammunition. He'll use it to make you look like a murderer."

It was dark now, and cold. They headed back.

AT THE house, lights were blazing. On the deck Malik, Farid, J.T., and Rosalie were raising glasses. Jenna ran to embrace her brother. Farid joined in the hug. The lawyers wore the easy smiles of warriors whose battle was won.

In a corner Laila stood quietly with a handsome, weather-burned young man. "My friend David Christiansen," she said to Jenna. "We just stopped by to thank you."

"For what?"

"For telling the truth."

THE next day at noon Jordan Chiles went before the cameras to announce that a grand jury had indicted Amira Badir al-Rashad, alias Jenna Sorrel, on a charge of second-degree homicide.

Boyle called. "This is it. We're going in now. Otherwise Chiles is likely to show up with a television crew and handcuffs." He instructed them to meet him at a rest stop on the interstate.

From there they drove to the courthouse in Boyle's car. There was a crowd, police, trucks with satellite dishes, signs supporting Jenna. Chants. Cheers.

"I took the liberty of letting a few people know we were coming," explained Boyle. "All right now, we march in like we own the place."

Someone opened the car door, and Jenna stepped out to a surge of cheering from the crowd. Then she was racing for the courthouse door, with her hand in Brad's, Sam Adams Boyle hustling in front of them like the old fullback he undoubtedly was.

Epilogue

Aftermath

JORDAN Chiles's last important public achievement was to convince a judge that no bail should be set for the defendant in the case of *People* v. *Rashad*. Two days later he was overwhelmed at the polls by a thirty-three-year-old corporate lawyer and former public defender named Jennifer Faye Edmondson.

Sam Adams Boyle blasted Chiles in court and in the media for waging a vendetta against the Badirs. With much less sound and fury he opened negotiations with Jennifer Edmondson.

"It'll take a little time," he told Jenna, "but it's the only way—and the best way."

"How long?"

"Worst case, three months—that's when Edmondson takes office. Best case, if we can steamroll Chiles, three or four weeks."

"What then?"

"A plea of some kind. With luck, there won't be any more jail time. Even if there is, I can guarantee that it won't be much."

"That sounds good. Thanks, Sam."

"Just doing my job. So how are you holding up, kid?"

Jenna had to smile at "kid." Boyle had become distinctly avuncular as they had come to know each other. "I'm fine, Sam. Really."

The funny thing was that it was almost true. Unlike most new prisoners, Jenna didn't need to learn the trick of living one day at a time. She had lived that way before, in the women's quarters of the royal palace in al-Remal. True, in the palace she and the other women had access to every luxury, but psychologically the similarity was remarkable. When it came right down to it, the women in the palace had been prisoners, too.

The jail, at least the women's wing, wasn't especially grim. Essentially a small dormitory, it wasn't even crowded; Palm Springs was hardly a high-crime area. Most of the handful of inmates were single mothers who worked in minimum-wage jobs or survived on public assistance, very much like women Jenna had known at the free clinic in Boston. Their typical offense was shoplifting or writing bad checks. At first they treated Jenna like a celebrity. A housemaid named Latronia Parrish broke the ice.

"You that princess shot her husband?"

"Yes."

"What you shoot him for?"

"He was trying to kill my brother."

Latronia nodded. "What's it like bein' a princess?"

They all wanted to hear. After lights out, nudged along by a dozen questions, she began the story of her life. It went on for several bedtimes. They wept when she described the events in al-Masagin, gasped in disbelief about Alexandria, cursed the beating that had hospitalized Amira. By the time it had all been told, they treated her less as a celebrity and more with the respect due a survivor.

For all that, the loss of freedom was hard, and hardest of all was Jenna's inability to go to her son. Every day he was slipping further away from her—she could feel it—and there was nothing she could do. If only she could see him, talk with him, for just one moment. Wouldn't a word, a touch, be enough to make him remember, to change his heart?

MALIK was in his best mood of sunny optimism.

"Everything will work out, little sister, you'll see. With Karim, too. Maybe I'll find him and fly him out. You said he likes me."

Jenna was less certain. "A lot has changed for Karim, brother. Invite him if you like. But whatever you do, don't pull a stunt like you did with me."

He smiled guiltily.

"How's Laila?" asked Jenna.

"Fine." But he was suddenly more somber. "She'd like to see you again, you know, but I think she's nervous. And to be honest I've discouraged it. You know what a circus this thing has become."

"I agree. Please tell her it's okay."

"The truth is, I've suggested that she go back to France until this is over. I've talked with David about it. He'd go with her, at least part of the time." He smiled again. "I hate to admit it, but I like that young man. I think he's good for Laila."

Jenna felt a little better. One thing, at least, was working out. And it was a hopeful sign, too, that Malik and Laila were acting like father and daughter again. Not so long ago Laila had hated Malik— as Karim now seemed to hate Jenna.

Brad was in for the weekend as always, flying from Boston late Friday, returning late Sunday. Characteristically, he was more restrained than Malik in analyzing the Karim situation. "We knew it would be tough when we took this route. Karim was in a rebellious phase to begin with. It may get worse before it gets better—but it *will* get better. It's just going to take time. We need to prepare ourselves for the possibility that it may take a lot of time."

It was true, Jenna knew, but it wasn't enough. Even Brad's "I love you" as he rose to go wasn't enough—not here, not across a table in this harsh, sterile place, under cold fluorescent lights and the eyes of the guards. What she needed was his strong, gentle touch, his arms around her, his words whispered against her skin.

And she needed her son.

Then Jenna had an idea. She summoned Ryan, the redheaded detective. "Find Karim. Find him and talk with him. That's all. Just talk with him, find out what he's doing—how he's doing."

Ryan nodded. "Okay." He pulled out a notebook and pencil. "Give me the names of his friends—girlfriends especially. Addresses, phone numbers. Classes he was taking at school. Places he likes to hang out."

Jenna gave the best information she could.

"I'll go tomorrow," he said.

ONE look at Ryan's face told Jenna that she had been dreaming again, foolishly dreaming. "What happened?"

"I found him. That's the good news. It wasn't hard. He was

crashing at Josh Chandler's apartment. He let me in, very polite, but he didn't want to hear anything I had to say. He told me he'd made his plans and didn't intend to change them."

"What plans?"

Ryan looked straight at her, breaking the news. "He says he's going to al-Remal—permanently. He's just waiting for the paperwork to go through. Some confusion over his legal identity—supposedly some of his relatives, his father's people, are taking care of it. He said it wouldn't be more than a few days."

A few days. Her son would be lost to her in a few days.

"What did he say?" What did he say about me, she meant.

"He clammed up. Showed me the door. Politely, but there was no question I was being given the boot. I asked him to give it some thought, just take some time to think it over. He didn't even answer. I'm sorry, Jenna."

WITH Ryan's report Jenna's hope turned to desperation and what had been worry over Karim turned to torture. He was about to vanish from her life.

Then one evening the little television in the women's section brought the news that Karim al-Rashad, son of the victim and the alleged killer in the Ali al-Rashad case, had returned to his native land as an honored member of its royal family.

It was almost as if he had died. Jenna knew that she could never go to al-Remal, never. The other women, sensing her torment, tried to console her, but the pain was too deep.

Even the promise of freedom barely lifted her spirits.

"I believe we'll have bail fixed for you by Monday or Tuesday," Boyle told her with gruff satisfaction. "Ms. Edmondson is going to tell the court that her office intends to reduce the charge to involuntary manslaughter. If you plead guilty, she'll recommend a sentence of time served, probation, and community service. I recommend that you consider the offer very seriously. On the other hand, I happen to believe that you're innocent of any crime and that I can prove it in court. The decision is yours to make."

"I'll plead guilty," said Jenna. "I killed him. I didn't have to."

"Think about it for a day or two."

"No. I'm sure. Tell her today."

Boyle nodded and closed his briefcase. "You'll be out of here by this time Tuesday," he said.

The next few days were longer than all the others that had gone before. Jenna couldn't drive the past from her mind, couldn't separate it from the present. The run from Tabriz. Philippe dead. Years of hiding, lying, fear. All of it to keep her son, to protect him. And now she had lost him anyway, lost him to the place from which she had risked her life to take him.

Saturday. Visiting hours. A guard called Jenna's name. It would be Brad. She almost didn't want to see him. He would be bubbling about plans for going away together, and she had no heart for it.

But the person in the visiting room was Laila.

"Hello, Aunt Jenna. I—I'm sorry I didn't come sooner."

"Please, there's nothing to be sorry about. It's so good to see you."

"I got to thinking . . . about my mother, you know—my real mother—and what you did for her. And for me. I wouldn't even be here without you. I had to come."

"I know it was hard for you to come here. And you did. That's all that matters. But weren't you supposed to be in France?"

"I went somewhere else, Aunt Jenna. I went to see Karim."

"You did?" Jenna felt a surge of wild hope. "What happened?"

Laila shook her head. "I can't tell you what you'd like to hear. He's gone. There's nothing you could have done to hold him."

Jenna waited.

"It was David's idea," said Laila. "I was always talking about you and Karim, always saying, you know, what a shame. And one night David said, 'Look, no one this kid meets for the rest of his life is going to understand his problem like you do. Why not give him a call?' And so I did.

"At first he didn't want to talk. Then he did, but it was all . . . bitterness. Anger. I wasn't getting through to him. So the next day I flew to Boston. David came with me. Karim was packing. His visa had just come through. But I managed to talk with him some more. For hours, really." She shrugged helplessly. "I tried to show him what I had learned for myself, about my father. That it wasn't his fault—wasn't your fault. That both of you had done what you thought was best. Karim didn't want to hear that. I wouldn't have listened either, at that stage. But at least I planted a seed."

"Laila, whatever you did, I can't thank you enough."

"I didn't accomplish much." She looked at Jenna with deep sadness, then suddenly brightened. "But do you know what, Aunt Jenna? I think it'll be all right. I think he'll be back someday. He's no more a Remali than I am. The time will come when he'll long for home—his real home. And he'll be wiser then. He'll begin to understand why you did what you did. I'm sure of it. Don't give up hope."

"Laila." Jenna couldn't hold back tears. She couldn't help seeing, in her mind's eye, the other Laila, that night in al-Masagin. And now it had come full circle.

Laila smiled. "Don't cry, Aunt Jenna. Listen, I made Karim promise to stay in touch with me. I'll call him as often as he'll put up with it. That way it won't be as if he's totally disappeared." She spread her hand on the glass partition for Jenna's hand to meet. "It'll work out—you'll see. But now I have to go."

"But you just got here."

"Someone else waiting to see you. Bye. See you soon."

She hurried out, stopping just long enough to smile at Brad.

He sat at the partition and looked long and longingly at Jenna.

"I just talked with Boyle," he said. "It's done. You'll be out on Tuesday. Three more days."

"Good. Thank God."

"I talked with Laila, too. A remarkable young woman—no surprise, considering her family. Listen, we're going to have plenty of time for all those trips I've been talking about. I finally realized that they might not be what you want right now. Would you settle for a long weekend at Marblehead? We could take it from the top. Maybe I'll get it right this time."

"Yes," said Jenna. "Yes. That sounds good."

It did. It sounded very very good.

SOHEIR KHASHOGGI

"I love many of the traditions of my culture," says first-time novelist Soheir Khashoggi of her Islamic roots. "I may be against some of the teachings, but I can't change what's in my heart."

Growing up in Alexandria, Egypt, Khashoggi lived in a somewhat less strict household than is typical of fundamentalist societies. But like her heroine in *Mirage,* she learned early on that "boys had power and girls had none. We were not allowed to talk in the presence of men." And she had to wear the veil when she was visiting.

Khashoggi was schooled in Alexandria. By age twelve she was fluent in three languages, and during her teens won many prizes for both writing and art. After attending the American University in Beirut, she became an interior designer and a fine artist— and grew accustomed to Western-style freedoms. She subsequently moved to Saudi Arabia with her husband by an arranged marriage. But life in that fundamentalist world became intolerable, and she fled with her daughter to London. Helping her escape was her wealthy brother Adnan, whose lavish lifestyle served as a model for Malik's in *Mirage.* "I couldn't resist borrowing some details," she admits.

These days Khashoggi and her four daughters—three of them by a second marriage—divide their time between Connecticut and France. Her next book will be about Egypt in the 1930s.

ILLUSTRATORS

Ted CoConis: *Notorious*

Dan Gonzalez: *Snow Wolf*

Richard Williams: *The Cat Who Said Cheese*

Michael Dudash: *Mirage*

ACKNOWLEDGMENT

Pages 6–7: H. Armstrong Roberts

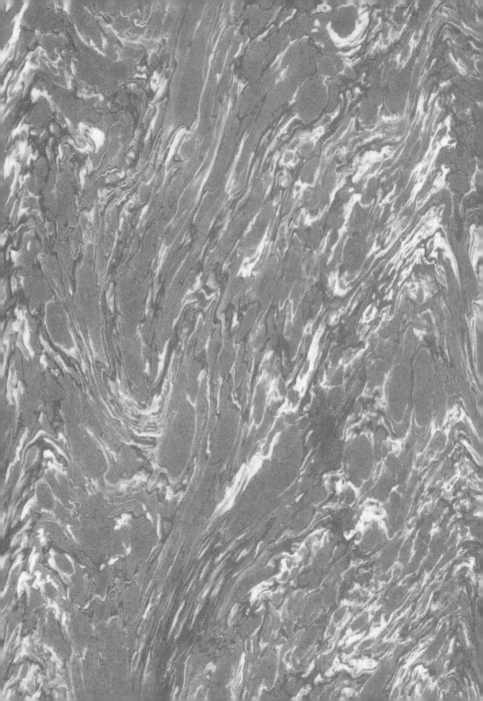